The Shadow Throne

ALSO BY DJANGO WEXLER

The Thousand Names

THE SHADOW THRONE

BOOK TWO OF THE SHADOW CAMPAIGNS

DJANGO WEXLER

A ROC BOOK

ROC
Published by the Penguin Group
Penguin Group (USA) LLC, 375 Hudson Street,
New York, New York 10014

USA | Canada | UK | Ireland | Australia | New Zealand | India | South Africa | China
penguin.com
A Penguin Random House Company

First published by Roc, an imprint of New American Library,
a division of Penguin Group (USA) LLC

First Printing, July 2014

Map illustration by Cortney Skinner

LIBRARY OF CONGRESS CATALOGING-IN-PUBLICATION DATA:

Wexler, Django.
The shadow throne / Django Wexler.
pages cm.—(Shadow campaigns; bk. 2)
ISBN 978-0-451-41806-7
1. Imaginary wars and battles—Fiction. 2. Fantasy fiction. I. Title.
PS3623.E94S53 2014
813'.6—dc23 2014004574

Printed in the United States of America
1 3 5 7 9 10 8 6 4 2

Set in Bembo
Designed by Elke Sigal

PUBLISHER'S NOTE
This is a work of fiction. Names, characters, places, and incidents either are the product of the author's imagination or are used fictitiously, and any resemblance to actual persons, living or dead, business establishments, events, or locales is entirely coincidental.

For Mom and Dad, as always.

ACKNOWLEDGMENTS

The advantage of writing the acknowledgments for the second volume in a series is that I can, in some sense, pick up where I left off. In the first volume, I wrote a little bit about the road that led to these books, and the people who helped me along it. Let me, then, briefly add to the list.

This time around, my invaluable history text was Simon Schama's *Citizens*. While the events of *The Shadow Throne* are not a particularly close fit with history, Schama's wonderful portrait of the French Revolution provided a storehouse of inspiration and detail that I have shamelessly raided.

Elisabeth Fracalossi continued in her task as alpha reader, a crucial role to fill for any writer. Cat Rambo heroically devoured the entire massive manuscript in a single gulp in order to talk it over with me when I'd gotten myself in a pickle. No less heroic are my beta readers, Konstantin Koptev and Lu Huan, whose feedback was, as always, invaluable.

At this point, we can take it as read that my agent, Seth Fishman, is accomplishing wonders. The rest of the team at the Gernert Company, Will Roberts, Rebecca Gardener, and Andy Kifer, has also done great, and it's thanks to them (and their hardworking coagents!) that we'll soon see *The Thousand Names* in French, German, Polish, and Italian.

My editors, Jessica Wade at Roc and Michael Rowley at Del Rey UK, were their usual incredibly talented and helpful selves. In particular, thanks go to Jessica for working literally up until the last day before her maternity leave, and to Michael for the apt suggestion that Marcus' life should be more like *Yes Minister*. Again, too, I'd like to recognize all the people at both publishers who help transform my Word document into an actual *thing* (or e-thing) and who don't get nearly enough praise.

Lastly, my heartfelt thanks to everyone who enjoyed *The Thousand Names* and took the time to talk about it: in e-mails to me, on Twitter, in book reviews, or in the multifarious corners of the blogosphere. You make it a lot easier to convince myself to get up in the morning and get to work.

The Shadow Throne

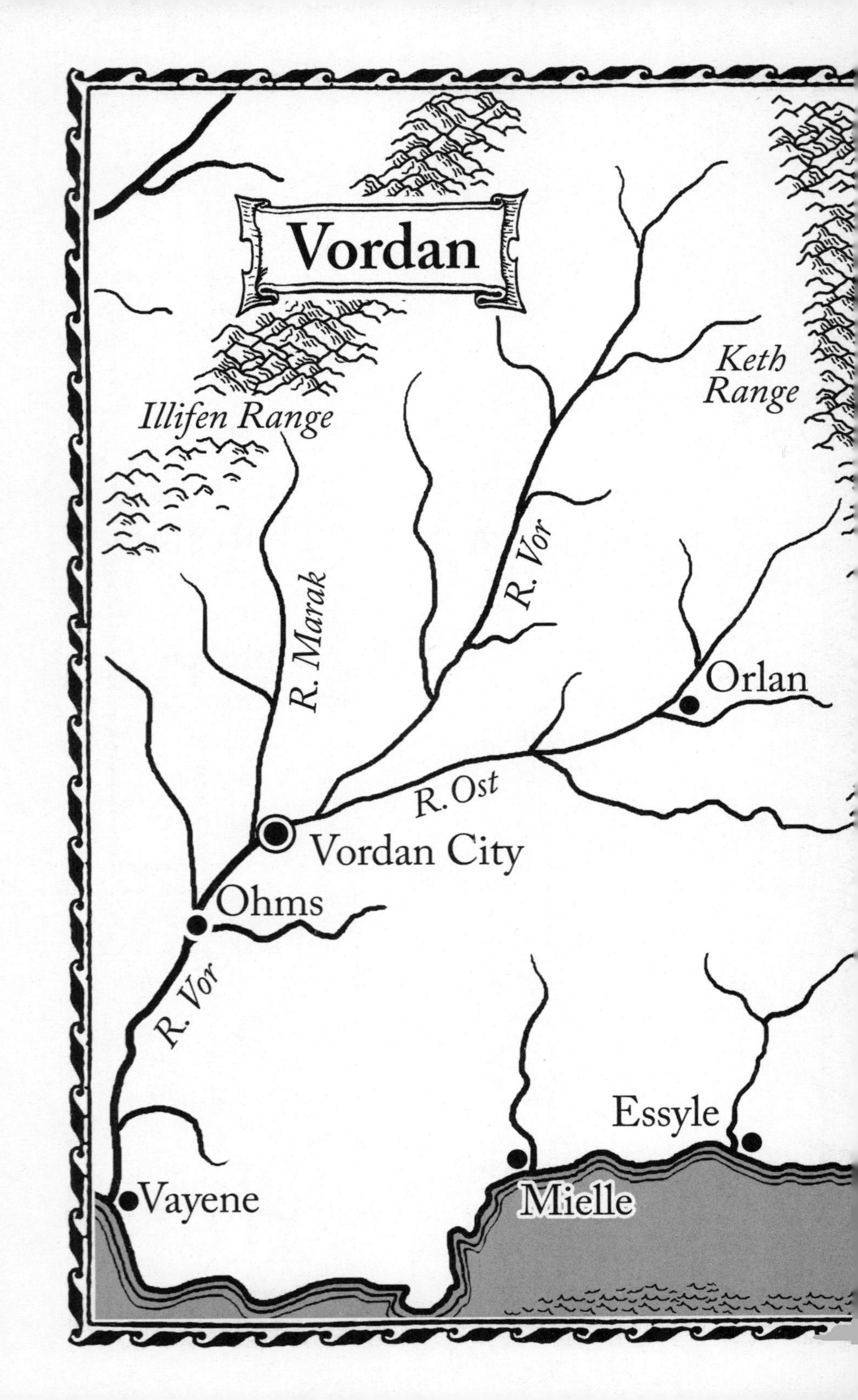

Vordan
Keth Range
Illifen Range
R. Vor
R. Marak
Orlan
R. Ost
Vordan City
Ohms
R. Vor
Essyle
Vayene
Mielle

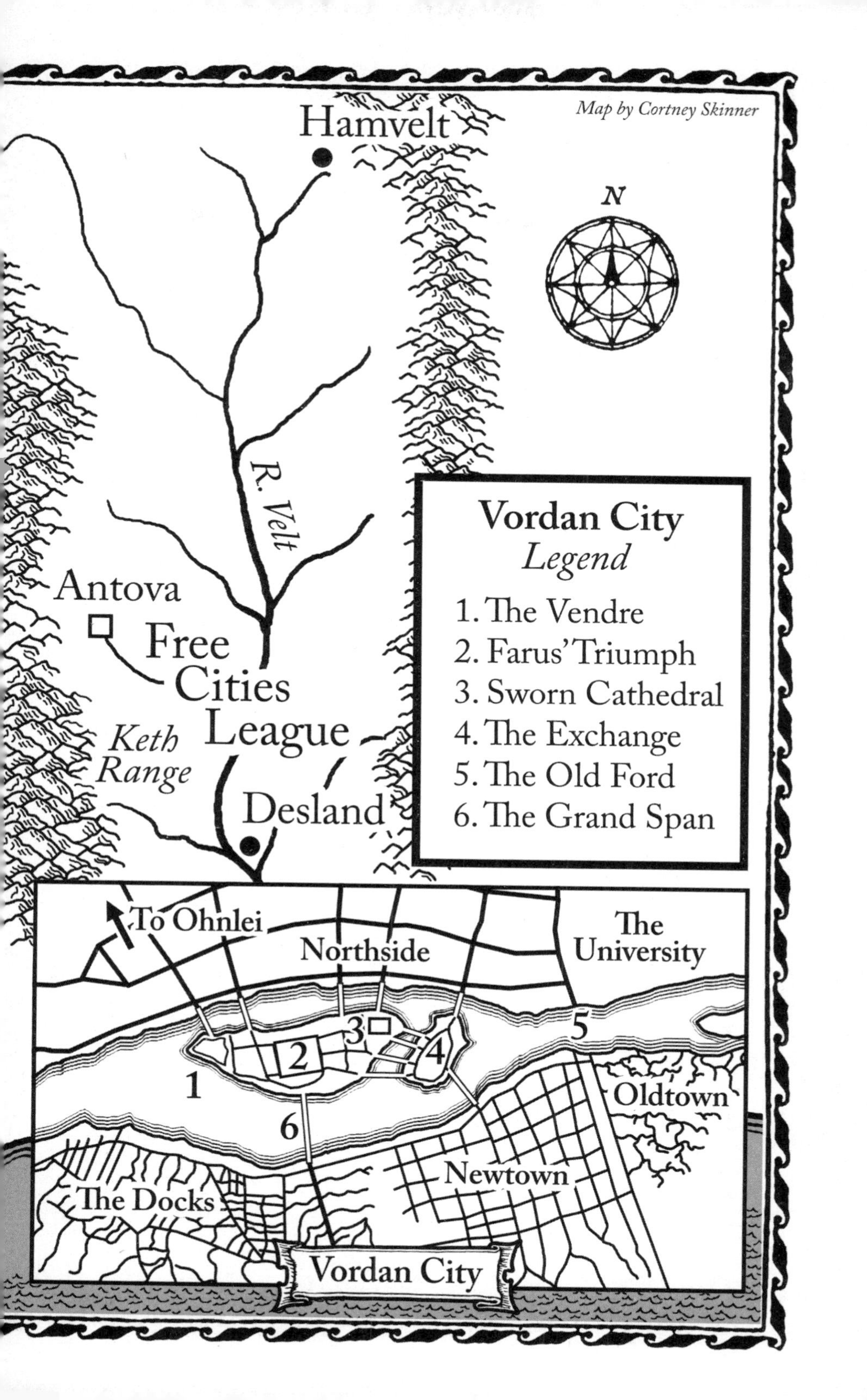
Map by Cortney Skinner
Hamvelt
N
R. Velt
Antova
Free
Cities
League
Keth
Range
Desland
Vordan City
Legend
1. The Vendre
2. Farus' Triumph
3. Sworn Cathedral
4. The Exchange
5. The Old Ford
6. The Grand Span
To Ohnlei
Northside
The
University
1
2
3
4
5
6
Oldtown
Newtown
The Docks
Vordan City

PROLOGUE

THE LAST DUKE

There were stories about what went on inside the Ministry of Information. The building—dubbed "the Cobweb"—was innocuous enough on the outside, another example of Farus VI's fondness for marble, classical columns, and elaborately decorated facades. Inside, the stories ran, it was a place of dust and shadows, full of hidden archives, rat-infested cells, and elaborate death traps. More than one adventure serial had featured some hero rescuing his lady-love from its forgotten oubliettes.

Duke Mallus Kengire Orlanko, Minister of Information and head of the Concordat, found all of this faintly offensive. In reality the Cobweb was lit by thousands of standing lamps, day and night, and a whole corps of junior servants was employed refilling oil and replacing wicks. There was no point in having the clerks ruin their eyesight trying to squint by candlelight, after all. And if one thought about it logically for a moment, it would be much *harder* to sneak into a brightly lit building bustling with activity than a moldering dungeon full of death traps. As for cells, there were a few, of course, but they were hardly rat-infested. Orlanko tolerated no vermin in his domain.

It was yet another example of the popular taste for colorful fantasy over prosaic reality. In Orlanko's opinion, if the Vordanai as a people could be said to have a fault, it was an excess of imagination outweighing proper sense. Not that the duke was complaining. He'd become an expert at playing on that imagination over the years.

His private office, at the top of the building, was a remarkably small and well-organized one. If an outsider had wandered in—though of course none were ever allowed to do so—he might have wondered where all the books and papers had gotten to. This was, after all, the heart of the Ministry of Information, the nerve center of the Concordat, the omniscient (again, in the popular imagination) secret police who knew everything about everyone. And yet here was the Last Duke himself, sitting behind a modest oak desk with only a few clipped bundles of paper, and not even a bookshelf to decorate the walls or a leather-bound tome full of dark secrets.

Again, the duke thought, a failure of common sense. What was the point of turning his office into a library? The whole *building* was his library, and all he really needed to do his business was the little copper bell on his desk. Ringing it would send in a clerk—there was always a queue of them waiting outside—who would silently accept the Last Duke's instructions and take them down into the archives, deputizing subclerks and sub-subclerks to break his order into manageable tasks. Files would be read, copied, summarized, and collated, until the original clerk returned to Orlanko's desk with another neat clipped bundle of paper. It was a machine for *knowing* things, for carrying out the will of the man sitting behind the desk, and Orlanko was immensely proud of it. Building it had been his life's work.

In that sense, Andreas bothered him. Not the man specifically, but the need for him, and others like him. Duke Orlanko wished that everything was like his Ministry, where he could just ring a little bell and speak a few words to set the whole vast apparatus clicking into motion. Beyond the walls of the Cobweb, unfortunately, things were messier, and required the employment of those who, like Andreas, had . . . special talents.

Andreas was in his middle thirties, with an average build and a forgettable face, both assets in his line of work. He wore one of the black, floor-length leather greatcoats that were the unofficial uniform of the Concordat. The coat had become a symbol. Parents frightened their children with it. This was useful, since if everyone knew what a Concordat agent looked like, it made it all the easier *not* to look like one when that was what was required.

Orlanko shifted in his special chair, which creaked slightly as hidden springs took up his weight. He adjusted his spectacles and pretended to notice Andreas for the first time, though the man had been waiting patiently for at least a quarter of an hour.

"Ah, Andreas."

"Sir."

"Any progress with your investigation of the Gray Rose?"

Some things were too delicate to trust to the machine. The Gray Rose had been another of Orlanko's special employees, one of the best, but she'd slipped the leash several years back and disappeared without a trace. As a matter of principle, the duke couldn't allow that sort of thing. Andreas had been pursuing her ever since, patiently following the faintest traces with a persistence that would have done credit to a bloodhound. Andreas, the duke sometimes thought, was a bit like an automaton himself.

"I have several promising leads, sir," Andreas said. "My people are following them up."

"You're still convinced she hasn't left the country?"

"The balance of evidence seems to suggest she remains in the city, sir."

Damn the woman, Orlanko thought. If she'd done the logical thing and fled beyond his supposedly all-powerful reach, he would have happily called off the hunt. She knew nothing that would damage him, not at this stage. But by remaining close by, she implicitly challenged his authority, and that could not be tolerated. It was an irritating waste of resources.

"Well, I'm sure your men can proceed without you for a time. There are other matters that require our attention."

"Yes, sir." Andreas waited patiently, hands crossed behind his back.

"Have you heard the news from Khandar?"

"Yes, sir. Colonel Vhalnich appears to have won a great victory. The Vermillion Throne is secure, and newly indebted to His Majesty."

"So the papers would have us believe," Orlanko said sourly. Vhalnich was already well on his way to becoming a popular hero. Such stories were usually exaggerations, but the duke's own agents reported that the broadsheets were, if anything, understating the case. "Vhalnich is on his way back here, apparently. He's expected any day."

"And the special asset you sent with him?"

"I've heard nothing." Orlanko's finger tap-tap-tapped on the report. "Which, in itself, speaks volumes. If we assume the worst, she's been eliminated."

"And the Thousand Names may be in Vhalnich's hands." A hint of animation entered Andreas' face. "Would you like him removed upon arrival?"

The duke stifled a sigh. If Andreas had a fault, it was a definite tendency to resort to drastic measures too quickly. It was an odd failing in someone so patient in every other respect. Orlanko suspected that Andreas simply liked to kill people.

"That would be a bit obvious, don't you think?" Orlanko shook his head. "No, Vhalnich will undoubtedly enjoy the favor of the king and the adoration of the mob. For the moment, we dare not touch him. But His Majesty is *very* ill. If he dies . . . we shall see."

"Yes, sir."

"We need to know what happened in Khandar, Andreas. If these Names our Elysian friends are so interested in really exist, and whether or not Vhalnich has them. Whether he even understands their importance." He leaned back in his chair, springs creaking. "Find out."

"Understood, sir."

"Vhalnich is a very clever man, and he'll be on his guard. Concentrate on the people around him. Nothing too obvious, of course."

"Yes, sir." Andreas betrayed only a hint of disappointment.

"And I may have another assignment for you soon, depending on how the king's health progresses. There are quite a few little cabals out there hoping to capitalize on the confusion. We have them all infiltrated, naturally, and there's nothing *terribly* dangerous. But a few well-timed disappearances should put the fear of God into them." Or rather, he thought, the fear of the Last Duke. That was better. "Make sure your people are ready."

"Of course, sir."

"That will be all."

Andreas ghosted out. Orlanko looked at the stack of reports, adjusted his glasses, and unclipped the top pile.

What nobody understood was how *hard* his job was. Riding herd on the city sometimes felt like trying to keep his seat on an unruly stallion. Yes, he knew about everything of importance practically before it happened, and yes, he could whisper a name and Andreas or someone like him would drag that person into a cell where they'd never see the light of day again. But really, what good was that? You couldn't lock *everybody* up. His task was much trickier—to make them forge a prison in their own minds, out of their own fears, in which they would lock themselves and throw away the key. He'd been working at it for years, and he liked to think he'd done a fair job. The black coats were part of it. The occasional vanishing, the odd body found floating in the river, those just helped to grease the hinges. Fear would populate every shadow with hooded figures, when even he couldn't possibly employ enough agents to do the job.

He wasn't afraid of conspiracies. No conspiracy could survive exposure and decapitation, after all, and he was an expert at both. But Orlanko had learned to feel the *mood* of the city, as though it were a single vast organism. Sometimes it was sleepy and complacent, when times were good and people were fat and happy. When times were lean, it was snappy and irritable, prone to sudden rages and panics. And the death of a king always put people on edge.

He could feel something coming. The city was like a dog growling deep in its throat, not quite ready to leap but not far from it. It was his job to calm it, with either a nice bloody steak or a well-placed boot. Which it would be, Duke Orlanko had not yet decided.

But once the king died, after the chaos subsided, he would finally have what he'd dreamed of all these years. A ruler who would *listen*.

She'll listen. Orlanko smiled to himself. *Or else . . .*

Part One

Chapter One

RAESINIA

The mirrored halls of the Royal Palace at Ohnlei were dark and quiet. Not silent, for the thousands of footmen, maids, gardeners, guards, cook and candle boys who made the great palace run could never really stop moving, any more than a heart could stop pumping. But they moved cautiously, avoiding loud footfalls on the marble floors and talking in low voices, and only a few candles flickered in the enormous braziers. The great black velvet drapes and carpets had not been hung, for the king had not yet died, but in a hundred cellars and storerooms they had been unrolled, aired out, and checked for wear.

Raesinia and her party clattered through the hush like a wild stallion in a glazier's. First came the princess' hard-soled shoes, *tak-tak-tak*, and then the heavy, flat-footed tromp of the trio of Noreldrai Grays who provided her escort. It gave everyone plenty of warning to form up and clear the way, so that her progress was marked by a bow wave of dipping heads from staff lined up on either side of the corridor. The occasional courtier sparkled like a precious stone among the pale blue of the Royal livery. Ordinarily, politeness would have obliged her to stop and exchange a few pleasant words with anyone of sufficient rank, but under the circumstances the nobles merely bowed their heads and let her by. No doubt they began whispering as soon as she turned the corner, but Raesinia was used to that.

The ground-floor apartments of the king were reached through a broad marble arch, carved with a frieze depicting King Farus VI in the act of smiting some armored foe. Raesinia's great-grandfather was everywhere at Ohnlei. He'd died decades before she was born, but she'd seen his narrow-cheeked, pointy-bearded countenance on so many statues, bas-reliefs, and portraits that he was as familiar to her as any of her living family. This one was actually not a particularly good likeness, she'd always suspected. The sculptor had given the king a squint, and he looked out at the viewer rather than keeping his eyes on the business at hand, as though to say, "Who are you, and what are you doing at my battle?"

Beyond the arch was a grassy courtyard, roofed over with great sliding panes of glass that could be opened to let the air in when the weather was good. Here the king, in better days, would receive guests or dine with his favorites. It was surrounded by a colonnade and a terrace floored with marble, from which a dozen oak-and-gilt doors led to the king's private chambers and the residences of his servants and guards. A dozen of the latter were scattered around the courtyard, not just the somber-uniformed Noreldrai Grays but Armsmen in their forest green coats and white trousers and Royal Army grenadiers in Vordanai blue and polished brass. Guarding the king was a great honor, and none of the three services was willing to leave it to the others.

In the middle of the lawn, looking a bit incongruous, was a polished oak dining table surrounded by high-backed chairs. Raesinia had eaten there many times with her father, in the company of the mightiest nobles of the land, surrounded by a veritable swarm of servants and flunkies. Now the long, mirror-smooth surface was nearly empty. At the far end sat a gray-haired man, back hunched from a lifetime of bending over the beds of his patients. He got painfully to his feet as Raesinia approached, in spite of her urgent gesture.

"Good morning, Your Highness," he said, with as much of a bow as his stiff back could muster. "I hope you are well?"

He had a Hamveltai accent, which turned "well" into "vell." Raesinia nodded.

"As well as ever, Doctor-Professor Indergast," she said.

He peered at her over the top of thin-rimmed half-moon spectacles. "I ought to have a look at your diet," he said. "Some days it seems to me that you are not growing up properly. Your mother was nearly as tall as I when she was nineteen, you know."

Raesinia, who had to look up slightly to meet the stoop-shouldered doctor's gaze, gave a careful shrug. "Perhaps, someday. But we have more important things to worry about at the moment. I got a message to come at once—is he all right?"

"His condition has not changed, Your Highness," Indergast said. "I am sorry to have worried you. It is only that he is awake, and asked to see you."

Raesinia's heart gave a weak flop. Her father slept more than he was awake, these days, and sometimes he was delirious with pain and fever. She'd spent many hours at his bedside, holding his hand, but he hadn't often known she was there.

"I'd better go and see him, then," she said, "before he falls asleep again."

"Of course, Your Highness. Pay no mind to me." He gestured at a huge book, which lay open on the table where he'd been sitting. "I was only paging through a volume of Acheleos that the Grand Bishop was kind enough to lend me, to see if he had anything useful to tell us."

"And does he?"

"Alas, no. Like all the ancients, he has many theories but very little practical advice."

"You'll figure something out. You always have."

Doctor-Professor Indergast ran one gnarled hand through his wispy hair. He had been personal physician to her father since before Raesinia had been born. Some at the court wondered why the king needed a foreign doctor to attend him, but Raesinia had come to love the old man. He'd pulled the king back from the brink more than once, when no other doctor at the University would have dared even make the attempt.

"I'm honored by your trust, Your Highness," he said, but his expression was grave. "I beg you, though, not to place too much faith in my poor skills." He paused, then added quietly, "Miracles are the department of His Grace the Grand Bishop."

Raesinia set her lips but said nothing. She gave the old man a nod and swept past him, toward her father's bedchamber.

"The Grand Bishop is with him now," Indergast said from behind her. "As is His Grace the duke and the rest of the cabinet."

She faltered but didn't break stride. This wasn't a matter of an ailing man wanting to see his daughter, then. If the king had summoned his ministers, then he had something official to say. Raesinia breathed a silent thanks to Indergast for the warning, told her bodyguards to wait outside with the rest of the king's protectors, and slipped in the door.

The king's bedchamber was small by the standards of Ohnlei, which meant that it wasn't quite large enough to host a tennis match. The royal bed was enormous, though, its four oak posts practically trembling under the weight of silks and velvet hangings. In the center of it, drowning in a sea of covers and embroidered cushions, the king was visible only as a disembodied head surrounded by expensive fabric.

A group of well-dressed men stood at the end of the bed, huddled together for mutual support. The Grand Bishop of Vordan, prevented from huddling by the voluminous folds of his crimson robes of office, affected an ecclesiastical aloofness a little ways off.

It was apparent to Raesinia that she had walked into the middle of an argument, though one that might not have been obvious to anyone who hadn't spent their lives at Ohnlei. It was the kind of roundabout, exquisitely polite disagreement carried on by men who are aware that their opponent could, technically, have them executed.

"I'm certain Your Majesty has considered the matter carefully," said a large, thick-bearded man at the front of the huddle. This was Count Torahn, the Minister of War, his soldier's physique running to fat beneath the careful tailoring of his court uniform. His normally florid complexion was practically aglow now. "But I wonder if you have given a thought to the situation from my position. We are speaking of a young and talented officer, showing great promise, and to remove him to what is, after all, an interior post . . ."

"So promising that you sent him to Khandar?" said the king. It made Raesinia's heart break just to hear him, his voice reduced from the confident baritone she remembered to a wheezy, petulant rasp.

"Where he has achieved great things," Torahn said smoothly. "And, in due time, if his career is not interrupted—"

"I'll leave that to his judgment," the king said. "He may choose to decline the post."

"But he will not, Your Majesty." This was from the Minister of Finance, Rackhil Grieg. He had always reminded Raesinia of a ferret, with a narrow face and beady, wary eyes, an effect that was not helped by his unfortunate choice to wear his ratty brown hair long at the back. Torahn shot him an ugly look when he spoke up. Grieg was a commoner, unique on the cabinet, and the others resented him for it. He owed his advancement entirely to the patronage of the Last Duke, and was therefore widely considered to be Orlanko's creature.

"After all," Grieg went on, "an offer from Your Majesty is an honor not to be lightly refused. Even if it went against his judgment of what was best for the service, would he not feel obligated to accept so as not to dishonor Your Majesty with his refusal?"

"That's true," Torahn said, recognizing a good line of attack like a proper soldier. "For any officer of the Royal Army, Your Majesty's wishes must be placed above any doubts or personal concerns."

"Does that include you, Torahn?" the king snapped, with a little of his old vigor.

The Minister of War bowed deeply. "I am only attempting to bring to Your Majesty's attention aspects of the matter that may have escaped your notice. We will, of course, abide by Your Majesty's ultimate decision."

Even from across the room, Raesinia could read the expression on her father's face. She decided the time had come for an interruption.

"Excuse me, gentlemen." Raesinia bobbed her head in the direction of the ministers, then curtsied deeply toward the bed. "Your Majesty, you sent for me?"

"I did," the king said. "The rest of you, out. I would speak to my daughter alone."

Raesinia stepped aside so the assembled notables could file past her. The Grand Bishop murmured something sympathetic in his heavy Murnskai accent as he went by, and Torahn dismissed her with a glance and a perfunctory nod.

Only the last one to leave caught her eye. He was a short man, no taller than Raesinia, and his bulging waistcoat made him look very nearly round. The crown of his head was bald, but a wild ruff of hair behind his ears and around the back of his skull made up for it, giving him the look of a classical philosopher. The most remarkable thing about his appearance, though, was his spectacles. They were enormous, each lens almost a handsbreadth in diameter, and so thick and curved that they provided only the most distorted vision of the face behind them. Strange, twisted blobs of nose- and cheek-tinted color moved and twisted as he turned his head, but when he looked straight at you, as he looked at Raesinia now, his eyes would suddenly appear magnified disconcertingly to five times their normal size.

It would be easy to dismiss this funny little man, and many had done so, always to their sorrow. His Grace Duke Mallus Kengire Orlanko, Minister of Information and master of the Concordat, was always ready to embrace any advantage, even that offered by his own innocuous appearance. Raesinia was not fooled. The Last Duke was widely agreed to be the most dangerous man in Vordan, and she had spent enough time at the palace to know that this was, if anything, an understatement. She wasn't certain there was a more dangerous man in all the world.

Today he favored her with only a brief smile and a little bow before continuing on his way, shutting the bedroom door behind him. Raesinia went to the bed, which was so big she was forced to climb up onto it to reach her father. He extracted one hand from the constricting comforters and reached out to her, and she took it between both of hers. It was thin and light, like a songbird in her palm. His bones seemed as brittle as twigs, and his skin was papery-dry.

He turned his head in her direction and blinked watery eyes. "Raesinia?"

"I'm here, Father." She gripped his hand a little tighter. "It's good to see you awake."

"For a change." He coughed. "Every time I wake up, I think of a thousand things to do, in case this time is the last. But I'm always exhausted before I can get through one or two." He closed his eyes and let out a rattling breath. "I'm sorry, Raesinia."

"Don't speak that way, Father," Raesinia said. "This may be the beginning of an improvement. Doctor-Professor Indergast—"

"Doctor-Professor Indergast is honest with me," he interrupted. "Unlike the rest of the fools and flatterers, or that great whale in red."

"He is very skilled," Raesinia insisted. "Better than any other doctor in Vordan."

"Some things are beyond skill." The king squeezed her hand and opened his eyes. "But I did not call you here to argue."

Raesinia ducked her head, and there was a moment of silence while the king composed his thoughts. Finally, he said, "Do you know Count Janus bet Vhalnich Mieran?"

"Only in passing," Raesinia said, blinking in surprise. "He was at court three years ago, I think. We spoke briefly."

"You do not know much about him, then?"

"Just that he went to Khandar to suppress the rebellion, and that he's been doing well. Why?"

"His mission to Khandar has been a success. A complete success, in fact, beyond anyone's expectations. Even our good Minister of Information seemed surprised, and you know how rare an event that is." He gave a dry chuckle, which turned into another cough. "I've summoned him back to Vordan. He's on his way as we speak. When he gets here, I'm going to make him the Minister of Justice."

Raesinia was quiet. Plans rearranged themselves at the back of her mind, new information slotting into place. She kept her expression neutral.

"I'm sure he'll do well there," she said, after a moment. "But—"

"But what does this have to do with you?" The king sighed. "I have to look ahead, Raesinia. Think about what you'll be left with after I'm gone. Orlanko has too much influence on the cabinet already. Grieg is in his pocket, and Torahn is heading in that direction. Count Almire has made a career of avoiding politics. If Orlanko puts one of his own in Justice as well, he'll be king in all but name."

"If you don't trust Orlanko, get rid of him," Raesinia said, unable to keep a bit of heat out of her voice. "Better yet, have him executed."

"If only it were that simple. The Borels would never allow it. And, like it or not, Orlanko may be all that has kept us afloat since . . ."

He trailed off, eyes losing focus and staring away past the ceiling. But Raesinia could finish the thought on her own. She'd been only thirteen at the time of Vansfeldt, the battle that had cost Vordan its war with Borel and its crown prince in one disastrous afternoon. Her father had been sick then as well, too sick to go to the front as he felt he ought, and though his illness had waxed and waned since then, she wasn't sure his spirit had ever recovered.

The king blinked and shook his head weakly. "Tired. I'm so tired, Raesinia."

"Rest, then. I can come back later."

"Not just yet. Listen to me. Count Mieran is . . . more than he seems. I had hoped . . ." He swallowed. "I had plans. But I am running out of time. I think . . . I *think* you can trust him. At the very least, he is no friend of our Last Duke. He will help you, Raesinia." Tears glistened in the royal eyes. "You will need all the allies you can get."

"I understand, Father."

"It will be hard for you. I never meant for this to happen." His voice softened, as if he were drifting away. "None of this. You were supposed to have . . . something else. Not this. But . . ."

"It's all right, Father." Raesinia leaned over him and kissed him, gently, on the cheek. His attendants had bathed him in rosewater, but the perfume was unable to cover the sick-sweet scent of rot wafting from the royal flesh. "Everything will be all right. Now rest."

"I'm sorry," he said again, eyes slowly closing. "My little girl . . . I'm sorry . . ."

Raesinia's own quarters were in a faux-medieval tower named, inelegantly, the Prince's Turret. Most of its rooms had been shut since the death of her brother,

Dominic, and Raesinia preferred to live simply in a few chambers on the ground floor. She had the keys to the whole place, however, and it was easy enough to unlock the servants' stairs and slip up, past silent sitting rooms and parlors with furniture covered in dust sheets, and emerge on the roof.

Strictly speaking, she did not have to be naked to accomplish what she was about to do. There was no point in ruining a perfectly good dress, though, and it appealed to her sense of melodrama. Raesinia had decided long ago that this was a defect in her character, that in the same way a coward lacked moral foundation and a drunkard strength of will, there was something in the pit of her soul that gave her an unhealthy weakness for sappy gestures and romantic poetry. Alas, the acknowledgment of this flaw did little to help excise it, and periodically it got the better of her.

The sun had set behind the forests to the west, but dark crimson light still stained the sky in that direction, painting the scattered clouds the color of blood. All around her were the lights of Ohnlei, neat rows of lanterns marking the avenues and byways, clusters of more distant lamps picking out the dark hulks of the Ministry buildings. Most of these had gone dark already as the clerks retired for the evening, but as always the Cobweb was a blaze of light, and smoke puffed merrily from its many chimneys. The Ministry of Information ran in overlapping shifts, it was said, like a coal mine, and there were clerks in the deep basements who had never seen the sun.

Farther to the south, across the intervening belt of royal parks and carefully tended wilderness, a deeper, ruddier glow marked the edges of the city of Vordan. Raesinia stared for a long time in that direction, as the wind whipped around her and raised goose bumps on her bare skin. It was a warm July night, but four stories up the breeze still carried a chill.

Only a single lantern burned atop the Prince's Turret, and no guards waited there. It was just a circular expanse of slate surrounded by an irregular raised lip meant to suggest a real castle's crenellations. In better times, the prince might have used it to breakfast in the sun, but Raesinia was certain no one but she had been up there in years. The pigeons that infested Ohnlei like lice on a beggar had stained the stones white and gray.

For her purposes, the important feature of the roof was what it overlooked. The Prince's Turret formed the northeasternmost corner of the great rambling palace, and it was well away from any of the heavily trafficked areas. Looking down, Raesinia could see a raked gravel path four stories below, and beyond that a low stone wall marking the edge of the gardens. The only windows that looked onto it were her own, and she kept the curtains drawn. Squads of Noreldrai Grays patrolled the perimeter in a slow procession, but they only passed at twenty- or thirty-minute intervals, and the torches they carried made them visible from a long way off.

One of these squads had just passed out of sight, and Raesinia gave them a count of two hundred to get safely around the corner of the vast, irregular building. She stepped up onto the lip of stone, staring out over the darkened trees beyond the edge of the grounds, and forced herself to stand straight, with her arms at her sides.

She felt as though she ought to say something, to mark the occasion, although there was no one to hear.

"I wish," she said, "that there was a better way."

Raesinia extended one foot, let it hang tingling for a moment in midair, then tumbled forward off the wall and into darkness.

She'd always pictured the few seconds of fall telescoping into an eternity, time stretching like taffy as the wall of the tower rushed past and the wind whipped across her bare skin. In fact, she was barely aware of it, a single blurred moment of weightless, involuntary terror before the crashing pain of impact. Her shoulder hit the ground first, shattering the bone instantly, and an instant later her skull impacted so hard on the gravel it shattered like an egg. The princess' body twitched once, feet pushing weakly at the gravel, then lay still and broken in the gathering twilight.

Deep inside, in the darkest pit of her being, she felt something stir.

Raesinia wished she could faint. Some of the ladies at court were given to fainting, and she had always considered it a useless affectation in that setting, but she had lately come to appreciate that it was simply the body's way of trying to spare its occupant some grief in a difficult time. Unfortunately, in her current state, she seemed to have lost the knack, and so she could feel the grinding of bone against fragmented bone in her shoulder, the slow seep from the cracks in her skull, and the drip of blood from where innumerable bits of sharp gravel had driven themselves into her back.

She had become somewhat indifferent to pain over the years. Repeated demonstrations had made her acutely aware that there was her body, currently lying in a broken heap in the gravel, and *herself*, somewhere else entirely, and that pain and all sensations of that kind were simply signals from one to the other, as one ship might warn another of a dangerous reef via semaphore flags.

Still, she couldn't quite banish her discomfort, and she directed a silent, metaphorical glare at the magical binding and demanded that it quit lazing about and do its job.

It emerged languidly from the depths of her soul, yawning like a sleepy tiger coming out of his cave. Raesinia imagined it casting about to see what she'd done to herself *now*, heaving a sigh at the extent of the damage, and reluctantly setting to work. She knew it was ridiculous to anthropomorphize it so—it was simply a process, after all, no different from that which consumed wood and phlogiston to make fire, or turned exposed iron into rust. But after living—if that was the word—for four years with the thing wrapped around her soul, she couldn't help feeling as if it had moods and feelings of its own. She imagined it looking in her direction with hooded, reproachful eyes before it set to work.

Her skull shifted, as though under invisible fingers. Chips and fragments of bone reassembled themselves like a jigsaw puzzle, knitting back together into a seamless whole. The rents in her skin drew closed, like someone stitching up a seam. Her shoulder was next, torn muscles reknitting, arm straightening as the bones snapped into place. She felt an unpleasant stirring along her back, and as soon as she was able she heaved herself up onto her knees and listened to the quiet *click-click* as bits of rock that had been forced deep beneath her skin dug themselves out again and clattered to the ground.

Within a few minutes, she could stand. The binding had restored her to the state she had been in before she stepped off the roof, plus or minus a layer of grime and a few pints of blood smeared on her skin or soaking into the turf. As best she could see it was the state she would be in until the long-postponed Day of Judgment finally came to pass. The same state, in other words, that she'd been in four years ago, before she had died the first time.

Sothe appeared out of the darkness. She had a way of moving that was so quiet she seemed to materialize from nothing, like a ghost, with equally terrifying effect. In this case, her aura of menance was diminished by the fact that she wore the long blue dress and gray apron of a palace lady's maid, and was carrying a fluffy towel. Even in this attire, though, she had a formidable air, tall and slim as a blade, dark hair cut short as a boy's, and sharp, aquiline features.

As far as the world was concerned, Sothe was Raesinia's maid and personal attendant. That was true, but her duties went considerably further than that. Raesinia knew that before entering her service Sothe had been highly placed in Duke Orlanko's Concordat, though she was closemouthed about what exactly had prompted her depature.

"There has to be a better way," Raesinia said. "I mean, this is ridiculous."

It was easy enough to get into or out of the palace during the day, when a steady stream of delivery carts arrived to feed its vast appetite. Unfortunately, during the day the princess royal needed to be seen. By night, the grounds were closed off and patrolled, which had forced Raesinia to devise this somewhat unorthodox method of escaping unseen.

"It has the virtue of being unexpected," Sothe said.

"We should knock out those ridiculous leaded glass windows and put in something I can open. Or at the very least get the gardeners to put a planter here. Fill it with dirt and grow something soft. Lavender, maybe. Then I wouldn't come out of it smelling like blood and brains."

"The gardeners might wonder," Sothe said, "why it looked like something had fallen on their plants from a great height."

As she spoke, she dragged one foot back and forth across the gravel where Raesinia had landed, erasing the small crater and burying the bloodstains. Raesinia sighed and rolled her shoulders, feeling a few errant splinters of bone click back into place. She wiped the worst of the blood off her skin and handed the towel back to Sothe, who accepted it without comment and offered Raesinia a folded silk robe. Thus at least minimally attired, the princess led the way away from the house and out into the woods, Sothe ghosting along behind her.

"Any trouble tonight?" Raesinia said, pushing aside an overhanging branch.

"None at all." Sothe frowned. "The man Orlanko has assigned to you is . . . inattentive. I ought to write him a reprimand."

"I hope you'll refrain, for both our sakes."

"I don't know," Sothe said. "I might enjoy a bit more of a challenge."

Raesinia looked over her shoulder at her maid, but her expression was unreadable. That was the trouble with Sothe—she never smiled, and it was almost impossible to tell when she was joking. Raesinia was fairly sure this was one of those times, but not completely certain. Sothe did occasionally complain that soft living was taking the edge off her skills, and she'd been known to take extreme measures to stay in practice.

The forest they were traversing was as much a work of artifice as the manicured gardens of the palace. It had been carefully tended and sculpted by generations of gardeners into the very epitome of what a forest ought to be, with tall, healthy trees spreading leafy branches, and no irritating undergrowth or unexpected deadfalls that might tangle the footing of an unsuspecting courtier. It was therefore easy going, even with bare feet and by moonlight, and before long they'd reached one of the many little lanes of packed earth that wound through the woods. Here a carriage was waiting, a battered one-horse cab. An elderly gray mare waited in the traces, munching contentedly from a feed bag.

Sothe attended to the horse while Raesinia climbed inside. Gathered on the battered wooden seat, with Sothe's usual attention to detail, were her necessaries: more towels and a jug of water for a more thorough cleaning, pins for her hair, and clothes and shoes for the evening. As the carriage lurched into motion, Raesinia set about effecting her transformation.

By the time the regular clicking of the wheels over cobblestones indicated that they'd reached the city proper, she was ready. No one from the palace would have recognized her, which was of course the idea. Her normally shoulder-length hair was pinned up and tucked under a short-brimmed slouch cap, and she'd traded the silk robe for cotton trousers and a gray blouse. It was a boyish outfit, although she doubted anyone would mistake her for a boy. That wasn't the point. Rather, it was the kind of thing a girl student of the University might wear—comfortable and casually defiant of custom. In the taverns and eateries of the Dregs, it was as good as a uniform.

She'd originally wanted to change her name, but Sothe had advised against it. Responding properly to a false name took a good deal of training, and there was always the chance of slipups. Besides, there were thousands of girls named Raesinia in the city, all roughly her age, products of a brief fashion for naming children in honor of the newborn princess. So she became Raesinia Smith, a good solid Vordanai name. Raesinia had spent a few interminable court sessions daydreaming an elaborate backstory for her alter ego, complete with parents, siblings, aunts and uncles, family tragedies, and bittersweet young loves, but somewhat to her disappointment no one had ever asked.

The clicking slowed and stopped. Raesinia checked herself over in the hand mirror Sothe had thoughtfully provided, found nothing out of the place, and opened the carriage door to step out into the Dregs.

She was immediately assaulted by a blast of heat and a blaze of light. It was well past sunset, but the streets were as crowded as if it were noon, and nearly as bright. The torches and braziers burning in front of every open establishment were traditional, as were the lanterns carried by some passersby, but Professor

Roetig's new-pattern gas lamps outshone them all with a steady, unceasing radiance, standing tall atop their high steel sconces. They gave an oddly manic cast to the whole scene, as though the scurrying nighttime revelers were flouting some celestial law.

Carriages were rare in that part of town, and those that were visible were all hired cabs. The three or four miles of Old Street that ran across the front of the University were mostly fronted by shops and drinking establishments catering to the student body, but above and behind these places of business were innumerable second- and third-floor rooms and tumbledown tenements. Here lived those scholars not wealthy enough to secure living space on University grounds, alongside the hawkers, publicans, and prostitutes who worked on and around the nearby streets.

Raesinia loved the Dregs because it was a contradiction in terms. It was on the north side of the river—that was to say, the correct or fashionable side—and only a stone's throw from the respectable brick-fronted town houses of Saint Uriah Street. And, in theory, the students of the University were mostly the scions of gentle families, or else the very best and brightest the lower orders had to offer. On the other hand, that student body consisted almost exclusively of young men, and wherever young men gather together with money in their pockets, an industry will arise, as if by magic, to provide them with what they need in terms of wine, women, and song. The paradox gave the whole area a kind of reputable disreputability that attracted exactly the sort of person Raesinia was looking for.

Most of the taverns and restaurants had signboards displaying their names and painted crests for the benefit of the illiterate, in accordance with ancient tradition, but in more modern times some bright storekeeper had come up with the idea of erecting a flagpole, cantilevered diagonally out over the heads of the pedestrians, to fly the banner of his establishment. Like any good idea, this had been rapidly copied, and so the gaslights shone on rows of hundreds of triangular flags, now hanging limp in the hot, windless air. Tradition had grown up surprisingly quickly here as well, giving the flags a uniform shape and design—three simple bars of horizontal color, different combinations marking the various shops to the eyes of the cognoscenti.

A trained observer could gather quite a bit from those colors. In a crowded market, the wine sellers had specialized, and by now their particular combination of colors marked them as surely as a count's heraldry. The top bar usually represented the political affiliation of the clientele, or at least the primary language spoken within. The University drew its students from half the continent, and so while the majority of the flags Raesinia could see were topped by solid Vordanai blue, she could also spot the muddy red of Borel, the yellow of Hamvelt, the dove gray of Noreld, and even a few spots of white for lonely Murnskai scholars, hundreds of miles from home.

Nor were the triple-striped emblems confined to the flags. Quite a few of the young people on the street wore armbands blazoned with the symbol of their preferred establishment. Others showed the colors as a band around their hats, or, in the case of the more well-heeled students, in jeweled pins on their breasts or at their collar. Thus one could tell at a glance who was who, since where someone drank conveyed a great deal about his views and affiliations, and Raesinia's practiced eye automatically sorted the crowd into Republicans, Utopians, Redemptionists, and a hundred other factions, sects, and splinter groups.

The pin she wore at her own collar was a delicate butterfly wrought in silver, its wings colored in blue, green, and gold. She sought out the flag that matched it, and found it floating lazily over the warm updraft from a torch stand. The windows of the Blue Mask blazed with light, and as she walked toward it she could smell the familiar cocktail of sawdust, charring meat, and cheap liquor. Raesinia looked over her shoulder at Sothe.

"You *can* come in, you know," she said. "You don't need to follow me out in the dark like some kind of voyeur."

"Safer not to," Sothe said. "You know I'll be nearby if you need assistance."

"Suit yourself." Privately, Raesinia thought Sothe simply preferred lurking alone in shadowy corners to sitting with friends by the fire, but it wasn't worth the argument. She squared her shoulders, pushed aside the curtain that blocked the doorway—the door was wedged open to admit the summer air—and went inside.

The common room of the Blue Mask was a miasma of wood smoke, tobacco fumes, and delicious-smelling steam wafting from a couple of big cauldrons over the fire. The tables were crowded tonight, and the pair of serving maids were having difficulty threading their way past the tight-packed patrons. In other taverns, in other places, there might have been games of dice or cards, discussions of merchant shipping or criminal enterprise, even poetry and literary criticism. Here at the Blue Mask, the overriding obsession was politics. Raesinia could hear a half dozen arguments in progress, overlapping and occasionally interrupting one another in a nonstop babble of voices.

"—the natural rights of man demand—"

"—you can't just *assume* equity. You've got to—"

"—don't give me 'natural rights.' I—"

"—Voulenne says—"

"—the parliament in Hamvelt resolved to do something about—"

"—Voulenne can suck my cock, and so can you—"

Raesinia breathed this atmosphere in with the air of a creature returning to its natural environment, or a man surfacing after a long dive. A few patrons noticed her, and waved or shouted inaudibly in her direction. She waved back and threw herself into the throng, working her way past the crowded tables and stepping nimbly out of the way of wildly gesticulating limbs.

Here and there a catcall followed her, but she was used to that. Barely one in a hundred University students was female, and while the ratio was somewhat redressed by visitors who didn't actually attend the school, Old Street still felt like the eye of a raging storm of indiscriminate masculine humors. When she first came here, Raesinia had taken such things personally, but she'd since come to understand they were more of an automatic reaction, like dogs barking at one another when they meet in the park.

At the rear of the common room was a flimsy door, leading to a short corridor off which there were a number of dining rooms where one could talk with at least the illusion of privacy. Raesinia headed for these and knocked twice on the second door along. Inside, a barely audible conversation was suddenly silenced.

"Who is it?" someone said, a bit muffled.

"It's me."

The door opened, slowly.

"We ought to have a secret knock," someone said from inside. "It's not a proper conspiracy without a secret knock. I feel stupid just shouting, 'Who is it?'"

"You and your secret knocks," someone else said. "And codes and signals with dark lanterns and God knows what else. If you had your way we'd spend all day memorizing the damned things and never have time to get anything done."

"I just think it adds tone, is all. You wouldn't catch Orlanko's people just shouting, 'Who's there?' through the damned door—"

"Raes!"

Something small and fast-moving hit Raesinia around the midriff, and a pair of arms locked behind her and made a spirited effort to squeeze the air from her lungs. For Raesinia this was actually not much of a handicap, but she staggered under the impact of the ballistic hug and had to throw an arm against the doorway for support. She hoped that Sothe, no doubt watching from somewhere, would not conclude that she was under attack and charge in with guns blazing.

"You did it!" her assailant squealed. "You did it, you did it, you did it! It worked!"

"Did I?" Raesinia managed, in a croak.

"Cora," someone said, "I think Raes might be in a better state to appreciate the news if you let her breathe."

"Sorry."

Cora detached herself reluctantly, like a barnacle peeling away from a ship's hull. She still had to look up to meet Raesinia's eyes, but only just. Cora was fourteen, with the gangly, broad-shouldered frame of a girl still growing like a weed. She had straw-colored hair bound back in a thick ponytail and a face that looked like the site of a pitched battle between freckles and acne. She had a tendency to bounce on the balls of her feet when she was excited, and she was bouncing now, her green eyes blazing.

"And close the door," Faro said, from the direction of the sofa. "Unless you want to share our secrets with everybody in the common room. Honestly, you'd think that none of you had ever been part of a cabal before."

The back room was a bit cramped but cozy. The fireplace was cold and dead, but the night was quite warm enough already. The battered old sofa and chairs had been dragged from their ordinary positions into a rough circle. Faro had claimed the entire couch for himself, legs propped up on one arm and head hanging off at the other, upside down. It was a testament to Faro that he could make even this awkward position look graceful, if not particularly dignified. He was a slender youth, with short dark hair and a face like a hatchet, dressed in well-tailored gray velvet.

Behind him, Johann Maurisk—whom, for reasons Raesinia had never quite understood, everyone addressed by his family name—paced beside the window. He was as thin as Faro, but where Faro was lithe and graceful, Maurisk had the sunken-eyed look of a desert hermit. He was constantly in motion, walking back and forth, toying with his shirt or rapping out an unconscious rhythm on the windowsill with long, bony fingers.

Cora stepped back, took a deep breath, and made a visible effort to get control of herself.

"It worked!" she said. "I mean, I knew it would work, if everything went the way you said it would, but now everything has, and I'm having a hard time believing it. Do you have *any* idea what's going to happen when the markets open again on Monday?" She giggled. "The whole Exchange is going to be swimming in coffee beans! I know at least three firms that have been hoarding for months, waiting for bad news, and now I hear they're clearing out the warehouses. You won't be able to sell the stuff for two pennies a bushel!"

"I'm thinking of putting up nets below the Grand Span," Faro said. "We could fish the jumping bankers out of the river and go through their pockets."

Maurisk slapped the windowsill and turned to glare at Faro, who smiled back impishly. Maurisk appeared to completely lack a sense of humor, which left him ill at ease in Faro's company.

"I take it the news has reached the market, then?" Raesinia said.

"This afternoon," Cora said. "We saw De Borg himself strutting about like the top peacock, rubbing everyone's faces in it."

"And we did well?"

Cora gaped, made speechless by this colossal understatement. Faro, grinning upside down and head lolling like a corpse, said, "Quite well, apparently. I don't pretend to understand the specifics of it, but I gather we've just about hit the jackpot."

"It's not *that* complicated," Cora protested. "I bought De Borg's paper at ten pence, on a ninety-five-point margin, and as of close today it was back to par. After fees and so on, that gives us a return of about a hundred and eighty to one."

Truth be told, Raesinia didn't follow the specifics, either, but she trusted Cora's assessment. *She's a prodigy, after all.* That last number made her sit up and take notice, though. Raesinia was no financier, but she could multiply, and a hundred and eighty to one meant that the little pool of money their circle had laboriously accumulated had been transformed overnight, as if by alchemy, into a substantial fortune.

"I'm not really recommending it," Faro said, "just throwing the idea out, really, but you realize that we *could* just take the money and run. Go to Hamvelt and live like princes for the rest of our days." He looked around the room, from Maurisk's burning eyes to Raesinia's guarded ones, and sighed. "Fair enough. I'm just saying."

"It's not about the money," Raesinia said.

"Of course it's not about the money," Maurisk said. "I've always said money is only a distraction. We should be out there"—he stabbed a finger at the window—"raising the awareness of the common—"

Faro laughed and slid off the couch like a cat, landing in a crouch and rolling his shoulders before straightening up.

"I think awareness is not our problem," he said. "Everyone is perfectly *aware* of what's going on. They just don't see anything they can do about it."

"Then we need to tell them—" Maurisk began.

"In any case," Raesinia said, raising her voice before the usual argument could get started, "we're on our way."

"We certainly are," Faro said. "Though God knows to where." He slapped his thighs. "This calls for a drink, I'd say. Let me go and get something."

He went out, and Raesinia turned to Maurisk. "What about Ben and the doctor? Are we expecting them?"

"Not tonight," he said, with a glower. "They're in Newtown. Reconnaissance, Ben calls it, though he wouldn't tell me what he's expecting to find."

Cora waggled her eyebrows and gave a lewd giggle, and Maurisk snorted. This was a joke; neither of the last two members of their cabal was likely to be found in any of the South Bank's notorious brothels.

"Well, I've got news. I suppose we can fill them in later." Raesinia paused as the door opened and Faro returned, with two bottles under each arm. "I've had word from my contact at the palace."

"Oh?" Cora perked up. "Anything I can take to the Exchange?"

"I'm . . . not sure. The king is going to name Count Mieran to the Ministry of Justice."

There was a pause. Faro uncorked one of the bottles and started setting up mugs on a side table.

"This is the same Count Yonas or some such who has been smiting the heathens so heroically in Khandar?"

Raesinia nodded. "Count Janus bet Vhalnich Mieran."

"And what do we know about him?" Maurisk said.

"Not much," Raesinia admitted. "But there's no love lost between him and Orlanko."

"That's got to be good for us, then," Cora said. "The enemy of my enemy, and all that."

"I don't know," Faro said. "I've found that most of the time the enemy of your enemy can be relied on to stick a dagger in your back while you're busy with the first fellow."

"We'll see soon enough," Maurisk said. "It's Giforte who really matters. If Count Mieran puts someone new in as head of the Armsmen, it'll tell us a bit about what he plans. If he promotes Giforte instead—"

"Then I'll drink another toast," Faro said. "Giforte is a crusty old fart with more breeding than brains. Not that there's any shortage of such around His Majesty."

"Long may he reign," Cora said, and the others echoed her automatically.

"Here," Faro said. "Better to do that with wine in hand."

Maurisk glared at him while Faro distributed the mugs, then looked up at Raesinia.

"Was there anything else?" he said. Maurisk was a teetotaler, yet another point of contention between him and the hard-drinking Faro.

"Not at the moment," Raesinia said, accepting a mug herself.

Maurisk's habitual scowl deepened. "Then I will say good evening."

He went for the door, dodging Faro's attempt to offer him a mug, and let it bang closed behind him. Faro stared after him for a moment, giving his best impression of an abandoned puppy, then laughed and turned back to the others. "And I will say good riddance." He took a long sip from his mug and swallowed thoughtfully. "Honestly, Raes, what possessed you to bring him into this?"

"He's smart, and he believes in taking the country back from Orlanko," Raesinia said. "And he takes it seriously." She brought the mug to her lips.

The wine was actually rather good, Raesinia thought. In spite of its run-down appearance, the Blue Mask kept a good cellar. The unwashed floors and ratty furniture were a deliberate affectation, an act; situated as it was on prime real estate beside the University, the rent on the Mask was probably higher than many noble town houses.

An act. Raesinia stared into the depths of her mug, letting the conversation drift around her. Faro talked enough for three, anyway, pretending to flirt with Cora and laughing hugely at his own jokes.

It's all an act. Raesinia Smith was an affectation, just like the Blue Mask. So, for that matter, was Raesinia Orboan, the delicate, empty-headed princess she played at Ohnlei whenever formal ceremonies demanded it. She might have been real, once, but she'd died four years ago, coughing her lungs out in a bed stinking of piss and vomit. What had risen from that bed was . . . something else, an imposter.

She felt the binding twitch, ever so slightly. It wouldn't let her get drunk—she suspected it saw the inebriated state as a problem to be corrected like any other. Once, as an experiment, Sothe had procured a gallon of potent but awful liquor and Raesinia had downed the lot in a single sitting. All it had produced was a powerful need to visit the toilet.

There were only three people in Vordan who knew what kind of creature lurked underneath her masks. One was Raesinia herself, and another was Sothe, whom she had come to trust with her life. The third was the Last Duke, Mallus Kengire Orlanko. It was Orlanko who had intervened when Raesinia ought to have died. He'd called in his backers, Sworn Church priests in black cloaks and glass masks, and they had done *something.*

At the time, Raesinia hadn't appreciated the brilliance of it. Now she understood all too well. The king had no sons, not since Vansfeldt, so what better way to keep the future queen under your thumb? Let even a whisper of the truth escape—that the princess was cursed, damned, not even human—and the mobs would be howling for her head, with every priest in the city egging them on. When the king died . . .

Long may he reign. Raesinia took a pull from her mug. But he wouldn't; anyone could see that. Already the city lived in fear of the duke's Concordat, and the tax farmers squeezed the common folk to pay the Crown's debt to Viadre. When her father died, Raesinia would ascend the throne, but Orlanko would be king in all but name. His northern allies would come seeking their rewards, and no doubt Raesinia would find herself married to some Murnskai prince, while Borelgai profiteers looted the kingdom and Sworn Priests burned the Free Churches.

And so Raesinia Smith had built her little conspiracy, step by step, lying to everyone. The depth of her betrayals—not telling Cora and the others who she really was, breaking her father's confidences—roiled her stomach, but there was no other option. If Orlanko found out she wasn't the empty-headed, pliable princess he thought she was . . .

Cora laughed, and Faro grinned. Raesinia looked away from them and stared down into her mug. *It's not a betrayal, not really. We all want the same thing.* Power in Vordan for the Vordanai, and the end of the Last Duke. No more tax farmers, no more Borelgai bankers muscling honest merchants into poverty. No more disappearances in the night and mysterious bodies floating in the river. No more screams from the depths of the Vendre.

It was the right thing to do. She knew it was. Even Father would understand that, wouldn't he?

Chapter Two

MARCUS

"By the third day, we were pretty much used up, and those big naval guns were knocking the place to pieces around our ears," Marcus said. "If the colonel hadn't turned up when he did, I doubt we could have held on until nightfall. Even as it was, things got pretty heated. I had to go out myself—"

He stopped. *And Adrecht saved my life, and lost his arm.* Adrecht, his best friend, who had later tried to kill him, and who was now a set of slowly bleaching bones somewhere in the Great Desol. *Along with quite a few others.*

Count Torahn, Minister of War, knew none of this. His jowly face was alight with vicarious martial excitement. "Splendid, Captain. Absolutely splendid. Have you thought about writing up your experiences in the campaign? Colonel Vhalnich will submit his official report, of course, but it's important to have as many perspectives on the thing as possible. I'm sure the *Review* would jump at the chance if you did them a little monograph."

Marcus tried not to grimace. "Thank you, sir. I think Giv—uh, Captain Stokes was trying his hand at writing something about it when I left." He didn't add that Give-Em-Hell's memoir, titled *Across the Desert with Bloodied Saber,* seemed to be turning into more of an epic than a monograph.

"Wonderful. I look forward to reading it," Torahn said. He glanced over his shoulder. "I've always said that a properly led Vordanai force should be a match for any army in the world, eh?"

This last was directed at the other end of the little anteroom. Duke Mallus Kengire Orlanko sat in an armchair, stubby legs barely reaching the ground, flipping idly through an enormous leather-bound ledger. He looked up, spectacles catching the light from the candles and becoming two circles of pure light.

"Indeed, Torahn," he said. "You have certainly always said so. Now if only our soldiers could learn to walk on water, the world would truly be within our grasp."

It was hard for Marcus to believe that this was the infamous Last Duke, Minister of Information and master of the dreaded Concordat. He looked more like somebody's cheerful old grandpa, at least until he turned those oversized lenses in Marcus' direction. Then his magnified, distorted eyes became visible, and they seemed to belong to some other person altogether. Not a person, even. Eyes like that belonged on something that lived at the bottom of the sea and never ventured out of the shadows.

You sent Jen to me. Marcus matched the duke's gaze as levelly as he knew how. *You sent her and told her to do whatever she needed to do.*

He'd always known Jen had worked for the Concordat, but somehow he'd allowed himself to believe—*What? That she could fall in love with me?* At the very least, he'd thought she'd finally been honest with him. Then, that awful night in a cavern full of monsters, she'd thrown it all back in his face and revealed herself to be something much more than a simple agent. *Ignahta Sempria*, the Penitent Damned, the demonic assassins serving an order of the Church that was supposed to have disappeared more than a hundred years ago.

Marcus had tried to kill her, in the end, but Jen had brushed aside his best efforts. Only Ihernglass, in some way that Marcus still didn't understand, had been able to use the power of the Thousand Names to bring her down. When he'd left Khandar, she still hadn't awoken, and Janus wasn't sure she ever would.

"Are you certain?" she had said. "Are you—"

Count Torahn was saying something, but Marcus had missed it entirely. He smiled at the Minister of War and wondered how to politely ask him to repeat himself, but a click from the door saved him the embarrassment. Janus slipped quietly out of the king's bedchamber.

"Well," the Last Duke said. "I take it congratulations are in order."

Count Colonel Janus bet Vhalnich Mieran bowed formally. For his visit to the Royal Palace he'd put on a formal uniform Marcus had never seen him wear before, a cross between his usual blues and something more appropriate for a courtier. It included a long, thin cape, which fluttered elegantly as he moved, and was trimmed in the bloodred and Vordanai blue that were his personal colors as Count Mieran. In his ordinary dress blues, giltless and patchy from repeated washing, Marcus felt like a beggar by comparison.

"Thank you, Your Grace," Janus said. "I will do my utmost to be of service to His Majesty."

"Gave it to you after all, did he?" Torahn said. "I argued against it, you know. Nothing against you personally, you understand, but it didn't seem a proper post for a military man. I'd hoped to use you elsewhere. Still, I suppose the king knows best."

"I'm sure he does," Janus said.

Marcus felt as if he'd come to class to find everyone else had studied for a test he didn't know was on the schedule. Janus, as usual, had explained nothing, either during the uncomfortable journey or since they'd arrived at Ohnlei. He must have been able to see the confusion in Marcus' face now, however, and he took pity on his subordinate.

"The king has honored me with his trust," Janus said. "He has named me to the cabinet as Minister of Justice, to oversee the courts and the Armsmen."

There was a shuffling sound from one corner. Representatives of all three of the organizations tasked with protecting the king's safety were on hand, standing at attention so quietly that Marcus had nearly forgotten they were there. There was a sergeant from the Noreldrai Grays, big and imposing in his dark uniform and tall cap, and an impeccably uniformed grenadier from the Royal Guard. In addition, there was an Armsman, in a somewhat more ornate version of the dark green uniform worn by these officers of the law. At Janus' words, he had stiffened up and saluted.

"Speaking of the Armsmen," Orlanko said, as Janus nodded and signaled for the guard to relax, "their captaincy is vacant at the moment. If you'd like, I can have my people prepare dossiers on some suitable candidates. I believe Vice Captain Giforte has been serving in that role since the previous minister's passing, but he—"

"Thank you, Your Grace," Janus interjected, "but that will not be necessary. My choice is an easy one. Captain d'Ivoire will assume the post."

"He will?" Orlanko's magnified eyes shifted.

"I will?" Marcus said.

He looked at Janus and caught a flick of his eyes. Marcus didn't have Fitz Warus' effortless ability to understand his superior's unspoken commands, but he was slowly getting the knack of reading the colonel's expressions. This one said, *Later.*

"A good idea," Torahn said. "That's the trouble with the Armsmen these days. Too many layabouts at the bottom, too many lawyers at the top! A good, honest soldier will shake things up a bit. And you could hardly do better than the captain here."

Marcus wasn't foolish enough to believe that the Minister of War had taken *that* much of a liking to him in their few minutes of conversation. This was another salvo aimed at Orlanko. Marcus felt like a fisherman rowing between two foreign men-of-war, caught in a conflict he understood next to nothing about, crouching to keep his head beneath the gunwales as broadsides flashed back and forth overhead. Whether this one had hit the mark, he had no idea, but Orlanko brushed it aside.

"I'm sure the captain will do a fine job." The Last Duke closed his ledger and heaved himself onto his feet. "And now I must be going. You may rely on my people, of course, for any information your new duties may require." He gave a very slight bow. "I look forward to working with you, Count Mieran."

"Likewise, Your Grace," Janus said. "Your Excellency, if you will excuse me as well. I have much to do."

"Of course," Torahn said, then wagged a finger genially. "Don't think this gets you out of writing me a proper report!"

"I wouldn't dream of it," Janus said. "Come, Captain."

The Armsman beside the door saluted again as they passed. The anteroom let onto a corridor leading out the back of the king's suite, opposite the much larger entrance to his formal audience chambers. Like all the hallways at Ohnlei, it had been decorated within an inch of its life, in this case with a pattern of tiny bas-relief eagles whose eyes were tiny, sparkling mirrors. Candles flickered in cleverly concealed braziers.

"Sir—" Marcus began.

"Jikat," Janus said quietly.

This was a word in Khandarai, of which there were probably only three speakers within a hundred miles. It was an ancient and expressive language. The word "jikat" meant "quiet," but more than that. A literal translation might read "the silence we observe in the presence of our enemies."

Enemies? Marcus said nothing.

"Back to our rooms," Janus said. "Everything should be ready by now."

The invisible, omnipresent administrative apparatus of Ohnlei—the *true* rulers of the kingdom, Marcus sometimes suspected—had assigned Janus and his staff to a cottage not far from the palace, on one of the many curving gravel roads that wandered through the grounds like a plate of dropped noodles. "Cottage," in this context, referred to a two-story stone-and-timber building, elegantly appointed and self-sufficient in the matters of kitchens, baths, and so on, with its own staff and caretakers. This one was called Lady Farnese's Cottage. Marcus had gathered that the kings of Vordan were in the habit of building these little houses for their friends, mistresses, and favorite courtiers, and once these original inhabitants died or fell from favor, they were repurposed as housing for guests of the court.

Small squads of Noreldrai Grays patrolled the grounds, mostly for the look of the thing, but they were met at the front door of Lady Farnese's Cottage by a pair of soldiers in an unfamiliar uniform, cut like a Royal Army outfit but with the same red-on-blue trimmings Janus was wearing. Marcus guessed that these must be men in direct service to Janus in his capacity as Count Mieran, and this impression was shortly confirmed. One of the pair, a lieutenant by his shoulder stripe, stepped forward and saluted, and Janus made the introductions.

"Captain, this is Lieutenant Medio bet Uhlan, of the First Mierantai Volunteers. Lieutenant, Captain Marcus d'Ivoire, lately of the First Colonial Infantry."

"Honored, sir," said Uhlan, speaking with a gravelly upcountry accent. He was a young man, clean-shaven and handsome, with a crispness to his stance and salute that Marcus found depressingly keen. "Thank you for taking such good care of the young master."

"For the most part it was him taking care of me," Marcus said. "But it's good to meet you in any case."

"You've made the preparations as I asked?" Janus said.

"Yes, my lord." Uhlan saluted again. "Everything is in readiness."

"Good. Let's go inside."

The cottage had a serviceable parlor, suitable for entertaining guests, and another pair of Mierantai guards stood at attention as they entered. When Uhlan shut the door behind them, leaving his companion on guard outside, Janus gave a small, contented sigh.

"Here, I think, we may speak freely." He glanced at Marcus. "The Last Duke knows everything that goes on in the palace, so you should always assume you are being overheard. The same holds for most of the rest of Ohnlei. We're only a mile from the Cobweb, after all, and he'd be a poor spider if he didn't know what was going on in his own lair."

"But not here?"

"Here Lieutenant Uhlan and his men will keep watching for stray eyes and ears. They've already swept the house for hidey-holes—did you find any, by the by?"

"Yes, my lord," Uhlan said. "One trapdoor and a tunnel through the foundation, and a spot outside where the moldings make a sort of ladder leading to a way in through the roof. We've closed them both, as you instructed."

"And the staff?"

Uhlan grimaced. "It took some argument before they agreed that you could provide your own household, but we managed. I've sent to Mieranhal for our people, but it will be a few days before they arrive."

"Mieran County is too remote and too insular for our friend Orlanko to infiltrate easily," Janus said to Marcus. "I thought it best to import a few people we know we can trust."

Marcus didn't feel quite so blasé about it, but if Janus wanted to trust in Uhlan and his crew, he had little choice but to do likewise. He nodded.

"Where's Lieutenant Ihernglass?" Janus said.

"Upstairs," Uhlan said. "And asleep, I believe."

"Just as well. It's been a long journey, and I won't need him until tomorrow." He gestured at an armchair. "Sit, Captain. Lieutenant, would you ask Augustin to bring us some refreshments?"

"Of course, my lord."

Marcus settled himself into the chair, wincing at a protest from his lower back. It was a legacy of the hell-for-leather carriage ride from the coast, two days of misery in a jolting, bouncing wooden box, trying valiantly to hold on to his lunch.

It had, indeed, been a long journey. Preparations had been under way to bring the entirety of the First Colonials back to Vordan, but when Janus had received the news of the king's illness, he hadn't wanted to wait. He'd commandeered the fastest ship in the harbor by the simple expedient of asking the captain how much gold it would take to convince him to dump his current passengers and cargo and make for Vordan, then offering him half again as much for the quickest passage he could manage. The ship, a sleek Vheedai frigate, had made the run in less than half the time it had taken the lumbering transports on the way out, at the cost of running full-sailed through a blow Marcus had been certain was going to sink them.

Then, instead of turning west for the mouth of the Vor and the slow plod upriver to the capital, the colonel had led them ashore at Essyle and paid another hefty sum to arrange a stagecoach. Riders galloped ahead of them, bearing instructions to have fresh horses ready and waiting, and so the wheels of the coach had barely stopped turning from the coast to the capital. Even the famous Vordanai mail coaches didn't run by night, but Janus had paid for spare drivers as well as spare horses, and the broad highway of the Green Road was smooth enough to traverse by torchlight. As a result of all this effort, their little party had covered the three hundred miles from Essyle to the outskirts of Vordan City in a bit more than thirty-six hours, which Marcus was certain had to be some kind of record.

The few hours of sleep he'd managed to snatch between their arrival and the royal summons had not made up for the previous few days, and Marcus couldn't blame Lieutenant Ihernglass for taking the opportunity to rest. He himself found the overstuffed armchair dangerously comfortable, but a certain anxiety kept him from drifting off. Janus favored him with one of his flickering smiles.

"I imagine you have questions, Captain? I'm sorry I couldn't explain earlier. It wouldn't do to tip our hand."

"I can think of a few," Marcus admitted. "What did the king say to you? And what did you mean about making me head of the Armsmen? You know I don't know the first thing about running a city—"

Janus held up a hand. "Let me begin at the beginning. I believe I've had the opportunity to explain that Duke Orlanko and I do not always see eye to eye?"

"I'd gathered that, yes."

"Our success has placed him in a difficult position," Janus said, with another half smile. "He doesn't know what happened in the temple. All he knows is that his gambit to obtain the Thousand Names and to destroy me has failed, and that his assassin has not returned. At the same time, the victory has given me a certain popularity with the commons as well as favor with the king and the Minister of War."

"I can see how that would vex him." Janus had yet to explain just what was so damned important about the set of ancient steel plates he called the Thousand Names. Having gotten a glimpse of the world of demonic magic firsthand, Marcus wasn't certain he wanted to know.

"Indeed. However, by returning without the rest of the Colonials, I have placed myself at a disadvantage. Apart from you, Lieutenant Ihernglass, and Lieutenant Uhlan and his men, there is no one in the city I can fully trust.

Whereas for Orlanko this is his home ground, mapped and quartered, and he can call on legions of informants and all the power of the Concordat."

Marcus frowned. "In that case, why the damned hurry to get here? We could have taken the transports with the rest of the Colonials."

"Unfortunately, waiting that long would mean giving away the game before it began."

Janus sat back in his chair as Augustin entered, bearing a tray with a teapot and cups. The sight of the old manservant reminded Marcus of how much he missed his own adjutant, Fitz Warus. He'd been forced to agree when Janus suggested that Fitz be left behind to supervise the transfer and loading of the Colonials; Val had command by seniority while Marcus was away, and that kind of organizational detail had never been his strong suit.

When he was equipped with a steaming cup of tea, Janus continued. "You know the king is very ill."

"You told me he was dying."

"He is, though that is not yet widely known. When he dies—which cannot be long delayed, I'm afraid—the crown passes to the princess royal."

Marcus accepted his own cup from Augustin, ignoring the man's faint scowl. Augustin had never approved of his master's putting so much trust in Marcus.

"All right," he said. "So Raesinia becomes queen."

"It's been more than three hundred years since Vordan has had a queen regnant, and we've never had one so young. Things are going to be . . . unsettled."

"From the sound of it," Marcus said, "the Last Duke has matters well in hand."

"That is exactly the point," Janus said. "There is considerable unrest in the city. Orlanko is not well liked."

"Nobody likes the man who has to crack heads to keep order," Marcus said, omitting for the moment the fact that Janus proposed to put him in exactly that position. "And there's usually someone willing to cause trouble whenever an excuse comes up. I remember the riots after Vansfeldt."

"This may go beyond mere rioting. There are plans for full-scale insurrection."

Marcus snorted. "You can't be serious. We haven't had a real revolution since Farus IV and the Purge."

"Times are changing, Captain. How long has it been since you've spent time in the city?"

Marcus reckoned backward, and felt suddenly old. He could remember leaving home for the last time, waving to his little sister as his carriage lurched into motion, the familiar old house vanishing around the corner . . .

He clamped down hard on that line of thought, before it could lead him into familiar darkness. "Not since I left for the College, I suppose. Nineteen years."

"Since Vansfeldt, things have been different. After the end of the war, Orlanko all but threw in his lot with the Borelgai, and their influence has only grown since then. Borelgai merchants rule the Exchange, Borelgai bankers run the Treasury, and Borelgai Sworn Church priests preach on the streets. There is nothing that so arouses a people as an infestation of foreigners." Janus raised an eyebrow. "As you and I have good reason to know."

Marcus grinned wryly. "Fair enough. Nobody likes the Borels. How does that lead to revolution?"

"Nobody believes that Raesinia will be able to rule in her own right. When she takes the throne, it will be Orlanko who takes power. And as far as the people are concerned, that means the Borelgai will have finally completed the conquest they began ten years ago. Rising against the rightful king is one thing. Rising against a queen perceived as a foreign puppet is quite another."

"I hate to seem callous," Marcus said, "but what of it? If all this is true, Orlanko must be well prepared by now."

"Indeed. In fact, I'm certain he's planning on it. The revolt will be bloodily suppressed, and the subsequent crackdown will cement his control. Then there will be no stopping him." Janus cocked his head. "You see now why we had to hurry? If the king had died while we were en route, we would have arrived too late to take a hand in matters."

"Balls of the Beast," Marcus swore. "No offense intended, Colonel, but I'm not sure I *want* to take a hand in matters. You make it sound like Vordan is as bad as Ashe-Katarion, and you remember how that turned out. Maybe we should have stayed in Khandar."

"That might have been an option for you, Captain, but not for me. If Orlanko consolidates his power, he will have no more reason to fear me. A mere ocean would not be enough to blunt his reach." Janus did not appear particularly discomfited by this thought, but Marcus thought of Jen, glowing with coruscating, unnatural power, and shuddered. "Besides," Janus went on, "I have a duty to my king, and my future queen."

"So, what did the king tell you? Giving you Justice when there's going to be fighting in the streets seems like setting you up for disaster."

"Fortunately, the situations are not exactly analogous," Janus said. "The king has always been aware of Orlanko's ambitions, of course. He asked me to serve as a counterweight on the Cabinet. To protect Raesinia, and try to ensure that she gets a genuine chance to rule in her own right."

"He doesn't ask for much, does he?" Marcus muttered.

"He's desperate," Janus said. "And he knows that Orlanko has ways of getting to even the best people. He needed someone who already had the Last Duke's enmity. The fact that our victory in Khandar has gained us something of a reputation is all to the good."

"All right," Marcus said. "Fair enough. So, what's the plan?"

"I'm still working on it," Janus said, with another fast smile.

"What?"

"We've been here less than a day, Captain. All my information is weeks old. It will take time to receive new reports from my sources, and more time to formulate a course of action."

"Wonderful," Marcus growled.

"One thing is for certain, however. We must discover the depth of the connection between the duke and the Priests of the Black. That may shed light on . . . a great many things."

Are you certain? she'd said. Marcus nodded slowly. "How?"

"Putting you at the Armsmen was the first step. The more friends we have among the city authorities, the better."

"Making me captain doesn't put the Armsmen in your pocket," Marcus said. "Not if we're talking about fighting in the streets. When both sides wear the same uniform, the chain of command can get a little . . . confused." An image of Adrecht came to him, scared and defiant, clutching the flap of his empty sleeve.

"Of course. And I have no doubt the Armsmen are liberally salted with Concordat agents. But you will do what you can. In the meantime, you will have the legal authority to investigate the activities of the Black Priests, once we uncover them."

"Do you think that's likely? With Orlanko's backing, I imagine they'll be well hidden."

"I have a lead that may prove fruitful. You get accustomed to your new command, and I will do what I can. For the moment, I suggest you get some sleep. A rest in a real bed will do wonders for your disposition."

After all this, Marcus thought, *I'd better learn to sleep with one eye open.*

"Before you do," Janus said, sipping his tea thoughtfully, "you might wake Lieutenant Ihernglass. I would like to have a word with him."

WINTER

She awoke from a warm, jumbled mess of a dream. The feel of a body pressed against her, soft skin, fever-hot, and delicate fingers running across her. Lips pressed against hers, hesitantly at first, then with mounting enthusiasm. Hot breath against her neck, her hands running through long red hair, spiky with the sweat of their exertions. Green eyes, boring into her like daggers.

Jane. Winter groaned, half-awake, and opened her eyes. The air was stuffy and smelled of dust, and she lay in the peculiar semidarkness of a room with heavy curtains drawn against the daylight. The bed underneath her was titanic and sinfully soft, and she was surrounded by a nest of silk pillows. The one beneath her head was damp with sweat.

Ever since that horrible day at the Desoltai temple, she'd traded one set of nightmares for another, though. The new ones had begun as a vague feeling of confinement, of being trapped in darkness while distant voices droned on and on. On the journey from Khandar, they'd gradually sharpened until she could nearly make out the words. She knew, somehow, that these visions welled up from the pit of her being, where the thing Janus had called Infernivore slumbered like a quiescent predator digesting its meal.

Dreams of Jane were almost a relief, a familiar ache in her chest. Jane, whom she'd fallen in love with and then abandoned to an awful fate. Whose memory she'd fled across a thousand miles of ocean to escape.

And now I'm back. Under a different name, wearing a different identity, but . . .

The knock at the door came as something of a relief. Winter tried to sit up, but the deep feather bed thwarted her efforts, and she ended up half rolling, half flopping until she got to the edge. The knock repeated.

"Lieutenant Ihernglass?"

It was Captain d'Ivoire. Winter managed to escape from her mattress, kicked off the ensnaring sheet, and got to her feet.

"I'm awake," she said. "Just one moment."

There was a full-length mirror in one corner, a luxury she'd rarely had in Khandar. Winter went through an automatic self-examination to confirm that her male disguise was intact. While Janus knew the truth of her gender, Captain d'Ivoire did not, and there would be servants and guards as well. She found that she was still wearing her uniform, though a couple of buttons had come loose as she tossed and turned. Apparently she had barely managed to get her boots off before collapsing.

She fixed the buttons, adjusted her collar, and tugged a bit at her cuffs. Once she felt reasonably presentable, she went to the door. Doors with proper latches—that was something else to get used to. Khandarai mostly made do with curtains.

Captain d'Ivoire was waiting in the corridor. There were dark circles under his eyes, and Winter sent up a silent prayer of thanks that the colonel had let her sleep. D'Ivoire looked about ready to fall over.

"He wants you," the captain said. No need to specify who "'he" was. "Downstairs, in the parlor."

"Yessir."

"If he needs me, I'll be over"—he gestured vaguely toward the doors to the other bedrooms—"there. Somewhere."

"Yessir."

He staggered off. Winter stepped out into the hall and shut the door behind her, looking around curiously. She hadn't gotten much more than a cursory look at the cottage when they came in, tired as she'd been. Now, making her way down the stairs, she let its fundamental *weirdness* sink in. It was huge, ceilings far higher than necessary and corridors far broader, and what wall space wasn't occupied by vast paintings was taken up by glass-shielded braziers, ablaze with candles even in the middle of the day. The art was mostly moody, sweeping landscapes, with the occasional nautical scene thrown in for variety, all set in fantastically carved gilt frames. The carpet underfoot was thicker and softer than her army-issue bedroll.

The only place she'd ever been that was anything like this was the palace in Ashe-Katarion, and that had been partially burned and entirely looted before she'd gotten there. The orphanage she'd grown up in—Mrs. Wilmore's Prison for Young Ladies, as the inmates had referred to it—had once been a noble's country house, but any vestiges of luxury had been obliterated by decades of careful effort on Mrs. Wilmore's part. The casual opulence on display *here* took her breath away.

She could hardly believe they were actually at Ohnlei. The Royal Palace and its grounds had always seemed semimythical to her, like the heavens the Khandarai believed were somewhere up among the clouds. The stories of the king and its other inhabitants had felt no more real than those same heathen myths. The idea that it was a physical place that you could simply drive to in a carriage was something she was still getting used to.

The parlor was a large room downstairs with no obvious function, containing a couple of bookshelves, a fireplace, several armchairs and a sofa, and a few fussy little tables. Janus sat in one of the chairs, feet propped up on an ottoman, reading from a thick sheaf of paper. He looked up as Winter entered.

"Ah," he said. "Lieutenant. You rested well, I hope?"

"Very well, sir." After weeks aboard ship and days in a rattling coach, just lying *still* felt like an unimaginable luxury. "Captain d'Ivoire asked me to tell you that he's gone to bed."

"Just as well. It's been an exhausting day for everyone." Though if exhaustion had any effect on Janus himself, it didn't show in his face. "Have a seat."

Winter settled herself cautiously into the chair opposite Janus, and Augustin glided in with tea.

"I should start out by telling you the same thing I told the captain," Janus said. "At Ohnlei, the walls quite literally have ears. You should always assume you're going to be overheard. I've brought down some of my own men from Mieran County, men I trust, and so this cottage is probably secure for the moment. You may speak of anything *relating to our mission*."

He hit the last few words with peculiar emphasis, and his gray eyes drilled into Winter. She took his meaning easily enough. *"Men I trust," eh?* She supposed that trusting someone not to betray your confidence was one thing, and trusting him with the secret of the Thousand Names—and Winter's involvement with it—was quite another.

"I . . . understand, sir." She paused. "What *is* our mission here?"

"Much the same as it was in Khandar, at some level. The king has appointed me Minister of Justice."

Winter wasn't sure how to respond to that, so she decided to play it safe. "Congratulations, sir."

"Thank you, Lieutenant," Janus said politely. "But I fear the problem it presents is considerable. The city is close to the boiling point, and getting closer as the king's health worsens. I am expected to ride herd on it with no time to prepare, and no way to know who among my subordinates may be working for my . . . enemies."

This last, again, carried more than its surface meaning. As far as Vordanai politics was concerned, Janus was opposed by Duke Orlanko and his allies, but only Winter and a few others knew it went deeper than that. The revelation of the true nature of Jen Alhundt had shown that there were more sinister forces at work. Feor, the Khandarai priestess Winter had rescued from the Redeemer cult, had called them the Black Priests.

"I understand, sir." Winter sipped her tea thoughtfully. "And I appreciate the difficulty."

"Accordingly, I'm afraid I will be leaning quite heavily on you and Captain d'Ivoire, at least until the rest of the Colonials arrive."

Bobby, Winter thought automatically. And Folsom, Graff, Feor, and the rest. Not to mention the nondescript wooden crates full of steel tablets, engraved with the secrets of centuries. "I'll help however I can, sir."

"I'm going to take you up on that," Janus said, with just a hint of a smile. "I have a task for you."

Something about his tone made Winter's skin crawl. *I'm not going to like this, and he knows it.* "A task, sir?"

"One of the primary centers of unrest in the city is the Southside Docks. There's a . . . society, you might call it, of dockworkers and other menials who have been responsible for an increasing number of violent incidents. They call themselves the Leatherbacks."

"I see," Winter said, though she didn't.

"The Armsmen have attempted to suppress this group, with no success. Much of the Docks is a rat's warren, difficult to penetrate and search, and the Leatherbacks enjoy the tacit support of the residents. The occasional arrest and, I may say, brutal example has not dampened their ardor. A more subtle approach is required."

"Subtle, sir?"

"Infiltration, Lieutenant. We need to know more about this group. Our friends at the Concordat claim to have placed several agents among them, but given the lack of success, we have to assume they are either withholding or deliberately falsifying the information they pass along. I need someone I can rely on."

"Someone—you mean *me*, sir?" Winter almost laughed out loud. "I'm sorry, but do you really think I would be able to blend in with a gang of burly dockworkers?"

"Ah, but I haven't told you the most interesting part," Janus said. His half smile returned, and he leaned forward in his chair. The bastard was enjoying this, Winter thought. "The Leatherbacks have an inner circle that appears to be composed entirely of women."

"What?" At first Winter was occupied trying to picture a band of revolutionary dockworkers taking orders from fishwives in skirts, so it was a moment before the real import of his words struck home. "*What?* Sir, you can't be serious!"

"You don't think you can pass as a woman?" Janus said, eyes flicking to the front door, where the guards were waiting. "I understand it's something you've done before."

"I don't . . . I mean . . ." Winter paused and sucked in a long breath. "Even if I could . . . pass as female, that doesn't mean I'll be able to just waltz in and join up! These women are all Southsiders, aren't they? I won't . . . look anything like them, sound like them, or anything!"

"I agree that you are not the spitting image of a fisherman's daughter," Janus said, eyes sparkling. "Fortunately, there is another way. In the district adjacent to the University, colorfully known as the Dregs, there is another center of unrest. The students are notorious for preferring talk to action, however, and now and then one of them gets fed up and crosses the river to join the Leatherbacks. I believe you could present yourself as one of these pilgrims quite easily, and it would provide a useful explanation of why you lack friends or connections."

"But . . ."

Winter couldn't say what she wanted to say. Not just because of the guards, who didn't know her secret, but because she had a hard time even putting it into words. *He wants me to . . . to put on a* dress *and walk down the street in broad daylight?* The notion filled her with a sort of instinctive revulsion, born of two years of terror at the thought of being *found out.* To just throw off that mask, after so long . . .

She swallowed hard. "I . . . appreciate the trust, sir. But I'm not sure I could do it."

"I appreciate that it's difficult for you. But you would be, after all, only putting on a disguise. Once the current crisis is surmounted, you can simply . . . take it off."

"I . . ."

"And I hope that *you* appreciate," Janus said, leaning forward in his chair, "how important this is. There is no one else I can trust with this. And when I say that the fate of the kingdom may rest on what we do in the next few days or weeks, understand that I am not simply being melodramatic."

Winter closed her eyes and said nothing. Her throat felt as if it had fused into a solid mass, blocking her breath.

"There's another thing," Janus said. "Before we left Khandar, you asked me for a favor. Locating an old friend of yours, I think."

"Jane." Winter's eyes opened. "Have you found her?"

"Not just yet. But I suspect we're on the right track."

"She's alive? She's not—"

"As far as we know." He held up a hand. "It may take some time. I just wanted you to know that I hadn't forgotten the matter."

Winter stared at the colonel's face, so apparently guileless, wearing a half smile that never touched his bottomless gray eyes. He would never stoop to anything so straightforward as an obvious quid pro quo, but the implication was clear enough. *Remember,* he was saying, *what I can do for you, when you think about what you will do for me.*

In the end, Winter reflected, not without some bitterness, what choice did she have? She'd saved Janus' life in Khandar twice over, but in doing so she'd placed herself at his mercy. There was nothing for it but to go along, and hope like hell he knew what he was doing.

"I can . . . try," Winter said, around the knot in her throat. "I still don't think they'll accept me, but if you want me to, I'll try."

"That's all I ask, of course," Janus murmured.

CHAPTER THREE

RAESINIA

One advantage of the palace's state of premourning was that it was considered normal for the princess not to emerge from her tower for long periods. Overcome with grief, obviously. Or so Raesinia had managed to convince Sothe, in any case. While her maid hurried back to Ohnlei to tell visitors that the princess was feeling unwell, Raesinia was able to walk the city in daylight for the first time in months. Sothe worried about leaving her alone, but as Raesinia pointed out, what could really happen to her?

Besides, she was spending the day in the company of Ben Cooper, and it was hard to imagine anything bad befalling her with him around. Ben was a tall young man with sandy hair, broad shoulders, and a lantern jaw, who looked a bit like a classical depiction of one of the more muscular saints who spent their time smiting the unrighteous. In addition to these physical attributes, nature had blessed him with a sunny, honest disposition and a strong sense of justice, which as far as Raesinia was concerned was about as good as hanging a giant "Kick Me" sign around his neck. Spending too much time around him made her feel intensely guilty, both because she had to lie about who she really was and from the puppy-dog eyes he directed at her whenever he thought she wasn't looking.

Her other companion was cut from a different cloth. Doctor-Scholar George Sarton looked as though he had been born to skulk under rocks. He was actually nearly as tall as Ben, but he made himself seem short by hunching his shoulders, walking with a strange, crabwise gait, and cringing whenever someone looked directly at him. He spoke with a helpless stammer that practically invited mockery. It was Ben who had recruited him, of course, recognizing in the miserable-looking medical student a remarkable mind waiting to be put to good use.

Faro completed their party, dressed in his usual gray and black and wearing a rapier as current fashion dictated. Raesinia wondered idly if he knew how to use the thing, or if there was even a blade inside the elegant chased-silver scabbard.

"And you still can't tell me what we're going to see?" Raesinia said to Ben.

"Don't want to prejudice you," Ben said. "I need to know if you see the same thing I do."

Raesinia shrugged. Truth be told, she was simply enjoying the freedom from the stuffy corridors of the palace. They were walking across Saint Parfeld Bridge, newest of the many spans over the Vor. It was a bright summer day, and the bridge offered expansive views in both directions, as well as a river breeze that cut through the July heat. Upstream, to Raesinia's left, she could see the spires of the University loom above its wooded hillsides on the north bank, and the low bulk of Thieves' Island lurking around a slight bend in the river like a smuggler's ship. Downstream were the enormous marble-faced arches of the Grand Span, and beyond that the endless fields of warehouses and brick tenements that faced the docks. The river was crowded with traffic in both direction, little water taxis driven by two or four burly oarsmen darting among the big, flat-bottomed cargo boats.

They had just walked through the Exchange, where the day's business was beginning to heat up. Ahead of them was Newtown, a perfectly regular grid of paved streets and imposing four-story brick cubes, whose original Rationalist design was now barely visible under the accumulated debris and damage of nearly a century of habitation. The broad, easy-to-traverse streets had been turned into a maze by a profusion of vendors, spontaneous outdoor cafés, and simple accumulations of trash. Something as simple as a stuck wagon could start the process—leave one in the street, and before the week was out, someone would be using it as a platform to sell oranges, while another enterprising merchant put up a cloth lean-to from the side to start a fortune-telling business and a poor mother tried to raise two children underneath. The looming facades of the apartment buildings were pitted and torn, half the facing bricks looted for building material or washed out in the rain, and plastered over with posters, notices, and painted slogans.

"This place gives me the creeps," said Faro. "It's the grid. It makes me feel like everyone has set up shop in a graveyard."

"It's l . . . l . . . logical," Sarton said. He was nearly always referred to as "Sarton" or "the doctor," but never "George." "Or it ought to be, if it were p . . . p . . . properly organized."

"Come on," Ben said. He led the way down the granite steps at the Newtown end of the bridge and into the chaotic swirl of traffic.

The first to accost them were the sellers of papers, pamphlets, and other ephemeral publications. These were mostly boys of eight or nine, who rushed about in enormous flocks toward whoever looked as though they had money and knew how to read. Densely printed sheets of newsprint, folded and emblazoned in one corner with a little caricature of the author for easy identification, could be had for a penny.

Raesinia passed by the Weeping Man, the Shouting Man, and the Kneeling Man, but much to Faro's annoyance she stopped and bought a copy of the Blacksmith's latest and one from the Hanged Man, who was always good for a laugh. The sight of her purse brought a new flood of pamphleteers, all shouting at the top of their lungs about the superiority of their product. She doubted any of the ragged street children could read what they were carrying, but it was a moot point, because she couldn't understand any of them in the cacophony.

Ben bought a couple of papers that were written by friends of his, and Sarton took a pamphlet full of new woodcuts of interesting vivisections. Faro, meanwhile, swatted any of the youngsters who got close to him, which provoked a whole gang of them to start tugging his clothes and trying to pinch him. They only veered off when some sharp-eyed scout spotted a two-horse coach coming over the bridge, and the others ran after him like a wheeling flock of starlings.

"Newspapers," Faro said bitterly. "Why they bother to print them is beyond me. Does anyone actually read the things?"

"You ought to be kinder," Ben said. "Most of them are on our side, after all."

"So they claim. I think they're just a pack of cowards."

Raesinia opened the Hanged Man's paper. A quarter of the sheet was a woodcut cartoon, entitled "Life at Ohnlei." On one side a Hamveltai doctor—recognizable as such by a ridiculously tiny short-brimmed hat—worked on a crowned, bedridden figure amid flying sprays of blood. At a table in the foreground was the instantly identifiable Duke Orlanko, short and round with huge spectacles, sitting in front of a plate of tiny, starved corpses with protruding ribs. He had one of them on his fork, inspecting it distastefully. Beside him stood Rackhil Grieg, angular and vulpine, with the caption HAVE TWO, YOUR GRACE. THEY'RE SO *SMALL* THESE DAYS.

In the background a rotund Borelgai with a fat drunkard's nose and a bristly beard had his pants around his ankles and was having his way with a weeping young woman in a circlet, who Raesinia supposed was meant to represent herself. It was not, she thought, a very good likeness. She passed the paper to Ben without comment, and he showed it to Faro.

"I'm not sure I'd call that cowardice," Ben said.

"It's easy enough to talk big when you're hiding in some basement and paying kids to sell this drivel in the streets," Faro said. "That's the kind of person who takes one smart step to the rear when the time comes to actually *do* something."

"Orlanko has sent publishers to the Vendre before," Ben said.

"When one of them does something so stupid he can't pretend to ignore it," Faro said. "The Last Duke is no fool. The easiest way to get people to pay attention to someone is to lock him up."

It's true, Raesinia reflected. Orlanko was no fool. *He only drags people off to the Vendre to make a statement.* If one of these papers made him angry, there would just be an . . . accident. Late night, wet bricks, another body floating in the river. Or else—and this was the possibility that gnawed at her—a man would go out for a walk and never come back. He'd end up in the Vendre, all right, but not in a tower cell where anybody would ever see him again. The dungeons under Vordan's most notorious prison were rumored to be both noisome and extensive. The thought of Concordat thugs in black leather cloaks turning up at the Blue Mask and dragging them away—dragging Cora away—made it hard for Raesinia to affect Ben's casual confidence, or Faro's studied nonchalance.

"Ben," she said, interrupting their argument, "what was it you wanted us to see?"

"Oh! This way." He pointed. "I only hope they're in the same place."

They walked along the grid, two streets down and one street over. Ben gently guided Sarton whenever they made a turn, since the medical student had become absorbed in his new reading material. Finally, they reached a place where two large streets crossed and made a little square, in the center of which a flat-bedded wagon had been parked to make an impromptu stage. It was surrounded by a crowd, mostly Newtowners in their ragged cotton trousers and coarse brown linen. There was a man on the stage in a black evening coat and three-cornered hat, cutting a dashing if somewhat antiquated figure. The people in the front rank of the crowd were shouting something at him, but Raesinia couldn't make it out from her position at the rear.

"So, what are we looking at?" said Faro.

Ben pointed. A sign on the edge of the stage read BARON DE BORNAIS' POTENT CURE-ALL, followed by a lot of smaller type listing the many afflictions this product was supposed to address. Faro followed Ben's gaze and rolled his eyes.

"Something wrong with you that you haven't told us about?" Faro said. "I think you might as well drink bathwater and call it a magic potion."

"Forget the potion," Ben said. "Listen to the sales pitch."

"It doesn't look like anything much so far," Faro said. "I hope you aren't suggesting we invest in this fellow. No offense, old buddy, but you should leave the market games to Cora—"

A murmur rippled through the crowd, followed by a respectful silence as the man on the stage—presumably de Bornais—began to speak. This in itself was odd, since in Raesinia's experience it was not in the nature of a crowd of Vordanai to listen quietly to anyone who wasn't actually a priest. De Bornais' presentation seemed to be pandering of a quite ordinary sort, which made it hard to explain the rapt attention.

"Ben . . . ," she said.

"Wait," Ben said. "This isn't it, not yet."

"—how many of you are sick?" de Bornais said. There was a wave of muttering from the crowd. "How many of you are afflicted? How many of you have the doctors given up on? How many of you can't afford to even visit the damned bloodsuckers?"

This last drew a louder rumble than the others, and de Bornais went with the theme. "I'm taking an awful risk coming here, ladies and gentlemen. They don't want you to hear about this, oh no. All those Borel cutters and the fancy robes up at the University"—he mimed a swishing, effeminate gait—"they would just about shit their britches if they heard about me. Might want to shut me up, I wouldn't wonder. Because what I have here . . ." He paused, smiled, revealing a glittering gold tooth. "But I don't expect you to take *my* word for it."

The crowd let out a collective sigh. De Bornais bowed and stepped aside as another man climbed up from behind the stage. He was tall and broad-shouldered, with a shock of wild black hair and an enormous bristling beard. He was dressed in leather trousers and a vest that hung open to the waist, making it obvious that he was well muscled and apparently in rude health.

"My name," he said, "is Danton Aurenne. And I was not always the man you see before you."

Raesinia blinked. He had a fine, carrying voice, but it was more than that. It cracked like a whip across the crowd, *commanding* attention, locking every eye to his face.

He spoke at some length, starting with his childhood on the streets of Newtown, his mother's struggles, and his diseased and generally malformed state at young adulthood, with particular attention paid to the more horrifying symptoms. From there he recounted his near starvation, unfit for one job after another, finally washing up in a church hostel for the dying. Where, of course, he met de Bornais, and his amazing tonic—

It was an absurd story. Ridiculous. It wasn't even a masterpiece of the spoken word; it sounded as though it had been written by someone with only a middling command of Vordanai and very little imagination. And yet—and yet—

The words didn't seem to *matter.* The rolling power of that voice put the audience into a trance by the force of its delivery alone. Every man, woman, and child in the crowd was rapt. Raesinia found that she could barely even remember what had been said, moments after he'd said it. All that mattered was the plight of poor Danton, and his rescue by the astonishing philanthropy of the brilliant de Bornais, and the fact that she was being invited, *exhorted* to purchase a vial of this miracle elixir at the incredible price of only one eagle and fifty pence. It was practically giving away the secrets of life, which only showed you the kind of person de Bornais was.

She felt something inside her twitch. The binding perked up, very slightly, one predator raising an eyebrow at the sight of another stalking quietly across the plains.

Raesinia blinked.

"Good, isn't he?" said Ben, grinning.

"God Almighty." Faro shook his head, as though he felt drunk. "What the *hell* was that?"

"He's got his symptoms all m . . . m . . . mixed up," said Sarton. He'd looked up from his pamphlet only when Danton started talking. "And I wouldn't be surprised if he had an early case of the red wind. In childhood—"

Ben cut him off. "You see why I brought you here, right?"

"Just because the man can sell snake oil," Faro said, shaking off the effects, "doesn't mean he's going to be any use to *us*."

Raesinia shook her head. She was still watching the stage, where de Bornais had reappeared with a crate full of glass vials. Coins were flying out of the crowd and landing on the stage with a noise like hail.

"Do you see the girl at the edge of the stage?" she said quietly. "The one with the twisted leg."

"Nervasia," Sarton said. "Caused b . . . b . . . by deficiencies in the diet in infancy."

"She's lived with that her whole life," Raesinia said, watching the hobbling, wretched creature. "This morning she knew as well as you do that she'd live with it until the day she died. Now she's ready to hand over what is probably her life savings."

"In exchange for a vial of sugar and river water," Faro said.

"She's not buying an elixir," Raesinia said. "She's buying *hope*." She took a deep breath and glanced at Ben. "And a man who can sell hope to a girl like that can sell anything to anyone."

Ben was nodding. Faro frowned.

"Come on," Raesinia said. "I think we need to have a chat with him."

They waited on the edge of the square until de Bornais had sold every last vial. At that point he, Danton, and two porters left the square, de Bornais promising that he would return the next day to help those who hadn't been close enough to the front of the line.

"He does this every day," Ben said. "Sometimes it's the same people in the crowd."

"I guess they think that twice the dose will do twice the good," Faro said.

"Do you know where he goes afterward?" Raesinia asked Ben.

"There's a tavern around the corner. Last time I was here he spent a while in there."

"Right."

There was no sign marking the tavern, but none was really necessary. Even so early in the day, there was a steady stream of customers headed for the door, coming off odd-hours shifts or just slaking a midday thirst. Raesinia followed Ben through the swinging door into a gloomy, smoke-filled space. It was on the ground floor of one of the old apartment blocks, and looked as though it had originally been an apartment itself. The proprietors had knocked out the internal walls, boarded up most of the windows, and set up shop behind a wooden board balanced on a set of barrels. The tables were a mix of battered, scavenged furniture and knocked-together substitutes, and small crates served for chairs.

Unlike the Blue Mask and its fellows, who wore their disreputability like a costume for a masked ball, this place was honestly, solidly disreputable. Really, Raesinia thought, it didn't even rise to that level, since that would imply that it had a reputation. It was just one anonymous boarded-up apartment among many, where men traded small change for temporary oblivion. She'd visited Dockside taverns after shift change, full of drunken shouting workers spoiling for a fight, but there was none of that sense of danger here. The people around the makeshift tables just looked tired.

De Bornais and Danton sat at a table in the corner, with the two porters at another nearby. A few faces looked up to regard Raesinia and the others, but without much interest. Only the proprietor, a rat-faced man with a long mustache, took any extended notice. Raesinia stepped out of the doorway and beckoned her companions close.

"I need to get this Danton alone for a few minutes," she said. "Can we detach de Bornais?"

"I could engage him in a discussion on the m . . . m . . . merits of his treatment," Sarton offered. "But—"

"He's more likely to run from a real doctor than talk to one," Faro said. "Swindlers like him live in fear of someone turning up and demanding answers."

Raesinia thought for a moment. "All right, here's the story. Faro, you're the young son of some merchant, and Ben is your manservant. You've heard from belowstairs about this elixir, and now the master's taken sick, so you want to secure a supply. Buy him a few drinks and imply you're willing to make a pretty substantial contribution."

"Got it," said Ben, then sighed. "Why do I always end up as the manservant?"

"Because you don't know how to dress properly," said Faro, shooting his cuffs and inspecting them for lint. "Come on. Just follow my lead."

"What are you g . . . g . . . going to say to Danton?" Sarton said, as the two of them sauntered over to the table.

"First we need to find out what de Bornais gives him. Is that story of his genuine, or is he just a paid shill?"

The lingering power of Danton's oration insisted that the story was true—it *had* to be true; how could anything so obviously heartfelt not be true?—but the cynical part of Raesinia's mind suspected the latter. She kept her eye on Danton as Faro oiled up and engaged de Bornais in conversation. Faro's talent as an actor was considerable—it was one of the reasons they'd brought him in to their little conspiracy—and his warm handshake and extravagant gestures fit his role as a gullible young man from the moneyed class perfectly. De Bornais seemed to be taking it in, but Danton showed little interest in anything but the pint of beer in front of him. Bits of froth were clinging to his ferocious side whiskers.

"There we go," Raesinia muttered, as de Bornais got to his feet. Faro took him by the arm and steered him in the direction of the bar, leaving Danton alone at the table. "You keep watch from here. If Faro looks like he's losing his grip on de Bornais, warn me."

Sarton ducked his head, obviously pleased to have been given a position of responsibility. Raesinia left him by the door and headed for Danton. A few eyes followed her. In her University-tomboy getup, she didn't look particularly feminine, but women of any kind seemed to be a rarity here. Raesinia ignored the gazes and sat down on the crate de Bornais had vacated. She'd timed her arrival for just after Danton reached the bottom of his pint, and he looked up from it to find her smiling at him.

"Can I buy you another one of those?" she said.

Danton blinked, looking down at the empty mug, then back up at her.

"Another beer," she repeated, wondering how much he'd already had to drink. "More."

"More," Danton agreed happily. Raesinia waved at the sour-faced proprietor, who set to filling another mug from a barrel on the bar.

"I listened to your speech," Raesinia said. "We were all very impressed. Is it a true story?"

"'S a story," Danton said. Up close, his voice had the same quiet rumble, but it lacked the authority he'd displayed on the stage. "I'm supposed to tell it. Jack gave it to me."

"Jack—you mean de Bornais?" His face was uncomprehending, and she tried again. "The man who sells the medicine?"

This time he nodded. "Yes. Jack. He's a good fellow, Jack." This last had an odd singsong rhythm, as though he were repeating something he'd heard many times. "He shows me what to do."

"How much does he pay you?"

"You shouldn't worry about the money." This, also, sounded like a pat phrase. "Jack takes care of everything."

Raesinia paused, rapidly reassessing her position.

"Does Jack," she said slowly, "tell you what to say? When you're out on the stage, I mean, talking to everybody."

Danton dipped his head. "Mmm-hmm. He told me a story, and I tell it to people. It's good to share stories."

Raesinia stared at him. *What the hell are we dealing with here?* Danton wasn't just drunk—he seemed almost feebleminded. If she hadn't seen him speaking to the crowd herself, she wouldn't have believed he was capable of anything of the sort. *So he's—what? Some kind of idiot savant?* She watched him grab the new mug of beer in both hands and take a long drink. *But if he can repeat whatever someone tells him . . .*

A plan was just beginning to form when a heavy hand descended on her shoulder. She looked up into the thickset face of one of de Bornais' porters, whose eyes widened in comical surprise.

"'Ey," he said. "You're a girl."

She twisted to face him, brushing his hand aside. "What about it?"

De Bornais himself arrived, sidestepping Faro and hurrying to the table. He yanked the beer out of Danton's hand and slapped him, hard, like a mother smacking a squalling toddler. Danton blinked, his eyes beginning to water.

"You know you're not supposed to talk to anybody," de Bornais said. "I've told you a hundred times. Say it. What are you supposed to do?"

"Drink m' beer," Danton mumbled. "Not talk to anybody."

"Right." He spun to face Raesinia, who had wormed free of the porter. "And what the hell do you think *you're* doing?"

"I thought—" Raesinia began, but de Bornais waved her into silence, glaring at the porter standing beside her.

"Sorry, boss," the big man said. "I didn't catch what she was up to."

"All I want—" Raesinia tried again.

"I know what you *want*," de Bornais said. "The same thing they all want. They want to tell my friend a sob story and get a free dose, because he's too good-natured to know any better. It's a good thing he has someone to look out for him—that's all I have to say. If I left him alone this city would pick him clean in an hour." He nodded to the porter. "Get her out of here."

Faro had drifted over behind Raesinia, hand hovering near the hilt of his ridiculous dress sword. Ben followed, looking uncomfortable. The second porter, sensing trouble, left the bar and took position flanking de Bornais, while the unfortunate proprietor cringed behind his bar.

"All I want," Raesinia repeated, "is a few moments of your time. I have a proposal for you."

"My time is valuable, *miss*."

Raesinia could see Faro bridling at de Bornais' sneering tone, and she put up a hand to restrain him. Her other hand dug in her pocket and came out with a new-milled fifty-eagle gold piece. The smooth gold winked in the tavern lamps as she flipped it to de Bornais, who picked it out of the air and held it in front of his eyes as though he didn't believe what he was seeing. The gold represented enough money to buy the entire contents of the bar several times over.

She raised an eyebrow. "How much of your time will that buy me?"

De Bornais' eyes narrowed.

The closest thing to privacy the tavern offered was the tavern-keeper's bedroom, a miserable space crammed behind a door in the back barely big enough for a straw mattress and a chest of drawers. Raesinia had slipped him an eagle to let them use it, and de Bornais' two porters stood an uneasy watch outside, opposite Faro, Ben, and Sarton.

"All right," de Bornais said. "This had better be good."

"We saw Danton's speech outside," Raesinia said. "My friends and I were very impressed."

"Of course you were. He's a damned genius."

"I was curious about the . . . terms of his employment."

De Bornais smiled nastily. "Oh, I see where this is going. You're not the first to come sniffing around, you know."

Raesinia did her best to give a carefree shrug. "It's only natural. When a man has a talent like that, it seems to me he could charge whatever he liked."

"Maybe. But you talked to him, didn't you? Danton's . . . special. A bit touched." De Bornais put on an unconvincingly sad expression. "I take care of him, you see? He's practically a brother to me. I knew his mam, and when she was dying, she asked me, 'Jack, please take care of our Danton, because you know he can't do anything for himself.' I make sure he's okay, and he helps out however he can."

"Yes, I saw how well you take care of him," Raesinia deadpanned.

De Bornais had the decency to blush, rubbing his knuckles. "I don't like having to do that. But like I said, he's a bit touched. It's the only way to get him to understand sometimes. He doesn't blame me."

"You don't pay him?"

"He wouldn't know what to do with it." De Bornais patted the pocket where he'd tucked her coin, and gave a nasty smile. "So it's no good, you offering him money. He's got everything he needs, and he does whatever I tell him."

"If that's the case," she said, "perhaps *we* could come to some kind of arrangement."

"Don't be stupid," de Bornais said. "You were there today, weren't you? Then you saw the kind of money I'm making."

"But not for long, I'll bet," Raesinia said. "You must move around a lot."

"Of course." He gave a sickly grin. "Have to spread the good news."

And stay out of the way of angry customers, Raesinia thought.

"What if you were to let us . . . hire Danton, and we guaranteed your income? Think of it as a vacation."

He chuckled. "I don't think you appreciate the kind of money we're dealing with here—"

He stopped as she undid the first two buttons on her overshirt and reached down past her collar. In an inner pocket, held tight against her side, there was a sheaf of documents, and after a moment's thought she selected one of these and withdrew it. It was a folded sheet of thick, expensive paper, startlingly white in the gloom, and she snapped it open in front of de Bornais.

"Can you read, Baron?" By his eyes, she saw that he could. "Good. This is a draft on the Second Pennysworth Bank for ten thousand eagles, payable to the bearer with my signature. Do you think that would be sufficient?"

"I . . ." He looked from the bill to her face and back.

"Is the choice of institution not to your liking?" Raesinia patted her pocket. "I have others."

"No." De Bornais' voice was a croak. "No. That will be . . . fine."

De Bornais emerged from the back room, all smiles, waving the anxious porters away. Raesinia followed, catching Ben's eye, and nodded. They followed de

Bornais to Danton's table, where the big man was at work on a third mug of beer.

"Hello, Jack!" Danton said, suds frosting his wild beard. "You want a drink?"

"Er, no, thanks. Not right now." De Bornais looked nervous. "Listen, Danton. You like stories, right?"

"I like stories!"

"This young lady"—he gestured at Raesinia—"has some stories she wants you to tell. Do you think you could help her out?"

Danton nodded vigorously, then hesitated. "What about you, Jack? Don't you need my help?"

"It's all right. I've got to go on a . . . trip. Just for a while. But she's going to take care of you in the meantime, and you do whatever you can to help her, you understand?"

"All right." Danton took another pull from his beer, apparently unconcerned.

Raesinia stepped forward and extended her hand. "It's good to meet you, Danton. I'm Raesinia."

Danton stared at her hand for a moment, as though unsure what to do with it. Then his face split in a huge grin. "Just like the princess!"

"Right," she said, as they shook hands. "Just like her."

"So you bought him?" Cora said.

"I didn't *buy* him." Raesinia had been fighting a queasy feeling all afternoon that this was exactly what she *had* done, like some Murnskai lord trading field workers for coach horses. She had her justifications all ready. "He needs someone to care for him. We're just taking over that task for a while so he can work for us. After everything's finished, we can send him wherever he wants."

"I see," said Cora. "So you *rented* him."

Raesinia nodded sheepishly. "If you like."

"For *ten thousand eagles*." The teenager's eyes glowed, as they always did when she was talking about money.

"We can afford it," Raesinia said defensively.

"It's not a matter of being able to afford it," Cora said. "I'm just wondering what it is this man brings to the cause that's worth the price of a decent-sized town house."

"You didn't hear him."

They looked down at the object of their conversation, who looked back at them with guileless blue eyes. Raesinia had spent the afternoon in slow, careful conversation with him before bringing him to meet the others in the back room of the Blue Mask. Danton himself had proven to be amiable, willing, and uninterested in anything but the prospect of beer and food. Currently he was working his way through a pint of the Blue Mask's best with the same enjoyment he'd shown drinking the slop from the nameless Newtown bar. Around him were gathered all the members of the little conspiracy: Raesinia, Cora, Faro, Ben, Sarton, and Maurisk.

"Well?" Cora said. "Let's hear him, then."

"Yes," Maurisk said, briefly pausing in his pacing beside the window. "Let's." His sharp tone made it clear what he thought of this entire enterprise.

"We may need some time to get ready," Ben said. "He'll need some coaching, obviously. And—"

"No," Raesinia interrupted. "He won't. Danton?"

"Hmm?" He looked up from his beer and smiled. "Yes, Princess?"

Faro raised an eyebrow. "Princess?"

"Because of the name," Raesinia said, trying to sound amused. "Danton, do you remember the story I told you this afternoon?"

"I do. I like stories."

Maurisk snorted and stalked back to the window.

Raesinia ignored him. "Do you think you could tell that one to everyone right now?"

"Of course!"

He set his glass carefully on the floor and got out of his chair. Standing, he made for a somewhat intimidating figure, almost as big as Ben, with wild, unkempt hair and ragged clothes Raesinia hadn't had time to replace. His face went slack, eyes slightly unfocused, and Raesinia held her breath.

Then he began:

Where are you, thief? Step into the light, sir
Like an honest highwayman, show yourself
And I'll spit into your skull, match my sword
Against your scythe, and show you the power
Of a man wronged, and sworn to black revenge . . .

It was Illian's Act Two speech from *The Wreck*, the darling of every would-be actor and dramatist, a tirade against Death that built to a roaring, frenzied crescendo. Raesinia had heard it before, probably a hundred times, often from men reputed to be among the finest actors of the age. But it seemed to her that no command performance at the palace had ever matched this one. She could *feel* Illian's rage, the crawling frustration of revenge denied, marooned on a deserted island while the murderer of his true love sailed away to a hero's reward. Danton himself seemed to vanish, subsumed by this creature of anger and hatred, a wild tiger thrashing helplessly against the bars of its cage until it was bloody with the effort.

Her breath came out in a hiss, unnoticed, only to catch again when he came to the climax. Illian, despairing, hurled himself from the promontory, all the while daring Death to lay a skeletal finger on him. Raesinia could feel the air rushing all around her, and the shocking cold of the final impact.

"From this world, or from the next, I will have—"

Danton stopped. *Illian hits the water; the lights go down; the curtain falls. Intermission while they change the sets for Act Three.* Raesinia let out a long, shaky breath. Danton smiled at her, flopped back into his chair, and reached for his beer.

"Brass balls of the fucking Beast," Maurisk swore.

"I'm inclined to agree," Faro said. "How long did it take to teach him that?"

"No longer than it took him to say it," Raesinia said. "He can't read, but if you start telling him a story, he remembers *everything.* He had it word-perfect, first try, and it was"—she shivered—"like that."

Cora was huddled in her chair. Sarton was staring at Danton, unblinking, and Ben at Raesinia with something like admiration. There was a long silence.

"So," Faro said, "is he a wizard? A demon? That can't be natural. How does he *know* how to say it?"

Maurisk snorted again. "Don't start that Sworn Church nonsense—"

"I don't care if he is," Raesinia said, cutting off the argument. "Sorcerer, demon, whatever you can think of. We *need* him. He can be the symbol we've been looking for." *Besides,* she thought, *I'm not exactly in a position to look down on a little magical assistance.* She wondered if Danton's binding had been forced on him, as hers had been, and felt a pang of sympathy for the man.

"Maybe," Maurisk said. Something new had entered his voice. He was seeing the possibilities.

"We'll need somewhere for him to stay," Raesinia said.

"I can find something," Faro said, staring.

"Good." Raesinia hesitated. "Do you think you could also . . . clean him up a bit?"

"He does have a certain lunatic-beggar charm, doesn't he?" Faro smiled. "I'll take care of it."

Raesinia turned. "Ben, you find us a venue. Somewhere not too public, not yet. And with plenty of ways out in case something goes badly wrong. Maurisk, Sarton, you're in charge of the text. You're writing for the masses, so go easy on the classical allusions, and remember that not everyone knows *Rights of Man* by heart."

Cora looked up. Her eyes were red, and her cheeks streaked with tears, but she was grinning now. "Can I sell tickets? We'd make a fortune."

"We already have a fortune."

"*Another* fortune." The girl shrugged. "All right. Maybe later."

By the time they broke up, it had gone three in the morning. The air was still as damp and warm as a laundry, and the street was scarcely better than inside. The members of the conspiracy left one at a time, going their separate ways, except for Faro, Cora, Raesinia, and Danton.

"All right," Raesinia said to Danton. "I'd like you to go with Faro. He'll find you somewhere to sleep, and make sure you get plenty to eat as well. Please do what he says until I get back."

Danton nodded amiably, wobbling a bit. He'd put away an astonishing amount of beer over the course of the evening. "Sure. Okay, Princess."

Raesinia winced inwardly. She'd told him to stop calling her that, but the admonition had gone through his mind like lead shot through custard, without leaving much of an impression. "All right. Faro, you're going to be okay?"

"No problem." He smiled and sauntered out, with Danton following like an obedient puppy.

Raesinia turned to Cora. The teenager had washed her face, but her eyes were still red.

"Are you all right?"

Cora gave a vigorous nod. "Fine. It was just that speech. I'd never heard anything so . . ." She shook her head. "Do you really think it's magic?"

"I have no idea, and I don't care if it is." Raesinia smiled. "Have you never seen *The Wreck*? We'll have to take you sometime. Leonard Vinschaft is doing Illian at the Royal now, and I've heard he's amazing."

Even as she said it, Raesinia wondered if she would get any pleasure out of the show. After all, how could another rendition compare to Danton's?

Good God. She stared after him for a minute while Cora put on her coat. *He's a weapon, isn't he? A bomb that we're going to set and prime, light the fuse, and hope we've found the right place to stand . . .*

The two of them left the room and said their good-byes in front of the Mask. Raesinia waited until Cora had turned the corner, then said, "When I tell you what happened to me today, you're not going to believe it."

Sothe materialized out of the shadows. She'd traded her maid outfit for her working blacks, drab and almost invisible in the darkness, bunched tight to her body with leather cords so that no hanging fabric would betray her with a whisper.

"There's news from the palace," Sothe said.

Raesinia's breath caught in her throat. "My father?" *Too soon, it's too soon. We're not ready!* Those were her first thoughts, followed promptly by a crushing wave of guilt. *My* father *is dying, and all I care about is—*

"No," Sothe said. "Vhalnich has arrived."

"Already?" Raesinia frowned. "I thought he wasn't expected for another few weeks at least."

"Apparently he left his command and made a faster crossing."

"How is the Cobweb?"

"Buzzing."

Raesinia smiled in the darkness.

Chapter Four

MARCUS

Marcus had never really understood the point of inspections by senior officers. It certainly made sense for a sergeant to turn out his men now and again to make sure everyone's kit was in order, but the deficiencies of individual rankers were generally beneath the notice of a captain. At the War College, he'd known some officers who liked to play the martinet, find some tiny deficiency and fly into a frothing rage to show that they weren't to be trifled with, but Marcus had privately considered such performances to be more trouble than they were worth.

He would gladly have dispensed with the whole ritual, but the men seemed to expect it, and so he found himself walking along a line of well-turned-out Armsmen an hour or so after officially taking over his new command. At his side was Vice Captain Alek Giforte, who'd served as acting commander since the dismissal of the previous Minister of War. The vice captain seemed to know the name and service record of every man in the unit, and he kept up a running commentary as Marcus went along the lines, accepting stiff salutes and dispensing nods and smiles.

"That's Staff Gallows, sir." "Staff" was apparently a position in the Armsmen equivalent to "ranker," named for the tall wooden staves they carried that served as both weapon and badge of office. The man the vice captain had pointed out was tall and broad-shouldered, standing at rigid attention, a pair of unfamiliar decorations glittering on his chest. "He won the Blue Order for his bravery in breaking up a riot in the Flesh Market in 'oh-five."

Gallows pulled himself up even straighter, and Marcus felt that something was expected of him. He cleared his throat.

"Well done," he said. When that didn't seem to be enough, he added, "Glad to have men like that on the rolls."

"Yes, sir," Giforte said, guiding Marcus down the line. "This is Sergeant Mourn, the longest-serving sergeant in . . ."

And so on. The unfamiliar green uniforms gave Marcus the odd feeling of being in a foreign land, a visiting dignitary inspecting the local honor guard. He kept adjusting his own uniform, which was uncomfortably tight and encrusted with gilt buttons and bits of dangling gold braid. At least it had a loop for a proper sword so he could wear his familiar cavalry saber.

When, at last, they reached the end of the line, Marcus let Giforte dismiss the men. They trooped out in single file, leaving the two officers alone.

"Thank you, Vice Captain," Marcus said. "That was very . . . informative."

"Of course, sir." Giforte stood with his hands behind his back, the picture of alertness. He was an older man, with gray at his temples and shot through his neatly trimmed beard, and his face had the lined, leathery look of a man who'd spent most of his life outdoors. Marcus was still trying to figure out what to make of him.

"So," Marcus said, when Giforte didn't seem inclined to offer anything further. "Do I have . . . an office, or something like that?"

"Of course, sir," the vice captain said. "This way."

They were in the Guardhouse, a rambling ruin of a building on the grounds of the Old Palace. Farus II, son of the Conqueror, had built his stronghold just outside Vordan City, the better to keep his eye on his fractious nobles. His great-grandson, Farus V, had desired something grander and more detached from city life, and had moved the court and the center of government to the manicured gardens of Ohnlei. The Old Palace had been stripped of anything valuable and allowed to fall into disrepair, but the Guardhouse—once the headquarters of the king's personal guard—had proven a convenient base for the Armsmen.

Marcus' new office turned out to be on the top floor, with an excellent view of the overgrown hedges and scrub that had once been the palace grounds. Giforte stepped in front of him to open the door, putting his shoulder against it and pressing hard.

"There's sort of a trick to it," he explained as it groaned open. "It sticks in the summer, so you've got to press it and lift a bit."

"I'll keep that in mind," Marcus said, going in. The office was cleaner than he'd imagined for a place that hadn't been used in months. There was a desk, an enormous oak thing dark with layers of polish that had to be a hundred years old. On its gleaming surface were several neat stacks of paper, thick with ribbons and seals. Otherwise, the room was empty, without even a bookcase. It didn't look like a place anyone had spent any amount of time in.

Giforte stood beside the door, hands behind his back. Marcus walked over to the desk, pulled out the ancient chair with a squeal of rusty casters, and sat down. He looked at the papers, fighting a mounting sense of déjà vu.

"What's all this?" he said.

"Documents for the captain's approval," Giforte said. "Duty rosters, punishment details, reports from each of the subcaptains, incident summaries—"

"I get the picture."

Marcus took the top document off the pile. It was a warrant for the arrest of a Vincent Coalie, on charges of housebreaking and theft. At the bottom right was the seal of the Armsmen, a hooded eagle pressed into green wax. Below it was a signature that Marcus could just about make out as Giforte's.

He flipped through the next few pages. Giforte's name was on most of them.

Marcus looked up at the vice captain, who was still standing in rigid silence. "And I need to read all these?"

"If you like, sir," Giforte said.

"And . . . approve them?"

"Yes, sir."

"What if I find something I don't approve of?"

Was that just the tiniest hint of a smile at the corner of Giforte's lips? "You can inform me, of course, and I will investigate the matter at once."

"I see." Marcus paused. "May I ask you a personal question, Vice Captain?"

"Of course, sir."

"How long have you been with the Armsmen?"

"Nearly twenty-three years now, sir."

"And how many captains have you served under?"

Giforte paused, as though calculating. After a moment, he shrugged. "Fifteen, I think. But I may be forgetting one or two."

Marcus thought he'd finally gotten a handle on what was happening here. It was an old, old army game called Manage the Officer, discovered by subordinates everywhere when called on to deal with a superior who was in over his head.

At first, he'd wondered if Giforte's stiff attitude was concealing bitterness that he himself had been passed over for the top job. Looking at the stacks of papers, though, Marcus understood that Giforte was exactly where he wanted to be. Captain of Armsmen was a *political* appointment, made and dismissed at the whim of the king or the Minister of Justice. *Fifteen in twenty-three years.* With such frequent changes, it was no wonder that the vice captain, a solid, dependable lifer, had accumulated all the actual authority.

He expects me turn up for the inspection, glance through all of this, and then scurry back to Ohnlei to get on with my life. Marcus gave a rueful smile. *More fool him. He doesn't know I haven't got a life.* And if Janus was correct, Giforte's carefully tended organization was going to be turned upside down. Marcus felt sorry for the man.

"All right," he said aloud. "I'll take a look. I'm sure you have better things to do than stand there and watch me read."

"As you wish, sir," Giforte said. "Staff Eisen will be posted outside the door, should you require anything."

After three hours, the notion of scurrying back to Ohnlei was definitely starting to look more attractive, especially since green-vested scribes had already come in twice to add new piles before Marcus had even finished the first one. He ran his finger along the lines of an incident report, frowning at the cramped handwriting and twisted grammar of someone as uncomfortable with the written word as himself.

"—a small crowd having gathered to hear the speech of the orator Danton, a band of pickpockets belonging to the Red Snip crew claimed the right to work in the area. This being the case, the Gnasher crew took offense, saying it was their territory, and the two groups commenced to fighting. Staves Popper and Torlo restored order, and the following injuries were reported—"

Marcus shook his head and flipped the page onto the finished pile. He wasn't sure what he was looking for, exactly, only that he didn't intend to command the Armsmen and not know what they were doing. He had to admit, though, that the task was daunting. He pictured something like the period when command of the Colonials had been forced on him—after all, the Colonials mustered more than four thousand fighting men, while the Armsmen had only a bit over three thousand. But the Colonials had mostly kept together, doing one or two things at a time, and thus didn't require much in the way of complex administration. The Armsmen, by contrast, were spread all over the city in a complicated web of patrols, stations, and details, each of which generated a stream of paper that flowed up the chain of command. He guessed there were probably as many scribes copying out reports and signing off on expenses as there were Staves on the streets.

There was a knock at his office door. Another scribe, he guessed, with another load of paper. *There must be some way to get Giforte to sort this stuff.* But the vice captain obviously wanted to see Marcus snowed under. Marcus gritted his teeth and shouted, "Come in!"

Staff Eisen, a pleasant young man with a scruffy beard and dirty blond hair, opened the door and saluted briskly. He brandished an envelope.

"Got a message for you, sir," he said. "From His Excellency. One of his men delivered it personally."

Marcus found his heart leaping at the prospect. A good excuse to get out from behind the desk and away from the mountain of papers would be welcome. He accepted the envelope from Eisen and broke the seal, finding two scraps of notepaper inside.

One read:

> Captain—the inquiries I mentioned earlier have borne some fruit. I believe this to be the location of a cell to which our sleeping friend reported. I suggest you take an armed guard when you investigate, and be very careful with any prisoners you take. Good luck.—J

The other had an address that Marcus didn't recognize. He folded the note and put it in his pocket, then looked up at Eisen. "Could you fetch the vice captain, please?"

It was a few minutes before Giforte came in. His features were composed—if he was irritated at being called in, he didn't show it. *He must be used to a new captain making a show of being busy for a few days.*

"You called, sir?"

"Yes." Marcus handed him the note with the address. "Do you know where this is?"

Giforte frowned slightly. "Yes, sir. It's in Oldtown, a couple of blocks from the ford. Why do you ask?"

"I'm going there on an investigation. Orders from His Excellency the minister. Could you lend me a couple of men who know the way?"

"The Armsmen are at your disposal, Captain." Giforte saluted. "With your permission, I'll accompany you myself. Let me put together an escort. A dozen men should be sufficient."

"I don't need to stand on ceremony, Vice Captain. Just yourself and Staff Eisen will be sufficient."

"Ah," Eisen said. "I'm not sure . . ."

"What Staff Eisen means to say, sir," Giforte said, and Marcus recognized the patient tone he'd gotten so often from Fitz, "is that standing orders are not to go into Oldtown in groups smaller than six. And it would be best to take a carriage."

Marcus looked between them and sighed.

The carriage was a big one, painted in Armsmen green with the hooded-eagle crest on the sides. Marcus and Giforte sat inside, while Eisen and a pair of Armsmen waited on the roof, and another squad of eight Staves followed behind. Marcus hadn't asked for stealth, but he'd hoped at least for subtlety. This was about as subtle as a bullhorn.

Rather than splash through the muddy ford, Giforte directed the carriage to take the Grand Span to the South Bank and then follow the River Road east to Oldtown. The driver, another Armsman, didn't require any further directions, which left Marcus and Giforte sitting awkwardly in silence as the carriage rattled down cobbled streets and clacked over flagstones.

"So." After five years in Khandar, living in the tight circle of the Colonials, Marcus found his small-talk reflexes a little rusty. "Tell me a bit about yourself, Vice Captain."

"What would you like to know, sir?" Giforte said.

"Are you a family man?"

"Widower, sir."

Marcus winced. "Any children?"

"A daughter." A hint of real emotion was visible for a moment in the vice captain's face, but it was quickly suppressed. "We've lost touch."

"Ah." And that, Marcus thought, was the end of that. *Hardly my fault if he doesn't want to hold up his end of the conversation.*

Probably Giforte thought it wasn't worth getting too chummy with a captain who might be gone with the next cabinet shake-up. *Actually, it might be downright dangerous.* Marcus looked at the vice captain's bland smile, and wondered how much he knew about affairs at Ohnlei. *If he knows that Janus and the duke are enemies, then he may expect me to be gone sooner rather than later.*

He pushed aside the curtain and looked out the window as the carriage bumped down off the bridge and turned onto the packed dirt of the River Road. The chaotic sprawl of the Docks soon gave way to the grid of symmetrical towers that was Newtown, stained and blackened by smoke and weather. The River Road was kept reasonably clear of obstructions—he remembered a duty rota assigning squads to the job—but the side of it was lined by carts, stalls, and tents, with vendors shouting at the top of their lungs to draw people out of the stream of traffic. The combination of obvious poverty and manic entrepreneurial energy reminded Marcus of Ashe-Katarion before the Redemption.

A flash of green drew his attention, and he saw a small crowd gathered some distance up the street. Two crowds, really. In the center, a man in a white robe was speaking to a small group. Surrounding this inner circle was a ring of Armsmen, staves held sideways to hold back a much larger and dirtier crowd that watched the proceedings with a sullen air, shouting unintelligible abuse. Another pair of Armsmen patrolled inside the ring, watching for any attempt to force through the line or throw things at the speaker. When one man raised a rotting cabbage high, they pounced and clubbed him to the ground.

The speaker held something out at arm's length, and the inner crowd fell to their knees. Marcus caught the glint of gold. The jeers of the outer crowd increased.

Marcus drew Giforte's attention to the scene as the carriage went past, and the vice captain glanced at the window and grimaced. He shook his head.

"Sworn Priest," he said. "Borelgai, by the beard. They're always preaching down here."

"Why does he have a whole squad protecting him?"

"His Majesty's orders are that the Sworn Priests should be free to offer their teachings unmolested. We're charged with enforcing that." He watched Marcus for a moment, considering, then added, "It was part of the peace treaty. After Vansfeldt."

A hundred and fifty years ago, Farus IV had thrown in his lot with the League cities in their rebellion against the Sworn Church of Elysium. The subsequent war, waged simultaneously against the Murnskai legions and a cabal of his own horrified nobles, had come close to costing Farus his crown. The last bloody flames of that revolution had taken a generation to die out, and atrocities committed on both sides had given the Vordanai people an abiding distaste for the power of the Sworn Church. The Great Cathedral of Vordan had been sacked and left in ruins to guarantee that none of the new Free Church parishes that were rising from the ashes could lay claim to leadership of the others.

The Borelgai had been having their own civil war at the same time, with opposite results. Their king had lost his head for heresy at the hands of an ecclesiastical court sent from Elysium, and since then the interests of the Borelgai throne and the Sworn Church had been tightly entwined. Fifteen decades had served to cool the hatred enough that the Sworn were no longer officially banned from Vordan, but they had never been allowed to preach in the streets, much less with an official Armsmen escort.

After the war. That would have been just about the time Marcus was leaving for Khandar, at the conclusion of the War of the Princes. He'd gone straight from the disastrous Vansfeldt campaign back to the War College in Grent, two hundred miles from the capital, and he hadn't paid much attention to politics in those days in any case.

"He didn't look like he was having much success," Marcus said.

"There's always a few Sworn around. Foreigners, mostly, and some of the very poorest." Again, Giforte gave him an evaluating glance, deciding how much he should say. "All I know is it's a headache for us. They're always stirring up trouble."

Marcus nodded. What Janus had told him about fighting in the streets seemed a bit more plausible now. The Crown's debt to the Borels was one thing; only merchants cared about that. But foreign priests by the side of the road, with Armsmen protecting them . . .

"It's getting worse, too, now that this Danton is telling everyone the Borelgai are the source of all their problems."

"Danton?" Marcus said. That name had come up a few times in the reports.

Giforte waved a hand. "Just a rabble-rouser. He's been making waves since last week, but he isn't saying anything we haven't heard before. We keep an eye on that sort to make sure they don't try anything stupid."

"What does he want?"

"The usual. Down with the Last Duke, Vordan for the Vordanai, that sort of thing." Giforte, watching Marcus' expression, carefully did not express his own opinion. Marcus suppressed a smile. *He really does have this down to a science, doesn't he?*

Glancing out the window again, Marcus saw they had left the towers of Newtown behind and entered Oldtown, the most ancient of Vordan City's districts. The architect Gerhardt Alcor's grand project to rebuild the city along rational lines had ended with his death, leaving a stark divide in the middle of what had once been a uniform rat's warren of mazy, twisting streets and tumbledown half-timber houses. Nowadays the boundary was called the Cut, a street running south from the Old Ford as straight as a knife wound. On the Newtown side, Alcor's perfect grid of cobbled roads stretched out until it met the Docks; across the way, there were only medieval cowpaths and meandering lanes. Here and there a stone-walled church loomed amid the sea of flaking plaster and whitewash like a bastion.

Farus V had sponsored Alcor on the theory that a rational city would breed a better class of citizen, but Marcus could see no evidence of this. The residents of Oldtown were hard to distinguish from those of Newtown, perhaps a little bit more frayed in their attire and more desperate in their poverty. When the Armsmen carriage turned off the River Road and began threading its way into the depths of the maze, the streets cleared as if by magic, and every window was covered by a curtain. Here and there a group of young men made a point of not moving, glaring at the vehicle and its escort with undisguised hostility.

"They're not fond of us, are they?" Marcus murmured.

"Don't take it personally, sir," Giforte said. "Take it from someone who's been at this for a long time. Whenever times get bad, we become very unpopular." He pointed up the street. "There's your address, sir."

It was a two-story house in the old style, plaster rotting and flaking from around the timber frame. The narrow windows were boarded up, but a small curl of smoke rising from the chimney indicated that someone was in residence.

"Did His Excellency indicate what we were likely to find here?" Giforte said. "Anything dangerous?"

"I'm not sure." If they had someone like Jen in there, a dozen men weren't going to be nearly enough. *Janus wouldn't have sent me here if he thought that likely, though.* "Get someone around the back. I don't want anyone sneaking out."

Giforte nodded. As the carriage came to a halt, he opened the door and stepped out, already shouting orders. Their escort fanned out, two men slipping around either side of the house. Eisen hopped down from the carriage roof and hurried over, eager to impress.

"Want me to go in first, sir?" he said.

"I'll go first," Marcus said. "Eisen, take five men and follow me. The rest of you, make sure nobody gets past us."

"I'll join you," Giforte said.

"Vice Captain—"

"No offense intended, sir, but it would be an embarrassment to lose my new commanding officer on his first day on the job." Giforte's expression told Marcus it would be pointless to argue.

The small contingent of Armsmen edged up to the door, a slab of ancient, scarred pine with several peeling layers of whitewash. The latch was broken, and the door hung a half inch open, so Marcus simply prodded it with his foot. It swung inward, creaking, revealing a single shadowy room with a table, a few chairs, and a fire barely glowing in the hearth. Rickety-looking steps in the rear led up to the second story.

"Hello?" Marcus said, stepping over the threshold. Giforte was close behind him, followed by Eisen and another Staff. "I'd like to have a word."

A wooden groan and clatter gave him a half second's warning. He caught something huge in motion to his left, and reflex drove him into a dive, pulling Giforte with him. The thing—a wardrobe, one of the ancient oak constructions that was taller than Marcus and weighed as much as four men—toppled across the doorway, catching the door and pushing it closed as it came down. Eisen had the presence of mind to dive forward alongside his superiors, but the second Staff tried to jump the other way and didn't make it before the door slammed. The wardrobe hammered him to the floor, his surprised shout ending in a nasty crunch.

Marcus pushed himself up at once, clawing for his sword. By the light of the dying fire, he could see a man standing on a wooden crate, recovering from the shove he'd given the wardrobe. He was tall, and impressively bearded, dressed in crude homespun and rags, with a cutlass and a pistol thrust into the scrap of rope he used as a belt. Marcus didn't want to give the man time to use either, so he rushed him, dragging the heavy cavalry saber out of its scabbard.

The bearded man drew his pistol, but Marcus thrust at his face as he pulled the trigger, making him jerk back. The weapon went off with an earsplitting *crack* and splinters rained down from the ceiling. Before his opponent could draw his cutlass, Marcus aimed a kick at the corner of the crate he was standing on, rocking it backward and spilling the man to the floor.

"Sir!" Giforte said. "Down!"

Marcus spun. Giforte was standing beside the dresser, trying to shift it, while Eisen had retrieved his staff and moved to help Marcus. Another man had appeared on the stairs, bare-chested and hairy, holding a pistol in each hand. Marcus dove for the rickety table, catching Eisen around the knees and dragging him down as well. The first shot caught the young Staff in the forearm, spraying blood against the dresser, and the attacker dropped the empty weapon and shifted the other to his right hand. Giforte grabbed Eisen's staff dropped by the dead Armsman, moving surprisingly quickly for a man of his age, and ducked as the second pistol went off. The ball *pinged* off the dresser and ricocheted up to punch into the ceiling, producing a shower of plaster.

"Behind you, sir," Giforte snapped, popping back up and charging toward the stairway, staff in hand. Marcus rolled and regained his feet in time to block a downward cut from the bearded man's cutlass. Steel rang against steel, the blade of the cutlass sliding down to catch on the saber's guard. The man shoved, grunting, trying to force both blades into Marcus' face. He was big and broad-shouldered, and Marcus quickly realized he wasn't going to win a contest of strength.

Instead he faded sideways, pulling his sword away and letting his opponent's force carry him forward. The bearded man turned it into a spin, cutlass whipping around at head height, but Marcus had anticipated the move. He ducked, his own weapon swinging low and catching his assailant below the knee with bone-cracking force. The man screamed, his leg buckling, and as he fell Marcus delivered an upward stroke across his chest that left him lying on the floor in a spreading pool of blood.

Marcus turned, looking for Giforte. The bare-chested man had met his charge head-on, grabbing the staff before the vice captain could swing and using it as a bar to push Giforte into the wall. He was of a similar size to his late companion, and Giforte's face had gone white with the effort of keeping the staff from being pressed against his throat. Marcus ran at them, arm drawn back for a brutal downward cut, which the man only noticed at the last moment. He half turned, taking the blade at the base of his neck, a blow hard enough to break bones. When he staggered backward, the saber came free, and blood exploded from the wound. The bare-chested man took one more step backward, groaning, then collapsed to the floor.

Silence fell, and Marcus could hear his own rapid, ragged breaths. Giforte still held the staff in front of his face, unmoving. His eyes were closed, and his throat worked rapidly.

"Vice Captain?" Marcus said. "Are you all right?"

There was a long pause before Giforte opened his eyes, blowing out a deep breath. "I'm fine," he said. "Eisen? Jones?"

"I'm all right, sir," Eisen said, voice a little shaky. "Right through my arm. But I think Jones is dead."

A moment's investigation showed that he was right. Marcus tried to shift the huge wooden thing off Jones, the other Armsman, but found that he couldn't even budge it. Opening the wardrobe door, he found the whole thing was stuffed with sacks of bricks. *It must weigh a ton.*

He indicated the bricks to Giforte.

"They were waiting for us," the vice captain said.

"Or waiting for someone," Marcus said. "There might be a lookout upstairs."

They looked at each other, sharing the image of a man with a pistol trained on the stairs, just waiting for someone to ascend. Marcus took a deep breath.

"I'll take a look," he said. "See if you can get this door open."

"Sir—"

Marcus was already crossing the room, bloody saber still in hand. The right move would have been to wait until the others could get inside, but one man was dead already; he couldn't stomach the idea of sending another into what might be a trap. He stopped at the bottom of the stairs and looked up. Light flickered against the flaking plaster of the roof. *Someone has a fire lit.*

He paused, considering his options, then raised his saber and took the stairs at a run, hoping to startle anyone who might be waiting into a hasty shot. The wood creaked alarmingly under his boots, but he cleared the last step and immediately threw himself sideways, out of the line of fire, landing in a crouch.

The second floor was another large room, this one unfurnished except for three dingy straw pallets. At one end of the room was a heavy iron cauldron, with a merry firelight coming from inside it. Standing next to it was a young man in worn leathers, in the act of dropping a small bound notebook into the flames.

"Don't move!" Marcus growled, hurrying over. The young man raised his hands, no surprise evident in his features, and stepped back. A glance into the cauldron confirmed Marcus' fears. It was a mass of glowing paper. *Those bastards downstairs were buying time.*

"You're under arrest," he said, awkwardly aware that there was probably a proper way for an Armsman to arrest someone, and that he didn't know it. "Keep your hands up and don't try anything."

The young man smiled. He had a thin, expressive face, with a neat beard on his chin but smooth cheeks. When he spoke, Marcus could hear just a trace of a gravelly Murnskai accent.

"I wouldn't dream of it," he said, and smiled a little wider. "It's good to meet you, Captain d'Ivoire."

CHAPTER FIVE

WINTER

In an effort to calm her jangling nerves, Winter was trying to make an inventory of all the things that were making her anxious. This didn't *help*, but once she'd started she found she couldn't stop.

First and foremost was the dress, or "the damned dress" as she thought of it. It had been uncomfortable to begin with, but she'd assumed that it wouldn't take long before old habits reasserted themselves. Now it had been two days, and while she was able to go for minutes at a time without thinking about it, sooner or later she would turn around quickly or get hit by a gust of wind, and the feel of the long skirt's fabric brushing against her legs would have her grabbing for it in a panic.

The top was nearly as bad. It was by no standards indecent, but the short sleeves and billowing fit made her feel half-naked. The figure it draped was, while not generous, still clearly that of a young *woman*, and every time Winter caught sight of her reflection in a shopwindow she had to fight a powerful urge to find something with which to cover herself. She even found herself missing the tight pinch of her self-tailored undershirts. At least she still had a hat, even if it was a slouching felt thing instead of the brimmed officer's cap she'd grown used to.

Second—or maybe it was part of the first—was the constant dread of impending *discovery*. Winter had lived for two years among the men of the Royal Army, knowing that any slip that led to someone finding out her true gender would lead to her being locked up and sent home at the very best. Walking around a crowded city, dressed like this, was worse than walking around naked.

She felt like the most brazen of whores, shouting out her most closely held secret for all to hear. The apparent unconcern of those around her would be shattered at any moment by—someone, some authority, who would drag her away somewhere to answer for her crimes.

Third was the more mundane anxiety that she was not getting anywhere with her assigned task. She had given herself a day of simply walking around in her new garb, getting used to the idea. She'd somehow expected to attract stares from every eye, as though the news would race out ahead of her that here was *Winter Ihernglass*, dressed as a *girl*! In fact, nobody paid her the least attention, aside from a few street vendors who took her relatively well-washed appearance to mean that she had money.

Walking through the streets of a city unobserved was a new experience for Winter. A few vague early memories aside, she'd spent her entire childhood at Mrs. Wilmore's and had gone more than a decade without venturing farther from the old manor house than the neighboring estates. Then she'd run away to Khandar. The Colonials had had the run of the city before the Redemption, but their uniforms and skin color meant they would always be objects of attention.

It was something they'd all gotten used to, and she'd stopped noticing the feeling until it was suddenly gone. Here she was just a girl, one among thousands, a little out of the ordinary for this neighborhood but no more so than dozens of others. She felt as if some sorcerer had turned her invisible.

The second day, she'd resolved to get down to work. Janus had supplied her with plenty of coin, and she'd rented a room at a hostel, then set about canvassing the town for some sign of the Leatherbacks, the revolutionary group she was supposed to be joining. This proved to be less than successful. Winter found that while people didn't pay her any mind walking by, the minute she opened her mouth she was irretrievably marked as an outsider. Quite apart from her not knowing any of the locals, her voice lacked their twanging accents, and she was so ignorant of the local dialect that she found some of the patois borderline incomprehensible.

The district was loosely referred to as the Docks, a poorly defined area covering roughly half of Vordan's Southside. It was bounded in the north by the bank of the Vor and in the south by Wall Street, a broad thoroughfare that was all that remained of Vordan's medieval city wall. There were more houses beyond Wall Street, but that was widely agreed to be where the Bottoms began, a swampy, unhealthy district that even the Docks looked down on. In the west the river and the street met at the southern water battery, forming a section of city shaped like a wedge of cheese. To the east, though, the Docks gradually petered out, residential buildings, shops, and wine sinks gradually transforming into the warren of dirt roads and vast warehouses that surrounded the Lower Market.

Life in the Docks had three poles, one of which was those warehouses. Every day, thousands of tons of goods—produce, meat, cereals, animal fodder, and other foodstuffs for the most part—were brought into the city via the Green Road from the south, the wagons forming a line miles long down the swamp-bound causeway. Thousands more tons—almost anything that could fit aboard a ship, including silk and coffees that had originated in Ashe-Katarion—entered the city from the west, shipped upriver by barge from Vayenne at the Vor's mouth or from another city on one of the river's many tributaries. More barges, narrower and shallow-drafted, brought stone, cheeses, and wool from upriver. All of these things needed to be moved from boat to wagon, wagon to boat, boat to warehouse, or any combination of the three, and a substantial portion of the people living in the Docks made their living doing exactly that.

The second pole was the Fish Market, hard against the river. People who worked in the Fish Market were easily distinguishable by scent, and mostly lived in their own section of the district known as Stench Row. Every morning before dawn the fishermen laid out the day's catch, and representatives from kitchens all over the city, from the noble estates to the lowliest slop houses, came to browse. Thriving if whiffy businesses at the edges of the square processed the rotten rejects and unwanted organs into various forms of fertilizer or pig slop.

On the southern side of the Docks was the Flesh Market, which Winter had learned was not nearly as vile as it sounded. It was simply a large square where farmers from downcountry could come to hire extra hands, and as such waxed and waned with the seasons. Right now, at midsummer, business was booming as the planters hired help in advance of the autumn harvest. Farmhands were traditionally paid their first week's wages in advance, and the presence of large numbers of young men with money in their pockets had encouraged the growth of a complex network of brothels, wine shops, and feuding gangs of thieves.

All of this Winter had been able to discover in the first couple of days, just by wandering around and observing who went where. That there were discontent and revolutionary activity going on, too, was beyond a doubt, because everywhere she looked there were posters and painted graffiti inveighing against the king, the Last Duke, the Borelgai, the Sworn Church, the tax farmers, the bankers, and any other group that could conceivably hold any power. One intense-looking young man had given her a pamphlet claiming that there was a conspiracy among the greengrocers to take over the city, which even as an outsider Winter had to say sounded a little unlikely.

What she *hadn't* been able to find was any evidence that the Leatherbacks existed outside of popular fantasy. The broadsheets sold at street corners for a penny were full of their doings, how they'd robbed this shop or beaten up that Armsman, but details were suspiciously few. There were certainly no Leatherbacks chapter houses, no signs saying "Revolutionary Conspiracy This Way!" and by the third day Winter had started to wonder what Janus had been thinking to give her this assignment. She'd spent a lot of time and quite a bit of his money in wine shops and taverns, buying rounds all through the evenings and pumping her new best friends for information, but no one had been able to tell her anything beyond vague rumors.

Nevertheless, focusing on the task at hand had calmed her down a bit, as had the reflection that it could have been much worse. Since that horrible night in the ancient temple in Khandar, she'd played host to a *thing*—a demon, the Church would have it, though the Khandarai word was *naath* or "reading"—that Janus had named Infernivore. A demon that ate other demons, that had torn the power right out of the body of the Concordat agent Jen Alhundt. Winter could feel it, deep in her mind, waiting like a river crocodile, placidly but with the coiled-spring potential for sudden violence.

She'd been certain, when Janus insisted she accompany him on the breakneck voyage home, that it was Infernivore he really wanted. Winter had expected him to be sent into battle against Black Priests and supernatural horrors; her current task, while it went against the grain, was certainly better than *that*.

Now she was sitting in a tavern that fronted on the River Road, which was as close as the Docks came to an upscale area. It was a big establishment, built to serve the evening rush of workers coming off their loading shifts, and at midday there were only a scattering of patrons. The plank floor was covered in sawdust (easier to sweep up spilled beer, not to mention blood and vomit) and the round tables were big, heavy things on wide, solid bases, unlikely to get smashed in the event of roughhousing. The mugs and flatware were of the cheapest clay kind, the sort that would start to flake and fall apart after a few washes, but Winter suspected they rarely survived that long. Clearly, the tavern-keeper knew his clientele.

Winter had one of the tables to herself. Most of the rest of the customers were women, sitting in pairs or small groups and talking quietly. A few older men or odd-shift workers congregated near the fire, where a desultory dice game was in progress. A bored-looking serving girl brought Winter a plate of something she claimed was beef, boiled into unrecognizability and floating in its own juices inside a rampart of mashed potatoes. She attacked it voraciously. Two years eating either army food or Khandarai cuisine had given her a longing for good old-fashioned Vordanai fare, and she'd discovered the tavern meals here in the Docks were exactly the sort of bland, brick-heavy stuff she'd eaten as a girl at Mrs. Wilmore's. The beer was good, too. The Khandarai made good wine and liquor, but what they called beer was, at best, an acquired taste.

She hadn't intended this to be an intelligence-gathering stop. That usually came later in the day, as chairs filled up and the drink started to flow freely. She barely looked up at a nearby rustle, and nearly choked on a mouthful of beef when a woman flopped into the chair beside her with a flounce of colorful skirts.

"Hi," the woman said. "You're Winter, right?"

Winter sputtered, grabbed for her beer, and gulped frantically. The woman waited patiently while she swallowed, and Winter used the opportunity to look her over. She was a girl of eighteen or a little older, with a broad, heavily freckled face and brown hair in a tightly pinned bun that exuded a halo of frizzy, escaping strands. She wore a long skirt with a red-and-blue pattern and a sleeveless vest, exposing pale-skinned arms and shoulders already showing a hint of red from the summer sun. Her button nose was peeling, and she scratched it absently.

"I'm Winter Bailey," Winter said, when she'd recovered. That was the name she'd given in the course of her investigations, and she didn't see any point in denying it. "May I ask who you are?"

"I'm Abigail," the girl said. "You can call me Abby. Everyone does. Do you mind if I have a drink?"

"I don't think you need my permission for that," Winter said, buying time.

"A drink *here*, I mean. I'd like to talk to you." Before Winter could answer, Abby waved at one of the serving girls and pointed to the mug in Winter's hand, then held up two fingers. "I hope you'll join me."

"Much obliged," Winter said. She looked down at the remains of her meal and decided she wasn't hungry anymore. "Would it be fair of me to ask *how* you know my name?"

"Perfectly reasonable, under the circumstances," Abby said. She gave a smile so sunny Winter could almost feel the warmth on her face. "You've been asking questions about the Leatherbacks, haven't you?"

Winter froze. But, again, she could hardly deny it. She reached for her mug, took a sip, and nodded cautiously.

"And you're obviously not from around here," Abby said.

"Neither are you." Abby lacked the characteristic Docks accent.

"True! I suppose that makes us strangers together." The serving girl arrived with two more mugs, and Abby took them and set one in front of Winter. "Now, either you're a Northside girl who has gone chasing the wrong rumors—"

Winter was about to speak up, since that was exactly what she was claiming to be, but Abby went on quickly.

"—*or* you're a spy. Armsmen, Concordat, something like that. Although, no offense, if you were Concordat I would expect you to do a better job of blending in."

"So I clearly can't be a spy," Winter said. "I'm too incompetent."

"You can't be a *Concordat* spy," Abby corrected. "I wouldn't put it past the Armsmen to send some clueless girl over to the Docks to ask silly questions. Or you could be a very *good* spy, *posing* as an incompetent one to get your targets to let their guard down. *That* sounds more like Orlanko to me."

"What does this have to do with you?"

"We were curious which it was. Had a little money on it, in fact. So I thought, well, the quickest way to get an answer is always to ask directly."

"So you want to know if I'm a spy?" Winter said.

"Exactly!"

"I'm not a spy."

"Ah," Abby said, "but that's exactly what a spy *would* say, isn't it?"

Winter raised her mug, found it empty, and took a long pull from the new one Abby had ordered. The girl matched her enthusiastically.

"All right," Winter said cautiously. "I've answered the question. Now what?"

"What do you know about the Leatherbacks?"

"Only what I've heard," Winter said. "They stand up to the Concordat and the tax farmers, try to help people. And that the inner circle is all women."

"Not many people know that last part," Abby said. "Or else they don't believe it. So you just decided to come down here and try your luck?"

"I was at the University," Winter said, feeling a bit more comfortable. This part of the story she'd practiced. "My father owned an apothecary northside. We weren't rich, but he saved everything he could to send me there. He didn't have a son, you see, and I was supposed to carry on the family business."

Abby nodded appreciatively. "Go on."

"I don't know all the details. But Father got involved with a tax farmer named Heatherton." This, Janus had assured her, was a real person. "He fell behind and got into debt, then got further into debt trying to dig himself out. Eventually Heatherton turned up with a warrant that said he owned the shop, and Father went to prison. They tossed me out of the University as soon as my tuition dried up." She tried to put a little quaver into her voice, as though she were only remaining calm by dint of much effort. "I'd heard stories, and I had a little money left, so I thought . . ."

"You thought you'd come and ask for help?"

Winter shook her head. "That would be silly. I know I'm not going to get the shop back, or even get Father out of prison. I just wanted to . . . *do* something. To hurt them. To help someone else, if I could. I don't know." It wasn't hard to feign embarrassment. "Maybe it was a stupid idea."

"You'd be surprised what can come out of stupid ideas," Abby murmured.

"Are you one of them, then?" Winter said. "Is it true about the Leatherbacks?"

"Some of the stories are greatly exaggerated," Abby said. "You might say I'm an associate member."

"Can you get me a meeting with them?" Winter let a touch of her real eagerness creep into her voice. She thought it would be in character.

Abby sighed. "Are you sure that's what you want?"

"I've been down here for days," Winter said. "They have my *father*. Of course it's what I want."

"You know the story of Saint Ligamenti and the demon, right? 'Be careful what you wish for.'"

"If I remember the story," Winter said, "Saint Ligamenti tricks the demon and sends it back to hell."

"It depends on which version you read," Abby said brightly. "All right. Are you going to finish that, or are you ready to go?"

Winter looked down at the plate, a sudden unease sitting poorly amid the boiled meat and mashed potatoes in her stomach. "Let's go. I've lost my appetite."

"How did *you* join the Leatherbacks?" Winter said, as Abby led her away from the crowded River Road and into the dense tangle of plaster-and-timber buildings that housed the population of the Docks. Aside from a few major thoroughfares connecting the market squares, there were no official streets, just a wandering warren of alleys established by consensus and tradition. With the sun well up and no clouds in the sky, washing lines had sprouted from every doorway and window, like fast-growing creepers adorned with fluttering, colorful flowers. They had to pick their way carefully to avoid getting a face-full of someone's underthings when the wind blew the wrong way.

"By doing a lot of really stupid things and getting very lucky," Abby said. "Honestly, what I *deserved* was to be found floating naked in the river with my throat slit. It must be true what they say about God looking out for idiots and children."

That stymied Winter for a while, conversation-wise. Abby led confidently but apparently at random, taking this turning or that without a second thought, making wide circles when a more direct route seemed available. Winter wondered if it was all for her benefit, to keep her from remembering the way to some secret hideout. If so, it was wasted effort—Winter had been lost the moment they left sight of the river. *Maybe Abby is just lost, too.*

"I ran away from home, if you can believe it," Abby said eventually. They separated to pass to either side of a fishmonger gutting his latest acquisitions into a bucket in the middle of the street. "I didn't even have a good reason. We're a good family, plenty of money, nobody taking a switch to me or anything like that."

"What happened, then?"

"I had a difference of opinion with my father. His ideas are . . . old-fashioned."

Winter did her best to sound sympathetic. "Marriage?"

"Politics."

Abby stopped in a tiny square where five of the little streets came together, and looked around. She selected the narrowest one, a thin dirt lane squeezed so tightly between two houses there was barely room for two people to pass each other. Winter looked at it dubiously.

"Come on," Abby said. "This way."

"Where are we going, exactly?" Winter said, hurrying a little to keep up.

"Right here." Abby turned around, in the center of the alley, and gave her sunny smile again. "One of the things I learned pretty quickly was not to follow strangers down narrow alleys, even in the middle of the day."

A change in the quality of the light told Winter that there was someone behind her, blocking the mouth of the alley by which they'd come in. Another shadow loomed across the exit. She considered her options. The buildings close on each side meant it was unlikely she'd be able to scramble past an attacker, and she wasn't a good enough climber to get up the pockmarked plaster walls before someone got a hand on her. The damned dress would make running difficult, too. She had a knife, stashed in her waistband beside her coin purse, but the only thing she could think to do with it was take Abby hostage. That didn't seem like a good option; the girl looked fleet and spry, and in any case Winter wasn't sure she could cut her throat in cold blood.

Instead she smiled back and kept her hands carefully at her sides. "I hope it wasn't too painful a lesson."

There were footsteps in the dirt behind her. Two men, it sounded like. A quick kick to the groin or stomach might get her past one, but that would leave the other, with no room to get around. *A nicely planned ambush, I must say.*

"I really don't know who you are," Abby said, "but you certainly were never a University student. We have close contact with the people there. At the same time, I meant what I said about the Concordat."

"That you think I'm a spy?"

"That I think you're not competent enough to be one of Orlanko's." Abby shrugged. "This is your chance to come clean. If you're working for Big Sal or one of the other dock gangs, we're not going to hold it against you. Though they ought to know not to mess with us by now."

"I'm not working for Big Sal."

For a moment, Winter thought about telling the truth, but she held back. She wasn't certain how Abby would react, and there was always the possibility that this was some kind of hazing ritual. Admit defeat early, and at best she'd have to go back to Janus and tell him she'd failed utterly. At worst—she didn't want to think about at worst. *Better to stick to the story for now.*

"Have it your way," Abby said. "Don't squirm. You might hurt yourself."

A hood came down over Winter's face, smelling of leather and horses. Thick hands gripped her arms, and she felt herself being lifted into the air.

"I'm still not sure," Abby said, her words muffled by the leather over Winter's ears. "The Last Duke can't think we're *that* stupid."

"Could be an assassin," came another young woman's voice. "Come to kill the boss."

"How's she going to manage that tied up on the floor?" said another.

"You hear stories," said the first, darkly. "Some of the things that come out of the Cobweb aren't human."

Winter thought of Jen Alhundt, and shivered. *You have no idea how right you are.*

She was lying on what felt like threadbare carpet. After dragging her through the streets for some distance, with a little bit of spinning and doubling back for good measure, the men who'd carried her had delivered her to a doorway. They'd bound her hands, then departed, leaving Winter in Abby's charge. At that point she might have been able to make a run for it, but tied and blind she wouldn't have gotten farther than the nearest wall, so she'd allowed Abby to lead her through a building and up at least two flights of stairs. All around her, muffled by the hood, were the sounds of people talking, laughing, joking, swearing, as though they were passing through a barracks or a dormitory. The words were indistinct, but a couple of times someone hollered Abby's name in a friendly fashion. All of the voices Winter could make out were female.

After delivering her to this carpeted room, Abby had left for a minute and returned with these two other girls, who were apparently to make some kind of decision about her fate. It was, Winter thought, time to speak up.

"Is this how you treat all your guests?" She tried to put some bravado into her voice, but the leather hood somewhat spoiled the effect.

"What?" Abby said.

"I said," Winter began, but accidentally got a mouthful of leather and gagged at the awful taste. She spent a few moments coughing, the inside of the bag getting slick and hot with her own breath.

"Oh, take that thing off her," Abby said, exasperated. "She's not going to bite us, I think."

Someone loosened the drawstring at Winter's neck, and the bag came off. She drew in a great breath, thankful for even the dusty, stale air, then looked around curiously. They were in a small, unfurnished room, with only a rug on the floor and a boarded-up window. Candles burned and flickered in the corners. Abby had been joined by two girls of roughly her own age, seventeen or eighteen, dressed for labor in trousers and leather vests over linen blouses, with their hair tied up in colorful kerchiefs. The one on the left looked so pale she seemed about to faint, while the one on the right was enormous, a head taller than Winter, with the thick, muscled arms and ruddy complexion of someone used to serious outdoor work.

They hadn't searched her, which meant she still had the knife, but her hands were well secured. If they left her alone, she might be able to squirm around to the point where she could do something with it, but for now she settled for glaring at Abby.

"I said," Winter said, "do you treat all your guests this way?"

"We don't get many guests," Abby said. "We keep to ourselves, for the most part. That's part of what makes this so difficult."

"I'll do it," the smaller girl said eagerly. She took a knife from her belt, a thick cleaverlike kitchen blade with a glittering edge that spoke of many loving hours of honing. "She must be Concordat."

"If she's Concordat, we'd better ask Conner first," the big girl said thoughtfully. "He might not like it if she turned up dead."

"*I* certainly wouldn't like it," Winter said. "Especially since I'm not Concordat."

"Put that away, Becca," Abby said. "Nobody's killing anybody until the boss gets back. It shouldn't be long now."

Becca put the knife away with a certain reluctance. Abby looked from her to the other girl. "Chris, do you think you can watch her for a while?"

The big girl nodded. Abby and Becca went out and closed the door behind them. Winter didn't hear the click of a lock, but Chris settled herself deliberately against it and crossed her arms. Her posture dared Winter to try to get past her, but there was something off about her eyes. Winter thought there was *fear* there, and uncertainty, and something else she couldn't quite identify.

Winter rolled over until she got her legs underneath her and sat up, maneuvering awkwardly with her arms still bound behind her back. Chris' eyes followed her every move, as though she expected her to pounce like a mad dog.

"I'm not Concordat, you know," Winter said.

Chris grunted and shifted uneasily against the door.

"My name is Winter," Winter said. This got another grunt. "You're Chris? Is that short for Christina?"

"I shouldn't talk to you," Chris said. "If you're a spy."

"If I'm a spy," Winter said, trying to stay reasonable, "then you'll kill me, and it doesn't matter what you've told me. And if I'm not, then it doesn't matter anyway. Besides, is your name that important?"

Chris' lip twisted. Winter sighed.

"I'm just trying to pass the time," she said, honestly. "Waiting for someone to decide if they're going to kill you is . . . unpleasant." Her mind raced back to Adrecht's mutiny, and the look on Sergeant Davis' face as he tried to choose between rape and murder. With an effort, she pulled her thoughts back to the present.

"It's Christabel," Chris said finally. "After my mother."

"That's nice. I never knew my mother. She died when I was very young." This wasn't part of her cover story, but a bit of ad-libbing seemed to be called for. *It's the truth, anyway.*

"My mother died," Chris said. "Last year, of the root flu. And my da's in prison." Chris looked at her feet. "I tried to keep our patch going, with my brother and sisters, but last winter we nearly starved, and in the spring the tax farmer came. They took my brother for the army, and sent me and my sisters . . ." She stopped.

"I have a . . . friend in the army," Winter said, desperate to keep the conversation going. "He went to Khandar with the Colonials. Do you know where your brother ended up?"

"Somewhere to the east," Chris said. "He said he would send letters, but I never got any. James was never much for reading and writing."

"How long have you been here?" Winter said. "With the Leatherbacks, I mean. If that's who you people are."

"Don't try to trick me," Chris said, crossed arms tightening. "Don't think I'll let you get away with anything, just because I'm not as crazy as Becca. If you're a spy . . . if you came here to hurt the boss, I'll . . ."

"It's all right," Winter said, cursing mentally. "I didn't mean it like that."

But Chris had decided it was safest to say nothing at all. They sat in silence, Winter twisting her hands and worrying at the cord that bound them, until there was a knock at the door.

"Chris?" It was Abby.

"Yeah?"

"Is she still tied?"

"Yeah."

The door opened a crack. "The boss wants to talk to her alone."

"It might not be safe!" Chris protested.

"Don't tell *me* that. Come on. We can wait outside."

"But—"

"Chris." This was a third voice, an older woman. *The boss?* Something about it tickled the back of Winter's mind. "Get out of the way, would you?"

Chris opened the door, reluctantly, and stepped outside. Winter struggled to her feet, staggering a little, and waited.

Another woman came into the room and closed the door behind her. Winter's eyes went very wide.

That is not possible.

The boss of the Leatherbacks looked a year or two older than Winter herself, tall and buxom, dressed in the trousers and leather vest that seemed to be a uniform. Unlike the others, she left her hair unbound, cut man-short like Winter's own and clumped by sweat into a spiky mess—

—dark red hair, soft as silk, sliding through her fingers like liquid fire—

—green eyes that sparkled like emeralds in the sun—

—that lip-quirking smile, alive with mischief.

Not possible.

Jane took one step closer, then another, cocking her head as she examined Winter's trembling face. Winter felt frozen in time, like a mouse staring into the golden eyes of a cat, her whole body locked rigid. Her hands were still tied behind her, and she could feel her fingers curling over the cords and digging into her palms. Something thick blocked her throat.

Not possible . . .

Jane crossed the rest of the distance between them in two quick steps, grabbed her by both shoulders, and kissed her. Winter felt as if she were frozen in a block of ice, a marble statue. Jane's lips were soft and sweet, tasting faintly of mint, and the smell of her sweat catapulted Winter across time and space to a hedgerow behind the Nursery. Sweat, and mud, and a tentative touch—

Winter's reaction was instinctive. It couldn't have been anything else—her conscious mind was still too stunned to contribute, but the instincts built up over two years in hiding, terrified of this very scenario, did her thinking for her. Her hands were still bound, but by twisting her body she could get some leverage, and she pushed back against Jane's grip and drove her shoulder into the other girl's chin. Jane's teeth came together with a *clack*, and she staggered backward. Winter hooked one of her ankles with her own and turned the stumble into a fall, and Jane hit the threadbare carpet with a muffled *oof.* Winter backed up until she felt a wall against her shoulders, heart pounding as though it meant to explode.

I'm sorry. She couldn't get the words out. Couldn't get anything out. Couldn't even breathe. Her eyes filled with tears.

Jane rolled over and climbed to her knees, a trickle of blood smeared at the corner of her mouth. She fixed Winter with an unreadable look—*those green eyes*—and got silently to her feet.

Jane! I'm sorry, I'm sorry, I'm sorry . . . But her traitor throat was still locked closed. Jane turned and walked to the door, wobbling a little. It shut behind her with a slam that shook dust from the plaster, and Winter's legs gave way underneath her. She rolled onto her side and curled up on the carpet, unable to get her arms up to stanch the flow of tears.

Winter had no idea how much time passed. It could have been weeks. Something in her chest felt as though it had broken loose, a steel shard that drifted through her innards, tearing great ragged holes with every breath and every heartbeat. Her face was wet with tears, and her arms ached and were cramping.

There was a knock at the door. It took her a moment to realize that there was no one in the room but her, so she must be meant to answer.

"Yes?" she tried to say. It came out as a cough. She rolled off her side to a sitting position, spit a glob of phlegm onto the carpet, and tried again. "What?"

"It's me." Jane's voice.

"Oh."

"May I come in?"

Winter swallowed hard. She tried and failed to wipe her snotty nose on the shoulder of her blouse, and blinked tears out of her eyes. "Y . . . yes."

The door opened, slowly. Winter got a brief glimpse of Abby waiting anxiously in the corridor before Jane closed it again.

They stared at each other for a long moment. There was still a smear of blood on Jane's cheek, and a corner of her lip was already swelling.

"I—" Winter swallowed again. "I didn't mean to hurt you. I—"

"I should be the one apologizing," Jane said. Her eyes were bloodshot, Winter noted, as if she'd also been crying. "Coming at you like a horny sailor. You had every right."

"It's just . . ." Winter tried to gesture, but her hand only tugged weakly at the cord behind her back. "Do you think you could untie me?"

"Oh!" Jane's eyes went wide. "Goddamn. I didn't even think about that. Just a minute."

A knife appeared in her hand, so fast that Winter didn't see where she'd gotten it from. She put her other hand on Winter's shoulder, a tentative touch with fingers extended, and Winter obligingly turned round. The cord fell away, and Winter winced as sensation flooded back into her fingers and filled with pricking needles. Jane stepped back, formally, as though they were fencers at a duel, and made the knife disappear again.

"I had this . . . idea," Jane said, as Winter cautiously worked her fingers and felt her shoulders pop. "A fucking fantasy, more like. One day I'd be walking along, and I'd turn a corner, and you'd just be . . . right there. And I'd grab you, and kiss you, and then everything would . . . be all right. Just a dream, right? When I opened the door, I wasn't sure I was awake." She ran her hand through her spiky hair and gave an exasperated sigh. "That sounds like I'm making excuses. Fuck. No. I'm sorry. I shouldn't have done that."

"It's . . . all right," Winter said. "I didn't hurt you very badly, did I?"

"Busted my lip pretty good, but I've had worse." Jane shook her head, eyes locked on Winter's face. Winter took her sleeve in one hand and dabbed at her eyes, suddenly self-conscious. "I am awake, right? You're really here? This isn't some goddamned dream?"

"Apparently not," Winter said. "Though I think I may still be in shock."

"Goddamn. God*damn*." Jane shook her head. "They told me they'd brought in someone called Winter, and I thought . . . no. That's *not* the way the world fucking works." She swallowed, and her voice got very quiet. "I thought you were dead."

That caught Winter off guard. "What? Why?"

"I went looking for you. You weren't at Mrs. Wilmore's, and nobody knew where you'd gone. There was this rumor that you'd escaped, run away, and become a soldier or a bandit chief, but I never believed it. I thought for sure that you'd died somehow, and that withered bitch was covering it up. Did you really get away?"

Winter nodded. "I thought . . ."

"How? What happened?" Jane caught Winter's expression, and the eager tone in her voice fell away. "What's wrong?"

Three years of nightmares. Winter bit her lip. "I never thought I'd see you again. I didn't think you'd . . . want to find me."

"What?" Jane took a half step forward, then checked herself. Her cheeks

flushed, and her hands gripped the edges of her trousers and twisted the fabric. "Winter. Why would you say that?"

"It . . . it was . . ."

Winter's throat was blocked again. Her eyes filled with tears, and she wiped at them angrily with her sleeve. Jane swore under her breath, and after a moment Winter felt her standing close, inches away. She hovered, halfway to gathering Winter to her chest.

There was a long pause. Winter stepped forward, pressing her face against Jane's shoulder, and Jane's arms surrounded her with a tangible feeling of tension released. After a moment, Winter felt Jane's cheek resting on the top of her head.

"I like the short hair," Jane whispered, after a brief eternity. She rubbed her cheek back and forth. "It tickles."

Winter smiled shakily, face pressed into the leather of Jane's vest. *I have to say it.* She wanted to stay here, in the circle of Jane's arms, and never leave. *But if I don't say it, none of this is* real.

"It was my fault," Winter said, barely audible. "I was supposed to get you out. That night, when Ganhide . . . visited you. I was . . . I couldn't do it." That was the night that had haunted her dreams for years. The night she'd been supposed to escape with Jane, only to find that the brutish Ganhide had gotten to her first.

"You've been worried about *that*?" Jane squeezed Winter a little tighter. "Balls of the Beast. Winter, I was *crazy*. You know that, right? I mean, I told you to *kill* him if you ran into him."

"I couldn't do it."

"No shit you couldn't do it. You were what, seventeen? And if you *had* done it we'd probably both be hanged by now." Jane rubbed Winter's shoulder. "Come on. I was a teenager, too, and scared out of my wits. That 'plan' would have gotten us killed."

"I got all the way to the door," Winter said. The lump in her throat was melting. "I had the knife. Ganhide was *right there*. I almost . . ."

"Karis Almighty. Really?" Jane rocked her, gently, back and forth. "It's all right. It's all right."

"But . . ." Winter rubbed her face against Jane's vest one more time, then looked up. "I left you for him. I just *left* you there. How can that . . . how can you say that was all right? He took you away and—"

"Married me?"

Winter nodded, lower lip trembling.

"That was the plan all along, remember? One of my better plans, from when I was a little more in my right mind. I told you it would be easier to get away from some idiot husband than from Mrs. Wilmore and her crew of dried-up old cunts. I was out of Ganhide's place in less than a month."

She smiled, and that almost made Winter start crying all over again. It was the same Jane smile, crooked at one side, alive with intelligence and mischief. Winter let out a breath, and something else escaped with it, something she'd been holding in the pit of her stomach for three years. Her body felt light, as if she'd just shed a sixty-pound pack, and her limbs were as wobbly as after a long day's march. She shifted, to unpin her arms from her sides, and nearly fell over. Jane linked her hands at the small of Winter's back to keep her upright, and Winter let her own hands rest on Jane's shoulders.

"You really don't . . . hate me? You're not angry?" *Can you be haunted by someone who isn't dead?*

"Winter, listen to me." Jane matched her stare, eyes locked on each other. "I should apologize to *you*. I never should have asked you to do that. Hell, I wouldn't have done it myself. I'm sorry."

"You don't have to be sorry," Winter said. "I think we've both apologized enough."

Jane's smile returned. They held perfectly still for a long moment, still staring. Winter felt as though they were breathing in unison, as though animated by a single bellows. Jane licked her lips nervously.

"You have no idea how much I want to kiss you," she said, in a whisper.

"It's all right."

"You're sure? What I did before—I wouldn't blame you if you didn't—"

"It's all right."

Winter smiled, and when Jane hesitated a moment longer, she pulled herself up and kissed her instead. She still tasted of mint, and very slightly of blood from where she'd cut her lip. Winter's hand slid across Jane's back, up the nape of her neck, and twisted itself in her hair.

"Your hair looks nice short, too," Winter said, when they finally came up for air. Their faces were only inches apart, noses almost touching. "But I'm going to miss wrapping it around my fingers."

"You know what's strange? I miss brushing it. It was always such a chore, but it made me feel calm, sometimes." She shook her head. "It was that fucker Ganhide who made me cut it, you know. He said it only got in the way. Maybe I ought to grow it out again."

"You really just ran away from him?"

"More or less." There was an odd look in Jane's eyes, as though she was seeing something she preferred not to remember. She blinked rapidly, and it was gone. "But what happened to *you*? I couldn't find anything but rumors. It was like you'd dropped off the face of the earth."

Winter closed her eyes and let out an exaggerated sigh. "That," she said, "is a *long* story."

MARCUS

Vice Captain Giforte came into Marcus' office and dropped a stack of pamphlets on his desk, beside the piles of reports and cleaning rotas.

"This is becoming a real problem," he said.

"Good morning, Vice Captain," Marcus said mildly.

He sipped from his cup of coffee and made a face. For five years in Khandar, he'd put up with drinking coffee because there wasn't a decent cup of tea to be had in Ashe-Katarion for love or money. The supply of dried leaves Janus had brought along had been almost as much a boost to Marcus' morale as the two thousand extra troops. But now that he was back in Vordan, where the best tea in the world could be had on any street corner for a couple of pennies, he found himself missing the thick, dark coffee of Khandar. A Khandarai would have confused what the Vordanai called coffee with river water. Marcus set the cup down, regretfully.

"Good morning, Captain," Giforte said.

"You're fully recovered?"

"Yes, sir. It was only bruises."

"And you've made arrangements for . . ." Marcus realized, with a guilty pang, that he'd already forgotten the names of the Armsman who had died. He cleared his throat. "You've made arrangements?"

"Yes, sir. By the grace of His Majesty, families of men who fall in the line of duty are well provided for."

"Good." That was a new wrinkle. None of the men Marcus had commanded in the Colonials had had any family to speak of. "And Eisen?"

"He should recover fully, sir. He expressed a desire to be back on duty as soon as possible. I believe he wanted to thank you for saving his life."

"Let him take as much time as he needs." Marcus scratched his cheek. "Now. What are these?"

"Broadsheets and pamphlets, sir. All printed since last night. Take a look."

Marcus flipped through the stack, looking at the front pages. The inking had a smudged, hasty look, with lots of big blocks of barely readable text. They differed in what they considered important, but the phrase "One Eagle and the Deputies-General" appeared in nearly every headline. Marcus tapped it and looked up at Giforte.

"What does this mean?"

"'One Eagle' refers to the traditional price of the four-pound loaf, sir. It's over four eagles now. And the Deputies-General was the assembly that first offered the crown to Farus the Conqueror after—"

"I know what they *are*, Vice Captain. Why have they got everyone so worked up?"

"It's Danton," Giforte said. "That's his new slogan. Cheap bread and political reform."

"Fair enough. So what's the problem?"

"He's drawing big crowds, sir. Bigger every day. People are starting to take notice. They say the Exchange is getting skittish."

"I don't think protecting people from falling share prices is in our jurisdiction."

"No, sir," Giforte said. "But I'm starting to hear talk."

"Talk from whom?"

The vice captain's features froze into a grimace. "Leading citizens, sir."

Ah. In other words, someone's been leaning on him. Marcus himself hadn't been in place long enough to attract that kind of pressure—presumably it was easier to ignore him and go straight to the man with the real authority. "Has Danton done anything illegal?"

"Not that I can see, sir. Although we could probably come up with something if you wanted to have a chat with him."

"If he hasn't done anything wrong, then I don't want to worry about him just yet." Catching the vice captain's expression, he sighed. "I'll pass your 'talk' on to the minister. He can decide whether there's anything to be done about Danton."

"Yes, sir." Giforte looked relieved to have passed the burden up the chain of command.

"Is there anything else pressing this morning?"

"Not particularly, sir."

"Good." Marcus pushed his coffee away. "I'm going to have a chat with our prisoner. See if a night in the cells has done anything to loosen his tongue." Giforte's interrogators had questioned the man; they'd taken all evening, to no avail.

Giforte's face froze again. He could give Fitz a run for his money, Marcus thought, in the carefully-not-saying-how-stupid-you-are-sir department.

"Are you certain you want to do that yourself, sir?" the vice captain said. "My men are more . . . experienced with that sort of thing. He'll talk eventually."

"The minister wishes me to ask some questions that need to be kept as quiet as possible," Marcus lied. "If he's uncooperative, I'll ask His Excellency if I can brief you."

"As you say, sir. Be careful. We searched him thoroughly, but he may still be dangerous."

Marcus remembered a discordant tone, like the world tearing apart, and ripples in the air that shattered solid stone statues like toys. *You have no idea.*

The majority of the prisoners kept by the Armsmen were distributed among several old fortresses in the city, more convenient than the old palace grounds. The city's most notorious prison, the Vendre, belonged to Duke Orlanko's Concordat, but some of the most dangerous Armsmen prisoners went there as well. The cells in the Guardhouse were for captives of special interest, who had to be kept separate from the general prison population for one reason or another. Marcus had directed that the young man they'd taken in the Oldtown raid be kept in a cell as far as possible from any others, with a guard on his door at all times. So far, he seemed utterly mundane, but Marcus didn't want to take chances.

The guard was waiting in front of the solid iron-banded door, and he saluted at Marcus' approach.

Marcus nodded acknowledgment. "Has he said anything?"

"No, sir. Not a peep. He takes his meals readily enough, though."

"All right. Let me in. Then make sure we aren't disturbed until I call for you."

"Yessir." With another salute, the green-uniformed Staff turned a key and swung the door open. Inside was a small room, divided in half by iron grillwork. There were no windows, and an oil lamp hanging from a wall bracket provided the only illumination. A small hatch at waist height provided a way that food and water could be passed in without unlocking the cell door.

Marcus' half of the room was empty. The other half had a cot with a sheet and a lumpy pillow, a bucket, and a three-legged stool. The prisoner, now dressed in black-dyed linens, sat beside the grille, looking comfortable. He glanced up as Marcus entered, and smiled.

"Captain d'Ivoire," he said, in his faint Murnskai accent. "I thought I would see you eventually."

Marcus shut the door behind him, the latch audibly snicking closed. He regarded the young man for a long moment, then shook his head. "Have you got a name?"

"Adam Ionkovo," the young man said. "Pleased to meet you."

"How did you know my name?"

"You featured centrally in the reports from Khandar. There was even quite a good likeness."

"Whose reports?"

Ionkovo waved a hand. "The reports His Grace the duke was good enough to share with us, of course."

"Then you don't deny it. That you work with the Concordat. That you're one of—"

"The Priests of the Black?" Ionkovo nodded. "No, there doesn't seem to be any reason to argue the point. Though of course I am not an ordained priest, merely an . . . adviser."

The Priests of the Black. Jen Alhundt, the Concordat liaison who had become Marcus' lover, had turned out to be a member of that order, long thought extinct. More than a member—one of the *Ignahta Sempria*, the Penitent Damned, with powers that Marcus could hardly comprehend. His stomach crawled as he looked into Ionkovo's bright, beaming eyes.

"Why did your men try to kill us?" Marcus said, after a moment.

"They weren't 'my men.' They were protectors assigned to us by the order, and they took their assigned duties very seriously. I advised them to surrender, but . . ." He spread his hands. "I'm sorry it had to come to bloodshed."

"So am I."

Silence fell again, stretching on until it became awkward. Ionkovo scratched his chin and yawned.

"Come, now, Captain," he said. "We both know why you're here. Save yourself a lot of trouble and just ask your question."

"This was a mistake," Marcus said. "I shouldn't have come here. How could I possibly trust anything you tell me?"

"If you won't ask, I will." Ionkovo leaned forward. "Our reports said you were very close to Jen Alhundt. But we have no record of what happened to her, in the end. Perhaps you would care to enlighten me?"

"I'm not telling you anything."

"No? I worked closely with her for years. We were practically family. It's only natural to ask about family, don't you think?"

He'd hit the word "family" a little too hard. *Or did he?* Marcus glared through the bars, anger mixing with a roiling uncertainty in the pit of his stomach.

A lifetime ago, when Marcus had been only a boy going through his first round of education at the War College, a fire had ripped through the d'Ivoire estate. His mother, father, and little sister had lost their lives, along with most of the servants. It had been an accident, they told him, a tragic, stupid accident that had destroyed his life when it had barely gotten started.

Except . . . Jen had as good as told him it *wasn't* an accident. That there was some truth, buried in the burned-out wreckage, that he'd been too young and too blinded by grief to see. She'd been doing her best to enrage him, and he'd tried to dismiss it, but . . .

Are you certain? she'd asked. It nagged at him, like a half-lifted scab he couldn't help picking at, no matter how much it hurt. *Does he know something?*

"You want to ask, Captain," Ionkovo said. "It's written in your face. How about a trade, then? Answer my question, and I'll tell you the truth." He spread his hands. "What's the harm? It's not as though I'm going anywhere."

The truth. It was tempting, so tempting. *He certainly* isn't *going anywhere. What would be the harm?* But something deep in Marcus' soul stopped him. He'd disobeyed orders even to come down here; telling Ionkovo what he knew of that horrible night in the temple would be a betrayal of Janus' trust he wasn't sure he could live with. Slowly, he shook his head.

Ionkovo leaned back, his face hardening. "Fair enough. Let me ask you something else, then. Did Jen just lead you on, or did she actually let you fuck her?"

Marcus' head snapped up, color rising in his face. *"What?"*

"Ah, I see that she did." Ionkovo's smile had changed to a predatory leer. "I ask only out of professional interest. I'd guessed that with a simple man like yourself, she would stick to the most basic methods."

"That's enough."

"You're a lucky man, Captain. Jen is very skilled." His smile widened. "I can attest to that personally."

"Shut *up*." Marcus slammed a hand against the grille, producing a ringing, metallic tone and a stinging pain in his knuckles. "We're done here."

"If you like. My offer remains open."

"I hope it entertains you," Marcus said. "As far as I'm concerned, you can stay here until you rot."

Ionkovo chuckled. Then, as Marcus thumbed the latch, he said, "May I offer a suggestion?"

Marcus pulled the door open, teeth clenched.

"You did answer a question, after a fashion, so I owe you something. Call it a show of good faith."

Marcus wanted to slam the door in his face and keep walking, but the nagging at the back of his mind wouldn't let him.

"What?" he said, through clenched teeth.

"Have you been back to your old estate? Since . . . well, you know."

"No," Marcus said.

"It might be worth your time to have a look. Just for nostalgia's sake."

Marcus paused, deliberately, then stepped through the door and slammed it behind him. The Armsman outside saluted nervously.

"No one is to speak to him without my permission," Marcus growled. "Not Giforte, *no one*. Understood?"

"Ah, yessir."

"Good."

Part Two

ORLANKO

Duke Orlanko tossed the broadsheet onto his desk, where it bumped a stack of paper and sent the crisp white sheets sliding a few inches across the wood. To those who knew him, the gesture was as emphatic as if he'd put his fist through a window in a rage.

"'One Eagle,'" the Last Duke read, "'and the Deputies-General.'"

Andreas stood, in his long black coat, as impassive as ever.

Orlanko tapped his finger on the paper, smearing the ink slightly. It was still warm from the printer's. "As though the two were somehow connected."

"Nonsense," Andreas offered.

"It's brilliant nonsense," Orlanko snapped. "The poor of this city are cynical enough not to trust someone who promises nothing but cheap bread and times of plenty. But toss in a bit of mumbo jumbo about politics, just enough to sound confusing, and the rabble will believe anything. Most of them wouldn't know the Deputies-General if it convened in their outhouse, but they'll shout for it in the streets because it means bread at an eagle a loaf."

"Yes, sir," Andreas said.

"What do we know about this Danton?"

"Almost nothing."

"'Almost' nothing?" Orlanko controlled his temper with an effort. "The man must have come from somewhere."

"Of course," Andreas said. "But nobody knows where. We got a few bits and pieces about some kind of adopted brother named Jack, but he seems to have left the city. As far as anyone knows, Danton appeared out of thin air that day in front of the cathedral."

"And since then?"

"He stays at the Hotel Royal, near the Exchange. Keeps to his rooms and only comes out to give speeches. The staff brings him his meals."

"Who visits him?"

"Only couriers."

"You've followed them, I assume?"

Andreas nodded. "He receives a great many every day. They all come and go from the Exchange Central courier office."

"Have you traced the messages back from there?"

"We don't have the men. That office handles ten thousand messages a day."

Orlanko drummed his fingers on the broadsheet, heedless of the ink smearing under his palm. "Someone is trying to hide from us, Andreas. Like a snake in the long grass."

"Yes, sir. But I can't set a man on every trader in the Exchange."

"Even if we could, it would be a bit obvious."

This attempt at humor, feeble as it was, went completely past Andreas' head. "Yes, sir." He paused. "May I offer a suggestion?"

Orlanko cocked his head. This was unusual, coming from Andreas. "Speak."

"This business with the couriers, sir. It reminds me of the Gray Rose."

"She had contacts at the Exchange Central?"

"No, sir. But it's the *kind* of trick she liked. Hiding a tree in a forest, if you like."

Orlanko considered. If the Gray Rose *was* involved, that meant the matter went a great deal deeper than he'd thought. On the other hand, Andreas had been working on the Gray Rose case so long he was developing an unhealthy obsession with her, and had a tendency to see her fingerprints on anything mysterious. He was a fine operative, diligent and extremely persistent, but analysis was not his strong point.

"I'll take that under advisement," Orlanko said. "For the moment, focus on Danton's backers."

"Backers, sir?"

"Staying at the Hotel Royal costs money. Couriers cost money. Printing these"—he tapped the broadsheet again—"costs money. He must be getting it from somewhere. Find out where. If it's his own, find out where it comes from. If someone is bankrolling him, I want to know who. Understood?"

"Perfectly, sir. I may need to borrow some clerks from the finance section."

Orlanko waved a hand and settled back in his chair with a chorus of squeaking springs. "Take whoever you need."

"Thank you, sir."

"I received your report on that other matter, incidentally."

"Vhalnich, sir?"

"Yes, our friend Count Mieran. It seemed . . . thin."

"All the relevant information was included, sir."

"Unfortunate that the accounts are so contradictory."

Andreas shrugged. "Matters in Khandar were apparently quite confused."

"You say that Vhalnich brought two officers back with him aboard the fast packet, Captain d'Ivoire and a Lieutenant Ihernglass. I've met the captain. What's happened to this lieutenant?"

"It's not quite clear, sir. Vhalnich hasn't given him any official orders, but he hasn't been seen for several days."

"Away without leave, perhaps?"

"If so, no one has reported it to the Minister of War."

"An oddity." Orlanko frowned down at his hand and wiped it on his sleeve. "But we have too many oddities lately, and the situation is approaching a crisis. See what you can find out."

"Of course, sir."

The Last Duke took a large gold watch from his pocket and snapped it open. He liked clocks and watches. There was something about the sight of all those little wheels, rushing around and around in perfect order, that made him feel . . . peaceful.

"And now, Andreas, you must excuse me," he said, and snapped the watch closed. He levered himself out of the chair with another chorus of squeaks. "I have an appointment."

Even here, deep beneath the Ministry where only a few were permitted to tread, the halls were clean and free from damp or pests. They were not well lit, but that was unavoidable, since candles or torches required menials to tend to them, and no menials were trusted enough to work down here. He'd considered having gas laid on, but the main city lines were still miles from Ohnlei, and the expense would be colossal.

Perhaps, he thought, after the coronation, the Crown might be persuaded to bear the expense.

For now he carried his own lantern. He opened an ornate wrought-iron grate with a black iron key from a pocket on the inside of his shirt. The lantern made the shadows of the bars stripe the corridor beyond, canting back and forth as it swayed in his hand. The grate opened with the squeak of well-oiled hinges, and Orlanko continued down the hall, his padded shoes shuffling on the flagstones.

He didn't like this place, or the alliance it represented. It represented a certain untidiness in the nature of the world. Only weakness had forced him to resort to it. But the Last Duke was nothing if not pragmatic, and he had long ago committed himself to using whatever tools were necessary.

Nine hundred years ago, when Elleusis Ligamenti had laid down the foundation stones of the Elysian Church, he had ordained that it would be ruled by a council of three, each the head of an order with distinct responsibilities. The Pontifex of the White concerned himself exclusively with spiritual matters, the relationship of Man to God, and the moral well-being of the Church's flock. The Pontifex of the Red was responsible for the physical maintenance and upkeep of temporal Church power and authority, and its relations with the secular world and its rulers. And the Pontifex of the Black's remit was the endless quest against the demons of the world, as enjoined by the Savior Karis' *Wisdoms*.

As the Church's dogma had become the law of the land, the power of the Priests of the Black had expanded until they had become a vast and terrible inquisition obsessed with the discovery of doctrinal heresy as well as supernatural evil. In their obsession with destroying the demons of the world, they began to make use of the supernatural as well, recruiting fanatics who volunteered themselves for eternal punishment by playing host to a demon in order to help the Church's crusade against evil. These were the legendary *Ignahta Sempria*, the Penitent Damned.

It was this overreach by the Black Priests as much as anything else that had provoked the great schism between Free and Sworn churches, and in the aftermath of the wars sparked by that terrible rebellion the Black Priests had been greatly reduced in power. Bit by bit, they had died out, until the death of the last Pontifex of the Black had officially ended the order. To the extent that they thought about it at all, most modern people viewed this as ancient history.

After all, they would say, everyone knew there wasn't *really* any such thing as demons.

Brother Nikolai was waiting on the other side of the second grate. There was no key to this one, so it could only be unlocked from the inside, by Brother Nikolai or one of his successors. In his more whimsical moments, the Last Duke wondered what would happen if Brother Nikolai were to suffer an apoplectic fit and die without anyone noticing. Presumably they would have to smash the grate down, if only to retrieve the body.

Brother Nikolai wore soft black robes that fell in deep folds from his shoulders and shrouded him in silence, like a patch of moving shadow. His dark hair was bound in a thick queue, in the Murnskai fashion, but the most striking thing about him was the mask that obscured his face. It was a flattened oval with narrow slits for the eyes and mouth, surfaced with a thousand tiny chips of black volcanic glass, like a dark gem with innumerable facets. A tiny spot of light from Orlanko's lantern was reflected in each facet, so Brother Nikolai's face was alive with a thousand pinprick fireflies that danced and wove in unison as the lantern swung from the duke's hand.

He was a Priest of the Black. Or a subpriest, or sub-subpriest, or something similar. Orlanko had never been able to parse the arcane hierarchies of Elysium, but he assumed that Brother Nikolai must be fairly lowly to be given such a dull assignment. He was something like a lighthouse keeper, for a very peculiar lighthouse, one that lived in the dark below the Cobweb.

"Brother," Orlanko said, with a polite nod.

"Your Grace," Brother Nikolai returned, and opened the grate. Beyond it the corridor ended in a pair of facing doors. One led to the little room where Brother Nikolai lived, studied, and prayed. The other held his charge.

Orlanko followed the priest and waited while he worked the lock on the cell door. Besides Orlanko's lantern, the only light was from a candle in Brother Nikolai's room. No illumination came from the prisoner's cell, as she had no need of any.

Brother Nikolai opened the door and stepped aside. "You are punctual as always, Your Grace."

The duke favored him with a thin smile and stepped inside. The cell was generously sized, and though spare it was kept scrupulously clean. A bed and a privy were the only furniture the prisoner required.

She sat cross-legged in the center of the room, a girl not past her early twenties with short, dark hair and the pallid skin that came from years without sunlight. Her robe was similar to Brother Nikolai's, but gray. In front of her was an open book, which she was carefully passing her finger across, line by line, as though she were painting.

Brother Nikolai had once explained the procedure. The priests began with two young people. Any pair who shared a strong bond would work, lovers or even very close friends, but Black Priests preferred siblings so they could begin work at an early age. Twins were ideal. Once the pair had been chosen and carefully studied to ensure that they were free of physical or mental defects, they were both given the name of a demon to read.

From that moment forward, the two would be as one, two minds melting into each other under the vile creature's irresistible pressure. The pairs would undergo training and instruction together, and then eventually one of the two would be shipped in great secrecy to some hidden outpost of the Priests of the Black, like this one, while the other remained in the endless dungeons under Elysium. Then they would wait until they were needed, to throw the voice of the pontifex across thousands of miles in an instant, receiving reports and delivering instructions.

There was a danger in this, of course. If the member of the pair who went abroad fell into the hands of the Church's enemies, additional bonds might be created, additional minds added to the loop, with potentially disastrous results. The research theologians of the Black Priests had determined that eye contact was necessary for this procedure, and so whichever of the siblings was sent away had them removed, for safety's sake.

The girl raised her head at the sound of Orlanko's entrance, and the light of the lantern played for a moment on her pale, empty eye sockets. The Last Duke gritted his teeth at a sudden wash of nausea and set the lantern down, leaving her mutilated face mercifully in shadow.

"Hello, Your Grace," she said. She had a lilting voice with a singsong Murnskai accent.

"You recognize the squeak of my shoes?" Orlanko said, venturing a slight smile.

"Oh yes." She shrugged. "But that is no great feat, since only you and Brother Nikolai ever open that door."

Orlanko glanced at her book, which lay near where he'd set the lantern. It was a copy of the *Wisdoms*, of course, a special one made for the blind, with thickly embossed letters that could be discerned by a passing finger. The Black Priests taught the children to read in this way, after they were bonded, so that their souls might receive some measure of grace. The pages of this one were almost blank, the painted letters worn away by the passage of her fingers.

"Would you like a new one?" he said.

"A new what?"

She couldn't follow his gaze, of course. "A new copy of the *Wisdoms*. Yours seems to be worn out."

She shrugged again. "No, Your Grace. I know the words by heart anyway." She shifted slightly, robe rustling. "His Eminence is arriving."

"Very well." The Last Duke drew himself up a little, though of course there was nobody to see in the little cell.

The girl's face twisted slightly, her mouth gaping like a landed fish's for a few seconds. Then—and this was the part of the procedure that the duke always found most disturbing—a new voice emerged. Her lips moved to shape the syllables, but the sound was that of a man, his voice thick, breathy, and heavily accented. The words of the Pontifex of the Black, spoken in some dungeon fifteen hundred miles away, flashed across the continent by magic to emerge in this tiny cell.

"Orlanko," the pontifex said.

"I'm here, Your Eminence."

"My time is short," the pontifex said. There was a breathy rasp to his voice that sounded unhealthy. Brother Nikolai had once told Orlanko that the pontifex had survived a pox in childhood that had badly damaged his lungs. "What do you have for me?"

"Less than I would like," Orlanko said. "Vhalnich has not made any overt moves since returning from Khandar."

"Has he had any contact with the princess?"

"None. The only time they have met was at a reception, where I was present personally."

"And he brought nothing back from Khandar?"

"Only two of his officers," Orlanko said. "And we're keeping track of them."

"Then whatever he discovered must be with the rest of the regiment. They're still aboard ship?"

"Yes, Your Eminence." Orlanko frowned. "You're still assuming he found something."

"The agent we provided had spoken one of the Greater Names. The demon she hosted should have been a match for anything Vhalnich could do." The pontifex sounded annoyed, though Orlanko was never certain how much faith to place in communication by this strange channel. "The fact that she has not returned means that he discovered something in Khandar of considerable power."

"So you've said," Orlanko said. Privately, he thought that the pontifex placed too much faith in his precious *Ignahta*. Magic or not, anyone could be killed, or even suborned. "Do you have any idea what it was?"

"A demon, of course. A powerful one. The question is whether he called it himself or trusted it to some ally. And what *else* he may have found."

"My agents have already told us a great deal. When the Colonials land, they will provide a full report. They should have ample opportunity to gather information during the crossing."

"Good. We have worked too long for this to risk it at this stage. How fares the king?"

"Poorly. Doctor-Professor Indergast says it is a matter of weeks, at best."

"Then proceed as planned. And find out what Vhalnich is up to, and what his connection is with the princess."

"It could be a coincidence," said Orlanko.

"I don't believe in coincidence," said the pontifex.

There was another moment of gulping silence, and then the girl said, "He's gone, Your Grace."

"Thank you." The duke picked up the lantern. "Please inform Brother Nikolai if you require anything, and we will provide it."

"Thank you, Your Grace, but I am content."

Brother Nikolai closed the cell door and the grate behind him as he left, heavy iron bolts clacking home in their brackets. Orlanko's mind was otherwise occupied. In spite of what he'd said, he didn't believe in coincidence, either. *Something* had happened in Khandar, something supernatural, and Vhalnich's return mere weeks before Raesinia's coronation had to be deliberate. The mysterious colonel was planning something, and the princess was part of it.

Somewhere there was a weak link, a loose thread that would tell him what Vhalnich was up to. Sooner or later, Andreas or one of the others would find it.

And then, Orlanko thought, *I'll make Vhalnich regret the trouble he's caused me.*

Chapter Six

WINTER

"The thing you hafta understand about the Docks," Jane said, "is that the people here don't want t' fight."

Winter smiled to herself. She'd listened to Jane's accent shift as they came down out of the apartment tower, thickening into a good approximation of the dockworkers' dialect. Even her gait was different, widening into the rolling swagger affected by boatmen and those around them. Winter wondered if Jane was even aware of the changes. *She always had a talent for fitting in, when she cared to.*

"'Cept for a few fucking loonies," Jane went on, "everybody just wants to do their thing in peace and quiet, make enough to eat, maybe get drunk now an' then. But none of 'em want to get fucked over, not by each other and not by the fucking tax farmers. So they work themselves up to a brawl now and then, but they don't really *mean* it. Not like those bastards from Oldtown, who only do a bit of work when they can't find something to steal."

Jane's band of young women lived in a dilapidated four-story building, which had once been the offices of a defunct shipping company. Jane had claimed it, according to Abby, by driving out the gangs of squatters and vagrants who had been living there previously. Abby had given Winter a little tour, and Winter had been surprised both by how orderly the whole thing was and by how many people were living there. There had to be several hundred girls at least, ranging in age from Jane and herself down to children of ten or twelve. Winter, amazed, had asked where they had all *come* from, but Abby had been evasive.

Now they were out on what Jane called her "rounds." Winter had been allowed to descend without a bag over her head, which she supposed meant that she was now at least an honorary member of the gang. So far, so good, at least as far as her mission from Janus was concerned.

Janus. Winter gritted her teeth at the thought. *He had to know. He* had *to.* This whole project, sending Winter to infiltrate a gang of women dockworkers, made no *sense* unless he'd known. Janus was a good enough judge of talent to know that Winter was no spy—witness the way she'd made a hash of things. Sending her here was futile, unless Janus already knew that Jane was at the heart of these Leatherbacks.

And if he knew, *why didn't he tell me?* She couldn't decide if it had been a shrewd move on his part, given her probable reaction, or else had been the colonel's twisted idea of a joke. Janus did have a decidedly odd sense of humor at times. *Either way, I owe him a solid kick in the arse.* She glanced at Jane. *Or else my abject gratitude. One or the other. Maybe both.*

It was still a little hard for Winter to believe that Jane was *here*, that the girl who had figured so prominently in her dreams for three years was actually standing beside her. With her long hair gone, dressed in trousers and dock-workers' homespun, it sometimes felt like this profanity-spewing young woman was someone else entirely. Then something would catch Winter's eye—her face in profile, that wicked smile, a certain cast of the eyes—and her heart would give a sickening lurch, and she'd be ready to break down in tears all over again.

Jane's rounds, it turned out, consisted of walking an irregular circuit of the streets around her base. This took considerably longer than it might have, since everyone they met on the street seemed to know her, and every third person stopped her to exchange a few words. Jane introduced Winter whenever she had the chance, but to Winter the dockmen and their names quickly became a blur. They had a certain sameness about them—big, weathered men, tan and wiry from years of heavy work in the sun. They had names like Bentback Jim, Reggie's Teeth, Bob the Swine, and Walnut.

This last was a true giant of a man, bigger even than Winter's Corporal Folsom, with wrinkled skin tanned dark as leather and a grin that showed shockingly white teeth. He was called Walnut, Jane explained, because he liked to eat the nuts, and, more important, because he could crush them in his fists. Walnut, hearing this, laughed delightedly and demonstrated with a couple of nuts from a nearby bowl. He tightened his grip until they broke, with a crack like a pistol shot.

"'Ave you seen Crooked Sal this morning?" Walnut said, picking the meat from the bits of shell in his palm with surprising delicacy.

"Not yet," Jane said. "Why?"

"He was gettin' pretty hot last night," Walnut said. "Something about his daughter and George the Gut."

"Fuckin'—" Jane loosed a string of profanity that Winter couldn't follow, which made even Walnut raise an eyebrow. "Is he still going on about that?"

"Said he was going to go over there and slit George open to see what his gut was made of," Walnut said. "Course, he was sopping drunk at the time. But it sounded like he meant it."

"I'll sort him out." Jane turned on her heel and stalked away, and Winter had to hurry to keep up.

"Fucking Sal and his fucking daughter," Jane muttered.

"I take it you know them?" Winter said. "You seem to know everybody."

"Sal's an ass. And his daughter's a little idiot who likes to make trouble. I mean, why else would she move in with George the Gut? It's not like he's anything to look at."

"So, what are you going to do?"

"Find Sal and talk some sense into him. His girl's seventeen already. If she wants to spend her time fucking ugly eel fishers, that's her own business." Jane paused. "You don't have to come, if you don't want to. Sal's not really dangerous, but if he's started working himself up to something, he may be half-drunk already." She glanced at Winter and looked away, almost bashful. "All this . . . fighting and so on. You're not—"

Winter almost laughed but restrained herself. She hadn't told Jane her story yet, and so Jane's image of her was still the proper little girl from Mrs. Wilmore's, who had to be painstakingly cajoled into the slightest disobedience.

"I can take care of myself," Winter said. "Or at least manage to stay out of the way."

Jane gave her an odd look but didn't protest. They set off down the rambling Docks alleys at a more rapid pace, and Jane acknowledged the shouts of greeting from the people they passed with only a grunt and a wave. Their course tended generally downhill, and every now and then one of the straighter streets gave Winter a view of the river, glittering in the sunlight and aswarm with small boats. A few large cargo galleys were tied up to piers or making their way slowly upriver, like languid whales among schools of smaller fish.

When they were a few hundred yards from the waterfront, Jane turned into a narrow alley that passed between two stout brick warehouses and then into a back-lot no-man's-land full of small wooden dwellings. Jane headed for the closest on the left-hand side, a shaky-looking two-story construction that looked as though it had grown like a mushroom rather than been built to any plan. The windows had rag curtains instead of glass, tied up in bundles to admit any passing breeze, and the door was wide open in the summer heat. Jane took advantage of this to walk right in, with Winter following somewhat diffidently behind her.

The bottom floor of the house was one large room, arranged around a firepit. A big, solid table stood beside it, smelling distinctly of fish, with a heavy carving knife embedded in it point-down as if it were a butcher's block. A fat yellow cat, lazing in a patch of sunlight, rolled over and hissed at Jane, fur bristling.

The young man standing at the table had very nearly the same reaction. He looked to be about sixteen, thin and gangly, with a peach-fuzz mustache and a few stray wisps of beard.

"Your da upstairs?" Jane said, without preamble.

The boy puffed out his chest, though he'd retreated to put the table between himself and the intruder. "What if he is?"

"Don't be a fool, Junior. Do I look like the fucking Armsmen to you? Go and fetch him."

He deflated a little. After pausing for a few moments, just to show that he didn't *have* to do what Jane told him, he ran to the rickety staircase at the back of the house and clomped halfway up it. "Da?"

"'M busy," came a voice from above, like a drunken saint speaking from on high. "Tell 'im to go away."

"Da, it's Mad Jane!"

"Mad" Jane? Winter caught Jane's eye with a questioning look. Jane gave her best mad smile and waggled her eyebrow conspiratorially. The shared, instantaneous understanding was so powerfully familiar that it made Winter wobble, weak at the knees. *Right.* She kept her hysterical giggles to herself. *Mad Jane. I'm surprised we never called her that at Mrs. Wilmore's.*

The boy scurried out of the way as someone much heavier clumped down the stairs. This, presumably, was Crooked Sal, a man in his forties with only a fringe of stiff gray hair remaining around a bald, shiny pate. For once, no explanation of his sobriquet was necessary; Sal's nose looked as though it had been broken at least a dozen times, and it zigzagged like a wandering stream. He wore a leather vest that left his arms and hairy chest bare, and smelled of old fish. Behind him, perching halfway up the staircase, was a boy of twelve or thirteen.

"You here to stick your nose in my business?" Sal roared.

"That's right," Jane said.

"Not a good habit," he growled. "You keep putting that nose where it don't belong and it'll end up looking like mine."

"Fortunately, nobody can bear to damage my good looks," Jane said. "Now, what is this bullshit about you and George the Gut?"

"Fuckin' George the pus-ridden Gut is havin' his way with my virgin daughter!" Sal said. "I've got every right to show him the color of his kidneys!"

Jane scratched the side of her nose. "Iffie's a nice girl, but you're going a bit far there, aren't you? The way I heard it, Iffie climbed through his window in the middle of the night."

"She's still my daughter," Sal said. "An' he shouldn't have put his grubby hands all over her."

"I'm hardly an expert on daughters," Jane said. "But did you ever think this is what she wants? Getting a rise out of you? Remember what happened with Tim the Lad? Or Steve Shake Eye? Or that Hamveltai sailor you chased off?"

Sal's face twisted. That had touched a sore point, obviously, and he fell back on good old-fashioned rage. "Get out, you stupid bitch! Take your big mouth out of my house before I break your pretty face for you!"

"Not until you promise me you're not going to run off and try to carve up poor George."

"I know who I'm going to carve up!"

Sal reached across the table and wrapped his hand around the handle of the carving knife. Before he could jerk it out of the wood, Jane did her knife trick again, blade flashing into her hand as though she had summoned it into being. In the same motion she reached out, lazily, and laid the edge of the blade against the apple of Sal's throat. Sal froze.

"I would think real fucking hard before you do that," Jane said. Her eyes moved. "And you, Junior, I would think even harder."

The older boy had been edging toward the confrontation. He paused, and Winter passed unnoticed behind him. There was a heavy iron poker by the stairs, and she edged in that direction, ready to grab it if Jane lost control of the situation. Glancing over her shoulder, she saw the younger boy fumbling with something—there was a *click*, menacingly familiar—

Winter reacted instinctively. She grabbed the poker in one hand, spun, and swung it around into the barrel of the pistol the kid had just cocked. He pulled the trigger just before the metallic *clang* of the impact, and she saw the flash of the powder in the pan, followed by the shatteringly loud report of the gun going off. By that time, her blow had knocked it well away from its intended target, and the ball *pocked* into a wall, throwing off splinters.

Sal was so surprised he let go of the knife and bulled forward, and Jane had to retreat hastily to keep him from cutting his own throat. He whirled to face the stairs, where the younger boy was cowering and clutching his stinging hand.

"Jim!" he roared. "What the *fuck* do you think you're doing?"

"She was going to hurt you, Da!" Jim screeched. "She had a knife, and—"

"I am going to give you such a *fucking* thrash—"

Sal took a couple of steps toward the stairs and his cowering son, then stopped, because Jane had grabbed his arm from behind. He started to turn but halted when he felt the prick of her knife between his shoulder blades.

"You're more of a fucking moron than I thought, Sal," said Jane. "Were you planning to bring that thing to George's?"

Sal had the grace to looked embarrassed. "George has got three sons. They might've been armed."

"And if they had been? You'd have killed one of 'em? What for?"

"I just thought—"

"Thinking is the last thing you were doing. Now, you listen to me, Salmon Bellows. I have had *enough* of this, do you hear? When Iffie comes back—and she *will* come back, once she figures out you're not going to pick a fight with George—I want you to have a nice long talk with her. A *talk*. If I hear that she's walking around with bruises, I'm going to come back, and you and *me* will have a talk. You understand?" She nodded at the boy on the stairs. "That goes for him, too. It's your own damned fault for leaving a loaded pistol lying about. You get all that?"

"I—" Sal began, but Jane did something to his arm, and he moaned. "I get it. I get it!"

"Good." Jane backed off a step and made the knife disappear again. "Hell, tell Iffie that if she really likes George so much, she ought to marry him. That ought to bring her running back right away."

Sal, to Winter's amazement, laughed and shook his head. His sons laughed with him, timidly, and at this reminder he turned on them with another roar.

"And as for *you*, Jim, I'm—"

Jane cleared her throat pointedly, and Sal paused.

"I'm going to have a talk with you," he finished. "A *long* talk. Now go to your room and stay there."

Jane took her leave, and Winter followed her back out into the alley. They said nothing until they'd gone round a bend and out of sight of the little shack. Jane sighed and rubbed her temples.

"Goddamn that kid. Scared the piss out of me." She squeezed her eyes shut for a moment, took a deep breath, then looked up at Winter. "Are you all right?"

Winter flexed her hand, which still tingled from the transmitted impact of the poker. "Nothing serious. I'll be fine."

"Fucking kid. Could have killed someone."

"I think he wanted to kill *you*, actually."

Jane chuckled. "I gathered that. Nice swing with the poker, by the way. Have I thanked you yet?"

"Not as such."

"Thanks." Jane ran a hand through her hair, mussing it further. "Sorry. It's not every day a kid a head shorter than me tries to fucking shoot me in the back."

"You could have fooled me," Winter said, honestly. "I figured this was all in a day's work for Mad Jane."

"Don't *you* start," Jane muttered. "It's bad enough that Sal and the rest started calling me that." Catching Winter's smirk, she changed the subject. "What about you, anyway? What happened to the girl who was too afraid to throw a bucket of shit at Mary Ellen Todd? Did you take lessons in swinging a poker?"

"Not . . . exactly," Winter said.

"You said it was a long story."

"It is."

"Well," Jane said, "we've got a ways to go yet."

By the time they made it back to Jane's building, late in the afternoon, Winter had gone through most of the last three years. It had been a halting narrative, punctuated by Jane's conversations with various merchants, fishwives, and other Dockside inhabitants along her route. A few times she'd had to stop while Jane was called on to solve some minor issue, such as one house's tendency to lean onto another's property and what that should mean for rents, or the matter of some rancid fish that somehow got packed into a shipment. Each time, the participants seemed to look to Jane for judgment as a matter of course, and accepted her ruling with more grace than Sal had done.

These gaps helped Winter keep her story straight. She told the truth, more or less, but left her personal involvement in events deliberately vague, and omitted any mention of Feor, Bobby's healing, or that last awful night in the temple under the Great Desol. After a short internal struggle, she also decided to say nothing about what Janus had sent her to do. *I still need to figure that out myself. I can always fill Jane in later.*

Jane listened, her eyes going wider and wider, until by the end of the trip she was ignoring the friendly greetings that met her at every corner to concentrate entirely on Winter. When they stopped outside the barred gate of her building, she stopped and glared.

"You're serious about this, aren't you?" Jane said. "You ran away from Mrs. Wilmore's and joined the *army*, like some girl out of a ballad?"

Winter nodded.

"And then you served in fucking Khandar with *Vhalnich*?"

"I didn't *mean* to," Winter said. "I went to Khandar because I thought it would be a good place to hide. It's not my fault they decided to have a revolution right after I got there."

"You really did it," Jane said. "I do not *fucking* believe it!"

With a happy shout, she grabbed Winter and hugged her roughly, and after a stunned moment Winter hugged her back.

"God," Jane said, "and here I was pretending *I* was the tough one, when you've been marching around fucking Khandar and eating monkey brains."

"No monkeys in Khandar," Winter said, a bit muffled. "Beetles, though. They like to eat beetles. And there's these sort of snakes that live in the canals. They pack them in mud and bake them—"

"Please stop," Jane said. "I've just worked up a healthy appetite and I'd hate to ruin it. Does your diet still extend to cows and pigs?"

"Not often enough," Winter said. "Mostly we ate mutton. I never want to see another sheep as long as I live, alive *or* boiled."

"Come on, then. You can sample the unique Vordanai delicacy I call 'pork roast pretty rare on one side and fucking black on the other,' because Nellie in the kitchen is still learning and tries her best." Jane shook her head. "I can't wait to tell the girls you were in *Khandar.* They're going to have fits."

"*No!*"

The word came out of Winter with such force that it surprised both of them. Jane went quiet.

"You can't tell anyone," Winter said, only now becoming aware of the risk she was taking. *If word gets* out *that there's a girl-in-boy's-clothing in the Colonials, I'll never be able to go back.* The thought of wearing dresses for the rest of her life brought her close to the edge of panic, and her collar suddenly felt tight and hot. It hadn't even occurred to her that she might not be able to trust Jane. "Please." The word was all she could manage.

There was another strained silence. Jane coughed.

"Well," she said. "It's your story."

"Thank you." Winter felt her throat unclench. "I'm sorry. I should have . . . said something. I'll explain—"

"Don't worry about it," Jane said. "In here we don't ask about what happened to anybody if they don't want to talk about it. Saves a lot of tears." She smiled. "I guess we'll have to entertain the girls with the story of how you saved my life from little Jim Bellows."

Winter's smile was weak, but grateful. "I don't know if he could have *hit* you, to be honest. Except maybe by accident."

"You're probably right," Jane said. "But we don't have to tell *them* that."

Supper was a drawn-out affair in Jane's— *Apartments? Barracks? Commune?* Winter wasn't really sure what to call it. The knocked-together kitchen and dining room weren't big enough to hold all the girls at once, so they turned up in shifts, while a relay of cooks came and went in the kitchen under the uncertain supervision of Nellie-who-tries-her-best.

The dining room—fashioned from several adjacent offices by knocking down any inconvenient walls—was a churning flock of eating, talking, laughing young women, dressed in a bewildering variety of clothes that had all come from the bottom of someone's ragbag. They ate off a menagerie of clay and wooden crockery, with flatware gathered from a thousand junk shops and rubbish bins. As far as Winter could tell, small groups turned up whenever they liked and ate their fill, then left to make room for others.

Jane presided over it all like a medieval baron, sitting at an especially tall table with a small group of the older girls. Winter had a seat to one side of her, which got her a few uncomfortable looks from some of the others, but Jane immediately launched into the story of what had happened at Crooked Sal's, and that broke the ice. Abby, who seemed to serve as a kind of second-in-command, sat on Jane's other side. Among the others, Winter recognized Becca and Chris from when she'd been captured, and was introduced to a short, soft-spoken girl named Min and a ramrod-thin woman closer to her own age called Winnie. These four, with Abby, seemed to serve as Jane's lieutenants, and Winter's presence at the high table apparently meant that she'd been added to their number.

The food was everything Jane had promised or threatened. It was plain and plentiful, with more meat and fish than Winter had seen in her years at Mrs. Wilmore's *or* her time in the army. There was plenty of bread, too, great piles of steaming round loaves.

Winter ate her fill, and more. Her army time had taught her that the availability of food was always touch-and-go, so it was always best to stock up when one had the chance. Jane also attacked her plate with gusto, though she carried on a whispered conversation with Abby throughout the meal. Winter restrained her curiosity, though she couldn't help noticing that Abby left in the middle of dinner, leaving behind a half-full plate.

Once she'd taken the edge off her hunger, certain questions presented themselves irresistibly to Winter. Jane was fully occupied in her role as master of the house, shouting across the room to this girl or that and occasionally roaring with laughter at the responses. Min reported on the day's activities—her responsibilities seemed to focus on the care and feeding of the younger girls—and Jane listened and gave occasional instructions.

Where does it all come from? These girls ate better than she ever had in the army, and the food was certainly better than the gray slop produced by Mrs. Wilmore's kitchen. *How does she pay for all this?* For that matter, where had the girls themselves come from? *Abby said she'd been taking in orphans and strays, but that can't be* all *of them.*

As supper wore on, Winter started to worry. *Janus sent me here for a reason, after all, and he's Minister of Justice now. Maybe Jane's running a gang of thieves.* A gang of thieves that included a cadre of chattering, happy twelve-year-olds seemed unlikely, but Winter's experience was limited. The feral children of Ashe-Katarion had certainly included their share of thieves, but she couldn't picture them sitting around a table like this.

Another thought occurred to her, and Winter bit her lip. There was always *one* way for a group of young women to earn a living, after all. *Surely not. Jane would never be involved in something like* that. Her friend's morality had always been a bit selective, but surely there were some lines she would never cross. *Never.*

By the end of the meal, she was feeling decidedly uncomfortable. The conversation flowed all around her, but she was no part of it, like a rock sticking out of a smoothly flowing stream. It felt all too much like being back in Davis' company, as the "Saint," collecting her meager ration and wolfing it down in silence while the men around her joked and boasted about their drinking and whoring. The jokes were different, of course, but the feeling of camaraderie—from which she was excluded—was the same. She poked morosely at the congealing bits of fat and vegetable left on her plate.

A hand descended on her shoulder, and she looked up to find Jane smiling down at her.

"I'm about done," she said. "Let's go upstairs."

"I've got—" Winter began.

"Some questions." Jane gave a little sigh, and her smile faded. "I know."

Jane's room was on the top floor, in one corner of the building, where windows caught the sun from two sides. They arrived to find Abby tugging the door closed with one finger, awkward because she was carrying a thick wad of clothing in her arms.

"Sorry," she said, edging to the side of the passage to let them pass.

Winter got the feeling that Jane's room had been enlarged from its original state in the same way the dining room had, by pulling out interior walls, but here some effort had been made to disguise the fact. A half dozen rugs of different fabrics and vintages overlapped on the floor, and a heavy oak table in one corner was strewn with papers. The walls were hung with colorful fabric to disguise the crumbling plaster. A couple of heavy trunks, lids open, comprised Jane's wardrobe, and an enormous mattress meant for a four-poster bed simply lay on the floor, covered by a clean but threadbare sheet.

"My palace," Jane said, spreading her hands. "Do you like it?"

"I spent two years living in a tent," Winter said, closing the door behind her. "Just sleeping indoors feels like a luxury to me." She hesitated. "Nobody's going to—"

"Sit with a glass pressed against the door? Don't worry."

Winter relaxed a little. "How long have you been here?"

"Just over a year," Jane said. "It seems like longer."

"You've certainly made yourself comfortable."

"I'm good at that." Jane winked, and went to a small cupboard standing on its own beside the big table. She withdrew a corked bottle and two slightly dusty glasses and waggled them suggestively at Winter. "Drink?"

Winter nodded. While Jane poured, she went to the window and twitched the curtain aside. Summer's late evening sun was just setting, staining the muddy, sooty streets of the Docks with a pattern of red and black. Candles and torches burned here and there, but not many. The view was to the north, and Jane's building was taller than those around it, and so Winter could see all the way to the river and beyond. The Island was a blaze of light in the distance, like an enormous ship.

Jane stepped up behind her, quietly, and pressed a glass into her hand. Winter sipped without looking, and was pleasantly surprised. *Of course, any Vordanai wine would taste good next to that Khandarai stuff.* She made a face at the memory.

"No good?" Jane sipped from her own glass. "Not the *best* vintage, I'll grant you, but—"

"It's fine." Winter turned. "I have to ask. What are you *doing* here? Where did all these people come from? How do you manage to feed them all?"

"It is a bit odd, when I come to think about it." Jane turned her glass back and forth, staring at it. Winter noted, absently, that much of the swearing had dropped out of her vocabulary now that they were alone. "It's . . . like yours. A long story."

"I think we have time," Winter said.

"I suppose so." Jane took a deep breath. "Most of the girls are from Mrs. Wilmore's, like us."

"What?"

"I went back, after I ran away from Ganhide," Jane said. "I had to hide for a while, until they gave up looking for me, and I sort of got to thinking. I'd got away, all right, but there were all those girls still there, and the same thing was just going to happen to them—they'd be married off to the first brute of a farmer who came asking."

"So you went back."

"I went back."

"And staged an . . . escape?" There had to be three hundred people in the building. Winter tried to imagine them all sneaking out of Mrs. Wilmore's, one at a time, hiding from the proctors and the mistresses . . .

"In a way," Jane said. She scratched the back of her head and reddened slightly. "More like a revolution, actually."

"A revolution? But how did you keep from getting caught?"

"I didn't." Jane swallowed the rest of her drink with sudden decision. "When

I first got there, I was hiding in the hedges and so forth, but the more I watched the more I thought . . . why bother? I mean, you were there. It's not as though Mrs. Wilmore had a fucking battalion of guards on the premises."

"But . . ."

"I know." Jane shook her head. "When I first went back, I was so frightened. I spent days trying to figure out how to get in without the proctors seeing me. It all went to shit when I tried it, of course. I practically walked into one after five minutes. I was ready to run for it, and she was shouting, and suddenly I thought—she's nothing! Just a little girl with a sash! She probably wasn't fifteen, a little stick of a thing. I just pushed her out of the way and kept going."

"Didn't she fetch the mistresses?"

"Of course. But by that time I had a little while to talk to the girls in the dorms. So on one side there were five old women with willow switches, and on the other a couple of hundred angry girls." Jane grinned. "They took one look at us and locked themselves in their offices."

Winter couldn't help laughing. It was true, when you thought about it that way. Mrs. Wilmore's moral authority had always been so overpowering she'd seemed like a deity from antiquity, living on a mountaintop somewhere and dispensing favor or thunderbolts according to her whims. But, of course, she was human like anyone else. *Just a bitter old woman.* Even at Winter's distant remove, it was a tremendously liberating thought.

"And you just walked out," Winter said.

Jane nodded. "We just walked out. I told the girls I would take care of anyone who wanted to come with me. Some of them stayed behind, some of them just bolted and disappeared, and the rest . . ." She waved a hand at the building below them.

This must have been after Bobby escaped. The corporal had been closemouthed about her time in Mrs. Wilmore's institution, but she surely would have mentioned *this.*

"You had all this ready for them?" Winter said.

"What? Oh no. God, it was fucking awful for a while. We spent a week sleeping in the swamps past the Bottoms, staying up half the night with torches and cudgels to keep the thieves and rapers away. I had no idea what I was doing. All this came later."

Winter laughed again. That was Jane all over—do something bold, brilliant, beautiful, and have absolutely no idea how to handle the consequences. *Dive in first and worry about how deep the water is later.* She drained her own glass, looking around for the bottle, and it was a moment before she realized Jane had gone silent.

"Jane?"

She was staring at her hands, rolling the empty glass from one to the other. A single crimson droplet spiraled round and round just short of the rim, never quite escaping.

"Sorry," Winter said. "I shouldn't have laughed. It must have been terrible."

"What? Oh." Jane shook her head. "It's all right. It is pretty fucking funny, when you think about it. I was just—running, from one thing to the next, trying to stay one step ahead of the Armsmen and the thieves and just plain starvation. With a couple of hundred people suddenly looking to me to keep them safe and figure out where their next meal was coming from."

Winter winced in sympathy. Her thoughts went back to her first mission with the Seventh Company, d'Vries' idiot scout, and the sudden crashing realization that everything had descended on *her* shoulders. Screams and powder smoke, the crash of muskets and thrashing, terrified horses . . .

"I nearly left them," Jane said, very quietly. "In the swamp. I was standing guard, and I thought, I could just *leave*. Then none of this would be my problem anymore."

"You didn't, though."

"I wanted to. I wanted to, so badly. Or else to just wander out into the bog, get lost, step in some sinkhole, and just let it swallow me. It didn't seem *worth* it."

There was a long silence. Jane turned the glass round and round. Tentatively—it had been a *long* time since she'd touched another human being of her own free will—Winter extended a hand and let it rest on Jane's shoulder.

"You did it, though. You won." Winter patted her in a way she hoped was reassuring. "You beat Ganhide, and Mrs. Wilmore, and all the rest. I mean, look at this place!"

"You don't understand," Jane said. "I didn't—I thought—"

She swallowed hard. Winter, uncertain, said nothing.

"I wasn't looking to start a revolution at Mrs. Wilmore's," Jane said. "Not really. I was looking for *you*."

Oh. Winter blinked.

"Every day, after I ran away from Ganhide, I thought about you stuck in that place and . . . what they would do to you, eventually. I *had* to go back. But it took so long—I needed to hide, and then . . ."

"I was gone by the time you got there," Winter said.

Her throat clenched under a sudden, crushing wave of *guilt*. All this time, she'd felt like a traitor for her failure to set Jane free on that last night. She'd cursed herself as a coward. *But what happened afterward* is worse. *I ran away to Khandar like all the demons of all the hells were after me. I never even* considered *going back to look for Jane, helping her get away from Ganhide, or all the other girls I left behind. I just ran until I found somewhere I thought no one would ever find me.*

"It's good that you ran away," Jane said, still staring at her glass and oblivious of Winter's moral crisis. "I wouldn't have wished you another minute in that fucking place. When I got back there, though, and they told me that you were gone, and *no one* had any idea to where . . ." Her grip tightened on the glass, as though she meant to shatter it against her palm.

"I'm sorry," Winter said, in a whisper.

"No. I told you, I don't blame you for anything. You did what you had to do."

"I'm sorry." It felt like all Winter could do was repeat it. "Jane, I'm—"

"Would you stop apologizing?"

"But—"

Jane turned, grabbed both of Winter's shoulders, and jerked her close. Winter shut her eyes and cringed, in automatic expectation of a blow, but received a kiss instead.

It went on for a long time. She could taste the wine, smell the sweat on Jane's skin, feel a tickle where a tear had run down Jane's cheek and ended up hanging from the tip of Winter's nose. Jane's hands slid down to the small of her back, drawing them together, and Winter could sense the warmth of her through layers of leather and linen.

Jane finally pulled away, breathing hard, but she kept her arms wrapped tight. Winter's whole body tingled, and her head swam as though she'd had considerably more than one glass of wine.

"It's all right," Jane said. "You're here. That's all that matters now."

Winter, staring into those hypnotic green eyes, nodded.

Eventually the moment ended, as all moments do. A muscle in Winter's leg, weary from the long day of walking around the city, chose that moment to register its complaint with a vicious cramp, and Winter stumbled and nearly fell. Jane took her weight and swung her toward the mattress, where Winter sat with a thump. Jane flopped down beside her, stretching her arms above her head and arching her back like a cat.

"God," she said. "Just talking about it makes me feel better, you know?"

"I should . . ." Winter shook her head, still dizzy. The softness of the mattress was suddenly unbelievably attractive. "Sleep, I think. It's been a long day. I don't suppose you could spare a bunk for me?"

Jane looked at her sidewise. "I can have them make up a room. There's plenty of space."

"Thank you."

"Or," Jane said, "you could stay here."

"Here?" There was a long, stupid moment while Winter cast about the room to see if there was another bedroll tucked away somewhere. Then, belatedly, she understood. "Oh. Here, with you."

Jane smiled again. "Here, as you say, with me."

Some part of Winter wanted to. Her body fairly ached where Jane had been pressed tight against her, in ways that had nothing to do with hours of walking around town. But she couldn't stop the panicky feeling that welled up when she thought about it, the ground-in need to *flee* from even the possibility of contact.

"I . . . can't," she said, after a moment.

Jane nodded levelly. Winter searched her face.

"It's not that I don't want to," Winter said. "I do. I mean, with you. Just not . . . now. It's hard. I'm sor—"

"I told you to stop apologizing," Jane said. "It's all right, really."

"I'm just . . . tired." Winter took a deep breath and got a grip on herself. "Just give me some time to get used to things."

"Of course." Jane stood up and extended a hand. "Come on. We'll find you a room."

Winter took her hand, tentatively, and allowed herself to be led out into the hall, wobbling like a drunk on her way home from the tavern.

She barely remembered the room they'd put her in, or undressing. It might have been the best night's sleep she'd ever had, dark and silent and blessedly free of dreams.

MARCUS

The heavy Armsmen carriage rumbled down Fourth Avenue, toward the intersection with Saint Dromin Street. Marcus twitched aside the curtain to look at the houses going by and wondered what the hell he was doing.

Here, at least, he didn't require an armed escort. This was the far north of Northside; too far from Bridge Street and the Island to be truly fashionable, but well insulated from the teeming crowds of Southside and the poverty of Oldtown. It was a neighborhood of big, low houses with well-landscaped grounds, with flower gardens and small groves of birch and willow. The buildings were set back from the street, behind screening trees and gravel drives flanked by stables and carriage-houses. The people who lived here were moderately well-to-do merchants, as Marcus' father had been, or the upper crust of well-payed artisans and professionals.

Marcus was accompanied only by his driver and Staff Eisen, fresh from the cutters' care. The young man looked only a little the worse for their attentions, with his left arm neatly trussed in a linen sling and swathed in bandages. Looking at him reminded Marcus of Adrecht, who'd lost an arm to a similar wound at Weltae-en-Tselika. He suppressed a shudder.

"You're certain you want to take up your duties so soon, Eisen?" Marcus said. "If it's a matter of money, I can make sure—"

"No, sir. I mean, yes, sir, I am, and it's not about money. I don't like sitting around, sir." He touched his bound arm. "The cutter told me it wouldn't be a problem. No bones broken. Not much of a wound at all, really. I oughtn't to have passed out."

"Just shock," Marcus said. "It happens, if you've never been shot before. Not your fault. And you still didn't have to come all the way out here with me."

"Vice Captain Giforte assigned me to look after you, sir," Eisen said, as though that explained everything.

Marcus wondered if the Staff's enthusiasm was genuine, or if he was simply buttering up the new captain. He'd never been good at telling the difference. Another new problem—nobody had bothered to cozy up to him in Khandar. He shook his head and looked out the window again.

"Did you grow up in the city, Eisen?"

"Yes, sir," the Staff said. "Not so far from here, as a matter of fact."

"Really?" Marcus glanced at him. A position in the Armsmen, especially starting from the bottom, was an odd choice of career for the son of a wealthy family.

Eisen cleared his throat. "Servant's boy, sir. My mother was a housemaid; my dad was a coachman. I used to help out with the dogs until I got sick of it and signed up to wear the green."

"I see." Marcus paused. "How old are you?"

"Twenty-three, sir."

That would have made him four at the time of the fire. Just about Ellie's age. The carriage lurched as it turned the corner onto Saint Dromin Street, revealing—

History. The street unrolled in front of him like a memory, as though it had been days instead of years. The landmarks of his childhood flashed past the windows—the beech he'd fallen out of when he was ten and nearly cracked his head open, the raspberry bushes where he'd found a mother cat watching her kittens, the stretch of cobbled street where he'd first learned to ride—

He rapped on the wall, and the carriage slowed to a halt. Before he was quite aware of what he was doing, he'd hopped down, with Eisen following awkwardly behind him.

It even *smelled* the same. Marcus took a deep breath, inhaling the mixed scents of cut grass from the lawn and fresh dung from the horses in the street. Carriages rattled past, giving the Armsmen vehicle a wide berth, and a few pedestrians looked at him curiously. Marcus ignored them.

"A long time since you've been home, sir?" Eisen said, at his shoulder.

"Nineteen years," Marcus said. "Give or take."

Eisen gave a low whistle. "Think you can still find your way around?"

"Of course." Marcus pointed. "Our place was just up this way, past those beeches."

There were three of the trees instead of four, and they were a bit larger, but there was no mistaking them. They'd belonged to the Wainwrights, whose children had played with Marcus nearly every day in the precious few hours between lessons and dinner. Veronica Wainwright had been the first girl he'd ever kissed, in the darkness behind her father's woodshed, the day before he left for the College at sixteen. There had been tears in her eyes, and he'd promised he'd come back and marry her when he finished his training and became an officer.

He hadn't thought about that in years. Hadn't thought about *any* of it, in truth. After the fire, he'd walled off that whole section of his memories, shut them away and thrown away the key, hoping to keep out the pain. Coming back here had opened it all up again, and he was surprised to find that it didn't hurt as badly as he remembered.

Marcus hurried down the street, past the beeches, until what had been the d'Ivoire estate came into view. Two visions of it competed in his mind. One was the real thing, as he'd last seen it, with ivy creeping up the stone walls and the ancient leaded glass his father preferred to the modern kind. The other was something he'd constructed in his mind over the intervening years, a blackened ruin of scorched beams and tumbled stone.

Instead he found himself looking at another house entirely. It was squarer, larger, higher-ceilinged than his old estate, with big single-pane windows and a high, arched doorway. The grounds were the same—even the ancient oak, its limbs spreading above the roof—but someone had replaced the house itself with an imposter. Marcus stared at it for a moment, blinking.

Of course it's different. He'd been stupid. The old place had burned, but prime land in Vordan City never went idle for long. Someone else had bought the property, cleared the ruin, and put up their own house. He'd had the vague idea that he could poke around, discover something in the wreckage that everyone else had missed, but of course that was ridiculous. *After this long, it's not even wreckage anymore.*

Ionkovo told me to come here. Why? The Black Priest agent might have just been having a laugh at Marcus' expense, of course. *But he doesn't seem the type. He wanted me to find* something.

"So what the hell am I doing here?" Marcus said.

"Sir?"

He shook his head and looked at Eisen, embarrassed to have spoken aloud. "Nothing. I thought there might be something left, but that was stupid."

"I'm sorry, sir. It must be difficult."

Marcus turned, scanning the surrounding houses. "I can't imagine many people still remember much of the fire, either." *So what's the* point*?* He felt like going back into the cell and throttling the smirk off Ionkovo's face. *He knows something, but all he'll give me is riddles.*

"Are you looking for information on what happened, sir?"

"I suppose." Marcus shrugged, feeling defeated. "I'm just not sure there's anything to find."

"I think," Eisen said, "I may have an idea."

The Fiddler occupied a dignified space at the corner of Fourth Avenue and Saint Dromin Street. It was not a tavern or a wine shop but a true public house of the old school, less a business establishment than a club for the respectable men of the neighborhood. The building was old brick, patchy with overlapping repairs, and twined here and there with climbing ivy. The front door was open, but Eisen, leading the way, stopped beside it and pointed with his good hand.

"You see, sir?"

Marcus peered closer. A small brass plaque, much tarnished, read 17TH ROYAL VOLUNTEER FIRE COMPANY, HEADQUARTERS. EST. 1130 YHG.

"My uncle was in the Twenty-fourth Company," Eisen said, "over by the Dregs. He always said it was mainly an excuse to spend evenings away from the family. Not as many fires as there used to be, north of the river. But he told me every company has one old bastard who's been a member for fifty years and can tell you every house that ever burned down on his watch."

"Worth a try," Marcus said, though privately he thought it was a bit of a thin reed to hang any hope on. "Let's see if we can find them."

Eisen led the way into the common room. It was a long way from the Khandarai taverns Marcus was used to, with a feel closer to a family sitting room—big, solid tables, polished to a blinding sheen, and genuine carpet underfoot instead of boards and sawdust. Marcus paused, embarrassed, and backtracked a step or two to make use of the boot scraper by the door.

It was midafternoon, and only a few of the tables were occupied, mostly by small groups of older men who looked as though they never left. Eisen went to the bar, a vast expanse of scarred wood dark with resin and polish, and talked for a moment with the bespectacled gentleman behind it. When he came back, he was smiling.

"We're in luck, sir. He knew exactly who I wanted to talk to. Come on."

They went through a doorway into another room, lined with bookshelves bearing weather-beaten, mismatched volumes. There were more tables here, but only one was occupied, three men sitting at a big round table much too large for them. Another small plaque marked it as reserved for the Seventeenth Company.

Two of the men were younger than Marcus, in their twenties, but the third matched Eisen's description almost exactly. He was bent over a tall pint glass, head bowed as though his neck didn't want to support its weight, and the fingers that curled around the drink were stick-thin and mottled with liver spots. The dome of his head rose through a crown of snow-white hair, like a mountain pushing up past the tree line. When Marcus stood in front of the table and cleared his throat, the old man looked up, and his deep-sunken eyes were dark and intelligent.

"You're the Seventeenth Fire Company?" Marcus said, feeling awkward.

The old man pursed his lips but said nothing. One of the younger men got to his feet, taking in Marcus' uniform, and nodded respectfully.

"We are, though we're not on duty at the moment," he said. "Is there a problem?"

"I'm not here officially," Marcus said. "I was just hoping I could have a word about an . . . incident. Something that happened quite a while back."

The young man looked at his older companion, who caught Marcus' eyes and held them for a moment. When his voice emerged, it was surprisingly deep and smooth, as though polished by the years.

"You're the new captain of Armsmen, then? D'Ivoire."

Marcus nodded. The two young men exchanged a look—they obviously hadn't recognized his rank.

"I wondered if you might come around," the old man said. "You may as well sit down."

"Staff Eisen," Marcus said, "would you please buy these gentlemen a drink?"

"Of course, sir." Eisen extended a hand, and with a last look at Marcus the two young men followed him. Marcus pulled back one of the heavy chairs and sank into the ancient, cracking leather.

"Marcus d'Ivoire," he said.

"Hank," the old man said. "Or Henry, if you're feeling formal. Henry Matthew."

"You said you were expecting me?"

"Just a thought." The old man shrugged. "I saw your name in the broadsheets, and I figured you might come looking. It's been a long time."

"I've been away," Marcus said. "Khandar."

Hank nodded. "And it's not like there was much left for you to come back to. It was a terrible business."

"You were there?"

"I was. That was back when I went out on calls. Now I sit here and let the young'uns buy me drinks, and tell stories." He tapped his half-empty glass, and gave Marcus a crinkly smile. "Not a bad life, to be honest. But yes, I was there."

"What happened?"

"Didn't they tell you about it?"

"Not much. Only that it was an accident, and that nobody . . . got out." Marcus' voice hitched. He swallowed hard, irritated.

Hank peered at him kindly. "You want a drink?"

"No, thank you. Just tell me what happened."

"Well. It's not easy to say. When a house burns, 'less everyone's asleep, usually somebody notices. They run from the flames and come out the other side, you see? Sometimes if a place is a real tinder trap, it'll go up all suddenlike, and sometimes there's no other way out and people get trapped. That's bad luck."

Marcus remembered the Ashe-Katarion fire, the swarms of determined people pressing tighter and tighter to get through the gates into the inner city, or throwing themselves into the river to drown instead of burn. He swallowed again. "I'm not sure what you're getting at."

"The d'Ivoire place—your place—it was old, but it wasn't a tinder trap. It took time to burn. And there were plenty of doors. So how come nobody got out?"

Marcus shook his head. He didn't even know if the fire had been during the day or at night, he realized. No one had volunteered any information, and he'd been just as happy to avoid the details.

"When we got there," Hank went on, "it was obvious there was no saving the place. I led my boys in as soon as we could, but that fire burned hot. We never found more than bits and pieces of the folk who lived there." He caught Marcus' eye and shook his head. "Sorry. Shouldn't have said it like that. What I mean is the fire was odd."

"What do you mean, odd?"

"As best we could tell, it started in three places at once. Oil lamp by the front door, fireplace near the back door, spark in the straw by the stable door. Three doors, three fires. That's *real* bad luck."

There was a long silence.

"You're sure about that?" Marcus said, voice dull.

"There's no *sure*, with fires. But I had a look, and I talked to the people who were around. I'd been at this twenty years, even then."

"Why didn't you tell anyone?"

"I did." Hank's wrinkled face was a mask. "Went to the Armsmen, said I thought it was passing strange. They bounced me around for a while, and finally somebody told me they didn't want to hear it, and they didn't want anybody *else* hearing it, either. I got the message."

"You're telling *me*," Marcus pointed out.

"It never sat right with me," Hank said. "And they were your people." He smiled slyly. "Besides, him that told me to shut my mouth, you outrank him now. I reckon it's your right to know, don't you think?"

"Outrank—" Marcus stopped, abruptly. "I see."

"For what it's worth, I'm sorry."

"Don't be," Marcus murmured, his mind a whirl. "You've been . . . very helpful."

Giforte. It had to be Giforte. The vice captain had been effectively running the Armsmen since well before the time of the fire. Captains came and went, but Giforte stayed on, bending to the winds of politics and keeping the ship running.

Hank told him the fire wasn't an accident. Couldn't have been an accident. Someone killed them. His mother. His father. Ellie. Ellie!

Marcus realized he was holding his breath, hands clenched tight. He forced himself to relax.

It wasn't an accident. The thought ran around and around in his head. *Not an accident. Murder.* Three doors, three fires. *Cold-blooded murder.*

Someone had murdered his little sister, barely four years old. He wanted to scream.

Who?

Giforte knew. Or at least he knew *something.* But he had no reason to tell Marcus anything. There was nothing like proof, just the ramblings of one old man. The vice captain's position was secure; the Armsmen couldn't run without him, and he knew it. *No wonder he's been so cagey around me. I thought it was just about the politics, but he must have been wondering if I'd found out.*

There was another option. *Ionkovo's "trade."* The Black Priests' agent obviously knew enough to send Marcus here, and he might know the rest. But he would want something in exchange. *Which is obviously why he sent me here in the first place.* The very fact that he wanted to know so badly what had happened in Khandar implied that telling him was dangerous.

I could ask Janus . . . There was a certain comfort in the thought of appealing to the colonel. But that would mean revealing that he'd talked to Ionkovo in the first place, and Marcus wasn't sure how Janus would react to that.

Hell. Anger squirreled around inside him, searching for a target, finding nothing. He tasted bile.

"Sir?" Staff Eisen said.

Marcus blinked and came back to himself. He was standing outside the

Fiddler, facing the ivy-covered brick wall, one hand pressed flat against it. When he let it fall, bits of grimy mortar clung to his palm.

"It's all right," Marcus said. "I'm all right."

"Did you find out what you wanted, sir?" Eisen said.

Marcus squeezed his eyes shut and shook his head. *I have no idea.*

Chapter Seven

RAESINIA

Raesinia's candle had burned down to a stub, floating in a saucer of molten wax. Her hand was splotchy with ink, and there was a spot on her index finger where the pen had rubbed it raw that would be a blister tomorrow.

Or, at least, it would be if she were a normal, living person. She set down the pen and felt the binding twitch, and the itchy pain was replaced with a cool numbness. The red spot faded away as though it had never been, leaving plain, unblemished skin.

She'd been working on the speech for nearly six hours straight. After they'd found Danton, Sothe had insisted she spend a day at Ohnlei, putting in appearances and playing the dutiful daughter. Raesinia hated it. Her grief was a palpable thing, a tight, hot ball in her throat, but *parading* it in front of everyone made her feel like a fraud. She'd visited her father's bedside with Doctor-Professor Indergast, but the king hadn't awoken. His breathing was terrifyingly weak under the duvet.

I'm sorry, Father. She'd spent a long time by the bedside, gripping his hand. *I'm sorry I have to lie to you. I'm sorry I can't stay.* Then, once darkness fell, it was time for another fast trip down from the top of the tower so Sothe could smuggle her into the city.

Raesinia didn't get tired anymore, in the normal sense of the word, but she was still subject to a kind of mental exhaustion. Too many hours of concentration left her feeling as if her eyeballs had been boiled in tar. She grabbed her elbows behind her head, arched her back, and stretched, feeling tiny pops in her shoulders and all up and down her spine.

Out of the corner of her eye, she saw Ben raise his head, eyes surreptitiously locked on her breasts. Raesinia hurriedly unbent and crossed her arms over her chest with an inward sigh. Ben's infatuation, which she had regarded at first as a curiosity, was getting more and more problematic. He tried to act like the soul of courtesy, even when it meant getting in her way, and he was more insistent that she not expose herself to anything that might be dangerous. Raesinia, who went out of her way to do anything that *was* dangerous on the ground that it was better for *her* to be in the middle of it than anyone else, was left in an awkward position.

And what if he just comes out with it? She'd seen a look in his eye a couple of times that seemed to indicate he was on the verge of a confession of love, and only a hurried change of subject had distracted him. If he ever managed to spit it out—*Then what? Break his heart, and risk him leaving the group?* That didn't sound like Ben, but Raesinia didn't have much experience when it came to men and romance. *Or else . . . play along? How?* That possibility was just a blur in her mind, a vaguely unthinkable gap. *I don't think I could fake love well enough to fool him.*

It would have been easier for all concerned if she had actually fallen in love with him. She wasn't certain she was still capable of that, though. Aside from Cora, he was probably her best friend among the conspirators. She could see, objectively, that he was kind, honest, idealistic, even handsome. But love? No.

Maybe the binding sees love as an illness, like drunkenness, and purges it before it has a chance to settle in. She wouldn't mind that, on the whole. As far as she could tell, love was mostly good for making people act like morons.

Oh well. She looked down at the paper, where the ink had dried by now, and picked it up carefully to add to the stack. *That should do it.*

"Finished?" Ben said.

"I think so," Raesinia said. "You two will have to look it over."

Maurisk, who had his own portable writing desk set up in a corner of the room, gave a derisive snort.

"You already decided not to use my version," he said. "So I don't see what good my advice will do."

"We all agreed that your version was excellent," Raesinia said, trying to be soothing. "It would have done credit to a University symposium. It's just that the common people aren't up to your level, that's all."

Not to mention that your version was three hours long. Raesinia had no doubt that Danton could make an exhaustive history of the practice of banking in Vordan sound riveting, but she personally wouldn't have been able to stand it.

"We should be educating them, then, instead of lowering ourselves to the lowest common denominator."

"You're still sore about the slogan," Ben said.

"'One eagle and the Deputies-General,'" Maurisk said, and sniffed. "What does that even *mean*? Our grievances go far beyond the price of bread, in any case, and it's no good calling for the deputies without saying what you want them to *do*."

"It's caught the popular attention," Raesinia said. "And you've been writing those broadsheets. That's what will educate people in the end."

"If you'd let me give a proper speech, instead of letting that lummox do everything, we might be farther along now," Maurisk said. "He doesn't read what I write properly."

Raesinia wanted to point out that Maurisk's writing was as dry as week-old bread crusts, but she refrained. The door opened and Faro came in, the noise of the common room of the Blue Mask following him for a moment before he shut the door behind him. He'd covered his customary finery with a heavy black cloak, and carried a thick leather satchel under one arm.

"God," he said, "I never want to do that again. I felt like everyone on the street was watching me."

"You look ridiculous in that cloak," Maurisk said. "You might as well carry a sign saying 'I'm up to no good.'"

"I'd be happy to," Faro said. "Much safer than one saying 'I'm carrying enough money to buy a small city.' Besides, it's essential. Cloak-and-dagger work, you know? Cloak"—he pushed the cloak back, revealing a steel gleam at his belt, opposite where he normally buckled his sword—"and dagger! I wouldn't feel properly dressed otherwise."

"You didn't have any problems?" Raesinia said.

"Not unless you count the pounding of my heart." Faro handed her the satchel. "I still don't see why we couldn't have all gone, in daylight."

"We would have been noticed." Raesinia undid the tie and riffled through the contents. *Everything seems to be in order.*

"I thought we *wanted* to be noticed," Faro said.

"Not until tomorrow morning," Raesinia said, retying the satchel. "All right. I'll take this on to Cora."

This, as expected, drew a protest from Ben. "I really wish—"

She cut him off. "I know. But let's face it: I'm a lot less threatening than you are. We don't want to spook anyone. I'll be perfectly safe." She couldn't tell them that, in addition to her own personal immortality, she'd have Sothe riding escort. "You concentrate on going over the speech and getting Danton ready for tomorrow."

"All right." Ben got to his feet and met her by the door, catching her off guard. He wrapped his big arms around her in a tight hug, crushing her against his chest. "Be careful."

Raesinia forced herself to relax, waiting patiently until he let go. She fussed awkwardly with her hair for a moment, then turned to the others and nodded.

"See you in the morning." She paused. Something more seemed needed. "This is going to work. I can feel it."

"He's getting too forward," Sothe said, from the darkness beside the Blue Moon's entrance.

"Who? Ben?" Raesinia didn't bother to ask how Sothe had been watching. Sothe seemed to know everything. "He's harmless."

"He's besotted with you." Sothe fell into step beside Raesinia. "That can be dangerous if you let him take liberties."

"Given everything we're involved in," Raesinia said, "I think Ben is more or less the least of my worries, don't you?"

Sothe frowned but didn't answer. She led Raesinia around into an alley beside the tavern, where one of Vordan's ubiquitous hired cabs was waiting. The driver tipped his hat respectfully, which Sothe ignored, vaulting into the carriage and turning to help Raesinia up after her. She rapped on the wall, and a snap of the driver's reins coaxed the horses into motion.

This wasn't a new cab, so they clacked and jolted over the cobbles. Raesinia patted the satchel again, to make sure it was still there, feeling an echo of Faro's anxiety. It was an awful lot of money. Certainly enough to kill for, or try to, if anyone knew what they were doing.

"I'm worried about our security arrangements around Danton," Sothe said after a while, apropos of nothing.

"I don't think he's a target," Raesinia said. That had been preying on her mind. Danton went along cheerfully enough, but he'd never *asked* to be a part of any of this. "He's too public a figure now. If he were arrested, or someone took a shot at him, the backlash would be worse than anything Danton himself could accomplish. That was the whole point of bringing him out in the open."

"I'm not worried about *him*. I'm worried about us. It'll be obvious that someone is pulling Danton's strings, and Orlanko will be looking."

"I thought your trick with the couriers was supposed to cover that." Once they'd ensured that a steady stream of uniformed couriers was coming and going from Danton's hotel suite, it was easy to slip an extra one through, letting the cabal members come and go without being followed.

Sothe waved a hand dismissively. "It won't hold for long. It makes it too obvious we have something to hide. He'll figure out a way through, depend on it."

"It doesn't have to hold for long," Raesinia said. "Just long enough. My father is not getting any stronger."

"Nevertheless—"

A splashing sound from outside drowned her out for a moment. They'd been following the Old Road south from the Dregs, avoiding the bridged section of the river around the Island. Just south of the University, the road ran across the Old Ford, a wide stretch of river that was only ankle-deep in places, made more passable over the years by the addition of large, flat stones to form a sort of causeway. The barrier to river navigation this created required a time-consuming portage for most vessels, and according to legend this blockage had been the original seed that had sprouted into the city of Vordan itself.

Beyond the ford lay Oldtown, a tangle of timber-and-plaster buildings and mazy cow paths. It was a hard place to find your way around during the day, much less in darkness. This cabby apparently knew his business, however, and once the carriage had splashed out of the ford it picked up a little speed and proceeded confidently into the curving streets.

Raesinia glanced at Sothe. "All right. You're worried. What do you want to do about it?"

"I'd like to take a little more overt action against a few of Orlanko's watchers."

Raesinia winced. With Sothe, "overt action" usually meant "body parts floating in the river." "Won't that just draw his attention?"

"We've already got his attention. That goes double after tonight. I want to slap his hand, make him think a little harder before he sticks it out again."

"Well. Security is your bailiwick." Raesinia had been amazed at how naive the rest of the cabal could be. Perhaps she was paranoid, or perhaps she just knew Orlanko. Ben and Maurisk appeared to think that they could get away with giving false names and speaking in low voices. Without Sothe running interference, she was sure they'd all have ended up in the Vendre long ago. "Do what you need to do, but be careful."

Sothe snorted. "I don't need *you* telling *me* to be careful."

The carriage came to a halt, and a rap from the driver indicated that they'd arrived at their destination. Raesinia opened the door and hopped down, looking back at Sothe. "Where will you be?"

"About." Sothe waved vaguely. "I'll be close if you need me."

"Just don't do anything precipitous. We can't afford for this to get out of hand." Raesinia hesitated. "And if anything *does* go wrong, make sure to get Cora out of there first."

Sothe grimaced, but she could see the logic in this. *After all, she can always fish me out of some drainage ditch if it comes to that.* Cora *could get hurt.* Sothe nodded, and Raesinia turned to face the building she'd been driven to.

It was a big one, by Oldtown standards, two stories high and as long as several ordinary houses. It had once had real glass windows, too, though these had long ago been covered over with boards and canvas tarpaulins. Its stone walls and the brass double-circle bolted over the doorway identified it as a church. A few crumbling statues that might have been saints before the local boys had made a game of throwing stones at them perched over the gutters.

The big double doors at the front were tightly closed, but a side door was invitingly open, shedding a warm orange glow into the shadowed street. Raesinia picked her way toward it, carefully; the streets of Oldtown were packed earth, liberally sprinkled with horse dung. She could make out sounds from inside as she got closer. A group of people were singing, not particularly well but with considerable spirit.

The church—the Third Church of the Savior Karis' Mercy, as the blackened metal letters on the door proclaimed—was the domain of a Mrs. Louise Felda. Her husband, Father Felda, had been the Free Priest to the Third's congregation for well over forty years. Technically, he still was, though his declining energies in his old age had restricted his duties. As he became bedridden, his wife had taken over his duties, until she was more fully in charge than he had ever been.

Mrs. Louise Felda was a large and vigorous woman who looked like a giantess beside the shriveled form of her husband. Nowadays, she split her time between making sure his needs were cared for and bringing her idea of Karis' mercy to the people of Oldtown, as best her resources would allow. This meant beds for the sick and the desperate, helping hands for those who weren't right in the head, and warm meals for as many as she could manage. Raesinia had often thought that the city could do with more priests along the lines of Mrs. Felda.

Cora had grown up here, taken in as a soot-stained little girl and put to work helping the mistress wash bedding and change dressings. When she got older, she'd gone to work as an unofficial courier in the Exchange, delivering messages for pennies as the business of the nation clattered around her. That was where Raesinia had found her, back at the very beginning, when all she had was a vague notion and a burning need to do *something* . . .

Raesinia shook her head and walked through the door. The interior of the old church was one enormous room, its wooden internal walls long ago torn away to expose the massive supporting beams that held up the roof. Here and there, small sections were partitioned off by hanging curtains to provide a bit of privacy. Bedrolls lined both walls and covered about half the available floor space at one end of the building, while the other end had a huge hearth and kettle and a table big enough to seat twenty, stacked high with dirty, mismatched crockery. A group standing in front of the fire was the source of the impromptu concert, which had segued from a hymn about Karis' mercy to a bawdy song about a young man who couldn't locate his belt buckle. The lyrics of the latter were mercifully obscure.

There were more people about than Raesinia had seen on her previous visits. A big crowd had gathered in the open space between the table and the beds, standing in small groups and talking to each other in low tones. They looked considerably more hale than Mrs. Felda's typical strays, who were usually crippled, elderly, insane, or all three at once. These people, though obviously poor, were mostly young men and women, with the occasional child huddling against its mother's skirts.

Cora was hovering near the edge of the crowd, talking to a group of women in colorful skirts and shawls. She caught sight of Raesinia and hurried over, looking agitated.

"Raes," Cora said. "You made it."

"No problems," Raesinia said.

"And you've got . . ." Cora's eyes flicked to the satchel.

"I've got everything we need." Raes eyed the crowd. "Are you *sure* we should go through with this?"

"None of these people know who we really are," Cora said. "Even if one of them talks to Orlanko, we won't be in danger."

"I'm not worried about *us*," Raesinia said. "I'm worried about *them*. If it goes wrong tomorrow, we could have a riot on our hands."

"This was your idea, Raes." Cora looked at the floor. "It's the best chance we have of really hitting them where they'll feel it without getting anybody killed in the process."

"I know, I *know*." She'd been the one who talked them all into the plan to begin with. Somehow, though, she hadn't imagined coming face-to-face with the people who were going to be on the sharp end. Risking her own life—not that she was *really* risking it, a traitorous part of her mind supplied—was one thing. *But we're crossing the line here. No going back after this.*

"It'll be all right," Cora said. "We're going to have Danton ask everyone to stay calm. You know how convincing he is."

Raesinia nodded. There was an odd gleam in Cora's eyes, she thought. The girl's genius had made this plan possible, and she was clearly eager to see it to fruition.

"I suppose we've got to do *something* with these letters," Raesinia said. "You're certain we don't have any trouble here?"

"Oh yes. I know half of these people, and that half knows the other half. They're mostly friends and relations of our regulars."

"Where's Mrs. Felda?"

"Upstairs." Cora looked a little embarrassed. "I haven't told her all the details. I don't think she wants to know. Better for her if someone comes asking."

"Okay. Let's get started."

Cora called for attention, and the assembled people stopped their whispering and looked up at her. Raesinia jogged over to the big table and clambered up on it to give herself some extra height, wishing they'd been able to bring Danton in to handle this part. She was used to lots of eyes on her—life at Ohnlei had been good training for that—but she knew she didn't cut a terribly imposing figure.

"Um," she began, and gritted her teeth. "Hi. I'm Raesinia Smith. I'm going to assume that Cora's filled you in on the basics."

"Only that we've got t' go over t' the Island tomorrow," someone shouted. "An' that we'll get some money."

"That's about the shape of it," Raesinia said. She set the satchel down, undid the laces, and extracted a single thin sheet from the stack inside. "This is a letter of deposit on the Second Pennysworth Bank for a hundred eagles. If you queue up at the bank and hand this over, they'll give you a hundred eagles."

"No, they won't," someone shouted. "Goddamned Borel bankers wouldn't give a stiff like me the time of day."

"If you show them this, they *have* to give it to you. It's like a contract. If they break their word, none of the other banks will trust anything they've written." Raesinia flourished the letter. She wasn't sure how many people in the crowd could read, but it *looked* impressive enough, with a gilt border and embossed seal in the Borelgai colors.

"So that's it?" someone near the front said. "We just got to take that paper and walk up to this bank? Sounds too damned easy to be worth a hundred eagles."

"Together," Raesinia said. "That's important. Everyone has to go together. We're going to gather at Farus' Triumph before the bank opens, and Danton will make a speech, and then we'll all go to the bank."

The mention of Danton's name sent a buzz through the crowd. Raesinia was surprised. She didn't think his calls for the Deputies-General would have much resonance in Oldtown, where even an eagle a loaf might put good bread out of reach. Clearly, though, a few of those present had heard him speak, and the power of that voice had touched them out of all proportion to their understanding of what he'd said.

Dear God. He could make himself king, if he had half a brain to call his own. *Thank Karis we got to him before someone else did.* She gave a guilty wince at the thought but pushed it away.

"Why're you givin' away money?" said another, sharper voice. "What's in it for you?"

Raesinia glanced at Cora, who shrugged helplessly. Staring out at the crowd, Raesinia fumbled for an answer they'd accept.

"Because every one of these letters means money out of Borel pockets," she said. "Vordanai money, back to the Vordanai people where it belongs!"

This got a ragged cheer. Raesinia was no Danton, but, she reflected, it was easy to get a good response when you were handing out cash.

"Now," Cora said, "let's form a line. Remember, you need the letter to get the money, so make sure you keep it safe and don't get it wet . . ."

Raesinia entered Farus' Triumph from the west, having taken a circuitous route over the Saint Vallax Bridge. Sothe had insisted that the members of the cabal not arrive as a group, and that they keep their distance from Danton unless something went badly wrong. Raesinia could see the sense in that—Orlanko's eyes would be everywhere—but it gave her an itchy sense of powerlessness, as though the thing she was about to unleash was already out of her control.

Which it is, of course. She might be able to stop Danton from giving his speech, but what the crowd would do then was anybody's guess.

Farus' Triumph was one of the many great public works—including Ohnlei itself—erected by Farus V in honor of the military achievements of his late father, made possible by using the vast resources that Farus IV had expropriated from the dukes and other rebellious nobles.

It was a huge stone-flagged square, a quarter mile across, built in the very center of the Island. The square had four subsidiary fountains at the center of its four quadrants, boxing in one great central monster of statuary and foaming water. An equestrian statue of Farus IV, rearing with sword in hand, formed the centerpiece, while closer to ground level a ring of saints looked up at the king adoringly while various nymphs, water sprites, and the occasional swan spouted streams of water into a broad reflecting pool.

On the north side of the statue the pool was split by a stone staircase leading up to a flat disc that went all the way around the column, above the nymphs but well below the dead king. This had been the rostrum from which Farus V had loved to speak to the multitudes, at least until the ruinous expense of his projects had nearly wrecked the state and turned the commons against him. Since then, tradition had made the platform available to anyone who wished to speak publicly. The implicit understanding was that nothing treasonous or blatantly commercial was permitted, on pain of the displeasure of the Armsmen and the Last Duke. Danton's speech today would push the boundaries of both, Raesinia thought, but Orlanko would have plenty of reasons to be angry anyway.

From the northwest corner of the square, Raesinia could see that the space was beginning to fill up, though from this distance it was hard to tell how many were Cora's friends-of-friends from last night and how many were simply confused onlookers. There was a fair number of Armsmen as well, conspicuous with their head-tall staves and dark green uniforms.

She made a half circuit of the square, dodging touts and street vendors. In addition to the purveyors of food and drink, the pamphleteers seemed to be out in particular force today. Raesinia recognized several of her own broadsheets, along with quite a few others that had picked up the banner. ONE EAGLE AND

THE DEPUTIES-GENERAL! blazed in huge type across half the papers she saw, along with DOWN WITH THE SWORN!, NO OATHS TO ELYSIUM!, NO MORE FOREIGN BLOODSUCKERS! and a great deal of anti-Borelgai raving.

The latter made Raesinia more than a little uncomfortable. The arrogance and general foreignness of the Borelgai, along with their dedication to the Sworn Church and domination of the banking and tax-farming establishment, made them an easy target for heated rhetoric. Some of Danton's speeches had played on that theme, though Raesinia had done her best to keep the focus on the Church and the bankers rather than the Borelgai nation. Unfortunately, her efforts had not been enough to prevent a deep vein of anti-Borel sentiment from exploding upward along with the outpouring of anger they'd been hoping for. In particular, a great many young men of Vordan, having grown up with their fathers' bitter stories of the War of the Princes, seemed to think that the best thing to do would be to go another round and hope to even the score.

Near the northeast corner of the square was a café, with wrought-iron tables and chairs set up in a jealously guarded bit of street space. One of these tables was already staked out by Ben, who sat with a cup of coffee by his side and his feet propped up on a second chair. Raesinia drifted over idly, as though she'd happened to see someone she knew, and he gave her a smile and gestured to another seat.

"Getting busy over there," Ben said. "Anyone following you?"

"I don't think so," Raesinia said. Actually, Sothe was following her, which meant that any tail Orlanko had assigned would be having a bad time. "You?"

"Not that I could see." He checked his watch. "Fifteen minutes to show-time, assuming Danton stays on schedule."

"That's up to Faro."

"Maurisk and Sarton are camped out at the Exchange. I think Maurisk is still sulking because you took out that piece explaining the essential inequity of fractional-reserve lending."

"He means well." Raesinia sighed. A flash of movement caught her eye. "Here comes Cora."

The teenager was visibly excited, bouncing across the flagstones as though she might be ready to take flight with any step, though bags under her eyes told of a night without sleep. Raesinia didn't know whether the rest of the cabal ever wondered how she herself was able to stay up nights, sometimes for days at a time, with no ill effects. *Maybe they think I'm a vampire.*

"I think it's going to work!" Cora said, too loudly. Raesinia winced, but the noise of the crowd would probably cover any casual conversation. "Look at all these people. It's *got* to work!"

"No way to tell, until Danton does his thing," Raesinia said. "Are you all right?"

"Just a little tired," Cora said, flopping into a chair. "After this is over I think I'm going to sleep for a week."

"After this is over," Ben said, "I intend to get very, very drunk."

"*If* we get away with it," Raesinia said. "I don't think they allow liquor in the Vendre."

"We should get closer," Cora said, bouncing back up from her chair and peering at the fountain. "Don't you think we should get closer? We won't be able to hear anything."

Raesinia glanced at Ben. "I think it would be appropriate to join the crowd at this point, don't you?"

He nodded. The inner circle of onlookers, those who'd known what was going to happen this morning, was now surrounded by a much larger crowd that had seen the gathering and wandered over out of simple curiosity. All around the square, people were leaving the cafés and heading inward, so as to be close enough to catch a glimpse of whatever had attracted the attention of so many people. The conspirators did the same, Raesinia and Ben strolling casually while Cora raced ahead.

They found a spot near the outer edge of the throng with a decent view of the central column, and Raesinia took a moment to assess the character of the crowd. The air was abuzz with the expectation of *something*, but there was less anger than she'd expected. Nearer the center, the mass of people were mostly poor workers, students, women, and vagabonds, but on the outskirts there were a fair number of middle- or upper-class types who wanted to see what the spectacle was about.

That was good, in Raesinia's book. Anything that decreased the risk of outright violence. The specter of a riot, with the inevitable casualties and arrests, still haunted her. *Not to mention that if the Armsmen have to shut down the Exchange, this will all have been for nothing.*

A flurry of shouting and scattered cheers at the front of the crowd told them something was happening. Eventually a solitary figure emerged onto Farus V's rostrum, dressed in a dark, sober coat and a respectable hat. Faro had done wonders with Danton—he'd trimmed the wild beard and slicked back his hair, then taken him on a round of the Island's best tailors and haberdashers until he looked every inch the reputable man of business. He was almost handsome, in a rough sort of way, as long as you didn't spend a minute talking to him to discover he had the mind of a five-year-old.

"My friends," he said, spreading his arms wide to encompass the crowd.

Even though she knew what was coming, Raesinia couldn't help shivering as that voice rolled over her. It echoed across the square with effortless power, slicing through the buzz of a thousand conversations and silencing them mid-sentence. It rang with stentorian authority off the cobbles and made the shop-windows rattle in their frames. It wasn't the voice of a rabble-rouser or the shrill screech of a fanatic, or even the rolling, practiced tone of a veteran preacher. It was the calm, knowledgeable voice of a man of the world, sharing a few facts of life with a beloved but impetuous companion. Raesinia half expected to feel an avuncular hand patting her firmly on the shoulder.

"My friends," Danton repeated, as the murmur of the crowd died away. "Some of you know me. Some of you have no doubt heard my name in the paper. To those who are strangers, I will begin by saying that I am Danton Aurenne, and a little bit about why I have been compelled to speak."

"Compelled" was a nice touch, Raesinia thought, as the speech rolled onward. She'd written it, apart from a few of the more technical flourishes, but seeing it in her own hand on an ink-splattered page and hearing it ring out across a mob of thousands in the middle of the Triumph were very different matters. Raesinia's heart beat faster as Danton picked up the pace. He seemed to have an instinctive feel for the material—*God knows he doesn't* understand *it*—and gradually let his slow, measured delivery take on more emotion and power as he went along.

Banking, he said, was an old and honorable tradition. There had been bankers in Vordan as long as there had *been* a Vordan, helping people through bad times with loans, providing safe haven for surpluses in good years, showing restraint and compassion to debtors whose luck had gone sour. Danton's father—an imaginary figure, of course—had instructed him in that way of doing business, and when he'd come to manhood he'd fully intended to follow that ideal.

When Danton paused, the whole square was hushed, as though everyone present were holding their breath at once.

"But things are different now, aren't they?" he said.

An incoherent mass of shouts and cheers answered him, until he cut it off with a gesture. Then he explained just *how* things were different. The bankers had changed, and the banks had changed with them. They were foreigners now, outside the community of which they had once been pillars. Interested only in how much profit—how much of the sweat and toil of good, honest people—they could drain out of Vordan entirely. Parasites, sucking the lifeblood of a country like a gang of swamp-bound leeches. The bankers and the tax farmers—Raesinia was proud of how she'd slipped that conflation in—were to blame for all the ills of Vordan. If not for them, there would be work for everyone. Bread would be an eagle a loaf again.

"One eagle!" someone shouted, and it quickly became a chant. "One eagle and the Deputies-General! One eagle and the Deputies-General!"

"The Deputies-General," Danton mused, as though it had just been suggested to him.

It would be the answer. Representatives of the people, working together in confraternity to solve the people's problems, under the august blessing of the Crown. But it wouldn't happen unless they *made* it happen.

"But," Danton said, "we must hit them where it stings. 'Burn down the banks,' they tell me. 'Burn down the Exchange.' But what's the use in that? The workers in the bank are Vordanai like you or me, and they'd be thrown out of work. The farmers who sell their food on the Exchange are Vordanai, like you or me. The Armsmen are Vordanai. Would you force them to arrest their own brothers? No. Our enemies are not *things*, not mere assemblies of iron and stone, vaults and marble floors. Our enemies are *ideas*.

"So, what can we do?"

He reached inside his coat and drew out a slip of paper. When he unfolded it, gilt lettering flashed in the sun.

"This is a bill on the Second Pennysworth Bank. It represents a promise to pay the bearer one hundred eagles. A promise—that's all a bank really is, in the end. Promises." He held the paper out at arm's length, between two fingers, as though it were a stinking dead fish. "So we can do *this*."

His other hand emerged from his coat pocket holding a match. He struck it on the stone of the column, and it flared brilliantly for a moment, provoking an intake of breath from the crowd. Danton held it to the corner of the bill, and it grudgingly took fire, curling up toward his fingers and gouting thick black smoke.

"This is what their promises are worth, when all is said and done," Danton said. As the flames licked toward his fingers, he let the bill fall, blazing as it drifted to the stone. "And we have to make them see it, too."

He turned his back on the still-burning bill and walked off the rostrum. Faro would be waiting for him on the steps, ready to hustle him out of the square. In the meantime, the crowd waited in stunned silence for a few long moments, not quite realizing that the speech was over. Then, as if on cue, it erupted in a single voice, a throaty combination of a roar of triumph and a scream of rage.

At the center of the tight-packed mob were the vagrants from the Third. They'd waited patiently for Danton to appear, but now that he was done, they were eager to receive their promised reward. They began to shove their way through the crowd in a body, headed east, for the bridges that connected the Island with the Exchange. The rest of the crowd parted to let them pass, then filled in behind them, dragged onward by curiosity and the power of Danton's voice. It was like a comet falling to earth, with the vagrants at the head and everyone else as the trailing, blazing tail, aimed directly at the Vordan headquarters of the Second Pennysworth Bank.

"My word," Sarton said, looking down from the balcony. "There m . . . m . . . must be a thousand carriages down there."

Faro, uncharacteristically, had thought ahead and reserved a balcony suite in the Grand, one of Vordan's finest hotels. It overlooked the Exchange and happened to have an excellent view of the granite-and-marble facade of the Second Pennysworth Bank. So Raesinia, leaning on the balcony rail, had a box seat at the grand spectacle of one of mankind's classic debacles: a run on the bank.

The Exchange was actually larger than Farus' Triumph, but not nearly as impressive. It was simply a large, open, irregular space, dirt-floored and rutted with cart tracks. On a normal day it would have been scattered with clusters of men seated at tables or behind portable desks, with flags fluttering behind them on little poles like the pennantry of medieval jousters. Other men milled around them, running from one station to another, shouting incomprehensibly and receiving shouts or hand signals in return. Cora had explained it to Raesinia, once: each station was a gathering of those interested in buying or selling a particular thing or class of thing, with the seated men representing the large, established firms and the ones who shuttled back and forth their prospective customers. Hundreds of millions of eagles changed hands here daily, in some ethereal way that involved nothing so concrete as a handshake. A shout, a thumbs-up, or a nod of the head was enough to start a chain reaction that, hundreds of miles away, might cause a ship to be loaded with goods and sent off around the world.

And Vordan was only a distant third among the great commercial cities, Cora said. The Bourse in Hamvelt was bigger, and the mighty Common Market of Viadre was large enough to swallow them both together with room to spare. Cora talked about the Common Market of Viadre in the same dreamy way that a priest might discuss the kingdom of heaven.

Today, though, all that had been roughly overturned, the tables knocked aside, the traders driven away by the mob. The banks ringed the periphery of the Exchange, their templelike construction seeking to impress a sense of their permanence and majesty by sheer force of architecture. The Second Pennysworth was one of the newest among these, a Borelgai transplant, and its building was the grandest of all. A queue—if something so disorderly could be dignified with the name—stretched from its doors and wound out into the Exchange, until it lost its identity and dissolved into a sea of pushing, shouting men.

Carriages were normally banned from the Exchange, but today none of the rules seemed to apply. They had begun to arrive not long after Danton's speech, and as the hours passed the trickle had become a flood. Moreover, the vehicles that turned up had been getting grander and grander, sporting coats of arms and liveried footmen, until it seemed that half the nobility of Vordan was crammed into the market.

Somewhat at the head of the line were the vagrants Cora and Raesinia had handed out bills to the night before. They had served as the pebbles that, tossed onto a snowy slope, dislodge a growing, rolling avalanche of ice and dirt that flattens villages in the valley below. Raesinia watched with an odd mix of awe and terror as the thing she'd created roared onward, devouring everything in its path.

It was all about fear, Cora had explained. Banks were built on trust, and the antithesis of trust was fear. Even with the profits she'd made, they didn't have enough capital to hurt a behemoth like the Second Pennysworth. But a little priming of the pump, combined with the magic of Danton's voice, meant they didn't have to.

Inside the bank, some poor manager was watching his worst nightmares come true. In theory, anyone who held one of those bills was entitled to turn up at the door, whenever they liked, and demand actual clinking metallic stuff in exchange. The bank's very existence was predicated on its ability to meet these promises. In practice, of course, only a few people would do this, but every banker lived in fear of the day that the people who had entrusted him with their money turned up en masse to demand it back. For the Second Pennysworth, that day was today. Every man in the queue had a bill he wanted paid *now*, for fear the bank would not be around tomorrow to pay it. Every bill had to be met with coin from the cashiers, with strained, frozen smiles. But there was not enough coin in the vaults for everyone, and the crowd knew it.

Shortly after opening, a Second Pennysworth official had come out to proclaim, nervously, that the bank was completely sound and no one had anything to worry about. He'd even tried a little joke, to the effect that if people wanted to set fire to bills of his bank, that was completely all right with him, since it would after all only make it sounder.

It hadn't helped. Everyone knew that bank managers only said things like that when they were worried; when the banks actually *were* sound, they sat in their offices and met complaints with an angry, scornful silence. Everyone in the Triumph had heard Danton's speech, then watched a squadron of determined-looking people march across to the Exchange and head straight for the Second Pennysworth to turn in their bills. That was enough for many, and the sight of the queue stretching out past the doors tipped the balance. The bank had become a sinking ship, and no one wanted to be the one left without a lifeboat.

"There's a line at the Crown, look," Cora said. "And another at Spence & Jackson. It's spreading."

"Of course," Raesinia said. "If a respectable institution like the Second Pennysworth can go down just because someone gives a speech, then what other bank could be safe? Much better to cram your coin in a sock and hide it under your mattress."

"I should have invested in socks," Cora said. "Or mattresses."

Raesinia patted her on the shoulder. "Sorry. This must be hard for you to watch."

"Not . . . exactly." Cora looked momentarily shifty. "It has its advantages."

Raesinia quirked an interrogative eyebrow. Cora sighed.

"I was going to tell you," she said. "But there wasn't time."

"What did you do?"

"Nothing much. You know how I had to buy all those bills so we could give them away?"

Raesinia nodded.

"Well, I had to have *some* kind of a cover for why I wanted so much Second Pennysworth debt, or else people would have figured out something was up. So I arranged to *sell* Pennysworth bills at the same time, to make it look like we were just moving some investment around."

"But if you sold the bills—"

"I *arranged* to sell them in the Viadre market. They're not due for another three days. It takes time to ship the things to Borel, after all."

"But you haven't got the bills anymore. We gave them away."

"Right." Cora smiled. "Actually, when I saw the prices, I ended up selling a lot more than I ever bought."

"So what you're telling me," Raesinia said, struggling to follow, "is that someone is going to be very angry with you when it turns out you've sold merchandise you can't deliver?"

"Oh no!" Cora looked genuinely surprised at the idea. "No, you don't understand. Once the bank collapses, the bills will be practically worthless. I'll just buy the purchasers out of their contracts at a couple of pennies on the eagle. They might still be angry, but I think most of Viadre will be in a panic once the news of this gets there."

"So . . . ," Raesinia prompted.

"We get to keep the money from the sales," Cora said, in a speaking-to-children voice. "But we don't actually have to deliver anything."

"So you've made money."

Cora nodded.

"A *lot* of money?"

She nodded again, a little hesitantly. "I didn't think I should do it without asking you first, but we didn't have very long, and if I'd taken the time to track you down, the market would have closed . . ."

"Cora," Raesinia said, taking her hand. "Come with me."

Cora's face was a mask of panic as Raesinia dragged her through the balcony doors and into the suite. Sarton was still watching the crowd, but Ben was there, and Faro had brought up a canvas sack full of bottles. When he saw Raesinia, he picked up a glass flute full of sparkling white and waved it in her direction.

"Raes!" he said. "Come on! We're celebrating!"

Raesinia took the flute from Faro and presented it to Cora.

"You deserve it," Raesinia said. "After we win, I'm going to ask the deputies to make you Minister of Finance."

I really will, Raesinia thought, as the teenager sipped the bubbly wine. *God knows she couldn't be worse than the last few men who've gotten the job.* Her father had many fine attributes, but paying attention to eagles and pennies was not one of them, and his Treasury heads tended to be chosen for their political connections rather than their competence. Then there was Grieg, one of Orlanko's minions, who'd spent the last five years building the tax farm into his private empire. *A little girl would make for a nice change of pace.*

"By the way," Faro said, "I had to stash Danton in the front bedroom. We'll have to figure out some way to get him out without anyone noticing."

Raesinia rounded on him. "You brought him *here*?"

Faro shrugged. "His room at the Royal was mobbed after the speech. I couldn't think where else to put him." He caught Raesinia's expression. "Relax. Nobody saw us come in."

And how the hell would you know? Faro had a high opinion of his own skill and daring, but Raesinia had her doubts. *He's certainly no Sothe.*

Ben patted her on the shoulder. "Relax, Raes. It's just until the storm passes. Have a drink, would you?"

Raesinia sighed, but accepted a flute and sipped at the wine for form's sake.

They still don't take it seriously. Cora had the excuse of youth, but the rest of them . . . *Why am I the only one who seems worried?*

Some time later, they'd emptied half the bottles, and the crowd on the Exchange was finally dispersing under the stern eyes of dozens of Armsmen.

The Second Pennysworth had suspended payments just before noon, admitting to the world that it couldn't make good on its promises. That was the turning point Raesinia had fretted over, the instant where the crowd might turn into a mob and exact violent retribution. Fortunately for all concerned, the gradual gentrification of the panic over the course of the morning meant that by the time the bank actually failed, a good proportion of those waiting in the queue were of the well-bred classes. There were shouting matches, a little shoving, and the occasional swooning or fit of hysterics, but it was no longer the type of crowd to start hurling bricks through windows. By then, too, the Armsmen were out in force, responding with unusual rapidity to the developing crisis. Raesinia had watched the lines of green form and thicken throughout the morning, and sent up a silent thanks to whoever had organized the usually lackadaisical defenders of the peace.

Sarton and Maurisk had left shortly thereafter, the former to whatever he did in his free time—nobody seemed to know—and the latter to bash out a broadsheet about how the bankruptcy of the Second Pennysworth proved the essential bankruptcy of Borelgai-style finance. Back in the suite, Ben and Faro were playing some kind of game that involved dice and many, many glasses of wine. Cora was dozing on the sofa, curled up like a cat. Raesinia found herself wandering out of the living room and into the little anteroom, where doors led to the pair of bedrooms and the tiny private kitchen.

One of the bedroom doors was open a few inches, and a wan light shone from within. Raesinia went over and found Danton sitting on a neatly made bed, still wearing his hat and boots. He looked up, his face splitting into a broad, childlike grin.

"Hello, Princess!"

Raesinia slipped into the room and eased the door closed. "Hello, Danton. What are you doing in here?"

"Thinking," Danton said.

"Thinking about what?"

He blinked at her, as though that question made no sense. After a moment, he nodded at a half-full glass flute on the nightstand. "Faro gave me some stuff to drink, but I didn't like it."

"No?"

"Too many bubbles. They went up my nose." He wiped his nose with the back of his hand. "Is there any beer?"

God Almighty. A surge of guilt broke across Raesinia like a tidal wave. *Look at him. He doesn't understand any of this. He didn't choose this. We're just using him, and we're going to end up getting him killed before it's all over.*

You're just using all of them, her conscience taunted her. *Danton is no different from Ben, or Faro, or Cora. They're just tools to get what you want. If one or two of them get broken along the way, what's the difference?*

They all chose this, though. Maurisk, Sarton, Ben, even Faro. They have their own reasons for being here.

And Cora? She doesn't have any idea what she's getting into.

Raesinia swallowed hard. Danton was still smiling at her. It was hard to reconcile this childlike expression with the man he'd been—or appeared to be—standing on the column in Farus' Triumph. *Does he know what he's doing?*

"Danton," she said, "that was a good . . . story you told this afternoon."

"Did you like it, Princess?" His joyful tone made her heart lurch sickeningly. "There were a lot of people listening."

"There certainly were." She hesitated. "Did you understand it? The story, I mean. Do you know what it means?"

Again the look of incomprehension, as though what she'd said was a contradiction in terms. "It's a story, Princess."

"But . . . the people listening. What did they think it meant?"

"People like stories. They like to shout, but it's good shouting."

Raesinia's binding, the demon in the pit of her soul, gave an odd little twist, as though it were turning over in its sleep. *Probably getting rid of the last of the alcohol,* she thought regretfully. It would have been nice to let her consciousness dissolve in bubbly white wine for a while, like the rest of the cabal. *Or even to be able to put my head down and take a nap.*

"I'll see if Faro brought any beer," she said.

"Thank you, Princess!"

She'd only opened the door a fraction when she heard the knocking. Someone was rapping at the outer door of the suite, only a few feet away. *But nobody is supposed to know we're here.*

Probably just the hotel staff. She fought off incipient panic and smiled at Danton. "I'll be right back. You just stay here and . . . think, all right?"

"All right!"

He settled himself on the bed, and Raesinia went back into the hall and shut the door behind her. Loud voices were coming from the sitting room, where Ben and Faro were still at their gaming. She didn't think anyone else had heard the knocking.

The outer door had no convenient peephole, as a lower-class hotel might have. Raesinia frowned, then settled her weight against the door, bracing her legs against any attempt to force it open.

"Yes?" she said, barely loud enough to be audible. "Who is it?"

"Raesinia? Is that you?"

"Sothe?" Her maidservant/bodyguard had been adamant about keeping herself hidden from the other members of the cabal. "What are you doing here?"

"Are you alone?"

"For the moment. Everyone's out by the balcony."

"Good. Open the door."

Raesinia took her weight off the door and thumbed the latch, letting it open a few inches. She kept her boot wedged against the base so that a sudden push from the outside wouldn't throw it wide open. Sothe was visible through the resulting crack, and Raesinia relaxed and opened the door the rest of the way.

"Good," Sothe said. "Voices are easy to fake. Now help me with her."

The open door revealed that Sothe was standing beside a young woman in the smart gray-and-black livery of the hotel. The woman's head was resting on Sothe's shoulder, and it was obvious that Sothe's arm around her waist was the only thing keeping her up. At first Raesinia thought she was stumbling drunk, but as Sothe shuffled into the suite her limp, dangling limbs made it clear she was completely unconscious.

Raesinia stood aside and pressed the door closed behind them.

Sothe, surveying the suite, nodded toward the bedrooms. "Are those empty?"

"Danton's in one of them."

Sothe's expression tightened into a frown.

"The other one should be."

"Good. Get her legs."

Raesinia grabbed the mystery woman about the ankles and lifted her feet off the floor. Together they manhandled her into the second bedroom, and Sothe maneuvered her onto the bed and let her fall. Her head thumped heavily onto the covers.

"Sothe," Raesinia said, "who is this? And what's wrong with her?"

Sothe glanced back out into the suite and shut the door behind them. "What's wrong with her is that she's dead." She indicated a detail Raesinia had missed: the leather-wrapped hilt of a long-bladed stiletto, sticking out of the woman's left side just below her armpit. "As for who she was, I can't tell you precisely"—Sothe made another knife appear in her hand, as if by magic—"but she was definitely Concordat."

Raesinia was silent for a moment. Sothe immediately set to work, sawing through the waistband of the dead woman's skirt and then slitting it in two down the length of her leg, peeling her clothes off like a University savant removing the skin from a new specimen.

"You're *sure* she was—" Raesinia began.

Sothe sighed. She tore the skirt aside with a rip of fabric, revealing a leather strap around the corpse's thigh, which held several thin blades in cunningly designed sheathes. Sothe pulled one of these out and sent it humming across the room to bury itself in the wall with a *tick* a few inches from Raesinia's ear.

"Throwing knives are not a common accessory for hotel maids, even in Oldtown," Sothe said, "much less maids at the Grand. She was Concordat."

"All right," Raesinia said. The knife in the wall was still buzzing slightly. "Did you kill her?"

"Of course I killed her."

"Can I ask why you're stripping her naked?" Sothe had started slitting the woman's blouse up toward her collar.

"Because I'm looking for something, and we don't have a lot of time." Sothe jerked the dead woman's undershirt up like an impatient lover, pawed at her breasts, and grinned in triumph. "Got you. Some things never change."

"Sothe . . ."

Sothe held up a hand, bending over the body. She came up with a long, thin, flat paper, curved where it had been pressed against the woman's skin.

"Pockets are too risky," Sothe said. "And you have to keep it on you. Some of the men used to keep it up their arseholes, but I always preferred sticking it on somewhere intimate with spirit gum." She frowned down at the body. "I wonder who's teaching them that trick now."

"What is it?"

"Cipher. One-use, good for a couple of hundred words. The only other copy is with some clerk under the Cobweb." Sothe unfolded the packet into a small square of onionskin paper, then folded it back up and tucked it away. "It's how she was going to report in."

"Ah. So you're going to send in her reports?"

"Just one report. They burn the cipher after use. Keeps it secure." Sothe shook her head. "I'll try to salvage something out of this."

"Salvage something? Have you seen the crowd outside?" Raesinia felt a little of her excitement returning. "Sothe, it *worked*. We brought down a bank. *That* will hit the Borels where it hurts—"

"I don't mean the banks. You brought Danton *here*. Do you know how many people are following him right now, after the speech he gave? Now they know he came to a hotel room, and they're going to ask who else was there. That's all they'll need." Sothe shook her head bitterly. "How many times did I tell you to *keep away from him*? We can't afford to let Orlanko tie the two of you together."

"Faro brought him," Raesinia said defensively. "He didn't have anywhere else to stash him. I should have realized they couldn't go back to the Royal. We could have made other plans—"

"We can worry about fixing the blame later. Right now we have to get you out of here."

Raesinia nodded, trying to focus. "Does Orlanko have anyone else watching the place?"

"There's two men in grooms' uniforms stuffed into a hayrick in the stables," Sothe said grimly. "I think we're clear for the moment, but that won't last. You have to come with me."

"What about the others?"

"Warn them if you like," Sothe said. "Just don't take too long about it. After that, they're on their own. We need to split up anyway."

"If the Concordat ties them to Danton—"

"If Orlanko figures out that *you* aren't the wilting dove he's been led to believe you are, he'll clap you in irons until your father is dead and he's got you safely married off, and this whole project is for nothing," Sothe said. "Now come on. I've got to get you away before I can clean up here."

"All right," Raesinia muttered. She looked down at the body. "Don't you think you should . . . cover her, or something?"

Sothe rolled her eyes and grabbed the trailing edge of the blanket, folding it back over the half-naked corpse. Raesinia hurried out to the living room, hoping fervently that Ben and Faro were still sober enough to walk.

Chapter Eight

MARCUS

Marcus had a distinct sense that he'd been here before.

The trappings were different. He was in his office in the Ministry of Justice, instead of the vast, ruined throne room of the Prince of Khandar. The incomprehensibly formal Khandarai had been replaced by furious Vordanai, and the elaborate gilded wigs by floppy-brimmed hats with one side tied up, as current fashion apparently demanded. But the air of outraged privilege was the same, the sense that the world had been rocked out of its normal, comfortable course, and that someone was going to have to *do something about it.*

"I want his goddamned head—you hear me?" shouted a middle-aged count with a florid face, who had apparently fortified himself for this meeting with several bottles of wine. "Damned *merchant*"—he pronounced the word as though it were something vile—"thinks he can put something over on his betters! Well, I'm not going to stand for it!" He was waving a paper, too fast for Marcus to read, but from the gilt edging he assumed it was a Second Pennysworth certificate. "If the king was well he wouldn't stand for this nonsense!"

There was a murmur of agreement from the rest of the nobles, about a dozen or so of whom were packed into the office. They had a certain sameness about them, partly because they were all dressed almost identically, and partly because they were all cousins or second cousins twice removed or something similar. The fat, drunk one had nominated himself the spokesman, by virtue of being willing to say out loud what all the rest were thinking.

"My lord," Marcus said, "as I've said before, we are investigating the matter, and I assure you that—"

"Investigating? Investigating! Damn you, I want to see a hanging by sundown!"

"If I may, Harry?"

A young man with a good deal more composure touched the fat count on the shoulder. He subsided a little and shuffled out of the way, allowing the young man to step in front of Marcus' desk. He was a handsome fellow, with a neatly trimmed beard and immaculate dark hair. The fashion that made the others look faintly ridiculous actually gave him the intended air of nonchalant daring.

"I don't believe we've met, Captain," he said. "I am Count Alan d'Illphin Vertue."

"Captain Marcus d'Ivoire," Marcus said, a little warily. He was staying behind his desk for the distance it provided, and the opportunity to duck behind it if they started throwing things. "Forgive me for not offering you a seat, my lord, but—"

Vertue waved a hand graciously. "And I likewise apologize for the demeanor of some of my companions. Obviously, yesterday's events have left tempers a bit high."

"Perfectly understandable, my lord," Marcus said. "I hope you understand that the Armsmen are doing all they can in the matter."

"Of course." Vertue smiled coldly. "Under ordinary circumstances, Captain, I would positively insist that the normal affairs of commerce be permitted to take their course. This is Vordan, not Imperial Murnsk, and we cannot expect royal intervention every time the vicissitudes of the market produce a minor catastrophe." The tiniest flick of his eyes at the fat drunk, who was now muttering quietly to a couple of the others. "However."

"However?"

"What we have in this case does not fall within the ordinary bounds of commercial activity, Captain. This man, this Danton, has engaged in a deliberate conspiracy to undermine the soundness of an otherwise reputable financial institution. He has produced a panic through tricks and inflammatory rhetoric. The markets are unsettled, and rightly so, for who knows what his motives are and where he will strike next? If the Armsmen were to take the matter in hand, it would be greatly reassuring to everyone."

"By 'take the matter in hand,' my lord, may I assume that you want me to arrest Danton?"

"It seems the most expedient method," Vertue said. "At the very least he should be detained until his true motivations are determined."

Marcus gave a "my hands are tied" shrug. "Unfortunately, my lord, we must operate according to the law, which dictates that it must be the other way around. If we believe Danton to be guilty of a crime, then of course we will arrest him, but until then . . ."

Vertue smiled, but it was a thin smile, stretched like rubber pulled to the breaking point. *I wonder how much he's on the hook for,* Marcus thought.

"Surely," the count said, "under the circumstances, extraordinary measures are called for? Especially given the uncertainty of the political situation."

Meaning that nobody knows when the king is going to drop dead. Marcus put on a bland smile of his own. "Extraordinary measures are not my prerogative, my lord. I suggest you speak to the Minister of Justice and the rest of the Cabinet. If my lord the minister issues me instructions to proceed, I will certainly carry them out as swiftly as I am able."

There was a long moment of silence, broken by the muttering in the back ranks. Vertue eyed Marcus, as though assessing whether there were any other levers he could apply. Finally, he gave a curt nod. "As you say, Captain. I will do as you suggest."

"I wish you every success, my lord."

Vertue turned, and after some effort was able to corral the rest of them out of the office. There was a distant shout from the fat man—"His head, damn you! His head!"—that was cut off when the door closed behind them. Marcus blew out a long breath and counted to three. There was a knock at the door before he got there.

"Eisen?"

"Yes, sir."

"Come in."

Staff Eisen entered, a thick wad of papers tied with string under his good arm. He shifted awkwardly, unable to salute, and Marcus waved him forward with a slight smile.

"Did you hear most of that?" he said.

"Couldn't help it, sir." Eisen deposited the papers on the desk, straightened up, and offered a belated salute. "Apologies for eavesdropping."

"The way they were carrying on, I imagine half the building heard. What did you think?"

"I was impressed, sir. Where did you learn to talk to nobility like that?"

"It was on the syllabus at the War College," Marcus said. "I think I'm a bit rusty. I feel like I've been washing my mouth out with soap."

"Won't Vertue go straight to the minister?"

"Let him. He won't get in to see him today, that's for certain." He tapped a sheet of paper on his desk. "Count Vhalnich is meeting with the Cabinet, and requests my presence. I doubt he'll be up to receiving guests. I'll make sure he knows Vertue is coming."

Eisen nodded. "He won't be angry with you for putting them off?"

"I doubt it," Marcus said. Janus was capable of many things, but Marcus didn't think he'd hang one of his subordinates out to dry. Not unless he had a very good reason, anyway. "By the way, I haven't heard of this Count Vertue, but I feel as though I should have. Or at least he *acted* as though I should have. Any idea why?"

"No reason you would have, sir. They're not a military family."

"Important, though?"

"Very rich, which is more or less the same thing. Their lands are in the Transpale, on the northern coast. About as far as you can go in Vordan before you get to Borel. Young Vertue's half Borel on his mother's side, and he's married to one of them, too."

"And I imagine they have banking interests."

"So I've heard, sir."

"That figures," Marcus said. He turned his attention to the files. "What have you got for me?"

"Service records and incident reports, sir. For the men who were on the scene the night of the fire, and . . . uh . . . the vice captain."

Eisen squirmed, obviously uncomfortable. Like most of the Armsmen, he had a deep respect for Giforte, and going behind his back like this obviously made him uncomfortable. Having looked through a few years of records already, Marcus was beginning to see why. Giforte's attention to detail and sympathy for the men under his command were apparent in his reports, and his steadying hand had guided the Armsmen through the chaos of court politics and short-term captains. *Hell, I would have been glad to have him in the Colonials.*

It wasn't the man's character he was looking into, though. He needed *something*—either something to tell him why the vice captain had put off the investigation, or else something he could use as leverage to make Giforte tell him. The latter prospect made Marcus deeply uncomfortable, but not as much as the alternative. Sometimes he thought he could feel Adam Ionkovo staring at him through three stone floors, waiting for Marcus to take his bargain.

"Sir?" Eisen said.

"Hmm?" Marcus had untied the string and idly flipped through the first of the files.

"I'm certain if you just *asked* the vice captain—"

Marcus shook his head. "Not yet."

"What if he notices the activity in the archives?"

"If he asks you directly, you don't have to lie," Marcus said. "Otherwise, you're just doing private work on my direct orders. Nothing wrong with that."

"Yes, sir," Eisen said, unhappily. Marcus sympathized with him—confusion in the chain of command was every soldier's nightmare. *But I have to know. And since Janus doesn't seem inclined to help me*—the colonel hadn't found the time to come and speak to Ionkovo himself, or even send Marcus any instructions—*I'll use whatever I've got at hand.*

He picked up the stack of files and unlocked the cabinet under the old oak desk, where the rest of the material he'd gathered was collected. Once the new acquisitions were secure with the rest, he dusted off his hands and stood up.

"I'll go through these later. Right now I've got to attend to His Excellency and see what urgent task he has in store for me. Keep an eye out for anything else that might be relevant."

"Yes, sir." Eisen hesitated. "Good luck, sir."

Janus had an office at the Ministry of Justice, of course, but it was primarily for ceremonial purposes. He worked out of the cottage on the palace grounds where he'd established his household, and he'd already turned the dining room table into an impromptu writing desk. Stacks of notepaper were arranged across it in crosshatched piles, which Janus flipped through repeatedly in between every word he put to paper. A silver tray by his left hand gradually filled up with wax-sealed outgoing correspondence, and a servant periodically came and substituted an empty tray for the full one.

Guards in Janus' red-on-blue livery surrounded the building, standing at attention beside the doorway and prowling the exterior in squads of four. There were more of them about than Marcus remembered. He recognized Lieutenant Uhlan, who favored him with a crisp salute as he passed through the doorway.

"Sir?" Marcus said.

Janus stopped writing and laid down his quill, carefully, on an ink-stained steel tray provided for that purpose. He stretched his right hand, fingers spread, and Marcus could hear pops from his knuckles. Only then did he look up. To Marcus' surprise, he seemed somewhat the worse for wear. Even in the desert temple, Janus had never shown signs of strain, but now there was a hint of red around the edges of his huge gray eyes, and his chin and upper lip needed shaving.

"What is it, Captain?"

"You asked for me, sir. The Cabinet meeting."

"Ah." Janus squeezed the bridge of his nose. "Yes, of course."

He smiled, but the usual sparkle was absent from his eyes.

Marcus coughed. "Forgive me for saying so, sir, but you look . . . tired."

"I suppose I am," Janus said. "I'm not sure when I slept last."

"Two nights ago," said Lieutenant Uhlan, unexpectedly. "And then only for three hours."

Marcus looked up and met the lieutenant's level gaze. A certain understanding passed between them, the shared feeling of men tasked with keeping a superior from absentmindedly killing himself. Marcus suppressed a smile.

"Two nights," Janus mused. "Well, I will rest once the Cabinet meeting is finished with. In the meantime, I have a great deal of work to do."

"May I ask a question, sir?" Marcus said.

"Certainly, Captain, though I reserve the right not to answer."

"Isn't the Last Duke going to read all your letters?"

"Another monograph I must write, if I ever find the time. 'On the Methods of Enciphered Communication,' perhaps?" Janus watched Marcus' incomprehension and smiled again. "Never mind. Suffice it to say, there are ways of baffling our friends in the Ministry of Information. The duke's influence is all-pervasive and his clerks are diligent, but his methods are somewhat unsophisticated. I suspect that power has made him complacent." He glanced at the table and sighed. "Unfortunately, these techniques require a considerable effort on my part."

That wasn't much of an answer, but Marcus nodded anyway. Janus got up, stretching, and retrieved his coat. It looked as rumpled as he did.

Once they were outside, with the guards at a discreet distance, Marcus leaned close and spoke quietly. "I wanted to ask you, sir, about the prisoner."

"Which—ah. Yes. The prisoner."

"I wondered if you might care to talk to him."

Janus let out a long breath. "Eventually, Captain. Matters are moving more quickly than I anticipated, thanks to this Danton. We are walking a very narrow bridge, and I cannot afford a misstep now. We will have time to pry out the secrets of the Black Priests when things are more . . . settled."

Jen's voice, mocking Marcus from the back of his mind. *Are you certain?* He wanted to protest but swallowed the urge. "Yes, sir. Speaking of Danton, I should fill you in on what happened this morning."

He told the colonel about Vertue as they entered the palace through a side door and walked down its apparently endless hallways, whose decor alternated between glass-and-mirror confections and baroque wood-and-gilt monstrosities. The faces of dead kings were everywhere, chiefly in the form of Farus IV, crowned in glory, looking on in beneficent approval at the mighty deeds of his son Farus V. Later monarchs had added their own touches, though, and in addition to the heads of state a veritable swarm of second sons, daughters, wives, and more distant relatives stared down at Marcus from every wall. There was even a picture of the Khandarai Court, though it bore only the faintest relation to reality. As far as Marcus could remember, the Vermillion Throne had not been attended by rearing stallions and roaring lions, much less dragons and hippogriffs.

At the grand archway that marked the entrance to the Cabinet wing, they encountered a young woman coming in the other direction, followed by a liveried maid and a squad of guards. She stopped when she saw Janus, who bowed deeply. Marcus followed his example.

"Princess," Janus said. "It is an honor."

Marcus looked up sharply as he straightened. The girl was small and delicate, with a round, lightly freckled face and tied-back curly brown hair. She wore a loose-hanging green dress of multilayered silk, gathered in a foamy collar at her slender throat but leaving her arms bare. Thin jeweled bracelets flashed at her wrists.

This *is Princess Raesinia?* He'd have guessed her for a teenager at first glance, though he knew the princess had been preparing to celebrate her twentieth birthday before the king had taken ill. She looked as frail as spun glass, and her head barely came level with his chin. He couldn't imagine this fragile creature as a queen. *No wonder Orlanko has taken so much power for himself.*

"Count Mieran," she said, her voice surprisingly strong. "It is a comfort to have you at court. My father thinks very highly of you."

"His Majesty honors me with his trust." Janus' gray eyes caught and held Raesinia's. "I only hope to be able to perform the services he asked of me."

The princess blinked and nodded. Something had passed between her and Janus that Marcus couldn't follow.

After a moment's silence, Janus gestured at Marcus. "May I present my captain of Armsmen, Marcus d'Ivoire?"

Raesinia inclined her head, silk rustling. "Captain. I have heard tales of your exploits in the Khandarai campaign."

"All exaggerated, I'm sure," Marcus said, following Janus' lead. "I'm honored to serve my lord Mieran."

"I imagine you've been quite busy of late."

Marcus wasn't sure what to make of that. He sipped coffee to cover his confusion.

"With the near riot in the Exchange," she went on. "And the problems at the banks." Catching his look, she flashed him a quick grin. "Even princesses can read the broadsheets, Captain. And I'm not *entirely* impervious to rumor here in my ivory tower."

"Of course, Your Highness. And to answer your question, yes, we've been very busy keeping the peace. Especially during your father's illness, public order is paramount." Marcus lowered his eyes. "We all hope for his swift recovery."

"Long may he reign," Janus murmured, and the princess' guards echoed it in a low chorus.

"Long may he reign," Raesinia agreed. "And I am sure I'm keeping you gentlemen from important business. If you'll excuse me."

She nodded again, getting another deep bow from Janus and Marcus, and glided past.

"She's lovely," Marcus said, when she was out of sight. That seemed safe enough.

"Indeed," Janus said. "And . . ." He shook his head. "Later. Come on, they're waiting for us."

"I don't see what all the fuss is about," said Count Torahn.

Marcus suspected he was being deliberately obtuse to needle Grieg. If so, it worked. The Minister of Finance was almost visibly steaming under his high, tight collar.

"After all," Torahn continued, "it's just a bank. These things happen, eh? Market goes up, market goes down. Everyone knows the only proper thing to do is keep your nose out and leave it to those who know about such things."

Grieg made a visible effort to control himself. "Speaking as one of those 'who know about such things,' I wish more gentlemen would follow your advice. However, under the circumstances, the Second Pennysworth is not 'just' a bank. It is—"

"—a *Borelgai* bank," Orlanko cut in. "And that makes this a political matter."

"Exactly," said Grieg. "The solvency of this government depends on our ability to tap the Viadre markets to borrow against future revenue. That, in turn, depends upon the conviction of the Borelgai that we are willing to do *whatever* is necessary to safeguard their investments. As such, this affair represents a serious threat to the Crown." He turned from Torahn to Janus, who had been silent thus far in the proceedings. "I call on the Minister of Justice to take appropriate measures."

A frown flickered across Orlanko's face, there and gone again in an instant, like one of Janus' smiles. It was impossible to read his eyes behind those enormous spectacles, but Marcus saw the slight inclination of his head toward Grieg. *Puppet not dancing properly, is he? Strings get tangled up?*

"I would advise against any . . . precipitate action," Orlanko said. "Danton Aurenne has become an extremely public figure. The reaction of the commons might be unpredictable."

"Where did this fellow come from, anyway?" Torahn complained. "I'd never heard of him until the broadsheets started shouting about this Deputies-General nonsense. Could he be a spy?"

"If so, he's an exceptionally poor one," Orlanko said, with a hint of strained patience. "Seeing as he's brought himself so thoroughly to our attention. Our investigation into his background is still proceeding."

"I'm not worried about his background," Grieg snapped. "I'm worried about what he's going to do next. I'm already hearing rumblings from over the straits. And His Most Esteemed Lordship the ambassador has already been to see me and made himself clear most emphatically on the subject."

"I'm not saying nothing should be done," Orlanko said. "I'm saying we must be cautious, in order to avoid provoking a backlash worse than the initial problems. There are better ways to deal with Danton than tossing him in prison."

Or tossing him in the river, Marcus added silently.

"Such as?" Grieg said.

"Buy him," the Last Duke said bluntly. "Everyone has a price. Find out what his is, and give it to him."

Grieg snorted. "He was *giving away* Second Pennysworth bonds to help start the panic. I don't think a bit of coin will turn his head."

"Not all prices are measured in eagles," Orlanko said. "Perhaps he craves some honor from His Majesty. Or an introduction at court. Or"—he paused significantly—"a seat on the Cabinet."

Grieg looked pale and angry.

There was a long silence, which Torahn broke with a loud *harrumph*. "Make him Minister of State, I say. Almire hasn't bothered to turn up to a meeting in years, and that just means more work for the rest of us."

Grieg and Orlanko both ignored him, preferring to glare at each other. They broke off and looked up only when Janus gently cleared his throat.

"Surely," he said, "the issue is whether Danton has committed a *crime* or not."

Both Grieg and Orlanko seemed stunned by this assertion, and Marcus suppressed a laugh.

"After all," Janus said, "we are a nation of laws. Freedom from arbitrary arrest was one of the rights Farus IV fought the Great Purge to win."

"Indeed—" Orlanko began, but Janus spoke right over him.

"Danton has given a speech in the Triumph. That is not, as far as I am aware, a crime. There is a long precedent of tolerance there, except in cases of direct incitement to treason. Speaking against a foreign bank can hardly be treason, I'm sure you'll agree."

"It can be treason if it goes against the interest of the government—" Grieg said.

Janus ignored him, too. "Danton has also distributed a large number of Second Pennysworth bills to underprivileged citizens, in a laudable act of charity. This, too, is not a crime. We should always encourage the most fortunate among us to extend a hand to the least."

Orlanko was smiling now, and Grieg clenching his teeth. Janus put on a thoughtful look.

"And yet," he said, "the combination of these two acts and the content of his speeches certainly makes it appear as though he is engaged in a deliberate attempt to defame or injure a commercial enterprise, namely the Second Pennysworth Bank. And that, I'm afraid, *is* a crime. It remains to be proven, of course, but there are certainly grounds for an arrest, and I'm sure the truth will come out in the trial—"

"Don't be stupid," Orlanko snapped. "Arresting him is bad enough, but if you bring him to *trial* the streets will go mad."

"I have no choice, Your Grace," Janus said. "I'm charged with upholding the laws of Vordan. I swore an oath to the king to that effect."

Now Grieg was smiling. Orlanko looked from him to Janus, and Marcus could picture the tiny gears behind those glass lenses whirring at phenomenal speed.

"Captain," Janus said.

"Sir!" Marcus came to his feet and saluted crisply. He could tell when he was being used as a prop, and thought he might as well play the role to the hilt.

"You are to take Danton Aurenne into custody as soon as possible, along with any other individuals who may have contributed to his conspiracy. He is to be given all due rights and processes. Is that understood?"

"Sir, yes, sir!"

"Don't be foolish." Orlanko turned to appeal directly to Marcus. "Captain, you must know what will happen if you arrest Danton. It is your Armsmen who will be on the front lines in the event of rioting. I urge you to reconsider."

Marcus kept his face calm with an effort, but inside he was grinning savagely. "With respect, Your Grace," he said, "I take my orders from the Minister of Justice, not from you. I also swore an oath to the king. If you would like them changed, I suggest you take the matter up with my lord Count Mieran."

Something played at the corner of the duke's mouth, but his eyes remained invisible blurs behind his spectacles.

"Well," he said, "if the Minister of Justice has quite made up his mind, I have preparations to make. If you'll excuse me, gentlemen."

All eyes followed Orlanko as he rose stiffly and left the room. He nearly ran into a footman in the act of knocking on the door on the way out, and pushed past him without a word. The footman, red-faced, stepped to one side and then met the assembled gazes of the most powerful men in Vordan with evident embarrassment.

Janus rescued him. "Yes? Did you have something for us?"

"Yes, my lord," the man said, bowing deep. "Doctor-Professor Indergast begs an audience with the Cabinet." His eyes flicked after the vanished Orlanko. "Shall I tell him the meeting has ended?"

Grieg started to say something, but Janus overrode him. "His Grace has departed, but the rest of us are still here. Bring him in."

The footman bowed, withdrew, and returned a moment later leading an old man in the silver-threaded black robes of a University professor. Indergast had only a wispy remnant of silver hair, and he walked hunched over, as though there were a great weight on his shoulders. When he raised his head to look around the room, however, his sunken eyes were sharp and intelligent.

"Doctor-Professor," Janus said. "Welcome. I regret that we have not had the chance to meet before this."

"Count Mieran," Indergast said, with a faint Hamveltai accent. He ducked his head. "Forgive me if I do not bow, but I am afraid I might not be able to straighten up again."

"Of course. Please, take a seat."

"No, thank you, my lord. I will not keep you long."

Janus nodded. "You have news for us, then?"

"I do."

"Good news, I hope," Torahn drawled.

"I'm afraid not, my lords." Indergast cleared his throat. "The malignancy in His Majesty's left armpit is on the verge of reaching the major vessel there. If it is not removed, it will kill him within a few weeks, at the longest, and much of that time he will be in terrible pain. If he is to be saved, I must operate within the day."

Janus looked across the table at Torahn and Grieg. The former shrugged, while the latter would not meet his gaze.

"Then you must operate, of course," he said. "Is there anything you require?"

"It is not as simple as that," Indergast said. "His Majesty is not a young man, and the malignancy has greatly weakened him. There is a chance—a very good chance, I'm afraid—that he will not survive the surgery, or that he will lack the strength to recover."

There was a long silence. Torahn coughed.

"Seems clear enough," he said. "If you operate, he might live. If not, he'll die for certain. Better to throw the dice, eh?"

"Has His Majesty expressed an opinion?" Janus said.

"Regrettably, he has not been conscious for some time," Indergast said. "I waited as long as I dared, hoping to put the question to him, but now I believe he will not wake until after the surgery, if at all. I have therefore come to you, my lords."

"His Majesty was never one for letting go of something if there was a chance of making it come out right," Torahn declared. "He would have wanted to chance it."

"I must agree with the Minister of War," Janus said. He glanced at Grieg, who gave a brief nod. "Very well. Please proceed, Doctor-Professor. I wish you the very best of luck."

"Thank you, my lord," Indergast said. "As I have said, the prospects are dim, but if we have faith perhaps God will have mercy."

"One thing," Janus said. "The city is in a delicate state. I must insist that this news not spread any farther, and that no one be allowed to leave the king's chambers once you begin the operation."

"Yes," said Grieg fervently. "Wild rumors are the last thing we need."

"I understand," said Indergast. "I will begin the preparations."

They watched the old man hobble painfully out of the chamber. Once the door closed behind him, Torahn said, "The princess ought to be told, at least. Preparations need to be made, just in case."

"Don't be a fool," Grieg snapped. "If we start polishing up the funeral carriage, you don't think *that* will start a rumor?"

"Still, common decency and all that. The girl deserves to know about her own father."

"Agreed," Janus said. "But we dare not trust the information to a servant. My lord Torahn, if you would be so good as to visit Her Highness personally? And impress upon her the need for secrecy."

"Eh?" Torahn shrugged. "I suppose. As you say."

"In that case," Janus said, "I suggest we adjourn. As His Grace said, I'm sure we all have preparations to make."

Marcus held his tongue until they were out of the palace and walking across the lawns, with Janus' Mierantai bodyguards following a step behind. Finally, he leaned toward the colonel and murmured, "Are you sure about this?"

"Hmm?"

"Orlanko could be right. I don't know the city like he does, but things may get ugly."

"It's quite possible." Janus glanced at Marcus, just for a moment. "These are dangerous times. I am afraid I may be asking a great deal of you."

Marcus straightened up. "I'll do whatever I can, sir."

"I know," Janus said. "And believe me, I am grateful. If, sometimes, you cannot quite see the way clear . . ." His smile was there and gone again in an instant, like a lightning bolt. "Sooner or later we all must take something on faith."

"Sir," Giforte said woodenly, standing at attention in front of Marcus' desk.

Marcus eyed him thoughtfully, doing his best to keep any suspicion out of his gaze. He didn't think the vice captain would notice in any case, though. He was obviously working to keep hold of some strong emotion, and his stony mask was cracking at the edges.

"Yes, Vice Captain?" Marcus said. "Did you have some comment regarding your orders?"

Giforte took the invitation to speak, words escaping like steam from a boiling kettle. "Yes, sir. This is a mistake, *sir.* A critical mistake."

"These orders come from the minister himself," Marcus said.

"Perhaps the minister doesn't grasp the situation fully," the vice captain said. "If he were to come and speak with me—"

"The minister is very busy," Marcus said. "And I think he understands more than you think. These are his orders, and we will carry them out."

"If we arrest Danton, the streets will explode. We don't have the manpower to keep order."

"I assume the minister knows that."

"Then why won't you speak to him?"

"I gave him my opinion." Marcus shook his head. "He told me I needed to have faith."

"*Faith*, sir?"

"One of his little jokes, I think." Marcus sighed. "Look, Vice Captain. We don't have a choice. Take whatever men and equipment you need, and do whatever's necessary to keep our men safe. But I want Danton behind bars as soon as possible. Understood?"

"Yes, *sir.*" Giforte saluted, textbook-perfect. "Excuse me, sir. I have preparations to make."

"Send me a report when he's taken."

Giforte saluted again and left the office. Marcus leaned back in his chair and rubbed his forehead with two fingers.

It would be so much easier if I could trust him. Giforte was competent and conscientious. But Marcus, struggling through the files Eisen had brought him, had found at least a trace of what he'd been looking for. Other incidents, other *accidents*, where the Armsmen's investigation had been only perfunctory. Not so unusual—there were accidents in the city every day—but these were cases where the Armsmen involved had wanted to dig deeper, only to end up stalled at Giforte's desk. As far as Marcus could tell, none of the previous captains had even noticed.

So when he doesn't want to arrest Danton, is he really worried about riots in the street? Or is there someone else pushing on him from the other direction?

He tapped one finger on the desk for a long minute. Then he shook his head, retrieved the stack of files from his cabinet, and resumed his painful search of the archives.

Chapter Nine

WINTER

Jane had organizational matters to discuss with Min and her other lieutenants in the morning, which she none too subtly told Winter would probably only bore her. She detailed Abby to escort Winter to breakfast. Something passed between the two of them that Winter couldn't quite catch, but Abby accepted the task without arguing, and led the way back downstairs toward the makeshift dining room.

"What you told me," Winter said, "when we first met. About how you came here. Was that true?"

"What?" Abby looked over her shoulder and looked thoughtful. "Oh. Yes, I think so."

"So you didn't come here from Mrs. Wilmore's?"

"Ah. She told you about that, did she?"

Abby stopped beside a half-open door, through which Winter could see a half dozen young teenagers getting out of bed. The place was organized much like Mrs. Wilmore's had been, with girls divided up roughly by age group and again into "dorms," though here there were only separate hallways. The ones she thought of as lieutenants were the oldest, closer to her and Jane's age, and they served the role of proctors and organizers. Someone, somewhere was spending some effort to keep things ticking over in an orderly manner—there was a list of names and times tacked to the bedroom door, which looked like a rota or duty roster.

"She did," Winter said. "I'm still having a hard time believing it."

Abby laughed. "I said the same thing, when I first got here. To answer your question, no, I was never at the Prison, and I've heard enough about it to be glad of that. After Jane set up shop here in the city, she started to take in strays. You'd never know it to look at her, but she's a sucker for a sob story. Runaways, orphans, ex-prostitutes, all sorts of people. Only girls, though, and mostly those too young to look out for themselves. I think we're nearly half and half now, between them and the original group from Mrs. Wilmore's."

Abby started walking again, and Winter followed. They passed more doors, open and closed, and a couple of gangs of chattering young women brushed past them on the way to breakfast.

I have to ask, Winter thought. It wasn't as if she was *spying*, since she hadn't decided what she would report to Janus. *If he ever even comes asking.* She was just satisfying her own curiosity. *Besides, it can't be spying if Abby is practically giving me the tour.*

"The thing I don't understand," Winter said, as they stood aside to get out of the path of a gang of charging twelve-year-olds, "is how you keep this up. Who *pays* for all of this?"

"The building was abandoned. We fixed it up ourselves, mostly—"

"Jane told me. But what about the food? The clothes? You must have four hundred people here."

"Three hundred sixty-eight," Abby said, and shrugged. "Keeping track of that sort of thing is my job. Jane doesn't have much of a head for numbers."

"Three hundred sixty-eight, then. Food for that many doesn't come cheap, especially if you always eat the way we did last night."

"It's true. Jane always says some of the little ones need more meat on their bones." Abby smiled, looking oddly sad, then quickly shook her head. "Most of the girls work in the area, once they're old enough."

"Work at . . ." Winter trailed off.

"Odd jobs." Abby shot her a look that showed she understood perfectly what Winter didn't want to mention. "We send them out in groups, which keeps them safe, and the local tradesmen all know us."

And they knew that laying a hand on one of them would earn a visit from "Mad Jane." "I can't believe you're supporting a place like this on 'odd jobs,' though."

"No, we're not. The bulk of the money comes from our . . . other activities."

Before Winter could follow up on this, they reached the dining room. Abby was greeted by waves and calls from a dozen quarters, but she made her way toward a group of older girls at one end of the tables, and Winter trailed behind her. They sat beside a small cluster who were bent over the table, all trying to read a broadsheet at once.

"Hey, Abby," said one, a short, plump girl with brown ringlets. "Have you *seen* this?"

"No," Abby said. "Is it Danton again? What did he do this time?"

"He only brought down a *bank*," said a younger blond girl with crooked teeth.

"A *Borelgai* bank," said another.

"There was nearly a riot in the Exchange," the first girl said. "All the nobles were trying to get their money out, and they didn't get the jam of carriages cleared up until after midnight!"

Winter managed to maneuver a look at the paper. Large type blared SECOND PENNYSWORTH FAILS AFTER DANTON'S DENUNCIATION! Beside the broadsheet was a pamphlet, bearing a crude woodcut she assumed was supposed to be Danton and the title ONE EAGLE AND THE DEPUTIES-GENERAL! DOWN WITH THE SWORN CHURCH AND THE BOREL PARASITES!

"Let me introduce you," Abby said. "This is Molly, Andy, Becks, and Nel. Girls, this is Winter."

The four of them looked up from the paper and seemed to notice Winter for the first time. Winter, suddenly shy, managed a little wave.

"Winter, as in *the* Winter?" said Nel. She was the one with the teeth.

"Winter the Soldier?" said Andy, an older girl with pretty black ringlets and pale skin.

"I don't know," Abby said, smiling. "Why don't you ask her? I'm going to get something to eat."

She left Winter standing awkwardly in front of the four of them, who continued to gape at her as though she were some weird deep-sea fish someone had hauled up onto the dock.

"Well?" said Molly, who was the first one who'd spoken. "Are you?"

"Am I what?" Winter said.

"Are you Winter the Soldier?" said Andy. "From the story."

That rang a very tiny bell with Winter. Bobby had talked about it, hadn't she? *The story that went around after I left . . .*

"Are you four from Mrs. Wilmore's?" Winter said.

Three of them nodded. Becks, who was small with stringy, mouse brown hair, was taking the opportunity to study the papers.

"Everyone told stories about Winter," Andy said. "How she ran away from the Prison and joined the army."

Molly looked at her crossly. "Jane doesn't like people telling that story."

"Because she couldn't find her when she went back," Nel said. "After the fire."

Fire? Winter opened her mouth to ask, but they'd moved on.

"But if she's *here*," Molly said, "then she has found her again, hasn't she?"

"If it's the same Winter," Andy said. "There are a lot of Winters around."

"I don't really know the story," Winter said. "But I'm pretty sure it's completely wrong. I *am* the same Winter who was at Mrs. Wilmore's with Jane, though."

There was a collective indrawing of breath.

"Then you didn't escape and join the army?" Andy said.

"I escaped," Winter said. "But no, not the rest." *Best to start thinking up a cover story . . .*

"I always liked the one where she became a bandit queen," Nel said. "Did you become a bandit queen?"

Winter laughed. "No, I didn't do that, either."

"Listen," said Becks, looking up. She had spectacles on, with one wire arm broken off and replaced with a bit of wood and string. "It says Danton is going to give another speech today! In Farus' Triumph, like before."

Winter immediately lost her place as the most fascinating thing at the table, which was all right with her. Abby returned a few moments later with a pair of plates and glasses. The plates were loaded with potatoes, sliced and fried in pork dripping, with a pair of fat, greasy sausages guarding the flanks. It was the kind of serious food that Winter would have happily killed for while on the march in Khandar, and it temporarily absorbed her full attention. In the background, she was vaguely aware of the girls debating the merits of Danton's platform, whether a mandated price for bread would work and if the Deputies-General could really accomplish anything.

"We ought to go," Becks said, as Winter was scrubbing the last of the grease from her plate with a slice of potato. "I want to hear what he has to say."

"Absolutely," said Nel.

Molly looked uncertain. "You think it'll be safe?"

"Oh, come on," said Nel. "It's the *Island* in the afternoon, not the Bottoms at midnight. And with this"—she tapped the paper—"there'll be Armsmen all over the place."

"There was nearly a riot in the Exchange," Molly said. "This time people might get angrier."

"That was only because they weren't getting their money back from the bank," Becks said. "We don't have to go anywhere near the Exchange."

Andy decided to appeal to a higher authority. "Abby, what do you think? Is it safe to go and see him?"

Abby, in the middle of cleaning off her own plate, took a thoughtful moment to chew and swallow. "Probably," she said. "Let me talk to Jane. I may want to come along, too."

As though the name had been an invocation, another girl appeared behind them, short of breath. "I've got," she gulped, "a message. Jane wants to see you."

"Me?" Abby said.

"You and Winter," said the messenger. "Upstairs." She hesitated. "She sounded mad."

Mad Jane. Winter suppressed a chuckle. Even her own people were half in terror of her.

"Well." Abby pushed her plate back. "It looks like Jane has decided to bring you into the fold. Come on. I'll explain on the way."

"And you'll ask about seeing Danton?" Andy said.

"I'll ask."

"Do you know anything about the tax farmers?" Abby said, as they navigated through the tide of late arrivers to breakfast.

"No," Winter said. Her cover story had mentioned one, but the colonel's briefing hadn't had any details. "Except that Danton seems to be against them."

"Everyone's against them. See, back before the war, everyone knew where they stood with taxes. Each district had a royal customs officer to collect duties, and if you didn't want to pay you just had to bribe him or sneak your stuff through in the middle of the night. It worked for everybody."

"Except, presumably, the Treasury," Winter said dryly.

Abby shrugged, as if this was of no great importance. "After the war, the Crown needed money to pay off the debts to the Borels, and Orlanko put Grieg in charge. Instead of appointing some dullard count to do the job, he had the bright idea to sell the warrant to collect taxes in a particular district to the Borels in lieu of cash up front on the debt."

"And the Borels don't take bribes?"

"That's not the half of it. The old royals didn't get to keep what they taxed out of people. They just got a stipend from the Crown in exchange for turning over the lot. So they were never very enthusiastic about their jobs. But the tax farmers need to make enough money to cover what they spent on the warrant, plus profits to satisfy their investors."

"Investors?"

"Oh yes," Abby said bitterly. "I hear shares of tax farm companies are the hot thing on the Viadre markets. Some of them even trade on the Exchange. They don't care if they leave people enough to eat, or how many heads they have to break to get what they want. People here tried to fight back, but the farmers just sent bullyboys with their collectors and made sure the Armsmen weren't going to listen to any complaints." She rubbed two fingers together suggestively.

"I think I get the picture. What does that have to do with you, though?"

"This was before I got here, but they say Jane was drinking in one of the river taverns, listening to the fishermen bitch and moan. They're hit the worst, you know. They're supposed to pay a tax on every load, see, and in a good day a boat might take five loads. So the tax farmer says, you owe for five loads. And if the fisherman says he only took three, the farmer says, well, then you must be trying to smuggle the other two, so you owe for five. So if you have a bad day, or you have to stay home because your kids have the flu, or *anything*—"

Abby caught Winter's eye and took a deep breath.

"Sorry," she said. "It just makes me angry. That's how I ended up here in the first place. Anyway, the fishermen were complaining, and Jane asked them why they didn't do something about it. To make a long story short, they had a few more drinks, and then the whole pub went down to the nearest tax farm office and torched the place." Abby smiled. "That was when the tax farmers found out the Armsmen are happy to take bribes to stay *out* of the Docks, but it's much more expensive to get them to come *in*."

"So Jane started fighting the tax farmers?"

"Not all by herself," Abby said. "She got people organized, like a general. After a while things settled down. We let them take enough to get by, they don't get greedy, and nobody's head gets broken. And the locals, uh, express their gratitude." She waved back toward the dining room. "That's where most of this comes from."

"These are the Leatherbacks I heard so much about, then," Winter said.

"Yeah. I don't know how the name got started, but the fishermen wear those leather aprons, and eventually we started wearing them, too."

"'We'? You mean the girls here go out and *fight*?"

"Not all of them," Abby said. She was grinning. "Just the older ones. And Jane never *made* anyone go. They just didn't want to let her go off by herself."

I suppose I'm hardly one to complain about girls fighting. Still, she hadn't joined the army with the expectation of actual combat. Everyone said Khandar was supposed to be a nice, safe, boring post at the end of the earth. The rest of it just sort of . . . happened.

"I'm just amazed you get away with it," Winter said.

"Like I said, most of the tax farmers got the message after a while. They've got better things to do than bash their heads against a wall. And we don't see much of the Armsmen around here."

"What about Orlanko? I thought he was supposed to know everything."

Abby's steps slowed slightly. "That's . . . more complicated. The head man in the Concordat for this part of the Docks is named Phineas Kalb. He and Jane have an arrangement." Abby looked at Winter and sighed. "He makes sure we don't turn up in the reports, and every couple of weeks he comes by and some of the girls . . . entertain him."

That took a moment to sink in, like a bomb with a slow-burning fuse, but when she caught the meaning, Winter exploded. *"What?"*

She said it louder than she meant to, and the girls passing them in the corridor looked over curiously. Abby grabbed her by the sleeve and pulled her into the nearest open doorway, which led to a storeroom half-full of sacks of potatoes. Winter rounded on her.

"You're telling me Jane *sends* girls off to . . . to *pleasure* some secret policeman?" Winter was practically vibrating with rage, though she couldn't have said at whom. *At Abby? At Jane? After what happened to* her, *I can't believe it.* "I *don't* believe that."

"Jane told me you wouldn't understand," Abby said. "The girls *volunteer* to do it."

"Sure," Winter said. "They volunteer if they want to keep getting fed. I've heard this story before." *No better than goddamned Mrs. Wilmore.*

"No," Abby said. "Winter, listen to me. Before we all found out about this, Jane was doing it herself. We practically had to hold her down to let someone else go in her place. She's . . . still angry about that."

Winter paused in mid-rage, uncertain. Abby took the opportunity to kick the door to the storeroom closed, then rounded on Winter.

"Listen." There was a catch in her voice, and her eyes glittered with unshed tears. "I know you and Jane go back a long way. God, if I've heard her talk about you once, I've heard it a hundred times. But you haven't been here for the past year, all right? You look at this now"—she thumped the wall, quite hard—"and it all looks so neat and tidy, and you don't see what it took to make it this way. What we *all* had to do, but Jane more than anyone. So if she wants to move you in like a long-lost . . . sister, that's fine, that's her choice. But don't you *fucking* dare think you can sit in judgment of her."

There was a long pause. Winter had faced down many things—Feor's enormous *fin-katar*, a horde of screaming Redeemer cavalry, the leering face of Sergeant Davis that still featured in her nightmares—and by those standards this skinny teenager, hands balled into fists, eyes red and gleaming, was not much of a threat. But . . .

She's right. Winter closed her eyes. *I wasn't here. I didn't come back for her. Jane did what she had to do, not just for herself but for all these people, while I ran away and hid in a hole until someone came and dragged me out.* She let out a long, shaky breath.

"I'm sorry." Winter opened her eyes to find Abby wiping her face on her sleeve, still trembling. "Abby. I'm really sorry. I . . . wasn't thinking."

"It's all right." Abby blinked away a few stray tears and managed a smile. "I shouldn't have blown up at you. I haven't been myself lately."

To Winter's surprise, the scene in Jane's room looked like a conference she might have found in Janus' tent outside Ashe-Katarion, albeit only if all the officers had been in drag. Jane sat at her big table, which was half-covered by a hand-drawn map of the Docks, each crooked alley surrounded by carefully penciled notes and annotations. Becca and Winn sat on one side of the table, Min and Chris on the other. There were two conspicuously empty seats, one to either side of Jane.

"Took you long enough," Jane grumbled.

"Sorry," Abby said. No trace of her rancor remained, except for a slight reddening of the eyes. "We had to finish up at breakfast."

She took a seat at Jane's left hand, and Winter slid into the chair that was obviously meant for her, feeling uncomfortable all over again. Apart from Abby, she'd barely exchanged a word with any of Jane's lieutenants. For the most part they kept their eyes on Jane, but Winter found herself the subject of the occasional sideways glance. *Not hostile so much as curious,* she decided. *I can hardly blame them. I don't have any right to be here, really.*

"We have problems," Jane announced, once everyone was seated. "More accurately, one problem, and his name is the Most Honorable Sir Cecil fucking Volstrod."

"Bloody Cecil," said Winn. She was a tall, skinny woman, her well-muscled arms crosshatched with thin white scars.

"A tax farmer," Abby said to Winter. "One of the worst."

"I take it you filled her in?" Jane said.

"More or less." Abby and Winter exchanged a look.

"Bloody Cecil kept our peace for a while," Jane said, "but he was never happy about it. We all remember what happened last time he tried to throw his weight around."

Winter was about to say that *she* didn't, but from the way everyone around the table looked down, she thought she probably didn't want to know.

"Unfortunately," Jane said, "Bloody fucking Cecil has apparently been playing the markets with company money, in the hopes of raking off a bit more for himself." She tapped a folded note in front of her. "Or so we are led to believe, anyway. Thanks to Danton and his pack of idiots, Cecil is in something of a bad spot right now, and he doesn't have long to get out of it. That means he's coming to the Docks, tonight, for a bit of impromptu smash-and-grab, and he's bringing every hired leg-breaker he can get his hands on."

"You're not kidding there," said Min, reading another note. Her role seemed to be managing papers and organization. Winter found it hard to imagine her fighting. "Jenny in the Flesh Market says he's got nearly a hundred men already."

There was a low murmur around the table. Jane frowned.

"I don't care if he has *two* hundred," she said. "If we sit this one out, it means we can't protect the people here when push really comes to shove. Fuckers like Cecil will be all over us. We have to stop him."

"If we call in every favor we can manage, I doubt we could come up with more than sixty men willing to stand up to Cecil," Abby said. "That's not going to be enough."

"We've got a few muskets," Chris said, hesitantly. "If we set some of the girls up on the rooftops, we could—"

"No muskets," Jane said. "A little brawling is one thing. If word gets out that tax farmers and dockmen are fucking shooting at each other, the Armsmen will be all over us."

There was a long, depressed silence. Winter cleared her throat. "Do you know the route they'll be taking?"

Jane cocked her head. "More or less. They'll have wagons, so they won't be able to get through the alleys."

"And do you think Cecil himself will be coming with them?"

"Definitely. If he can't come up with some quick coin, he's fucked. He'll be here."

Winter wondered whether this was what Janus had had in mind when he'd sent her here. Somehow she suspected not. *Though, with Janus, who knows?*

"Then," Winter said, "I have a suggestion . . ."

The street was alive with flickering shadows, swinging to and fro with the motions of the torch-wielding men and the rocking of the lanterns on the wagons. It looked as though an army of dark spirits were walking to either side of the tax farmers' thugs, projected against the fronts of the buildings, slipping in and out of view but always keeping in step.

Aside from Bloody Cecil's men, the street was deserted. Jane had made sure that news of the incursion got around. Winter only hoped that their own preparations had not also become common knowledge. The convoy was three empty wagons drawn by four-horse teams, to carry the booty, followed by a single two-horse coach with dark-uniformed footmen on the running boards. Around the vehicles, the mercenaries maintained a loose guard, walking in small groups clustered around the torchbearers. Snatches of conversation drifted past her, and occasional coarse laughter.

She was forcibly reminded of a little fishing village beside the Tsel, and a column of brown-uniformed Khandarai marching in good order into a hellish cross fire. These hirelings had nothing like the discipline of the Auxiliaries, though, and were armed with truncheons and staves instead of Royal Army–issue muskets. On the other hand, Winter's own allies were similarly poorly equipped. *At the Tsel we didn't have any girls in the company, though. Aside from me, of course. And Bobby, come to think of it.*

Not all of the Dockside fighters were escapees from Mrs. Wilmore's Prison, though. A crowd of rough-looking men in long, front-and-back leather aprons had turned up in response to Jane's call. Walnut was among them, and to Winter's surprise so was Crooked Sal, equipped with a pair of thick oak truncheons and apparently looking forward to having his nose broken one more time. Jane's contingent included twenty or so of the girls from her building, among them Chris, Becca, and Winn. They looked tougher and more professional than Winter had expected.

"I don't like it," Jane muttered.

"Don't like the plan?" Winter said. "It's a little late to say so now."

"Not the plan. Abby. She should have been back by now."

Abby had gone off with Molly, Nel, Becks, Andy, and a small cohort of younger girls to see Danton's speech in Farus' Triumph. Jane had agreed to the expedition, with misgivings and a firm injunction that they be back before nightfall. The sun was now well down, and there had been no word from them.

"We'll be fine," Winter said. "All the barricade crew has to do is make a lot of noise, then keep their heads down."

"That's all right for *us*, but what about her?" Jane cursed and shook her head. "I shouldn't have let them go."

Winter put a hand on her shoulder. "She'll be fine, too. Let's stick to what's in front of us, shall we?"

Jane forced a smile. "Right." Her face softened with some genuine humor. "You and me, waiting to put one over on some officious prat. Just like the old days, eh?"

"Given how most of those adventures ended, I hope not."

"We didn't *always* get caught."

"It just hurt like blazes when we did," Winter said. "I think I still have marks on my arse."

"I'll have to check some time," Jane said. Before Winter could do more than sputter, she peered around the corner. "Nearly there. Should be seeing us any minute now . . ."

"Brass Balls of the Beast! What the fuck do you think you're playing at?" The swearing came from the front of the convoy. The light of lanterns had revealed that the street was blocked by a shoulder-high barricade of wooden junk—torn-up carts, tipped-over tables, planks from fishermen's stalls, even an upside-down boat that for Winter brought back further memories of Khandar. Behind this barrier, a few dozen men waved their makeshift weapons at the tax farmers.

Winter and Jane were in an alley down the street from the roadblock, which put them behind the carriage that brought up the rear of the convoy. From that vantage, they could get only glimpses of what was happening through the press of shouting, angry mercenaries, but the sounds made it clear enough. A torch rose briefly, then fell in a descending arc, accompanied by a hoarse shout of pain. Winter guessed someone had tried to mount the barricade and gotten a bash on the head for his troubles. The general racket increased as both sides began shouting at each other.

One of the thugs ran to the carriage and rapped at the door. The footman opened it, just a crack, letting the orange light of another lamp fall on the man's face.

"Boss, there's some locals in the street. They don't want to let us through."

The voice from inside cracked like a whip with the weight of hereditary privilege, beneath a heavy, rasping Borelgai accent. "Of course they don't want to let us through! Why do you think I brought so many of you lads along, for the company?"

"Yeah," the mercenary said, dubiously. "But they don't look like they're going to move."

"Then fucking move them! I want these wagons rolling again in ten minutes."

"Right."

The door closed. The mercenary drew his truncheon from his belt and slapped it against his palm a couple of times, testing the weight. Winter didn't blame him for hesitating. Hundred men or no hundred men, climbing over a barricade against an enemy who knew you were coming was not going to be a pleasant experience, especially for whoever was first in line.

"Right!" he said, louder. "Boss wants this shit out of the way double quick! Form up. We'll go over all at once!"

Very good, Winter thought. *Stick to nice, obvious tactics. Just charge on ahead. Nothing up my sleeves . . .*

She felt, oddly, at home. Almost at peace. This was a battlefield, of sorts, and there was going to be a battle. Admittedly, a battle between a couple of hundred sweaty, shoving men armed with clubs, but still a battle, even if it went as she hoped and produced no serious casualties. She'd never thought she could miss such a thing, but being here now felt *right*, in a way that nothing had since she'd taken ship in Khandar.

I wish I had the Seventh here with me, though. She imagined Bobby, Graff, and Folsom shouting orders, and a hundred musket barrels swinging into line to bear on this rabble of leg-breakers for hire, bayonets gleaming in the lantern light. *They'd piss their britches.*

"Time?" said Jane.

When did I get to be in charge? She'd proposed the plan, but it was still Jane's army. Winter peered at the milling thugs. "Almost. Wait until they make their first rush."

A few seconds later, a wave of shouts indicated that the attack had begun. Splintery crashes, curses, and screams of pain quickly followed.

"Now," Winter said.

Jane put two fingers in her mouth and produced a sharp, piercing whistle, which was answered by shouts from the deeply shadowed alleys all around them. Packs of men and girls burst out, weapons raised, all heading for the carriage at the rear of the column. No sooner had the sound died away than Jane joined the rush, and Winter scrambled after her. She glanced dubiously at the club they'd given her, which looked suspiciously like a table leg, and wished she'd brought her sword.

Most of the mercenaries were up at the front of the column, struggling to clear and dismantle the barricade. Only a half dozen men remained around the carriage, while a good twoscore of Jane's people were closing in on them. Their calls for help were drowned under the shouting from the fight up the street.

On the side of the carriage Winter and Jane were approaching, there were three thugs, plus the liveried coachman on the running board. One of the mercenaries took to his heels as soon as they emerged from cover, and the other two instinctively put their backs against the carriage and raised their cudgels. Winn was the first to reach them, armed with a long staff. It was obvious she'd done this sort of thing before; she came in with a yell, poking at the thug's face, but when he came forward to meet her with a clumsy overhand blow she faded sideways and whipped the reverse end of the staff around into his ankles. He toppled with a screech, his weapon bouncing into the dirt.

Jane was not far behind her, ignoring both mercenaries and going straight for the carriage door. The second thug started to aim a swing at her back, but before it connected Walnut was on top of him. The big man grabbed the cudgel at the top of its arc and yanked it out of the thug's hands, then hammered the mercenary against the carriage with one weighty fist.

By the time Winter had made it to the carriage, Jane had the door open. Steel gleamed in her hand as she did the trick with the knife again and dove inside, and an outraged shout swiftly turned into a scream. Winter spared a moment to look at the footman, who was clinging to the rail with his eyes closed and didn't seem inclined to start trouble. One of the Leatherbacks had dragged the driver down from his box and taken the reins, trying to calm the skittish horses. Up the street, the sounds of the melee continued, although there was more wooden crashing now than shouting. The barricade squad was supposed to have run for it once they heard Jane's whistle.

A man appeared in the carriage door. He was tall and thin, in an elaborate black suit with tails and silver threading, covered over by a voluminous fur jacket. His hair was wild where his hat had been knocked away, and the silver line of a knife gleamed at his throat. Jane's face came into view beside him, grinning savagely.

"After you, most honorable sir," she said. "But slowly, if you please."

A round of cheers went up from the Leatherbacks. Winter noticed some of the mercenaries from the front of the column drifting back to see what was going on. She ran back to Jane, who was prodding Bloody Cecil down to the street.

"Come on," Winter said. "If we don't get them to call this off soon, people are going to get killed."

"You'll all hang for this!" said Cecil, who was not entirely current on events. "I am a duly credentialed enforcer of the king's taxes! This is rebellion against the crown!"

"Shut the *fuck* up," Jane said, jabbing him hard in the ribs with her free hand. Cecil wilted. "You have no idea how much I would like to slit your throat right here. Now come on and say only what I tell you to say, you understand?"

Winter followed Jane toward the front of the convoy. The Leatherbacks had formed up between two of the carts, and the mercenaries were drifting into a rough line opposite them. A good deal of shouting was being exchanged, but thus far no actual blows. The thugs had the numbers, but they weren't being paid to fight pitched battles. It didn't help that Walnut was in the front line, hefting a stick the size of a fence post.

Jane pushed Cecil through the line, flanked by Winn and Walnut, with Winter bringing up the rear. A murmur ran through the mercenaries when they saw their employer in such a state. Jane's grin widened.

"Listen up!" she said. "I want you all off the street in the next fifteen minutes. This expedition is over. Cecil, tell them."

"Don't listen to her!" Cecil shouted. "I am a *knight* of Borel! These scum would never dare harm me. Take them!"

Jane glanced at Winter and rolled her eyes.

"Do you know who I am?" she said. There were a few answering shouts from the mercenaries, but mostly silence. "These are the Leatherbacks, and I'm *Mad* Jane. Do you really want to tell me what I wouldn't dare to do?"

More muttering, on all sides, and a long silence from Cecil. Walnut passed the time by bending his enormous cudgel between his fists, so the wood creaked ominously.

"I think," Cecil said, "we had better do as she says. After all, she is a known and dangerous criminal. I think—urk!"

"That's about enough," Jane said. "Quiet."

The thugs were already taking Cecil's advice. Beating up helpless families, or even brawling in the open with drunken dockworkers, that was one thing, but bringing a fight to an armed gang that meant business was quite another. And, as Winter heard one of them point out, they wouldn't get paid *anyway* if their employer had his throat slit. Better to make the best of a bad business and get out without anything broken. In a few minutes, the street was empty, except for a few groaning casualties.

For a moment, the Leatherbacks looked at one another in stunned silence, not quite able to believe the ease of their triumph. Then someone raised a weak cheer. It was followed by a more energetic shout, then another, until the whole street was roaring with victory. Winter found herself surrounded by a crowd of smiling, yelling men, trying to shake her hand or clap her on the shoulder.

"Someone needs to help the injured," she said. "And we should probably make sure all those thugs have really gone."

Her voice was drowned under the tumult. Winter shrank back from the adulation, but behind her were only more excited Leatherbacks, who gripped her arms and screamed excitedly in her ear. Winter bit her lip, so hard that she drew blood, and twisted the hem of her shirt between clenched fingers.

Jane came to her rescue.

"I don't know about *you*," she shouted, cutting through the babble. "But *I* need a *drink*!"

A Leatherback named Motley, whose face was half-covered by a plum-colored birthmark, turned out to be the owner of a nearby watering hole. Casks of beer and barrels of wine were rolled out of the back room, an assortment of mugs and glasses were produced from somewhere, and the celebration commenced in earnest.

Winter was surprised to see the girls from Jane's party joining in as heartily as any of the dockworkers. Some of the men looked a little awkward around these women-in-men's-clothing, but the majority seemed to take their behavior in stride. Chris, pale face flushed red with drink, already had a small court of admirers attempting to match her drink for drink, and Winter had spied Winn dragging a blushing younger Leatherback up the stairs in the back to some private rendezvous. Becca was playing a knife-throwing game in the corner, and by the clink of coins and the groans of the spectators doing rather well.

In truth, Winter could have done with a drink herself. She had to think hard to remember the last time she'd been truly drunk—in Ashe-Katarion, with Bobby and Feor, the night before the city burned. She'd happily have split a bottle with Jane, but the presence of all these strangers made her too nervous to do more than sip from a mug of beer, which in all fairness was quite awful.

Jane herself barely indulged. She sat at a table near the door, fielding congratulations and enthusiastic, table-slapping declarations of eternal gratitude, but she kept glancing between the street outside and the door to the storeroom. The latter was where they'd stashed Bloody Cecil, bound and gagged. As for the former, she'd sent one of her girls running back to check with Min for news of Abby, and no messenger had yet returned. It was obviously preying on her mind.

Winter received quite a few congratulations, too. More than her fair share, as she saw it. Jane had put it about that the whole plan had been her idea, when in fact she'd only contributed the ruse with the barricade and the idea of grabbing Cecil himself to end matters quickly. *And it's not like that was a stroke of genius, either. Engaging an enemy in front while you turn his flank is about the oldest trick in the tactical book.* If Janus had been here, no doubt he would have somehow argued Cecil's men into laying down their weapons and turning out their pockets.

In spite of her protests, the good wishes continued, growing increasingly incoherent as the night wore on. It was a warm summer night, and the air soon grew hot and smoky with the fire, the candles, and the close-packed heat of so many excited people. The smell of spilled beer mingled with the odor of unwashed bodies, smoke, and piss to produce an almost visible miasma. Winter felt herself passing into a bit of a daze as the excitement washed out of her, leaving her drained and shaky. She mechanically shook hands or accepted shoulder-buffeting clouts of endearment, nodding and smiling and pretending not to hear the questions about where she'd come from or how she knew Jane.

Movement by the door caught her eye, and she shook herself back to wakefulness. The crowd had cleared out somewhat, some to weave their way to their homes, others to the upstairs rooms. A contingent of hard-core drinkers had pushed their tables together, and matters had degenerated into tavern songs. Winn and Chris were among them, belting out the lewd verses as loudly as anyone. In one corner Walnut sat with a young woman on his lap, lips locked and one of his broad hands exploring under the hem of her shirt. His size made her look like a doll by comparison.

And Jane had gotten up and gone to the storeroom. She emerged a moment later leading the gagged Cecil by his bound hands, and dragged him toward the front door. A few of the revelers noticed, and they shouted encouragement at her. Only Winter seemed to see Jane's expression—not merry at all, but furious, and full of cold determination. As Jane headed out the front door, Winter struggled to her feet and went after her.

The air of the street outside was refreshing after the dense stink of the tavern. Jane had paused to change her grip to the back of Cecil's coat, the better to prod him along, and she glanced over her shoulder when Winter emerged. Her eyes narrowed, but she said nothing. She forced the tax farmer into motion, and Winter followed behind.

They walked for several minutes in silence, except for the occasional whimper and groan from Cecil. Jane answered these with vicious jabs, and eventually he kept up a steady pace. Before long they reached the broad mud-churned stretch of the River Road, which they had to pick a careful path across to avoid the puddles and mounds of dung.

On the other side, the Vor stretched calm and dark into the distance. The western tip of the Island was directly in front of them, a blaze of lights stretching high into the air. It took Winter a moment to see a silhouette, and when she did, she shivered; that was the crumbling spire of the Vendre, aglow tonight for who knew what sinister purpose of the Last Duke's.

Upstream of the big piers where the cargo barges unloaded was an accumulation of smaller quays, knocked together from whatever bits of wood were at hand. These were home to the water taxis, smaller fishing vessels, and other little boats, and Jane steered Cecil in their direction. They clumped down across the muddy flood zone and out onto one of the piers. The far end was surrounded by a trio of deep-keeled rowboats tied to a post. Here Jane finally stopped and with a bit of effort forced Cecil to his knees.

Winter had watched all of this in silence, but she took a step forward when Jane's knife appeared in her hand.

"Jane—"

"Quiet," Jane said. There was something in her voice Winter hadn't heard before. It was nearly a snarl. She bent over and cut the gag off Cecil, though she left his hands bound. "Bloody Cecil. You've had a nice long time to think about what you've done, haven't you?"

Cecil took a few ragged breaths, then shuffled around on his knees so he could look up at Jane. "What do you want from me? Is it money? I can pay you whatever you want. Just don't—" The knife was suddenly at his throat, and his Adam's apple bobbed as he swallowed hard and closed his eyes. "Don't kill me."

"Jane," Winter said. "What are you doing?"

"Winter, please shut up and listen. Cecil, do you remember a night in February, when your men came looking for salt taxes? They went into Vale's preserved-fish shop and started smashing up the place."

His eyes, terrified, darted from Jane to Winter and back again. "I don't—I don't remember! We've raided hundreds of shops. How am I supposed to remember each one—" It occurred to him that this might not be the best tack to take, and he clamped his mouth shut.

"Some of my people decided to put a stop to it," Jane went on. "I think it was Becca who took them down there. Vale's married to her older sister, you know. There wasn't time to gather up anybody from the neighborhood, so they went down there themselves, just a dozen girls. I'm not sure Becca realized it was *your* people they were dealing with. The other tax farmers would back off if you said you were from Mad Jane's place, but not your men. Not this time.

"Well. There was a bit of an altercation." Jane grinned, showing her teeth. "A bit of a *fucking* fracas, you might say. Becca got her arm broken. The others got scrapes and bruises. It didn't help Vale one bit, but otherwise, you might say we got off lightly. Except one of the girls didn't get away. Somebody must have grabbed her, and when our people scattered, nobody noticed she was gone.

"We found her when we went to clean up in the morning. Your men had taken turns with her, half the night, it looked like. Then, when they were finished, they cut her throat like a hog and left her on a pile of rotting fish."

Winter felt her fists clench tight. Jane's voice was deceptively calm, but there was something tight underneath, like a gut string wound round over and over until it hums on the point of snapping.

"I . . ." Cecil hesitated. "You can't mean . . . That wasn't *my* fault. I didn't tell them to kill anybody!"

"Her name was Sarah," Jane said, her tone flat and dangerous. "She was seventeen. She was one of mine. She had a copy of the *Wisdoms* that she read from every day, until it was practically falling apart. She liked to eat broccoli raw so it would still have some crunch. There was a boy she was sweet on, one of the fishermen's sons, but I don't think he knew she existed. She wanted to . . ." Jane's voice cracked. "She was one of *mine*. And you raped her, cut her throat, and *tossed her into a pile of rotten fish*."

"*I* didn't do anything!" Cecil said, his Borelgai accent getting harsher as he grew terrified. "I didn't—*bhosh midviki*—you can't blame *me* for what some *ghalian* Vordanai thugs did!" He drew in a deep breath. "You know the kind of people I have to work with. They're the scum of the earth. I don't have a choice!"

"They wouldn't have *been* there if you hadn't sent them," Jane snapped. "If you'd been reasonable like all the other fucking tax farmers."

"And your Sarah wouldn't have been there if it wasn't for *you*," Cecil said. The blood was rising in his face. "*Blani* Mad Jane. You run around the Docks like you're some sort of hero from a fairy tale, and these idiot girls just follow your example. Have you ever thought they might be better off if you'd left well enough alone?"

"I *help* them."

"Like you helped Sarah? Instead of staying in her father's house minding her own business like a young woman should be doing, she was out trying to fight grown men with a stick! And look what happened to her." Cecil's thin face twisted into a snarl. "*Blani ga taerbon midviki*. You're going to kill me, I can see it. But I won't let you pretend to be a saint while you do it."

"You're right about one thing," Jane said. "I'm going to kill you—"

"Jane!" Winter said.

Jane paused, the knife half-raised, as though she'd forgotten Winter was there. Without looking round, she said, "I let you come because I thought you ought to know why I was doing this. But I shouldn't have. Go back, Winter. You don't have to live with this."

Too late for that. "You can't kill him."

"Why not? Are you going to stop me?"

"If I have to."

Jane turned around, finally, the knife still held in front of her. She'd unconsciously dropped into a fighter's crouch. "You don't mean that. Just go."

"I won't." Winter spread her hands. "You know that killing him won't help anyone."

"It'll help Sarah."

"Sarah's dead. Come on, Jane. You're supposed to be the smart one."

Jane stared at Winter, eyes as wide as a hunted animal's, searching for a way out. "He deserves it."

"*You* don't."

"You don't understand. I . . ." Jane shook her head savagely. "And who are you to tell me what to do? Did you never have to hurt anybody in—"

Winter cut her off hurriedly. "I did, *in battles*. I've killed . . . I don't know how many. But they were armed, and trying to kill me. He's a *prisoner*."

"Does that matter?"

"It has to!" Winter bit her lip. "Besides, he's wrong. You *know* he's wrong."

"Of course he's fucking wrong. What does that have to do—"

"Sarah volunteered. Abby told me that. Everyone who helps you, who does what you do, they all *choose* to do it. Do you think they didn't know they might get hurt in the process?"

"I . . ."

"You don't need to kill him to prove your point. You *don't*, Jane. Please." Winter took a cautious step forward and grabbed Jane's arm, easing around the quivering point of the knife.

Jane said something too low for Winter to hear. Then, before Winter could ask her to repeat it, she spun around, breaking Winter's loose grip, and planted a kick solidly in Cecil's midsection. The Borelgai coughed and toppled backward, sprawling on the end of the pier. A further kick from Jane encouraged him to roll over, and he dropped six inches with a *thud* to the bottom of one of the little boats. The momentum set the craft bobbing out into the river, restrained by a single taut line. Jane sawed at this with the knife for a few moments until it broke with a *snap*, then put her foot on the gunwale and shoved the boat out into the river.

"If I ever see you in the Docks again," she said, "I will kill you. Slowly. You understand? Find yourself a ship and go back to fucking Borel, or jump off a bridge for all I care. But your work in Vordan is *over*."

Cecil responded with a stream of Borelgai profanity as the boat drifted farther from shore, out into the sluggish current. "*Blani fi'midviki!* How am I supposed to go *anywhere* with my hands tied behind my fucking back?"

Jane wound up, paused to judge the distance, and sent the knife whirling end over end toward the boat that was rapidly vanishing into the river darkness. There was a *thok* as the blade bit into wood, and a screech from Cecil.

"And I'm sending you a bill for the fucking boat!" Jane called after him, as he disappeared.

She stood staring after him for a long moment, hands clenched and vibrating with tension. Winter stepped up behind her, uncertainly, and tried to put a hand on her shoulder, but Jane spun away from her touch and stalked back up the pier. She sat down on a post and crossed her arms, curling up as though she wanted to withdraw inside herself.

"I'm sorry," Winter said.

Jane muttered something indistinct.

Winter paused. "Jane?"

"I said go fuck yourself." Jane raised her head. "You should leave. Go home. Back to wherever you came from. Just leave me here with the rest of the scum and *go*."

"No," Winter said. Her heart hammered double time, and tears stung her eyes.

"Just *go*."

"I won't. Never again."

"Fuck," Jane said quietly, and curled up again. "Nobody fucking listens to me."

Winter sat down beside her, on the soggy wood of the pier, and waited. Even back at Mrs. Wilmore's, Jane had suffered from foul moods. Winter had learned that the only remedy was silence. She always resurfaced, eventually.

The city was quiet at this time of night. The ever-present sounds of distant crowds and thousands of plodding horses and rattling cartwheels were absent. Instead Winter could hear the quiet lapping of the river, and the slow creaks and groans from the tied-up fishing fleet. A distant whistle sounded, where an Armsman needed assistance. Somewhere, a dog barked.

"She was one of mine," Jane said. "She followed me because she believed what I told her, that I could keep her safe. I *told* her that. And I brought her here, and she . . . she died."

"I know."

"No, you don't," Jane snapped. "You don't understand what it's like. I have a *responsibility*, and I . . ."

Winter eased closer. When Jane didn't flinch away, she slipped an arm, gently, around her shoulders.

"You're wrong," she said. "I *do* understand. I may be the only one here who does."

Winter thought about the ambush by the river, the charge up the hill with Auxiliary cannonballs coming down all around them, the long march through the wasteland of the Great Desol. And, deep in her heart where she hardly dared acknowledge it was real, the last desperate square in the darkness under the temple, with green-eyed corpses clawing at them from every side. *And the looks on the men's faces when I turned up. The* relief, *as though now that I was there everything was somehow taken care of.* Just the memory of it slammed her like a fist in the gut. She'd gotten them out, in the end, but . . .

. . . but not all of them.

Something else twitched, down in the depths of her mind. A flick of the tail, a tiny gleam of light on ivory fangs, something to remind her that the viper was still coiled comfortably in its hole. The other thing she'd acquired that night, aside from nightmares. *Infernivore.*

Jane had relaxed, letting her arms fall to her side and her head rest on Winter's shoulder. They stayed like that a long time.

"We should get back," Winter said, eventually. "The others will be wondering what happened to us."

"And coming to all the wrong conclusions, no doubt," Jane said. Her grin was back, mad and infectious. She bounced up from the post, grabbing Winter's hand and pulling her to her feet through an elegant twirl. When the turn brought their faces close, Jane leaned in and planted a kiss, light and fast.

"Come on," she said. "It must be nearly dawn."

They expected to find Motley's tavern nearly deserted, as the sun was indeed making its presence known on the eastern horizon by the time they made their way back. Instead it was packed, both with Leatherbacks and those of Jane's girls who had not returned home. They looked as though they had assembled in haste; one of the girls had obviously been rousted out of bed and was wearing nothing but a bedsheet, coiled round her like a winding shroud.

All attention was focused on one younger girl at the center of the crowd. Winter recognized Nel, her spectacles askew, her clothes dirty with soot and torn in places. She looked close to tears, but her eyes lit up the moment Jane came in.

"Jane!"

The whole crowd turned to look at them, their collective stare freezing Winter and Jane in their tracks. Jane blinked.

"What? What in the hells is going on?"

"They took her," Nel said, fighting back sobs. "They took all of them. I tried to help, but all I could do was hide. Then the Armsmen had closed the bridges, and I couldn't find a way through. I tried . . ."

She broke off, snuffling.

Jane stepped forward. "Calm down. Who took who?"

"They took *Abby*. And Molly and Becks and the others."

Crooked Sal spoke up. "The Armsmen have arrested Danton, and the Concordat are rounding up everybody who might have had anything to do with him. I heard they took nearly a hundred people from the big speech, and now they're all over the place taking people for who knows what. Everybody's locking themselves in and barring the doors."

"They took them to the *Vendre*," Nel wailed. "Everyone said so."

Jane stood stock-still, trying to process this. Winter stepped up beside her.

"They can't just arrest people for listening to speeches," she said, then looked around at a ring of worried faces. "Can they?"

"The Last goddamned Duke can do anything he wants," said Chris, and spit on the floor. "With the king dying, who's to stop him?"

"Everyone knows no one who goes into the Vendre comes out again," Winn said.

"Except at night," said Becca. "In pieces."

"The king is ill," said Walnut, "and the princess is a child, and sickly besides. The duke is in charge, if anyone is. And the duke works for the Borels and their Sworn Church. After what Danton did, I'm sure his masters have applied the whip. No wonder he reacts like this."

Winter bit her lip. A thought had occurred to her, but she didn't like it. *If anyone can help Abby and the others, it's Janus.* He was Minister of Justice, after all, and an enemy of Orlanko's. *But he might not be able to. Or he might not* want *to.* God alone knew what Janus would decide. And if he *did* help, that meant revealing to Jane and the others that she'd been sent here as a spy.

"Winter," Jane said. "Come on."

She turned on her heel, heading for the door. Winter, distracted, took a moment to catch up.

"Wait!" Sal called after her. "Where are you going?"

Jane turned, her eyes glowing dangerously in the firelight. "Where the *fuck* do you think I'm going?"

Walnut stood up, unfolding himself to his full, massive height like a collapsible easel setting up. "Then I am coming with you. It's not only your girls who have been taken."

Jane looked from him to Winter and back again, then gave a curt nod. This time, when she started for the door, everyone in the tavern scrambled to follow.

MARCUS

"Hello, Captain," Ionkovo said. "That is you, I take it?"

Only a single candle burned in the cell under the Guardhouse, casting a weak pool of golden light and throwing the long, angular shadows of the bars across the far wall. Adam Ionkovo lay on his pallet in a pool of darkness, only his eyes marked by the faint, shivering reflection of the flame.

Marcus stood in the doorway, half wanting to slam the door and stalk away. Instead he slipped inside and shut it behind him.

It had been hours since Giforte left with a strong escort of Guardsmen, hours with no word as the sky slipped from blue into a deep, bruised purple. He'd spent as long as he could stand reading through the files, rubbing at his eyes as he read, cross-referenced, and investigated. Looking for *something*, some clue that he was increasingly convinced wasn't there. Giforte was too careful; the reports were too vague. Maybe Janus would have been able to make something of the stack of oddities and exceptions, some brilliant leap of logical deduction, but it was beyond Marcus.

When he couldn't take it anymore, he'd locked the files in his cabinet and started wandering the halls. The big old building was nearly empty, the clerks and scribes on a skeleton crew for the night shift and most of the on-duty men out in the city. Marcus had circled the top floor without meeting anyone, peering out through blurry old glass windows. A brilliant sunset blazed in the west, but when he looked to the east the sky was blotted out by dark, heavy clouds, spreading like a stain as they approached.

In the end, he'd found himself here, in the one place he shouldn't be, speaking to the man he'd been forbidden to talk to. The man who knew—*maybe!*—what he needed so badly to hear.

"It's me," Marcus said.

"I keep expecting a visit from your Colonel Vhalnich," Ionkovo said. "So far he has disappointed me."

"He's a busy man these days," Marcus said. "The king's made him Minister of Justice. I'm afraid he hasn't got time for you."

"Or you?" Ionkovo said. He sat up, angular face coming into the half-light.

He's just needling. There was no way the prisoner could know what was going on outside. "I came to ask if you're willing to talk."

"I'm happy to *chat*, Captain, but if you mean am I willing to tell you what you want to know . . ." He shrugged. "My offer still stands."

"I'm not going to take your *bargain*," Marcus said.

"Why not? Whose interests are you really serving, Captain?"

"Vordan's. The king's."

"I see. And has Colonel Vhalnich reported what happened to Jen Alhundt to the king, do you think?"

Marcus shifted, uncomfortably. "The king is ill."

"To the Minister of War, then. Or the Minister of Information. Or anyone." Ionkovo smiled, the shadows making his face a death's-head. "We both know he hasn't. He went to Khandar looking for the treasure of the Demon King. You think that was part of his official orders?"

Marcus said nothing. The candle was guttering, the room growing darker. Shadows seemed to *flow*, gathering around the man in the cell.

Ionkovo's smile widened. "So, who are you really serving, when you keep his secrets? The Crown? Or Janus bet Vhalnich? What has *he* done, to deserve such loyalty?"

"He saved my life," Marcus muttered. "Several times. He saved *all* our lives, out in the desert."

"That makes him a good soldier. But you should know as well as anyone that good soldiers don't always do the right thing."

Adrecht. Marcus stared at the dim figure. *He knows, of course.* The mutiny and its aftermath would have been in the reports.

"Let me suggest something to you, Captain," Ionkovo said. "You know who I am, who I work for. What they stand for. And, unlike everyone out there"—he waved a hand widely—"you know the truth. Demons are *real*, not fairy stories. Magic is *real*, and it can be deadly.

"Now consider my order. Because people no longer believe, we must operate in secret. Because our enemies are powerful and utterly without mercy, we must use whatever methods are available to us. But can you really say we are wrong, and Vhalnich is right? Why seek the Thousand Names if he does not intend to use them, as the Demon King once did?"

"He is my superior officer," Marcus said. "Appointed by the Crown."

"A Crown that knows nothing of his plans," Ionkovo said. "If you discovered Vhalnich was planning to murder the king, it would be your duty to stop him, superior or not. How is this any different? He betrays not just his country, but humanity itself, to our great and common enemy."

Sooner or later, Captain, we all must take something on faith.

Marcus opened his mouth to speak, hesitated, and stopped.

Why did I come here? Was this already in my mind?

"I . . . ," he began, and stopped again. "I don't—"

Someone knocked on the outer door, fast and loud. Marcus had ordered that he was not to be disturbed, and the sound made his heart do a double somersault. He turned his back on Ionkovo and yanked the door open to find Staff Eisen in the doorway, panting.

"Sir," he gasped. "We've had a runner from the city."

"What's happened?"

"Riots, sir. After the vice captain arrested Danton, people were gathering in the streets. The Concordat has been arresting the ringleaders, but it only makes them angrier."

Of course it does! Marcus wondered what the hell Orlanko was thinking. "Is Giforte back yet?"

"He's taken Danton to the Vendre—"

"To the *Vendre*? Why?"

"He judged it would be safer, sir. It's a fortress. Between the men he took along and the garrison, it can hold off an army."

Marcus stared at him, a sinking feeling in his guts. The Vendre. A fortress, to be sure, but a fortress on the tip of the Island, within easy reach of an angry mob. *And run by Orlanko's people. I don't like this one bit.*

"Can he bring Danton here?" The Guardhouse was less defensible, but at least it wasn't in the heart of the city.

"No, sir. That's why he sent a runner. There are enough people in the streets that he doesn't want to risk it."

"Balls of the Beast," he swore. "All right. Gather up anyone you can find here who can hold a musket. We're going down there."

"Yes, sir!"

Marcus strode away, letting Eisen close and lock the cell door behind him. He was aware of a certain lightness in his step, in spite of the crisis. Or, perhaps, because of it—Eisen's report had banished all thoughts of Ionkovo and Janus, reducing the world to simpler terms. His men were in danger, and for the moment Marcus d'Ivoire knew exactly where his duty lay.

Part Three

ORLANKO

The Cobweb was always brightly lit on the inside, but tonight even the facade was ablaze with lights.

The Last Duke had put out the word, and the army of shadows sallied forth. Alone or in groups, on horseback or riding in great armored wagons, each according to his particular assignment, they formed a river of lanterns, glittering steel, and dark, flapping coats stretching from Ohnlei toward the city.

It was another advantage, the duke reflected, of the uniform, the black coat that was so embedded in popular imagination. The Concordat employed two scribes and bean counters for every spy and assassin, and on a night like tonight manpower was in very short supply. And yet take the lowliest junior analyst, a half-addled boy who'd never been trusted with anything more than adding up columns of figures; swaddle him in that sinister black leather, and he was suddenly *Concordat*, a terrifying instrument of the will of the all-knowing and all-powerful Orlanko. Never mind that if you gave him a sword, all he'd be able to do was cut himself. People came along quietly, goaded by the phantoms in their own minds. It was remarkable.

Of course, there were some assignments that couldn't be trusted to dressed-up scriveners. Orlanko paged through the first of the reports that were already flooding into his office, and looked up expectantly as Andreas entered.

"Sir. You summoned me."

"I did. Your report says that you have identified Danton's backers."

"Only in part, sir. I have a source in the group, but his information is limited."

"But you know where they meet."

"I believe so, sir."

"And you think they'll be meeting tonight?"

"Almost certainly, sir. The minister's arrest of Danton has set the city buzzing."

"Vhalnich," Orlanko said bitterly. "He was supposed to be taken care of in Khandar."

"Yes, sir." Andreas' voice was neutral.

"In your report," the duke said, "you recommend not taking immediate action against this . . . cabal."

"Yes, sir. I believe there is another layer, to which only the senior members have access. My source claims their funding was obtained via speculative investments, which is obviously nonsense. There must be another entity, with deep pockets, standing behind them. If we let them have free rein for a while, we will eventually discover it."

Orlanko tapped his fingers on the desk. That was certainly the conventional procedure. Once you had a hook in the prey, it was always best to let them have their head for a time, especially once they became aware the forces of authority were breathing down their neck. It was always interesting to see where they bolted.

But this was hardly a normal time. *The ship is close to the breakers,* the duke thought. *If we can navigate the narrow passage, then it will be clear sailing, and there will be plenty of time to run down any rats.*

"Take them," he said. "Tonight. Use as many men as you need. I want as many as possible alive for interrogation. Bring the source in as well, and keep him with the others. You never know what he might hear."

Andreas bowed slightly. "Yes, sir." He hesitated. "There may be a complication."

"Oh?"

"You know several of the agents following the group were found dead, the day of the bank run."

"Obviously they became careless. These are desperate men and women."

"Yes, sir. I received a final report from one of those agents, with a promising lead that turned out to be a dead end. When our people analyzed the report, there were irregularities in the text. I now believe it to be the work of—"

"The Gray Rose," Orlanko said, not bothering to keep the weariness out of his voice. "This has become an obsession with you, Andreas."

"It is the only logical explanation, sir. And the consequences are alarming. If our ciphers have been compromised—"

"I designed our ciphers myself," the duke said. "Part of that design ensures that any individual cipher falling into enemy hands does not affect the security of the whole."

"I know that, sir. But if it *is* the Gray Rose, her knowledge of our procedures makes us vulnerable. I think—"

"It makes no difference one way or the other," the duke snapped. "You know where this cabal is meeting. Go and take them. If the Gray Rose shows herself, you have my permission to kill her."

Andreas looked, for a moment, as though he wanted to argue, but his face quickly returned to its customary blank mask. He bowed deeply, worn leather coat flapping about his ankles. "As you say, sir. I will proceed directly."

As Andreas padded out, the duke looked back at the report he'd been reading, fighting a rising sense of irritation and, most annoyingly, nervousness. Things really were coming to a head, in more ways than one. *Vhalnich. It all turns on Vhalnich.*

Vhalnich had decided to arrest Danton, a move guaranteed to send the streets into convulsions. Orlanko didn't understand what the new Minister of Justice was playing at, which for the master of the Concordat was an uncommon and distinctly unwelcome feeling. There hadn't been time to stop him, so Orlanko had done the next best thing.

If Vhalnich wants the city brought to a simmer, we'll see how he likes it when the pot boils over. The Concordat agents fanning out through the city were bringing in every agitator, every troublemaker, every printer of libelous broadsheets or licentious pamphlets. They'd begun at sundown and were working until dawn, gangs of black-coated men riding through the streets, breaking down doors, hauling terrified men and women in nightshirts out of their homes and off to the black, hulking walls of the Vendre.

There would be clashes, even deaths. It would only enhance the effect.

The streets will burn. *There will be riots, looting, disorder.* Afterward, it would be easy to put the blame on Vhalnich. After all, his arrest of Danton had been the spark that ignited the powder magazine. Besides, the maintenance of public order was the responsibility of the Armsmen and the Ministry of Justice. They *needed* the goodwill of the public. All the Concordat needed was fear.

Then, when the king died—which Orlanko's analysts assured him would happen tonight or tomorrow, Indergast's best efforts to the contrary—there would be a new ruler. The one thing he'd been missing for his whole career, the capstone of his power. A *tame* head to wear the crown, a queen who would do what she was told. Once she was in place, Vhalnich could be dismissed from his post and all the prisoners released, to transform the public's wrath to joy. Danton would moderate his message, or else he, too, could be replaced in time. Orlanko would take great pleasure in delivering a lesson to Rackhil Grieg on the nature of *loyalty*.

And Vhalnich, some dark night, would vanish. He would be trussed up like a lamb for slaughter and delivered to the Priests of the Black. That would satisfy the pontifex and, Orlanko thought, be a suitably satisfying way of disposing of the man.

There was a way through the passage; he could see it. It was narrow and lined with roaring breakers, but it was there, sure enough. At the other end, the queen and the city would praise his name, as the man who held Vordan together in its moment of crisis.

A slow smile spread across his face as he contemplated the prospect.

For tonight, then, let the city burn.

If there had been a real eagle overhead that night, as opposed to a heraldic one, it might have been forgiven for thinking that Vordan *was* burning.

The air had the hot, muggy quality of a laundry, the moisture a nearly perceptible fog that felt like breathing soup. The heat kept people from their beds, robbed them of their good humor, made tempers fray. Children stripped down and played by the riverbanks, jumping into the water from the docks or, for the more adventurous, from the bridges. In Farus' Triumph, thousands had gathered for Danton's speech. Fights were already breaking out when the Armsmen arrived, with Orlanko's snatch squads close on their heels.

All over the city, streets emptied in panic at the sight of phalanxes of men in dark leather coats, marching to doorway after ill-fated doorway. Children screamed as the black-coats broke down doors with sledgehammers, and women shrieked as their homes were ransacked. Trouble began almost immediately. A printer of seditious pamphlets attempted to flee rather than go to the Vendre, and fell out a second-story window to his death. A man accused of nothing more substantial than speaking against the tax farmers in a tavern fired a pistol at the Concordat agents sent to round him up; he missed, but the enraged secret policemen stabbed him a dozen times and left him to bleed on his own doorstep. Women were forced out of bed and paraded through the streets in their nightshirts. Dark, armored wagons shuttled back and forth, hauling their sobbing cargo to the prison.

Most of the city was dark, at first, as fearful Vordanai doused their lamps and candles in the hopes that the Concordat's wrath would pass them by. Here and there, though, sparks of light remained. The Dregs, outside the University, were a ribbon of light. There, in taverns and wine sinks under a hundred colored flags, students and intellectuals of every stripe shouted and cursed, drank and hurled glasses against the walls.

They grew more heated as the news trickled in of fresh atrocities, real and imagined. A dozen women raped in Oldtown. Twenty Free Church priests mutilated for speaking blasphemy in the eyes of Elysium. Fifty men shot down in cold blood in a Bottoms shantytown. Hundreds more Concordat men on the way—no, they were Borelgai mercenaries, hired by the banks, smuggled into the country by the Last Duke to secure his position and dressed up in Concordat coats. No, they were *Murnskai*, Black Priests sent to cull the heretics at last.

At the other end of the city, in the Docks, another knot of lights glowed. It was faint at first, but like a coal feeling the breath of the bellows, it grew brighter by the moment. It spread, tracing the mazy paths of the streets and back alleys around the fish shops and warehouses, outlining the river and filling the squares. Torches, hundreds of torches, and candles, tapers, flaming brands, and bull's-eye lanterns. It was a river of flame, and it began to flow, slowly but inexorably, draining toward the River Road and east along the bank to the base of the Grand Span.

Once across the river, the flaming river met with other tributaries—from Newtown and Oldtown, from the Dregs, even from the prosperous and orderly districts of Northside. The torches swirled, eddied uncertainly, and finally turned decisively west, to break like a wave outside the craggy black walls of the Vendre.

CHAPTER TEN

RAESINIA

By the time she got away from Ohnlei, Raesinia was nearly frantic. Things were happening, out in the city; the streets had taken fire. But she'd been stuck in her room in the palace until nearly dawn, greeting a steady stream of high-ranking messengers sent from her father's sickroom, all coming to assure her that no news had yet emerged. They all knew he was going to die, of course, and all of these counts and other scions of nobility were eager to get their foot in the door with the new center of power. Raesinia greeted each one less courteously than the last, until she finally couldn't stand it any longer. Sothe had put it about that the princess had gone into hysterics and been put to bed with a sleeping draught, and the two of them had escaped.

It was hard, not staying with her father. But Indergast wouldn't let her be in the room with him, and in any case she thought that if he knew the whole story, he would approve. The good of the country and the Crown came first, even before family. Raesinia closed her eyes in a brief, silent prayer. *One more day, Father. I know you're in pain. Please, just give me one more day.* Even the thought made her feel guilty.

The first light of day was just showing in the east, but torches and lanterns were still burning up and down the Dregs. All the cafés were packed, colored flags hanging limp in the hot, dead air, and armbands, sashes, and other proclamations of allegiance seemed to adorn everyone who passed the windows of her carriage. Raesinia put the string in her pocket and fingered the blue-green-gold butterfly pinned to her shoulder. She hadn't seen anyone in those colors so far, and she was beginning to worry.

There were broadsheets and pamphlets everywhere, their smudgy ink still wet. Every hack writer and handpress in the city seemed to have sprung into action, and the boys who usually sold papers for a penny were giving away stacks of them to anyone who wanted to read. Anything more than an hour old was tossed aside in favor of the latest news, so the carriage wheels rattled and crunched down a street paved with discarded paper. Raesinia wondered how much paper there *was* in the warehouses of Vordan, and what would happen when it ran out.

She caught sight of the sign of the Blue Mask, but the density of the crowd increased, slowing the carriage's pace to a crawl. Frustrated, she kicked the door open and hopped down into a swirl of excited, arguing young men. She edged around a contested space, where a wild knot of Utopians were arguing with a Rationalist sub-sub-subcommittee, and managed to make it to the edge of the street, up against the windows of a café. From here, she could see the blue-green-gold flag of the Mask, hanging in a long row with all the others.

Sothe materialized at her side. One nice thing about Sothe, Raesinia reflected. You never had to worry about waiting for her to catch up.

"This is a madhouse," Raesinia said. "Half the University must be out here."

"And more besides." Sothe sounded grim. "This isn't safe. We should go back."

"We created this, Sothe. We can't go back now. Besides, we'd never get the carriage turned around." Raesinia tried to force a note of cheer into her voice, though she had to shout to be heard over the tumult. "Come on. Let's see if the others are still here."

They picked their way, slowly, through the crowd. Every faction and sect seemed to be out in force tonight, striving to take control of this critical moment with all the volume they could muster. Reunionists preached the virtues of a united Church, Republicans had taken up Danton's call for the Deputies-General, and a thousand splintered bands of Utopians shook worn copies of Voulenne's *Rights of Man* at one another. Gangs of Feudalists, with their antique flags, shouted at phalanxes of Monarchists, refighting the battles of Farus IV that had been dead and buried before Raesinia was born. And everywhere the papers, with huge, jagged type, letters in different styles, random splashes of ink from malfunctioning presses, anything the printers could think of to draw the eye. More carriages had gotten stuck and been abandoned by their passengers. The drivers sat playing cards on the boxes, resigned to waiting until the crowd broke up. Judging by the reek of horseshit, some of them had been there for a while.

After ten minutes of making progress only by vigorous application of her elbows, Raesinia broke into the clear. The street in front of the Mask was empty in a wide half circle around the doorway, as if it had been enchanted with an evil charm. The interior was dark, and it took Raesinia a moment to realize what was wrong—the big, expensive single-pane windows had been shattered and lay in glittering fragments all around.

"Oh God." Raesinia took a step forward, automatically, and felt Sothe's restraining hand on her arm. "What the hell happened?"

She looked around, wildly, and grabbed a hapless Individualist by the wrist. He squawked as she dragged him into the cursed, empty circle.

"What happened?" He stared at her, blankly, and she raised her voice. *"What happened here?"*

Her victim, a freckled boy with sandy brown hair and a bewildered look, glanced at the broken windows and shook his head.

"Concordat," he said. "They raided quite a few places before the street really filled up. After that people started running them off."

"Raided? What for?"

"How should I know? I heard they were just rounding up whoever they could find and hauling them off to the Vendre." He brightened. "See, it proves the fundamental illegitimacy of collectivist ruling structures that, in a crisis, they must always resort to coercive measures or violence. A truly just polity would emerge *spontaneously* from—"

Raesinia left him to babble and grabbed for Sothe. "Orlanko's people were *here*. They found us."

"We don't know that for certain," Sothe said. "Other cafés were hit as well. But it's possible." She frowned. "I told you we couldn't keep them off forever."

"We have to find them," Raesinia said.

"Don't be foolish," Sothe said. "*If* they were taken, they're on their way to the Vendre."

"We *have* to find them. You know what happens to people in there!"

Sothe fixed Raesinia with a withering look. "Of course I do. And I know what Orlanko will do to *you* if he discovers you're involved."

"But . . ." Inspiration struck. "They know me, don't they? When he starts asking for information, they'll give him a description, and Orlanko will be able to put the pieces together if anyone will."

"They might not talk," Sothe said, but she looked unhappy.

"Everybody talks, eventually. You told me that, Sothe."

"I know."

"Then let's go! If all the streets are as crowded as this one, they can't have gotten far. We can—"

"Stage a rescue? Have you got a bag of bombs under your skirt you didn't tell me about?" Sothe shook her head, a calculating look in her eye. "I'll go. You stay here."

"You know *I* won't be in danger—"

"You will be," Sothe said. "You may not be able to die, but if you get caught, we lose everything."

"What if they catch *you* and make you talk?"

Sothe smiled grimly. "Believe me, I have plans against that contingency."

"But—"

"Besides, I'll move faster without you. Just *stay here.* Stay in the crowd, and keep your head down. I'll find a way to get word to you as soon as I have news." She glanced at the ruined Mask. "And stay away from this place. It may be watched."

"Sothe . . ."

"We don't have time to argue about this."

"I know." Raesinia took a deep breath. "Just . . . bring them back, all right? And be sure to come back yourself, too."

"I'll do my best." Sothe gripped Raesinia's hand for a moment, squeezed, and let it fall. "Remember. Stay where there's a crowd, and don't do anything to get their attention."

Raesinia nodded, her throat suddenly thick. Sothe turned on her heel and stepped into the crowd, slipping through the packed street like a ghost. She was lost to sight in moments.

Beast, Raesinia swore, alone in a semicircle of clear cobbles. *Balls of the fucking Beast.* She'd always known this was a possibility, of course. The whole conspiracy had been a desperate throw of the dice. Once it became clear that her father wouldn't live out the year, she'd had no other choice. Only a popular uprising against the Last Duke could free the kingdom of his malign influence, and so she'd set about creating one. *But it wasn't supposed to happen like* this. *What possessed Vhalnich to arrest Danton? I thought he was smarter than that.*

The sound of someone calling her name made her jump. It was accompanied by a wooden crash and a lot of swearing. Raesinia turned and saw a light flickering somewhere inside the ruined coffee shop.

"Raes!" The voice was hoarse, desperate. It was Ben. *Oh, hell. "Raes!"*

Raesinia spit a curse and ran inside the Blue Mask.

The common room had been comprehensively destroyed. Every table lay in splinters, the chairs had been kicked to pieces, and the intricate bronze-and-copper coffee apparatus on the bar lay in twisted metal fragments. Broken wine bottles were everywhere, and the smell of the stuff, slopped on the floor and soaking into the rugs, made Raesinia's head spin. It was mixed with the reek of urine from a smashed chamber pot, and the gritty, earthy smell of powder smoke.

The light was coming from the back, where the conspiracy had held their meetings. Raesinia passed through the smashed door and hurried across the wine-stained footprints. The door to their room was broken, too, and the table they'd sat around had been overturned. Ben was standing by the window, peering carefully around a jagged rim of shattered glass.

"Ben?"

He turned around, narrowly avoiding cutting his arm open on the remains of the windowpane. "Raes!"

She barely had time to brace before he was on top of her, both arms wrapped around her in a bear hug. His lantern, hanging forgotten in one hand, swung wildly and clipped her painfully in the small of her back, but she managed not to make a sound. Her feet briefly left the floor, and his scratchy, unshaven cheek was pressed against hers.

"Thank God," he was saying. "Thank God. I thought they'd got you."

"Ben. I'm fine. Please." He didn't show any sign of letting go, so Raesinia wriggled her arm loose and pried him off. "Ben! I'm fine, really. What happened? Where are the others?"

His eyes, bloodshot and teary, took a moment to focus on her, and he swallowed hard. "I haven't seen Sarton. Maurisk is in some kind of meeting with the other groups. They're trying to decide what to do, but when I left they weren't getting anywhere. I lost Faro somewhere in the crowd, but he's okay, I think. Cora . . ."

He paused.

"What happened to Cora?" Raesinia said, the pit in her stomach yawning wider.

"They took her," Ben said. "The Concordat. I was across the street when they got here, a dozen men. They broke the door down, smashed the windows, and started chasing people out of the place. They must have been here for *us*. They just let everyone else get away. A couple of them were searching, smashing everything, and then they brought Cora outside and put her in a wagon. I wanted . . ." His fists clenched. "I wanted to *help* her. But there was nobody on the street then. And I wanted to warn you, and the others—"

"It's all right," Raesinia said. Her stomach felt sick—not a sensation she encountered much anymore—but Ben was clearly on the point of hysteria and needed reassurance. "We'll find her. Ben, listen. I have an idea. Once things calm down—"

"Actually," said a voice behind them, "you'll see her much sooner than that."

There were two men in the shattered doorway, in shabby trousers and slouch caps. They looked like University students, but the one in front carried himself in a fighter's crouch, and his compatriot held a cocked and loaded pistol. Raesinia froze.

"What?" said Ben, slightly slower on the uptake. "Who are you?"

"They're Concordat," Raesinia said. "I imagine they were waiting for us."

"Very good." The leader inclined his head slightly. "I am Andreas, and I do indeed serve His Grace the Minister of Information. You are Benjamin Cooper, I believe, and you are the mysterious Raesinia with all the bright ideas. Please don't try anything heroic. My companion is an excellent shot." His face was blank, but there was something hot and bright in his eyes, as though he wished they *would* try something. Raesinia risked a glance over her shoulder and saw another pair of figures through the window, waiting in the alley outside.

"What do you want?" Ben said.

Andreas shrugged. "His Grace would like you to answer a few questions. If you'll come with us, I assure you that you will not be harmed."

Fuck. Raesinia ran through scenarios in her head. *Fuck, fuck,* fuck. Andreas obviously hadn't recognized her on sight, but if she was taken to the Vendre, it would only be a matter of time. A quick escape might work, but it would leave Ben behind. *And Sothe is halfway to the Vendre herself by now.* She spit a silent curse at herself for ignoring her maid's advice. *Of* course *Orlanko would leave someone to watch the place. Oh, saints and martyrs.*

Now what?

Her eyes flicked to Ben and she found him looking back at her. Raesinia's heart gave a sickening lurch as she realized he was about to do something stupid.

No, no, no, I'll think of something. Don't—

"Raes, run!"

Ben threw himself forward, head lowered like a bull. He covered the distance to the doorway surprisingly quickly for someone of his bulk, but not quickly enough to prevent the Concordat agent from pulling the trigger. Raesinia saw blood spray from Ben's back, but the impact wasn't enough to stop him, and he crashed into the gunman with all the momentum he could muster and slammed him against the opposite wall, sending the pistol clattering to the floor.

Andreas spun sideways, slick as an eel, still blocking the corridor leading to the front room. Raesinia forced herself into motion, hard on Ben's heels. She bounced off the corridor wall, faked one way, and darted the other, trying to slip past the Concordat agent's outspread arms. He followed her easily, and as she tried to squirm by he grabbed her by the wrist, yanking her back toward him. His other hand went to her elbow, palm out, forcing her arm into a painful lock and pushing her to the floor.

At least, that's how it would have worked on any normal human being. Raesinia let him pull her around, gritted her teeth, and kept coming. Something in her elbow went *crunch*, and then the bones of her forearm broke with an audible *snap*. The second of surprise this bought her was enough to deliver a quick kick to the back of Andreas' knee, folding his leg up around the blow and sending him toppling to the floor. Raesinia met his jaw with one of her knees on the way down for good measure. She heard the *clack* as his teeth met, and his hands slipped off her shattered arm.

Ben was still on his feet, barely, with the other Concordat agent slumped against the wall in front of him. The front of his shirt was slick with blood, as though someone had hit him full in the chest with a bucket of red paint. She grabbed his arm with her good hand and pulled, and he stumbled into motion, but the movement sent fresh waves of red into his already sodden clothing.

The common room of the Mask was shattered and empty. By the time they reached the front door, Ben was weaving, and his legs gave out after they'd taken a few steps into the cobbled street. Raesinia tried to support him, forgetting that she had only one arm to do it with, and they both went down in a tangled, gory heap. Raesinia pushed herself up one-handed, letting Ben roll onto his back.

He gasped for air and tried to speak, but his voice was so thin she had to bend close to hear.

"Run," he said. "Raes . . . run . . ."

Instead she shouted for help. A few eyes had already turned their way, but it took a moment for the crowd to realize what was happening. Then a woman screamed, high and shrill, and people surged forward in an effort to find out what was going on. Raesinia looked up at the Mask and thought she saw Andreas, framed in the rear door of the common room. He was gone almost at once. *They won't dare,* she thought. *Not in the crowd, not tonight. Stupid, stupid, stupid. I should have listened to Sothe. Oh, Ben . . .*

"A doctor!" she said, to the first young man whose attention she managed to catch. "I need a doctor. Now!"

But, turning back to Ben, she saw it was obvious that he had passed beyond the help of any earthly medicine. Blood pulsed from the hole in his chest with every heartbeat, but the stream was weakening into a trickle even as she watched. His lips moved, and she bent close to hear.

"Raes . . ." His breath was ragged. "I . . . I l . . . lov . . ."

"I know." Her eyes were rimmed with tears. "You weren't exactly subtle about it, Ben. Who did you think you were fooling?"

She leaned across his body, gore squishing in their clothes, and pressed her lips to his. His mouth was full of the warm, coppery taste of blood.

By the time she straightened up, even the trickle from his wound had ceased. Raesinia climbed wearily to her feet, her own shirt dripping and ruined, her face smeared with red. She straightened her arm and felt the binding going to work, broken ends of bone snapping together like a pair of magnets, the ruined joint rebuilding itself as muscles reknit around it.

She was surrounded by a ring of nervous onlookers, not wanting to get too close to the gory spectacle but pressed near by the mass of those behind who wanted to see. Raesinia touched the butterfly pin at her shoulder, leaving a smear of blood over the colors.

"This man was just murdered by a Concordat agent," she said. Quietly at first, then again, louder. "This man was just *murdered* by a Concordat agent!"

I'm sorry, Ben. Whether or not she'd returned his love, he'd been her friend; one of her only friends, if she was being honest. Though, in an odd way, she thought he would approve of being used as a symbol. *He would understand that we need to keep moving forward.* Later, in private, there would be time to mourn.

"Who is in charge here?" she said, shouting to be heard over the babble that had broken out. She raised one red-stained hand to point a finger, scanning round the circle. "Who's in charge?"

"There's a council," someone offered. "At the Gold Sovereign."

"They're not really in charge," someone else said. "They just like to argue."

"The notion of someone being in 'charge' is fundamentally illegitimate," said a third, "and indeed emblematic of a failed notion of the management of human affairs—"

"Take me there," Raesinia said. When this failed to produce an effect, she swung her arm, spattering the first rank with thickening drops of Ben's blood. *"Now!"*

They took her to the council. First, though, she consented to an offer from a stout middle-aged woman who turned out to be a proprietress of a nearby boardinghouse, and went for a quick sluice-down and a change of clothes. She emerged, not exactly clean—her hair was a fright, in spite of several washes—but not looking as if she'd just stepped out of a slaughterhouse. The only clothes the woman had been able to find to fit her was a young girl's sundress, pale green linen with foaming lace sleeves that Raesinia had torn off and thrown away. She kept the three-color butterfly pin, now filmed with crusty red.

The Gold Sovereign was an ostentatiously expensive café on the corner of the Old Road and Second Avenue, done up in a faux-baroque style complete with gilded plaster columns in the facade. Its blue-red-silver flag proclaimed it a bastion of the Monarchists, and Raesinia knew by reputation that it played host to gatherings of those University students who moved in the most elevated social circles—the children of counts and other noble relatives, with a leavening of families who had been wealthy long enough to merit a kind of quasi-nobility. Even in the current state of emergency, the place had maintained an air of reserve, and two footmen in long coats and white gloves stood beside its door, to keep out the rabble.

Faro was also standing by the door, tapping his foot and fiddling nervously with the grip of his dress sword. The crowd was thinner here, and he saw Raesinia coming up the street and hurried to meet her.

"My God," he said. "Raes, are you all right? They told me something happened—"

"Who else is here?" Raesinia said.

"Maurisk is inside. I heard a rumor that Sarton was picked up outside his apartment, but no one seems to know for certain. I haven't seen him. And you know they arrested Danton yesterday."

"They snatched Cora from the Mask," Raesinia said, her voice carefully controlled. "And Ben is dead."

"Oh no. You're certain?"

She wanted to scream at him, *I practically took a bath in his fucking blood—of course I'm certain!* With an effort, she kept her tone level. "I was with him. We went into the Mask to see if anyone was still there, and Orlanko's people were waiting for us. He helped me get away, and got shot in the process."

"Balls of the Beast," Faro swore quietly.

"My thoughts exactly."

"What the hell do we do now? They obviously know who we are. Maybe if we got out of the city—"

That seemed a little cold to Raesinia, but Faro had never been one to worry about others when his own skin was endangered. For all that, Raesinia felt sorry for him. In spite of his protests that he was just as serious about the cause as any of the others, he'd always treated the conspiracy like a game, and now things were in deadly earnest.

"Don't fool yourself," Raesinia said. "You can't get far enough, fast enough that Orlanko won't find you."

"Then we might as well turn ourselves in now and save him the trouble," Faro said. "Once all this dies down—"

"We can't let it," Raesinia said. "I know we planned on having more time, but this is *it*, Faro. If we can't pull it off now, we never will."

"But . . ." He gaped at her. "We're not ready. We've barely even *started*! We were going to arrange the Deputies, and contact the Armsmen, and get Danton to talk about . . . I mean . . ."

"We're out of *time*." Raesinia took a deep breath. "The king is dying. Soon. Tonight, maybe."

"Saints and martyrs. If that *girl* gets on the throne, it's all over. Orlanko might as well put the crown on himself."

"I think she'll listen to us," Raesinia said dryly. "*If* we can show her that the people won't stand for Orlanko and his Borelgai allies running things. That means today, while they're still angry. I don't know what the duke thinks he's doing with all these arrests, but he's got half the city up in arms."

"There's a rumor it's the new Minister of Justice's doing. Apparently Orlanko didn't want Danton arrested, but this Count Mieran overruled him."

"That has to be a lie," Raesinia said. *Father said I could trust him.* "I mean, from what I've heard of Count Mieran, he and Orlanko hate each other. And it was definitely a Concordat team waiting for us at the Mask."

Faro shrugged. "I've heard more stories tonight than I care to count. It doesn't really matter one way or the other, though, does it? What are we actually going to *do*? We haven't got anything prepared. We don't even have any way to get to our money without Cora. What does that leave? Send Maurisk in to argue politics with the duke?"

"We need *them*." Raesinia waved a hand at the street, now outlined in the soft light of the rising sun. The crowd had only grown larger since daybreak, a new wave of early risers mixing with those who'd been unable to sleep. "This mob is in the wrong place. If we could get them over to the Vendre—"

"What? We'd storm the walls?"

"We could threaten to. Pressure them into letting Danton go."

"That's pretty thin, Raes."

"Look at it from their point of view. How are they going to get rid of us?"

"Canister," Faro said promptly. "Double load at thirty paces. There'll be arms and legs all over the square."

"Even Orlanko wouldn't dare. The whole city would turn on him."

"Are you certain enough that you'd be first in line?"

"I would."

Easy for me to say. Though she had to admit she'd never been dismembered. She wondered what would happen. *Would my arms and legs grow back, or would I have to go around and collect them?*

Faro threw up his hands. "What's the use in talking about it? You haven't been listening to them argue in there. I don't think you could get this lot to agree that the sun rises in the east, and that happened not ten minutes ago." He shook his head. "I want to help Cora, too. But we're not going to do it by climbing the walls of the Vendre."

"Danton could get them to do it."

"Danton could talk them into forming a human pyramid so he could drive over the walls in a cart," Faro said. "But we haven't *got* Danton. That's the whole problem."

"Let me talk to them."

She brushed past him, and Faro fell in behind her. He waved to the footmen, and they held the door of the Gold Sovereign open to admit her.

"Raes," Faro said.

"What?"

"Ben. He's . . . really dead?"

She closed her eyes. Her lips still tasted faintly of blood. "He's dead."

"Damn." He repeated it under his breath, like a mantra. "Damn, damn, damn . . ."

The common room of the Gold Sovereign looked as if it belonged in a castle somewhere. The walls were covered with embroidered heraldry, dominated by the Orboan eagle, interspersed with polished swords, axes, and other weapons, each of which presumably boasted a storied history. There was even a suit of armor, complete with halberd, standing sentry by the stairs in the back. A huge fireplace filled one wall, dark and cold now in the summer heat, and high-backed chairs in the old medieval style were arranged in loose circles around polished marble tables. The general impression was that one had stepped into a duke's sitting room from four hundred years ago, and the only concessions to commerce were the discreet bar in one corner hosting assorted liquor and the coffee-making paraphernalia.

The way the current occupants were carrying on made Raesinia hope that all those weapons were securely bolted down. The "council" looked as though it might dissolve into a brawl at any moment. The various factions seemed to have settled into three rough groups under the pressure of their mutual antipathy, dragging the chairs together to maintain maximum separation from one another.

The largest group, closest to the bar, was easy to identify by their expensive, fashionable costumes. These were the Monarchists and their allies, the guardians of the old order, in their natural habitat here in the Sovereign and plainly resenting the newcomers. Quite a few of them were armed, though mostly with gilt- and gem-encrusted dress swords like Faro's. They aped the styles that were fashionable at court, but to Raesinia, who had seen the real thing, they looked too young and too uncertain in their finery, like children playing dress-up in their fathers' wardrobe. There were, she was not surprised to find, no women among them.

Maurisk's presence at the head of the second group identified them as the Reformers and associated sects, who wanted to tinker with the social order but not smash it entirely to pieces. They were well dressed, too, but in more sober clothing befitting their mostly commercial origins. Maurisk caught Raesinia's eye, and she tried to smile, but his expression remained grave.

The third group, by process of elimination, was the Radicals, including the

Republicans, the Individualists, and any number of other flavors of wild-eyed freethinkers and devotees of Voulenne. They were the most varied collection, by far, looking almost like an artist's depiction of a cross section of Vordanai society—everything from noble finery to mendicant's rags seemed to be represented. There were women among them, too, mostly the rare female University students whose dress Raesinia had affected. Unlike the other two groups, the Radicals still wore the badges of their individual cafés, taverns, and gathering places, and their rear ranks seemed to be engaged in a continual low-grade grumble of argument.

The shouting match that had been in progress when the door opened trailed off as Raesinia and Faro came in, and all eyes were suddenly on them. Raesinia searched the faces of the Monarchists, suddenly nervous. It was just possible that one of them had met her in person, at a party or a court function, and she held her breath waiting for a sudden shout of recognition. It didn't come.

"Another one for the loonies, then?" said the young man sitting at the head of the Monarchist cluster. There was a titter of laughter from behind him.

"She's with me," Maurisk said, setting off a storm of chatter in his own faction. "Raesinia, come here."

"I see," said the Monarchist. "Will little girls be allowed in the new Deputies-General, then?"

"I'm not here to join anyone," Raesinia said, a little too loudly. "And I'm not here to argue."

"Then why *are* you here?" the Monarchist said. "Not for coffee, I assume?"

She waited for the laughter to die down. "Might I have your name, sir?"

He inclined his head. "I am Alfred Peddoc sur Volmire, at your service."

Raesinia turned to the Radicals, who seemed to be represented by a young man in slightly shabby linen and a woman all in baggy, shapeless blacks. "And you?"

"Robert Dumorre," he said, flicking his eyes to the woman. "We all call her Cyte, but—"

"Cytomandiclea," she said. Her hair was pulled back in a tight bun, and she'd used something to darken her eyes. It made her look more adult, but Raesinia suspected she was actually no older than herself.

"I," Raesinia said, "am Raesinia Smith. A half hour ago, a Concordat agent tried to kill me. One of my dearest friends was shot, and died in my arms. For all I know, he's still lying there." She took a long breath as a chorus of whispers ran through the room. "I would wager that everyone here knows someone who was arrested last night. I am here to ask you what you're going to do about it."

"Speak for yourself," Peddoc snapped. "You have my deepest sympathies for your loss, of course, but if your friends came to the attention of the Ministry of Information I think you've been moving in the wrong company."

"The kind of company that cares about the truth," Cyte said. "The kind of company that—"

"She has a point," Maurisk said. "This isn't just a few madmen disappearing. I don't know how many have been taken, but it's got to be hundreds at least. And I've heard worse things, Free Church priests—"

"Rumors," Peddoc snorted. "His Grace does what he must to restore order."

"He's taken *Danton*," Cyte said.

Raesinia caught the troubled expression on Peddoc's face. In spite of his haughty pretensions, the fact that he and his friends were here at *all* said something, and Raesinia suspected he was more disturbed than he let on.

"Danton was . . . causing trouble," Peddoc said, finally. "I'm sure he was taken in for his own safety. In any case, everyone knows it was the Armsmen who arrested him, not His Grace the duke. If you want to blame someone, blame this Count Mieran."

"Don't be a fool," said Cyte. "You think some count fresh from Khandar can take a step at Ohnlei without Orlanko's approval?"

There were murmurs of approval at this, even from among the Monarchists. Raesinia wasn't sure she wanted to encourage this notion of the duke as an all-powerful bogeyman, but for the moment she would use what she had. She nodded at Cyte and said, "You must have seen what's happening outside. Those people are waiting for someone to lead them."

"That's what we've been trying to do," said Dumorre. He had the deep, commanding voice of a stage actor. "If our friends here would stop quibbling over every minor point."

"We wouldn't need to if *you* could come up with a declaration of principles that didn't double as an attack on the very foundations of society," Peddoc said. He turned to glare at Maurisk. "And if your lot would agree on what they actually wanted."

"The Deputies-General, to start with," Maurisk said, but he was almost immediately overwhelmed by cries from behind him. Raesinia heard "Representation by classes!" "Respect for the public purse!" and considerable argument about vetoes and powers before Maurisk managed to reestablish silence with a baleful look.

"We're not going to get *anything* by staying here," Raesinia said. "You all know the king may be dying. If we let this chance slip away, and Orlanko consolidates his control, there'll be no stopping him. You"—she looked at Maurisk and his fractious backers—"will lose your best chance to change things. And you"—this was to Peddoc—"will end up with a Vordanai queen with Borelgai hands wrapped around her throat!"

She rounded on Cyte and Dumorre. "And *you* have a choice. You can stay in here and argue about what Voulenne would want, or you can actually try to make something happen. I know what Danton would tell you, even if it wasn't him they'd locked up."

It was working; she could feel it. She'd written Danton's speeches, after all, and everyone here had heard them. While she lacked the orator's awesome personal magnetism, her words echoed the ones he'd spoken well enough to call him to mind. Peddoc's eyes were still wary, but the mass of young men behind him were less restrained, and there were even a few attempts at a cheer.

"That's all well and good," Dumorre said. "But if we don't have some kind of declaration of principles, how do we know what we're fighting for? It's one thing to say we want to cast down Orlanko—"

"No one said anything about casting anyone down," Peddoc said. "Perhaps His Grace needs to be persuaded to accept a . . . quieter role, but I don't think—"

"Orlanko doesn't matter," Maurisk said. "Once we establish the Deputies-General—"

The room dissolved into babble.

Faro touched Raesinia's shoulder and leaned close. "I warned you."

"We're so close," Raesinia muttered. "They know they have to do *something*."

"They're worried about being played for fools," Faro said. "It's a lot to risk, after all, if you don't know what you're going to be getting."

Raesinia's eyes found Maurisk. He shrugged uncomfortably, as if to say, *What do you expect me to do?*

On the other side of the room, Dumorre had gotten out of his seat and advanced on Peddoc, while several of the Monarchists had their hands on their swords. The actual content of the argument was all but inaudible under the babble of voices. But Cyte was looking directly at Raesinia, wearing a thoughtful expression.

"I have an idea," Raesinia said. "Faro, is there a room upstairs we could use?"

"Probably. But—"

"Grab a pen and paper and meet me up there. Tell that Cyte girl that I want her opinion on something, and see if she'll come up, too."

Faro looked doubtful. "Are you going to try to draft something yourself?"

"In a way. I think I know something they can all agree on."

"If you say so." Faro looked around at the scene of barely restrained violence and shook his head. "I think it'll take a miracle."

The news took some time to filter out of the Gold Sovereign. There were more arguments as various parties explained the Declaration to one another, got things wrong, compared rumors and counterrumors, and generally milled about. Some bright soul managed to hurry to a printer's shop and get to work setting the brief document into type, and once the presses were rolling, more accurate arguments spread up and down the length of the Old Road. Maurisk, Peddoc, Cyte, and Dumorre all spread the word to their followers, and small groups formed up, then became large groups as more and more people drifted in.

By the time the sun had reached the meridian, the mob was in motion. A vast procession, stretching down the Old Road to Bridge Street, and running from there to the Saint Vallax Bridge and across to the Island. Raesinia, walking amid the boisterous crowd at its head, could look out over the river to the Island's western tip, where the black walls of the Vendre were waiting.

Faro and Maurisk walked beside her. They had filled Maurisk in on Ben's murder and Cora's abduction.

"You should have told me sooner," Maurisk said. "You know I want to help her, Raes. It's just the others—"

"I know." None of the faction leaders had particularly firm control over their flock. "We've got them moving. That's the important thing."

Faro shook his head. He was holding a copy of the Declaration, whose ink was still wet. "Only by storing up a lot of trouble for the future."

"We can deal with the future when it gets here. Right now . . ." She shrugged.

"How did you know they would agree to this?" Faro said, flapping the paper.

Raesinia took it from him and looked it over, smiling to herself. It was only a few paragraphs long, and said nothing about principles, vetoes, taxation, or even the rights of man. Instead it laid out two simple demands: that Danton and the other prisoners taken to the Vendre be released, and that the king allow the assembly of a preliminary Deputies-General, consisting of the signatories and other eminent citizens, to debate all the questions to be addressed.

"Well," she said, "first of all, I showed it to them one at a time. So for all they knew, the others would sign, and if they got left out they'd end up without a seat at the table."

"That was clever," Faro allowed. "But still!"

"Think of it this way," Raesinia said. "You've got a gang of students who spend all their time arguing with each other in coffeehouses and wine shops. What's the one thing they can all agree on?"

"I wouldn't have thought there was anything," Faro said.

"That they like to argue," Maurisk said.

Raesinia smiled. "Exactly. So if you want to get them to agree to something, promise them the chance to argue on a really grand stage."

Faro chuckled dryly. He dropped back to walk beside Raesinia, letting Maurisk get a little ahead of them, and bent to speak into her ear.

"I know you're angry about what happened to Ben," he said, "and I know you want to help Cora. But you're not going to be able to stop this now. You realize that, don't you?"

"I know," Raesinia said, quietly. "We're in it until the end."

"I hope you know what the hell you're doing."

Raesinia's smile faded. "So do I."

CHAPTER ELEVEN

MARCUS

The gray light of dawn filtered into Saint Hastoph Street, dispelling the shadows. With them went Marcus' hope that the fires that had glowed all night outside the walls might be some kind of bluff. The mob, glimpsed as specters amid a sea of torches, gained an alarming solidity, a mass of people spreading from shore to shore of the narrow island and stretching back through the side streets toward Farus' Triumph. Marcus estimated there were several thousand he could see, and who knew how many more hadn't been able to push to within sight of the walls.

It was Fort Valor all over again, except instead of a few battalions of Royal Army musketeers and a half battery of artillery, Marcus had forty-odd badly frightened Armsmen and a contingent of guards from the Ministry of Information of highly dubious reliability. And the mob below showed none of the Khandarai reluctance to attack—Marcus could see a half dozen ladders already under construction, and the men on the parapets had to duck bricks and other missiles.

The outer wall of the Vendre was a good thirty feet high, so it took a strong arm to loft a brick over the top of it. There were plenty of strong arms down there, though, and one of the Concordat men had already suffered a broken arm, while one of Marcus' had nearly been knocked from his perch by a ballistic cabbage. At least here, unlike at Fort Valor, there was a proper fire step, so the men could crouch behind the parapet and be shielded from below.

For all its sinister reputation, the Vendre was as obsolete a fortress as Fort Valor had been. Originally built to supplement the water batteries that were Vordan's primary defense against a river-borne attack from the south, its seaward walls were thick and honeycombed with embrasures. The landward fortifications were something of an afterthought, a simple stone wall to enclose an inner court and provide an outer line of defense. When the dawn of modern artillery had spelled the doom of stone-walled forts all across the continent, the Crown had turned it over to the civil authorities, who had put it to work as a prison.

Marcus' current troubles hinged on a technicality. As a prison, the Vendre was under the command of the Minister of Justice and the Armsmen, and as captain of Armsmen Marcus ranked anyone in that organization except for Janus himself. However, the Armsmen had long ago seconded use of the structure to the Minister of Information, and so the everyday command and garrison of the place was drawn from the ranks of the Concordat.

The man who now presented himself to Marcus was, therefore, nominally under his command. He wore a captain's bars at his collar himself, however, and his look and bearing said that he considered Marcus, at best, an equal. He wore a curious outfit, something like a Royal Army officer's uniform but in black instead of blue, with silver buttons and trim, and covered by one of the black leather greatcoats of which the Concordat was so fond. He offered no salute, and Marcus gave him none in return.

"Sir," the man said. His face said that he considered this quite enough of a concession. "I apologize that I was unable to meet with you earlier."

"It's quite all right," Marcus said. "We've all had a busy night. I'm Marcus d'Ivoire, captain of Armsmen."

"Yes, sir. Captain James Ross, at your service."

"May I ask to what unit you belong, Captain Ross?"

"Ministry of Information, Special Branch. Sir."

"Special Branch. I see." Marcus had never heard of such a thing, but he'd been away from Vordan a long time. "How many men do you have here?"

"Seventy-eight in total, sir. I need a few to watch the prisoners, but I can spare at least forty for the walls."

That was as many men as Marcus had in total, which made him uncomfortable. He didn't like the thought of being in the power of this "captain" with his black coat and his shiny boots. "Let's hope it doesn't come to a fight."

Ross glanced out into the street, noting the ladders. "Small chance of that, I think. But we shouldn't have any trouble." He looked thoughtful. "In fact, I'd wager if I put a dozen sharpshooters up here, we could make the street too hot for them. Rabble never have any stomach for casualties. Shall I send for them?"

"No, Captain." Marcus frowned. "Let me make myself clear. Our duty is to secure the prison and the prisoners, not to end the riots. I fully expect the Minister of Justice and the rest of the Cabinet will resolve these difficulties soon. Until they do, we will make every effort to avoid bloodshed of any kind."

Ross' eyes were hooded. "I understand, sir."

"How many prisoners do you have at present?" Giforte had put Danton in a room in the tower, but Marcus hadn't yet had a chance to visit the dungeons. Concordat wagons had been coming and going all night, until the mob outside had blocked the streets. Marcus and his small contingent from the Guardhouse had nearly been too late; they'd slipped in just before Ross barred the gates. Marcus guessed he was now regretting waiting so long. He looked like a man used to being in charge.

"We don't have an exact count, sir, but I'd say a bit over five hundred. We've got the men separated out from the women and children, and everything's under control." Ross caught the look on Marcus' face and misunderstood it. "Don't worry, sir. We know how to manage our affairs here."

"Why, exactly, do we have children in the dungeons?"

"Couldn't say, sir. Not my place to ask. Every group was properly signed for by Ministry authorities." He ventured a sickly smile. "I just keep them behind bars, sir."

Marcus glanced down at the ladders. It would be another hour or so at least before they were prepared to make an assault, if that was what they were planning.

"Would you take me to the keep, Captain Ross?" he said. "I think I should make an inspection."

The keep was an irregular, lopsided structure, several stories high where it faced the water but only a single story aboveground on the landward side. Men in Concordat black lined the parapet above the ironbound doors, armed with muskets and swords. They all straightened up and saluted at Ross' approach, like a line of scarecrows.

Inside, the first floor was largely open. It had once been laid out with rows of long wooden tables and benches, to provide Orlanko's scribblers with somewhere to do their paperwork, but at some point in last night's confusion these had all been pushed to one side or stacked. Scraps of paper and pools of spilled ink were scattered across the stone floor.

"Normally we admit prisoners through a postern gate, or through the water gate," Ross explained, as he led the way to the staircases at the rear.

"With the volume we received last night, we had to start bringing them right down the main staircase. I apologize for the mess." His eyes flicked upward as they passed the ascending steps. "That leads to the tower rooms, where your man Giforte is holding Danton. Down this way is the dungeon."

Marcus stopped and bent to examine something caught in a crack between two flagstones. It was a tiny book, a child's version of the *Wisdoms* with large print and engravings. It had gotten soaked, and the back cover and half the pages were gone. Marcus pried the sad little thing up and looked at it thoughtfully.

"Sir?" Ross said, looking over his shoulder.

"It's nothing." Marcus pocketed the book. "Lead on."

More black uniforms stopped and saluted on the steps. The air smelled of leather and shoe polish, and, as they descended, increasingly of damp stone and mud. The stairs came to a wide landing, and Ross waved a hand.

"Is there anything in particular you want to see, sir? There are three levels of cells here. The first are the old dungeons, where we keep the usual prisoners, and—"

"Where have you put the people who came in last night?"

"On the lowest level," Ross said, and started down again. "We don't normally use it, because of the damp, but there's a lot of space. It was originally meant to be a powder magazine, but it's below the level of the river, so no one has ever been able to figure out a way to keep it completely dry."

Marcus felt a bit like a hero in a fairy tale, descending into some hell to battle the minions of darkness. The stairs wound down and down, lit at regular intervals by oil lamps. Ross' promised damp soon appeared, in puddles on the steps and a slimy film on the walls. Here and there, tiny clusters of mushrooms had emerged.

When they reached the bottom landing, a three-man detail was waiting for them. Their leader ignored Marcus, saluted Ross, and said, "I'm glad you're here, sir. There's been a bit of an altercation. The prisoners found out that one of the men was a Sworn Church deacon, and some of them tried to beat him."

Ross frowned. "I should see to this, sir. Do you want to join me?"

"I'd like to see the women's quarters, if you don't mind."

There was a look on Ross' face that Marcus didn't like. "Of course, sir. Lieutenant Valt, would you show the captain the way?"

Valt was taller and stockier than Ross, but uniformed with the same attention to detail. He, at least, saluted smartly, and led Marcus at a quick pace through the murky corridor. Watching him splash through the puddles, Marcus wondered how much effort it took every morning to keep those boots shiny. *Where does the duke* find *all these eager young inquisitors?*

"They're in here, sir." They turned a corner onto another corridor, with three doors on either side. Each door was flanked by a pair of guards, and there was a shuffling and a flapping of coats as they all turned to salute. "Each of these rooms has a couple of dozen."

"You don't have individual cells for them?"

He shrugged. "All the cells are occupied. This is the overflow. Once things quiet down, I imagine they'll be moved elsewhere."

Marcus nodded, trying to look thoughtful, and walked down the corridor. As he passed the second door, he heard a thin sound that might have been a scream, heavily muffled by wood and stone.

"This one," Marcus said. "Open it."

The guards looked at Valt, who nodded. When the door was unlocked, it revealed a small room whose floor was a single enormous puddle. Steady drips from the ceiling joined trickles on the walls to form a murky brown liquid. There were no windows and only one lamp, casting long shadows against the wall.

Most of the inmates huddled on the small stretch of dry stone by the door. Just in front of the doorway, a young woman was on her knees, hunched over, while a man in a black uniform stood astride her and was in the process of delivering a vicious blow to the side of her head. He'd stopped in midswing at the sound of the door, and turned awkwardly to see Marcus and the lieutenant framed against the light from the corridor.

"Ranker?" Valt didn't sound upset, only curious. "What's going on?"

"Feeding the prisoners, sir!" the Concordat man said. He indicated a large bowl of boiled beans. "Then this one attacked me, sir!"

"She didn't—" said a young voice from the crowd, before someone clamped a hand over the speaker's mouth.

"Try not to be unnecessarily rough with them, Ranker," Valt said mildly. "Remember that an injured prisoner is an additional burden."

The ranker clambered off the woman, straightened up, and saluted. "Yes, sir! Thank you for the reminder, sir!"

Valt turned to Marcus. "Did you want to interrogate the prisoners, sir?"

Marcus' eyes were on the young woman. She got to her feet, slowly. Her blouse had been torn to shreds, and he got a glimpse of small, pale breasts, mottled with bruises, before she pulled the scraps about herself and shuffled back to the corner.

"No," he said, making an effort to keep his voice level. "Let's go back upstairs."

"Good to see you, sir," Giforte said, as Marcus took the stairs to the tower two at a time. He almost looked like he meant it. Whatever his worries about Marcus, the crisis had clearly shaken his equilibrium. "Are they at the wall—"

"Not just yet," Marcus said. "Get together some men you think you can trust and get them down to the dungeons. Tell Ross we're taking over security on the lower levels. Tell him . . ." He thought for a moment. "Tell him I think his men will be better than ours if it comes to a fight, and I want them on the walls instead of guarding doors. That should make him happy."

"Yes, sir."

"And find something to help keep the prisoners out of the water, or half of them are going to be down with a chill before tomorrow evening. Those tables on the main floor, maybe. Break them apart. You can use the scraps for firewood. I want a fire in each room, you understand?"

"Yes, sir. What about—"

"*Now,* Giforte!" Marcus found a chair and sat down heavily, resting his forehead in his hands. "The rest can wait."

Giforte saluted and slipped out. Marcus tried to slow his breathing and calm the pounding in his skull.

What the hell *was Janus thinking?* The same question might apply to the Last Duke, of course, who had to know what the conditions would be like in the Vendre once he'd tripled the number of prisoners. But for all Marcus knew, Orlanko wanted the prisoners to suffer for some malignant reason of his own, whereas he was certain—fairly certain—that Janus wouldn't countenance such a thing. *Janus didn't know Orlanko was going to order so many arrests.* But he *had* known what would happen if Danton was taken.

Faith, he says. Marcus had kept faith once before, waiting in a Khandarai church while cannonballs rang off the walls like bells. That time, Janus' arrival had turned his desperate last stand into a glorious victory, though the cost had been higher than Marcus cared to think about.

Is he going to come and rescue me this time as well?

Giforte slipped back into the room. They were in one of the tower chambers, a much lighter and airier space than the dungeon, with high ceilings and gun slits that threw lines of sunlight along the floor. It was unfurnished except for a couple of chairs and a table made from a plank and a pair of barrels. Dust motes danced and spun in the lances of light.

"I've sent the messages, sir."

"Good." Marcus rubbed his forehead with two fingers, but the pounding only got worse. He sighed. "Have you gotten anything out of Danton?"

"No. He's got some sort of idiot act going. All he does is ask me to find the princess and if I can bring him beer."

"Saints and martyrs. You'd think he'd know what's going to happen if that lot outside tries to storm the walls."

"I've tried to tell him."

"Well, make sure we keep a few men up here, too. If Ross gets his hands on Danton while he's still playing games, it'll be red-hot pokers and thumbscrews."

"He's that bad?"

Marcus paused. He was spared the necessity of answering this by the arrival of Staff Eisen, breathless from a sprint up the stairs.

"Sir!"

There was only one thing it could be. "I'm on my way."

The ladders were ready, but the mob was not storming the parapets. Not yet.

"Whoever's in charge up there," a voice boomed from below, "come out! We want to talk to you!" A background roar from the crowd added punctuation.

Ross caught up to Marcus and Giforte at the base of the wall.

"We don't need to negotiate with them," the Concordat officer said. "It may be a trap. If they've got a decent shot with a rifle somewhere—"

"I'll take the chance," Marcus said. "Feel free to stay here."

"But—"

"They outnumber us five hundred to one, Captain. I think it's worth making the effort to talk, don't you?"

Marcus hurried up the narrow stone staircase to the fire step, Giforte and Ross close behind him. The orders he'd given Giforte had already been carried out, and half the Armsmen on the wall had been replaced by black-coated Concordat troops. All were armed, and Marcus suddenly wondered if his impulsive act of chivalry had been such a good idea. *One shot would be one too many.*

"Ross," he said, when they reached the top. "Make sure your men know they're to fire on my command, and not before. Anyone who takes an early shot will have the Minister of Justice to answer to."

"Yes, sir." Ross went to talk to his lieutenants, and Marcus stepped up to the parapet and looked down at the crowd.

Ominously, it was considerably better organized than it had been this morning. Six enormous ladders had been completed, and each lay near the base of the wall in the midst of a knot of people. The crowd was a mixed bag of fishermen, laborers, menials, and even women, but the ladders were conspicuously flanked by a crew of burly dockworkers, who looked more than capable of lifting them into position. Everyone in the teams by the ladders had acquired some kind of weapon, too, though this amounted to little more than wooden clubs or improvised spears. Here and there a sword gleamed, looted from who knew where.

In the center of this impromptu siege party stood an enormous man in a fisherman's leather apron, flanked by a pair of young women. He was the one who'd spoken, his deep voice easily cutting through the excited babble of the crowd.

Marcus took a deep breath and cupped his hands around his mouth.

"I'm in command," he said. "This is an illegal armed gathering. I'm going to have to ask you to disperse!"

Ripples of laughter ran through the crowd. The big man spoke briefly to the women, then said, "I'm afraid we still have business here!"

"What do you want?"

"Open the gates and release your prisoners! If you offer no resistance, you and your men can go in peace."

"My orders don't allow that," Marcus said. He saw Ross returning out of the corner of his eye. "However, if you would like to nominate a delegation to come in and negotiate, perhaps we can reach an accommodation?"

This seemed to cause some confusion. The two women fell into a heated conversation, with the giant listening intently. Marcus watched nervously. *If I can get them talking, I can buy time.* And time was all he could hope for—time for the government to do *something*, either decide to give in to the mob's demands or summon the nearest Royal Army unit to crush them. *Either way, it won't be on* my *shoulders.*

"No point to negotiating," the big man said, coming out of the huddle. "Either open the gates or we'll open them for you." He put his head to one side. "You're an Armsman, aren't you? We have no quarrel with you. Do you really want to die for Orlanko's dogs?"

Not at all, as it happens. Marcus glanced back at Ross, who was beckoning urgently.

"Ranker Hans is an excellent shot," he said. "He's certain he can pick off the leader at this range."

"And how would that help?" Marcus said.

"It would throw them into confusion! Then a few volleys into the teams by the ladders—"

"Hold your fire until my command."

"But—"

"Armsman!" said the man outside. "We would like an answer."

Marcus glanced at Giforte, but the vice captain was looking away, down the line of Armsmen and Concordat soldiers. The men in green looked decidedly shaky, crouched against the parapet with muskets in hand. Most of them had probably never fired a shot in anger.

"I can't let you in," Marcus shouted. "If you would just agree to talk—"

"Forward!" the big man shouted.

The crowd answered with a roar. Marcus could make out cries of "Danton!" "One Eagle and the Deputies-General!" and "Death to the Last Duke!" amid the general tumult. The dockmen hoisted the ladders and hurried toward the wall, with the armed bands following close behind.

"Sir!" Ross said.

Militarily, Marcus knew, he had already played things poorly. The men at the parapets ought to have been firing this whole time, forcing the attackers to stay beyond musket range and giving them a broader strip of no-man's land to cross when the assault finally came. As it was, it could go either way. The defenders were grievously outnumbered, but it took more nerve than most green troops possessed to climb a thirty-foot ladder while balls whizzed and men fell all around you. A few volleys might break them. *Or just make them angry enough to get up here and crack all our heads open.*

If he gave the order to fire . . .

He would be remembered for it, he realized. No matter how things came out. *Marcus the Butcher, who ordered his garrison to fire into the crowd.*

The young woman with red hair had dashed forward to join one of the ladder teams. The other one was still staring up at him intently, as though she recognized him.

Balls of the Beast. I can't do it, can I?

These were his own people, fishermen and porters and shopkeepers whose only grievance was with the men in black who had taken hundreds of their husbands, wives, and children in the middle of the night. *Hell, if I didn't have this uniform, I might be out there myself.*

Once he'd come to that realization, he felt surprisingly calm. His objective, finally, was clear. *Buy as much time as I can, without actually killing anybody.* In which case, it was obvious what to do.

"Sir!" Ross said again, then turned away to address his own lieutenant. "Prepare to—"

"Back!" Marcus shouted. "Fall back from the wall. Back to the keep!" He turned full circle, making his voice loud enough to be sure the attackers below heard as well. "Everyone, fall back!"

"You can't be serious!" said Ross.

"The keep is more defensible," Marcus said blandly. "I don't want to risk men in an engagement here."

All around him, the Concordat men hesitated, but the Armsmen needed no urging. They headed for the stairs and the inner courtyard. The men in black, left with only half a garrison, were forced to follow.

Giforte, Ross, and Marcus were the last ones atop the wall.

Marcus held out a hand. "After you."

"This is treason, *sir*," Ross said coldly. "You may be certain I will report this to His Grace."

"Feel free." Amid cheering from below, one of the ladders *clacked* against the parapet. "But perhaps we should continue this conversation elsewhere?"

Ross spit an oath and took the stairs two at a time. Marcus, still looking down at the crowd, said, "He didn't fall and break his neck on the way down, did he?"

"No, sir," said Giforte.

"Pity." Marcus took a deep breath. His headache was clearing at last. "Come on."

WINTER

The man Jane summoned to deal with the door was called Grayface. This was not, as Winter originally guessed, because he was of Khandarai descent, but rather because he was a blacksmith with a habit of leaning too close to his fires and coating his face with ash and smoke. He was a stout man, not as big as Walnut but broader about the belly, and while his face was not gray at the moment it was nonetheless a bit terrifying. His eyebrows had gone long ago, and his cheeks and forehead were cratered with burns where stray sparks had landed.

"S'not too hard to make a ram," he said, hands resting on his belly, in the confident tones of someone offering a professional opinion. "What you do, see, is get yourself a big iron pot. Or half a big kettle will do in a pinch. Then you find a nice big log, slip your pot over the end, and get it nice and hot while you hammer it into place. When it cools off it'll shrink and grip the wood tight."

"It'll have to be a damned big log," Walnut said, "if you want us to put a dent in *that*."

That was the door to the keep, a solid-looking portal of oak banded with iron for strength and set deep in the stone with no visible hinges. It certainly looked formidable enough, to the untrained eye, but Winter had never considered it a serious obstacle, as the design of the fortress meant it couldn't be properly defended.

If the Island as a whole was shaped like a squeezed lemon, the Vendre occupied one pointed end, covering a roughly triangular patch of land with its tip aimed downstream. The keep had the same triangular design. The two outer walls, facing the river, were three stories high and studded with gun slits and now-empty embrasures, and from their rear an awkwardly shaped slate roof sloped down to meet the single story on the landward side. There were no gun slits in those two rectangular towers facing the wall below.

In short, there was no way for the defenders of the fortress to harass an enemy once they were in the courtyard. And, as Janus had proven at the fortress in the Great Desol, there was no door strong enough to hold off an opponent with time, manpower, and tools. Jane's forces were short on cannon and powder but long on willing hands and strong backs, so a ram seemed like the best bet.

What bothered Winter was what would happen after they broke the door down. Walnut and the others didn't seem to have thought that far ahead, and Winter didn't want to undermine Jane's authority, so she quietly caught her friend's eye.

". . . probably need at least twenty men on it," Grayface said. "Call it thirty, to be safe. Figure two feet per man, we need a beam maybe thirty feet long."

"Right," Jane said. "Do it. You're in charge. Walnut, make sure everyone gives him everything he needs."

Grayface blinked. "Where am I supposed to get a beam that long?"

"Plenty of houses out there," Jane said. "Find one with a nice long roof beam and take it."

"That'll take *forever,*" Grayface said, squirming under unaccustomed responsibility. "We'd have to pull the tiles off and brace—"

"Only if you care whether the roof falls in," Walnut said.

"You want me to tear down someone's house?" the blacksmith said.

"I want you to do whatever you need to do to get it done quickly." Jane glanced at Walnut, who nodded and took Grayface by one arm.

"Come on," he said. "I saw a Sworn Church up the street that looks like it has just what we need."

"Try to make sure nobody's hiding inside," Winter called after them. She couldn't tell if they heard.

Then she and Jane were alone, or as alone as they were likely to get. The inner court of the Vendre was full of laughing, shouting people. It had been home to a few small wooden stables and other structures, but the rioters had vented their anger on these and the remains had been appropriated for the giant bonfires that were starting to take shape in the street outside. Food was on its way, and drink had already arrived or been liberated from closed shops nearby. A carnival atmosphere was taking hold, and there was a general feeling that with the retreat of the Armsmen from the walls, it was all over but the shouting. The great mob was drunk on a sense of its own power, as though the easy victory had made it immune to potential consequences.

Jane was in charge, inasmuch as anyone was. At least, she could give orders, and most of the time they were obeyed. Min, the soft-spoken girl who'd organized cleaning rotas back at Jane's headquarters, had set to arranging bands of fighting men with the same enthusiasm, with the rest of the Leatherbacks helping to round up work crews and get people pointed in the right direction. There had been a little bit of laughter at the expense of "Mad Jane's Girls," but it hadn't lasted long.

"Well?" Jane said. "What's the problem?"

Winter blinked. She hadn't thought her worry showed in her face. "Why do you think there's a problem?"

Jane laughed. "Come on. You have the exact same expression you did when you were trying to talk me out of throwing rotten eggs at Mistress Gormenthal, or stealing Cowlie's underwear. I used to think of it as your 'But, Jane!' face. 'But, Jane, we'll get in trouble!'"

Winter forced a smile. "Far be it from me to be the killjoy."

"But," Jane prompted.

"But," Winter said, "I think you're not taking this seriously enough."

Jane's smile vanished. "Seriously? I just told them to start wrecking houses so we can get through that door. That isn't serious?"

"The door isn't the problem. If they fight—"

"They won't," Jane said. "If they were going to shoot, they would have done it at the wall. It doesn't make any *sense* to start now, when they're in a far worse position."

"I'm not sure that they *are* in a worse position. If we have to fight our way into that thing, it'll be a nightmare. If it comes to that, people are going to get killed. A lot of people."

"We knew that this morning, and it didn't stop us."

"That was then. Now everyone's acting like we've already won."

Jane frowned, then looked carefully at Winter. "There's something else you're not telling me."

Winter nodded, reluctantly.

"The Armsmen captain. It looked like you recognized him. Is that it?"

"His name is Marcus d'Ivoire," Winter said. "He commanded my battalion in Khandar."

"Did you know him well?" Jane leaned forward eagerly. "Do you think you could talk to him for us? If we could make him understand—"

"What?" Winter blinked. "No! No, you don't understand. He doesn't know about"—she gestured down at herself, dressed in trousers like Jane but still marginally feminine—"about me. I couldn't talk to him without explaining what I was doing here."

"Sorry." Jane shook her head. "I got ahead of myself. *Do* you know him, though?"

"A little bit. More from hearsay than anything else. We weren't friends."

"What's he like?"

"Tough. Not the most imaginative soldier, but stubborn. When he was fighting on the Tselika, he was ready to slug it out to the last man rather than give up the position he'd been ordered to hold. And he practically worships the colonel."

"The colonel?"

"Count Mieran. The Minister of Justice."

"Ah." Jane looked speculatively at the door. "So you think he has something up his sleeve."

"Not . . . exactly. I just don't think he'll give up easily."

"He gave up the wall, didn't he?"

"He had the keep to fall back to. If we really push him into a corner . . ."

Winter saw the door splinter in her mind's eye, collapsing inward, cheering Leatherbacks rushing over the wreckage. And, inside, a makeshift barricade of furniture studded with musket barrels, dozens of muzzle flashes, the merry zip and zing of balls ricocheting from stone and the *thwack* when they found flesh. The blood, and the screams.

"You really think he'd do it?" Jane said.

"He obviously doesn't *want* to, or he'd have done it at the wall," Winter said, trying to clear the nightmare vision. "Tactically, you're right—it would have been a better move. But if the colonel has ordered him to hold Danton, then at some point he'll have to fight."

"Damn." Jane glared at the door. It was odd to think that there were men behind it, as remote as though they were on the moon, besieged and besiegers separated by only a few feet of solid oak and iron. "We'll try to negotiate, once we have the ram ready. Maybe we can convince him to see reason. But you know we're running out of time. Somebody up *there*"—she jerked her head north, toward Ohnlei—"will have to do something eventually."

"I know." Winter let out a long breath. "There's one bit of good news."

"What's that?"

"If Captain d'Ivoire is in charge in there, then Abby and the others are all right."

Jane tried not to show it, but there was relief in her face. "You think so?"

"If they made it here in one piece, he'll have made sure they stayed that way. The colonel once told me that when it comes to women, Captain d'Ivoire missed his calling as a knight-errant."

Jane laughed out loud. "I suppose that *is* good news."

If he is *in charge.* Winter bit her lip. There had been men in black coats as well as Armsmen green on the battlements.

This line of thought was interrupted by the arrival of a young woman wearing one of the aprons that served the Leatherbacks as impromptu uniforms. Winter didn't recognize her from Jane's councils—a number of the wives and daughters of the dockmen had invited themselves along on the march, following the example of Jane's hellions. Jane, pragmatic as ever, had deputized them and put them to work.

"Sir—that is—ma'am—Jane!" The girl was doubled over and out of breath, hands gripping her thighs. "I've got—a—"

"Give it a moment," Jane said.

"Yes, sir." The attempt at military airs made Winter smile; she wondered if this girl had read some of the same books she had, before fleeing Mrs. Wilmore's. When she'd gotten her breath back, the messenger straightened up. "There's more people arriving in the street! Hundreds of them!"

Winter whistled. "I wouldn't have thought there was anyone *left* in the Docks."

"They're not from the Docks," the girl said. "Not *our* people. A lot of 'em look like nobs, though they don't all dress like it. Viera said she thought they were from the University. They came down over Saint Hastoph Bridge."

"Did they say what they wanted?" Jane said.

"They said they were here to help. A lot of 'em are talking about Danton."

Danton. Winter knew Jane had never had much use for the demagogue, but he had a considerable following among the dockmen. *And apparently on the Northside as well.*

"Well," Jane said, "I suppose we can always use more hands." She glanced at Winter. "Maybe if we put a few respectable citizens in the front line, the Armsmen will be less likely to fire."

"Beg your pardon, si—ma'am," the girl interrupted, "but there were a bunch of them asking to see whoever was in charge here. One of 'em dressed real nice, too. I think he must be a count."

"Well." Jane straightened up, and a look passed between her and Winter. "We can't keep *nobility* waiting, now, can we?"

RAESINIA

Alfred Peddoc sur Volmire had lost his reluctance about the march shortly after it began. It transpired that he had spent a couple of years at the War College before deciding a soldier's career wasn't for him, and that extensive martial training now apparently qualified him for leadership of what he persisted in referring to as "our campaign." He'd even acquired a sword from somewhere, which he slashed through the air as he walked as if cutting his way through imaginary enemies.

He'd gathered around him a knot of others who had some pretensions to military expertise, or who had read a lot of books on the subject, or merely had become enthralled with the idea. They'd almost immediately started to argue about what to do next, but fortunately they weren't so much leading the mob from the Dregs as they were being carried along by it, like a bubble on a stream. Everyone knew where they were going, after all, and the angled towers of the

Vendre were clearly visible once they'd cleared the final row of houses flanking Bridge Street.

Maurisk and Dumorre walked nearby, deeply engaged in an argument over whether a republic would serve its people better than a monarchy, and under which set of assumptions about human nature. Raesinia found herself walking with Faro, who had stuck to her like a shadow since they met outside the Gold Sovereign, and Cyte, the woman who with Dumorre represented the Radicals. Ahead, behind, and all around them, a flowing mass of humanity packed the road. The houses they passed were boarded up tight, the inhabitants either fled or cowering within. No Armsmen were in evidence.

Eventually Raesinia said, "Cytomandiclea?"

"Yes?" said Cyte. She'd been sweating, and the dark makeup around her eyes was starting to run, leaving streaky black lines on her cheeks where she'd wiped them.

"I mean, why? I'm assuming you picked the name."

Cyte looked at her suspiciously, not sure if she was being made fun of.

"She was a queen of the Mithradacii," Cyte said. "When all the other chiefs wanted to submit to the Vanadii, she fought them one after another in single combat and killed them all. Then she led her people against the Vanadii, men and women both. This was about a thousand years BK."

"What happened?"

Cyte shrugged. "They were slaughtered. One of the Vanadii chiefs stabbed her and then they rode their chariots over her, again and again, until there was nothing left but bloody mud. All the Mithradacii men were executed, and the women and children were taken by the Vanadii as thralls. We're all descended from them, you know. They say if you have blue eyes, you have Mithradacii blood in you somewhere."

"That's . . . quite a namesake. Do you ever wonder if the other chiefs might have been right to want to give in?"

Cyte shrugged again, looking a little uncomfortable. "It's just a story. She might not even have really existed."

"What's your real name?"

Her eyes flashed fire. "That *is* my real name."

"Sorry. I'm just curious." Raesinia looked up ahead. The head of the crowd, with Peddoc at the tip, was just passing over the bridge to the Island. "I'm named after the princess, of course. Boring. I always wish I had a better story to tell."

"The original Raesinia was a great woman," Cyte said. "She was the older sister of the last pagan king of Vordan. They say she could heal the sick and know by magic if someone was lying to her, and her brother made her the chief judge for the whole country."

"What happened to her?"

Cyte sighed. "After the Conversion, she was executed as a sorceress by the Priests of the Black. After Farus IV threw out the Sworn Church, the Orboans decided she was a heroine and revived the name. They claim to be descended on one side from the old pagan kings."

"I'd never heard that."

"They don't talk about it as much these days." Cyte glanced sidelong at Raesinia, a slight flush showing on her cheeks. "Sorry to rattle on. Ancient history is my field."

"You're at the University?"

She nodded. "This is the end of my first year. And probably my last, if my father hears about this. But after hearing Danton speak, I couldn't just sit in the library anymore." She waved at the mass of people. "Look at this. This is happening *now*. It's not some theoretical debate on the nature of government." Her eyes flicked to Dumorre. "This is *real*. This is history, before it *is* history." She smiled, and for a moment both her youth and the basic prettiness of her face under the severe hairstyle and smudged makeup showed through. "It's like if Cytomandiclea decided to have her battle right outside my window, I couldn't live with myself if I just stayed inside because I was afraid of getting hit by a stray arrow."

Raesinia looked at her and wondered how she would feel if she knew that Danton was an illiterate with the brains of a child, and that every word of those speeches had been written by a few part-time conspirators in a back room of the Blue Mask. Or if she knew that Raesinia was deliberately fomenting this revolt against the government that she would—very soon now—be the nominal head of. Or if she knew that Raesinia wasn't even *alive*, technically, but an abomination born of a demon's magic, created by an alliance between the Last Duke and the Priests of the Black. Or—

She felt as though the layers of lies were dark water, rising all around her, thick and sludgy as syrup. It wouldn't be long before they rose so high they closed over her head.

But then, I don't really need to breathe, do I?

"Are you all right?"

"What?" Raesinia realized she'd been staring into space. "Oh yes. Sorry. Just thinking."

"I'm sorry that your lover died. I don't know if I had the chance to say that before."

"Excuse me? You mean Ben?" Raesinia felt her own cheeks color. "He wasn't—we didn't . . . get that far. But thank you."

"We'll make the Last Duke pay for every—"

She stopped as Faro came over to them. They were at the footing of the bridge now, just a short walk from the Island. Saint Hastoph Street ran directly in front of the Vendre's walls, and from this vantage Raesinia could see that it was already full of people. For a moment she wondered how the head of the column had gotten over so quickly; then the reality of the situation dawned.

Faro opened his mouth, but Raesinia pointed before he could speak. "Who are those people?"

"A mob from the Docks," he said, after taking a moment to regain his composure. "And more, I think. Someone named Mad Jane led them here after the news got out that Danton was taken, and they've been laying siege to the Vendre."

Cyte gave a shout of delighted surprise, and Raesinia felt a little weight lifting from her heart for the first time since she'd held Ben's corpse in her arms. *The whole* city *is rising.* It might actually work, in spite of the blown timing and the ruined plans. *And then he won't have died for nothing.*

Faro didn't look nearly so excited. "Peddoc started giving orders as soon as he arrived, and they aren't very happy about it. Someone went to get this Jane and arrange a meeting. We need to get down there before he makes a complete ass of himself."

Cyte shot Raesinia a conspiratorial glance and rolled her eyes.

"I strongly suspect," Raesinia said, "that we may be too late."

She was right. Before they arrived—indeed, before Faro had even gotten there with the news—Peddoc had managed to make an ass of himself, and by the time Raesinia and the others had shoved their way across the bridge and through the crowded streets to the outskirts of the prison, he'd contrived to turn what ought to have been a friendly meeting into something just a hair short of a brawl.

At the top of Saint Hastoph Street, where the bridge touched ground on the Island and the wall of the Vendre began, the column had come to a halt. This news had been slow to reach the rear of the mass, and so people were packing tighter and tighter onto the bridge to try to see the obstacle. Raesinia and Faro had to push their way through, and Cyte, Maurisk, and Dumorre followed in their wake.

When they finally reached the head of the group, they found a narrow clear space separating the marchers from a crowd of dockmen and angry-looking young women, packed shoulder to shoulder across the street like a line of battle. In the space between the two sides, Peddoc and his coterie of militaristic admirers faced off against a huge man in a leather apron.

The confrontation was happening in plain view of the wall of the prison. Raesinia looked nervously to the parapet, and was reassured to see it was lined with more Docks rebels. The two lines were yelling incoherently at each other, and it was only once she broke free of the crowd and approached Peddoc that she could hear what was going on.

"—I don't mean to be *rude*," Peddoc was saying, "but there is a proper way to conduct a siege, which you would know if you'd had military training as I have. It's only natural that we follow the plan—"

"Who's this lot, then?" said the big man, catching sight of Raesinia and the others.

"Ah." Peddoc straightened up and looked unhappy. "These are my"—he caught a furious glare from Maurisk and Dumorre—"colleagues. The other members of our council. Though, as a trained military man, I have taken the lead on the actual direction of our campaign."

"Well, I'm Walnut," the man said. "Jane's on her way. Does anybody want to tell me what the hell you all are doing here without going on about lines of circumcision?"

"Lines of *circumvallation*," Peddoc said. "It's a basic military concept for sieges—"

"We're here for Danton," Cyte said, which drew looks from both Maurisk and Dumorre.

"Not *just* Danton," Maurisk said. "We're here to take back the Crown for the people."

"To give the Crown *to* the people," Dumorre said, "returning government to its proper—"

Raesinia fished out her copy of their Declaration and held it aloft. The others lapsed into a sullen silence.

"We're here to free the prisoners," she said. "And to ask the king to acknowledge the Deputies-General, *at which these other points will be debated*."

"All well and good," Peddoc said. "But as the problem for the moment is a military one—"

There was a shuffle in the ranks of the dockmen, and after a moment two women emerged from the crowd. One was tall, with disheveled red hair and green eyes aglow with manic energy. The other, plain-faced with white-blond hair cut almost military short, stayed a step or two behind. It was easy for Raesinia to guess which one was "Mad Jane," but she named herself anyway.

"I'm Jane," she said. "And this is Winter. Walnut, who are these people?"

"They seem to be in charge," Walnut said.

"All of them at once?"

"As best I can tell."

"We're a council," Peddoc said. "And I—"

"We didn't agree to be a council," Maurisk interrupted. "That implies that we have equal votes."

"Voting should be proportional to representation," Dumorre said. "Which means nobody should be listening to Peddoc."

"I think you'll find," Maurisk said, "that support for the reasonable center—"

"We'd have to carry out a census," Dumorre interrupted.

"It's not a matter of votes!" Peddoc said. "I have the experience—"

Raesinia stepped forward as they fell to arguing, and silently handed the declaration to Jane. She and Winter scanned it briefly, then looked up at her.

"And who are you?" Jane said.

"Raesinia," Raesinia said. "I'm here because one of my friends was shot dead by a Concordat assassin last night, and because I think more of them are being held in *there*."

"And the Deputies-General?" Jane said.

Raesinia jerked her head at the bickering council behind them. The corner of Jane's lip quirked.

"In other words," Jane said, louder, "you're here to help."

"Exactly!" said Peddoc. "Listen. You've obviously been doing quite well, for amateurs, but if we're going to take the Vendre, then a siege on modern scientific principles is obviously called for. The first step is the establishment of a line of circumvallation to prevent outside assistance from reaching the invested position. We can start by digging a trench across—"

"Contravallation," said Winter.

Peddoc and Jane both looked at her. She shrugged uncomfortably.

"Lines of contravallation protect the besiegers from attack by outside forces. Lines of circumvallation guard against sorties of the garrison. You've got them backward."

There was a long silence.

"I always got those confused on exams," said someone in the back of Peddoc's retinue. "Cost me a few points with old Wertingham."

"Well," Peddoc said, trying to recover his momentum, "we'll need both, obviously. And—"

"And you're proposing that we dig a trench?" Winter said. "Here?"

She stomped her foot, and everyone looked down. Like all the streets on the Island, this one was cobbled.

"Well," Peddoc said again, more weakly, "obviously—"

"There's also the fact that the Vendre sticks out into the river," Winter went on. "So your lines are going to be underwater for about two-thirds of the length. But I was more concerned about another point. When you say you want to conduct a scientific siege, you mean by the Kleinvort method, I assume?"

"I . . . I think so," Peddoc said. "It's been some time—"

"That calls for a series of parallels to allow the attackers to reach close range, which seems superfluous in this case as we can already walk up and touch the walls without difficulty. More to the point, though, once the final parallel is established, the attackers must establish a breaching battery and effect a breach before making the final assault. Is that correct?"

Peddoc, mesmerized, simply nodded.

"Have you *brought* a siege battery?" Winter looked at Walnut. "You're taller than I am. Do you see any guns?"

Walnut shaded his eyes, theatrically, and stared out over the bridge.

"What my companion is trying to say," said Jane dryly, "is that we may be a *bit* beyond the textbooks here." She raised her voice. "And as for the rest of you! I want you to know that I could give a damn about this"—she shook the Declaration—"or your Deputies-General. But"—and now she looked down at Raesinia—"my friends are in there, and I intend to get them out. Anyone who wants to help with that is welcome. What you do afterward is your own business."

There was a long pause. Then, all at once, the council erupted with a hundred shouted arguments. Through the tumult, Raesinia caught Cyte's eye and smiled.

CHAPTER TWELVE

MARCUS

"What about the river?" Marcus said.

"I took a look at the docks this morning," Giforte said. He sounded gloomy. "There's one small pier and a couple of boats."

"How many men would they hold?"

"Call it a dozen each. Not nearly enough."

"Not for all of us, no." Marcus frowned. "I should have thought of that sooner. We could have sent to the shore and arranged a whole flotilla."

"There isn't *room* for a whole flotilla," Giforte said. "This place was designed to defend against an attack from downriver. Most of the wall goes right down to the waterline."

"What about the . . ." Marcus hesitated, not wanting to use the word "rebels." *Rebels* were crazed fanatics screaming for blood. *These are . . . something else.* "The rioters? Have they tried to block the crossing?"

"There's a few small boats out there, but they're just watching for now. I don't think they're organized enough to stop an armed force. Once they figure out we're trying to move people that way, though . . ."

Marcus could imagine it all too easily. Lumbering barges full of struggling prisoners, with every rowboat and fishing skiff on the river closing in around them. *Not good.* "And the ram?"

"I think they'll be ready by nightfall, or a little before."

The sun was already well past the meridian. That left four or five hours for Janus or the Royal Army or *someone* to come riding to the rescue. Once they started battering down the door, Marcus would have to choose one way or the other.

"Balls of the Beast." He groaned and rubbed his eyes. *How long since I slept? Twenty hours? More?* "All right. We need to start planning for contingencies. I want you to get fifteen men together, and—what the *hell* was that?"

The noise that had interrupted them had been a combination of a splintery wooden crash and an enormous metallic ringing, like the striking of the world's largest gong. It was followed by a great deal of swearing.

"I'm not sure, sir," the vice captain said. "It came from the main stairwell."

"I'm going to go find out."

He quickly dictated the rest of his instructions to Giforte, who saluted and hurried off. Marcus levered himself out of his chair with an effort, calves aching from too many hours of nervous pacing. He shrugged into his green uniform jacket—now rumpled and stained with sweat—and took to the stairs, navigating as carefully as an old man. The stone-floored fortress was unforgiving of slips and tumbles.

The noises were coming from below, and Marcus followed the main stairs down until he found them blocked by a knot of sweating, cursing men in Concordat black. They'd stripped off their leather coats and were wrestling some enormous object around the corner of the steps. Someone was trying to improvise a rope harness, while more men grunted and tried to lift from below. Standing at the top, above the fray, was Ross, who looked very pleased with himself.

"Captain?" Marcus said. "What do you think you're doing?"

"Ah!" Ross turned, beaming. "Sorry about the noise, sir. We found something down in one of the half-flooded levels."

"What is it?" Through the crowd of laboring men, Marcus could only get a partial view of the object they were lifting.

"A cannon. An eight-inch mortar, I think."

Marcus suddenly felt very cold. "I didn't think there were any guns left here."

"Neither did I, but this one must have been too much trouble to move. There aren't any bombs left, but it shouldn't be hard to improvise some canister. We'll set it up opposite the main doors. Then once they break through with their damned ram, they'll be in for a hell of a surprise!" He chuckled.

The image came to Marcus' mind's eye all too easily. Ross, he suspected, had never seen a cannon fired in anger.

"The recoil . . . ," Marcus began, weakly.

"Don't worry about it. We're setting up a position in the front hall, and we'll clear a space for this bastard once we get it up the stairs." Ross smiled. "You know, sir, I admit I was worried when you pulled the men back from the walls. But I'm man enough to admit when I was wrong. This is a much better position. As long as they have to come at us through those doors, we can hold out here until we can build a barricade out of corpses!" He seemed to be looking forward to this prospect.

This new, cheerful Ross was a change, and not a welcome one. Marcus muttered something noncommittal and hurried back upstairs, looking for Giforte. The vice captain had not yet returned, but there was a sergeant in Armsmen green there, shifting nervously from foot to foot. He saluted and came to attention as Marcus entered, sweat running into the crevices of his jowly face.

"Beg pardon, sir!"

"Yes?" Marcus snapped the word out more harshly than he'd intended, and the sergeant quailed. "What is it?"

"Sorry, sir. Didn't mean to interrupt, sir. Only there's been a bit of a disturbance with the prisoners, sir, and you asked to be kept informed—"

"What's happened?"

"A gang of them is kicking up a fuss. Bunch of young women. Saying they can help us, and that they want to talk to—" He broke off and looked around.

"Right." Marcus desperately wanted to sit in his chair, pull his cap over his eyes, and rest for a few hours. "You'd better take me to them."

"Begging your pardon, sir, but it was Vice Captain Giforte they were asking to see."

Marcus blinked. "Giforte? Did they say why?"

"No, sir."

"He ought to be down at the riverside dock," Marcus said. "Come on. We'll send someone to find him on the way."

The dungeon levels were as dank as ever, but the tables borrowed from the main floor gave the prisoners something dry to sit on. Concordat men still guarded the halls, but the cells themselves were watched by Armsmen, and the mood of the prisoners seemed much improved. Most of the cell doors were open, under a guard's careful eye, and Marcus saw the merry flicker of flames as the prisoners huddled round to warm themselves.

"Over here, sir," said the sergeant. He gestured to a room at the end of the corridor, where a closed door was flanked by a pair of musket-armed men. They saluted as Marcus approached, and one of them unlocked the cell with a key and stepped aside.

"Finally," said a young woman's voice, as he opened the door. "I—" She stopped as Marcus stepped into the doorway. A lone torch was burning in a wall bracket, and in its light Marcus could see a girl of eighteen or so, with frizzy, matted brown hair and freckles. She stood between the door and the rest of the prisoners in the cell, who were huddled in the shadowy corner.

"You're not my—you're not Vice Captain Giforte," she said.

"My name is Marcus d'Ivoire," Marcus said. "Captain of Armsmen. Whatever you have to say to the vice captain, you can say to me."

"But . . ." The girl trailed off, her lip twisting.

"Why don't you start with your name?"

"Abigail," she said. "Everyone calls me Abby." Then, reaching some kind of decision, she straightened up. "Listen. It's Jane who's leading the mob out there, isn't it?"

"I don't know if they have a *leader,* per se. The one shouting up to me was some sort of giant." Marcus frowned. "And you're remarkably well informed for someone who's been locked in a cell with no windows."

There was a cough from behind Marcus. "Sorry about that, sir," the sergeant said. "Some of the boys got to talking. Arguing, more like. It got a little heated. The prisoners must have overheard."

"The giant is named Walnut," Abby said. "If he's here, Jane is, too. Mad Jane, you must have heard of her."

Marcus shrugged and looked over his shoulder.

The sergeant nodded. "I know the name, sir. She leads a sort of gang in the Docks called the Leatherbacks."

"Do you have any idea if she's in charge outside?" Marcus said.

"Not that I've heard," the sergeant said. "Like you said, sir, it didn't look like they had a real strict chain of command."

"She's there," Abby said stubbornly. "She's the only one who could get the dockmen so worked up."

"Even if she is," Marcus said, "what does that have to do with you?"

"Jane and I are . . . friends. Have you tried talking to them?"

Marcus stiffened. "We offered to negotiate, but they didn't seem to be in the mood for conversation."

Abby nodded eagerly. "That's why you have to let me see her. I can get her to talk! She'll listen to me, and then . . . we can figure out some way out of this."

There was a long pause.

"What makes you think I'm looking for a way out?" Marcus said.

"Your men were talking about surrender," Abby said. "They're worried about what the mob will do to them if they lay down their weapons. If you'll just let me talk to Jane, I'm sure she'll agree to let you leave safely."

"Captain?" Giforte's voice came from the hall outside. Marcus turned and beckoned to the sergeant, who fell in behind him, pulling the door shut.

"Wait!" Abby said. "You have to let me see—"

The clang of the closing door cut off her words. Giforte hurried over, looking a little flushed, as though he'd run all the way. A couple of anxious rankers trailed him.

"You asked for me, sir?"

Marcus nodded, thinking hard. "You gave orders to prepare the boats?"

"Yes, sir."

Marcus turned to glare at the sergeant, who was sweating even harder. "What's this she was saying about surrender?"

"I . . . Sir, I mean . . . That is . . ." The man squirmed, took a deep breath, and straightened up. "It was just talk."

"What kind of talk?" Marcus paused, then added, "Tell me, Sergeant. I promise no one will be punished."

"Well . . ." He wiped his brow with his sleeve. "Some of the boys—not me, you understand—were saying that it didn't make much sense to fight once the doors get broken in. There's only a hundred of us, even counting the duke's bootlickers, and thousands of dockmen. Seems like a pretty foregone conclusion. And it seemed to us—to *them*—that anybody who fought back was likely to get his head bashed in. Some of the boys weren't too keen on shooting at them anyway. I mean, they're our own people, when all's said and done. So if we're going to lose *anyway*, it seemed like it might be best if we just gave up at the beginning. Less pain all around, you might say." He gulped for air, and added, "Not that I agreed with them for a minute, sir."

Marcus glanced at Giforte, who gave a small shrug.

An Armsman, Marcus always had to remind himself, was not a soldier. And even a Royal Army garrison would be considering surrender at this point, outnumbered hundreds to one with no relief in sight. It was the only sensible thing to do.

"There's a girl in there," Marcus said slowly, "who says she's a personal friend of one of the leaders of the mob. She thinks she can set up negotiations."

Giforte scratched his chin through his beard. "Not a bad idea, if it's true. *And* if she's not just trying to buy her own way out of here."

"She wanted to talk to you, specifically. Any idea why?"

"No, sir."

"Well. We can at least see what she wants from you." He nodded to the sergeant. "Open the door."

This time Giforte led the way into the cell, the torchlight laying long shadows across his face. Marcus followed behind. Abby was still waiting near the doorway, but at the sight of Giforte, she shuffled backward a step and looked at the floor.

"I'm Vice Captain Giforte," Giforte said. "What's your business with me?"

"Ah." Abby shuffled uncertainly, right hand gripping her left elbow behind her back. When she raised her face, Marcus heard Giforte's breath hiss. "Um. Hello, Father."

The doors in the Vendre were thick and heavy, as befitted a fortress, but not enough so to block out the shouting from the next room. Marcus sat on a stool in the corridor, feeling like a boy sent out of class for raising a fuss, and tried his hardest not to overhear. After a while, the yelling fell to murmurs and what sounded like occasional sobbing. He wasn't sure which state was worse.

I'm so tired. Marcus leaned his head against the wall behind him and closed his eyes, just for a moment.

"Captain."

Marcus sat up hurriedly, blinking. The door was slightly open, and Giforte stood diffidently behind it, not wanting to catch his captain napping.

"Sorry." Marcus stifled a yawn. "Is everything . . . all right?"

"For the moment." He pulled the door open wider. "You can come in."

Marcus climbed painfully to his feet, shoulders aching where they'd been jammed against the hard stone. Inside, Abby sat behind the table Marcus had been using as a desk, looking pale except for spots of color in her freckled cheeks. Her eyes were slightly red, but her expression was determined.

"My daughter tells me that she's been working with this 'Mad Jane' for some time now," Giforte said. "She's convinced that this woman is the one responsible for the mob."

Abby opened her mouth to speak but stopped at a glance from her father. Her cheeks colored further.

Marcus shifted awkwardly. "And what do you think?"

"I have no reason to disbelieve her. But sending someone outside to negotiate is extremely risky. There's no guarantee Mad Jane would remain friendly, or that she's even in control. Our men in the towers have reported a great many new arrivals in the last few hours."

"If I can talk to Jane," Abby said, "I'm telling you—"

"Abigail," Giforte snapped.

"Don't you 'Abigail' me," she said. "You can't treat me like a child."

Marcus cleared his throat to cut off the impending argument. "Young lady, would you mind if I spoke to your father in private for a moment?"

Abby sniffed and crossed her arms. Marcus touched Giforte on the shoulder and led him to a corner of the room, facing away from the girl.

"I know this can't be easy for you," Marcus said, in a low voice. "What do you want to do?"

Giforte looked pained for a moment. Marcus wondered if he'd been hoping the decision would be taken out of his hands. Eventually he let out a sigh.

"It's dangerous," he said. "But I think it's our best chance of avoiding a bloodbath. I . . ." He hesitated. "I'd like to suggest that I accompany her. If she can bring Mad Jane to a conference, better to have someone on the spot ready to talk to her."

For a moment, Marcus wondered if Giforte planned to use the opportunity to take his daughter and escape. *But no, not him.* Whatever his hidden connections, reading all those records had drawn a clear picture of the man, and he would no more abandon men under his command than Marcus himself would. He gave a quick nod. "If that's what you want."

"It is," Giforte said. "Thank you, sir."

Because there were no openings in the Vendre's landward face, Marcus had to ascend to the tower at the opposite end of the fortress to get a view of the proceedings. Even here all the gun slits and embrasures faced the wrong way, toward the rivers, so he had to take the stairs all the way up and pry open an old trapdoor to make his way up to the roof. It was a narrow stretch of flagstones, swept by a continuous wind from the river and long abandoned even by the sentries. The waist-high parapet was crumbling, and big chunks of the mortar had come loose and fallen four stories to slide down the sloping roof of the lower fortress.

Marcus leaned against one of the solider-looking blocks, trying to ignore the tingling in the soles of his feet every time the wind caught in his coat. He badly wanted a spyglass. There was a particularly fine one in his office at the Ministry of Justice, in fact, but he hadn't thought to bring it.

Far below, across the bulk of the fortress, Marcus could see the inner courtyard packed with rioters. Giforte had warned that it was no longer only dockmen in the mob, and even from this distance Marcus could see it was true. The crowd grouped up in tight bunches, as separate as oil and water, and while some of these wore the leather and gaudy colors of the South Bank workers, others had the darker, sober look of prosperity. Students, was Marcus' guess. Danton's speeches had always played well at the University.

He could tell by the reaction of the crowd when the big doors started to open. The mob took a few collective steps back in sudden shock. Then, seeing that this was not a desperate sortie, they surged back, and the background roar increased dramatically in volume. After a few moments a knot of people began to force its way out into the courtyard. Marcus could only guess that Giforte and his daughter were in the center.

The trapdoor gave a long, anguished scream of unoiled hinges. Marcus looked over his shoulder as Captain Ross came into view, his heavy boots clomping on the narrow wooden stairs. He was followed by a pair of musket-armed Concordat men. Marcus said nothing until all three had emerged onto the roof, their leather coats flapping like flags in the wind.

"Captain," Marcus said.

"Sir," Ross said. "Enjoying the view?"

Marcus raised his eyes beyond the courtyard. The sun was still an hour from the horizon, but the towers of the Vendre threw a long shadow across the Island, like the gnomon of a monstrous sundial. Already lanterns and torches glowed like tiny sparks in the courtyard, while in the streets beyond, the sullen glow of bonfires lit up the facades of the buildings and gleamed from the few unbroken shopwindows.

"Not really," Marcus confessed.

He looked back down at the courtyard. Someone had established a kind of order, clearing a ring around Giforte and Abby, who were now identifiable in the mob. They shared the space with a flock of young women, who were fighting with one another in an effort to be the first to hug Abby. An emotional reunion was apparently in progress.

"You released her." Ross followed his eyes. "One of *my* prisoners."

It wasn't a question. Marcus supposed he'd gotten the story from the guards downstairs.

"I didn't release her. I paroled her, on my own responsibility, to attempt to negotiate with the leaders of the riot." Marcus pushed himself away from the parapet and turned to face Ross. "And as *I* am in command here, she was one of *my* prisoners, Captain."

"Of course." Ross' lip quirked. "And what do you hope to accomplish with this . . . negotiation?"

"To see if there is any mutually acceptable way of settling their grievances, and to buy time for the Cabinet to come up with a solution."

"Some would say that an offer to negotiate is an admission of weakness."

Marcus shrugged. "You said yourself, Captain, that we could hold off an army here. What's the harm in keeping them talking?"

"None." Ross' eyes went cold. "Provided you actually mean to fight when the time comes."

"When the time comes—"

"Let me tell you what I think," Ross interrupted. He clasped his hands behind his back and looked thoughtfully out at the river. "I think you are a coward. I think you have no intention of doing your duty and defending this fortress. I think you are 'buying time,' as you put it, to prepare for your personal escape while you leave the rest of the garrison and the prisoners to fall into the hands of the mob."

Marcus felt as though he'd been hit in the face by a bucket of cold water. He'd grown used to the gibes of the Concordat officer, but—

"I suggest," he growled, "that you retract that statement."

"Why? It's only the truth. Or do you deny that your men are preparing boats for a getaway across the river?"

"Captain Ross," Marcus said, raising his voice. "You are relieved of your command, and I'm placing you under arrest for insubordination."

Ross glanced over his shoulder. One of the two Concordat men was staring down at the scene in the courtyard, but the other raised his musket to his shoulder and thumbed back the hammer. The barrel pointed squarely at Marcus' chest.

There was a long silence.

I should have expected that. God knew Ross had given him no grounds for trust. But this wasn't the Khandarai desert, with thousands of miles of sand and ocean between them and the Ministry of War. This was *Vordan*, where laws were supposed to mean something.

"Whatever you're doing," Marcus said, "you're going to regret it."

"I very much doubt that." Ross held out his hand, and after a long moment Marcus unbuckled his sword and handed it across. "His Grace always protects those who act in his interests."

"As does my lord the Minister of Justice."

"By the time this is over, I doubt Count Mieran will have much say in the matter." Ross turned to his second man. "Ranker Mills, what do you think?"

"Call it eighty yards," the man said, unstrapping his weapon. "No problem."

It wasn't a musket he was carrying, Marcus saw now. It was a longer-barreled weapon, slightly narrower, with a complex iron mechanism above the stock. A military rifle, he guessed. Probably one of the infamous Hamveltai Manhunters.

"Ranker Mills is an excellent shot," Ross said. "Once this Mad Jane shows herself, we'll have an excellent chance to dispose of her. It may break the morale of the mob entirely."

"Don't be a fool," Marcus hissed. "They're not going to break. They'll rush the door—"

"And we'll be ready for them," Ross said. "My men have the mortar in place, and we're well barricaded. It will be a slaughter."

He sounded pleased at the prospect. Marcus turned frantically back to the courtyard, where another group was working its way through the press to join Giforte and Abby. Jane and her companions, he assumed. Mills sighted carefully, tweaking the back sight of his rifle.

It was probably too far for anyone to hear him, but it was worth a try. Marcus cupped his hands to his mouth and shouted.

"Giforte! Jane! Up here—it's—"

A musket butt slammed against his jaw, slamming his teeth together with a *clack* and filling his head with shooting stars. He stumbled backward, grabbing at the parapet for support, and ended up flopping to the flagstones when his legs refused to support him. The Concordat musketeer stood above him, weapon raised for another blow.

"Not very smart," Ross commented. "Pick him up."

Marcus' head swam as they dragged him to the stairs. More Concordat men were waiting down below to take hold of his feet and lower him like a sack of potatoes. As they bound his hands behind his back and dragged him away, he heard the sharp *crack* of the rifle.

WINTER

"I think," Winter said, "that getting them started tearing down buildings may have been a mistake."

"We needed a timber for the ram," Jane said. "Besides, I didn't tell them to—"

She was interrupted by a drawn-out crash as the second story of an engraver's shop leaned drunkenly out over the street, wobbled, and collapsed into a pile of broken beams and brick dust. A cheer rose from the crowd, and before the rubble had settled, looters were swarming over the wreckage. Larger groups milled around, uncertain what to do next, until someone shouted that a handsome marble-fronted building up the street was the headquarters of a Borelgai fur importer. With a shout, the mob rushed in that direction.

"I didn't tell them to start pulling down the whole damned street," Jane finished, lamely. She gave a halfhearted shrug. "What am I supposed to do?"

"This was your idea, wasn't it?"

"Rescuing Abby and the others was my idea. Not all this . . ." She waved one arm to encompass the carnival of destruction and shook her head, at a loss for words.

Winter felt as though she should have been horrified, or even terrified, but a night without sleep and the stress of worrying about Jane made her simply numb. The rescue mission—or mob, or riot, or revolution, whatever it was—had grown beyond any possibility of control; that much was clear. She could feel the circle of her cares contracting, as it had done in Khandar when the Redeemer cavalry had come over the rise. The regiment, the country, the city, and even Janus would have to look out for themselves. Winter only had enough energy to concern herself with what was within arm's reach.

That meant, primarily, Jane. She'd been bouncing from one extreme to the other, alternating between a strange, manic energy and moments of black, vicious temper. The exhaustion Winter was feeling had to be a hundred times worse for her, with everyone looking to her for answers. Winter remembered all too well how draining *that* could be.

Another crash, from farther down the street, barely registered. The mob had quickly learned the best technique for demolition: a rope, tied tight around key beams, could be tossed out into the street and drawn by hundreds of hands until the whole front of a building came crashing down. Other groups were wandering about with sacks of broken bricks, looking for unshattered windows, or collecting scraps of wood to feed to the bonfires. Anything associated with the Borelgai or the duke was the target of special ire, and Winter had watched furious rioters feed thousands of eagles' worth of fur or fine fabrics to the flames.

Jane's Leatherbacks brought in scraps of information, but their picture of what was going on outside the immediate area was sketchy. The Armsmen had rallied on the east side of the Island, protecting the Sworn Cathedral and the bridges to the Exchange. As best Winter could tell, they seemed uninterested in challenging the mob west of Farus' Triumph, in spite of a few attempts by the North Bank rabble-rousers to gather a force to attack them, and she was happy to leave them be.

The sun was disappearing behind the buildings of the western skyline. Jane half turned, attention caught by some distant act of destruction, and its orange light caught her hair and made it shine like beaten gold. For a moment the sight of her took Winter's breath away.

"I didn't want this," Jane repeated. The shadow of the buildings reached out for her, snuffing out the fire in her hair, and she crossed her arms and looked down. "I just wanted . . ."

"I know." Winter slipped an arm around her shoulders. "It's all right."

Jane turned her head away. "I should never have let her go. Fucking Danton. I should have known."

"There's no way you could have known today was going to be the day Orlanko would bring the boot down," Winter said. "But it's *all right.* They'll be fine."

"What if they aren't?" Jane's jaw tightened. "What if they've hurt her? Or if she's . . ."

"I trust Captain d'Ivoire," Winter repeated. "He won't let anything happen to Abby or the others." *Though God alone knows who's going to protect* him *when we get to storming the place.*

Jane nodded, miserably, and took a shaky breath. She took Winter's hand in hers and squeezed. "Balls of the fucking Beast. I'm glad you're here."

They stood for a long moment in companionable silence, broken by the crackle of bonfires and the shuddering crunch of collapsing buildings. There was a distant scream, suddenly cut off. Jane frowned.

"At least the Borels had the good sense to run away when they saw us coming," Winter said. "Along with everybody else."

That got a weak chuckle. It wasn't strictly true, of course, and Winter suspected Jane knew it as well. Most of the buildings on the Island were shops or businesses, whose inhabitants had indeed fled at the approach of the mob, and the few residences were mostly abandoned as well. Jane had even used her Leatherbacks to conduct a few families to safety. Now, with the arrival of the Dregs contingent and thousands more from the Docks and the other poor quarters of the city, matters had gotten out of hand. *Most* of the inhabitants had fled, but Winter had carefully steered away from some groups of rioters who looked as though they'd been engaged in more than mere drunken destruction. Here and there, pathetic bundles hung from the lampposts, like gory decorations. Winter tried to keep Jane pointed in the other direction. *She doesn't need any more on her conscience.*

"We should get back," Jane said. "They must be nearly done with the ram by now."

"I wish you'd take the chance to sleep."

"You think I could *sleep*?"

Winter shrugged. "*I* could. It's been almost two days."

"That must be your soldier's instincts." Somehow they'd shifted to walking arm in arm, like a young couple strolling out for a night on the town. "Can I ask you something?"

"Of course," Winter said.

"Why Khandar? Why did you go so far away?"

There was a long pause. Winter swallowed hard.

"I wasn't . . . thinking clearly, after I ran away." Winter paused. "I had this idea that Mrs. Wilmore was some all-seeing monster, I think. Like the Last Duke, only worse. I felt like I had to get as far away as I possibly could, or else they'd come and drag me back."

"It's odd, isn't it?" Jane said. "I remembered her as this huge, evil person. But when I went back there, she was . . . nothing. Just a little old woman."

Winter nodded. They lapsed into silence again, and she couldn't help wondering what Jane was thinking. *If I hadn't been such a coward, if I hadn't run away, she might have found me again. Hell, I might have rescued her. If I hadn't—*

"That's Min," Jane said, raising her hand. Across the street, the slight girl waved back and hurried over. She was breathing hard.

"We need you at the gate," Min said. "Now."

"What's happened?" Winter said.

"Someone came out to negotiate. Abby's with him. But Peddoc and the others—"

Winter grabbed the girl's arm and dragged her into a run. Jane was already a half street ahead of them, and accelerating.

The courtyard of the Vendre was even more crowded than they'd left it, with both dockmen and University students pressing in as tight as they could without actually mixing with one another. In spite of the agreement between Jane and the council leaders, tensions between the groups remained high, and by the sounds of argument coming from the center of the yard, they weren't getting any better.

Winter broke away from Min as the girl pressed through the mob to join a crowd of Jane's Leatherbacks clustering around their leader. Winter herself stayed on the periphery, but she was close enough to catch Peddoc shouting.

"Of course it's a damned trap! This is the Last Duke we're dealing with! He lives and breathes treachery."

"Besides," said another councilman, "why should we negotiate? Just the fact that they're offering means they're at our mercy. We've finished the ram, and once we break down the door—"

"First of all," said another man that Winter didn't recognize, "I am Vice Captain Alek Giforte of the Armsmen. I am here on behalf of Captain of Armsmen Marcus d'Ivoire, and I do *not* answer to the Ministry of Information."

"Everyone knows this is a Concordat prison!" shouted a dockman from the crowd.

Winter was too short to get a decent view from the floor of the courtyard. She worked her way to the edges, where crates and barrels of supplies were stacked. Chris, who was already perched there, recognized her and obligingly gave her a hand up to share her vantage point. From there, she could see Giforte standing in the center of an angry circle of council people and dockmen. Beside him, a tight-packed mass of young women was centered on Jane, who was hugging someone tight. Winter sighed with relief when she recognized Abby.

I knew Marcus wouldn't let anything happen to his prisoners. She glanced up at the forbidding bulk of the fortress, now in shadow as the sun sank behind its towers. There were only a few men visible, up on the highest parapet and looking down at the scene below.

"Second," Giforte thundered, in the voice of a sergeant on a parade ground, "the captain is well aware that we are, as you put it, at your mercy. However, if you insist on storming the gates, we will be forced to defend them, and the waste of life will be enormous."

Winter, looking at the gate, was inclined to agree. *A narrow approach against prepared positions, with no way to outflank the defenders.* An attacking force might lose ten for one and consider itself lucky.

"The captain has asked me to speak to you to attempt to avoid this bloodshed. He recognizes that we are all, after all, Vordanai, and he is no more eager to begin the killing than you are." Giforte looked around. "In particular, he asked me to speak to the leader named Mad Jane. Is she here?"

"I don't see why—" Peddoc began, but Jane cut him off, emerging from the crowd of girls with Abby behind her.

"I'm Jane," she said, loud enough for everyone to hear. "And Abby tells me I can trust you."

There was an odd note of humor in Giforte's voice when he replied, "I'm glad she thinks so."

"So what terms does your captain propose?"

A hush fell across the courtyard, as everyone strained to hear what Giforte would say. In that instant, another voice floated down from afar, so distant as to be barely a murmur.

". . . Jane . . . up here! . . ."

Giforte started to speak, but Winter was no longer listening. She couldn't tell if anyone else had heard the distant warning, but all eyes but hers were on Jane and Giforte. Winter looked up, to the parapets of the Vendre tower, where—

"Jane!" Winter screamed, loud and shrill. Heads snapped around.

The *crack* of the shot was like a distant handclap in a crowded theater, almost inaudible. But Winter's whole being was tensed and waiting for the sound, and in her mind it was as loud as a cannon. Someone had fallen in the center of the crowd. Winter could no longer see Abby or Jane as the Leatherback girls closed in around them while the rest of the crowd opened outward like a blossoming flower. The courtyard began to fill with shouts and screams.

"There! Fire!"

Walnut's enormous voice cut through the babble. The Leatherbacks had brought a few muskets and carbines, and a few more had fallen into their hands when they took the courtyard. Jane had stationed men who had some experience with the weapons on the outer wall, to watch both the approach to the fortress prison and the towers. Now they fired a ragged volley, aimed at the parapet of the tower. It was too long a shot for a musket, nearly a hundred yards in the gathering darkness, but the roar and muzzle flashes were obvious to whoever was up there. Dark figures scurried for cover.

Winter jumped from her perch, twisting at the last minute to avoid colliding with a student scurrying for cover, and landed badly. One ankle gave way, and pain shot up her leg, but she forced herself back to her feet and sprinted as best she could to the center of the yard. Behind her, the musketeers kept up an enthusiastic but erratic fire, drowning out the screams. Ahead, the Leatherbacks had formed a tight, huddled mass, interposing their bodies between their leader and the shooter on the parapet.

That has to be eighty yards, Winter told herself. *No chance. Not in the dark. Even with a good rifle, that's too long a shot—Jane was moving—she can't—*

She came to the edge of the group and started prying surprised young women aside. Her voice of command would have been instantly recognizable to any soldier of the Seventh Company.

"Get out of the *fucking* way! *Now!*"

A path cleared. Someone was down, two people, and Winter's heart lurched at the sight of blood. It was everywhere, in dark spray patterns and a great pool soaking into the dirt.

Jane lay on her stomach, atop another girl. Her face was dark and slick with blood.

"Jane!" Winter fell to her knees and grabbed Jane's shoulder, pulling her up, dreading and praying all at once. *Please, please, please, God, not now, not—*

"Help her." Jane's voice sounded distant and tinny through the blood thumping in Winter's ears.

"Are you all right?" Winter rolled her over, roughly. There was blood everywhere, but she couldn't see an actual injury. "Jane! Can you hear me?"

"Fine." Jane spit a spray of blood. "I'm fine, damn it. Help *her.*"

Winter looked at the other girl for the first time. It was Min, lying on her back with one arm over her stomach and the other flung wide. The shot had gone through her neck, tearing a huge chunk of it clean away. She was still breathing, fast and shallow, but each gasp only bubbled blood in her ruined throat. Her eyes were very wide.

That there was nothing to be done was obvious, even to Winter. She turned back to Jane, who was trying to sit up.

"Help her," Jane said. "She's bleeding. Winter—"

"Lie still for a minute." Winter pressed Jane's shoulders to the ground.

"She pushed me away," Jane said. "When she heard you shouting."

Min made a gurgling sound, one hand clutching convulsively at the dirt. Finally, mercifully, she was silent.

"She . . ." Jane couldn't see Min, but her eyes were locked on Winter's.

"She's gone," Winter said. "We have to get you out of here. They might try again."

"Abby," Jane said. "Where's Abby?"

"I'm here." Abby knelt down beside them, grabbing Jane's hand. Winter took her other arm, and together they got her on her feet. The rest of the Leatherbacks closed in again, a shield of flesh and bone. Winter glanced up at the parapet. Walnut's men were still firing, but there were no figures visible.

Jane was looking down at Min's corpse. Her hand, sticky with blood, closed tight on Winter's arm.

"Get the ram," she said, very quietly.

"If we go in there," Winter said, low and fast, "more people are going to die. A lot more. We might be able to—"

Jane raised her voice to a shout that echoed across the square. "Get the *goddamned* ram!"

A thousand pairs of eyes took in her bloodstained features, and a roar rose as one from a thousand throats. The mob surged onward.

Chapter Thirteen

MARCUS

The house burned from the outside in, flame leaping across from the old, dry wood of the stable and around the front door, crawling along the walls and up onto the roof. Inside, the soft carpet in the front hall ignited with a *whoomph*, and the layers of gauzy window hangings Marcus' mother had loved floated up as they burned, like spiderwebs.

He knew it was a dream, but it didn't help. Marcus walked through the gap where the front door had been and down the hall. Fire raced along the old wallpaper, so he was moving down a corridor of flames.

People were running, shouting. Servants in livery or bedclothes rushed back and forth, trying to push through to the exit and falling back, defeated by the flames. Something near the back of the house collapsed with a rumble, and he heard screams.

All the faces were in shadow. Marcus hardly remembered them. He passed through the crowd like a ghost.

Another scream, from upstairs. This one was high-pitched and shrill, a little girl's wail of fear.

Ellie. Marcus started to run, in the strange, floating way of dreams, legs working but only making slow progress. He made it to the main staircase in time to see his little sister, dressed in a white nightshift, standing on the landing and staring wide-eyed at the spreading fire. The air was getting thick with smoke.

"Ellie!" The roar of the fire drowned Marcus' voice in his own ears. If Ellie heard, she gave no sign. She turned away from him and ran, back up the stairs.

He went after her, feet skidding on the landing, one hand grabbing the ball-shaped finial for balance as he had done a thousand times. When he reached the upstairs hall, he could just see her darting into her bedroom, white-blond hair flying out from under her cap. He went after her, passing his own room, the door still scarred around the baseboard where he always kicked it closed with his boots.

Ellie's room was a firetrap, thick with bed hangings, carpet, and velvet toys. Smoke already formed a thick blanket against the ceiling, tendrils creeping down the walls. Ellie, coughing, ran straight to the corner, where an enormous wardrobe painted in jolly greens and blues was standing.

"No!" Marcus said. "Ellie, don't—"

But she wasn't listening, or couldn't hear him—he hadn't been there, after all. She opened the wardrobe, climbed in, and pulled the door closed behind her, hiding from the flames and the choking, deadly smoke. Marcus crossed the room—it seemed to take an age, carpet pulling at his feet like taffy—and fumbled with the doorknob. When he pulled, something pulled back, so he had to lean away and use his full weight to prize the wardrobe open.

When it gave way, all at once, he fell backward. There were flames all around him now, the stuffed bears and rabbits burning like tiny torches, runners of fire streaking across the carpet. Marcus scrambled forward on hands and knees, pulling the wardrobe doors open wide—

There was nothing inside but ash. Fine, dark ash, slipping through his fingers like smoke and smudging gray against his skin.

For a long moment, Marcus stared at it, listening to the savage roar of the flames and the creaks and crunches of collapsing timbers. Finally, he got to his feet, and walked back to the stairs. The run that had taken an age passed in an instant, and a few steps had him back in the hall, wrapped in fire, looking out the front door into a square of darkness beyond.

There was a man standing there. Like the others, his face was a blank, anonymous shadow, but he wore a long, heavy coat, black leather flapping around him like dark wings.

Concordat.

Marcus opened his eyes. He sat in total darkness, wedged into a corner, stone flagstones beneath him and stone walls behind. All he could see was the faint vertical line of a gun slit, shining with faint, occluded starlight.

He felt as though someone had punched him in the gut, driving all the breath from his body. It was how he remembered feeling on that day, eighteen years ago, when they'd handed him the news. *No survivors.*

He hadn't been there, of course. A dream was just a dream. But that figure in the long black coat—

Orlanko. Something seemed to have come free in his mind during the night. *It had to be Orlanko.* He had no evidence, nothing he could take to a magistrate, but the pattern he'd seen in the old Armsmen files didn't make sense any other way. A powerful count could have leaned on the vice captain of Armsmen, or a criminal connection, or even a foreign spy, but Marcus hadn't found any evidence that Giforte's mysterious friend had ever wanted him to *do* anything. Just, every so often, to lose something in the shuffle, to stonewall an investigation until everyone forgot about it. *Whenever the Concordat wanted something to disappear.*

As far as he knew, his family had never meddled in politics, never done anything that might incur the Last Duke's wrath. But the rumors that swirled in Orlanko's wake said that it might not matter. Men had disappeared, it was said, for being opposed in business ventures to the duke's Borelgai backers, for owning too much of the king's debt, or simply for being witness to something better left unseen.

Something like that . . . Marcus felt a dull rage burning at the pit of his stomach. *Stupid, really. Would it be* better *if there was a good reason?* But the image of the Last Duke casually snuffing out lives on the shallowest pretext made him want to clench his hands into fists and batter a way through the wall.

The cold, impervious wall. Rage vanished, replaced by a sudden rush of despair.

His shoulders ached where they were jammed against the stone, and his neck had developed a crick. It was easiest not to move at all, but there was a pressure in his bladder that would not be put off, and eventually he was forced to lever himself to his feet. Ross hadn't dared take him down to the dungeons—that would involve going past too many Armsmen—so he'd improvised a cell from an empty room in the tower. It was an empty wedge-shaped stone space with a single door and a gun slit looking out over the river, lacking even the most basic prison amenities, like a hole to piss in.

He sighed. *Is it me, I wonder? Am I so incompetent a commander that my men have to keep locking me up?* He remembered sitting in a darkened tent, watched by Adrecht's cronies. *At least I'm not tied up this time.*

Marcus selected the corner farthest from where he'd been sitting and relieved himself, then made his way back and tried to ignore the smell. His eyes were adapting, and he could see faint lights through the gun slit. Putting his eye against it, he found that he had a narrow view of a slice of the river and, in the distance, the North Bank. Elaborate spires rose against the starlit sky: the strip of noble estates known as the Fairy Castles, each building more fanciful and less practical than the last. There were only a few lights showing at the windows tonight, and Marcus wondered how many nobles had already shown the better part of valor and retired to the country.

He was just contemplating whether he could piss out the gun slit when something blocked his view. He had a brief glimpse of a long, flowing black cloth, and then a sliver of face was looking in at him, heavily shadowed. Marcus took an involuntary step back, then stopped, feeling foolish.

"Captain d'Ivoire? Is that you?" It was a woman's voice.

Marcus didn't see any point in denying it. "It is. Are you . . ." He trailed off, shaking his head. Whoever it was was somehow suspended at least fifty feet over the jagged rocks at the base of the fortress wall, clinging to a sheer stone surface. He couldn't think of anything to say to someone in that situation.

"I wanted a word with you, Captain, but Captain Ross seems determined to prevent it."

"Well." Marcus gestured around the empty room. "I have a busy schedule, but I'll try to fit you in. Who are you?"

"You can call me Rose, if you like."

"Rose, then. And what did you want with me?"

"I heard," Rose said, "that Captain Ross has locked you up because you planned to surrender the fortress. Is that true?"

Marcus shrugged. "I wanted to come to terms."

"Why?"

"I swore an oath to protect the king and people of Vordan," Marcus said. "I didn't like the idea of firing grapeshot into a crowd of those people on behalf of the Last Duke."

"It would be fair to say, then, that you're not an ally of Orlanko's?"

Marcus spread his hands. "I'm locked in here, aren't I?"

Rose seemed to consider this. Marcus blinked, and surreptitiously pinched his arm to make certain he wasn't still dreaming.

"Ross hasn't told your men that he's had you arrested," she said. "Do you think they'd break you out, if they knew?"

"I doubt it," Marcus said. "Ross has more men, and better weapons."

"Would they surrender, if you gave the order?"

"Probably. It would be better if it came from Vice Captain Giforte." Marcus hesitated. "Do you know—"

"Ross shot *someone* out in the courtyard. I don't know who, but they're awfully angry about it. They're bringing up the ram now."

Marcus closed his eyes. "If they break down the door, it'll be a massacre."

"I know." Rose paused. "If there was a way to stop it, and it meant surrendering the fortress to the mob, would you be willing to help?"

"Yes," Marcus said, without hesitation. "But I'm not sure what I can do from in here."

"We'll break you out, and you'll order your men to lay down their arms."

"Gladly," Marcus said. "If you can assure me that my men won't be harmed."

"I think I can manage that." Rose paused a moment longer, thinking. "All right. Sit tight, Captain. I'll be back."

Her face vanished. Marcus tried to get a look at how she was climbing the wall, but the narrow gun slit blocked any view but straight ahead. He gave up and shook his head.

"All right," he said, to the darkened room. "It's not as though I have any choice."

RAESINIA

"Raes?" It was Faro. "Are you awake?"

"Yeah."

This was one of those times that Raesinia wished she *could* sleep. The binding drained the weariness from her body, like any other injury, but she missed the refreshing feeling of waking up from a real sleep.

Or she thought she did, anyway. It had been so long since she'd died that she wasn't sure she really remembered. She wondered what it would be like fifty years from now, or a hundred, trying to recall that increasingly tiny slice of her existence when she'd been a human being like all the rest.

I'll find out. As far as she could tell, she didn't have any alternative.

Her makeshift shelter was just a triangular lean-to of carpet tied to a protruding window frame and weighed down with stray bricks. It provided her with a place to get away from the crowd, which had gotten increasingly violent since the shooting in the courtyard. The carnival atmosphere of the evening had evaporated, and the mob had separated into armed camps, clustered around their bonfires. Jane's Leatherbacks, the closest thing the Dockside contingent had to leaders, had already had to break up several fights between their people and the council followers.

The carpet twitched open, and Faro slipped in on his hands and knees. There was enough spare fabric to cushion the cobbled street, and Raesinia had found a torn feather pillow and a lantern somewhere. He looked around approvingly.

"Very cozy."

"Thanks." Raesinia sat up and yawned, for effect. "Did you talk to Abby?"

"It took a while to pry her away from Jane and Winter, but yes."

"And?"

"She hasn't seen Cora." Raes' disappointment must have shown on her face, because he added, "She said the women and children were kept in a bunch of separate cells, though. And she said that the Concordat troops were pretty rough on them, initially, but that Captain d'Ivoire stepped in and put Armsmen guards in place before anyone got seriously hurt."

"Captain d'Ivoire." The bluff, bearded officer she'd met with Vhalnich. Raesinia pursed her lips thoughtfully. "All right. That's something. What do you make of Mad Jane?"

"She doesn't seem all that mad to me. Her people have really taken charge. I think most of the crowd came here looking for Danton, but with him locked up Jane has been organizing everything. She's got a bunch of young women and dockmen working for her directly, and the rest seem to have a lot of respect for her."

"Any idea what her goals are?"

"No more than she told us: to get the prisoners out. Maurisk and Dumorre have been trying to explain to the Dockside people how it's their manifest destiny to throw off the ancient chains of servitude and assume their proper role in the running of the state, but it's an uphill battle. It sounds good when Danton's saying it, but coming out of those two . . ."

"Danton." Raesinia shook her head. That was another problem. "God only knows what they've made of him in there."

"They can't have really figured him out," Faro said. "Otherwise they'd have bribed him with a beer and sent him out to tell everyone to go home."

"We have to get him back." Raesinia ran a hand through her hair distractedly and winced as her fingers caught in the knots. Pure reflex, of course—she didn't feel the pain anymore. "We're running out of time. We got away because Orlanko has more important things to deal with, but Ohnlei can't let this go on forever. Sooner or later they'll send in the *real* troops."

She could only imagine the panic at the palace and the ministries. She wondered if her father was still alive, if Indergast's operation had saved him, or if he was dead and Orlanko was simply keeping the fact from the outside world. She wondered if she'd been missed yet—how long could one continue to be in hysterics? *That may be the least of our worries. If Orlanko has decided to bring the knives out for good and all . . .*

She needed to be in five places at once, and none of them was *here*, waiting outside this fortress. But Cora was in there, and Danton, and probably Sarton as well. *I can't leave them.*

"We won't have long to wait," Faro said. "Peddoc was arguing strategy with Jane, but they're bringing up the ram. Once they have the gate down they'll storm the place."

"Saints and martyrs. If the guards open fire—" Everyone had been so sure they'd surrender, but that had been before the rifleman had tried to kill Jane in the courtyard.

"It's a death trap," Faro said. "But they haven't got enough men to keep us out."

"And then it'll be a massacre on *both* sides."

Faro nodded. "They're already shouting, 'No quarter' in the courtyard."

"This isn't going to work. What if the guards start killing the prisoners? Hell, what if they decide to blow the magazine?" *There* was a gloomy thought. Raesinia imagined sitting up, alone, her skin a blistered ruin, amid the wreckage of half the Island and thousands of corpses.

"I know. But what else can we do? As you said, we're running out of time. If we wait around until they send in the army, things will be even worse."

"I need to talk to Jane. Can you set that up?"

"I can try," Faro said.

"Tell her . . . tell her I have a plan."

Faro blinked. "You have a plan?"

"No." Raesinia sighed. "But I might think of something by then. We have to do *something.* This is *our fault*, Faro, even if we didn't want it to end up like this. We wrote every word Danton said. I'm not going to let this turn into a bloodbath."

"All right," Faro said. "I'll do what I can."

He turned around and crawled out of the little shelter. Raesinia held the carpet up for a moment after he went, looking out at the fire-studded darkness.

She'd always known that her path would provoke some kind of confrontation. Once they'd started using Danton, that had become a near certainty. But she'd always imagined it as being . . . more civilized, somehow. *A gathering of statesmen. Eloquent arguments in marble halls. Perhaps a few mass demonstrations to peacefully show the will of the people.* Orlanko and his cronies would be forced out, but . . .

Not like this. Not mobs with battering rams, shouting, "No quarter!"

Either she'd overestimated her ability to control the situation or underestimated the viciousness of Orlanko and those underneath him. *Or, most likely, both. Damn, damn, damn.* She could feel Ben hovering nearby in the darkness, smiling gently.

What did you expect, Raes? A peaceful revolution?

"Raesinia."

The voice came out of nowhere. Occupied as she was communing with ghosts, Raesinia started, getting tangled in the hanging carpet and nearly bringing the whole makeshift thing down on top of her.

"Who—" she got out, before realization dawned. "Sothe!"

Her maidservant appeared from the shadows, like a patch of mobile darkness. Raesinia extricated herself from her shelter and scrambled to her feet.

"Are you all right?" Raesinia said. "I shouldn't have sent you on by yourself. I didn't know things had gotten this bad."

"I'm fine." Sothe's voice was grim. "And if I had known how matters were going, I never would have left."

"I'm sorry." Raesinia looked down and shook her head. "Ben's dead."

"I know. The story is all over the city."

"Where have you *been*?"

Sothe nodded over her shoulder at the dark bulk of the fortress, looming near invisibly against the skyline. "In there."

"You've been inside? Did you see Cora?"

"Not personally, but the prisoners seem to be well treated so far," Sothe said. "That may not last, though. Do you know Captain d'Ivoire?"

"The Armsman? I've met him."

"Pulling back from the wall was his idea, and he's put Armsmen on guard duty instead of Orlanko's thugs."

"He seemed like a reasonable man. Do you think he'd be willing to surrender?"

"Willing, yes. Able, no. The Concordat captain has him locked in the tower. He's getting ready to blast whoever goes through that gate into bloody ruin. They dug up a *cannon* from somewhere, and they're setting up barricades for a room-to-room fight all the way to the dungeons."

"Saints and martyrs," Raesinia swore. "That'll be bloody murder."

"If we go in through the gate, it will."

Raesinia had known Sothe a long time. "You've got another way in. *Please* say you've got another way in."

Sothe nodded. "There's a dock below the tower. D'Ivoire had men on it, but this new captain has pulled them off to man the barricades. I think we could get a small boat in without the sentries on the parapets noticing."

"How small?"

"Four or five."

Raesinia frowned. "How much could they accomplish?"

"I have an idea how to go about it." Sothe hesitated. "It's . . . risky. You would have to come with us."

"Me?" Raesinia blinked. Sothe was usually insistent that Raesinia keep herself *away* from possible dangers, in spite of her supernatural invulnerability, for fear that her secret would be exposed. "I mean—I'm willing, of course. But why?"

"We need someone Danton will trust. That means one of the cabal. And the only one of *them* I trust is you."

"The others are trustworthy," Raesinia protested.

"Princess," Sothe said softly. "Please."

"All right." Raesinia sighed. "I started this whole thing, didn't I? It's only fair."

Sothe looked unhappy but said nothing. Raesinia took a deep breath and blew it out.

"All right," she repeated. "What's the plan?"

"That's it," Raesinia said. "It's risky, but it sounds a hell of a lot better than storming a barricade in the face of muskets and canister."

The leaders of the riot had prudently moved to the far side of the outer wall, in case any Concordat marksmen decided to try their luck with another shot. On top of the wall, a squad of amateur musketeers kept watch on the parapet, occasionally loosing a volley when one of them spotted a creeping shadow or errant cloud.

The ram itself, an ugly thing with a cold-hammered iron head that resembled a lumpy knuckle, was being borne through the gate and into the yard on a tide of shouting, angry men. Behind it, the mob was filling up the courtyard, heedless of the threat of sharpshooters on the towers. Men with makeshift weapons pressed to the front, eager to be the first through the doorway when the breach was made.

Jane, Abby, and Winter sat on boxes in front of a small fire built of bits of scrap from demolished houses, surrounded by a group of young women in the leather aprons that seemed to be some sort of uniform or mark of distinction among the Docksiders. From the council only Cyte was in attendance, sitting cross-legged beside the fire. Maurisk, Dumorre, and the others were presumably off haranguing the crowds, and she'd seen Peddoc and his followers positioning themselves in the vanguard, eager for glory.

Jane looked at her two lieutenants. Winter, chewing her lip, nodded slowly.

"I don't know anything about the layout of the fortress," she said. "But even without artillery on the inside, getting through that door is going to be a bloody business, and they can make us repeat it at every barricade. If they *have* found a gun somewhere, it could be a disaster."

"We don't know they've found one," Abby said. She glanced at Sothe, who stood at Raesinia's shoulder. "All we have to go on is the word of this . . ."

"Rose," Sothe said. "Call me Rose."

"Rose," Abby said. "For all we know she could be Concordat."

"I'll vouch for Rose," Raesinia said.

"And who vouches for you?" Abby countered.

Jane shrugged. "She has a point. You and your people turned up late to the ball. That leaves plenty of time for Orlanko to get his agents in place."

"What do we have to lose, though?" Winter said. "Raes and . . . Rose have said they'll be going themselves. If it's a trap and Concordat soldiers are waiting on the dock, how does it hurt us?"

"You wanted three volunteers," Abby said. "It would hurt *them*."

"If we storm the doors, a hell of a lot more than that are going to die," Winter said. "Even if we win. I think it's worth the risk." She paused, then added, "I should go."

"Don't be an idiot," Jane said. "If any of us is going in there, it's me." But both Abby and Winter were shaking their heads.

"We need you out here," Abby said. "If this is going to work at all, they can't start the attack on the doors yet. You're the only one who can hold everyone back, if anyone can."

"But—" Jane began.

Winter cut her off. "That leaves two."

Raesinia nodded. "If he's willing," she said, "one of them should be Vice Captain Giforte. Rose talked to Captain d'Ivoire and he thought that most of the Armsmen would surrender if the vice captain were giving the orders."

Abby's face hardened at the suggestion, but she said nothing.

"I don't suppose you want to explain how you 'talked' to Captain d'Ivoire in the middle of a fortress full of Orlanko's men?" Jane said to Sothe. Sothe only shrugged, and Jane gave an irritated sigh. "Okay. I don't like it, but if Winter wants to go . . ."

"I'll be the last one," Abby said. "If . . . if the vice captain is going, I ought to—"

"No." Jane grabbed her arm, as if to hold her in place. "I need one of you here to keep things in line. Besides, you just got *out* of there."

"And left the others inside!"

Abby turned to Jane, and the two locked gazes for a long moment. Abby subsided, looking weary.

"I'll go."

Everyone turned to look at Cyte, who thus far had said nothing. She flinched at the sudden attention, then straightened up. Her black makeup had smeared and run until there was nothing left but dark streaks from her eyes across her cheeks, like savage war paint.

"Are you certain?" Jane said.

"Someone from the council ought to," Cyte said. "Would you rather I went to fetch Peddoc?"

Raes winced and nodded. Jane looked from her to Winter, who frowned at Cyte, but said nothing.

"Well. We should get started." Jane put her hands on her knees and got to her feet. She glanced at Winter. "And if you're not back by daylight I'm going to break down that door and come in after you."

"I'll find us a boat," Winter said. "Raes, you see if Giforte is on board."

"He will be," Abby said gloomily. "He's got a stubborn streak a mile wide, but when it comes to his men . . ." She sighed. "Take care of him, would you?"

Raes nodded. "I'll do my best." She held out her hand for Winter to shake. "Meet you at the waterfront?"

Winter nodded, and shook it. Or *nearly* shook it. As their fingers came together, something leapt between them, like a spark of static electricity. Raesinia felt the binding come to sudden, thrashing life within her, emerging from its torpor and winding itself tight around the core of her soul. Her whole body hummed with the energy of it, ready to fight, run, or do anything in between. She'd never felt anything like it, not even remotely, and from Winter's widening eyes she'd gotten some echo of the same sensation.

The binding couldn't control Raesinia's actions, but in a dim and distant way it could make its wishes known. It wanted her to back off, to run, to take a swing at Winter with the nearest available weapon, and most of all on *no account* did it want to touch her. If Raesinia hadn't known better, she would have sworn the damned thing was terrified.

WINTER

"You're sure you're all right?" Cyte said.

"Fine," Winter muttered. "I just . . . thought of something."

In truth she wasn't sure *what* that had been. Sometimes it was easy to forget the spell she'd carried since that night in the temple; that she *would* carry, if Janus was to be believed, until her death. *Obv-scar-iot*, the Infernivore, the demon that feeds on its own kind. For the most part it was not a demanding passenger, and Winter felt only its occasional twitch and rumble deep in her being, like a trickle of smoke from a cave that betrayed the presence of a fire-breathing dragon.

As she'd reached to shake Raesinia's hand, the Infernivore had awoken. She'd felt it reaching out, straining at the leash, pulling taut whatever arcane lashings bound it to Winter. Winter felt the sudden conviction that if she'd touched the girl and exerted her will, *obv-scar-iot* would have surged across the gap between their souls and devoured whatever magic hid inside Raesinia, leaving her comatose like Jen Alhundt, or worse.

But that means she has *some spell to devour.* Where had a teenage revolutionary gotten her hands on such a thing? According to Janus, the only remaining sorcerers in the civilized world were those in the service of the Priests of the Black, who had set themselves the task of exterminating all others. He'd mentioned that there was such a thing as a rogue talent, someone who enchanted himself without outside intervention, but the colonel had not been forthcoming with the details. *So Raesinia is either one of those or an enemy agent.*

Either way, Janus would have to be told. That was for later, though. *Assuming we survive.* A proper agent might have dropped everything to report this surprising intelligence to her master, but Winter was not about to abandon Jane and the others. *If I die, Janus will just have to take his chances.*

"I'm fine," Winter repeated, aware that she'd spent too long staring into space. "Sorry."

"It's all right." Cyte met her eyes only briefly, then returned her gaze to the cobbles when she saw Winter looking back.

"I don't think we've been properly introduced," Winter said. "You're Cyte, I think? I'm Winter."

"It's Cytomandiclea, really," Cyte said. "But Cyte is fine."

"After the ancient queen?"

Cyte looked up, blinking. "You've heard of her?"

"I used to read a lot of history." History, particularly *ancient* history, was one of the few subjects on which Mrs. Wilmore's expurgated library had had plenty of materials. Winter and Jane had spent a lot of time there, hiding from the proctors, and she'd acquired quite a broad, if patchy and uneven, education. "Jane always loved her. She has a thing for noble last stands."

"Really?" Cyte shook her head. "I thought I was the only one in the world who bothered with that stuff. At the University, only third-raters go into pre-Karis history."

"You're a third-rater, then?" Winter smiled, to show it was a joke, but Cyte's face went dark.

"I'm a girl," she said. "Girls are automatically third-rate, at best."

There was a pause, and then Cyte relaxed a fraction, running a hand through her dark hair.

"Sorry," she said. "Old wounds, you know?"

Winter nodded and pointed the way down to the riverbank. "We'd better see if we can find those boats."

The crowd thinned out as they got farther away from the gate, but here and there small groups congregated around a fire or sent dancing shadows out from a swinging lantern. As the Vendre passed out of view behind a line of town houses, the deadly serious air of the riot dissipated somewhat, and some of the previous sense of revelry returned. Here, the doors had been smashed open and the houses ransacked, sometimes for valuables but mostly for liquor, and groups of younger dockmen were passing these finds around. Some of them were even singing, though rarely in the same key. None of the student-revolutionaries from Cyte's group seemed to have made their way this far south.

"How old are you?" Winter asked, abruptly.

"Twenty." Cyte looked at her curiously. "Why?"

Twenty. Winter felt as though her time in Khandar had aged her by a decade. She was only two calendar years older than Cyte, but for all that the University student felt like a *girl* to her, which made Winter the adult. It was an echo of what she'd felt for the men of her company, back when Captain d'Ivoire had first put her in command. *Though most of* them *were younger than Cyte.*

"I just . . ." Winter shook her head. "You don't have to do this. I know how you feel, but—"

"I doubt it," Cyte said darkly. "And I know I don't *have* to. I volunteered, same as you."

"I'm not sure you know what you're getting into, is all," Winter said. "Have you ever been in a fight?"

"Once or twice."

"A real fight, with someone trying to kill you? And you trying to kill them?"

Cyte pursed her lips, silently.

"Do you know how to use a weapon?"

"I've studied with the rapier," Cyte said stiffly. "Four years now."

"With padded tips and paper targets," Winter said.

"I see," Cyte grated. "And I suppose you've killed a dozen men?"

"Not a dozen," Winter said, "but one or two." *Or three, or four.* She tried to count but couldn't keep track. *Do green-eyed corpses count?* "I'm not saying you're—"

"I don't care what you're saying," Cyte said. "I volunteered. I'm going. I can take care of myself."

"I didn't say you—"

"Here's a dock," Cyte said. She vaulted a rope and walked carefully out onto the stone quay. "Do you think these boats will do? Or do we need something bigger?"

Winter put her hands in her pockets, gave a little inward sigh, and went after her.

Chapter Fourteen

WINTER

Clouds were rolling in from the east. That was good and bad; it would hide them from any watchers on the parapets, but it made even finding the dock under the Vendre's walls far from a sure thing. Fortunately, Rose's sense of direction was apparently not hampered by either the darkness or the current. She and Winter rowed in tandem, as gently as they could manage, pushing the little boat closer and closer to where the fortress blotted out the sky. Behind them sat Cyte and Raesinia, with Vice Captain Giforte huddled uncomfortably in the rear.

The wind was a bare breath on her cheek, and the gray surface of the Vor was glassy smooth. The sheer walls of the prison rose above them like a cliff, darkness broken here and there by the faintest lines of light, reflections of firelight through the gun slits. Winter held her breath as they came close. Here even Rose's instincts were not enough to guide them, and she was forced to let a trickle of light out of her hooded lantern. By its faint gleam, she saw piles of jumbled rocks where the wall met the river, worn smooth by centuries of wind-driven swells. And, so small that she would have missed it from any farther away, a narrow passage between them, leading to a low, vaulted passage under the wall.

They began rowing again, slipping nearly silently through the gap into a long, watery tunnel. The air stank of mold, and streaks of dried slime on the walls charted the rise and flow of the river. Winter stared ahead, trying to discern the outlines of the dock in the gloom. She reached for the lantern to let out a little more light, now that they were out of view of the sentries on the walls, but Rose's hand slammed down over hers. The boat bumped against one dripping wall and rocked to a halt.

"There's a guard," she whispered, nearly inaudibly. "A light, anyway. Shut the lantern."

Winter did so, blinking in near-total darkness. Near, she found, but not quite. There was another light somewhere, around the curve of the corridor, and it speckled the water and the damp walls with tiny reflections. *How the hell did she see it, though?* Winter looked back at Rose to find her tugging the laces off her boots.

"I'll take care of it," she said. "I'll bring the light forward when it's safe to move in."

Giforte shuffled forward, making the boat rock and rasp ever so slightly against the wall. Winter thought Rose winced.

"One of mine," the vice captain said in a hoarse whisper, "or one of theirs?"

"No way to know." Rose shrugged out of her jacket and pulled her thin undershirt over her head in one fluid motion. Giforte gave an embarrassed cough, though it was so dark that all Winter could make out were silhouettes. "Does it matter? One scream and we've had it."

"Just . . ."

"I'll do my best." Rose stepped out of her trousers, folded them neatly, and handed the bundle of clothes to Winter. It was heavier than it should have been, and she could feel several hard, flat metal shapes through the cloth. "Hang on to these."

Rose slipped lithely off the boat and into the water with barely a splash, setting the little craft to rocking once again. Her legs cut the surface once, and then she was underwater. Winter couldn't see where she came up.

"She works for you?" Cyte whispered to Raesinia, incredulously.

"More or less," Raesinia said.

"Quiet." Winter was straining her ears for the sound of a gunshot, or even a scuffle. There was nothing.

"What if she doesn't signal?" Cyte said. "How long do we—"

"She'll be fine," Raesinia said. "Trust me."

A moment later, a bright light came on, glinting off the water. Winter started paddling forward, first one side and then the other, while Raesinia took up the other paddle and helped fend off the walls. After a few dozen yards the passage ended in a larger chamber with a protruding stone dock. Rose sat on the end of it, naked and dripping, holding a lantern in one hand and a rope in the other. She tossed the latter to Winter, who hauled the boat alongside and tied it off.

"Any problems?" Raesinia asked, as they stepped carefully onto solid ground.

Rose shook her head, accepted the bundle of clothes from Winter, and dressed. She moved with a total unselfconsciousness that reminded Winter of Jane. In the lantern light, Winter could see that she was a good deal more muscular than she looked when dressed, and that her skin was covered with thin white lines. A star-shaped lump of scar tissue marred the inside of one breast, and her arms were practically crosshatched with old wounds. Giforte pointedly looked away, and after a fascinated moment Winter did likewise.

The body lay at the base of the dock, under a black leather coat that covered it like a shroud. Winter walked over to it and found it was a young man, dirty and bearded, with a single puncture wound just below his ear.

"He had a pistol," Rose said, coming up behind her and holding the weapon out by the barrel. "Make sure it's loaded."

Winter checked the pan and the barrel and confirmed the pistol was charged, then wedged it somewhat awkwardly in her belt. She already had another pistol there, and an old cavalry saber on her hip. It felt better than she wanted to admit to be carrying weapons again. Raesinia had refused any armaments, but Giforte carried a sword and pistol and Cyte had a rapier. Rose had fended for herself.

Once their little party had gathered in the light of the lantern, Rose gestured at the corridor leading back from the dock.

"From here it's not far to the main stairs. Two levels up from here is where they've got the new prisoners. Then there's another three levels of ordinary cells before the ground floor. Captain d'Ivoire and Danton are in the tower above that. I don't expect to see anyone on the stairs, now that Jane has started making threatening noises with the ram, but there'll be guards on the cells.

"Raes and I will go and find Danton. Vice Captain, most of the men guarding the prisoners were your people. Do you think you can convince them to stand down?"

"If they know what's good for them," Giforte growled.

"Winter, Cyte, go with him, in case there are some Concordat soldiers mixed in. We'll break the others out and come down to meet you."

"What if you run into trouble?" Winter said.

"Then you're in charge. Do whatever you need to." Rose lifted her lantern. "Let's go. And remember to stay as quiet as you can."

The first turn of the spiral stairs was completely dark. Rose crept ahead while Winter followed with the lantern almost completely shut, leaving just enough light for the others to see the steps. After they crossed the first landing, more light began to leak down from above. Rose held up a hand, shuffling up the steps at the center of the spiral, until she'd gone just barely out of sight. She edged back just as quietly, frowning.

"Two men on the landing," she whispered. "Armsmen. I can't take both quietly. Either one of you can take one"—she glanced at Winter, then at Giforte—"or we can try it your way."

"Let me talk to them," Giforte said.

"Just don't make a lot of noise." Rose glanced at the ceiling. "The Concordat people have got to be close."

Giforte nodded, straightened his back, and went up the steps with a reasonable approximation of parade-ground swagger. The others followed, keeping a half turn back. On the landing, the two green-uniformed Armsmen lounged against the wall on either side of a doorway. They straightened up at the sound of footsteps, but the sight of Giforte's uniform confused them for a crucial second while he stepped into the light and gave them a good look at his face. They started to salute, but Giforte waved a hand.

"Keep quiet," he barked in a stage whisper. "Both of you."

"Yes, sir!" said the man on the left, coming to attention so stiffly he vibrated. His companion, older and wider of girth, squinted suspiciously at the group now coming into view up the stairs.

"Sir?" he said. "Beg your pardon, sir, but we were told you had tried to surrender the fortress to the rebels, and were to be detained on sight."

"Circumstances have changed, Sergeant," Giforte snapped. "I had direct orders from Captain d'Ivoire to begin negotiations. When Ross found out, he tossed the captain in a cell and took over."

"Fucking Ross," the younger Armsman said. "I always said he was a snake."

"But . . ." The sergeant hesitated, looked at the four young women.

"Representatives from the leaders outside," Giforte said. "I've agreed to release the prisoners on this level, who were in any case illegally detained by the Ministry of Information. In exchange, we've been guaranteed safe passage away from the fortress. Captain d'Ivoire and I will take all responsibility to the minister and the king."

That was enough for the sergeant, who saluted. "Sir. Yes, sir!"

"Where are the rest of our men?"

"About half are here watching the cells, along with two or three blackcoats. The others are up at the barricade. Ross wanted to pull everyone off, but we had orders from the captain himself to guard the prisoners."

"What about the prison levels above us?"

"Empty up to the ground floor. Ross has got everyone waiting for the big break-in. I think he still has men on Danton up in the tower, though."

"Right." Giforte glanced over his shoulder. "It sounds like you should have a clear path until you get to the tower."

"I can handle a few guards," Rose said. "Raes, stay a half turn behind me. Let's go."

"The problem here is going to be breaking the news to the rest of the Armsmen without anyone raising the alarm," Giforte said.

"Uh . . . I don't mean to interfere, sir," said the sergeant, "but I don't think Ross will surrender on your say-so. And he's got a lot more men than we do."

"One thing at a time." Giforte looked at Winter. "Any ideas?"

"What's the layout of this level?" Winter said.

"There's a sort of anteroom through here," the sergeant said, indicating the door. "After that passages run in either direction. One way is where we've got all the women and kids. The other is the men."

"How many people in the anteroom?"

"None, now," the Armsman said. "We were using it as a break room, but Ross called everyone up."

"Perfect. Vice Captain, you wait in there. Sergeant, you go down to the cells and ask one of your friends to step out for a moment. Say that Ross is asking for reports on the prisoners, or something like that. Once they get the picture, send them back and get another one."

"What about the Concordat people?" Giforte said.

"I don't think it'll be hard to convince our fellows to hold a gun on them," the sergeant said. "Hell, I've been itching to do it myself."

"Cyte and I will watch the stairs," Winter said. "I want every one of those guards to see nothing but green uniforms."

Giforte nodded decisively. "Come on, Sergeant. Let's spread the news."

"We can keep a better watch about a half turn up," Cyte said. "That way we can keep an eye on the next landing."

Winter nodded agreement, and they started up the steps as the three Armsmen disappeared into the dungeon. Oil lamps flickered in wall brackets, casting uneven shadows. After the door below closed, a deep silence returned, broken now and then by muffled muttering.

"What if something goes wrong?" Cyte said, quietly.

"Then we'll hear the screams," Winter said. "Or the gunshots."

They settled down to wait. Winter knew from experience that time stretched like taffy in situations like this one, turning minutes into endless hours. She wished she had a pocket watch so she would know when to really start worrying. *Although, in the end, what good does worrying do?*

There was a sound from above, faint at first but getting louder. Footsteps on the stairs, and the sound of voices raised in conversation.

"They're coming down," Cyte said. Her voice was tight.

"They may not come down this far. Maybe they're checking the cell blocks."

"What if they do?"

Winter let out a long breath. "Then we take them. As quietly as we can."

"Take them." Cyte put her hand on the hilt of her rapier, testing the grip. "Right."

Turn around, Winter willed the footsteps. *Go back upstairs. You'll live longer, and so will I.*

Two pairs of black boots became visible around the curve of the stairs, followed by the flapping tails of two black leather coats. Winter drew her saber and waited another heartbeat, then rushed them.

Two Concordat soldiers, both with shouldered muskets, came into view. Running up the steps robbed Winter of most of her speed, and the soldier on the right had a split second to react. He brought his musket up crosswise, ready to parry a cut at his chest or hit her with the butt. Winter, breathing hard, caught him off balance by stopping several steps short and whipping the heavy blade around in a low cut that caught him on the inside of the knee. The joint practically exploded, the soldier's leg bending stomach-twistingly sideways, and he toppled past Winter and started rolling downward.

She barely had time to sidestep the injured man before the other one came at her with a bellow, musket raised in both hands over his head like a club.

Winter blocked the swing and nearly lost her weapon and her footing from the force of the blow. Before he could take advantage and shove her down the steps, Cyte came into view, rapier extending in an awkward fencer's lunge on the uneven footing. The thin blade went into the man's armpit, found a gap between his ribs, and sank smoothly nearly to the hilt. He fell backward with a gurgle, dropping his musket, and the hilt of the rapier was jerked out of Cyte's hands.

Winter looked over her shoulder to see what had become of her own victim, but her head snapped back around when Cyte shouted her name.

"Winter! Up there!"

Looking up, Winter got a glimpse of a third man, a quarter turn behind the other two and already taking to his heels. She swore and vaulted the corpse of Cyte's victim, clawing for the pistol at her belt. There was no time to check the pan again. Just a moment to level and fire—*and even if I hit him, they'll hear the shot*—

She pulled the trigger. The weapon went off with an earsplitting *bang*, and she saw the man's coat flutter, as though a passerby had given it a tug. But the ball missed his body, cracking wildly off the stone wall beyond, and before Winter could reach for her other pistol he was up the stairs and out of sight.

"Balls of the Beast," Winter said. She turned back to Cyte. "There's going to be more of them in a minute. Come on, back to the landing."

"I . . ." Cyte gestured weakly at her sword, which was still embedded in the Concordat soldier. His hands scrabbled wildly at the air, and blood bubbled in his mouth.

Winter grabbed the hilt, planted her foot on the man's side, and yanked the weapon free as he shuddered and died. She handed the thin blade back to Cyte, still slick and red, and pulled another pistol and a pouch of ammunition from the body. Then she grabbed the girl's free hand and pulled her down the steps to the landing, where there would at least be flat ground to fight on.

Her own victim was there, head cracked and leaking blood from his tumble down the unyielding stone stairs. She pushed him aside and turned to Cyte.

"Are you all right?" Winter said.

"Fine." Cyte was staring at the sword in her hand as though she didn't know how it had gotten there. "I'm fine. I just . . ."

"I know," Winter said. "But you have to focus."

Winter hated having to act so *hard*. It made her feel like Davis, someone who could cut men down and laugh about it later in his cups. *But there's no* time.

The man she'd shot at would make it back up to the others on the ground floor, and surely they'd send a larger force—

"Cyte. Cytomandiclea." The sound of her assumed name seemed to bring the girl back to herself a little. "Do you know how to load a pistol?"

"N . . . not really. I've never . . ."

"Shit." Winter went to the door and hammered on it. "Giforte? Are you in there? They're on their way down!"

There was no response. Winter cocked an ear at the steps and fancied she could hear the pounding of many feet. She grabbed Cyte and pulled her up against the inner wall of the spiral.

"Stay here until they get close," Winter said. "You don't want to give them a target if they decide to shoot at us. And stay on the landing, away from the stairs. It's no good giving them high ground to fight from."

"But . . ." Cyte's mind was catching up with events at last. "There's too many! They'll kill us."

A rational debater would have told her that this was, after all, what she'd volunteered for. Davis would have just screamed at her. Winter shrugged, patted the girl on the shoulder in what she hoped was a reassuring manner, and went for the dead soldier's musket. This *was* loaded, and wonder of wonders, the fall had not knocked open the pan and spilled the powder. Winter cocked it, went to one knee at the bottom of the stairs, and settled down to wait.

She didn't have to be patient long. A clatter of boots preceded the arrival of the Concordat troops, coming down the stairway two by two. Winter took aim before their heads came into view, tracked their motion for a moment, and fired. The musket's report was even louder than the pistol's, and the weapon delivered its familiar kick to her shoulder. This time her aim was better, and one of the leading black-coats was punched off his feet to sprawl bonelessly on the steps.

Winter tossed the musket aside and threw herself flat. As she'd expected, the keyed-up soldiers returned fire, filling the stairway with a deafening cacophony of thunder, broken by the *zip* and *zing* of ricocheting balls. Smoke billowed from the barrels and locks of their weapons, puffing around them like a localized thundercloud. It hung motionless in the still air, and the men came charging through it with tendrils of gray clinging to their coats, brandishing their bayonetted muskets like spears.

All that kept Winter alive through the next few moments was the fact that the bayonet, so impressive in glittering ranks on an open field, was far from an ideal weapon for close-quarters combat in a stairway. She pushed herself to her feet as they pounded toward her, and faded to the left as the first pair closed. The man on that side came at her at a run, stumbling slightly as he leapt off the last stair and hit the landing, intending to run her through like a lancer. Winter's parry caught the musket barrel behind the bayonet with a *clang* of steel on iron, forcing his arm wide. His momentum carried him into her, and she brought the curved hilt of her weapon around and slammed the pommel into his face with all the force of his running start behind it, bowling him over as if he'd run into a clothesline at a gallop.

The second man, more cautious, checked his run and thrust his bayonet at her as she stepped clear of the falling body. Winter twisted away from the point and slashed wildly at him, but the length of his weapon kept him at a safe distance. He backed up and tried again, and this time she barely caught the wicked point of the weapon with her saber and battered it aside. Her clumsy return stroke cut only air. She backpedaled, acutely aware that there were only a few steps of flat ground behind her before the downward stairway resumed.

Out of the corner of her eye, she saw another Concordat soldier vault the body of the first and try to cut around to her right. He'd overlooked Cyte, who'd been pressed tight against the wall on that side. She brought her rapier up and lunged, this time with perfect form, as though on a fencing strip. The tapered point went through the soldier's leather coat, into the small of his back, and emerged somewhere in the vicinity of his navel.

He screamed, which made Winter's opponent look aside for a split second. Winter half turned to get past the point of his bayonet and grabbed the barrel of the musket with her free hand, yanking it out of his distracted grip. He looked back just in time to see the downward saber slash that opened him from sternum to hip.

Four men were down in the space of as many seconds. Winter let the musket fall and raised her eyes, expecting another charging musketeer. Instead she found herself staring into the barrel of a pistol.

Oh. Logical, under the circumstances, especially if you were willing to let your comrades charge forward into the fray while you lined up your shot. Time seemed to telescope, on and on. She could see the two-day stubble on the man's face, the glint of a captain's bars on his chest where his coat hung open. She could see the open pan of his weapon, ready for the descending flint to strike a spark.

There was always a chance. Pistols loaded in haste misfired, or failed to fire at all. A malformed ball might emerge at an odd angle, caroming harmlessly away. Springs broke, clamps failed, flints went spinning off instead of properly sparking. Even at close range, it was easy to miss a target, especially for an inexperienced marksman. But Winter had a sudden certainty that none of those other chances were going to break her way this time. The man's finger tightened on the trigger—

Then his eyes crossed, as though puzzled, and he toppled forward. The pistol went off, ball zinging off the steps, but the Concordat captain kept going, beginning a boneless tumble down the stairs that ended with him sprawled facedown at Winter's feet. A heavy knife—almost a cleaver—was embedded at an angle in the back of his skull as though it were a butcher's block.

Rose, farther up the stairs, was straightening up from her throw. She caught Winter's eye and smiled.

Behind Rose came Raes and an older man Winter didn't recognize. She assumed this was Danton, although nothing about him suggested the charismatic leader. His shirt was stained with sweat, and his hair was wild and unkempt from days in captivity. His expression was one of beatific satisfaction, however, and one of his hands gripped one of Raes'. Winter wondered if there was something between the two of them. *It would explain her insistence on coming along.*

"Is that all of them?" Rose said, stepping carefully among the bodies on the landing. She knelt beside the man Winter had laid out with the pommel of her sword, produced a knife from somewhere, and stuck it almost gently into the side of his head, just forward of his ear. He shuddered and died without a sound.

"A . . . all." Winter shook her head, trying to banish the vision of the pistol trained on her head and the certainty that she was about to die. Her heart hammered wildly, and something unpleasant roiled in her stomach. *Now is not the time, damn it.* "Yes. That's all the ones who came downstairs. But I was expecting more of them."

"It turns out there were a few Armsmen locked up next to the captain," Rose said. "They've got the next group pinned down at the ground floor landing for the moment."

"Not for long," said another voice, accompanied by the rapid clatter of boots. Captain d'Ivoire came into view, looking odd in the unfamiliar green Armsman uniform, a musket in one hand. "We don't have enough men to really stop them, but after the first volley they've gotten cautious. We're going to have to fall back if they make a serious push."

Somehow Winter had not thought this far ahead. She stood on the landing, bloody saber in hand, and felt the captain's eyes tracking toward her with the same feeling of awful premonition that she'd felt watching the pistol come to bear. If he recognized her—*more to the point, if he recognizes me as a* woman—

Then what? The fear of discovery, ground in over long years, made Winter's blood sing. *But who would it actually harm? I could stay with Jane and the others. Tell Janus to find someone else to fight his damned battles.*

It would never work, of course. If nothing else, she could never rid herself of the Infernivore; as Janus had pointed out to her, what felt like a lifetime ago, that meant she was involved whether she liked it or not. *Besides,* another part of her mind insisted, flooding her with guilt, *there's Bobby to think of. And Feor, and Graff and Folsom, and everyone else in the Seventh.*

All this flashed past her mind's eye in the instant between when the captain started down the stairs and when he met her gaze. Their eyes met, just for a moment, and she thought she saw something change in Marcus' expression. It was gone an instant later, though, and he was moving on, pushing past Raes and Danton toward the door to the cells.

Energy flowed out of Winter like water out of a barrel with the bottom knocked off. She wiped her saber roughly on a fold of Concordat uniform and returned it to its sheath, legs wobbling like a drunk's. She found Cyte still standing by the man she'd killed. She'd managed to keep her rapier in hand, this time, but she was staring at the bloodied weapon as though she wasn't sure what to do with it.

"Are you all right?" Winter said. This time, it took only a moment for Cyte's eyes to clear. *It gets easier every time, doesn't it?*

"I . . . I think so." She looked down at herself, astonished to be intact. "Did we win?"

"Not yet."

"What happens now?"

Winter struggled to remember the plan Raes had outlined. It had been a bit vague on that point, but . . .

"I think," she said, "that's up to Danton."

The anteroom on the prison level was crowded to capacity and beyond. The guards' table had been dragged against the outer door as a stage and impromptu barricade, with Winter, Raesinia, Danton, and the others standing in the doorway and Giforte and the rest of the Armsmen making a thin line on the other side.

Beyond them were the prisoners. Captain d'Ivoire had ordered the cells thrown open, and the liberated abductees filled the room and backed up out into the corridors. The angriest among them, mostly from the male contingent but including a number of women as well, had pushed to the front of the crowd and were engaged in a shouting match with the captain, who stood on the table trying to argue with them.

"Look," he said, his voice already going hoarse with the effort of trying to make himself heard over the babble. "I know you don't have any reason to trust me. But my men are going to be with you. Some of them are fighting upstairs right now to give us this time to argue! *I* am going to be with you. And if we don't disarm those Concordat soldiers, hundreds of your fellow citizens are going to be gunned down!"

"We should start by stringing you up!" someone shouted.

"Bloody Armsmen!"

"If we fight Orlanko's men, they'll just kill *us* instead!"

"I heard it's a bunch of dockmen at the gates," said someone with a Northside accent. "Are we supposed to sacrifice ourselves for a gang of lazy stevedores?"

Winter badly wanted to punch this person. From the sound of it the sentiment was shared by many in the crowd, and the ensuing scuffle threatened to engulf the entire room in chaos. Marcus shouted for order. The air was thick and close with the scent of too many unwashed bodies.

At Winter's side, Raesinia was speaking quietly to Danton. The orator sat cross-legged with the same stupid smile on his face, nodding absently as the girl read to him from what looked like prepared notes. He reminded Winter of nothing so much as a little boy not paying attention to a lecture from a parent.

She stepped away from the table, into the cooler air of the corridor, where Cyte stood with her back to the stone. Her eyes were closed, and her face was flushed under the smears of black makeup.

"What's going on?" she said.

"The captain is trying to argue them into taking the Concordat positions from behind. I don't think it's going as well as they'd hoped."

"What about Danton?"

"Raes is still coaching him." Winter shook her head. "He's not what I expected."

There was a long pause. Marcus' pleading was drowned out by an angry roar from the crowd.

"This wasn't . . . what I expected," Cyte said.

"No?"

"More blood, for one thing." She gave a little shudder. "I always pictured . . ."

"I know," Winter said. "Like in an opera. You swing the sword, someone falls over. Maybe a little stage blood on your hands." She looked down. They'd moved the Concordat corpses out of the way, but the flagstones were still stained red and brown. "No matter how much you imagine, it's never enough."

"I thought it would be harder, to kill somebody."

"I know."

"You tried to talk me out of coming." Cyte opened her eyes. "Thank you."

"It didn't work."

Cyte gave a weary shrug. "The effort has to be worth something."

"All right!" said Raesinia, behind them. "You've got all that?"

"I've got it, Princess," Danton said. "Afterward—"

"Afterward you can have whatever you like, Danton," Raesinia said, with a glance at Winter and Cyte. "But those people are waiting to hear your story."

"Okay."

Danton got to his feet. Raesinia smoothed the front of his ruined shirt and tugged on his cuffs for a moment, then gave up.

And then Danton—changed.

It was astonishing to watch. He straightened up, altered his stance, ran a hand casually through his hair. A moment earlier he had given every appearance of amiable dullness—on the verge of idiocy, Winter would have said. Now his eyes were full of fire, and he moved with an obvious sense of purpose. Captain d'Ivoire stepped aside and the orator mounted the table and raised his hands for silence. To Winter's amazement, he got it, or as close to silence as a crowd of that size could manage. The shouts and arguments snuffed out like candles in the wind as he cast his gaze about the room.

"You might want to move down the stairs a bit," Raesinia said to Winter. "There are going to be a lot of people coming this way in a minute."

Winter and Cyte stepped away from the doorway, and Raesinia came to stand with them. Rose, so still and quiet Winter had forgotten she was there, came with her.

"You really think he can convince them?" Winter said in a low voice.

"Call it a hunch," Raesinia said.

"Brothers!" Danton began. "And here, in this pit, we are truly brothers. I say to you . . ."

The crowd of roaring, cheering men surged up the stairway like water bursting from a broken dam. They passed the tiny group of Armsmen fighting a rear-guard action and hit the Concordat troops opposing them with the force of a tidal wave. The soldiers who had loaded muskets fired them, and here and there in the mass a man went down, but these were pinpricks on the flanks of the great beast that was the mob. The black-coats were bowled over, disarmed, grabbed by many hands, and borne in triumph down to the cells, while the rest of the crowd pushed on toward the front gates.

With the death of Captain Ross and the roar of the mob outside, the Concordat soldiers manning the barricade were in a fragile state of mind. The firefight at the stairs had put them on edge, and the swelling chorus of shouts coming up the corridors only heightened their anxiety. Some of them turned around to see what was coming, and a few had the presence of mind to fire. No one thought to try to wheel the great mortar around, with its massive load of canister, until it was far too late. The enraged crowd was on them.

Squads of women sat on the soldiers to keep them down until they could be safely detained, and the older children scurried about picking up the fallen muskets. A gang of men set to work heaving the huge iron bar away from the door. It opened to reveal the astonished besiegers clustered around their ram, huddled together with weapons raised in expectation of a trick or sortie.

A few minutes later, the crowd inside had dissolved into the crowd outside. Cheers spread from the gate like ripples on the surface of a pond radiating out from a dropped stone, until the entire island seemed to ring with hoarse shouts of joy and triumph, peppered by the *pop, pop* of muskets fired jubilantly into the air.

The Vendre had fallen.

CHAPTER FIFTEEN

RAESINIA

"Raes!"

"Cor—"

Raesinia didn't have time to get the word out before the girl hit her at speed, knocking the wind out of her and hugging her so tightly she had trouble sucking in another breath. Raesinia let this go on for a while, but eventually she tapped Cora on the shoulder, indicating that a slight decrease in pressure would be appreciated. Raesinia didn't really *need* to breathe, but it was difficult to talk without air in her lungs.

"Cora," she got out, once she was able. "Are you all right?"

"More or less," Cora said, still pressed close against Raesinia's shoulder. "They were a little rough when they tied us up."

"They didn't . . ." Raesinia hesitated, and Cora gave her a squeeze.

"I'm fine. The black-coats were threatening some of the women, but the captain replaced them with Armsmen before anything came of it."

"Thank God." Raesinia had been having waking nightmares of finally taking the prison, only to find a pile of mangled corpses, in spite of what Abby had told her. "Have you seen Sarton? We heard he was taken as well."

"I saw him just now," Cora said, and made a face. "He was walking around on the old prison levels. They have machines there for . . . well, for a lot of unpleasant things. You know Sarton and machines, though, whatever they're for."

"I know." The ghost of a smile crossed Raesinia's lips, then vanished. "Cora . . ."

"What about the others?" Cora looked up. Her hair was a rat's-nest tangle, and her eyes were red from crying, but there were no tears there now. "Were they arrested?"

"Maurisk is downstairs, arguing with someone, I suspect. Faro as well." Raesinia closed her eyes. "Ben . . . Ben's dead."

She felt Cora's hands tighten on the back of her shirt. "He . . . you're sure?"

"I was with him. He saved my life." That was a lie, of course, but she thought it a kind one under the circumstances. "Orlanko's men tried to kill us both."

"Ben . . ." Cora swallowed hard. "God. I never thought things would get this bad."

Guilt made a lump in Raesinia's throat. "Neither did I."

There was a long silence. Eventually Cora loosened her grip and stepped away. They were in one of the Vendre's tower rooms, long disused and empty except for dust and an ancient table and chairs. Raesinia went to one of the latter and sat down, gingerly, half expecting it to collapse. It let out a groan, but held for the moment.

"What the hell *happened*?" Cora said. "The guards wouldn't tell us much. Just that there was a mob attacking the prison."

"They arrested Danton," Raesinia said. "The Armsmen did, I think, but afterward the Concordat must have thought it was time to make a clean sweep. They picked people up all over the city."

"I know," Cora said. "I was at the church in Oldtown. We sent everyone out the back when we saw them coming. I was going to try talking to them, but they just kicked in the door and grabbed me before I could say a word."

Raesinia nodded. "They're onto us, obviously. It was bound to happen eventually. I just didn't think the Last Duke would try something like *this*. He's supposed to be smarter than that."

"But where did this riot come from?"

"All over. A woman named Mad Jane brought a huge gang of Docksiders over because they'd taken some friends of hers. I went to the Dregs and helped Maurisk round up the students and hangers-on. And once it got started people showed up on their own. I think half the city must be down there now."

Cora shook her head. She glanced at the gun slit in the wall, where a faint gray light was just starting to make itself felt against the glow of the candles.

"It's nearly morning," she said. "What happens now?"

"I don't know." Raesinia shook her head. What she wanted more than anything else was *time*. Time to let emotions cool, time to gather the scattered members of her cabal and make a proper plan, time to get her own head in order. Time to mourn Ben the way he deserved. But she was equally aware that she was not going to get it. Half the city might be gathered in the streets, but they wouldn't stay there for long. Something was happening, and it was happening *now*, whether she wanted it to or not.

If we don't get control of it, someone else will. Right now the fall of the prison had produced a triumphant atmosphere, but the anger was still there. *And God only knows what's happening at Ohnlei. If Father is dead, then Orlanko will be trying to take control.* There were too many variables, too many possibilities. *Maybe I can leave Cora and Maurisk in charge here, and—*

There was a knock at the door. Cora started and spun.

"It's me," said Sothe.

"Come in," Raesinia said.

Cora looked surprised but said nothing as Sothe slipped in and shut the door behind her. Raesinia gestured wearily from one to the other.

"Sothe, you know Cora. Cora, this is Sothe. She's an . . . agent of mine. She's been working with us since the beginning. I trust her with my life." *Or the nearest equivalent.* "We couldn't have taken the prison without her."

Cora frowned, then bowed in Sothe's direction. "Then I don't know how to thank you."

"No need to thank me," Sothe said, with a glance at Raesinia that told her they'd have words later. "It's part of my job, after all."

"What is your job?" Cora said, curious.

"Chambermaid," Raesinia said. Sothe suppressed a smile. Cora looked between them and shook her head.

"They're planning a grand council downstairs," Sothe said. "To arrange for something along the lines set out in your declaration."

"Who's invited?" Raesinia said.

"Everyone from the old council, plus you, 'Mad Jane' and some of her people, Captain d'Ivoire, and some representatives of the merchants and traders. All sorts have been turning up, and everyone's demanding a place at the table." Sothe paused. "They're going to want Danton to make a speech."

"That can be arranged," Raesinia said. "I'll need some time to work out what we want him to say."

"Before that," Sothe said, "there's something else we need to talk about."

"Oh?"

"All of us." Sothe's expression was grim. "The cabal. Alone."

The sun was coming up, but the morning light had revealed the hovering clouds to be heavy black thunderheads. They swept across the city like a conquering army, plunging it into shadow. It was still hot and dry, but the wind that whipped across the Vendre's parapet was thick with the scent of rain. Distant, warning grumbles echoed across the river like the coughing of far-off cannon.

Raesinia sat on the stone parapet, her back to a crenellation, one leg dangling over the long drop to the rocks and the river below. Cora stood beside her, when she managed to stand still. Mostly she paced, arms crossed over her chest, hugging herself tighter when the wind gusted. Sothe, expressionless and impassive, waited between them.

One by one, the other conspirators made their appearance. Maurisk's eyes were dark with fatigue, but his expression was triumphant. Faro had found time to change clothes, and was now back in his fashionable courtier's outfit, complete with dress rapier. Unlike Maurisk, he seemed to be full of nervous energy, and glanced from Sothe to Raesinia and back again. Last to arrive was Sarton, who seemed none the worse for wear from his captivity.

"Raes, what's going on?" Maurisk said, breaking the silence. "I've got work to do. They're holding the council meeting this evening."

"And who is this?" Faro said, indicating Sothe.

"This," Raesinia said, "is Sothe. She's what you might call an adjunct member of the cabal."

Faro blinked. "What is that supposed to mean?"

"It means that I work for Raesinia, but I don't make myself known to any of you," Sothe said. "I help keep the Concordat looking in the wrong direction."

Maurisk's face clouded. "Then you've been doing a bang-up job, I *must* say."

"I don't like this," Faro said. "You should have told us, Raes. Letting her in on the secret put all of us at risk. We have a right to know what you're doing."

"I trust her," Raesinia said. "I've known her for longer than I've known any of you."

"But *I* haven't," Maurisk said. "Faro's right. Why not let us know?"

"Because," Sothe said, "I work for *Raesinia*. My job is to keep her safe. That includes keeping her safe from any of you."

That hung in the air for a long moment. Cora turned away, walking to the inner edge of the parapet and looking down at the still-thronged courtyard.

Sarton was still staring at the sky, but Raesinia, Maurisk, and Faro exchanged glances.

"Now I *really* don't like this," Maurisk said. He stepped forward to stand directly in front of Sothe. "What are you implying?"

"And," Faro said, coming up behind him, "why should we believe you?"

Thunder growled.

"There!" Sarton said. "Lightning!" He looked down at the others. "I'm sorry. You know how it is when you get your teeth in a p . . . problem. I've been spending some time looking at the arrangements here, and I think . . ."

He trailed off as he absorbed the tense atmosphere. Sothe cleared her throat.

"I imply nothing," she said. "I asked you all here because, by the night before last, I had become reasonably certain one of you was leaking information to the Concordat."

Maurisk snorted. "If one of us had been Concordat from the beginning, do you really think we would have gotten this far?"

"I didn't say the informant was leaking from the beginning. It began quite recently, probably after the Second Pennysworth riots. That was when Danton really became a problem, and I can only assume the Last Duke went looking for answers and found someone he could squeeze."

Faro was glaring at her, one hand on his rapier. "And you didn't think to mention this at the time?" He looked at Raesinia. "Ben's *dead* because we didn't know the Concordat was onto us. If we believe what she's saying—"

"It's a fair question, Sothe," Raesinia said. *You might have at least told* me.

"I said nothing because I wasn't certain," Sothe said. "Trust is paramount in a small group like this one. The mere accusation would have destroyed you, and I didn't want to risk that without knowing for sure who the informant was." Her eyes shifted, fractionally, toward Raesinia. "If that makes me guilty of Ben's death, I accept it."

"I don't believe a word of this," Maurisk said. He turned his back on Sothe and stalked away a few steps, then rounded on her. "The Last Duke would like nothing better than for us to turn on one another now. For all we know—"

"Sothe doesn't work for Orlanko," Raesinia said. "I'm certain of that, if nothing else."

"So *you* say," said Faro. He was still almost face-to-face with Sothe. "But you kept her secret in the first place. Why should we believe you?"

Sarton coughed politely. "If you kept silent because you didn't know for c . . . certain, the fact that you've told us now logically imp . . . plies that you *are* sure." Another rumble from the heavens nearly drowned out his soft, stuttering voice. "What happened?"

"The commander of the Concordat forces at the Vendre was Captain James Ross," Sothe said. "His files were well organized. Like many Concordat field agents, however, he failed to take seriously the regulations concerning the practice of keeping books of ciphers in physical proximity to encoded communications."

"You seem to know an awful lot about Concordat procedures—" Faro began, but Maurisk cut him off.

"You can read Ross' files?"

"Not all of them, but enough to know that I was right."

Maurisk's voice trembled. "And the identity of the informant?"

"Yes. The duke wanted to be sure he wouldn't be swept up in the purges."

"Don't tell me," said Faro, "that you're taking this seriously—"

Steel *zinged* as his rapier came out of its scabbard, faster than Raesinia would have given him credit for. Quick as he was, though, Sothe was faster. Her hand shot out and grabbed his, fingers interlocking like lovers' on a promenade, and something fast and painful happened. Faro let go of his sword and spun away from her, only to be brought up short when she kept her grip on his hand. Sothe's left hand had emerged from her waistband holding a long, thin dagger.

"Now," she said, "I hope—"

"Sothe," Raesinia said quietly.

There was a click. Even as he'd lost his sword, Faro's off hand had gone to his pocket and come out with a nasty-looking short-barreled pistol. He thumbed back the hammer and brought the barrel up to aim squarely between Raesinia's eyes.

"Your job is to protect her, isn't it?" Faro said, his voice tight with pain. "*Isn't it?* Then let go of me!"

Sothe locked eyes with Raesinia, just for a moment. Raesinia raised her eyebrows emphatically and nodded.

Better he point that thing at me than anyone else. Part of her was trying to process what was unfolding—that *Faro* had as good as signed Ben's death warrant—but the rest was still planning as calmly as ever. *All I need to do is make him pull the trigger.* He'd never get the chance to reload. Raesinia had watched Sothe split leaves with a knife at twenty yards, and she never had less than a half dozen blades on her person. *Come on, come on . . .*

Slowly, Sothe released Faro's hand. He stepped away from her, weapon still trained on Raesinia, and circled around until his back was against the waist-high parapet stone.

"You'll never get out of here alive," Raesinia said, conversationally. She heard a hiss of breath from Maurisk and a startled squeak from Cora, somewhere behind her. "You know that, don't you?"

"The hell I won't." Faro grabbed Raesinia by the arm and pressed the barrel of the pistol against the back of her skull. "Come on. Over to the trapdoor."

He pushed her, painfully, but she didn't move. "Then what?"

"Then I leave you all up here, bar the door, and get off the Island before anybody comes up here to let you out." He tugged again, and when she didn't move his voice turned almost plaintive. "Come *on*, Raes. Nobody needs to get killed."

"Ben," Raesinia said. "Ben got killed. Because *you* told Orlanko where to find us."

"I didn't know they were going to kill him! Everyone would have been fine if you'd just come along quietly."

"Raes . . . ," Maurisk said. "He's right. We'll catch up with this *bastard* later. It's not worth getting your head blown off."

"Please, Raes!" Cora's voice was high and scared.

"Answer me this, Faro," Raesinia said, implacably. "How much did it cost to buy you? A new pair of boots? One of those fancy swords you like so much?"

"Shut *up*. Move, damn it!" Faro tried to pull her after him, but Raesinia let her legs sag and ended up leaning against the parapet, facing outward, with Faro pressed up close behind her. Her knees pressed against the stone, and she felt a tingle in the soles of her feet as her balance shifted dangerously.

"Raes!" Cora shrieked.

Raesinia put her free hand on the parapet. "How much, Faro?"

"What the *fuck* is wrong with you?" Faro took a step back, spun Raesinia around so they were face-to-face, then pushed her back against the wall, his hand still tight on her wrist. The pistol was pressed tight against her forehead. "Are you trying to get yourself killed?"

More or less. Raesinia smiled. "How much?"

"They had my *family*," Faro hissed through clenched teeth. He pressed harder, levering her out dangerously over the edge. "My parents. My sisters. He told me he'd send them to me in pieces if I didn't go along. What in the name of the Savior was I supposed to do?"

He squeezed his eyes shut, blinking away tears. It was as good an opportunity as Raesinia thought she was likely to get.

She brought her free hand up and wrapped it around his wrist, feeling their shared center of balance rock against the parapet. At the same time, her knee came up, fast and hard, between his legs. The blow to his groin would curl him up, and she'd be able to force the pistol away from her head before he could fire.

That was the theory, anyway. Something felt wrong as soon as she started to move. Her knee got tangled against something hard between his thighs—*the damned* scabbard, *it got twisted when he turned around*—

The wooden sheath absorbed the force of her blow with a splintering crack. She got her hand on his wrist, but the pistol was jammed hard against her forehead, and she didn't have the leverage to shift it. She saw his eyes open and blink again, as slowly as if in a dream, and his finger jerked on the trigger. The hammer fell, sparking into the pan, and then—

Raesinia had never been shot in the head before. She felt a violent tug, as though someone had grabbed hold of her hair and yanked backward hard. In the same instant, her whole body went numb and all her limbs tried to pull inward at once, like a child instinctively clapping a hand over a skinned knee. With her knee between Faro's legs, caught on his scabbard, and one of his wrists in her hand, this had the effect of pulling him practically on top of her.

Something scraped against the small of her back. There was a high, thin scream—*Cora*—and Raesinia saw a dizzy, spinning view of the darkening sky. Something dropped out of the pit of her stomach, and then she was falling.

It was a long way to the rocky riverfront below. She had time to let go of Faro and push him away. Raesinia hoped, in the muzzy-headed way of one whose brain had largely been converted into a cloud of flying gore and splinters, that she'd gotten enough momentum to get away from the wall and hit the water, but as she spun the ground came into view and it became clear she wasn't going to make it. The base of the wall was a jumble of rocks, rounded off by the river at the waterline but still jagged above it.

Oh dear. This is going to hurt.

It turned out Raesinia *could* lose consciousness. All it took was driving a pistol ball through her brain, then smashing it to a red paste in a hundred-foot fall onto unforgiving stone.

She'd always wanted to have one of those out-of-body experiences sometimes described by seamen who'd been rescued from drowning, hovering above her corporeal form while a celestial chorus beckoned. It would have answered certain key questions raised by her postmortal state. But either those poor sailors had been telling stories or there was no choir of angels waiting for Raesinia. No army of demons, either, though. Just . . . nothing, a blank in her memory from the moment she'd hit the rocks. It was a little like waking suddenly from a deep sleep, but with none of the refreshed feeling from having rested.

The binding was still working furiously, pulling wounds closed and regrowing flesh to replace what was lost. It went about this process with a blind, idiot determination that reminded Raesinia of a swarm of ants, doggedly building and rebuilding their anthill every time some curious child kicked it over. There was no *intention* there, no thought, just the mindless response of an animal.

It couldn't understand, for example, when circumstances were unfavorable. As best Raesinia could tell, she was stuck on the edge of the skirt of rocks at the bottom of the Vendre's walls, with her head and shoulder underwater and her legs sticking up in a most unladylike fashion. Her lungs were full of muddy river water, and her heart was limp and still in her chest. But the binding had straightened the fractured bones of her arms, and she could move, after a fashion. When she brought her hands up to explore her face, she found a coin-sized patch on her forehead of smooth, freshly knitted bone, surrounded by a slowly closing knot of regenerated skin.

The most urgent problem was what she was stuck *on*. Her eyes weren't in working order yet, but she explored it with her hands. A splintery column of rock, freshly exposed by some underwater cracking, had driven itself some distance into her abdomen and caught there, leaving her hanging like a speared fish. As the gentle currents of the river moved her, she could feel it grate against her bottom ribs. The binding worked feverishly to repair the damaged flesh around the intrusion but could do nothing to push her off it.

Well. I suppose it's up to me, then. Raesinia flailed her legs for a few moments until she determined to her satisfaction that nothing could be accomplished with them. Her hands could reach the offending spike, but it was slippery and offered little purchase, and the angle was bad. Scrabbling and pushing at it earned her only torn skin on her palms, which the binding went to work repairing with—she liked to imagine—an exasperated sigh.

All right. Now what? She couldn't just hang here *forever.* There were people who went about picking up corpses, weren't there? Eventually someone would notice the upside-down body under the walls of the Vendre and send a boat out.

They would discover the Princess Royal of Vordan, her arse in the air, impaled on a spiky rock. She wondered if whoever did it would die of shock on the spot.

A moot point, though. *Sothe will get here first.*

She hung motionless awhile longer. Her eyes were beginning to clear, but there wasn't much to see, just the dark waters of the Vor. Her hair settled in long spiderweb patterns around her head, twitching this way and that in the weak currents. She felt a tug at her leg through a rent in her trousers. A scavenger, she assumed, and kicked her feet to indicate that she wasn't dead yet. *Or . . . well, whatever.*

Something splashed into the water nearby. Raesinia turned her head, but all she could see was a dark shadow in the murk, making its way along the rocks. A moment later it was beside her, a pair of hands groping gently along her body until they found the protruding chunk of stone. Whoever it was took hold of her, above and below the intrusion, and lifted. Dirty water flooded into the wound, and thick, dark blood flowed out. Raesinia pictured the binding sighing again, this time with relief, as it went to work knitting up the torn skein of her intestines.

Whoever it was pushed her away from the rocks, and someone else took hold of her hands and pulled. Between the two of them they managed to roll Raesinia over the low gunwale of a boat, to lie dripping and motionless on the bottom. She felt the boat rock as the figure who'd been in the water pulled itself back in.

This left Raesinia in something of a quandary. She could pretend to be dead for only so long. It might be Sothe, but it might not, and she dared not open her eyes to check. She opted to lie still, feeling her insides rebuilding themselves, and hoped that whoever they were, they would say something.

There was a long silence, in fact, broken by the splash of oars as the boat cleared off from the rocky walls of the Vendre and moved out into the slow, calm waters of the Vor. Eventually, though, the rowing sounds stopped, and strong hands took Raesinia by the shoulders and rolled her onto her back, letting her look up at her rescuers.

"I must say, Your Highness," said Janus bet Vhalnich, "you've looked better."

Raesinia sat up, her clothes squishing damply, and looked around. They were in a tiny rowboat, really too small for three. In the back was Sothe, an oar in each hand, resolutely refusing to meet Raesinia's eyes. In the front, Janus was stripped to a white shirt and trousers, sopping wet.

She opened her mouth to say something, but all that emerged was a thin stream of river water. Raesinia held up a finger to indicate he should wait, and Janus nodded gravely. She leaned over the edge of the boat and vomited up a mix of water and blood that went on for far longer than she'd expected. Then, feeling quite a bit lighter, she turned back to Janus and took an experimental breath. The binding tingled across her lungs, repairing the damage done by hours of immersion. Her heart started with a jerk, then settled reluctantly into its familiar rhythm, like an ancient machine squealing along a rusty track.

"I have," she said, and paused to cough a bit more water over the side. "I have been better. Considerably better."

"I trust that you'll recover?"

"I expect so." Raesinia felt a little giddy, either as a result of her rescue or because the binding hadn't created enough blood to replace all she'd lost. She looked down at her torn, bedraggled shirt, and sighed. "I think these clothes have about had it, though."

A smile flickered across Janus' face. He looked up at Sothe. "Back to the North Shore docks, then."

"Wait," Raesinia said, as the oars started to cut the water again. "I have to go back. The others—"

"Think you're dead," Janus interrupted. "Miss Sothe has been good enough to inform me of what happened. Your reappearance now might provoke suspicion, to say the least."

"She has?" Raesinia caught Sothe's eye and got a look that said, *I'll explain later.* She shook her head. "I could . . . think of something. Some miracle. It doesn't matter. I need to—"

"You *do not*," Janus said. "Matters have not proceeded *quite* according to plan, but the result seems satisfactory. Your presence here is no longer necessary."

Who the hell are you to tell me that? Raesinia's brain felt as though it still wasn't functioning properly. *He knows about me, obviously. How? How much has Sothe told him?*

"Besides," Janus continued, "you are urgently required at Ohnlei. The next act of the drama has already begun."

There was a long silence. Raesinia swallowed, tasting blood and river water. There was only one thing *that* could mean.

"My father?"

"I'm very sorry to tell you that the king is dead. Doctor-Professor Indergast did his utmost, but His Majesty's constitution was simply too frail to recover from the surgery, as he had in the past. He passed away in the small hours of the morning."

"I see," Raesinia said. It was news she'd been expecting on a daily basis for months, but it still felt like a steel-gauntleted punch to her gut. *He's dead. He's really . . .* "Is this widely known?"

"Not yet. The duke has been containing the information as best he can. But it will not stay quiet for long."

Raesinia nodded, trying to think. It felt as if her mind were in a fog.

Janus bowed his head, as low as he could. "As a noble of Vordan, as I once swore my loyalty to your father, I now offer it to you. I, Janus bet Vhalnich, the eighth Count Mieran, do swear to serve and protect Queen Raesinia of Vordan, though it means my life."

It was a standard oath, one she'd heard her father accept hundreds of times. Here and now, though, there was a strange solemnity to it, and Raesinia felt a chill that had nothing to do with the breeze or her soaked clothing. *Though it means my life.* It had already meant Ben's, and Faro's, and God knew how many others. *And more, before we're done.*

"You're right." Raesinia shook her head. She saw Maurisk's scowl, Sarton lost in his books, Cora sobbing, Ben gasping out his unrequited love with his last breath. "Back to Ohnlei." *And you are going to have a great deal of explaining to do.*

Thunder rolled overhead. A moment later, the rain began.

PART FOUR

ORLANKO

The grand bishop of the Sworn Church of Vordan was a big, soft man, made bigger by the fantastical crimson robes that hung in complicated folds around him, secured by jeweled clasps and tricks of embroidery. He looked like a flower, Duke Orlanko thought, an enormous, poisonous flower of the sort that grew in southern jungles and smelled of rotten meat. He spoke with a trace of a Murnskai accent, mostly audible in the way he attacked his hard *K*'s as if he meant to spit.

"The cathedral is full to bursting with my frightened flock," he said. "They have fled the rioting, and they bring most terrible, terrible stories. Sworn Churches pulled down, gold plate looted, icons used for firewood. Sworn Priests beaten to death and their corpses abused and hung from lampposts. Gently born women taken in the street like dogs, by gangs of a dozen men or more . . ."

The grand bishop's face was as red as his outfit, and he looked as though he were about to faint. The Borelgai ambassador, Ihannes Pulwer-Monsangton, sweating in his heavy furs, started up in his place. "I, too, have heard these stories. And now we hear that the Vendre itself has fallen, with the captain of Armsmen inside? The archdemagogue Danton and his followers have been freed, and bands of his men roam the city at will."

Orlanko looked around the Cabinet table. Count Torahn looked as though he were in shock, and Rackhil Grieg was staring at Ihannes like a starving man at a side of beef. The chair for State was unoccupied, as always, and in place of the Minister of Justice sat a pudgy man in the green uniform of an Armsman lieutenant, looking very uncomfortable.

It was this last that worried the duke. *Where the hell is Vhalnich?* It was too much to hope that the man had gotten caught up in the rioting and been himself killed, though the captain who'd been taken prisoner at the Vendre had been one of his creatures. *No, he's out there causing trouble.* And Orlanko would need to make his move soon; rumors of the king's death were already spreading, in spite of all his precautions. There were too many servants in the palace for even the Concordat to keep anything quiet for long.

"Before he, uh, left," the lieutenant said, "the captain instructed me to make every effort to secure the cathedral and the eastern half of the Island. We also have men in place on all the North Shore bridges."

"My analysts put the number of rioters at more than twenty *thousand*," Orlanko said, not without a hint of contempt. "If they were to storm the bridges, do you really expect your men to stop them?"

"My men will do their best, Your Grace," the lieutenant said. "Until we receive further instructions from the captain or my lord Mieran."

"No offense to our boys in green," Torahn said, "but the Armsmen are clearly inadequate for this crisis. We must summon the regiments."

Those words hung in the air for a long moment. Orlanko looked around the room—at his fellow Cabinet members, at the two foreigners, and at the small queue of courtiers behind them, waiting to present their grievances. Nearly everyone, he guessed, was thinking the same thing.

It had been nearly a hundred years since royal troops had entered the city, following a tradition upheld through the reign of four kings. The last time, when Farus IV had marched his triumphant legions across the Old Ford, had been the beginning of a civil war and the Great Purge. Every one of the carefully tended family trees in the room had branches that had been pruned during those tumultuous years, great-uncles and cousins who had died on one side or the other, or were simply caught in between. And there were more ancient families that had been extinguished by the vengeful king for their insurrection, including four of the five great ducal lines dating back before the time of Karis.

All but Orlanko's, who'd chosen the right side. One by one, every face in the room turned to him. The Last Duke cleared his throat.

"Do you think," he said carefully, "troops could arrive in time?"

Torahn nodded emphatically. "I smelled something in the wind when all this started, so I sent to the camp at Midvale to be ready to march on three hours' notice. That's a good forty miles from here, but the post can get there in a day's ride. There's a good road all the way. If I put a messenger on a horse within the hour, we can have eight hundred cuirassiers here by tomorrow evening, and six thousand infantry a day or two after that. Three at most, if the damned rain keeps up."

Ihannes caught Orlanko's gaze. "Eight hundred heavy horses would go a long way toward assuring His Supremely Honorable Majesty that the Vordanai Crown intends to do what is necessary to safeguard Borelgai interests."

There were mutterings of assent from the courtiers.

"It would be a momentous step," Orlanko said. "But if the sacrifice of our brave captain of Armsmen has accomplished nothing else, it has alerted us to the gravity of the situation. And yet . . ." He paused, as though consulting a mental document. "Only the king or a regent can order the Royal Army into action, I seem to recall?"

"If the king could speak," Torahn said, "he would tell us not to let the particulars of the law bind us at such a crucial moment."

"On the contrary," Orlanko said. "It is at such moments the niceties must be precisely observed, lest any hint of illegality taint our actions. Remember, my lord, we will be judged by history."

Another silence. Orlanko scrupulously did not look at Rackhil Grieg, who had been briefed at length in the Cobweb for just this moment. He would heal, eventually, but the duke trusted he would not forget again where his interest lay. And, indeed, he spoke up right on cue.

"The answer seems simple enough, my lords," Grieg said. "The king is incapacitated, and the princess has taken to her rooms. The Cabinet must propose a regent for the duration of the emergency. I nominate His Grace the duke."

Torahn shot Grieg a sharp look, then turned slowly to Orlanko. "A regency?"

"It honestly had not occurred to me," Orlanko drawled. "But if the Cabinet requires it, I shall of course be pleased to serve in that capacity, until the king recovers from his illness, or—"

"The king is dead," came a voice from the back of the room, among the crowd of courtiers.

Amid the sudden explosion of whispering, a wedge of green uniforms became visible, pushing their way through the crowd. Orlanko got to his feet, though with his small stature this did not assist him much.

"What's going on?" he said, loud enough to be heard over the growing babble. "Who's that?"

"Make way," bawled an Armsmen sergeant. "Make way for the Minister of Justice!"

Vhalnich. Orlanko forced a smile onto his face and sat back down. *Damn him. I should have been warned.* Concordat spies were in place all over Ohnlei, with instructions to report his movements, but apparently the man had evaded them somehow. His own Mierantai guard had established a cordon around his residence, and the backcountry soldiers had proven to be both competent and irritatingly unbribable.

Inside the flying wedge of Armsmen, Vhalnich walked beside another man, stoop-shouldered and fragile-looking. Orlanko's breath caught as he recognized Doctor-Professor Indergast. *How the hell did he get out of the king's bedchamber?*

"My lord Mieran," Orlanko said aloud. "I'm glad you could join us."

"I'm sorry to be late," Vhalnich said. "As you can imagine, the Ministry is in a bit of an uproar."

"And you have brought us the good doctor-professor," Orlanko said. "Who, I'm sure—"

"What you said about the king," Torahn snapped, interrupting. "Is it true?"

Indergast bowed his head, and the room went quiet as he spoke, everyone straining to hear the quavering words.

"It is. My lords, Your Grace, I regret to say that my skills have failed His Majesty in his last trial. I was able to remove the diseased mass, but the loss of blood and other strains overcame him. He is with the Savior now, until the end of time."

"I see," Orlanko said. He matched gazes with Vhalnich, whose wide gray eyes reflected the duke's spectacle-obscured stare. "The nation will mourn."

"It does not change the point at hand," said Torahn.

"Which is?" Vhalnich said, settling into his chair after helping the doctor-professor to a stool.

"We must have troops to put down the riots," the Minister of War said. "For that, we require a regent. The Minister of Finance has proposed His Grace the duke. Do you have any objection?"

"I am confused," Vhalnich said. "The king is dead, but we now have a queen, who is of age to rule in her own right. What need for a regent?"

"The princess," Orlanko said, "that is, the princess who was, and the queen who is, is clearly overcome by grief and the terrors of the moment. She has confined herself to her room these past three days. In time, perhaps, she will grow into her responsibilities, but for the moment—"

Vhalnich cut him off with a wave. The queue of courtiers was parting, of their own accord this time, like the bow wave preceding a ship. Leather creaked and silk rustled as they bowed.

Damn, damn, damn *Vhalnich! He planned this from the start.* Orlanko, no stranger to political theater, recognized the hand of an expert. None of it should have been possible, of course. *If the princess left her rooms, I should have been alerted immediately.* But he'd clearly underestimated Vhalnich's influence.

The duke forced a grave expression onto his face and sat calmly as a quartet of Noreldrai Grays trooped into the room and took up stations beside the door. For now, he had to ride out this farce.

Raesinia seemed even smaller and frailer than usual, swaddled in a tissue of gray silk and black lace, with fringes of pearls that clacked rhythmically as she walked. She was doing her best to look the queen, but her young appearance betrayed her.

He suppressed a smile. *Go ahead and put on your play. Let's not forget who has the upper hand here.* The people of Vordan would not long tolerate a queen who had made congress with a demon, and it would not be hard to arrange a public demonstration, should it become necessary.

"Orlanko," she said, with a nod. "Ministers. Honored guests. It is painful that we must interrupt this time of mourning with affairs of state, but the crisis will brook no delay."

"Indeed, Your Majesty." Orlanko inclined his head. "We were just discussing what measures to take. Count Torahn had offered the army's assistance in suppressing the rebellion."

"No." The single word rang out clearly, and a silence fell across the whispering courtiers.

Count Torahn cleared his throat. "With all due respect, Your Majesty, I believe there is no other way to restore order."

"Vordan City has gone four generations without feeling the tread of a soldier's boot," Raesinia said curtly. "I would not have the first act of my reign be to break that honored compact."

"Besides which," Vhalnich murmured, "the Royal Army is, by and large, recruited from the same unfortunates who have taken to the streets. Who's to say they would not simply join the mob?"

Torahn shot to his feet. "The loyalty of my soldiers is not in question! And as an officer yourself, you should be ashamed to make such an assertion—"

"Please." Raesinia raised a hand. "What Count Mieran meant was only this. These are not foreigners in the streets, or heretics, or even rebels. They are good citizens of Vordan, with legitimate grievances. Any man might hesitate to stand against them, without any implications to his loyalty to the Crown."

"They are a weak-willed mob," Grieg said, "in the sway of a demagogue."

"And what are their demands?" Raesinia said.

Vhalnich made a show of consulting a paper he took from his pocket. "To convene the Deputies-General to discuss the problems afflicting the nation."

"A call for the august body that conferred the crown on my respected ancestor in the first place can hardly be treason," Raesinia said. "I am inclined to grant their request. That will resolve the problem without the need for troops."

"Apologies, Your Majesty, but it will not," Torahn said. He was sweating. "The deputies of Farus the Great's time were the nobles and lords of the land, men who understood the order of things. Any body convened from this *rabble* will only impose impossible demands on the Crown, demands that will be all the harder to refuse once given royal sanction—"

Orlanko got to his feet. "Your Majesty. If you'll excuse me, I must attend to the latest reports from the Ministry."

"Of course," Raesinia said. She didn't take her eyes from Torahn, but Vhalnich met Orlanko's gaze. A smile flickered across the Minister of Justice's face, just for an instant.

It wasn't until he was back in the safe, well-ordered domain of the Cobweb that the duke once again began to feel secure.

Torahn might bluster and argue, but he would ultimately do nothing. And the princess—the *queen*—had obviously planned the whole affair with Vhalnich from the beginning. Orlanko had no illusions about what the "demands" of the Deputies-General would be. The mob was already tearing down Sworn Churches and hanging Borelgai from the lampposts, and who was more closely associated with the Borels and the Sworn Church than the despised Last Duke and his vicious Concordat?

It was a power play, nothing more and nothing less. Either Raesinia was smarter than he'd given her credit for, or else she was completely in Vhalnich's pocket. Whichever it was, the two of them planned to use the backing of the mob to push him out of the Cabinet and away from the throne.

Vhalnich. It has to be Vhalnich. Orlanko's fall might mean war with the Borelgai, a war Vordan could not hope to win, but such a sacrifice of life would not trouble a man like the Minister of Justice.

A thought struck him. Could Vhalnich himself bear a demon? The Pontifex of the Black had implied as much, in their last communication. At the time Orlanko had thought it unlikely. But if he really had found the Thousand Names, and invited one of the horrors into his own body . . .

Orlanko shook his head and clumped through the corridors, ignoring the passing analysts who scurried out of his way. He was breathing hard by the time he pushed open the door to his office and clambered up behind his desk. Once there, he slammed his hand on one of the little buttons, causing a distant bell to dance and jangle.

Contingencies, contingencies. Vhalnich wasn't the only one who held hidden cards.

The door clicked open, and Andreas entered noiselessly, dark coat flaring behind him like a living shadow.

"How the *hell* did Vhalnich get to the Cabinet room without my being informed he was even on the grounds?"

"We're investigating now, sir. It appears a number of our agents are in his custody."

"What?"

"His Mierantai guard rounded up our watchers and confined them in his cottage. It was quite a well-planned operation. No word escaped until we sent more men to investigate."

Orlanko glowered at Andreas, who took it stolidly.

"Of course, sir, it means that our communications have been compromised. He knew precisely who was assigned to him."

"I know, damn it." Heads would roll for that. The pasty-faced analysts who lived in the depths of the Cobweb and copied out books of numbers all day long had assured him that their codes were unbreakable. *We'll see how unbreakable they are.* But that would have to wait. "He's stolen a march on us, and we can't afford to play catch-up. I want you to call up the Special Branch."

If there was any emotion under the serene mask, it didn't show. Andreas bowed. "Of course, sir."

Orlanko made a face, as though he'd eaten something unpleasant, and stared at his pet killer. He sighed. "All right. Now we'll do things your way."

IONKOVO

A single candle flickered on the other side of the room, casting a dim glow across the windowless cell. The bars were outlined on the opposite wall, a striped pattern that danced and shivered on the rough stone surface.

Adam Ionkovo, lying on the scratchy straw-stuffed pallet, stared at the ceiling and let out a sigh.

He'd had high hopes for Captain d'Ivoire. But . . . no. Even a couple of conversations had shown him to be the kind of man whose blind, bulldog loyalty was impervious to reason. Neither bribes nor threats of eternal damnation would pry him loose from Vhalnich, not now. The bond between men who had fought together could tie them closer than lovers.

Did you get anything out of him, Jen? He was fairly certain his companion was dead. She bore an archdemon, after all. If she was alive, nothing could have stopped her from completing her mission. *But it's* how *she died that matters. Did Vhalnich find the Thousand Names? What powers has he unearthed?*

Oh well. If d'Ivoire wasn't going to talk, then it was pointless to remain here any longer. It was past time he was up and about.

The outer door rattled and opened a fraction. His guard, right on time with the evening meal. *Time to go.*

Ionkovo rolled off the pallet. Just in front of it was a thick, dark shadow cast by the table the candle was sitting on. The transition between light and darkness wavered as the flame shifted, and Ionkovo reached carefully over it to touch the floor where the shadow was constant.

"God save us," he muttered in Elysian. "The Penitent Damned."

The shadow *moved* under his fingers. It grew darker, black as ink, and rippled when he touched it as though his finger had brushed the surface of dark, still water. Ionkovo pushed himself forward just as the guard entered the room, diving into the shadow as easily as a seabird skimming to the ocean.

"The hell?" the guard said. He set the pewter plate bearing Ionkovo's nightly beans and crust of bread on the table and put a hand on his truncheon. "Ionkovo? Are you playing games with me?"

Ionkovo was always surprised at the reluctance of ordinary people to accept the evidence of their own eyes. There was nowhere to hide in the cell; ergo, it should be obvious that he was not in it. But the guard only edged forward cautiously, brow furrowed.

The candle threw the man's shadow on the wall behind him, larger than life. Its surface rippled, silently, and Ionkovo's arm emerged. His fingers curved into a claw, reaching for the Armsman's neck.

The man gave a strangled gasp as the grip closed, both hands automatically reaching up to pry the grip away from his throat. Ionkovo yanked hard, and the Armsman stumbled backward a step, then another. Then one more step, through where the wall ought to have been, and he fell into his own rippling shadow. The dark silhouette remained for a moment longer, then faded silently away.

Ionkovo released the guard and let him fall, screaming, into the endless void that was the no-place between the shadows. He pulled himself back out into the real world, out in the corridor, and let out a long breath.

There were no doubt a number of locked doors between him and the outside world. But it was the middle of the night, and most of the lamps were dark. The Guardhouse crawled with shadows.

Chapter Sixteen

WINTER

The halls under the Vendre were dark and nearly silent. Up above, the courtyard was ablaze with lanterns and torches, as the celebrations which had been put briefly on hold by the daylong rain got back under way. Down here, no one had been relighting the candles as they flickered out, and the roar of humanity outside was reduced to a faint buzz.

All the cells but one were empty. There had been some argument over this—in addition to seditious printers and disloyal merchants, the prison had held plenty of ordinary thieves, housebreakers, smugglers, and other scoundrels. In the end, though, there had been no way to tell them apart, so the newly enlarged council had voted to throw all the doors open.

Winter led the way toward that last cell, marked by the single lantern that hung in front of it. Abby, padding behind her, carried their own lantern, and raised it in greeting to the guard on duty. "Guard," in this case, was a generous term; it was one of Jane's Leatherbacks, a pimply girl of fifteen, who went goggle-eyed when she recognized her two visitors.

"Uh . . . ," she said, looking from Winter to Abby and back again. "Is something going on?"

"Jane wants them," Winter said, hooking a finger at the cell and trying to look casual.

"Of course!" She blinked. "I mean . . . nobody told me . . ."

Abby leaned closer. "Principa. *I'm* telling you, all right?"

"Right." The girl swallowed. "Let me get the door open."

They waited while Principa fumbled with the key and dragged the cell open with a screech of rusty iron. The cells up here were clean, Winter noticed, and lacked the sludgy pools of standing water of the makeshift pens on the lower level. *I suppose Orlanko believes in keeping a tidy dungeon.*

The two men who emerged both wore Armsmen green, though their uniforms were somewhat the worse for wear after the long siege. They stood blinking in the lantern light. Abby raised an eyebrow, glanced at Principa, and beckoned, and the men shuffled silently past her and back toward the stairs.

"Um . . . ," the guard said, standing in front of the now-empty cell. "What about me?"

"Stay here," Winter said. "I'll come and fetch you directly."

"Make sure Jane doesn't punish her," Winter said, once they were out of earshot.

"I'd punish her," said Giforte, "if she were in one of my prisons. Everyone knows you don't release a prisoner without written authorization, and never without a signature. That way everyone knows who'll catch hell if someone goes missing."

Abby laughed and touched her father's arm. "We'll have to bring you in to train all our jailers."

"Is this a prison break, then?" said Captain d'Ivoire. "Or has the council decided something?"

"The council can't decide what to have for breakfast," Winter said. "Jane feels you two would be safer elsewhere."

"She can't exactly let you walk out into the mob," Abby said. "They're ready to throw stones at anything in green."

Giforte winced. "What about the rest of my men?"

"Most of them have already gone home," Abby said. "The rest changed out of their uniforms and joined up with the riot."

"Danton has that effect on people, apparently," Winter muttered.

"In any event," Abby said, "it would be better for all concerned if you . . . slipped away. We've got a boat waiting down below."

Giforte frowned but said nothing. They walked in silence for a while, down the spiraling central staircase and past the landing where Winter and Cyte had fought the night before. The light of the lantern showed wide brown splotches on the stones, and Winter's gorge rose.

When they reached the bottom level, the gentle lap of water at the little dock became audible. Captain d'Ivoire stopped suddenly and caught Winter's eye.

"I think," he said, "we should give the two of them a moment alone."

Winter looked at Abby, who shrugged. She and Giforte continued on a short distance, while Winter and Marcus retreated to the stairwell. There was only one lantern, which faded to an almost invisible glow as soon as the other pair had gone around a corner. Winter put her back to the cold stone wall and waited. The captain was only the vaguest of shadows.

Shit. She'd known this was a bad idea. He hadn't recognized her the night of the raid, but since then he'd had plenty of time to think it over. *I should have sent someone else. Stupid, stupid—*

"Ihernglass," Marcus whispered. "It is you, isn't it?"

And there it was, stark as a skull. She took a deep breath. *What the hell do I do now?*

"I knew the colonel sent you on some secret mission," he continued, "but I hadn't imagined it would be anything like *this.* I don't want to blow your cover, so we don't have long."

Winter let her breath out and blinked. This was not how she'd imagined this conversation going. *If he tells me that he's always known I was a girl, I swear to God I'm going to scream.*

"I just thought," Marcus went on, oblivious of Winter's expression in the darkness, "that this might be a good opportunity. If there's anything you want to pass along to the colonel, I mean. It can't be easy to get messages to him."

There was a long pause. Eventually Winter shook her head, realized he couldn't see it, and said, "No message in particular. Just tell him what happened here, and make sure he knows I'm all right. I'll be here with Jane if he wants me."

"Right. I can't speak for the colonel, but you can take it from me you're doing a hell of a job." Marcus sighed. "Better than me, certainly. He sent me to guard a prison and I end up locked inside it. Twice."

"I think we made the best of a bad situation," Winter said. "And thank you. Sir."

Marcus' shadow nodded. "I know it can't be easy, even if being with Jane's lot means you get to wear trousers."

Winter paused, then ventured, "Sir?"

"Passing for female. Damned convincing. You'd have fooled me for certain, if I hadn't known better."

There was another long silence, this time while Winter tried desperately to fight down a spasm of mad laughter that seemed determined to burrow its way out from her lungs. She'd almost lost the battle when a frustrated shout from down the corridor brought their heads around.

"I think we've left them alone for long enough," Marcus said. "Come on, before they kill one another."

"Did you know about Abby and the vice captain?" Winter said. She covered her mouth; the laughter had transformed into hiccups. "Her being his daughter, I mean."

"I hadn't the faintest," Marcus said. "But he filled me in while we were in the cell. Apparently they don't get along."

"I will *not*." Abby's voice came to them at a volume usually reserved for opera sopranos playing to a full house. "Will you get in the damned boat?"

"That may have been understatement on his part," Marcus said.

As it turned out, no intervention was necessary. Abby stalked past them, lantern in hand, sending wildly swinging shadows up the walls of the corridor. She rounded the corner and, to judge by the light, stayed there. Winter and Marcus glanced at each other and continued on to the dock, where Giforte was already sitting in the little two-man rowboat.

"Let's get out of here," the vice captain muttered. He caught Winter's eye as Marcus carefully stepped from the dock, making the little craft sway alarmingly. "Please try to take care of her?"

"I'll do my best," Winter said. "Don't worry. Jane takes good care of all her people."

Giforte nodded, reluctantly, and took hold of the oars. Once Marcus had settled himself, Winter undid the line, and the little boat splashed and bumped its way out into the tunnel, bound for the friendlier docks on the North Shore.

Abby was waiting in the corridor, just out of sight of the dock. It was hard to tell in the bad light, but it looked as though she had been crying.

"Are you all right?" Winter said.

"Just furious." Abby dragged a hand across her face. "He always makes me that way."

"What did he want?"

"To go back with him, of course." She waved a hand. "It was all well and good my slumming it for a while—that's what he says *now*, though at the time he threatened to disown me—but things are getting *dangerous*. So I need to come home and be locked in a tower behind barred windows."

"I'm not sure I blame him," Winter said. "If I had a daughter, I don't think I'd want her out here. Hell, I'm not sure I want to be here myself, sometimes."

"He's a thickheaded old fossil," Abby said. "And I told him so. If anyone should be locked away, it's him. At his age he should be sitting behind a desk signing papers, not trying to hold a fortress wall against the notorious Mad Jane and her mob—what?"

Winter had started to chuckle, mixed with the occasional hiccup. She shook her head until she got control of herself again.

"Nothing," she said. "I'm in a strange mood, that's all."

"Come on," Abby said. "I need a drink."

Now, Winter reflected as they climbed the stairs, *I'm a girl pretending to be a boy pretending to be a girl. At least as far as Marcus is concerned.* Just the thought made her giggle. Janus probably planned it this way. She still hadn't figured out why he'd put her with Jane in the first place, unless it was purely to fulfill the request she'd made to him on the shores of Khandar. *I very much doubt that.* Not that Janus wasn't the sort of man to keep his promises, but she was certain he would find a way to arrange matters so that he himself derived some benefit. *I suppose I'm just too simple to see it. Though it would help if I knew what he wanted.*

On the first floor, they became aware of a new sound. At first Winter thought there had been some new attack, and that a melee was in progress. The crowd that occupied the Vendre courtyard had erupted, all at once, in a single vast roar that seemed to shake the castle to its foundations.

"What the hell is going on now?" Abby said.

"I have no idea," Winter said. "Let's find out."

No one ever claimed to have been the one who first delivered the tidings from Ohnlei, as if rumor had broken free of human constraints and flown free on shadowy wings.

Any story repeated so often was bound to be warped and distorted by the time it reached the end of the line, and a thousand lesser rumors swarmed in the wake of the great news. On two things, however, all the stories agreed. King Farus Orboan VIII was dead, and Queen Raesinia Orboan had assumed the crown. And, practically as her first act, she had called for the convocation of the Deputies-General to be held in the Sworn Cathedral.

Beyond that, the stories broke down, depending on whether the teller tended toward manic cheer or black pessimism. That night, there seemed to be no middle ground. No one could agree on what the Last Duke was doing, but everyone was happy to say what they'd heard: Orlanko was dead, killed by Count Torahn in single combat when he'd challenged the queen. Orlanko was locked in his own cells, where he'd killed himself in shame, or was being tortured with his own implements. He was gone, fled to his country estates, or had left the country entirely, to live like a prince on his ill-gotten gains in Hamvelt or Viadre.

Or he was gone, all right, but only as far as the nearest Royal Army base, to return with troops who would crush the upstart queen and her backers. Worse—they weren't even Vordanai troops, but an army of Borelgai mercenaries on the northern border and Hamveltai levies in the east, ready to break Vordan between them as they'd done in the War of the Princes. The legions of Murnsk were on the march, the uncounted horde of the holy emperor ready to destroy the Free Church stronghold once and for all.

Winter heard all these versions, and more besides. The queen had agreed to stand for election. The queen would marry Vhalnich, hero of Khandar, and give Vordan a new king. Prince Dominic had spent all the years since Vansfeldt pretending to be dead, but now he had returned to lead his people. The deputies would force the Borelgai profiteers and speculators to give up their villainous ways, and bread would be an eagle a loaf once again.

In the wake of the news came the crowds. The queen's pronouncement had turned the riot on its head; instead of thieves and murderers, the rioters were heroes who had taken the law into their own hands after sinister interests had tried to exploit the weakness of the dying king. People who hours earlier had been barring their doors and hiding the silver now flooded into the street themselves. Half the population of the South Bank seemed to be out, in spite of the late hour, and so many people tried to join the celebration on the Island that they ended up backed up onto the Grand Span. Before long the bridge was bright with bonfires and packed from edge to edge with shouting, happy people.

The Vendre itself remained under the control of the council, guarded by the Leatherbacks and others Jane thought she could trust not to run off and join the parties. It seemed oddly quiet compared to the roar from outside, like a cemetery in the middle of a bustling city. With her errand completed, Winter did not quite know what to do with herself. In spite of her exhaustion, there was no question of sleep, not until the celebration burned itself out. She went in search of Jane, and found her closeted with the council and some of the students from the Dregs. Winter settled for catching Jane's eye and giving her a little wave to indicate the prisoners were free, then wandered back downstairs.

The Vendre's main door was half-open, with a couple of Docksiders keeping watch. One of the pair recognized her and stood at attention, or at least a reasonable parody thereof. Winter almost burst out laughing again, but she bit it back and snapped a textbook salute before slipping out into the courtyard.

If there had been a carnival atmosphere before, things were now positively ebullient. One reason for this quickly became obvious: Now that the fighting was done, Vordan's merchants and vendors were taking up the challenge of supplying the crowd with all the food, and more important, all the drink, that it might be require. Bottles were everywhere, passing freely from hand to hand, and as she watched, a man pulling a handcart loaded with wine was mobbed by customers and relieved of his burden in a few minutes. He turned the cart around, pockets jingling with coin, and headed back for another load.

It seemed as though the entire city had decided to drink itself into an oblivious stupor. In the courtyard, some of Jane's Leatherbacks had formed a circle and were playing some kind of game, which involved a repeating chant and frequent pulls from any of several circulating bottles. Some of the girls, Winter thought, were too young for that sort of thing, but she was hardly in a position to complain. She spotted Cyte among them, dark makeup finally washed away, looking relaxed and comfortable and roaring with laughter. When she saw Winter, she beckoned her over, but Winter only shook her head and pointed out the gate, as though she had somewhere to go.

The street outside was a continuation of the same madness. Portable stoves had been hauled in, or improvised from boxes and wooden scraps, and a dozen enterprising vendors were hawking hot meals. It was far too loud for any shouts to be heard more than a few feet away, so they stood on boxes and raised what they had for sale above the heads of the crowd.

It reminded Winter of the markets of Ashe-Katarion. There she'd tasted roasted *imhallyt* beetle on the half shell (bitter and gooey), fried *dhakar* (a kind of centipede, spiced and crunchy) along with thick black bread, cornmeal cakes flavored with honey, and every conceivable product that could be made from any part of a dead sheep. The thought made her stomach rumble, but what was on offer felt strangely alien. Staring at the steaming sugar chestnuts, pork buns, and sizzling bacon sandwiches, she felt a pang of homesickness. Not for Ashe-Katarion, exactly, but for the camp outside it, for stale crackers and "army stew."

She felt as though she had spent half her life as a stranger among a strange people, only to return to the city of her birth and find herself a stranger there as well. In the middle of the jubilant crowd, Winter felt more alone than she had since . . .

Since Fort Valor. Since Captain d'Ivoire made me a sergeant, and I met Bobby and the others. She'd been alone before that, of course, when she wasn't being tormented by Davis and his thugs, but she hadn't really believed there was any other way she *could* be. The Seventh Company had changed that. But Bobby, Feor, and the others were still at sea, far away from here.

She suddenly wanted very badly to run back into the Vendre, pull Jane out of her meeting, and stay wrapped in her arms until the tumult in her head settled down. When she was with Jane, everything was simple.

Don't be silly, she instructed herself, sternly. Jane had been forced into quasi-leadership of this weird, leaderless coalition, and the last thing she needed was for Winter to have a breakdown and demand comfort. *There'll be time for that later.* She marched over to the closest vendor and bought a paper bag of sugar chestnuts, inhaling the sweet steam and popping one into her mouth as soon as they were cool enough to stand. It was crunchy and sweet, and she had to admit that as a snack it was an improvement on centipedes.

A large group had gathered in one of the nearby squares, and Winter drifted in that direction out of curiosity. She couldn't get close enough to get a view, but it sounded as though someone was giving a speech, and when she managed to catch a few words she realized it was Danton.

"The fourth duty of a citizen," he was saying, "is to at all times keep in mind the condition of the implements of labor given into his care—the land and its improvements, the seed stock and herds, the tools of his trade, and everything else that tends to the increase of his prosperity. It is his duty to his country to maintain and improve these tools, both for the sake of his own descendents and so that the nation as a whole shall progress toward a greater prosperity in accordance with God's design. However, this duty shall not conflict with the first, second, or third duties, and a citizen shall not . . ."

There was more in that vein, a great deal more. Winter wasn't sure she could have struggled through more than a page if it had been laid out in text. In Danton's great, booming voice, it had a certain ring to it, but it was still not exactly passionate stuff. And yet the crowd all around Winter showed every sign of being enthralled, standing in total silence so as not to miss a word of the great man's explanation of why, for example, potatoes were a superior crop to turnips and encouraging their growth was in the national interest.

Probably at this point he could be reading out of a dictionary and people would stand at rapt attention. Danton was certainly *capable* of a good turn of phrase—his speech to the prisoners on the night the Vendre had fallen had been stirring, even to Winter—but he clearly had not exerted his rhetorical talents here. She wondered idly which was the real Danton, the man of action beloved by the crowd or this intellectual with his obsession with potatoes.

Something tingled at the base of her spine. The Infernivore was restless, like an anxious child rolling over in its sleep. Ever since her near contact with Raesinia had roused the thing, she'd been more aware of its moods. Danton, apparently, made it nervous, and Winter slipped away from the crowd and back toward the prison.

Raesinia. Winter had wanted to get a message to Janus about her, telling him about the Infernivore's strange reaction, but the girl had been assassinated before she had a chance. According to those who'd been on the parapet, she'd been shot in the head by a Concordat spy, who had subsequently fallen to his own demise on the rocks below. After what she'd seen from Jen Alhundt in the Desoltai temple, Winter wondered if there wasn't more to it than that. *If Raesinia really was some kind of wild talent, maybe the Black Priests sent someone to eliminate her.* She decided she would have to tell Janus after all, if they ever had the chance to meet in private.

Behind her, Danton droned on. Ahead were the walls of the Vendre, where Jane would still be engaged in oh-so-important business. In between, the street was full of happy people, drinking toasts, singing traditional café songs, and even gathering round for impromptu dances. Someone had hauled out a fiddle and was playing it with more enthusiasm than skill, which suited the caliber of the singers perfectly.

Winter popped the last of the chestnuts into her mouth, balled up the bag, and wandered.

RAESINIA

At the door of Lady Farnese's Cottage, now surrounded by Janus' red-and-blue-uniformed guardsmen, Raesinia turned to address the small horde of servants and courtiers who had followed her from the palace proper. She took a deep breath, or tried to. The mourning dress was simple by court standards, but still uncomfortably stiff.

"I need to speak to Count Mieran on a number of important matters," she said. "I must ask you all to excuse me."

She jerked her head at Sothe, who stepped up to her side. Janus opened the front door, and a cordon of Mierantai stepped between the new queen and her followers. A babble of protest rose immediately, and Raesinia turned again.

"My lords, please. There will be time later for formalities, but the affairs of state will not wait. I thank you all for your concern."

Once she was inside, with the door shut behind her, she let out a sigh. *Is the rest of my life going to be like this?* It seemed depressingly likely.

"I'm sorry to impose on Your Majesty by asking you to come here," Janus said. "But I imagine you are no more eager to have our conversation reported to His Grace than I am."

"You think we're safe here?" Raesinia looked around. No guards or servants were in evidence, but that didn't mean much. Ohnlei was a labyrinth full of hidden doors and back corridors, ideal for eavesdroppers.

"As safe as I can make us," Janus said. "Miss Sothe has looked over my arrangements."

Sothe nodded. "Unless Orlanko has gotten a lot smarter since I left, I think we should be secure."

"Good." Raesinia paused for a moment, gathering her thoughts. "Then how about the two of you tell me *what the hell is going on*?" She glared at Sothe. "You never mentioned a *word* about knowing Count Mieran."

She was surprised how much that stung. Sothe was the one person Raesinia had placed her full trust in, unreservedly, and finding out that she'd been keeping secrets hurt badly. *I should have expected it, though.* Sothe came from a world of secrets.

"I assure you," Janus said, "our acquaintance is recent. After I heard about your . . . fall, I contacted her to offer my assistance."

"Then you knew—" Raesinia blinked. *Everything.* "How?"

"It would be best," Janus said, "if I began at the beginning. Please, have a seat."

He gestured. They were in the cottage hall, and beyond was an entertaining room with a sofa and chairs. Raesinia followed the count's gesture and sat down, carefully, on the sofa, the black dress folding and crinkling around her. Janus took the chair opposite, and Sothe remained standing.

"I would offer some refreshment, after what has been a very long night," he said. "But in Your Majesty's case, I gather that there would not be much point, and in any event I have banished the servants so we may speak in secrecy even from my own people."

Raesinia gave a curt nod. "Thank you. Now—"

"What the hell is going on?" Janus leaned back and smiled, just for a moment. "A fair question. For the sake of brevity, I will leave aside my own history and simply state that I am a scholar of the arcane and the occult. The dark arts, as some would have it. Demonology. Magic."

"That's a dangerous line of work," Raesinia said, determined not to let any surprise show on her face.

"Indeed. There are places where it flourishes, however. In the eastern League cities, chiefly, where the grip of Elysium is at its weakest. It was there that I went to further my studies, and it was there, three years ago, that your father's agents found me."

"My *father's* agents? Do you mean the Concordat?"

"Emphatically not. While the duke was, of course, a part of His Majesty's government, in this matter the king and the Minister of Information had . . . differing views. The man who contacted me had been well paid, through a very indirect route, to seek out someone with knowledge of the arcane arts and bring them before the king. Enormous precautions were taken to ensure that the Last Duke remained in ignorance."

"Why? What would my father want with a magician?" As far as Raesinia knew, her father had never believed in magic, like any sensible person of the modern age. If not for her own unique experiences, Raesinia doubted she would have believed in it, either.

"His Majesty wished to consult me on a very delicate matter." Janus coughed. "Not to put too fine a point on it, but he wanted to talk about you."

"About *me*? That doesn't make—" Raesinia shook her head, then froze. Her voice came out as a whisper. "He *knew*?"

"He did."

Raesinia's chest felt tight, as though the black dress had suddenly shrunk several sizes. *He knew.*

She had always been afraid of what would happen, should her father find out the truth of what had happened to her. She'd even constructed scenes in her mind, usually in the dead of night when her inability to sleep grated the worst. She pictured him having her dragged away in chains, to be imprisoned in some dark oubliette. Even executed, if he could figure out how. Burned at the stake. *After all, his daughter is dead. I'm something else. A demon.*

She swallowed hard. "He wanted you to . . . get rid of me?"

Janus shook his head. "He wanted a . . . cure, for lack of a better word. A way to reverse what Orlanko had done to you. In such a way that you remained alive afterward, of course."

Raesinia felt tears sting her eyes. She let her head fall forward into her hands, elbows on her knees.

He knew. She didn't want to sob in front of Janus. That was easy enough; she just stopped breathing. *He knew all along, and he wanted to help me. Oh God. Father. I thought . . . how could I have thought . . .*

He tried to tell me. "Count Mieran is more than he seems. You'll need all the allies you can get." He couldn't come out and say it, not with Concordat spies everywhere, but now the meaning was clear. *Oh, Father . . .*

"Your Majesty," Janus said, after a long silence. "If you like, perhaps we could—"

Raesinia squeezed her eyes shut, banishing the tears, and sucked in a long breath. The binding tingled across her, repairing the damage from her brief asphyxiation. She raised her head. "My apologies. Please continue."

Janus regarded her carefully for a moment, then nodded. "As you say. For some time, His Majesty and I carried on a correspondence, and I regret to say I was not able to be of much assistance. The Priests of the Black have been astonishingly effective at removing all traces of magic wherever their writ runs, and what remains is a pitiful remnant of what was once known. If the knowledge to do what His Majesty wanted existed, I told him, it was locked in the dungeons under Elysium." He steepled his fingers. "Then a bit of unexpected news opened up a new possibility."

Raesinia was starting to put the pieces together. "The rebellion in Khandar."

"Indeed. There have always been legends of the Demon King, who fled across the sea with his treasure trove, but nothing concrete. When I discovered that the Black Priests had tried several times to actually retrieve something from Khandar, though, I started to dig deeper. I became convinced that the treasure actually existed. The names—the bindings—of all the creatures captured by the Demon King. The Thousand Names of legend."

"And my father sent you there to find it."

"His Majesty took some convincing, as did his advisers," Janus said, with another flash of a smile. "The duke, for one, was deeply suspicious. But ultimately, yes."

"And?"

"The Names are real. We found them." Janus tossed the statement off, as though it were of no great importance. "By the time we did, however, we received word that the situation here had become critical. So I hurried back as soon as I could, and His Majesty named me to the empty seat on the Cabinet to assist you as best I could. I am honored to say that I believe he had come to trust me."

And will the Names work? Raesinia wanted to scream. Janus caught her expression and gave a little shrug.

"I do not know, yet, whether we'll be able to do anything for your condition. The Names must be deciphered and studied to see if something useful to you is among their powers, and I only had the chance to make a cursory inspection before I left Khandar. Once our current crisis is resolved, I will devote myself to it. But for the moment . . ."

Raesinia nodded. Somewhere deep in her chest, though, something had taken hold. A tiny mote of *hope*, that there might, somehow, be a way out. *Back to a normal life.*

"All right," Raesinia said. "I follow you so far. How did you end up talking to Sothe?"

"There's not much to tell," Janus said. "After your father gave me Justice, I began looking into the disturbances in the city. I got descriptions of all the potential leaders, and once I saw yours it wasn't hard to put the facts together."

There had to be more to it than *that*—the all-knowing Concordat hadn't been able to find her, after all!—but Raesinia didn't care about the details. "And Sothe?"

"Even easier. She's so close to you on the Ohnlei side that it was inconceivable that she not be a party to the deception, though I didn't understand the full extent of her involvement until she told me herself. I sent her a note, indicating what I knew and expressing a desire to help."

"It was waiting for me when I got back to Ohnlei, after you 'died,'" Sothe said. "I was frantic. I had to keep up appearances here, intercept Orlanko's watchers, and figure out how to retrieve you at the same time. When I saw this . . ." She shrugged.

"You just decided to trust him?" Raesinia was surprised. To say that Sothe was not a trusting person was a significant understatement of the facts.

"I went to talk to him," Sothe said, "since he knew the secret. I thought that either he'd end up on our side or I'd have to kill him, and in the latter case I wanted to get it over with."

There was a flash of surprise—not much, but definitely there—on Janus' face. "Well," he said after a moment, "I'm glad I was able to convince you."

"So, what happens now?" Raesinia asked, rubbing her eyes with the heels of her palms.

"I think we're almost through it," Janus said. "The announcement has gone out that you've accepted the Deputies-General, and the mob is ecstatic. When they present their lists of demands, one of them is certain to be a new Minister of Information and the elimination of the Concordat. All we have to do is be 'persuaded.'"

"Just like that?" Raesinia shook her head. "It's too easy."

"He has a fearsome reputation," Janus said. "But I must say he's proven to be only a mediocre opponent. He's badly overplayed his hand, and now he'll have to pay for it."

"He won't give up," Sothe said. "Not Orlanko. If there's a card left in his hand, he'll play it, and be damned to the consequences."

"That's what worries me," Janus agreed. "The Last Duke is finished. But now that he has nothing to lose . . ." He trailed off, staring past Raesinia and Sothe into the middle distance, then shook his head. "We will have to take precautions."

MARCUS

"The vice captain is here," Staff Eisen said from outside the door to Marcus' office.

"Send him in," Marcus said. His desk was clear of paperwork. He looked below it, to make sure the stack of files from the archives were still there. Evidence, in case he needed it.

The door stuck, as usual, then shuddered open. Giforte pulled it shut behind him, turned, and saluted.

"Vice Captain," Marcus said.

"Sir!" Giforte relaxed a fraction. "People have been trickling in, sir. We're still well below strength, but I think by tomorrow morning I should have at least—"

"I have a question for you, Vice Captain," Marcus said. "I want you to answer it honestly, if you can."

"Sir?" Giforte's face became a frozen mask.

He knows, Marcus thought. *He knows that I know.* Time to cut through all the secrets. He took a deep breath. "What is it that Duke Orlanko has over you?"

A long moment passed in total stillness. Marcus kept his eyes on Giforte, watching the man's face. His control was good, but not perfect. *If he tries to brazen it out . . .*

Then, all at once, his expression relaxed and his shoulders slumped. There was defeat there, but also relief, as though a great weight had been lifted.

I was right. Marcus had to restrain himself from pumping his fist in triumph. *I wonder if this is how Janus feels all the time.*

"I should have known I couldn't hide it," Giforte said. "I should have offered my resignation the day you took command."

"Now, *that* would have been a disaster," Marcus said. "It *is* the Last Duke, then?"

Giforte nodded, looking resigned. "He . . . it was my wife, to begin with. You've met my daughter. My wife never really recovered from the birth. Our local surgeons threw up their hands, so I wrote to doctors from Hamvelt, the best there are. One man said he could help, but the price he asked . . ." He shook his head. "I borrowed from a moneylender, but it was all for nothing. My Gwendolyn died before the doctor even arrived, and he refused to refund his fee. I was broken and penniless. I would have killed myself, if not for Abigail."

"And then Orlanko offered to help with the debt," Marcus guessed.

Giforte nodded. "I was too desperate to care what strings were attached. It wasn't long before he started making . . . requests. Certain investigations he wanted stopped, suspects he wanted released without further questions. Your family . . . that was one of the first."

"You didn't know about it beforehand?" Marcus said. "You weren't involved?"

The vice captain drew himself up. "Of course not! You . . ." He paused, and sagged again. "You have no reason to believe me, of course. But I'm not a murderer. I would never have done anything like that, whatever Orlanko told me. All he wanted was . . . no questions." Giforte shook his head. "When I heard you had been named as captain, I came close to panic. None of the other captains ever paid much attention, but you . . ."

Marcus exhaled slowly and leaned back in the squeaky old chair. "I went looking." *Though I might not have, if not for Adam Ionkovo.*

Giforte straightened up again. "Sir. I will draft my letter of resignation immediately. If the Minister of Justice wishes to offer charges, I am at his disposal."

"That won't be necessary."

"Sir?"

"I've been reading up on you," Marcus said. "Your tenure with the Armsmen has been excellent. I don't think there's anyone else I would want for the post."

"But . . ." Giforte swallowed. "What about Orlanko? He holds my debts. If he comes calling, and I don't obey—"

"The Minister of Justice will handle your debts," Marcus said. They hadn't discussed any such thing, but he was certain Janus would come up with a good solution. *This is too good a man to lose.* "And I don't think the Last Duke will be a problem for much longer. In confidence, I can tell you that the new queen is not a friend of his."

"She's going to unseat him? The Last Duke?" Giforte shook his head. "That's going to mean plenty of trouble. He's had three decades to dig in."

"That's why I need you," Marcus said. "We've got to get the Armsmen back together and providing some kind of order. And I suspect the Minister of Justice may have need of me, so a lot of that work is going to fall on you. I trust you'll be up to it."

Slowly, Giforte saluted, fighting a smile. "Sir. Absolutely, sir."

"Good. You'd better get to it."

And once this is over, Marcus thought, as Giforte saluted again and departed, *once the Last Duke has fallen, I'm going to dig through the Cobweb until I find the truth. And then he's going to pay for it.*

WINTER

The sun was lighting the eastern horizon by the time Winter returned to the fortress, at least half-drunk and feeling more maudlin than ever. She'd fallen in with a mixed band of Docksiders and University students, who were passing several bottles of middling-to-awful wine around a circle and debating the significance of the fact that the deputies had been summoned to the Sworn Cathedral. One faction held this to be a bad sign, indicating that the queen intended to continue Orlanko's policy of accommodation of the Sworn Church. Another group thought that it was a deliberate gesture in the opposite direction, a statement that the business of the Vordanai state was to be placed above the rights of Elysium and foreigners in general. Winter hadn't taken a side, and limited her participation to a couple of swallows whenever a bottle went past. They hadn't resolved the issue by the time she took her leave, and she suspected they'd be there until everyone involved had fallen out into a drunken stupor.

A mix of exhaustion and alcohol had Winter on the verge of that herself, and her steps were heavy as she dragged herself through the Vendre's courtyard and back to the big, half-open doors. She carried a sealed bottle in one hand, a present for Jane, who hadn't gotten the opportunity to get out and enjoy herself. The only question, Winter thought muzzily, was whether she would manage to deliver it before she collapsed into some corner. The chamber Jane had taken over had a bed, she seemed to recall. *That would be . . . convenient.*

She was vaguely aware of passing Leatherback guards, at the main doors and again on the stairs, but they all let her through with a wave. Winter answered with a cheery lift of her bottle, trudging up to the floor where the old prison staff had had their quarters and where Jane had made her own accommodations. At the top of the steps, she took a moment to compose herself, standing where a cool breeze came in by a gun slit and trying to shake the muzziness from her head.

Maybe I should just go to bed, and find Jane in the morning. She wasn't *that* drunk, but alcohol had formed a dangerous cocktail with the aftermath of too many nights without sleep and the loneliness of being by herself in the midst of the citywide revel. She felt fragile, on edge, and suspected the sight of Jane might bring her to tears. *I'll feel better in the morning.*

Good sense warred for a moment with sentimentality, but sentimentality gained the upper hand. Winter shook her head, feeling the world reel slightly. *I'll just see how she's doing. Jane's been up all night, too. She might need someone to . . . talk to.*

The door to Jane's room stood a few inches open, but there was no sound of conversation from inside. The council had apparently departed. *Hell,* Winter thought suddenly. *She's probably asleep by now. I'll just poke my head in and check on her.*

Wood creaked, and Winter froze, just beside the doorway. Something scraped against the floor, as though someone had pushed a chair. Listening closely, below the fading roar of the now-exhausted crowd outside, she could make out soft, quiet sounds. Quick breaths, the rustle of cloth, a faint sigh.

Jane?

She ought to have turned around, then and there. Every instinct Winter had was telling her to go back the way she'd come, to write the whole thing off as a drunken, maudlin fantasy. She fought them all and eased forward, setting the wine bottle on the floor so gently it didn't even make a click. The gap between door and doorframe was only a few inches away, and Winter leaned toward it, hardly daring to breathe.

Someone gasped. Jane said, very quietly, "Don't."

"It's been"—pause—"weeks. Seeing you every day"—pause—"and every night, I . . ."

This was Abby's voice. Winter finally got her eye against the crack in the door. She saw Jane, leaning on the big council table, her red hair damp and spiky with sweat. Abby was pressed up against her, arms wrapped around her waist. Her lips brushed a delicate trail of kisses from Jane's collarbone up into the hollow of her neck. Jane leaned her head back, like an animal offering its throat in submission, and her hands clenched the edge of the tabletop.

"I told you," Jane said weakly. "We can't. *I* can't."

"I know." Abby kissed the corner of Jane's jaw, then her cheek. "Just for tonight, all right? Just once. Please."

"Abby . . ."

"Call the guards, if you like. Throw me in the dungeon."

Abby kissed Jane full on the lips, and after a moment's resistance Jane's arms came off the table and wrapped around Abby's shoulders. Abby's hands roamed upward, running gently over Jane's flanks, her fingers tangling in the hem of Jane's shirt.

Jane moaned, very quietly, but Winter was no longer there to hear. She stalked away down the corridor, leaving her bottle by the doorway, eyes brimming with unwanted tears.

Chapter Seventeen

RAESINIA

For the moment, they were letting Raesinia remain in her chambers in the Prince's Tower. Eventually, she assumed, some court stickler for protocol would probably demand that she move over to the Royal Apartments, but that would require refurnishing, and the staff of the palace was fully occupied. So many of the more cautious nobles and their retinues had departed for the country as the riots had developed that the royal household had been left with a skeleton crew, managing a building that was suddenly vastly too large for its inhabitants. The task of putting the palace in its mourning garb was big enough to occupy an army, even without considering all the changes to the lists of precedence that would be required by so many departures and the consequent adjustments to social calendars, place settings, and so on.

Raesinia was happy to leave well enough alone. Sothe was adamant that her days of sneaking out to visit the revolutionaries were over, but it was nice to know that she still had her convenient-if-painful escape route from the tower. New rooms would come with a squadron of new servants, too, with all the complicated negotiations that entailed. Here in the Prince's Tower, Sothe ruled with an iron hand, and she had a very simple protocol—when Raesinia was present, Sothe met visitors at the door and no other menials were allowed to enter. The cleaning and laundry staff had learned to pounce on the room the moment Raesinia stepped out the door.

This morning, Sothe brought breakfast to her table, as usual, together with a stack of the morning papers. One advantage of being queen was that she could pay attention to current events more openly, without having to play the part of the brainless princess.

There was no news except the Revolution, as the papers were already starting to call it. Several woodcuts of Danton looked up at her, including a rather good profile in the *Barker*. The Deputies-General, scheduled to open today, had driven everyone into renewed frenzies of excitement. A more or less permanent camp of revolutionaries, centered on the occupied Vendre, was surrounded by a temporary mob whose size varied with the mood of the public. Today, Raesinia read, they occupied most of the Island, leaving only a small clear space around the cathedral in the hands of the Armsmen. The South Bank was boiling, and even the North Bank was starting to rumble, centered on the University and the Dregs.

Not all the news was good. Fresh water was becoming scarce on the Island, in spite of the best efforts of the merchants selling it at ruinous prices, so some of the gathered thousands had been reduced to drinking river water. The result was an epidemic of the bloody flux, which had already laid low hundreds and was claiming several victims a day. One paper even helpfully provided a cartoon, which showed Raesinia herself walking over the bridge to the Island in full regalia only to be met by a tidal wave of oncoming diarrhea.

In addition to disease, the prostitutes and thieves who gathered wherever there was a crowd to fleece were out in force, and with the Armsmen banished there was nothing to restrain their street feuds. Still, it looked to Raesinia as though everyone was behaving remarkably well under the circumstances, and the view of the papers seemed positive. The people believed in the deputies, which was exactly what the deputies needed in order to be effective.

The people also believed in Danton. Several papers reprinted the text of his latest speeches, beside columns calling for him to have some kind of a role in government even before the deputies had met. Or Raesinia should marry him, and make him king, so his wisdom could lead Vordan to a new golden age.

"Look at this nonsense," Raesinia said, rattling the paper. "He's telling everyone to stay calm, which is all well and good, but then he goes on and on about the nature of the social compact and the theory of a just monarchy. That's Maurisk's writing, obviously." She turned the paper over and rolled her eyes. "It goes onto the back, in small print. He never did know when to shut up."

Sothe didn't comment. Raesinia tossed the paper aside. "You delivered his speech for today?"

It had taken her most of the previous week to write, and Raesinia thought it was a pretty fine piece of work. As the keynote address to the new Deputies-General, coming out in Danton's glorious golden voice, it would go a long way toward setting the tone.

"I did. The others accepted that it was something you'd written before you . . . died." Sothe was frowning, and Raesinia thought she knew why. She decided it was better to bite the bullet.

"And? Did you see Cora?"

"I saw her."

"And?"

Sothe sighed. "Pri—my queen. I've said before that the farther you stay away from her and the others, the safer everyone will be."

"That's why I sent you to look in on her instead of going myself."

"It's still an unnecessary risk. I could be recognized, followed."

"We both know a dozen bloodhounds couldn't follow you across fresh snow."

"It's a possibility," Sothe insisted. "And I worry that you won't be content to simply 'look in' forever. It's better that you make a clean break, my queen."

"I just want to know if Cora is all right," Raesinia said. "Maurisk and Sarton can take care of themselves, but Cora's just a girl."

"She seemed fine," Sothe said, relenting. "She has taken your 'death' hard, but otherwise she appears to be in reasonable spirits. I believe Maurisk has been talking to her about the need to carry on, 'for Raesinia's sake.'"

Raesinia clapped her hands. "He's not completely clueless, then. Sooner or later, I want to find a way to bring Cora in."

"Much too risky. She'll recognize you, and then the secret is as good as out."

"Not if we asked her to keep it. Cora would never betray me."

"The same as Faro?" There was a long, painful pause. "I'm sorry, my queen. But the stakes are extremely high. Perhaps, in time, I might be able to find a way."

"Think about it," Raesinia said. "You've seen how talented she is with money. We're going to need all the coin we can get if we're not going to continue Orlanko's policy of mortgaging the kingdom to the Borels."

Sothe nodded, lips pursed. There was a knock at the door, and she got up to answer it. Raesinia read a few more paragraphs of Danton's speech, then pushed the papers away in disgust.

I'm going to have to have a talk with Maurisk. Then she remembered that she couldn't, not now and probably not ever. As far as Maurisk was concerned, Raesinia had fallen from the Vendre's walls with a bullet in her skull, dragging the traitor Faro to his death. A whole chapter of her life had ended, almost as though she *had* died. Rationally, she could agree with Sothe that it was probably for the best. Now that her father was dead and she was under greater scrutiny, sneaking out would be too risky; besides, the conspiracy had served its purpose. The will of the people, expressed through the Deputies-General, would give her the means to rid the country of Orlanko. With Janus as an ally on the Cabinet, she might be able to start putting things right.

Orlanko still held his trump card, the threat to expose her as demonically possessed. But the very power of that move would make him afraid to use it. Without being able to install himself as regent and thus as a clear successor to the throne, the result could only be chaos, possibly even another civil war. Raesinia's reign would have to be short, in any case, since eventually the public and the court would become suspicious of their unaging queen. *Unless Janus finds a solution in the Thousand Names. But I can't count on that.* She would have to marry someone she trusted to be the kind of king the country needed, the kind her father would have wanted and that her brother would have been. Then Raesinia could "die" with a clean conscience, and after that—something else. She had never allowed herself to think that far in advance.

Perhaps Janus himself is the king I need. He was certainly of a sufficiently noble line, albeit somewhat impoverished in recent years, that the people would accept him. He was intelligent, and a capable general, if his Khandarai exploits were anything to go by. And, of course, he already knew her secret, obviating the need for either a complicated subterfuge or a potentially dangerous confrontation. *And he's handsome enough, I suppose, in an arch sort of way.*

On the other hand, there was something about him that made her nervous. A sense of ambition, carefully harnessed but nonetheless visible just below the surface. She wondered if being king would be enough for him, or if he was one of those men whose thirst for power simply could not be slaked. The vision of Vordanai armies marching forth to conquer with fire and sword—with Janus bet Vhalnich at their head and Danton to fire their blood—was too plausible for comfort. That was not, she was sure, what her father would have wanted. His dreams of martial glory had ended with the cruel realities of Vansfeldt.

A problem for another day. There was a long, twisting road yet to walk before she arrived at a position where she could begin to contemplate that choice. *But it starts today, with the Deputies-General.*

Sothe reappeared. "Captain d'Ivoire is here, Your Majesty, with your escort."

Your Majesty. She wasn't sure she'd ever get used to that. "Send him in, and go and fetch the bits and pieces." Raesinia was already wearing the slim, plain black dress that was proper for a queen in mourning, but it wouldn't do to be seen in public without the appropriate accessories and a tasteful amount of jewels.

Bowing, Sothe went back to the door, and was replaced a moment later by Marcus d'Ivoire. The captain bowed as well, more formally. He was in the full dress uniform of the captain of Armsmen, dark forest green trimmed with silver and gold, with braids of army blue and silver at the shoulder to indicate he was a captain in a royal regiment as well. The only false note was the sword at his hip, which was a solid, weather-beaten cavalry saber instead of the jeweled rapier or small sword she might have expected.

"Your Majesty," he said, when she indicated he should rise. "You have my deepest sympathies."

"Thank you, Captain. And you have my gratitude for what you accomplished at the Vendre."

Marcus looked rueful. "I'm afraid I didn't accomplish much, Your Majesty. We surrendered the fortress, after all. And I spent most of the time locked in a cell."

"From what I have heard, you prevented a bloodbath. I was most gratified to hear of your escape."

"Some of the . . . revolutionaries," Marcus said carefully, "appear to have shared your gratitude. They gave me to understand that my further presence might cause difficulties. So I would not call it an *escape*, precisely."

"You're too modest for your own good, Captain."

"Only honest, Your Majesty."

Sothe came back in, with shoes, a shawl, and an assortment of delicate confections of gems and gold. Raesinia stood up and allowed these to be attached, and in the meantime studied Marcus' broad, patient face.

I would not mind marrying him, she thought, idly. *He seems like he would be kind. And I think he would make a good king.* Not that such a thing could ever come to pass, even if she'd been madly in love with the captain. He was a commoner, to start with, and the same gentle patience that she thought would be a useful trait in a ruler would see him eaten alive by the likes of Orlanko. *Where can I find a man who is both* capable *of ruling and good enough to do a decent job?*

When the fitting-out was finished, Marcus bowed again. "I'll go and alert your escort, Your Majesty."

"My queen," Sothe whispered, as soon as Marcus had gone out into the foyer. "Something is wrong."

"What?" Raesinia turned too quickly, setting her ornaments to clicking. "What do you mean?"

"I'm not certain." Sothe licked her lips, like a snake tasting the air. "Something isn't right. I can't—"

She quieted as Marcus reentered. He, too, looked perturbed.

"Your Majesty," he said. "May I ask a question?"

"Of course," Raesinia said, fighting a rising tide of anxiety in the pit of her stomach.

"Who usually guards your door?"

Raesinia blinked. "The Grays are charged with the security of the grounds. But the royal family is guarded by a company of Royal Grenadier Guards, and some of your Armsmen. There should be a few of each out there." She'd walked past them a thousand times.

"There's an escort forming up in the corridor," Marcus said. "But it seems to be only Grays. And when I looked out, I didn't see any Armsmen or Royals."

"That *is* odd," Raesinia said. "Perhaps they'll be joining us later on?"

Someone rapped at the door. A voice came from outside. "Your Majesty? Open the door, if you please. There's an emergency."

"Don't," Sothe said. Raesinia hadn't seen her move, but she was reemerging from her own room, a pistol in either hand, her long dress tied up above her knees to give her freedom of movement. "It's Orlanko."

"What?" Raesinia's anxiety was shot through with rage. "He wouldn't dare."

"We've overestimated his caution," Sothe said, positioning herself in the doorway. "Or his intelligence. But I'm certain those are his people."

"Get behind me, Your Majesty," Marcus said, surprisingly unfazed by this news. His saber rasped from its scabbard.

"Wait." Raesinia scrambled to her feet. "We can't be certain. Don't shoot anybody—"

There was a *thud* and a crunch of wood. Someone had rammed his shoulder hard against the corridor door. It was a light, decorative thing, not designed to endure that kind of abuse, and splinters flew from around the bolt.

"—oh." Raesinia's mind went blank. There was no excuse for doing *that* to the queen's chambers, even if the building was on fire. "Go ahead, then."

They were in the main room of her suite, with a couch and table providing the only cover. A door separated this room from the foyer, but it was no sturdier than the one in the corridor and would provide only a few seconds' respite. Instead of closing it, Sothe squared off in the doorway, staring across the open space of the foyer as though she were on a target range.

Another blow brought a great crash from the outer door, tearing the bolt out of the wood and sending splinters pinwheeling across the room. A man in a Noreldrai Grays uniform stumbled through it, and as he took a moment to straighten up and get his bearings Sothe shot him neatly in the head. He toppled backward against the doorframe, blocking the path of a second Gray who was struggling to get into the room. Sothe tossed her smoking pistol aside, switched the second one from left hand to right, and shot him, too, just as he was beginning to shout a warning. Then she drew a vicious, thick-bladed long knife into either hand, settled back on the balls of her feet, and waited.

"Your Majesty," Marcus said urgently. "We have to get out of here."

"Stay put," Sothe snapped. "We don't have a chance if they catch us in the open."

"There isn't time to explain." Marcus grabbed Raesinia's sleeve, but she yanked it away from him and set her jaw.

"I'm not leaving without her," she said.

"But—"

Marcus was interrupted by the ring of steel on steel. At least a half dozen Grays had cleared the two bodies and rushed across the foyer, only to pile up again at the inner door. They'd left their muskets behind and drawn their straight-bladed swords, but these weapons were still long enough that the narrow confines of the doorway offered no room to swing. The first one charged with his sword lowered point-first, like a lance, but Sothe's blade licked out and diverted the thrust so that it crashed into the decorative wainscoting and stuck there. Her off hand came up in an almost casual motion and drew a line across the guard's throat, which opened in a spray of gore. He gave a bubbling shriek and stumbled backward, clutching the wound, until one of his companions shoved him roughly aside and came at Sothe with leveled blade.

"You can't kill them *all*!" Marcus shouted, over the shouts of the attackers and the screech of blade against blade as Sothe blocked another thrust.

Yes, she can. Raesinia had never really had the opportunity to watch Sothe fight before. It was . . . *graceful* was not the word, precisely, or *elegant*, though the latter was closer. *Efficient*, possibly. Sothe fought like a master butcher carving a pig, no unnecessary flourishes or brutality, just the minimum number of strokes necessary to reduce her opponents to piles of quivering meat. The second Gray fared no better than the first, going down with a long gash in his inner thigh that fountained a quite astonishing amount of blood. Two more tried to come at her together, but she simply retreated a step, letting them tangle each other up in the doorway. One of them managed a clumsy thrust, which she sidestepped neatly as she lopped off his hand at the wrist.

"We just need to hold until help arrives," Sothe said, as this opponent fell back, screaming. She wasn't even breathing hard. "Orlanko can't have *all* the guards in the palace on his side—"

She checked an overhand swing from another Gray on one of her knives, falling back a step as he tried to force her down by main strength. Her other blade came up to gut him, but before it got there a pistol shot sounded from the foyer. Sothe's opponent stiffened for a moment, then went limp, sword dropping from his slack fingers. He fell forward, collapsing on top of her, and she had to catch him under the armpits to avoid being bowled over. As she tossed him aside and looked up, a second shot sounded, and Sothe grunted and spun as if she'd been kicked in the shoulder by a mule. The deadweight of the guard bore them both to the floor in a heap.

Raesinia screamed and tried to dart forward, but Marcus grabbed her with his free hand and shoved her back against the wall. Four Grays surged through the doorway, spreading out with drawn swords. Standing in the foyer, smoking pistol still in hand, was a young man in a long dark coat. He tossed the weapon aside and strode forward, black leather fluttering around his ankles.

He spared only a cursory glance for Raesinia and Marcus. Instead he went to where the dead Gray lay atop Sothe and rolled the guard off with the toe of his boot. Sothe was on her back, completely still, and from where she stood Raesinia couldn't tell if she was breathing.

"So," the man said. "The Gray Rose, run to ground at last." He glanced at the scattered corpses. "And with some teeth, after all. I commend you on a well-run chase."

He drove his boot into her stomach with sudden violence, and Sothe gasped and rolled on her side, curling into a ball. Blood squelched on the floor under her shoulder.

"And still a bit of life in you," he said. "Excellent. If you survive, His Grace will be very interested to hear what you have to say."

As he spoke, the four Grays had spread out into a loose semicircle around Marcus. He kept his saber moving and backed away until he and Raesinia were pressed against the wall. The Concordat agent gave Sothe another kick, almost playfully, and was rewarded with another gasp of pain. Then, with the air of someone attending to an unpleasant but necessary matter, he came to stand behind the ring of guards.

"She was wrong, as it happens," he said. "The Grays have been in the service of His Grace for some time, and the Grenadier Guards have orders not to interfere. Captain d'Ivoire's handful of Armsmen have already been rounded up. Ohnlei is ours, Your Majesty." He sketched a bow. "My name is Andreas. At your service."

"Orlanko has finally gone mad," Raesinia said. "This is treason."

"He'll hang for certain," Marcus said. "But you don't have to join him."

"Treason is a slippery thing," Andreas said. "It is, as they say, in the eye of the beholder, which means it depends on what people believe. And His Grace is an expert in that field."

"The deputies are convening as we speak," Raesinia said. "When I don't turn up—"

"The Deputies-General, as they so quaintly style themselves, are also being taken in hand." Andreas smiled. "Put down your sword, Captain, before you get hurt. I promise you, no harm will come to Her Majesty."

There was a long pause. The tips of five swords hovered in the air, twitching with nervous tension.

If she asked him to, Raesinia was reasonably certain that Marcus would fight and, in all probability, die. Ben had done the same. Even Sothe—she couldn't finish the thought. *Why are they all so eager to sacrifice themselves for me?* She wondered if she would do the same, if the circumstances were reversed, but of course the circumstances never *could* be reversed. *Not for me.*

I won't let him die. There's no point. She met Andreas' eyes, opened her mouth to speak, and hesitated. Behind the Concordat agent, one of the Grays was grimly winding a cloth around the stump of his severed hand, while another was checking on his fallen comrades in the foyer. And Sothe—

One of Sothe's hands was creeping across the floor, toward the hilt of one of her knives. It was only six inches away. Four. Her fingers twitched.

"I'll go quietly," Raesinia said, a little too loudly, "if you'll let the captain go."

Andreas shrugged. "We'll have to take him into custody for the moment, but I see no reason he could not be released once matters are settled."

"Your Majesty . . . ," Marcus began. His voice was thick.

"Captain. Please." She put her hand on his shoulder and went up on her toes, putting her lips as close to his ear as she dared. "Head left. The first door."

Marcus, she had to admit, knew how to play a role. His shoulders slumped, as though acknowledging defeat, and he let his sword point fall. "Yes, Your Majesty."

"Excellent," Andreas said, though he sounded a little disappointed. "Take them." He turned away from Raesinia, as if she didn't matter, and back toward Sothe—

Who was no longer there. The knife was a quicksilver blur, flashing across the room and burying itself to the hilt in the skull of one of the Grays on Raesinia's left, pinning his peaked cap to his head. Sothe herself was rolling toward the doorway and came up on her feet, graceful in spite of the spreading stain on her shoulder and the deathly pallor in her face. She'd already drawn another knife and flicked it at a second Gray, who had half turned at the uproar and took the blade in the meat of his cheek. He screamed and dropped his sword.

Raesinia ran. There were two doors leading deeper into her suite, but only one that made sense as an escape route. It led to the sitting room at the base of the tower, against the outer wall, with its wide leaded-glass windows. Sothe obviously had come to the same conclusion, since she'd taken care of the two guards in that direction. There was a ring of steel from behind her, and Raesinia risked a look over her shoulder to see Marcus parrying a halfhearted stroke from one of the two remaining Grays, backpedaling rapidly in her wake. Raesinia reached the doorway, grabbed the frame with one hand, and let momentum swing her into the room.

Andreas had drawn his own sword, but for a moment he seemed unsure what to do. Sothe took advantage of the confusion to vault the injured Gray in the foyer door, picking up a dropped sword as she went. A wild slash scattered the two confused guards near the outer door, and then she was through.

"Tell the Last Duke," she shouted over her shoulder, "that if he wants to catch the Gray Rose, he should send someone who will make a proper job of it!"

Andreas' lip twisted into a snarl. "I'll handle her," he snapped at the nearest Gray. "Kill the damned Armsman, and bring the queen to the Cobweb." Sothe was running down the corridor, and Andreas sprinted after her, well behind but gaining ground with every stride.

Marcus backed through the doorway, thrusting to drive back the Gray who tried to follow. Raesinia slammed the door in the guard's face before he could close back in, and shot the bolt, for all the good it would do.

"Sothe will be fine," she muttered. "I knew she would be fine. She's—"

"We may want to attend to our own problems," Marcus said. "We have to get to the gardens."

"The *gardens*? Why?"

"You'll just have to trust me." He grinned tightly. "Or if not me, then my lord Count Mieran."

After a moment's hesitation, Raesinia nodded. "All right. There'll be men on the path outside, but they may not be expecting us. You go through as soon as I've cleared the way."

"Your Majesty?"

There was a thud from the door. They didn't have more than a few seconds. Raesinia grabbed a heavy brass candelabra from the corner, hefted it thoughtfully, and looked at the windows. She'd often cursed those windows—if they'd only been proper modern windows, with a sash and a latch, she wouldn't have had to begin every night by throwing herself off the roof. She'd fantasized about this exact moment, if not under these precise circumstances.

Raesinia pivoted on the ball of her foot and brought the end of the candelabra around in a whistling arc. The delicate repeating pattern of colored glass shattered into thousands of razor-edged shards as the web of lead struts that contained it bent and splayed outward. She was surprised to see that it didn't give way entirely; a curtain of leadwork hung from the edges of the frame, like torn and tattered lace, with bits of glass still clinging to the edges. She brought the candelabra around again, and the second blow ripped through the soft metal and tore the whole thing away.

Marcus hurled himself through as soon as the frame was clear. It was a short drop to the gravel path outside, and he absorbed the fall with a crouch, then popped to his feet before the musket-armed Gray standing in his way could do more than raise his weapon. Marcus' saber caught him in the stomach and doubled him over, and a kick sent him sprawling. Raesinia dropped the candelabra and jumped through, her stupid court shoes twisting under her weight as she landed in the gravel. She kicked them off and started running, and Marcus lumbered into motion after her, the medals and ornamentation on his dress uniform clinking gently. Behind them, a shout had gone up, and she could hear gravel crunching under the feet of more Grays as they took up the chase.

The path curved around the back of the palace and cut up toward the edge of the gardens. Continuing on would bring them to the vast lawns that flanked the Ministry buildings, which she assumed was Marcus' intention. Instead he grabbed her hand as they passed a stone arch, which marked the edge of a set of walled and hedged gardens called the Bower of Queen Anne, planted by one of Raesinia's illustrious ancestors in honor of his deceased wife. These were a set of narrow walkways, planted round with hedges, connecting several little clearings set with garden furniture and wound through with carefully manicured streams and beds of flowers. There was another arch at the far end, near the main drive, and one more that led directly into the building. *But*—

"He'll have men out front for certain," Raesinia said. "We'll be trapped in there." She tugged her hand free of his and pointed out toward the lawn. "That way—"

"The Grays have a cavalry company," Marcus said. "We can't risk open fields. You said you would trust me, Your Majesty."

She grabbed his hand and followed him into the shadows of the walled garden.

Raesinia had not spent much time in the Bower of Queen Anne, but evidently Marcus had, or at least he'd done a thorough job of memorizing the layout. It wasn't exactly a hedge maze, but it had been designed to let small groups have private garden parties in little out-of-the-way spaces, and the hedged-in paths were always going through unexpected switchbacks and right-angle turns and branching at intersections marked with trellises of climbing roses. The hedges were tall enough to cut off the morning sun, so they ran through shadows except when the path curved to the east and Raesinia had to shade her eyes against sudden brilliance.

Marcus pounded through the first two intersections without even slowing down, and broke out through an archway onto an open section. Raesinia followed, working hard to match the captain's longer strides. For all his impression of stolidity, Marcus kept up a fair turn of speed once he got going, and it was only the binding's soothing passes through her overworked legs that let her keep up with him. Something went *pop* in her ankle—she'd rolled it jumping out the window—but the muscles and tendons reknotted before her foot came down again.

The Grays were not far behind them. A half dozen of them burst into the clearing when she and Marcus were halfway across, dodging through the garden furniture. Four of the guards kept running, but two dropped to their knees and leveled their bayoneted muskets.

"Halt!" one of them shouted, with a heavy Noreldrai accent. "Or we fire!"

"Bluffing," Raesinia gasped. "No good. To them. Dead."

Marcus nodded, swerved around an errant chair, and ducked through the arch at the other end of the clearing. Raesinia flinched at a shattering crack of musketry from behind them, but the shots had been aimed well over her head, and she heard the balls zing merrily past. Someone swore in Noreldrai before the curve of the hedgerow cut them off again.

It was hard to keep track of directions, but Marcus seemed to be leading them *deeper* into the Bower. She'd thought they would try to pass straight through, perhaps commandeer a carriage out on the main drive, but he kept turning back toward the palace. There was another exit there, but it would surely be guarded. *In fact, they could go around that way and cut us off—*

No sooner had she had the thought than they reached another triangular intersection as a trio of Grays turned up from the opposite direction. The guards were as surprised as Raesinia was, and pulled up short, but Marcus let his momentum carry him into them, narrowly avoiding being skewered on a protruding bayonet. He lowered his shoulder and knocked one Gray off his feet and into the man behind him, then came around with a wild swing of his saber that opened a long cut across the stomach of the third.

"That way!" Marcus gestured with his free hand toward the third branch of the intersection. "Get to the fountain!"

That seemed to be the only available direction, and Raesinia was already headed toward it. The word "fountain" filled her with an unexpected chill, though, and she struggled to remember why. Sparkling lights danced in front of her eyes—the binding was working hard to keep her legs functioning, and had no energy to spare for small matters like a lack of blood to the brain.

The two unwounded Grays disentangled themselves, retreating a bit from Marcus' furious swings, and were caught off guard when he turned his back on them and ran. Both raised their muskets, trying to get a shot off before he disappeared around a corner, but only one went off—the captain's bull rush must have knocked the second hard enough to spill the powder from the pan. Raesinia heard the ball zip by and crash noisily into the hedges.

She rounded the corner and felt flagstones under her feet instead of dirt. Ahead was one of the fountains in the classical style with which Ohnlei was so generously supplied. A broad, low pool, contained by a stone lip, fired jets of water against a stone pedestal that supported an equestrian statue of Raesinia's great-great-grandfather, Farus V. It was ringed by a circle of flagstones, already cracked and uneven in places where underground roots had wreaked havoc on the builders' perfect order. A low stone wall, backed by a more imposing hedge, cut the little clearing off entirely from the rest of the Bower.

The fountain. Raesinia realized, belatedly, what she'd been trying to remember. *There's only one entrance.* She skidded to a halt against the lip, and Marcus clomped and jingled his way to a stop beside her, panting hard. Raesinia had to remind herself to breathe, for verisimilitude.

"We're. Stuck," she managed. Marcus, bent over with his hands on his knees, was too out of breath to reply.

A few moments later, Grays started pouring into the clearing. They were disheveled from the long chase, sweating into their tailored uniforms, and most of them had lost their neat little caps. Half still had muskets, while the others had drawn their swords.

"That's about enough, *alvaunt*," gasped one, who had a sergeant's stripes on his shoulders. He took a deep breath and straightened up. "We got you, yes? Sword down, hands up. You come with us."

"Captain . . . ," Raesinia began.

"Marcus," he said, "under the circumstances."

"I appreciate what you've done. But this is enough, don't you think?"

Marcus let his sword fall. The clang of steel on stone echoed over the quiet babble of the fountain.

"I think you're right," he said. He was smiling.

The sound of boots on the flagstones behind them made a couple of the Noreldrai turn. The sergeant gestured angrily for them to keep their eyes on their prisoners, then spun to face the man who'd just sauntered through the archway.

"What in *volse* do you think you're doing?" he barked.

Janus, wearing his dress blues in place of the civilian costume of the Minister of Justice, put on an innocent expression.

"Going for a walk?" he said.

The sergeant snorted. "You can explain that to His Grace."

"I think it would be best," Janus said, "if you and your men would stack your arms and sit quietly against the wall."

"Excuse me?" The sergeant looked from Janus to his men. "Perhaps I speak your *kishkasse* language not as well as I thought."

"I just thought I would warn you."

The sergeant ran out of patience. He gestured with his sword, and the Grays advanced on Marcus and Raesinia. Two sword-wielding men sauntered over to deal with Janus, who wasn't even armed.

Janus sighed, and raised his voice. "In your own time, Lieutenant Uhlan."

Everyone froze, looking around to see whom he was addressing. In the same instant, two dozen long rifle barrels slid over the wall that edged the clearing.

Something hit Raesinia hard in the small of the back. It was Marcus, bearing her to the ground. He courteously put his other arm underneath her to cushion her fall against the flagstones, so she ended up pulled tight into a kind of embrace. The staccato *crack* of rifles at close range split the air, and billows of smoke filled the clearing with the scent of gun smoke. One or two blasts, closer to them, indicated that a few of the Grays had gotten a shot off, but in less than a half minute the burbling fountain was again audible.

"Very good, Lieutenant," Janus said, in a conversational tone. "Captain?"

Marcus relaxed his grip on Raesinia's shoulders. Raesinia took a deep breath—it had been like being hugged by a bear—and got a lungful of smoke, mixed with the scent of his sweat. She coughed, and wiped her eyes.

"Are you all right, Your Majesty?"

"Fine," Raesinia said, automatically. She'd skinned an elbow in the fall, but the cuts were already closing.

"No injuries, sir," Marcus said aloud.

"Nobody hit here, sir," said another voice, in a harsh accent Raesinia didn't recognize.

"Good shooting," Janus said.

There was another shot, not so close, but still loud enough to make Raesinia flinch. Marcus rolled off her, climbed to his feet, and offered her his hand. She took it, feeling a little unsteady. Another couple of shots drifted over the Bower, like distant handclaps. The clearing was wreathed in floating wisps of gun smoke, but she could see men in red uniforms climbing over the wall, long weapons in hand. The Grays were all down, either dead or keeping silent. The red-clad soldiers began to move among them while one bearing a lieutenant's bars hurried over, saluted Janus, then bowed deeply in Raesinia's direction.

"Your Majesty," Janus said, "may I present Lieutenant Medio bet Uhlan, of the First Mierantai Volunteers. His family has been in the service of the counts of Mieran for four generations."

"It's an honor, Your Majesty," Uhlan said, in what Raesinia assumed was a Mierantai accent. It sounded as if he spent his days gargling rocks.

"I owe you my life, sir," Raesinia said, a slight exaggeration for dramatic effect. "Thank you for your assistance."

Another couple of shots made both Uhlan and Janus cock their heads, listening carefully.

"Still just ours," Uhlan said, and Janus nodded.

"Quite a few Grays got shaken loose in the chase," he said to Raesinia. "They ended up wandering around the Bower, and the rest of Lieutenant Uhlan's men are rounding them up. We should give them a couple of minutes." He sighed. "I hope a few of them decide to surrender."

"We got the bulk of them at their barracks, when Orlanko's orders arrived," Uhlan said. "They were ready to fight their way out, but it turned out that some absolute bastard had soaked all the powder in the armory the night before." His grin was concealed behind a thick woodsman's beard, but his eyes twinkled.

Raesinia looked at Janus. "You knew?"

"Not for certain, but it's always wise to plan for contingencies." He frowned. "Though I must admit this seemed a fairly probable contingency. What our friend the duke does not understand is that a perfect record of treachery is just as predictable as one of impeccable loyalty. You simply must always expect to be stabbed in the back, and you'll never be surprised. Keeping faith occasionally would make him much harder to anticipate."

"Orlanko." Raesinia's hand twisted into the fabric of her dress, fingers tightening. "Do you have enough men to storm the Cobweb?"

"Not at the moment, I'm afraid," Janus said. "We have it blockaded, but there are too many tunnels and bolt-holes to cut him off completely. It's possible the duke has already fled."

"He'll hang for this, I swear." Her breath caught. "What about Sothe? Have you found her?"

"Her Majesty's maidservant," Marcus supplied. "She helped hold off the Grays. Last I saw her, she was running for it with a Concordat agent in hot pursuit."

"I haven't heard anything," Janus said. "But affairs are very confused at the moment. And, unfortunately, we have larger problems."

It was hard for Raesinia to tear her mind away from Sothe, but once she did she jumped to the obvious conclusion. "The deputies. Andreas—the Concordat agent who came to arrest us—said they were going to be taken in hand."

"It would be a foolish play to take the palace, only to lose it to the mob," Janus agreed. "And Orlanko is not *entirely* a fool. I suggest we proceed to the cathedral at once. Lieutenant?"

Uhlan was consulting with a pair of red-uniformed Mierantai who'd just entered the clearing. He looked up. "We're clear, sir. Got about thirty prisoners. Carriages are waiting in the main drive, and the sergeant commanding the Armsmen says he's with us."

"He'd damned well better be," Marcus growled.

"Don't be too hard on them," Janus said. "On days like this, it's never easy to know which way to jump." He and Marcus shared a look that spoke of some shared memory, and Marcus grunted. "Lead the way, Lieutenant."

Uhlan barked orders in his harsh, nearly unintelligible dialect, and the Mierantai formed up around them. Marcus drifted back as the column set off, until he was walking beside Raesinia.

"I'm sorry," he said.

"For what?"

"I could have told you earlier that this might happen." He nodded at Janus. "He insisted that I not say anything until Orlanko tipped his hand. I think he was worried you might panic. But if I'd said something, Sothe might"—he hesitated—"might not have gotten hurt. I can see she's . . . important to you."

Raesinia nodded, walking for a moment in silence. "I can hardly blame you for following orders."

"Still. I'm sorry." Marcus squared his shoulders, as though facing something unpleasant. "Whatever Orlanko had planned for the deputies may have happened already. Giforte is there with as many Armsmen as I could spare, but . . ."

"I know." Raesinia was thinking of Maurisk, Cora, and Sarton. Danton, Jane, Cyte, and all the rest.

"I hope we get there in time to do some good."

Raesinia nodded grimly. "So do I."

Chapter Eighteen

WINTER

In the hundred and twenty years since the Sworn Church had first been expelled from Vordan, the Sworn Cathedral had never played host to a congregation large enough to fill its echoing, vaulted hall. For years, when praying in a Sworn Church had been tantamount to being a traitor to the Crown, it had stood empty. Later, more tolerant ages had seen the Sworn Priests return, chase out some of the bats and rats who had taken up residence, and offer services to those few foreigners and die-hards who wanted them.

The War of the Princes and Borelgai proselytizing had brought a few more into the fold, but Winter was certain the gloomy old building hadn't seen a gathering like this in living memory. The Deputies-General packed the floor of the main hall—the moldy pews had been hauled outside to clear more space—and members of delegations searching for private space had invaded the warren of rooms, damp corridors, and drafty wooden stairways behind the altar that had once housed the massive administrative staff charged with overseeing the spiritual welfare of all of Vordan.

Giforte and a band of staff-wielding Armsmen were vainly attempting to keep order, but the most they could manage was to protect the floor of the main hall—which, it had been decided, constituted the actual chamber of the Deputies-General—from being invaded by crowds from outside. Eager to get a glimpse of what was going on, the spectators had found the stairs leading up to the old Widow's Gallery, a wooden-floored balcony that described a broad horseshoe shape around the back of the main hall, about thirty feet off the ground. Getting up took a bit of daring, since the stairways were in bad shape and the balcony itself was riddled with rotten boards, but it provided an excellent vantage point. From here, the adventurous could get a good view of the proceedings and, in spite of the best efforts of the Armsmen, throw chunks of floorboard at speakers they didn't care for.

Those proceedings were not, in Winter's opinion, worthy of all this attention. They had begun well enough, with the crimson-clad Sworn Bishop offering a nervous-sounding prayer, followed by a plea for fellowship and common sense from a pair of Free Priests. Once the clergy had departed, however, the wrangling over the agenda had begun. In fact, as best Winter could tell, things had not yet progressed to the point of arguing over the agenda; the deputies first needed to decide the order of precedence in which they would be allowed to offer points *during* the debate over the agenda, and this crucial discussion had thus far engaged the entire attention of all parties.

It was possible that this was taking an overly cynical view of matters. But in Winter's current mood, she was inclined to see everything cynically. The spectators on the gallery sat near the edge, as far forward as they dared test the rotten boards, while Winter paced in the back, lost in shadows.

Jane and Abby obviously had . . . something. Of *course* they did. When Winter listened to Abby talk about Jane, she could see an echo of the way she herself had felt all those years ago. Only willful ignorance had kept her from figuring it out sooner.

And, she thought, *that's for the best. It's only to be expected, isn't it? For all Jane knew, I was dead, or gone away never to return. Hell, I never planned to return. I wouldn't have asked to her to spend her whole life pining away for me. And since she did find someone, how can I expect her to just drop everything the minute I come back?*

All perfectly reasonable. *So why is it that whenever I close my eyes, all I can see is the two of them?* Jane's face, and the little sigh she made as Abby's lips touched her throat. Abby's hand, sliding up her flank, pushing up her shirt.

She might have told me. Winter bit her lip. *Either one of them might have told me.* But that wasn't really fair, either. Jane had made her intentions perfectly clear from the very start, and Winter had turned her down. *No wonder she's gone looking elsewhere.*

Wood creaked and popped under her weight. She found herself on the left-hand side of the horseshoe, near the end, where the balcony most closely approached the altar. The steps leading up to the altar had been adopted as speaking floor, with the silver and gold double circle dangling from its long, thin chain directly behind the speaker. Someone plump and well-dressed whom Winter didn't recognize was down there now, in the middle of what had obviously been a long address.

A small group of young women had occupied the very end of the horseshoe. Winter recognized Cyte, along with Molly and Becks from Jane's Leatherbacks, chatting amiably and apparently no worse for wear after their brief stay in a Concordat prison. The rest were a mixed group of Jane's girls and other young women from the South Bank who'd drifted up to have a look at the fun.

Before Winter could turn on her heel and stalk back in the other direction, Cyte noticed her and waved her over. Winter reluctantly picked her way through the chattering throng.

"Watch out for splinters," Cyte said.

"I'm a bit more concerned with the whole thing giving out underneath us," Winter said, sitting down carefully. "I don't think it's had a workout like this since the Civil War."

Cyte laughed. Her eyes were dark, Winter noticed. Not with makeup, this time, but the wages of interrupted sleep. Her face was thinner than it had been, and more worn.

"It never fails," Cyte said darkly. "Here come the scavengers."

"I'm sorry."

She indicated the fat orator, who was gesturing in the classical style and sweating profusely. "Look at him. A North Bank merchant, if I'm any judge, or maybe a banker. Never done an honest day's work. And *he* wasn't out in the streets when Orlanko turned his dogs loose. *He* didn't storm the walls of the Vendre. But now he's here, and we've got to listen to his self-righteous prattle."

"The queen called the deputies to represent all of Vordan," Becks offered. "Like it or not, that includes him and the other North Bankers."

"At least we're shot of the damned Borels," another girl said. "Those are the real bloodsuckers."

Cyte met Winter's eye. They got up together and walked a ways down the railing. Inquisitive glances followed them, but no one spoke.

"You know why they call this the Widow's Gallery?" Cyte said.

Winter shook her head.

"In the old days—the *very* old days, around the time of Farus the Conqueror—the Pontifex of the White decided that the churches had drifted too far toward being social centers instead of places for contemplation of the sins of mankind. He blamed it on unattached women, who were apparently smashing around society like loose cannons. So Elysium decreed that no women unaccompanied by a husband or male relative would be permitted to attend services.

"Of course, the women still wanted to come, and the local hierarchy was reluctant to lose their contributions. Some bishop came up with the idea that the women would subscribe funds for the construction of a balcony like this, so they could *watch* the service without being *at* it. And, since the unattached women who had money to spare were mostly widows, they called it the Widow's Gallery."

Winter forced a chuckle. "I'm glad I wasn't born in the eighth century."

Cyte tested the railing, found it sturdy enough to support her, and leaned against it with her chin in her hands. "Sometimes I feel like I was," she said, nodding toward the floor. "Look."

Abby was just standing up to speak in answer to the sweaty merchant. Aside from a few wives on the back benches, she was the only woman in the room.

"It was Jane who took the Vendre," Cyte went on. "She turned the mob into an . . . an *army*, practically. She sent us in to open the gates. Without that, the queen never would have given us the deputies! But if you look in the newspapers, you'd think Danton killed every Concordat soldier himself and cracked the doors of the prison with one blow of his mighty fist."

"People listen to him," Winter said. "He's a symbol."

"All he does is give speeches. Where is he *now*, when we need someone to shut these idiots up?"

"In his rooms, I think," Winter said. "He's supposed to have a big speech before lunch."

"More platitudes." Cyte snorted. "It should be *Jane* down there."

"The queen invited her," Winter said. "She sent Abby instead. This sort of thing . . ." She shook her head. "Jane isn't good at it."

"Did she send you, too?"

Winter colored slightly. "No. I'm here on my own."

There had been a few tense moments over that, back at the Vendre, which the Leatherbacks were still using as their temporary headquarters. After Jane had told Abby to speak for her at the deputies, Winter had announced that she was going as well. The expression on Jane's face—half-perplexed, half-hurt, with a tiny hint of guilt thrown in for good measure—was something Winter wished she could forget.

She'd made some excuse about wanting to be present at such a historic moment, which Jane hadn't bought. But Winter had been adamant. If she'd hung around the fortress, Jane would have cornered her eventually, and then there would be no avoiding the conversation she desperately did not want to have.

So I ran away. Again.

She swallowed and changed the subject. "What about you? You look a bit poorly, if you don't mind my saying so."

Cyte stared gloomily down at the floor below. "It's been a busy week."

"Be honest."

"I can't sleep. I keep thinking about . . . you know. That night, in the Vendre."

Winter nodded, sympathetically. "The first time someone tried to kill me, it was a while before I got a good night's sleep."

"It's not even that," Cyte said, lowering her voice to a whisper. "I was scared—I mean, of course I was. But . . ."

Winter waited.

"There was a guard I . . . stabbed. In the stomach, right through him. I barely even thought about it. He was going to kill you, kill me if he got the chance, and I just . . . did it." She brushed her hand against her leg, as though trying to wipe something away. "It was so *easy*."

Winter was silent. She tried to remember the first man she'd killed, but the truth was that she didn't know. In a battle—even the little skirmishes the Colonials dealt with before the rise of the Redeemers—you rarely knew if a shot had hit or missed. When someone fell it was anyone's guess if he'd been deliberately killed or clipped by a stray ball. In an awful way, that made it better. She'd felt like throwing up the first time she had to clean up a battlefield and bury a handful of enemy corpses, but there wasn't anyone she could point to and say, "I ended that man's life."

"I know you thought I volunteered for that on a whim," Cyte said, and raised a hand when Winter started to protest. "It's all right. You tried to talk me out of it, and I appreciate that. The truth is that I did my thinking before we even got to the Vendre. When we heard what the Concordat was doing, and people in the cafés started talking about marching, I thought . . . this is it. I told myself, 'If you're going out there, you have to be prepared for it. Are you ready to die, if that's what it takes? Are you ready to kill?' And I decided that I was, but it took . . . I don't know. It felt like a big thing to decide.

"And then, when it finally came to it, it was *easy*. Just a little thrust." She held out her hand. "Just like I practiced in front of the mirror. I barely even noticed what he looked like until afterward. I was too busy worrying if there was someone else behind him who was going to stick me with a bayonet. It was only afterward that I started to think about it, and I wondered, Is that what it's supposed to be like?" She closed her eyes and sighed. "Or is there something wrong with me?"

There was a long silence. Winter felt as though she were supposed to offer something here, some piece of worldly advice from a sergeant to a young soldier. But this wasn't Khandar, she wasn't a sergeant, and Cyte wasn't a soldier and was only three years younger besides. *And anyway, what the hell am I supposed to say to that?* She suddenly remembered rescuing Fitz Warus from Davis' cronies, cracking Will over the head with a rock just to get him out of the way. She'd killed him, it turned out, without thinking about it or even really meaning to.

If there's something wrong with you, it's wrong with me, too. But she couldn't quite bring herself to say it out loud.

"Excuse me," someone said. "Are you Winter?"

They looked up to find a bearded young man in the colorful clothes of a dockworker waiting with a polite air. He had an odd, gravelly accent, and something about the way he stood gave him a military bearing. She pushed away from the rail, brushing fragments of crumbling wood from her hands.

"I am," she said, cautiously. "Who are you?"

"Just a messenger." He took a folded page from his breast pocket and handed it to her. "Read it soon, and make sure you're alone when you do."

"Why? Who's it from?"

The young man's eyes flicked to Cyte, and he shrugged. "It's what I was told. Good luck."

"Good luck?" Winter echoed, baffled, but the messenger was already jogging back toward the stairs, raising little puffs of dust with every step. Winter looked down at the note, then over at Cyte.

"I'll be with the others," Cyte said, stepping away from the rail.

Winter unfolded the page. It bore only a few lines, in an elegant, aristocratic hand that made the signature redundant.

Winter—

Concordat action against the Deputies is imminent. I am on my way with help. Stall.

Janus

Her fingers tightened on the page, driven by a sudden, furious anger. *He drops me here for weeks, without so much as a word, and now he tells me Orlanko is on the way and I'm to stall? How? Start a goddamned circus to keep them occupied?* She glanced down at the hall floor, where Abby was still speaking, and fear replaced rage. *Oh, Balls of the Beast. If the black-coats show up here, it's going to be panic. What the hell does Orlanko think he's doing?*

She hurried back to where Cyte and the girls were waiting. Curious eyes followed her as she grabbed Cyte and dragged her away again, out of earshot of the rest.

"What?" Cyte said. "What's going on? Was that a message from Jane?"

Winter shook her head. Impulsively, she tore a strip off the bottom of the note, removing the signature, and handed the rest to Cyte.

"Who's this from?" Cyte said, glancing at the scrap in Winter's palm. Winter crushed it into a ball.

"Someone I trust," she said. *I think.*

"Then you really believe—"

"Yes."

"But that's insane. The queen invited the deputies here. It's *treason*."

"Be sure to mention that to the duke when you see him!" Winter snapped.

Cyte was quiet for a moment. Then she said, "What are we going to do?"

"I don't *know*. Give me a minute." She glanced at the pack of girls, all of whom were now watching Winter and Cyte instead of the dull proceedings on the floor. "Let's see if we can get them out of here, to start with. Once we're downstairs I'll try to find Giforte. There's Armsmen here—maybe we can organize a barricade." *And he owes me a favor.*

"Okay." Cyte blew out a deep breath. "I don't suppose you're armed?"

Winter shook her head again. "I didn't think I'd need it."

"Me, either. Saints and fucking martyrs." Cyte swallowed hard and straightened up. "Let's go."

Corralling the girls and convincing them that they needed to leave—and never mind why, lest someone scream and spark a panic—took longer than Winter would have liked. They got them moving in the end, though, and nothing untoward seemed to be happening as they trooped along the unsteady gallery, past other curious onlookers.

The main stairs to the gallery were at the bend of the horseshoe, near the rear of the main hall. On the far side, at the very end of the right-hand stretch, a small walkway led to a stone door letting on to the cathedral's warren of second- and third-floor rooms. Winter led her charges toward the stairs, letting Cyte watch the girls while she stayed a couple of strides ahead.

The stairway was a long switchback, and when they got there it was shaking under the tread of many feet. No one was descending from the gallery, though, which meant that a crowd of people was coming *up*. *Either some big group downstairs decided they want a better view, or else—*

Four men came around the switchback, standing shoulder to shoulder to block the stairway. They weren't immediately recognizable as Concordat—no black coats or shiny insignia, just plain homespun and worn tradesmen's overcoats—but all four wore swords, and something about their purposeful formation shouted trouble to Winter. She backpedaled up the steps, only to collide with Cyte and Molly coming in the other direction. The rest of the girls pressed them forward, still chatting obliviously.

"Back," Winter said. "Up the stairs. Go—"

Someone down below barked an order. Each of the four drew a pistol from under his coat.

One of the girls screamed. At the same time, shouts rose from the main floor, then cut off all at once at the sharp report of a pistol.

"I am Captain Richard Brack," boomed a voice, carrying beautifully through the high-vaulted chamber. "Of the Ministry of Information, Special Branch. And everyone in this room is under arrest!"

"Everybody on the floor!" drawled one of the four ahead of them. "All you girls, get down *now*!"

"Get *back*!" Winter shouted, pushing the screaming Becks up the stairs. The other girls needed little encouragement to flee, stairs creaking under their panicked footsteps. "Cyte! Go *that way*!" She gestured frantically to the right.

"I said *stop*!" one of the men repeated, stepping forward of the line and lowering his pistol to point directly at Winter. "We're with the Special Branch. What the hell do you think you're doing?"

Winter met his gaze, and there was a moment of contemplation. He held the pistol awkwardly, and his sword belt looked brand-new and poorly fitted. And there was something in his eyes—a bit of *fear*, she thought. This wasn't one of Orlanko's trained killers, Winter was certain. She doubted he'd ever fired the weapon he held.

Special Branch must mean the reserves. Not the regular Concordat agents, but some cadre of thugs and mercenaries summoned into service for emergencies. Men who were more used to bullying helpless civilians than to actual combat, who expected to command respect simply by virtue of *having* a weapon, without having to use it . . .

If she'd been facing an experienced soldier, what she did next would have been suicidal. But an experienced soldier would never have stepped so close to her in the first place. Winter's left hand shot out and grabbed the pistol around the hammer. The Special Branch man gulped and pulled the trigger, convulsively, but he'd hesitated too long, and the flint slammed down hard on the back of Winter's hand. This hurt like hell but produced no sparks. The thug's eyes broadened in comical surprise, and Winter brought her right hand up and delivered a hard blow to his wrist. His fingers opened automatically, and she plucked the weapon from his grasp. Before his companions realized what was happening, she reversed it, clicked the hammer back, and leveled it at his forehead. He froze.

"Fucking Beast," one of the others said, and three other pistols swung to bear on her.

"Don't be stupid."

Winter stepped back, carefully maintaining her aim, and climbed toward the shaky wooden walk. She desperately wanted to look over her shoulder, but if she took her eyes off the Special Branch men, the fragile moment could shatter. *Five steps? Four? Three?*

"There's no way out," said the man whose weapon she had taken. "We've got the building surrounded."

"No reason for *you* to get shot, then," Winter said.

That seemed to be the general opinion. They held their aim but didn't fire, and she kept backing up. Something creaked beneath her, and her groping foot couldn't find the next stair, throwing her dangerously off balance. Before she could trip, though, someone caught her from behind, and she heard Cyte's soft grunt. Winter steadied herself on the top step.

"The first head that comes up those stairs," she said, "gets a lead ball through the ears. Got it?"

Without waiting for an answer, she ducked around the corner, dragging Cyte with her. Jane's girls waited in a huddle against the wall. Down below on the main floor, she could see more of the Special Branch men moving through the crowd with weapons drawn.

"Come on," Winter said, shivering all over with released tension. She gestured with the pistol at the second-floor exit. "We may be able to get out that way. There has to be a back staircase." When none of Jane's girls moved at once, she let a touch of army sergeant into her voice. "Move!"

Floorboards creaked behind her as the Special Branch men came up the stairs. If she fired, they'd know she was unarmed and rush her; she closed the lock on the pistol, thrust it into her waistband, and ran for it. Cyte ran beside her, and together they chivvied the girls down the length of the Widow's Gallery like dogs herding a flock of geese.

The motion attracted some notice from the Special Branch men on the ground floor, but they had their hands full for the moment with the unruly crowd. Winter could hear several deputies competing to shout the loudest denunciation of Orlanko's "illegal and treasonous" actions.

They're brave, Winter thought. *Stupid, but brave.* Brack barked an order, and his thugs closed in around the offenders. Whatever reluctance they might have had to use their pistols did not apply to their fists, and the opposition was soon silenced.

By then Winter had reached the doorway at the end of the walk, stepping off the creaky wood onto the solid stone floor of the cathedral's upper stories. A corridor ran in both directions, with several doorways leading through it into dimly lit spaces, and Winter wasn't sure which way to go.

"Out, out, out," she muttered. "Which way is out?"

"Toward the back," Cyte said. "I know there's a door by the old kitchens, but they'll be watching it."

"Maybe we can get the drop on them." Winter gestured the girls to clear the doorway, and looked back down the walk. The four Special Branch men were following, but cautiously.

Someone tugged at her sleeve. It was Becks, red-faced but looking determined.

"I'm sorry I screamed," she said. "I was just surprised."

"It's fine—"

"But we can't leave! Not yet." Becks looked at her companions and got a round of nods. "We have to help Danton first."

"Help *Danton*?" Winter blinked. "Why?"

"He's up this way." Molly, standing behind Becks, pointed down the corridor. "We have to get him out of here."

"Orlanko let him get away once," Becks said, with a fifteen-year-old's certainty. "If they catch him this time, they'll kill him."

"Danton can take care of himself," Winter said. "I—"

"She's right," Cyte said. She met Winter's eye.

"You said yourself he's just a symbol," Winter said, quietly.

"Symbols can be important," Cyte said. "If we can get him out of the cathedral, Orlanko hasn't won yet."

The Special Branch men were getting closer. Winter hesitated a moment, then sighed. "All right. Stay close. They may have sent someone up from the back."

"I can see two of them," Cyte whispered.

"It sounds like there's at least one more inside," Winter said. "Maybe two."

"Three or four, then."

"Yeah."

Cyte swallowed. "We dealt with four at once in the Vendre."

"We were lucky." Winter looked down at the pistol in her hand. *One shot. No way to reload, even if I had time.* "And we were armed."

They stood in a narrow stone corridor, outside the entrance to a suite of rooms that had once served as some priest's living quarters. A couple of mismatched chairs and a folding table stood in the outer room, and a single lantern hung from a wall bracket. Another doorway led deeper into the suite, flanked by two men—not the Special Branch thugs, but real Concordat black-coats. As Becks had guessed, Orlanko was taking no chances with Danton. Beyond that doorway, some kind of altercation was taking place, and Winter could hear a muffled female voice shouting.

"We might be able to take one of them," Molly said. She and Becks had followed Winter and Cyte to peek into the suite, while the rest of the girls waited at the end of the corridor to watch for the Special Branch. "We could work together."

She sounded uncertain, and Winter didn't blame her. She doubted Molly and Becks put together outweighed one of the guards. Some of Jane's Leatherbacks were fighters, but those were mostly older girls, and these two were not among them.

Winter shook her head. "Stay here. If it goes wrong, run for it."

"But—" Molly began. Becks grabbed her arm and she fell silent.

"I'll take the one on the left," Winter said to Cyte. "You've got to keep the other one busy until I can get ahold of a sword."

"Okay." Cyte ran her fingers through her hair and blew out a long breath. "Let's go."

Winter drew back the hammer on her pistol, reflexively checked the powder in the pan, and stepped around the corner. The two Concordat guards took a moment to register her presence, absorbed in what was happening in the next room, and in the time this provided her Winter took a long step forward and shot the one on the left.

At least, she pointed the pistol in his direction and pulled the trigger. The powder in the pan flashed, but instead of a *bang* and a gout of smoke, the barrel emitted a noise more like *phut* and coughed a thin trickle of blue-gray vapor. Too late, Winter recalled the old pistoleer's maxim: The more critical the shot, the more likely it was to misfire.

Cyte was already coming around the corner, running at the man on the right. He started to shout something as she cannoned into him, wrapping her arms around him to trap his hands at his sides. Her momentum slammed him back against the wall with an *oof*, knocking the breath out of him.

Winter's own target clawed for his sword. She reversed the pistol and held it by the barrel like a club, hoping to get a blow in before he was ready, but he managed to get his blade out and drove her backward with a horizontal slash. She circled left, grabbed one of the wooden chairs, and sent it tumbling toward him, but he kicked it out of the way and pressed forward, forcing her to backpedal until she felt the wall against her shoulder blades. She tried for his head with the pistol, but he caught her wrist with his off hand, pinning her in place for a thrust.

Behind him, she could see Cyte's victim trying to break free, trapped arms straining. He lurched forward and managed to get his knee up into her stomach. She doubled over, and he slipped one hand free of her grip and tangled it in her black hair. Cyte screamed.

Molly's charge hit Winter's opponent in the small of the back, pushing his thrust wide to strike sparks off the stone wall to Winter's left. He let go of Winter and whirled around, sword humming dangerously through the air. Molly dropped flat, whimpering. Becks, coming up behind her, made a grab for the soldier's sword arm and missed, and his backhand cut opened a long gash on her arm and flicked a spray of blood onto the wall.

The two girls had distracted him long enough, though. Winter gripped the pistol in both hands and brought the iron-heeled butt down on his head as hard as she could. Something *crunched*, and he dropped bonelessly, sword slipping out of his grip to clatter on the floor. Winter scrambled to scoop it up, nearly cutting herself in the process, and came up just in time to see Cyte's opponent shake her off and send her crashing into a table. He turned round, saw Winter, and reached for his sword, but her lunge caught him in the stomach and he folded up with a groan.

"Saints and *fucking* martyrs," someone said, from the doorway. Winter spun to see two more Concordat soldiers. Behind them was a solid-looking door that they had apparently been trying to break down. Both went for their swords. Winter caught the one in the lead with a low cut as his blade came out of its scabbard, opening a bloody gash on his leg and sending him stumbling to the floor. The other one got his weapon out but backed away cautiously, toward the door he'd been pounding on. His fallen comrade had dropped his blade to clutch the wound on his leg, and Winter edged past him, coming almost into range of the fourth man. They stood, sword tip to sword tip, for a long moment.

"What the *hell* do you think you're doing?" the man snarled.

Winter thought about trying to explain but didn't see much point. She shrugged. The man was getting ready to say something else when the door behind him opened, quietly, and someone hit him over the head with a chair. That sent him sprawling forward, off balance, and Winter spitted him simply by remaining still with her weapon raised. He made a bubbling noise and slid off the blade to lie still on the floor.

Left eye to eye with Winter, holding the remains of the chair in her hand, was a girl about Molly's age, with blond hair and heavy freckles. She was breathing hard. Winter nodded to her, cautiously, and backpedaled into the outer room.

"Molly? Becks?" she said.

"I'm okay," Becks said, through clenched teeth. She sat on the floor, her wounded arm held out straight, while Molly busied herself tearing strips from a soldier's shirt to make a bandage. "It's . . . *uh* . . . not deep."

"Cyte?"

Cyte waved from the wreckage of the table and started pulling herself to her feet. A bruise was blooming on her cheek, but she seemed otherwise unharmed. "Sorry. He got away from me."

Winter nodded at them, a small knot in her chest untying itself. She turned back to the inner room, where the girl had emerged to kick the dropped weapons well out of range of the wounded soldier, who wisely remained curled in a silent ball on the floor. In the doorway behind her, Winter saw Danton, staring at the bloodied men with slack-jawed disinterest.

"Who are you?" the girl said. She was trying to keep her tone calm, but her breathing was fast and she seemed close to panic. Winter, realizing she still held a bloody sword, set it down for the moment and tried to sound reassuring.

"I'm Winter," she said. "I'm with Mad Jane. Are you one of Danton's people?"

"Something like that," the girl said. "My name is Cora. I came up here . . . when . . ."

Her eyes fell on the dead man, watching in horrified fascination as a pool of blood spread from where he lay facedown, and she trailed off.

"Cora," Winter said. The girl's head jerked up, her eyes full of tears. Winter held out her hand, and Cora took it tentatively. Winter drew her carefully past the bodies and into the outer room.

"Thank you." Cora knuckled her eyes. "I was watching from the gallery when the Concordat came in. I ran back up here to see if I could get Danton to move, but the black-coats blocked us in."

"We were on the Widow's Gallery. Special Branch men are all over the place." Winter glanced back down the corridor, to make sure the rest of the girls were still keeping an eye out. "We were hoping we could get out through the back."

Cora shook her head. "I poked my head down the stairs that way. They've got it blocked. But we don't need to get Danton *out.* We need to get him down to the floor."

"What? Why?"

"He has to speak," Cora said.

Cyte, on her feet now, came over. "What makes you think they'll let him?"

"I don't think they'll have a choice," Cora said. "He can be very persuasive."

Winter shook her head. "This is ridiculous. Orlanko has to have a hundred armed men out there. Danton wants to make a *speech* to them?"

"Have you seen him speak?" Cora said.

Winter paused. She had, back at the Vendre, and it was undeniable that the effect on his listeners had been nothing short of sensational. The mob of prisoners had taken the Concordat troops apart. *But we took them from behind, by surprise.* Even if he got a similar response out of the deputies, the Special Branch thugs were ready and waiting. The crowd might overwhelm them, but it would be a bloodbath.

Stall. That was what Janus had asked her. It might work. *If I can get him to play for time . . .*

"Let me talk to him," Winter said.

Cora shook her head. "He . . . doesn't like to talk to most people, up close."

"Just for a minute." Winter bit her lip. "If we're going to do this, I need to know he understands what he's getting into."

"I don't . . . ," Cora began. She paused. "You can try."

Winter nodded and went back down the short, bloody corridor. The door at the end was still open, and Danton was sitting in a flimsy chair, staring amiably at nothing. Several empty bottles stood by his feet. *Is he drunk? That would explain the vacant look.* He was well dressed, at least, in an elegant, understated coat with gold buttons, hair neatly combed and hat pinned in place. When he noticed Winter, he waved.

"Hello," he said.

"Hello," Winter said cautiously. "I'm Winter."

"Hello," Danton repeated, and laughed.

"Cora told me that you want to give your speech," Winter said, trying to get a read on his expression. "You know what's going on down there, don't you?"

"They're waiting for me to tell my story," Danton said, with a guileless grin. "I'm ready. Cora told it to me, and I'm ready."

"Your . . . story? I don't understand."

"I like telling stories."

Something is very wrong here. Was it some kind of act? Winter stepped up beside him, and he stared vacuously up at her, blue eyes empty of anything but simple curiosity.

"You could get killed," Winter said. "Do you understand that?"

He blinked, and smiled wider. "People like my stories."

"Stories . . ."

A cold suspicion spread through Winter. She reached out, deliberately, and put her hand on Danton's shoulder.

Deep inside her, the Infernivore stirred. It rose from the dark pit of her soul, winding out through her body and into her hand, sniffing the air for prey like a hunting dog. And in Danton, something responded—another presence, a bright, airy, colorful thing, recoiling in frantic terror. Infernivore halted, coiled to pounce, needing only an effort of Winter's will to spring across the narrow gap between them and devour the alien magic.

Danton sensed none of this. He looked up at Winter, still smiling. Slowly, she lifted her hand from his shoulder.

"I don't think we can get him to the floor," Winter said, reemerging into the outer room. "They'll be watching the stairs."

Cora nodded. "I think we can get to the gallery. I didn't run into anyone on my way here. It looks out over the main floor from behind the altar. Everyone should be able to see him."

"Wait," Cyte said. "You're going along with this?"

Winter nodded.

"What if someone takes a shot at him?" Cyte said. "Danton's *important*. He's the heart of . . . of all of this! He shouldn't risk himself."

Winter caught Cora's eyes, and a quiet understanding passed between them. *He's not the heart of it. He's just a . . . a tool.* Cora and her friends had been *using* him, or using the magic that coiled inside him. *Like the Khandarai used Feor, and Orlanko used Jen.* But, at this point, Winter didn't see any other choice.

"He wants to do it," she lied. "And I think . . . people will listen."

Becks, pale as a ghost but still excited, jumped to her feet. "*Everyone* will listen! Even the Concordat. I always said, if people would only *listen* to Danton, everything would work out!"

She stumbled, light-headed, and Molly caught her by the elbow and held her up.

Winter sighed. "All right. Cora, you lead the way to the gallery. Cyte and I will be right behind you. You girls stick close to Danton and give a shout if anyone comes up behind us."

The gallery was a small stone balcony that opened unobtrusively onto the great hall some thirty feet above the altar. The Widow's Gallery was open for the public to watch the proceedings, but the gallery provided a more private space for visiting priests and other dignitaries to observe the service. Since they were in the old priests' quarters, it wasn't far, and no Special Branch soldiers barred their progress.

A low stone railing lined the gallery, and Winter stopped Danton and the others at the doorway. She crouched and crept to the edge of the balcony, trying to get a sense of what was going on below.

The Concordat captain, Brack, seemed to have things well organized. The deputies sat on the floor in circular groups, surrounded by rings of Special Branch men with drawn pistols. A few black-coats prowled the gaps between them. Brack himself stood near the altar, and more soldiers waited by the exits and against the walls. She could see dark figures moving on the Widow's Gallery, across the way.

Just below Brack, a couple of black-coats with a big ledger were processing the arrestees. Small bunches were driven up to them by grinning Special Branch thugs, and the prisoners gave their names and were directed back to one group or another in accordance with instructions that Concordat men read from their book. Another man took down everything that was said. Brack wasn't paying much attention to the proceedings, though, and had eyes mostly for the big double doors at the back of the hall.

He's waiting for reinforcements, Winter realized. This operation was obviously an emergency measure, hence the hastily recruited Special Branch mercenaries. Sooner or later more of the Last Duke's men would be along to take the prisoners in hand. *Or maybe not. Janus said help was coming. And if Jane has heard about what's happened . . .*

Winter glanced back at Danton and shook her head. *We have to do the best we can with the cards we've got.* She crept back to the doorway. Cora was whispering urgently in Danton's ear, and he nodded occasionally to show that he was listening. Cyte, standing behind them, still looked disapproving. The girls were waiting in the corridor, clustered around Becks, who had apparently earned some kind of legendary status by nearly losing her head to a Concordat swordsman.

"Something wrong?" Winter said to Cora.

"Some last-minute advice," the girl said. "To suit the text to the circumstances."

"Is he ready, then?"

Danton bobbed his head happily. "I've got it."

"Go ahead, then. They're waiting." He shuffled past, and Winter caught Cyte's eye. "If they start shooting, help me drag him back into the corridor."

Cyte nodded, grimly. Winter, the Infernivore's hunger tingling in her fingertips, watched Danton walk onto the gallery. A change came over him as the crowd came into view—he stood up straighter, his gait became more confident, and he strode over to the rail and took hold of it with casual confidence. Before anyone below noticed he was there, he started to speak.

Winter had been afraid he'd begin his address with a bellow that would draw pistol fire from the soldiers, but Danton surprised her. His voice started nearer to a whisper, but a whisper that somehow echoed from the vaulted ceiling and cut through the low murmur of the Concordat scribes going about their work. Winter saw people look around, trying to figure out where the sound was coming from, and by the time they saw Danton he had already hit his stride.

"—the gathered representatives of the nation, assembled in the light of hope, are here to discover if the great issues of our time can be resolved, not through royal fiat or the horror of war, but rather by men of good sense coming together in friendship to discuss the things which divide them—"

There were some good turns of phrase there, and Winter—watching with new appreciation—wondered who had written them for the orator. He was pleasant, reasonable, somehow both unremarkable and spectacular. What he said was convincing, not because it was *him* saying it, but because it just made such good *sense*.

And yet . . .

At first Winter thought it wasn't working. He was good, but not *that* good. It was hard to believe that this was *the* Danton who had sparked all the trouble. She had a moment of panic, wondering if his magic had somehow failed.

Then she took in the slack-jawed expressions on the faces of Cyte and Cora beside her. The hall below had gone absolutely silent, every face turned up toward the gallery with wide, staring eyes. Danton's voice rose, his stentorian baritone ringing through the chamber. His hands came up, punctuating his address with sweeping, slashing gestures, as he moved from the high purpose of the assembly to the strength of the forces that would inevitably oppose it.

"They will slander us, they will bribe us, they will crush us underfoot and blast us with cannon," Danton boomed. "The corrupt forces that have infiltrated the state will bring against us every instrument at their disposal. But *I* am not afraid. Let them come! It only shows that *we* are what *they* fear, the people united to drive them from their filthy pits and into the unforgiving light of day—"

It's just me, Winter realized. The tingling feeling had spread from her hands throughout her body, as though all her limbs had fallen asleep and had pins and needles. She wondered if it was the Infernivore actively protecting her, or if its mere presence made her immune to the spell Danton wove with his voice. For one absurd moment, it made her feel *left out*, envious of whatever profound emotion everyone else was clearly in the grip of. She felt, suddenly, very alone.

But not *entirely* alone. Someone was moving, down among the sea of frozen faces. The Special Branch thugs had put their pistols away or simply let them fall, and stood side by side with their erstwhile prisoners, trapped like flies in amber by the power of Danton's voice. Even Brack and the other black-coats didn't seem to be able to move. But one man walked freely, threading his way through the mob toward the altar. He wore a full-length robe with long sleeves, but instead of the gray of a Free Priest or even the pure white of the Sworn preacher, he was in black from head to heel. His face was obscured by a black, faceted mask, which sparkled like glass in the light from the braziers.

Winter shot to her feet. "Look out!"

No one heard, of course. Not the enthralled people down below; not Danton, who seemed oblivious; and certainly not the man in black. His hand came out of his sleeve, holding a pistol.

"*Ahdon ivahnt vi, Ignahta Sempria.* In the name of God and Karis the Savior, we stand against the darkness."

Danton had reached his peroration. "We will fight them," he promised. "I will not let those who died at the Vendre have sacrificed in vain. I will lay my life down alongside theirs, in the name of Vordan and the queen, and I know that every one of you would do the same! If our determination remains unbroken, then we can never—"

Winter fumbled for her own pistol. But, of course, she hadn't thought to reload it when she had the chance.

The masked figure fired. Danton halted in midsentence, as the *boom* of the pistol echoed around the hall. The orator brought one hand to his chest and held it up, slick with blood. His face went slack, and he looked at Winter and Cora with a frown.

"I don't understand," he said, and toppled backward.

Smoke rose from the barrel of the masked man's pistol. He tossed it aside, turned to face the crowd, and spread his hands as if in benediction.

The mob went mad.

MARCUS

Marcus had never thought to find himself in the royal carriage of the king of Vordan. It was as opulent as he'd expected, but all the cushions and velvet couldn't manage to disguise the fact that it was, basically, a box on wheels, not that far removed from the meanest hired cab. He felt oddly disappointed.

It was certainly roomy, but it wasn't far into the journey when Marcus started to feel that it wasn't big enough. He sat on the backward-facing bench, sinking into the thick cushions, and Janus sat beside him. Opposite them, prim in her black mourning dress, was the young queen. Apart from an exchange of courtesies when they'd mounted, none of the three had said a word.

The carriage proceeded down the Ohnlei Road toward the city at an unhurried pace. Spread out in front and flanking it on either side were Janus' Mierantai Volunteers, followed by a tighter wedge of Armsmen. The Mierantai driver kept the horses to a walk to allow these escorts to keep pace.

Marcus had questions for Janus, but hesitated to ask them in front of Raesinia. After a few minutes, however, he decided anything would be better than more tense silence. He leaned toward the colonel and cleared his throat.

"Hmm?" Janus looked up. "Is something wrong, Captain?"

"I just thought, sir . . ." Marcus hesitated, glancing at Raesinia, but the queen was looking pointedly out the window. "I think you owe me some kind of explanation."

Janus' lip quirked. "I suppose I do, at that."

"Why arrest Danton? You must have known what would happen."

"It seemed the best way of bringing the anti-Borelgai feeling to a head." Janus leaned back in his seat. "It was also based on my reading of Orlanko. The duke has always operated from a position of strength, and he has a corresponding tendency to arrogance."

"So you stirred up the mob—"

"In order to turn them against the Borels and Orlanko," Raesinia said. "With the help of . . . revolutionary elements in the city. I must say I never thought Orlanko would go so far as to try to seize Ohnlei itself. Though *you* obviously did, my lord Mieran."

Janus waved a hand. "It was always a possibility. I thought it best to be prepared."

"I'd appreciate it," Raesinia ground out, "if, in the future, you would share these *possibilities* with me."

Marcus gave a hollow laugh. "Best of luck with *that*, Your Majesty."

Janus flashed a smile. Marcus leaned back against the velvet, trying to keep his head from spinning as he worked through the implications.

Eventually he said, "So, what happens now? If you would care to enlighten us."

"Now?" Janus shrugged. "Orlanko has attempted to capture the deputies, but we have enough men"—he tapped the window glass—"to overwhelm his hirelings. God willing, there's been no bloodshed, and we ought to be able to convince most of them to surrender. Then the queen will give the assembled representatives of the people the news of the duke's fall, and swear to abide by whatever decisions the deputies ultimately arrive at." He pursed his lips, thoughtfully. "After that, I suppose, we'll have to turn our attention to the financial situation. We dare not abrogate our debt to the Borelgai outright, but—"

Raesinia cut him off. "I'd feel better if we had Orlanko himself in chains. And I'm worried about Sothe."

"Unfortunately, the Cobweb is eminently defensible, and no doubt stuffed full of booby traps as well. I'm hopeful that Orlanko can be convinced to accept a comfortable exile, once it becomes clear he's lost. Digging him out by force would cost a great many lives." Janus covered his mouth and yawned. "Apologies. It's been a long few days. As for Miss Sothe, from what I know of her reputation, I suspect she will manage."

Raesinia frowned, but before she could say anything there was a rap on the carriage door. Janus leaned over and opened it. One of the Mierantai had hopped on the running board, and saluted with one hand while hanging on with the other.

"Sir! We're approaching the Saint Dromin Bridge, as you requested." He paused. "It looks like it's blocked, sir. There's a bit of a . . . mob."

"Here?" Janus frowned. "Stop the carriage."

The soldier relayed the command to the driver, and the carriage rolled to a stop. With the door open and the wheels still, Marcus could hear the sound of the mob, an indistinct murmur that put him in mind of the sea. They were stopped at the intersection of Saint Dromin Street and Bridge Street, and one row of buildings still blocked Marcus' view of the river to either side. Straight ahead, however, the street mounted the footings of the high, double-arched bridge, and the bridge was dark with the press of humanity.

The mob had sighted them, too. There was a collective roar, and those in the lead broke into a run. They packed the bridge from edge to edge, crowding dangerously against the railings. A complete cross section of the city of Vordan seemed to be represented: nobles draped in colorful silks, prosperous merchants in somber, well-cut coats, laborers in leather vests and ragged trousers, all the way down to vagabond wretches wrapped in patched homespun. The crowd that had besieged the Vendre had been mostly Docksiders, but here the South Bank residents were outnumbered by well-dressed North Bankers.

"They must have come from the deputies," Janus said, stepping out of the carriage and shading his eyes with one hand. "Most of them are in their Sunday best."

"Sir." Lieutenant Uhlan came forward, gesturing to his men. "Please move back."

Red-and-blue-uniformed Mierantai were forming a line in front of the carriage. The first rank of men knelt while another rank formed up behind them, and rifle barrels fixed with gleaming bayonets swung into position. There were enough of them to block the street in front of the carriage, but they made for a very thin line. Marcus was forcibly reminded of the Battle of the Road, watching a horde of Khandarai peasants charge the Colonial lines under the goads of their mad priests. That time, the line had held. *But in Khandar I had the Preacher and a battery of twelve-pounders.*

The sergeant leading the palace Armsmen caught Marcus' eye, looking for orders. Marcus grimaced and gestured him forward, and the green-coated men spread out uncertainly behind the soldiers. The mob was still coming, approaching the footing of the bridge, though their front ranks were slowing at the sight of all those rifles.

"Sir," Marcus said. "What now?"

Janus looked over his shoulder at Raesinia, who was just emerging from the carriage. She paused for a moment on the running board, looking over the heads of the Mierantai at the advancing mob.

"I take it this was not part of the plan?" she said.

"No," Janus said, calmly. "Something has gone wrong. Badly wrong, I should say."

"What do they want?"

"I have no idea."

Raesinia squared her shoulders. "Wait here, then. I'll go find out."

Janus flashed a smile. "You know I can't do that, Your Majesty."

For a moment Raesinia looked as though she might object, but in the end she only shrugged. "Do what you like."

Janus caught Marcus' eye, and they hurried forward to take up positions on either side of the queen. Lieutenant Uhlan barked an order and a narrow path opened through the disciplined Mierantai. Janus threaded his way through first, followed by the queen and Marcus.

The leading edge of the mob had come to a stop about a hundred yards away, where the bridge touched solid ground again. Those in front were hesitating to move closer to the threatening line of bayonets, while the mass behind who couldn't see pressed forward. The bridge's arch acted as a kind of amphitheater, and Marcus found himself looking up into rank after rank of staring faces. Every eye was on Raesinia as she came forward in the company of the two uniformed officers.

Some kind of a scuffle was taking place at the front of the crowd. Eventually three people forced their way through to emerge onto the bare cobblestones. It took them a moment to get their bearings, but before too long they squared off and walked out to meet Raesinia and the others halfway. In the lead was a young man with a bright green coat and a rapier on his hip, marking him as a noble. His two companions were more soberly dressed, and neither was armed. All three were disheveled from their trip through the mob, but the leader made an effort to brush some of the dirt from his coat before stepping forward to introduce himself.

"Your Majesty," he said, bowing very low. "I am Deputy Alfred Peddoc sur Volmire, at your service. This is Deputy Dumorre and Deputy Maurisk. We are here to speak on behalf of the Deputies-General."

Marcus saw Raesinia go stiff as a board, just for a moment. Whatever had afflicted her, she soon snapped out of it and inclined her head graciously.

"Deputy Peddoc. This is Count Janus bet Vhalnich Mieran, my Minister of Justice, and Captain of Armsmen Marcus d'Ivoire." She paused. "But I must admit to some confusion. I was on my way to address the Deputies-General, which I was under the impression was in session at the cathedral."

Peddoc hesitated. Maurisk was absorbed in studying Raesinia's face, but Dumorre stepped forward into the silence.

"The deputies came under attack. Mercenaries in the employment of the Minister of Information attempted to illegally take the entire assembly into custody."

"I take it the attack failed," Janus said.

"It was thwarted," Peddoc said, "by Deputy Danton Aurenne. He took the floor and made a speech so moving that everyone present threw down their weapons and embraced one another like brothers in the service of Vordan."

"Until he was assassinated," Maurisk said.

"Assassinated?" Raesinia stepped forward, and Marcus caught a slight hitch in her voice. "Danton is dead?"

Peddoc nodded solemnly. "He was a martyr to our cause, and his sacrifice will not be in vain. The Deputies-General *will* be established."

"Of course," Raesinia said. "But what are you doing *here*?"

"The deputies are nothing but a polite fiction so long as the Last Duke and his supporters control the city," Maurisk said. "His Concordat have terrorized us for long enough."

"I quite agree," Janus said. "In fact—"

"*As such*," Maurisk went on, cutting him off with a glare, "the Deputies-General will assume its proper place over *all* the essential functions of government. Until a proper vote can be taken, we must ask that all armed men, in whoever's service, submit to our authority."

"Y . . . yes," Peddoc said, glancing uncertainly at Maurisk. "Well. It seemed best, under the circumstances. We don't know how deep the Last Duke's influence extends, but it must be cut out, root and branch. All who surrender their weapons will be treated with courtesy. Your Majesty, of course, will accompany us as an honored guest."

"I can assure you," Marcus said, "my lord Mieran had nothing to do with the Last Duke—"

"That is for us to decide," Maurisk said. "And he would do well to remember that it was *his* order that led to the arrest of Danton and the fall of the Vendre."

"I have not forgotten," Janus murmured. "May I have a moment alone with Her Majesty?"

Maurisk looked sour, but Peddoc interrupted him. "I don't see why not."

Janus took Raesinia's arm—a shocking breach of protocol, under other circumstances—and the three withdrew a few steps.

"If we run," Marcus said, keeping his voice low, "we can make it back to the carriage. A few volleys will slow them down, and we ought to be able to get it turned around before—"

"Are you suggesting I should ask Count Mieran's men to fire on the crowd?" Raesinia said.

"They would, if Your Majesty required it," Janus said.

"I'm just suggesting an option," Marcus said. "I don't like the way this Maurisk is talking."

Raesinia had an odd smile on her face. "I don't, either. But I don't see what choice we have. Even if we make it away, Lieutenant Uhlan and his men would be slaughtered. And then what? Back to Ohnlei?"

"I'm forced to agree." Janus looked over his shoulder at the mob. "I . . . was not expecting this."

Coming from Janus, this was a shocking admission. Marcus let out a sigh. "Then we go along quietly?"

Raesinia nodded, decisively. She turned around and went back to face Peddoc.

"I want you to guarantee fair treatment for these officers and their men," she said.

"Of course," Peddoc said.

"We will hold them for a time," Maurisk said. "But when things are settled, they will be released."

"Very well." Raesinia drew herself up, though she still made for a tiny figure. "I place myself in your care, then. Count Mieran, would you ask your men to stack arms?"

Janus turned to address Lieutenant Uhlan. His orders were almost drowned out by the cheers of the mob. Shouts and hurrahs started at the front, where people could see what was happening, but they spread backward through the vast mass. Like sparks down a powder trail, the news and the exultation passed back over the bridge and spread outward in ripples, through the heart of the city.

Part Five

ANDREAS

The little cabin seemed dark and dead. Andreas, his booted footsteps inaudible on the soft, leafy ground, put his back to the trunk of a massive oak and checked his pistols, then paused a moment in thought.

The Gray Rose had led him quite a chase. That was to be expected, of course. He would have been disappointed by anything less. They'd left Ohnlei behind and climbed the forested slope at the edge of the gardens into the royal hunting preserve. This swath of ancient forest, untouched by axes since the days of Farus the Conqueror, was the domain of huge, spreading oaks and stands of skinny birches, with little underbrush to impede men or horses.

The ground was soft from the recent rain, but not muddy enough to show tracks. Fortunately, the Gray Rose was wounded, and Andreas had been able to keep her in sight. He'd stayed well back, conserving his own strength and letting her exhaust herself, not wanting to risk a pounce that might let her turn the tables on him. He had the highest respect for his quarry.

Orlanko would be furious, of course. The chase had taken all day, and the light that now slanted through the forest was the soft, golden radiance of late evening. But Andreas was confident the plans he'd laid would be enough to deal with the queen and the deputies, if the Gray Rose was not allowed to interfere. Besides, he'd been looking forward to this for years. Politics would keep. This was . . . personal.

As the sun sank lower, he'd closed the distance between them. The Gray Rose had slowed, worn down by distance and loss of blood. She'd seemed on the edge of collapse, in fact. He knew he would have to make an end of it before the light disappeared; wounded or not, she might be able to evade him in the darkness.

Then they'd crested a ridge and come into sight of this tiny cabin. It was a single-room log hut, roofed with crude shingles, and probably belonged to one of the Royal Gamekeepers. No fire was burning, though, and the little stable was empty. The Gray Rose had gone straight to the door, staggering and clutching her shoulder, and stumbled inside.

Until now, Andreas thought her flight had been random, but she'd obviously been aiming for this place, which meant that she'd prepared it in advance. He'd broken off his pursuit and done a long circuit of the little building, confirming that the door was the only way in or out. Then he'd closed to within a few yards of the door, behind the nearest tree, and listened. All he could hear was birdsong and the rustle of leaves overhead.

So it's a bolt-hole, he thought. *A hiding place. She'll have weapons, for certain. Booby traps, perhaps.* The Gray Rose hadn't looked in any condition for a fight, though. Now that she was run to ground, Andreas could go for reinforcements, but that would mean leaving the cabin unobserved for however long it took him to leave and return. He wouldn't put it past the Gray Rose to feign weakness and make a dash for it while his back was turned.

No. I have to finish this now. But carefully. He drew a pistol and edged around the tree, then sprinted to the cabin wall, flattening himself beside the door.

There was no lock, just a simple push latch. Andreas tried to get a view of the interior through chinks in the logs, but it was too dark to see anything. He crept up to the side of the doorframe and stared dubiously at the latch. Was that glistening just the recent rain? Or had some noxious substance been painted on for the unwary finger?

He retreated a few steps and cast about until he found a suitable stick. Then, shifting the pistol to his left hand, he put his back against the wall again and reached out with his makeshift tool to trip the latch. It took some fumbling, but he got it, and a shove with the stick sent the door creaking inward.

There was a *click* when the door had opened wide enough to admit a body. A moment later, a curved blade scythed around the doorframe with spring-driven force, ripping through the spot where an intruder would have been standing at groin height. Its arc continued through nearly three hundred sixty degrees, swinging all the way around to bury itself in the outer wall in a way that would have severely inconvenienced anyone standing cautiously to one side of the door as it opened. It smashed Andreas' stick to splinters.

He smiled and shifted the pistol back to his right hand.

Edging around the blade, he squeezed sideways through the door, not opening it any farther. His eyes scanned the floor for trip wires or caltrops, but nothing presented itself. The interior of the cabin was only dimly lit by the fading light from the doorway, but he could see the huddled shape of a human figure in the center of the dirt floor, beside a heavy stone cooking block. Next to it was a small pit, which looked as if it had been concealed under a dirt-covered board. Andreas, squinting, could make out a pair of pistols inside, but the figure made no move to take them.

Was that her? It was too dark to tell. But the rectangle of sun from the doorway showed a couple of brilliant scarlet drops on the floor.

"Did you get all this way, only to collapse on the threshold?" he said aloud. There was no response from the figure. He leveled his pistol at it and edged forward.

It certainly *looked* like a woman's body. It would be safest to shoot first and investigate later, but if the Gray Rose was lying in wait, that would leave him temporarily disarmed. Instead Andreas walked crabwise across the floor, scanning every corner of the cabin. No one was hiding in the shadows, and the body on the floor didn't move. When he was close enough, he reached out and nudged it with his foot. It shook, slightly, but did not respond.

He aimed his pistol, rolled the figure over, and stepped hurriedly back.

The body was . . . not a body. It was a giant doll, a mannequin stuffed with straw and dressed in a woman's coat. It had no face; where eyes and mouth should have been, there was an embroidered rose, in black and gray.

"Clever," Andreas said, turning slowly around. "But not clever enough, I think. You can barely stand. Can we not give up this contest?" He didn't seriously expect her to give in, of course. But the offer might provoke some kind of response.

At that moment, the *other* device that had been triggered by the latch went off. Ten barrels of black powder buried in the dirt floor of the cabin exploded simultaneously, converting the hut and everything in it into an expanding blossom of flame that rose into the canopy and shook burning leaves from the trees. The *boom* echoed through the hunting preserve, all the way to the distant walls of the palace.

ORLANKO

By the time he climbed up a stepladder and into the comfort of his private carriage, Duke Orlanko was sweaty and very out of sorts.

In hindsight, he'd stayed at the Ministry too long. Once it had become clear that Vhalnich's Mierantai had overcome the Grays—and how the *hell* had that happened?—the clerks of the Cobweb had begun their emergency preparations. Vital archives were evacuated, and the incinerators in the lower stories blazed as they devoured less important papers. It was in Orlanko's nature to prepare for all contingencies, and so there was a plan for everything, even the fall of the Cobweb itself. Nothing there was irreplaceable.

But Vhalnich's men had held back, and Orlanko had accordingly hesitated to order the final evacuation. Only when he'd gotten word from the deputies had he accepted that this round, at least, was definitively lost. The mob there had overwhelmed both the men he'd sent to secure them and Vhalnich's Mierantai, and by the time the news reached him they were only an hour from the gates of Ohnlei.

With some of Vhalnich's men still prowling the grounds, he couldn't leave by carriage. Instead he had gone out via another tunnel, which came up at a hidden post in the royal hunting preserve. Horses had been waiting for him and his guards, and from there it was only a short ride to the Midvale Road. The duke was an indifferent rider at best, though, and his small stature made mounting an undignified process. He cursed every minute they spent in the saddle, first trotting through the woods and then setting a faster pace up the road to where the carriage was waiting.

Halfway there, an enormous *boom* had broken the stillness of the forest. Orlanko, watching the column of smoke rising, was at a loss to explain it—it seemed to be coming from the middle of the hunting park, and there was no reason so much powder should have been stored anywhere near there. It was another inexplicable thing in a day that had been full of inexplicable things. Since the duke had prided himself for years on knowing everything there was to know about his city, this frustrated him beyond words.

Three vehicles waited for them, two big post wagons full of records and a black carriage with shaded windows for Orlanko himself. There were also two dozen mounted black-coats with carbines, and together with the squad that had escorted him from the Cobweb, they were enough to make Orlanko feel reasonably secure. He pulled himself into the carriage, muscles already complaining from the short ride, and sank into the cushioned seat.

Sitting opposite him were two figures in hooded brown cloaks. Brother Nikolai and his charge had been among the first to be evacuated from the Cobweb, bundled up to keep their identities concealed even from the Concordat. Orlanko dared not risk losing his link to the Priests of the Black, not now. But he felt his irritation rising at the sight of Nikolai's glittering black mask; the story he'd received from the floor of the deputies had been very clear on a few particulars.

"Your people have made a mess of things, Brother Nikolai," Orlanko snarled, as the carriage lurched into motion.

The priest shrugged. "It was not my doing, Your Grace, as you must know. But I believe His Eminence was eager to speak with you on that very subject." He patted the girl sitting beside him on the thigh. "Is he still there?"

She drew back her hood. A bandage of black silk was wound around her head, covering her mutilated eye sockets. "Yes. One moment." Then, in the harsh voice of the Pontifex of the Black, "Orlanko."

"Your Eminence," Orlanko said. "You have received the news, I take it?"

"I have," said the distant Pontifex. "I must say I am beginning to have doubts about your commitment."

"*My* commitment? I was promised a free hand."

"And you've been given one."

"Until today! It was one of your people that killed Danton and threw the mob into a fury."

"There was no other option," the pontifex said, the girl's mouth stretching oddly to speak his words. "He was possessed, as you should have been aware, and his demon was a particularly dangerous one. He needed to be eliminated."

"I had the situation in hand."

"I doubt that. I'm told your men were ready to go over to the rebels as soon as Danton started speaking."

Orlanko pursed his lips. He'd long suspected that the Priests of the Black had pawns in the city other than himself, but it was galling to get confirmation nonetheless. He was also uncomfortably aware that the pontifex was probably right. The Special Branch were, after all, nothing more than mercenaries, not like his own carefully trained Concordat men. *And if Danton had a demon . . .*

He regretted, for the first time, sending Jen Alhundt to Khandar. At the time, he'd been pleased to rid himself of the arrogant Church agent, but if there were demons on the loose, having one on his side would have been a comfort.

"Well," Orlanko said, after a moment of silence. "What's done is done. The mob appears to have turned on Vhalnich, so perhaps things are not as bleak as they appear—"

"They are bleaker," the pontifex snapped. "Vhalnich is no common enemy. He has the Thousand Names at his disposal. Now that you and your men have been driven from the city, there is nothing left to stop him from becoming another Demon King. Your failure runs deep, Orlanko."

Orlanko's fists clenched. *Someday, Your Eminence. Someday you will pay a heavy price for every slight.* He kept his tone calm.

"I am taking steps to retrieve the situation as we speak. By morning, I will be at Midvale—"

"Do whatever you think best," the pontifex said. He sounded dangerously dismissive.

"Your Eminence," Orlanko said, "I hope you understand that, in spite of our setbacks, we're still very close to achieving our goal. We can break this rabble, and once we have Raesinia in hand, everything will be under control."

"So you have always assured me," the pontifex said. "I am losing confidence in you, Vordanai. I will not allow another kingdom of darkness to be established on these shores, do you understand? So by all means, get matters in hand. Because, if you do not, I will be forced to take . . . other steps."

"I—" Orlanko began.

"He's gone," the blind girl said.

We're so close, the duke thought. *All these years, I've worked for this, and we're so close. If not for Danton and Vhalnich, it would have gone smoothly.* Now there would be fighting and bloodshed, but there was no helping that. *I will not let that pious old fool ruin everything I've built, either.*

The sun was just peeking over the horizon when the carriage and its accompanying wagons rattled off the Midvale Road and up a gentle slope to a high, grassy hill. From here Orlanko could see the town of Midvale a few miles off, a prosperous, tidy-looking community of a few hundred shingled houses. Closer to was the regular grid of long, low barracks that comprised the Royal Army camp. Midvale was the permanent camp of the Eighth and Tenth Infantry regiments, as well as the Osthead Cuirassiers. They formed a second town of seven thousand souls—not counting wives, servants, whores, and other hangers-on—that had grown up alongside the first, more uniformly laid out but not nearly so clean.

Another carriage was pulled up in the grassy parade ground, which by its luxuriant growth of weeds had not seen a great deal of parading recently. A squadron of cuirassiers was deployed around it, resplendent in polished steel breastplates and plumed helmets. A pair of them rode alongside Orlanko's carriage as it pulled in, and the Concordat troops spread themselves out among the cavalry.

In the center of the ring was Count Torahn, dismounted and standing by a folding table covered in maps. With him were several other officers Orlanko didn't recognize. The Concordat kept files on every military man of any consequence, but Orlanko didn't concern himself with any not likely to turn up at court. It probably didn't matter. The Midvale garrison was not considered a promising post in the army, and thus the men assigned to command it were likely to be nonentities.

He waited to get down until one of his men had placed the stepladder so he could descend without an undignified jump. Torahn and the military men looked at him coldly, as though he were something slimy that insisted on worming its way across the lawn instead of rotting quietly under a rock. And, in truth, Orlanko felt uncomfortable, here in the open, under the eyes of these big, haughty men with their gleaming spurs. He had always preferred to employ the small, quick, and clever. *But desperate times demand desperate measures, I suppose.*

"Your Grace," Count Torahn said. "I am pleased to see you unharmed. When we got no news from the palace, we feared the worst."

"Not the worst, thankfully, but bad enough," Orlanko said. "The city is in open rebellion, thanks to the traitor Vhalnich."

The colonels made noises of consternation, but Torahn cut them off with a gesture.

"The queen?" he said.

"A prisoner," Orlanko said. "She will be well treated, I think. The rebels claim to fight in her name. They need her to awe the common people."

Torahn frowned. "I hope they don't think to hold her hostage."

"I have a hard time believing any Vordanai would do such a thing," Orlanko said. "Rebels or not."

"True." Torahn glared at the three colonels. "In spite of my orders, it appears that preparations here have not yet been completed. It will be a day or two before we're ready to march, I'm told."

"The sooner the better," Orlanko said. "Every moment the rebels have to dig in works against us."

An icy look passed between Orlanko and the Minister of War. It was uncertain who ought to be giving the orders—as a duke, Orlanko had the advantage of rank, but the Ministry of War took precedence over Information, especially in a situation like this one. For the moment, neither chose to make an issue of it.

Orlanko turned to the three colonels. "Gentlemen. I have written a short statement, which I would like your officers to read to the men." He took a sheet of folded paper from his pocket and tossed it on the table. "In addition, I want to make sure every man in your regiments is impressed with both the importance of this operation and its legitimacy. Whatever their claims, the rebels have imprisoned our queen and taken illegal possession of the seat of Her Majesty's government. I want no wavering or vacillation when the time comes to confront the traitors!"

All three saluted and barked out assurances of their loyalty, but Orlanko was no longer listening.

If we can recapture Raesinia, he thought, *and clear Ohnlei of traitors, then we can reestablish order in the city.* He would need to apply the whip with a firm hand, especially in the seditious districts south of the river and by the University. *The mob thinks it has nothing to fear from Concordat. It must be taught otherwise.* He wondered what had happened to Andreas, and hoped he hadn't been killed. His talent for bloodshed would be useful in the days to come.

Most of all, though, it all had to happen *soon*. Too long, and the Borels might start to wonder if their loans would be repaid. Too long, and the Pontifex of the Black would act, and what form *that* action would take Orlanko hardly dared to imagine. *Time, time, all I need is time.* A few days, a few weeks, and the rebellion would be crushed. The queen would be taught proper obedience.

And Janus bet Vhalnich will be dying a slow, painful death.

CHAPTER NINETEEN

WINTER

Eight fresh bodies hung in front of the cathedral, roped by the neck and suspended from the rooftop crenellations. Four of them were Borelgai, three men still in their long fur capes and a woman in the shredded remains of an elegant dress. The other four, two men and two women, wore the drab clothes of Vordanai commoners. More Concordat, Winter supposed. The city seethed against the minions of the Last Duke, and more people were imprisoned as Concordat agents every day, on increasingly flimsy pretexts.

Armed men flanked the main entrance in the sashes of the Patriot Guard, Greens on the left and Reds on the right, regarding each other with mutually hostile stares. Winter, wrapped in the plain black sash of a deputy, was admitted after only a cursory inspection.

Inside, shouts and occasional bursts of violent applause indicated the Deputies-General was already in session. The entrance hall was crowded, deputies in their sashes mixing with spectators and supplicants. More Patriot Guards lined the walls, and another pair—one Green and one Red, of course—guarded the double doors leading into the great hall itself. Winter threaded her way through the crowd and, under the cover of a particularly loud burst of shouting, pushed the doors open and slipped inside.

The great hall of the cathedral was not really very well suited to be used for an assembly like this one. It was long and rectangular, arranged so that a single priest could stand at the altar at one end and look out over the rows of worshippers. At first the deputies had planned to put their speaker's rostrum in front of the altar, but some of the radicals had objected to the way this separated the speaker from the rest of the body—and thus, symbolically, from the body politic, beginning the process that could only end in the exaltation of an individual over the community—

And so on. In the end, in a pattern Winter was beginning to recognize, a compromise was reached that was clearly inefficient and pleased no one. Wooden bleachers were erected along one long edge of the rectangle, displacing various Sworn Church paraphernalia. The benches curved around when they reached the far end of the room, thus cutting off the altar from sight. The speaker was placed against the other long wall, a curiously lopsided arrangement that left him only a short distance from some of his audience and a long way from others. But he was very definitely *below* them, and in any case by the time the seats had actually been built it was too late to go back and redo everything.

In front of the altar, on the far right of the speaker's rostrum, the curved section of seats called the Bend was occupied by the Monarchists. They consisted of Peddoc and his ilk, offspring of powerful noble families, backed up by representatives of the larger merchants, Vordanai bankers, and other wealthy men. Opposite them, on the extreme left-hand side of the benches, were the Radicals, now a haphazard coalition of student revolutionaries, lowborn advocates of violent reform, and a few noble sons who had come under the seductive spell of Voulenne. Directly in front of the speaker was a large group variously called the Conservatives (by the Radicals), the Republicans (by the Monarchists), or simply the Center. This was not a cohesive group, but merely a collection of those who for whatever reason felt uncomfortable joining one extreme or the other, and was itself separated into subgroups based on class, shared interest, or simple association or friendship. Winter's own spot was with Cyte, Cora, and a few of Cyte's student friends who hadn't joined the Radicals.

Why she should be a deputy at all was something Winter had often wondered. The grounds for membership were poorly defined. Everyone who had been present on the day of Danton's assassination was invited, and a few more representatives had forced their way in by virtue of money or influence. Winter was theoretically there to represent Jane and the Leatherbacks, but Jane had given her no advice about what she was supposed to be doing.

In fact, she'd had only the briefest conversation with Jane since the assassination. They'd both attended the first meeting of the deputies after the queen's surrender, but a few hours of discussion, punctuated by shouting and the occasional hurled inkwell, had been enough for Jane. She'd retreated to the safety of her headquarters on the other side of the river. Winter spent those few hours sitting beside her in silence, with Abby hanging between them like a curtain. When Jane left, Winter had mumbled something about needing to keep a watch on things here. The uncomprehending pain in Jane's eyes made Winter want to vomit.

Since then, she'd felt duty-bound to attend these meetings, though increasingly that was because she had nothing else to do. Winter felt like she was drifting, alone and rudderless. Every day that passed was making matters worse with Jane, but she couldn't face the pain of ripping open the wound so that it might begin to heal. Her only other attachment was to Janus and Marcus, and they were languishing in the Vendre with other officers of the Armsmen and the Royal Grenadiers, while the deputies tried to figure out what to do with them. All that Winter had left was her tenuous friendship with Cyte, and a vague sense of guilt that forced her to sit through these noisy, tedious sessions.

Cyte mouthed a greeting when she caught Winter's eye, her actual words lost in the clamor of the deputies' debate. Winter awkwardly crab-walked along the rows of benches until she reached her friend's side and sat down between her and Cora.

"What's going on?" she said, into Cyte's ear.

"Same as yesterday," Cyte said. "They're trying to formalize the procedures for the final Deputies-General. Right now they're stuck on the veto. The Monarchists want the queen to have the right to veto legislation. The Radicals know they don't want a veto, but they can't seem to decide what they want the queen's role to be."

"What do you think?"

Cyte shrugged. "Gareth proposed a veto, overridable by a two-thirds vote in the Deputies. It seemed like a good compromise, but neither side was listening. I just wish they would get *on* with it." She sighed as there was a rustle in the Monarchist ranks. "And here's Peddoc to make his daily petition."

"Again?"

A shout of "Quiet!" came from the rostrum, and heavy thuds echoed through the chambers as the Patriot Guards on either side slammed the butts of their muskets against the floor. This eventually got the noise down to a level where a man could make himself heard, and Johann Maurisk, president of the assembly, laid his hands flat on his podium and cleared his throat.

How Maurisk had gotten himself elected president was another thing that was not clear to Winter. It had been in the first couple of days, when the heady mood of victory was still strong—if not for that, the deputies would still be arguing about whether they even *needed* a president. Maurisk's background was with the student radicals, but his well-known association with the martyr Danton gave him enough cachet with the Center to get his nomination through.

It certainly wasn't a job *she* would have signed up for, at any price. Maurisk seemed at home with the debates, though, which often ended up with president and deputy standing inches apart, shouting at full volume, spittle flying into each other's faces. While the Patriot Guards were nominally charged with defending the assembly, keeping the deputies from coming to blows had become an important secondary duty.

"The floor recognizes Deputy Peddoc," Maurisk said, in the resigned tones of someone who knows what is coming next.

Peddoc, dressed more colorfully and expensively than ever, got to his feet from his seat in the front row of the Monarchists. He raised his chin and extended one hand in the declamatory posture taught to rhetoric students at the University, in spite of the snickers and catcalls this provoked from the less educated members of the other parties.

"Brothers of the Deputies-General," he said, "we have won the city. But we cannot simply rest easy on our victory!"

"'Our' victory?" Cyte said under her breath. "I don't recall that he had much part in it."

Winter snickered. Peddoc continued.

"The villain Orlanko waits, only a few days' march to the north! Our scouts tell us the troops at Midvale are preparing to march. If we hope to retain what we have won, we must strike first! I propose that this assembly set aside all other business and call for volunteers for the Patriot Guard, for the purpose of moving immediately on the Last Duke's camp!"

The Monarchists were clapping and cheering before Peddoc had finished, and there was a little bit of applause from the Center, but the Radicals listened in stony silence. Their leader, a young man named Dumorre, got to his feet and heaved an exaggerated sigh.

"We've heard this story before, Deputy Peddoc," he said. "If Orlanko was going to march on Vordan City, don't you think he would have done it by now?"

That was a fair enough point, Winter thought. The deputies had sent scouts to Midvale, and while their amateur reporting was a bit garbled, the general picture was of a great deal of activity but no actual marching. Peddoc had been demanding action for four days now, and it was quickly descending to the level of farce. *Like a lot of other things around here.*

"Besides," Dumorre went on, "I think you know by now the main objection to your proposal. Who will command this force you want to assemble? And, once Orlanko is beaten, what is to prevent this commander from turning his men on the city?"

"I object to the insinuation that I would do any such thing!" Peddoc thundered.

"So you admit that you have yourself in mind for command?"

"Of course." Peddoc drew himself up. "May I remind you that I commanded the force that took the Vendre?"

That set both sides off, and the chamber erupted in a roar of claims and counterclaims. The Patriot Guards started slamming their muskets against the floor for quiet, but the Greens on the right were soon trying to outslam the Reds on the left, and they only added to the cacophony.

The Patriot Guard was emblematic of the deputies' problems. It had been formed in the immediate aftermath of the queen's surrender, when it became clear that *someone* had to maintain law and order. The Armsmen officers had been placed under lock and key, but many of the rankers were sympathetic to the revolutionaries, and they'd formed a growing corps of volunteers to keep the peace. In place of the Armsmen's traditional green uniforms, the Guards wore green armbands to denote their status.

Before long, though, other deputies had objected. The former Armsmen were too tied to the Monarchists and the Crown, and their loyalty was suspect. They'd formed their own guard, wearing red armbands, to protect the deputies from any attempt at coercion. The two groups had come to blows in front of the cathedral over who would have the honor of guarding the assembly, until the deputies had agreed to the creation of a Patriot Guard that would include both factions and answer to the body as a whole. Instead of armbands, they were to wear blue and silver sashes, the colors of Vordan.

That had lasted until some bright spark had added a thin strip of green to his sash. By the following day, every member of the Guard wore a similar patch of color denoting his allegiance, and Maurisk had been forced to decree that Greens and Reds would have exactly equal representation throughout the cathedral.

"I'd be almost tempted to let him go," Winter said, "if he could get any idiots to follow him. At least we'd be rid of them."

"It may come to that," Cyte said. "There's talk among the Monarchists that Peddoc means to march with anyone who's willing, resolution or no resolution. They say the Greens have a big cache of weapons they captured at Ohnlei."

"Oh." Winter wished she hadn't been quite so flippant. If Peddoc *did* march, anyone who followed him was liable to get killed. *Going up against regular Royal Army troops with* this *rabble would be madness.*

"Hell." Cyte ran her fingers through her hair and shook her head. "They're going to be at this all day."

"Probably."

"I'm going to find something more useful to do with my time," Cyte said. "Like trying to empty the river with a spoon. You coming?"

Winter shook her head. "I should stay. I'm supposed to be keeping an eye on this for Jane."

Cyte gave her an odd look, then shrugged. "As you like."

Winter sat through four or five more hours of debate before hunger forced her to venture out of the great hall. The square in front of the cathedral was thick with hawkers selling food and drink, but once she'd found something to eat, she couldn't bring herself to go back inside. They'd be at it for the rest of the day, and possibly into the night as well; sometimes it wasn't until one or two in the morning that the last arguing pair finally collapsed with exhaustion.

Instead she turned her steps toward home. Or at least what passed for home, in this strange world. She felt as though she'd stepped through a magic door into some kind of shadow-Vordan, where everything was upside down. *Though if it really was magic, Infernivore would have warned me by now.* Deputies had been assigned apartments on the Island; a large number of nobles and foreigners, especially Borelgai, had fled, leaving a surplus of vacancies. Winter's quarters were on the third floor of a narrow stone-faced building, whose monthly rent was probably higher than a year's salary for an army lieutenant. It had been lightly looted before she got to it, but they'd left a bed, table, and chairs behind, and that was enough for her purposes.

She trudged up the front staircase and paused in front of her front door. There was an envelope on the floor, labeled WINTER in a clear, careful hand. The post hadn't worked in days—the Post Office was technically an arm of the Ministry of Information—so someone must have hand-delivered it. Winter picked it up, curiously, and broke the plain wax seal on the back.

The note inside read:

Winter,

Please come. I need your help.

Jane

Under the signature was another line, which had been heavily scratched out. Below that, just the words "I love you."

"Fuck," Winter said, with considerable feeling.

An hour later, having shed the black deputy's sash, she was on her way to Dockside. A few adventurous cabbies were in the streets, but Winter had decided to walk, in the hopes that it would help her clear her head. It hadn't worked. All she could think about was Jane: Jane's smile, her soft red hair, her body pressed against Abby, her lips softly parting as Abby's hands curved over her breasts. Winter touched the note, a crumpled ball in her pocket, and bit her lip.

She passed through Farus' Triumph, still littered with filth and debris from the riots, and over the Grand Span to the South Bank. Lost as she was in her own thoughts, it wasn't until she got within a few blocks of Jane's building that she became aware of the change that had come over the streets. When Jane had made her rounds, every street had been alive with people and noisy with chatter, alleys crisscrossed by washing lines and swarming with children at play. Now they were empty. Only the occasional pedestrian crossed her path, head down and moving quickly, and there were no children about at all. In the distance, she saw a squad of a half dozen Patriot Guards swagger around a corner, muskets slung over their shoulders.

Winter's steps quickened. She wasn't as familiar with the streets around here as she might have liked. After the second wrong turn, staring at another street she didn't recognize, she stopped and ground her teeth. She hadn't been worried about getting lost, because anyone in the street could point her to Mad Jane's headquarters, but now . . .

A heavy hand landed on her shoulder. Winter spun away, instinctively, but another hand shot out and grabbed her wrist in an iron grip. Her off hand went to her belt, searching for a knife that wasn't there, but a moment later she recognized the tall figure and sighed with relief.

"Walnut," she said. "You scared the hell out of me."

"Sorry. Didn't want you running off." He let go of her arm. "Jane wants to see you."

"I was just trying to find her." Winter gave an embarrassed shrug. "But I think I'm lost."

"Come on. It's this way."

He walked by her side the rest of the way, which made Winter feel uncomfortably like a prisoner being escorted. There was something in the big man's attitude she didn't like; his expression was grimmer than she remembered, and he responded to her attempts at conversation with grunts. Winter was glad to see the familiar shape of Jane's old building when they turned a corner.

When Walnut knocked on the front door, it was opened by a very nervous teenage girl with a heavy wooden cudgel. She looked relieved to see Walnut, and her eyes went very wide when she caught sight of Winter. As they passed inside, Winter saw three more girls, similarly armed, all of them now whispering excitedly.

"I, um," the first girl said, "I'll go and get . . . somebody. Stay here."

She dashed off. Winter, Walnut, and the guards waited in silence for a few minutes. Somewhere nearby, a baby wailed.

A baby?

"Winter!"

It was Abby, naturally. Winter steeled herself and put on a neutral face. "Um. Hello. Jane asked me to come."

"I know. Thanks, Walnut. I'll take her upstairs."

Walnut nodded and let himself out. Abby beckoned Winter to follow and led her back through the building to the creaky old stairwell. When Winter had last been here, these lower halls had been dusty and seldom used, with the girls housed on the upper stories. Now the walls were lined with bedrolls, blankets, and makeshift mattresses, and all the people who were absent from the streets outside seemed to have made their way here. They were mostly young women, not the cheerful, well-fed girls Winter remembered but dirty, scared-looking things. A few boys were with them, too, and small clusters of old men and women, wrapped in blankets. All conversation stopped as Abby and Winter passed by, and all eyes followed them down the hall until they passed out of sight.

"Abby," Winter whispered, "what the hell is going on?"

Abby shook her head. "Jane can explain."

Reaching the stairwell, they climbed four stories to the top of the building and went into the old study Jane used as her war room. Jane was gathered around her table with Chris, Becca, and Winn, but when Abby and Winter entered she straightened up and made a shooing gesture. They all piled out, wide-eyed, leaving Winter alone with Abby and Jane.

"Jane—" Winter began.

"Walnut picked her up in the street," Abby said. "She was alone."

Jane paled and set her jaw. "Winter," she said carefully, "what the *fuck* do you think you're doing?"

"I *thought* I was coming to see you," Winter said. Her eyes flicked to Abby. "I got your note."

"And you walked here by yourself?"

Winter's cheeks heated. "I'm not a *child*, for God's sake."

Jane crossed to a chair and sat down, carefully, like an old woman sparing her creaking joints. Abby cleared her throat.

"The streets aren't safe," she said. "Not anymore. Three of our girls have been attacked, the last one in broad daylight not two blocks from here."

"Not to mention Billy Burdock's son," Jane said. "Sal fished him out of the river with his throat slit. And there's more missing."

Winter's skin crawled. "God. I didn't . . . I had no idea."

"Of course not," Jane muttered. "None of the goddamned *deputies* has bothered to come Southside and take a look around."

"I saw a squad of Patriot Guards," Winter protested. "Don't they patrol?"

Jane just laughed. Abby said, "The Guards are half the problem. When they're not harassing people, they're breaking into houses to look for spies and stealing everything that's not nailed down."

"Or fighting each other," Jane added.

"People are scared," Abby went on. "There's not enough food coming into the city, and men from Newtown and the Bottoms have been coming up to search for bread."

Winter looked around for another chair, found one, and sank into it. A moment passed in silence.

"Who are all those people downstairs?" she said, quietly, though she could already guess the answer.

"People from the Docks who didn't have anywhere else to go," Abby said. She turned her gaze on Jane. "But we can't keep them here. We're running out of food for ourselves, much less . . ."

"I know," Jane said.

"There's only enough left for—"

"I know," Jane grated. "Abby. Get out of here, all right?"

Abby looked at Winter, who managed to meet her eye without flinching. To Winter's surprise, Abby's expression was pleading. She mouthed two words at Winter.

Help. Her.

Then she slipped out, closing the door behind her.

There was a long, awkward silence.

"Winter," Jane said in a hoarse whisper. "Where have you been?"

Running away, Winter thought. *When you needed my help. As usual.*

"At the Deputies," she said. "I was supposed to represent us there . . ." It sounded weak, even to her.

"Do they even know what's happening here?"

"No," Winter admitted. "They've been debating whether the queen should have the right of legislative veto."

Jane gave another hollow laugh. "Oh. I can see why *that* would take priority."

"They mean well," Winter said, not sure why she was defending them. She reflected. "Some of them, anyway."

Jane lapsed back into silence.

"You said you needed my help," Winter ventured. "I got your note."

"I was waiting for you to come back," Jane said. "I keep trying to hold things together, but it's like . . . two fucking four-horse teams, pulling me in opposite directions. The people need help, my girls need help, but there's not enough *food* and everything's changing too fast. Half the fishermen have packed up and left, the stores are shut, nobody is willing to lift a finger for anyone else anymore." She looked up. "You remember Crooked Sal and George the Gut?"

Winter nodded.

"I thought I had gotten something through their thick skulls." Jane's eyes fell to the floor again. "Sal told someone in the Guard that he thought George was a Concordat spy. Last night a squad of Guard smashed up George's house and dragged him away."

Eight corpses, dangling from the cathedral. Winter wasn't sure if one of them had been George. She'd done her best not to examine them closely.

"I thought I had it together here," Jane said. "But it's coming apart in my hands, and I don't . . . I don't know what I'm supposed to do. I thought you would come help me." She swallowed. "I didn't think I'd have to beg."

"Jane . . ."

Winter wanted—wanted *so badly*—to get out of the chair, run across the room, wrap her arms around Jane, and never let go again. But the ghostly image of Jane and Abby hung before her, pinning her to her seat, stopping her voice in her throat.

There was only one way to exorcise it. It felt like taking a bone saw to a healthy limb, slashing the rusty, serrated teeth through soft flesh until they bit into the bone hiding beneath, bearing down until she heard the snap. Crushing a musket ball between her teeth, to stifle a scream.

"I . . ." Winter swallowed. "The night after we took the Vendre. I saw you . . ." Her throat was almost too thick to get the words out. "You and Abby," she finished, in a whisper.

Another silence, unbearably oppressive. Winter's breath came fast, and her heart thudded wildly in her chest.

"You saw that," Jane said, in a dull voice.

Winter nodded, not trusting herself to speak.

"And that's why you . . . stayed away."

"It's not what you think," Winter said. Words spilled out of her, suddenly, as though a cork had been pulled. "I realized the two of you must have been . . . together, before I got here. And I couldn't . . . I mean, I can't just walk in and expect you to . . . It was unfair. To both of you. You understand?" She paused, out of breath. *Please say you understand.*

"As soon as I knew it was you," Jane said, "I told her. She understood. I could tell that it hurt her, but she stood there and fucking *smiled*, for me. God. And then that night . . ."

Jane shot up from her chair, so fast she sent it skidding backward. Her hands balled into fists.

"I was drunk," she said. "So was she, I think. And I was lonely, and you . . ." She gritted her teeth. "I'd been sleeping alone. Since you got here. And she was . . . there. *Fuck.*" She whirled on Winter, green eyes full of fire. "What did you expect me to do?"

Winter held up her hands. "I told you! It wasn't fair of me to ask . . . anything. It's not fair." She hesitated. "I came here to apologize."

"You." Jane fixed her with a furious glare. "You came here to apologize."

"Yes."

"For what?"

Winter shifted uncomfortably. "For feeling . . . the way I did, I guess."

Jane paused, then ran one hand back through her hair, tugging at the spiky tufts.

"Fuck," she said. "Brass Balls of the *fucking* Beast. Karis the Savior's cock with bells tied round the tip." Having apparently run out of profanity, she put one hand over her mouth and shook her head. To Winter's surprise, her eyes were full of tears.

"*You* were going to apologize." Jane crossed the room in two quick steps and sat, cross-legged, at Winter's feet. "You thought you had to apologize to me."

"Jane?" Winter leaned forward. "Are you all right?"

Jane leaned her forehead against Winter's knees and sat there for a moment in silence.

"I don't deserve you," she said, in a whisper. "I don't deserve . . . someone like you."

Then she was sobbing. *Jane* was sobbing. Jane, who hadn't cried when she was locked in a cell, waiting for a man she didn't know to rape her and carry her off into bondage. For a moment Winter was paralyzed, staring in wonder as though the sun had risen in the west and water was flowing from the sea to the mountaintop. Then she slid out of the chair and onto the floor beside Jane and wrapped her arms around her. Jane buried her face in Winter's shoulder.

"I'm sorry," she said, voice muffled by the fabric. "Winter, I'm so sorry. I'm . . ."

"I told you," Winter said, her own voice quivering a bit. "You and Abby . . ."

Jane shook her head, cheek rubbing against Winter's shirt. "When I couldn't find you, I went a little crazy. Abby . . . helped me. We thought you were dead, and I tried to convince myself . . . that what I had with her was like what I'd had with you." She put her arms around Winter's waist. "When I saw you again, I realized I was wrong. So fucking wrong. I'm so sorry. It was stupid, stupid, stupid, I'd had too much to drink, and . . ."

She paused, swallowing hard. "No. No excuses. I'm sorry. I'm so sorry . . ."

Winter put one hand on Jane's head and tangled her fingers in her hair. The same silky red hair, now short and spiked with sweat, but still so familiar the gesture made her ache. She squeezed Jane tight.

"It's all right," she said.

They sat like that for a while, Jane's back quivering with silent sobs, Winter holding her and wondering if there was something else she should say. Eventually Jane lifted her head. She was a mess—eyes red, a trickle of snot running from her nose—but it made Winter smile.

"Do you think . . . ," Jane began, and stopped.

"Yes?" Winter said.

"Would it be all right," Jane said, "if I kissed you?"

"One moment." Winter worked one hand free and dragged the end of her sleeve across Jane's face, wiping away snot and drool. "All right. Go ahead."

Jane barked a laugh, then brought her hands up behind Winter's shoulders and pulled her close. Their lips met. Winter put her arms around Jane's waist, pulling her close.

As they came together, there was a single, awful moment of abject terror. The feeling that had come over her that first day, when Jane had kissed her without warning, surged through her body and told her to fight or to flee. Two years of flinching at every human touch, of listening to the crude jokes of Davis and his cronies and imagining what would happen if they *found out*, two years of waking up in the middle of the night with only the memory of fading green eyes. All these things came back to her, in that instant, and her body went taut.

Winter gripped Jane's shoulders so tightly she was sure it hurt. She broke away from the kiss and bit her lip, tasting the coppery tang of blood.

"Are you all right?" Jane said.

"I think . . ." Winter ran her tongue across suddenly dry lips and took a deep breath. "I think we should go to your room."

"My—" Jane blinked. "It's okay. You don't have to—"

"Jane. Look at me." Winter caught her eyes and held them. "I'm all right."

"You realize," Winter said, "that this doesn't solve any of your problems."

They lay in Jane's big bed, side by side. Winter felt trembly, boneless, as though she could dissolve into a puddle. A draft from the window played across her, pebbling her bare skin.

"We could leave," Jane said. "You and me. Leave the city, leave all of this. Go to Mielle, or Nordart." She grinned. "Or back to Khandar. You could show me the sights."

Winter laughed. "You don't mean that."

"No." Jane sighed. "I suppose I don't." She looked sidelong at Winter. "You'll help me?"

"I'll try," Winter said. Something had been working its way to the top of her mind, like a bubble rising to the surface of a pond. "And, actually, I think I have an idea."

Winter slept better that night than she had since the fall of the Vendre, feeling light and almost hollow, as if some barrier deep inside her had been broken to let a buildup of accumulated muck drain away. When she woke up the next morning, Jane still pressed tight against her, her head felt clear.

After wandering down to the great hall to find something to eat, Winter returned to Jane's room to find Abby fussing with Jane's formal outfit. Any remaining hint of jealousy at seeing the two together was quashed by the look of almost pathetic gratitude on Abby's face. Jane looked like her old self, full of energy, pacing back and forth as Abby laid out dark trousers, a gray waistcoat, and a coat that would have done credit to a prosperous merchant. Winter was impressed, and said so.

"You said I ought to dress the part," Jane said.

"I wasn't expecting you to have much on hand," Winter said.

Abby blushed. "I got most of it ready last night. I didn't think she ought to go to the deputies looking like . . ." She glanced up at Jane and coughed. "Like she usually does."

"I still don't think they'll listen to me," Jane said. "Why should they?"

"Because they're running out of other choices," Winter said. "You've heard the news, I take it?"

The news had seeped into the city, sometime last night, diffusing through the streets in the curious way that rumor had. It was as though everyone had learned it in a dream, and on waking only confirmed it with everyone else.

The news was that Orlanko's forces had broken camp. Seven thousand Royal Army regulars were on the march for Vordan. Counting the time it had taken the scouts to return with this information, it could only be another two days, perhaps three, before the Last Duke's men were at the gates.

Winter had expected panic, but when she and Jane left the building in the company of Walnut and a dozen armed Leatherbacks, the streets remained deserted. If anything, they were emptier than the night before, and Winter did not see another living soul out of doors until they reached the Grand Span. There small groups had gathered, a drifting current of humanity that flowed north, over the bridge and across the river. On the Island side, it met and merged with several smaller streams, bearing Winter, Jane, and their small group like a bubble on a stream. It was like a daylight replay of the march on the Vendre, but with no torches, no weapons, and none of the same sense of purpose. These people were frightened, not angry, and they didn't know what to do.

The stream entered Farus' Triumph on the south side, spreading out past the shuttered cafés. A large crowd had already gathered, forming a ring centered on the northwest corner of the square, where something seemed to be happening. Winter could see a single horseman moving about, above the heads of the crowd, and as they got closer she recognized his gaudy uniform. *Peddoc.*

"The deputies have failed us!" he was saying, his voice sounding thin above the murmur of the crowd. "There are good men in the chamber, but also fools, cowards, and even traitors. And there is no time now to sort the ore from the dross! That's why I'm calling on all true men of Vordan to do what must be done. Step forward! Be counted!"

By this point, Jane's escort of Leatherbacks had cleared a way through the crowd, and Jane and Winter could get a good view. Peddoc sat on the back of a stunning gray-and-white stallion, spurs gleaming, saddle every bit as polished and embroidered as his uniform. He rode at a slow walk around the edges of the clear space, holding the reins in one hand and gesturing with the other.

Behind him was a block of armed men, doing their best imitation of soldiers at attention. Some of them—mostly those who wore the green-edged sashes of Patriot Guard loyal to the Monarchists—managed reasonably well, although the spacing between ranks and files was ragged. Others seemed to have been grabbed off the street and issued whatever weapons were on hand. In addition to muskets, Winter saw shotguns and hunting pieces, pikes, ancient halberds, and crude spears.

More weapons rested in a great pile on a tarpaulin beside a couple of well-dressed men wearing black deputy's sashes. From time to time a man would break free of the edge of the crowd—sometimes pushed by those around him, sometimes breaking free of attempts at restraint—and make his way forward. The men in the ranks sent up a cheer each time this happened, which was echoed, a bit more weakly, by the crowd. The new volunteers reported to the two deputies, who issued them whatever weapon was on top of the pile and sent them to stand with the others.

"What the *hell* does he think he's playing at?" Jane said.

"He's going to march them against Orlanko," Winter said. It was idiocy, but it was the only thing she could think of. "He's been threatening to raise a force on his own for days, since the deputies wouldn't give him one. The news must have forced his hand."

"Balls of the Beast," Jane swore. "He's taking *this* lot?"

"Apparently. There may be more mustering in Northside." Winter counted the ranks with a practiced eye. Peddoc had assembled a thousand men, perhaps a bit more.

"Has he got a chance?"

"Against regulars?" Winter thought about the peasant horde, trying to storm the Vordanai line at the Battle of the Road, breaking in a welter of blood in the face of disciplined volleys of musketry and canister. "Not a prayer. Come on. We have to get to the Vendre."

They sent the Leatherbacks away once they reached the fortress-prison, now garrisoned by the Patriot Guard. The gates stood open, and the courtyard was a mass of confusion. Patriot Guards of both colors rushed about, talked in small groups, or shouted at one another. Winter guessed that Peddoc had sent instructions for the Guard to join his ranks, while the deputies issued contradictory orders. Judging by the ratio of colored sashes she could see, most of the Greens had sided with Peddoc, while the Reds were remaining at their posts.

No one stopped the two young women as they wandered through the courtyard, past the main door, and back to the main staircase. Jane gave a shudder as they passed over the threshold.

"I was hoping like hell I was done with this place," she said.

"Likewise," Winter said. "At least this time I get to come in the front door."

"And it's not full of black-coats."

"That, too."

Whatever one thought about Duke Orlanko, his Concordat had certainly made more effective watchmen than their replacements. Winter and Jane walked up the stairs without anyone giving them more than an odd look. On the upper levels, the confusion was less apparent, and at least the cells were each watched by a guardsman. Not knowing what floor they were bound for, Winter eventually collared a young Red and asked for directions, which he stammered out without thinking to ask who the visitors were and what they were doing.

"This is ridiculous," Winter said, as they climbed toward the third floor. "We could break someone out of this place with a gang of eight-year-olds."

Jane rolled her eyes in agreement. They walked down a short corridor and stopped in front of the door they wanted, which was guarded by an older man wearing a red-striped sash. He straightened up when he caught sight of them, bringing his musket to his shoulder and trying to pull in his sagging belly.

"We need to speak to the prisoner," Winter said, as he opened his mouth to speak.

"Ah . . . ," he managed.

"Deputies' business," she deadpanned.

He nodded. "I . . . that is . . . whose business, exactly?"

"I'm Deputy Winter Ihernglass," Winter said. "And this is Deputy Jane Verity."

The first name obviously meant nothing to him, but the second brought him up short. "Jane Verity? You mean Mad Jane?" His eyes flicked to Jane. "That's *her*?"

"That's right," Jane said, smiling in a way that was not particularly friendly. "Mad Jane."

He was sweating, but he managed a salute and started fumbling for his keys. "Let me get the door open, sir. Ma'am. Miss."

The room beyond was less a cell than a small bedroom, with a narrow gun slit for light and a worn but serviceable bed, desk, table, and chairs. At the desk sat Captain Marcus d'Ivoire, looking a little bit worse for wear. His uniform was creased and sweat-stained, his beard was ragged, and his cheeks carried a week's worth of stubble. Winter's stomach did a nervous flip at the sight of him, and before he could look up she grabbed Jane's arm and pulled her away from the door and the guard.

"You remember what I told you, right?" Winter whispered urgently. "About me."

"I think so," Jane said. "He knows you're *you*, but he thinks that you're dressed up as a girl to fool *me*." She smiled wickedly. "Maybe he's right, and you're just doing a *hell* of a job—"

"I know it's ridiculous, all right? Just . . . don't say anything. I'll work it all out later."

"Does he know that I know that he knows you are who he thinks you are?" Jane cocked her head, trying to think about that, and went cross-eyed. "Never mind. I'll be good."

"All right." Winter took a deep breath, smoothed her shirt, and stepped into the room. Jane followed and closed the door behind her.

"Good . . . morning," Marcus said, slowly. He looked from Winter to Jane, obviously trying to work his way through the same mental gyrations as Jane had done a moment earlier, and wondering what he should admit to knowing.

Winter decided she would never laugh at the plot of those penny-opera farces again. She gritted her teeth for a moment, then said, "Hello, Captain. This is Jane Verity. She knows I'm with the army, so speak freely."

"I see." Marcus blinked and scratched his ragged beard. "All right. Hello, Ihernglass, Jane." He paused. "You wouldn't be this 'Mad' Jane that everyone—"

"That's me," Jane said. "I think we met the last time I was in this place, but I don't blame you for being preoccupied."

"That's one way of putting it," Marcus said. "I'm assuming you're not just here to check on me? There seems to be some kind of commotion outside."

"Do you get any news in here?" Winter said.

"Not much. The guards let things slip sometimes, but it's mostly rumor."

Winter gave him a condensed explanation of what had been happening at the Deputies-General in the week since the queen's surrender. Jane also listened with interest, adding a few colorful expletives and comments on the situation in the Docks. By the end, Marcus was shaking his head.

"Saints and martyrs," he said. "I never thought it would get so bad."

"It gets worse," Winter said. "This morning we got the news that Orlanko's left Midvale with the Royal Army troops quartered there. Peddoc is out in the square right now gathering a force to go and meet him."

"To *meet* him? He must be crazy." Marcus glanced at the window, which looked to the north, out over the river. "Assuming the regulars will fight—"

"I think they will," Jane said. "At least, if we meet them armed, in an open field."

"So do I," Marcus said grimly. "It's going to be a slaughter."

"I had a plan," Winter said. "I thought we might be able to persuade the deputies to name *you* commander of the Guard, if Jane threw her weight behind you. A lot of people remember the way you acted at the Vendre, how you protected the prisoners. But Peddoc seems to have stolen a march on us."

"Peddoc," Marcus said to himself. "I knew a Peddoc at the College. Count Volmire's son. It's not him out there, is it?"

"I think so," Winter said.

"Hell. He was always a twit. Never made it through his lieutenancy."

"Now he's claiming command of the Guard based on his 'military experience,'" Jane put in.

There was a glum silence.

"What the hell do we do now?" Jane said.

"The deputies obviously can't stop Peddoc from leaving," Winter said. "Or they would have already. Once he's gone, though . . ."

"You think you can convince them to put Captain d'Ivoire in charge of the leftovers?"

Marcus held up his hands. "I'm touched by your confidence, but I'm not sure what you want me to *do*."

"I thought . . ." Winter took a deep breath, trying to ignore the sensation of the plan that had seemed so good this morning crumbling around her ears.

"If we could train the Guard, properly, I mean, we might be able to keep Orlanko out of the city."

"Vordan won't stand a siege," Marcus said, shaking his head. "Too many mouths to feed, and there aren't any *defenses*."

"Then what? Just give up?"

Marcus shrugged. "It's a possibility. Speaking as someone who'd probably lose his head, I'm against it."

Winter glanced at Jane, and her lips tightened. Speaking of people who would lose their heads . . .

"I'm open to suggestions," she said.

"Look. We both know that even if you'd managed to put me in charge, I wouldn't be able to stop Orlanko." He paused. "And we both know that if you *did* want to try, there's only one person I'd put money on."

Winter bit her lip. "Janus."

"Janus," Marcus said.

"Janus, as in Count Mieran?" Jane said. "The Minister of Justice?"

"He beat thirty thousand Khandarai with one regiment of infantry," Marcus said. "If you're looking for someone to put in charge, he's your man."

"I don't doubt that he's a genius," Jane said, in a tone that implied she doubted it very much. "But can we *trust* him? He's a noble, after all, and obviously he was close to the old king."

Winter and Marcus exchanged a look. Winter could tell the captain was thinking along the same lines she was, about the temple in the desert and the Thousand Names.

Can we trust him?

"I can't speak for the long run," Winter said, slowly. "But I know for certain that he hates Orlanko and the Borels."

Marcus nodded. "His head is on the block, too, if Orlanko returns."

"But I don't think the deputies would agree," Winter went on. "Janus is too popular with the mob."

"Even after he ordered Danton's arrest?" Marcus asked.

"In the streets they're blaming that on the Last Duke," Jane said. "Janus is still 'the conqueror of Khandar.' That counts for a lot right now."

"All right, he's a hero. So much the better, I would think," Marcus said.

"It means the deputies won't trust him," Jane said.

Winter nodded. "They were terrified of handing over leadership, even to someone like Peddoc, for fear that he would turn the Guard against them. As far as they're concerned, someone with Janus' reputation might try to set himself up as king."

"We need him," Marcus said. "Even if you could convince the deputies to put me in command, I wouldn't take it. Better to surrender than to fight and give Orlanko an excuse for brutality. If we had Janus . . ." He shrugged. "I would fight, if he thought it could be done."

"Maybe if we had him address the deputies?" Winter said. "He's not Danton, but he can speak when he needs to." She was thinking of the mutiny in the desert, and by his wince Marcus was, too. "But—"

"You're going at it backward," Jane said.

Winter and Marcus both turned to her.

"You're thinking of the deputies like a kind of collective king," she said. "But it's different. They have only as much power as the people are willing to give them. We don't have to *argue* them into it. We just have to convince them."

The commotion had calmed down by the time Winter and Jane left the Vendre. Those Guards who were going to join Peddoc had gone, leaving mostly Reds with a scattering of unconvinced Greens. A few of these had regained enough alertness to give odd looks to the two young women strolling out of the prison, and Winter smiled at them serenely.

As they passed out through the main gate, Jane said suddenly, "Do you really think this will work?"

Winter blinked. "It was your idea, wasn't it?"

"Not that part. Once Janus is in command, do you really think he can stop Orlanko?"

"If he can't, no one can."

Jane shook her head. "That's not good enough. Captain d'Ivoire was right. We *could* surrender."

"Assuming Peddoc loses . . ."

Jane snorted.

"If we surrender, Orlanko will certainly round up any traitors he can catch. That means you and me."

"We could get away." Jane grinned wickedly. "You escaped from Mrs. Wilmore. How much harder could it be to get away from the Last Duke?"

"And leave everyone behind? The Leatherbacks, your girls?" Winter hesitated only slightly. "Abby?"

"If we don't surrender, they'll fight, and maybe die. And if we lose, you know what Orlanko would do to the city."

It was all too easy to picture. Blue-uniformed soldiers in the streets, and black-coats smashing down doors, dragging people into the night . . .

"I don't want to pull everyone into that," Jane said, "just to save *our* skins. Not if you don't think we can win."

Winter thought about this for a long moment. "I'll give Janus this much. If *he* thinks we can win, then it's possible. And if he doesn't think so, he'd say it. I think the best we can do is put him in charge, one way or another."

"All right." Jane stretched and cracked her knuckles over her head, the old wicked smile creeping across her face. "Let's see what we can do."

Chapter Twenty

RAESINIA

The setting sun painted a pale crimson line through the gun slit in Raesinia's chamber on the top floor of the Vendre. It was a spacious room, and some effort had been made in the way of hangings and furniture to make it into a fit habitation for a queen. No amount of carpets or tapestries could conceal the thickness of the stone walls, though, or the fact that the door was locked from the outside and watched by the Patriot Guard day and night. The gun slit was not large enough to squeeze through, even for a prisoner like Raesinia who was willing to chance the four-story fall.

It was from just above here, after all, that she'd fallen with Faro.

She wondered if she could have avoided that, somehow. Was there some point on the twisting path where she could have taken a different turn, so that Ben wouldn't have been killed, Faro wouldn't have turned traitor? So that it wouldn't have come to *this*, waiting in a cell barely a week after her father's death. *Some history the reign of Queen Raesinia will make.*

Still. Better the Deputies-General than Orlanko. Better the mob than the Church and its demons. It was a small comfort, but it was all she had. If that *wasn't* true, if the people weren't better off, then everything she'd done was both monumentally selfish and ultimately pointless, given how it had ended up. She wasn't sure she could live with that.

Not that I have a choice in the matter.

There was a knock at the door. Raesinia sat up in bed. Servants came and went all the time, but they didn't knock. She'd had no other visitors.

"Yes?"

"I wonder if you have a moment to see me, Your Majesty," came a voice from outside. It took Raesinia a moment to recognize it as Maurisk's. He sounded hoarse.

"Of course," she said. "Come in."

She stood up and crossed to the table as he entered. There was a crystal pitcher of water there, and a bowl of fruit.

"I'm afraid I can't offer much in the way of hospitality," she said. "But help yourself."

Maurisk didn't smile. His thin face didn't seem made for smiles, and since she'd last seen him it had grown even less cheerful. His eyes were sunken and dark, almost bruised, and his cheekbones stood out sharply through his thin, pale flesh.

He was dressed more respectably than in their Blue Mask days, complete with the black sash of a deputy, trimmed with a band of cloth-of-gold. One hand tugged at the sash constantly, adjusting it this way and that. His lips were tight and cold.

He said nothing while the guard shut the door behind him, only stared hard at Raesinia's face. She felt herself flush under the scrutiny, and put on her haughtiest expression.

"Is something wrong?" she said.

"It's you, isn't it?" he said flatly. "Raesinia *Smith*. It was you all along. I got a look at you on the bridge, and I thought . . . But I wasn't sure."

Raesinia put a hand on the table to steady herself, and said nothing.

"I can see how you thought no one would notice," Maurisk said. He started to pace, as he had done a thousand times in the back room of the Mask. "After all, who actually meets the princess? Only courtiers at Ohnlei. So you sneak out in the middle of the night for—what, a bit of fun?"

"Fun?" Raesinia's cheeks colored. "You think I did this for *fun*?"

"Why, then?"

"For all the reasons I told you! Because if *someone* didn't stop him, Duke Orlanko was going to take the throne and end up selling the country to the Borels. Because my father was dying and there was nobody at Ohnlei I could trust." *Except Sothe,* she added silently, and felt her throat thicken. *Sothe, where are you?*

"But you couldn't trust us with who you really were?" He shook his head. "No, of course not. You never really trusted us. If you'd let us in on your plans, things might have gone differently."

"I did the best I could."

Maurisk laughed mirthlessly. "The world's most popular epitaph."

Raesinia glared at him, her fingers tightening on the tabletop. Maurisk reached the wall, turned around, and started back toward her.

"What happened, that night on the wall?" He stopped just in front of her and brushed the hair back from her temple. "I saw Faro shoot you. I *know* I did. And yet—"

"I had a . . . double." Raesinia had had plenty of time to think about her story. "Lauren. A girl who looked like me. We used her at court, sometimes, when I needed to get away. That last night, when Rose planned to unmask Faro, she told me I should stay behind and Lauren should go in my place. I didn't want to, but . . ."

"I guessed it would be something like that," Maurisk said. "So it's just another body to lay at your door. Along with Ben, and Faro, and poor, stupid Danton."

"We did what we needed to do. *You* know that." Raesinia waved a hand at the door and the Patriot Guard beyond. "All this was what you wanted, wasn't it?"

"Maybe that is why it vexes me," Maurisk said. "You . . . you *used* us. But, in the end, it came out right."

"Perhaps God has a sense of irony."

"Perhaps." Maurisk put his hand in his pocket, and she heard the crinkle of paper. "Or perhaps not. Orlanko is on his way back, you see, with seven thousand Royal Army regulars. A group of our men went off to try to stop them, and we've just heard the results of the battle." He shook his head. "If you can call it a battle. The deputies are terrified."

"What are they going to do?"

"I have no idea." He sighed. "That's why I came to see you. Tomorrow morning the deputies will meet, perhaps for the last time. They may want you to come out and take charge of the city yourself. Or they may decide we ought to hand you over to Orlanko and save our skins. Either way, I thought this might be our last chance to . . . talk."

"What do you want from me?" Raesinia said. "An apology?"

"You know, I have no idea. I thought I would come here, confront you, force you to break down and admit the truth. After that . . ." He shrugged.

"Are you going to tell everyone, now that you've got it?"

"I suppose I can't, can I? What good would it do now?" Maurisk stalked back and forth. "You ought to *pay* for treating people like they were . . . like they were *game pieces*, but the truth is we still need *you* for our game."

"Will you tell me something?"

He turned, eyes burning. "What?"

"Are the others all right? I know Danton died at the cathedral. What about Sarton, and Cora?"

Maurisk snorted. "You expect me to believe that you care?"

"Please," Raesinia said, quietly.

He paused, then shook his head. "They're all right. Sarton is working with the Guard on some secret project. Cora sits in the Deputies and doesn't say much." He scowled. "She loved you like you were her own sister, you know. If I told her what you'd done . . ."

Raesinia privately thought that Cora would be happy she was alive, rather than angry at being fooled. But for Maurisk, finding out that Raesinia had been putting up a false front all this time was only one more example of the base treachery of the people in power. Out of all the cabal, he had burned the hottest with the ideological fire of rebellion.

"Thank you," she said.

He gave a curt nod. "As you say. We'll see what happens tomorrow."

MARCUS

Marcus guessed their plan was working when his guards delivered a freshly laundered uniform, soap, and a razor. He spent an hour making himself as presentable as he could with a basin and a hand mirror, stripping off his old, sweaty things with considerable relief. The new uniform—that of a captain in the army, not the green of the Armsmen—didn't quite fit, but it was close, and when Marcus looked in the mirror and saw a neatly trimmed beard and white stripes on his shoulders, he felt closer to being himself than he had in a long time.

Not long after, a polite young Patriot Guardsman came to fetch him. Accompanied by a squad of a half dozen men, they left the Vendre and made their way to the cathedral. But not directly, Marcus noticed. That would have taken them through Farus' Triumph and Cathedral Square. Instead they circled around via Water Street and approached the cathedral from the rear, slipping in through an entrance to the long-disused kitchens. Marcus thought he could hear the roar of a mob, somewhere nearby, and he smiled.

The Deputies-General reminded him of his visit with the Prince of Khandar at Fort Valor—a desperate attempt to recreate the trappings of something important, but assembled in such haste that it was little more than a lick of whitewash over rotten wood. They clustered on half-built bleachers, carrying on a dozen arguments at once, while overhead crude blue-and-silver banners covered up the Sworn Church emblems carved into the walls. The altar was screened behind a curtain.

No one seemed to take any notice of him until the man at the rostrum called for silence. The guards on either side of him beat their muskets against the floor until everyone quieted down, but that only made the shouts of the crowd audible. They were muffled by the walls, but he could make out a rhythmic chant, repeated by thousands of voices.

"Captain d'Ivoire," said the president, a hollow-faced young man Marcus remembered vaguely from the fall of the Vendre. "I'm glad you could join us, and I apologize for the circumstances, and for your own confinement. I hope you understand."

"Of course." Marcus inclined his head. "I am always prepared to serve Vordan."

He scanned the rows of anxious faces on the bleachers until he found Iherngla ss. He was still in his feminine disguise—honestly, Marcus thought it wasn't terribly convincing, but he hadn't had the heart to say so—wearing a dark coat and the black sash of a deputy. When he caught Marcus' eye, he nodded, very slightly. Marcus worked hard to keep a straight face.

"It is good to see such loyalty in a military man," the president said. "I regret to say that many of your colleagues have chosen to betray this assembly, proclaimed by the queen herself and chosen by the people. You may have heard that several regiments of the Royal Army are on their way to the city as we speak."

"I have heard that," Marcus admitted.

"One of our own, the valiant Deputy Peddoc, took it on his own initiative to try to stop them. This assembly did not give its approval"—here the president glared at a cluster of deputies on the left—"and his actions were therefore illegal, but no one can question his courage, or that of those who marched with him. Unfortunately, it appears that they have been . . ." He searched for a word.

"Crushed?" Marcus said. The president winced but nodded. Marcus shrugged. "I'm not surprised. As a *military* man, I could have told you that taking an untrained militia into the field against heavy cavalry was foolish in the extreme. I imagine they broke at the first charge of the cuirassiers."

"So it would seem," the president said. "Captain, I hope you can see our dilemma. It is our charge to protect the people of this country, this city, against the foreigners who would usurp the throne and impose their taxes and religion on us. Those most capable of doing this are obviously the officers of Her Majesty's Royal Army. And yet—"

"You don't trust us," Marcus said.

"I would rather say—"

"Say what you mean. I don't fault you, because you're right. When it comes down to it, I suspect most officers would obey an order from the Minister of War over one from a self-appointed 'assembly' holding the queen hostage."

Someone stood up on the right side of the bleachers. "Her Majesty is *not* a hostage!"

"Is she free to leave, then?" Marcus said.

"She will be," the deputy said, "once our new constitution is written and the status of the deputies is confirmed. But 'hostage' implies that we might bring her harm, and I for one would resign from this assembly if that were even suggested!"

"That's how we can get rid of you, then!" said a voice from the left, followed by chuckles and shouts of disapproval.

"The status of the queen," the president cut in, "has yet to be determined. But I remind you that she *sanctioned* the deputies, voluntarily ceding power to the representatives of the people—"

"You can explain that to the colonels of those regiments, then," Marcus said. "I'm sure the Last Duke won't mind."

More laughter. The Guards slammed their muskets for quiet.

"And what about you, Captain d'Ivoire?" said the president, once the tumult had calmed. "Where do your loyalties lie?"

"With the queen and the nation, of course," Marcus said. "And the men under my command."

"That's a nicely elliptical response."

"Look," Marcus said. "We all know that's not the question you brought me here to answer. Why don't you come out and ask it?"

The president snorted. "As you wish. The suggestion has been put to this assembly that there is an officer of exceptional ability in the city, and that we ought to place our defense in his hands."

"And?"

"You served with him, I understand. In your opinion, is he all he is said to be?"

"That, and more," Marcus said. "I haven't read everything that's been written on the Khandarai campaign, but what I've seen in the papers if anything understates the case. Anyone who was there could tell you."

"People who were there are hard to come by," the president said dryly. "So you think he would be up to the task?"

"I would be willing to try it, under him," Marcus said. "And that's more than I can say for anyone else."

"But the more important question, Captain, is can we *trust* him?" The president waved toward the main doors. "He is . . . a hero. Beloved of the people. Will he accept the authority of the deputies? Or would he be another Orlanko, and seize power for himself?"

"I believe he is loyal to his queen and his country."

"That's not good enough!" said a deputy from the right.

"If he serves only the queen," said one from the left, "she might have the power to overturn everything we've accomplished—"

"Gentlemen!" Marcus said. "Could I ask you to open those doors?"

The Guardsmen looked at the president, who looked at Marcus for a long moment, then nodded. Two Guardsmen by the main doors pulled them open, and the sound of the crowd outside redoubled.

"You claim to represent the people," Marcus said, shouting to be heard over the noise. "Well, there they are! I think they've made their wishes clear." He looked up at the president. "Unless one of you would like to go out there and explain it to them?"

The president's sunken eyes met Marcus'. His lips tightened until they were white.

"It seems," he said, "that we have no choice."

"Vhalnich!" The roar of the crowd crashed through the cathedral like ocean waves. "Vhal-nich, Vhal-nich, Vhal-nich!"

"No," Marcus said. "I don't think you do."

On the way back to the Vendre, the Patriot Guard walked behind him, an escort instead of a prisoner detail. It was a subtle difference, but one that Marcus could appreciate. They left in the same roundabout manner they'd arrived, so as not to get bogged down, but Marcus could hear the cheers of the crowd as the good news was announced.

The look the president had given him before sending him off had been pure poison, though. *I'll have to tell Janus to watch out for that one.*

The Guards at the Vendre had gotten the news, too, and they stood aside as Marcus entered. Some of them even saluted inexpertly as he passed. He went directly to the third floor of the tower, where a large room directly underneath the queen's had been given over to the Vendre's second most important prisoner.

The guard by the door unlocked it and stepped formally out of the way. Marcus put his hand on the latch, hesitated, then knocked.

"Come in," Janus said.

Marcus opened the door. The cell was much like his own, though larger and slightly better furnished. Janus was sitting at a round table with a stack of letters. He signed the page under his hand with a flourish, set his pen aside, and sprinkled the ink with fine sand from a dish. Only then did he look up and favor Marcus with one of his there-and-gone-again smiles.

"Ah, Captain. It's good to see you."

"And you, sir."

Marcus felt as though it had been ages since he'd laid eyes on the colonel, but Janus behaved as though he'd stepped out of the room only moments earlier. He, also, was clean-shaven and in a fresh uniform, not the fancy courtier's getup but the plain blue field uniform of an army colonel. The silver eagles on his shoulders gleamed.

Janus put his letter carefully on top of the others. "You're here, I assume, to tell me that the deputies have decided to put me in charge of the city's defense?"

Marcus felt his mouth hang open for a moment. He closed it, firmly. "Someone's already told you, sir?"

"Not at all. The guards are very careful when they speak to me."

"Then—" Marcus gritted his teeth. "Don't tell me this was part of the plan all along."

Janus looked up at him, surprised. After a moment, he laughed. "Oh no, Captain. No, only simple logic. After the arrests, there were only two logical courses for the deputies to take, and one of them was to put me in charge."

"What was the other?"

"To have me executed, obviously. But if they were going to do that, they'd hardly send you to bring the news." He tidied the edge of the stack of letters, picked it up, and got to his feet. "Shall we go?"

In the corridor outside, they waited while the Guard fetched Janus' sword, and Marcus explained what he knew of what had been happening, including Peddoc's march and Orlanko's subsequent victory.

"It's too bad they didn't send for you sooner," Marcus said. "After what happened to Peddoc, it's not going to be easy to get people to fight."

"True," Janus said. "On the other hand, it buys us time."

"How so? There's nothing stopping Orlanko from marching on the city."

"He won't do that if he can possibly avoid it. Fighting in the city itself could lead to a long battle, and give his troops the chance to change their minds about their allegiance, not to mention causing considerable damage. Peddoc gave him exactly what he wanted, a nice quick victory in the open field. Now that he has it, he'll try to convince the deputies to surrender."

Marcus nodded. "That makes sense. Quite a few of them looked a little queasy with the way things are going. If Orlanko gave them an out, they'd probably take it."

"And end up on the scaffold just as soon as he got things under control. We need to make it clear to them that the Last Duke is not to be trusted, whatever he offers."

The guard returned, carrying not only Janus' thin sword but Marcus' battered old saber. He buckled it on and was surprised at how much better he felt with the familiar weight on his hip.

"Incidentally," Janus said, "I'm impressed that you managed to persuade the deputies to order my release so quickly. I was worried they might wait until it was too late."

"I had help with that, sir. Lieutenant Iherngl ass is still *on assignment*"—he waggled his eyebrows suggestively—"and he's made some very useful contacts. They were able to spread the notion that putting the hero of Khandar in charge would be just the thing."

"I . . . see." Janus had an odd expression for a moment, then shook his head. "You'll have to bring me up to date on the lieutenant's activities, but some other time. Are Lieutenant Uhlan and his men being held here at the Vendre?"

Marcus glanced at one of the guards, who gave an awed nod. Janus fixed the man with those huge gray eyes.

"Bring them down to the common room, if you would, and find me a candle and a stick of sealing wax." He flourished the stack of papers. "I have messages that need delivering."

"You wrote all those out on the assumption they were going to put you in charge, rather than execute you?" Marcus said, as they went downstairs.

"Indeed. I had time on my hands, so I thought I might as well get something accomplished. If they decided the other way, well, no harm done."

"No harm done." Marcus shook his head. "Don't take this the wrong way, sir, but you can be very odd at times."

Janus cocked his head. "Really, Captain? It seems perfectly logical to *me*."

An hour later, about a dozen of the Mierantai had been mounted on horses from the prison stables and sent riding in various directions, though to what end Marcus had no idea. The rest—almost a hundred men—had been returned their red-and-blue uniforms and their long hunting rifles. Lieutenant Uhlan led them out in a double column through the front gate, with Janus and Marcus strolling between them.

"The deputies asked me to bring you to the cathedral," Marcus said. "I imagine they want you to swear eternal loyalty and listen to speeches."

"I'm afraid I'll have to disappoint them," Janus said. "There is a great deal to be done, and time may be very short. Can I rely on you for a few of the more sensitive tasks?"

Marcus instinctively straightened to attention. "Of course, sir."

"First, you must deliver my regrets to the deputies. Tell them I would be honored if they would join me in Farus' Triumph tomorrow, an hour before noon, and that I will be more than happy to swear any required oaths there in public."

Marcus nodded. "They may not like that."

"If we survive the next few days, I'll happily take up the issue with them. For now, time is of the essence."

"Yessir."

"After that, get in touch with Lieutenant Ihernglass. Ask him to spread the word among his Southside contacts that the new commander will be giving a speech in the Triumph tomorrow. We'll want a crowd."

Marcus nodded. Privately he wondered what, exactly, Janus had in mind, but he knew better than to ask. The colonel would share his plans when he thought it was important, but he had a taste for the theatrical, and he loved to whip away the bedsheet at the last minute to show that the lady had vanished. It was a failing in a senior officer, Marcus thought, but as such things went, a fairly minor one.

"After that," Janus went on, "I need you to fetch the queen from the Vendre."

Marcus blinked. "The queen, sir? I mean . . . I'm not sure . . ."

"Lieutenant Uhlan will assign you a squad, but if the Guards give you any trouble, please direct them to me. And I would think you would be on familiar terms with Her Majesty after your adventure in the palace garden."

"That's true, sir. I'm sorry. It caught me by surprise, that's all." Marcus had a space in his mind labeled "Queen," and he couldn't quite make the waifish young woman he'd escorted from the palace fit into it. "Where would you like me to take her?"

"There's a manor house called the Twin Turrets on Saint Vallax's, not far from Bridge Street, that I happen to own. I'll send another squad there to make sure it's secure, and we'll use that as our headquarters. You can take Her Majesty there, and bring her to the Triumph in the morning."

"Understood, sir."

"After that . . ." Janus paused. "Your vice captain of Armsmen. Giforte, was it?"

"Yessir. Alek Giforte."

"What did you think of him?"

"He's . . . a good man, I think. Cautious. The men have—had—a great deal of respect for him. He's been vice captain a long time, and quite a few captains have come and gone. He more or less ran the place. But . . ."

Janus quirked an eyebrow. Marcus hesitated.

"He's been doing jobs for Orlanko. 'Fixing' things."

"Logical, I suppose," Janus said. "He'd need someone in the organization. I assume Orlanko had some hold over him?"

Marcus nodded. "Debt."

"Ah, the old standard." Janus fixed Marcus with a curious stare. "His credibility with the Armsmen would be an asset. Do you think we can use him?"

"I . . ." Marcus paused again. "I think his loyalty is in the right place, sir. But the Armsmen don't really exist anymore. Some of them joined up with the Greens, and they're probably Orlanko's prisoners. The rest are lying low, I would think."

"We're going to need them, Captain. Along with every other man in the city with any kind of military training. Track down Giforte and sound him out, see if he'd be willing to serve the queen against the duke. If you think he's trustworthy, have him start rounding up Armsmen. Not just the current ones, either. Any retired men who can still hold a musket would be welcome."

"I'll see if he's willing, sir. If he is, I think we can trust him. His daughter is part of the group associated with Lieutenant Ihernglass' contact."

"I see. Excellent." Janus clapped Marcus on the shoulder and smiled. "Off with you, then, Captain. We both have a great deal to do."

It was, indeed, a busy day.

Giforte was nowhere to be found. According to the servants at the vice captain's house, he hadn't returned since the day the queen had surrendered to the deputies. Apart from that, though, his errands went swimmingly. The deputies had been a good deal more polite than Marcus had anticipated, which he suspected had a lot to do with the twenty armed Mierantai who accompanied him. Their uniforms were a bit rumpled, but they were well disciplined and made a sharp contrast to the sloppy Patriot Guard. Afterward, he'd managed to pass the word to Ihernglass before hurrying back to the Vendre to retrieve the queen.

Retrieve the queen. Marcus shook his head. *Wouldn't Mother be proud? Me, escorting the queen. Sleeping under the same roof as the queen, even!*

The Twin Turrets occupied a very fine address, south of First Avenue and on the west side of Saint Vallax Street. It was a three-story stone manor set on a round, flat green, which was surrounded by a dense belt of colorful trees that mostly screened it from the view of its neighbors. The turrets that gave it its name were round and open-topped, rising from either end of the house and giving it a vaguely horned appearance. There had been surprisingly little looting and disorder on this side of the river, and along the front of the house the gardens were in full bloom.

It had obviously been locked up until recently, but by the time Marcus arrived the dust sheets had been taken off the furniture and a small squadron of staff was busy mopping the floors, hauling the art out of the attic, and generally making things presentable. Marcus recognized some of them from the Ohnlei cottage, more Mierantai imported by Janus from his home county. If they were intimidated at having the queen in the house, they didn't show it.

Now it was morning. Marcus' uniform had been thoroughly washed, dried, and folded overnight, and several of his shoddier pieces of kit, including his boots, had been replaced. His sword, old leather scabbard industriously buffed to a sheen it hadn't had in years, lay on top of the pile. It was the kind of quiet efficiency that reminded him of Fitz Warus, or for that matter of Janus' manservant Augustin. *I wonder if all servants are like that in Mieran County.* Or maybe, he thought, this was what it was like to be a noble—everything just *happened*, without your intervention or even your knowledge. It made him feel odd, as though the house were inhabited by helpful, invisible elves.

He came down from his bedroom—directly beneath one of the turrets, with a fine east view—and found the queen breakfasting in the dining room, attended by a servant and a pair of Mierantai guards. The table had been laid with an impressive meal, with a great river trout as the centerpiece, its head sitting in front of it on a separate plate and staring at Marcus with a resentful, fishy eye. It was buttressed by ham and bacon, buttered potatoes, diced eggs, and loaves of bread so steaming hot they could only have come from the house's own ovens. Marcus' stomach gave a growl at the sight of the food. The queen, he noticed, was only sipping at a glass of water and nibbling a heel of bread.

She was dressed plainly, in a sleeveless black dress with no jewels or ornamentation, her brown hair tied in a simple braid. Her pretty brown eyes were vague, focused on the middle distance, and Marcus could almost hear the brass wheels turning behind them. She looked for all the world like somebody's younger sister, a skinny girl in her late teens, perhaps a touch too serious for her own good.

As opposed to a woman of twenty, and ruler in her own right of one of the most powerful nations in the world. He shook his head, bemused. *Assuming that nation doesn't fall down around her ears in the next couple of weeks.*

"Are you going to join me, Captain?" she said.

They hadn't spoken more than a few words to each other on the way over, and Marcus was at a loss for how to begin. He cleared his throat. "Would that be proper, Your Majesty?"

"Seeing as we're not at Ohnlei, I think we can dispense with formal precedence. Besides, proper is whatever I say it is, isn't it?"

"As you wish." He bowed and pulled out a chair to sit beside her.

"And eat something, please. I don't eat much, and I would hate for the chef to feel like his work had gone unappreciated."

Marcus needed no urging on that score. His rations in the Vendre hadn't been a prisoner's bread and water, but they hadn't been much better. He helped himself to a slice of the trout—*what's the* point *of leaving the head there—are we supposed to eat it?*—and filled his plate with samples of the rest. Then he engaged in silent contemplation for some time while the queen watched, amused.

"Do all soldiers eat like that?" she said, when he'd cleaned his plate and started on a second round.

"Only when they've been locked up for a week," Marcus said, and then added hastily, "Your Majesty."

She smiled, took a small bite of her bread, and set it back.

"You're not hungry?" he said.

"I never eat much," she said. "Doctor-Professor Indergast says it may be an aftereffect of my illness, along with"—she gestured at herself and grinned ruefully—"my stature."

"I didn't know you were ailing, Your Majesty."

"I *was* ill. This was four years ago—you would have already been in Khandar, I think. For a while they were certain I would die, but by the grace of God"—she had an odd look—"I survived. I suppose a diminished appetite is a small price to pay." She waved at his plate. "Don't let me put you off *your* food, of course."

Marcus nodded, uncertainly, and looked down at this plate. It was still half-full, but his appetite had gone. He cut a bit more fish, for the look of the thing.

"They tell me that you're to escort me to some sort of gathering Count Mieran has planned for this morning," the queen said while he ate.

"Yes, Your Majesty. He asked for us an hour before noon."

"The last time you came to escort me somewhere, we ended up jumping out a window." She looked around the dining room, which was windowless and candlelit. "I hope that's not the usual procedure, with you."

"Ah . . . no, Your Majesty."

There was a pause.

"That was an attempt at humor, Captain. A poor one, I admit, but you might at least smile."

"I'm sorry, Your Majesty. I'm not accustomed to such lofty company."

She shrugged. "You needn't be so formal. Being shot at together creates a certain amount of familiarity, I think."

"I'll do my best."

"Do you have any idea what the count might have planned for us?"

"He mentioned that he was going to make a speech to the deputies, and that you might make one as well."

"I know. Fortunately, I've been composing one in my head ever since they locked me up. I spent last night writing it out."

"I hope you got some sleep as well."

"Enough for my needs," she said. "You don't know anything else about the count's plan?"

"The colonel," Marcus said, "that is, Count Mieran, is not in the habit of letting anyone know the whole of his plans."

"That must be irritating," the queen said, smiling very slightly.

"Sometimes. But it makes serving under him more interesting." Not to mention *dangerous*, but he didn't need to tell her that.

"Well. We'd best go find out, then."

Marcus pushed his plate back and got to his feet. "As you wish, Your Majesty."

"I wonder . . ." She hesitated. "Can I ask you something?"

"Of course."

"Have you heard from Sothe?" The queen set her jaw. "I'm certain she's alive, somewhere. But she might need help. I thought you might know something."

Marcus shook his head. "I've only been out of prison for a day and a half myself, Your Majesty, and the Armsmen have more or less disbanded. I don't have any information, but there's no reason I should. If you like, I can inquire with Count Mieran."

"Please do." The queen pushed herself back from the table and got to her feet. "Let's be off."

RAESINIA

A string of three carriages took them the short distance from the Twin Turrets to the edge of Farus' Triumph, across Saint Vallax Bridge. Raesinia sat in the center one with Marcus and a pair of guards, while the rest of the squad rode in and on top of the other two. Janus clearly remembered what had happened last time, and he'd ordered the escort to take no chances.

Perhaps he has a specific reason to be worried. Raesinia had heard a dozen versions of the story of Danton's assassination, but all agreed that the killer had worn a strange, glittering black mask. Most people assumed this was only the odd affectation of a lunatic—a man who had vanished in the midst of the crowd moments later—but Raesinia knew better. A mask like that figured in her darkest memories, reflecting the light of dozens of candles ringing her deathbed. The man who'd worn it had led her through an incomprehensible incantation, pausing every few moments as she coughed a little bit more of her life away. Raesinia, terrified and in pain, had done as she was told, even as she felt the binding trying to tear her soul to pieces. And when she'd finished . . .

The masks belonged to the Priests of the Black, the inquisitors of the Church, supposedly extinct for a hundred years. Where they'd struck once, they could strike again.

Of course, it would take more than a pistol for them to assassinate me. But getting shot in public would be extremely inconvenient, and it made her glad of Janus' precautions.

The sky was a brilliant blue, and the sun beat down with all the force of late summer. Farus' Triumph was crowded, as it had been when Danton made his speeches, but something in the air had changed. Those assemblies had possessed a palpable, crackling energy, leaping from man to man, cresting in wild waves whenever the great orator reached a crescendo. Today the people looked tired and suspicious, wilting in the heat. The enthusiasm had been replaced by *fear.*

They'd demanded Vhalnich, and now they had him. But, each man asked his neighbor, what could even Vhalnich really do? They had no troops, no weapons, just a few hundred fools in black sashes and a lot of empty promises, and bread was more expensive than ever. Wouldn't it be safer to hand the whole lot over to Orlanko? Hadn't things, some might say, been *better* under the Last Duke? Say what you like, he'd made things *work.* The Concordat might have been brutal, but they were certainly efficient.

With the windows closed, Raesinia could hear none of this, of course. It was only a story she constructed in her mind, watching the sour faces as the carriages rolled past and imagining the whispers that followed in her wake. Marcus was staring out the windows, too, though she guessed he was more focused on potential threats. She felt better, having him along. There was something very solid and reliable about the captain, although she still missed the comforting knowledge that Sothe was out there watching.

The crowd was densest around the central fountain with its speaker's rostrum. At Marcus' suggestion, they halted the carriages and disembarked, the Mierantai guard forming around the pair of them in a tight cordon. People drew back from the unfamiliar uniforms, and protected by this flying wedge of soldiers Raesinia and Marcus made their way to the base of the fountain, where a clear space had been carved out by a ring of Patriot Guards. There was a moment of tension as the Mierantai and the Patriots faced off, but Janus' orders had been specific. Most of the Mierantai peeled off, reinforcing the outer cordon, but four of the soldiers stayed with the queen and the captain as they passed beyond the ring of Patriots.

Inside the cordon of Guardsmen, the Deputies-General were milling around, staring up at the still-empty rostrum and fingering their black sashes. Raesinia saw Maurisk, his sash edged with gold, in the center of a knot of deputies. Winter and Cyte would be in there, too, she thought, but this wasn't the time to seek them out. *Let's see how the speech goes over first.*

A few eyes were turned in her direction, but for the most part people took little notice of her. There was nothing to mark out this girl in mourning dress as the queen. No great nobles or retinue attended her, just a few of Janus' men and one blue-uniformed captain. Marcus drew more stares than she did; Royal Army uniforms were an uncommon sight in the city.

The agitation of the crowd warned her of Janus' approach, accompanied by another wedge of Mierantai. There were even a few cheers, though these died quickly, like sparks falling on damp tinder. Janus himself strode ahead of his men, stopped in front of Raesinia, and bowed low.

"Your Majesty," he said. "Thank you for coming."

"It seemed polite," she said, "after your men rescued me from the Vendre."

His lip quirked. "Do you have your speech ready?"

"I do." It was written out on a few folded pages in her pocket. "Would you like me to start?"

"Please." Janus clicked open his pocket watch, frowned, and returned it to his pocket. "A reasonably brief address would be best."

"Why?"

He smiled again but said nothing. Raesinia exchanged a knowing look with Marcus, and shook her head.

"Captain," she said, "would you do me the honor of introducing me, and asking for quiet?"

Marcus bowed. "Of course, Your Majesty."

They started up the circular staircase that led to the platform halfway up Farus V's fantastic monument. It was, Raesinia noted inanely, quite high off the ground. For someone who had jumped from a tower roof on a regular basis, the little thrill in the pit of her stomach seemed ridiculous, but she felt it anyway. Two of the Mierantai stationed themselves at the base of the stairs, while the other pair followed her and Marcus up to the rostrum and waited just out of sight.

A startled, unsteady cheer rose from the crowd when she appeared, and people finally realized who they were looking at. For most of the people, she knew, this would be their initial look at the new queen. For the first time in her life, she wished that she were wearing something more impressive.

Marcus stepped to the edge of the rostrum and held up his hands, waiting for the cheers to die away. A hush fell over the square, a silence full of murmurs and rustles. When Marcus spoke, his words dropped into it like pebbles tossed into a bottomless pit.

"Welcome," the captain said, then cleared his throat. "I have the honor to present Her Majesty Raesinia Orboan, Queen of Vordan. May God grace her and Karis' favor protect her."

The archaic form was echoed, first by the deputies, then by the crowd, in a ripple of muttered words spreading out from the fountain. Marcus bowed low to Raesinia and stepped out of the way. She squared her shoulders and walked to the edge of the platform.

She'd never done this. Arguing in the back of the Blue Mask was one thing, with a few friends who were half-drunk and wouldn't hesitate to shout you down if they thought you were being a bore. Trying to convince the crowd in its gathered thousands, while they stared up in respectful, quizzical silence, was quite another. Raesinia felt her heart flutter, and she thrust one hand in her pocket and closed it into a fist around the folded copy of her speech. Down below, lined up at the edge of the fountain, the deputies waited. Maurisk's piercing eyes were in the front row, glittering with rancor.

"The Kingdom of Vordan," she said. She hated the sound of her voice, a little-girl voice, not the voice of a queen. At the moment, she would gladly have parted with her right arm for Danton's effortless, rolling baritone. *Concentrate on the words,* she thought. Those, at least, had always been hers.

"The Kingdom of Vordan is the only nation in the world that came into being through the will of its own people. In the year nine hundred ninety-two, the year of the Great Flood, the people of Vordan became fed up with the petty barons who liked playing at war better than serving their people. They elected the Deputies-General to speak for them. Those deputies went to the one baron whom the people trusted, the one ruler whose land had prospered, the man who had defended his people in times of war and cared for them in times of trouble. To this man, they *gave* the crown, and said, 'Please rule over us. Care for all the people, as you have cared for your own.'

"That man was Farus Orboan. Farus the Conqueror, we call him now, but it is important to remember that the deputies chose him before he won his fame on the battlefield. They chose him because they trusted him with the crown, *in the name of the people.* He would care for them, as a father cared for his children.

"The Sworn Church tells the King of Borel and the Emperor of Murnsk that they rule by divine right, that they are appointed by God and answer to no earthly authority. In Hamvelt and the League cities, rule is by the strongest or the richest, who think of nothing but lining their own pockets at the expense of others. Only here, in Vordan, do we understand that the Crown *belongs* to the people. My father understood that, and his father before him, and his father, all the way back to Farus the Conqueror. It is what has given us our strength in our most desperate hours. And my father taught me well . . ."

It wasn't a *bad* speech, Raesinia thought, as she worked her way through it.

She'd written most of it in preparation for her appearance at the opening of the Deputies-General, which the Last Duke had so rudely cut short. Some of the facts might not have stood up in the cut and thrust of debate at the Blue Mask—for example, the deputies of Farus I's day had been the wealthy landowners, and their main complaint had been that the barons were infringing their ancient rights of rent and taxation. But it carried everything Raesinia believed, everything she and her friends had worked for, everything Ben and poor Danton had *died* for.

And it wasn't going to work. She couldn't *make* it work. As she went on, the deputies kept watching, but she could *feel* the attention of the crowd wandering. Danton could have fired those words with the force of cannonballs, sent them flying out to smash everyone in the square right between the eyes and leave them dumb in wonder. Her father in his prime, though no Danton, could still have made the flagstones ring with lofty sentiments. But coming from her own lips, the words sounded weak, uncertain, pedantic. She closed her eyes for a moment, still speaking, trying to hold back tears of frustration.

We worked so long for this moment. I pushed them into it—Ben, Danton, Faro, all the rest. To get me here. And it isn't working. She took a deep breath, and began the peroration.

"When the people of Vordan once again called for the Deputies-General, Duke Orlanko and his allies saw it as a crime, an inducement to revolution. But how can that be? The people are *sovereign*. We rule in their name. How can a ruler revolt against himself? How can a call for the ancient representatives of the people be anything but the exercise of a God-given right?

"This is why I come before you today, as Queen of Vordan, in the humble acceptance of the right of the people to express their will through their gathered representatives . . ."

Something was happening, out at the south end of the square. The crowd swirled, some moving toward the disturbance, others fighting to get away. Raesinia could hear cheers, shouts, even screams, but nothing that made any sense. She trailed off, shading her eyes to see what was going on, and caught the glitter of steel.

Saints and martyrs. Are we under attack? She looked over her shoulder at Janus. He was standing at the back of the platform, in the shadow of the statue, looking down at his pocket watch. After a moment, he snapped it closed and looked up.

"Your Majesty," he said, "your timing is impeccable."

The crowd was parting, drawing back, but the cheers started to outnumber the shouts of alarm. Men in blue uniforms, a thousand strong, marched in a battalion column across the square. There was another column behind them, and another behind that, and between them came the great gray shapes of guns and their caissons. At their head snapped the Vordanai flag, silver eagle brilliant on a royal blue field, and beside it the battle flag of the First Colonial Infantry.

When the first rank reached the center of the square, just below the podium, the column halted. At a shout from their officers, a thousand men slammed the butts of their muskets against the flagstones of the square with an almighty clatter, then brought their free hands up to salute. A thousand voices spoke at once.

"God grace the queen!" they chorused, in the ancient formula. "And Karis' favor protect her!"

Janus smiled, just for a moment, and gestured at the crowd. Raesinia spun around and stepped to the edge of the platform, shouting the last lines of her speech.

"I, for one, do not plan to surrender these sovereign rights without a fight! Will you join me?" Looking down at the soldiers, she spread her arms and added, "Will you join *us*?"

The people began to shout. Here and there, she could distinguish a few words—"God grace Vordan!" or "God grace the queen!" The noise of the crowd grew and grew, from a murmur to a tumult to a full-throated roar that shook the square, rattling the windows in the shops and startling the pigeons from the rooftops. The soldiers joined in, until it seemed that the noise would shake the great podium to pieces. Raesinia closed her eyes and risked a smile.

Chapter Twenty-One

WINTER

"I don't know about you, but I'm going to join up."

"You never will. You're saying it, but you won't."

"I will!"

"Last time you told me there was no point going off to die for some nob."

"Yeah, but that was last time. This time it's *Vhalnich*."

"He ain't a nob?"

"He knows what he's doing, is all. *And* he's got some real troops to help. First Colonials, they said. You heard what they did in Khandar?"

"I heard a lot of things. That don't make 'em true."

"And you don't want Orlanko back here, either, with his goddamned Sworn Church and his Borel tax farmers."

"Yeah, but . . ."

"Besides, think about it. This time next week, a man in a blue uniform won't be able to buy his own drinks. And the girls—"

"Yeah, but you gotta be alive to enjoy it."

Winter, hands in her pockets, walked beside the pair of youths until they turned off onto a side street. She'd heard that conversation, or one very much like it, at least a dozen times since she left the cathedral.

The deputies had retreated from the cheering mob to the cathedral's great hall, locked in furious argument. The carefully negotiated alliances of the past week had all gone out the window, as though Janus' speech and the arrival of the Colonials had upset the checkerboard and spilled all the pieces on the floor. And, in a way, it had. Royal Army troops were in Vordan City for the first time in living memory, and that tipped the balance of power decisively in favor of the man who held their loyalty.

Radical, Monarchist, and Center split into a dozen competing bands. Some cheered Janus on, while others wanted to send a delegation to take command of the regiment and make sure it couldn't be used against the deputies. Still others argued against doing anything rash, or anything at all, for fear of provoking Janus before Orlanko was dealt with. Some argued that a true constitution needed to be written, clarifying the queen's position, before any action could be taken.

Maurisk alternately sat in silence and shouted, soothing the worried and beating back the more ludicrous proposals. Eventually he convinced the deputies to pass a resolution of support for Janus and the Colonials, which expressed, in a general way, their hopes that he would defeat Orlanko but didn't say anything terribly specific about what would happen afterward. Satisfied with this noneffort, the Deputies-General dissolved for the evening.

Winter had hired a carriage to take her to the Docks, but had been forced to abandon it after crossing the Grand Span. The streets were full of people, as if the passage of the Colonials had been a magic signal to come out of hiding. Everywhere torches were burning, men and women were talking and laughing, and children played in the streets and shouted with joy at the unexpected festival.

As she threaded her way through the crowd, Winter learned that there were more reasons for cheer than just the arrival of her old regiment. The Colonials had marched up the Green Road from the south, and they'd brought with them a considerable tail of carts and wagons. These belonged to the farmers and merchants of the area, who'd been frightened off from bringing their produce to the city by rumors of fighting. They'd flocked to the familiar blue uniforms, evidence that authority was being reasserted, and followed the Colonials to sell their wares. The road to the north was still closed, but this influx had helped to fill the food shortage and bring prices to more reasonable levels. Winter saw fresh vegetables, early apples by the barrelful, bushels of corn and sides of bacon, and the whole city seemed full of the smell of baking bread.

Jane's building looked like a castle just after the siege is lifted. The front doors were open, and people streamed in and out. Some of the injured were leaving, in the company of family and friends, and Winter witnessed a couple of emotional family reunions. A few Leatherbacks and some of Jane's girls were about, but they weren't going armed anymore.

Winter headed up to the big dining room, following the roars of laughter and the smell of food. A feast was in progress, and she entered to find the room in pandemonium. There were easily twice as many girls crammed into the hall as could actually fit around the tables, and all the chairs had been pushed out of the way. The guests ate with their fingers from a vast bounty: huge loaves of bread, roast chickens, hams and gravy, bowls of apples and berries. Nothing complicated, Winter noted with a faint smile. *Nellie tries her best.*

Jane sat at the high table like a king in a medieval court, surrounded by her lieutenants, exchanging shouted jokes with girls at other tables and roaring with laughter. Rather than fight her way across the room, Winter slipped around the edge, finding a table in the corner where the press of young women was not quite so solid. There was even an empty chair. She sat down and leaned back, just watching Jane, drinking in the sheer laughing wild *life* of her. Her hair was growing out, Winter thought, red spikes changing into a tousled mop that hung forward over her eyes and made her look younger.

No one took any notice of her, which was fine. She helped herself to an apple and half a roast chicken, pulling the bird apart with her fingers and licking them clean of the grease. She was vaguely aware of a conversation going on across the table from her, but it was only after she recognized Becks that she started to pay attention.

"—Jane would never let us!" Becks was saying.

"Not *us*," Molly said. "The older girls would go."

"What use is that?" said Andy. "*I* want to go. Able Tom says he's going to go, and he's only fifteen. I lifted a water barrel when he couldn't do it, *and* I beat him in a race."

"Vhalnich won't want the likes of Able Tom, either," Nell said. "He wants *men*, he said. Little boys don't carry muskets, and neither do girls."

"I could, I bet," Andy said. "And Becks wants to."

"I never said I wanted to," Becks said. "I just said we *ought* to. Nobody *wants* to go fight, but it's our duty as Vordanai."

"Do you think *Jane* will go?" Molly said. "Vhalnich would have to take *her*."

"He'd be stupid not to," Andy said. "Or Jess or Nina, or any of the older girls. They fought the tax farmers for a *year*. I'm sure they could fight Duke Orlanko."

"The other soldiers would never put up with it," Nell said, a bit huffily. "Girls *can't* be soldiers, I told you."

"Why not?" said Andy.

"They just can't!"

They just can't. Winter shook her head. *That ought to be a good enough answer for anybody. It ought to be a good enough answer for me.*

Big clay mugs of beer were circling, for anyone who wanted a swallow. Winter took a few gulps of the warm, thin stuff and sent it on its way. More girls scurried in, bringing more food and clearing away the remains. The air was hot and thick with the mixed smells of cooking and hundreds of unwashed bodies, leavened with smoke from the torches. It ought to have been choking and claustrophobic, but Winter felt comforted instead, as though the laughter and smell were wrapped around her like a warm blanket on a cold night. Someone was playing a fiddle, very badly.

"Winter, can I talk to you for a minute?"

She looked up. Abby was standing beside her table, shoulders hunched, arms crossed over her chest. She looked pale in the torchlight. Winter was still not entirely comfortable in Abby's company, but the room was too crowded to escape. She forced a smile and looked up with a noncommittal shrug. "Go ahead."

"Somewhere a little quieter."

With a last glance at Jane, Winter sighed and got to her feet. She followed Abby through the crowd and out into the corridor. Abby ducked through the first open doorway, which led into a small room with a half dozen bedrolls spread out on the floor. They were all empty now, and the candles were out. Only a little of the distant light from the torches in the main hall seeped in to break up the shadows.

"What were you doing there?" Abby said.

"Getting something to eat," Winter said, defensively. "Nobody stopped me."

"Not that," Abby said. She hugged herself tighter. "She's been waiting for you all night. Why haven't you gone to see her?"

"She looked happy. I didn't want to intrude."

"She won't really be happy unless you're there." Abby sighed. "Sometimes I'm not sure you understand how much you mean to her."

"I do," Winter said. *I think I do.* "Abby, what's wrong?"

"I haven't heard from my father," Abby said. "He's not at the house. He probably left the city after the queen surrendered, or went to stay with a friend, but . . . I don't know."

"If you're worried about him, find Captain d'Ivoire," Winter said. "He may know where to look."

Abby nodded. She was barely a shadowed outline in the dark, her eyes invisible. "But I can't leave. Not yet. I need to look after Jane."

"You need to start trusting her a little more," Winter said. "Jane can take care of herself, if anyone can."

"You saw her the other day," Abby said quietly. "She can take care of *herself.* The problem is that she tries to take care of everyone else, too."

"I know." Winter shook her head. "I'll look out for Jane."

"You won't let her do anything . . ."

"Stupid?"

Abby gave a weak chuckle.

"I'll do my best," Winter said. "Go and find your father. Or better yet, get some sleep. I only met your father briefly, but he struck me as being able to take care of himself, too."

"Thank you." Abby paused. "And thank you for helping Jane. I don't know all of what the two of you did, but all this . . ."

Winter held up her hands. "I only gave her a bit of advice. Jane and Janus did the rest."

Abby nodded, tiredly. She took a step toward the door, then halted. "What happens if we win?"

"What?"

"Suppose Vhalnich beats Orlanko. Then what? What happens to Jane and the rest of us here?"

"Why should anything happen?"

"I don't know," Abby said. "But I feel like it can't go back to normal, after this. What are *you* going to do?"

Winter shrugged uncomfortably. *Damned if I know.* "I'll figure that out when I get there."

Abby regarded her for a moment, a tiny gleam of light reflecting in her eyes. Then she swept out, leaving Winter alone in the darkness.

Winter didn't want to fight her way through the frantic, happy crowd in the hall, but she remembered seeing girls come in with fresh dishes from a door just behind where Jane had been sitting. She went in search of the kitchens and eventually found them by following the clatter of crockery. A half dozen girls were giggling together over an open bottle of wine. They looked up as Winter came in, but she ignored them. She found the door she wanted and eased it open.

The bad fiddler had been joined by a bad piper, who from the sound of it was playing an instrument she'd carved herself. The crowd clapped its hands to keep the beat, and as Winter came forward she saw that Chris had led some of the girls up on the tables and started to dance, heedless of the occasional chicken or bowl of berries that got kicked out of the way. Jane stood between Becca and Winn, clapping as loudly as anyone, and nearly doubling over with laughter when Chris stepped right off the end of the table and toppled into a sea of welcoming hands.

Winter stepped up and touched her on the arm. Jane looked over her shoulder, then spun around, grinning madly.

"Winter! When did you finally turn up?"

"Just now," Winter said. As the other girls began to turn to look at them, she grabbed Jane's hand. "Come with me."

There is a law of nature—one that Winter had previously been unaware of, but now instinctively sensed—that says that the more comfortable one is, lying beside one's lover with limbs entwined under a sweaty sheet, the more certain it is that one will eventually need to use the toilet. Winter held off as long as she could, but eventually she was forced to roll out of the big bed and pad across the chilly floor, navigating by moonlight.

When she returned, Jane had kicked off the sheet and lay on her back, hands crossed behind her head. She was gloriously naked, dappled in silver and shadow by the moonlight, and Winter stopped for a moment at the foot of the bed to stare at her in wonder.

Jane tilted her head. "Is something wrong?"

Winter clambered up on the foot of the bed and crawled up beside Jane, pressing up against her. Jane put an arm around her shoulders and pulled her in for a kiss, and Winter closed her eyes. After a moment, though, Jane pulled back.

"Something *is* wrong," Jane said. "Winter, please. What's going on?"

The knot in Winter's chest, so recently dissolved, tied itself tighter than ever. She swallowed hard. "Obviously you heard . . . what happened in the Triumph, this morning?"

"Of course I heard," Jane said. "Nobody talks about anything else. Vhalnich called for volunteers, and then the Colonials marched in—"

She stopped. Winter squeezed her eyes shut, as though expecting a blow.

"You're going back, aren't you?" Jane said.

Winter nodded, her face pressed up against Jane's shoulder. Tears were stinging her eyes.

"You don't have to," Jane said, after a moment. "You know that, whatever Vhalnich says. You can stay here with me."

"There's more to it than that." Winter wanted, for a moment, to tell Jane about the Infernivore and everything that had happened in Khandar, but she quashed the impulse. *She'd only think I'm crazy.* "I have friends there. More than friends. The men in my company . . . I have a responsibility." Winter opened her eyes. "You ought to understand that."

There was a long silence.

"I do," Jane said. "At least, I think I do. But . . . what happens afterward? If we win. Will you come back here?"

"I don't know."

"You have to come back." Jane sat up, looking down at Winter. She sounded almost panicked. "Winter, please. You *have* to. I lost you once, and by all the fucking saints I'm never doing it again. Please. Promise me."

"I don't *know*." Winter fought the urge to curl into a ball. "I don't know what's going to happen. Hell, I could be killed, or—"

"Don't talk like that. Please. If something happened to you, I don't . . . I don't think I could stand it. I don't know what I'd do."

"I'm sorry." Winter didn't know what else to say.

"You're always apologizing to me." Jane tried to smile, but even by moonlight Winter could tell it was paper-thin. "Have you ever thought that you should stop doing things that you need to apologize for, instead?"

"I don't . . ." Winter shook her head. "I don't have a choice."

"Of course you have a fucking choice! Everyone has a choice. You can stay here, and when Vhalnich comes looking for you we'll shove a musket up his arse and send him running. If anyone tries to take you, I'd—"

"You *know* it isn't like that. I have a responsibility to—"

"But not to me?"

"Jane." The tears were leaking out now, in spite of Winter's best efforts to stop them. "Don't do this. Please."

Jane rolled out of bed with a growl. Winter could hear her stalking through the room, floorboards creaking underfoot. There was a splash of water in the basin, and then the sound of shattering crockery.

Winter rolled over, facedown, burying her tears in the pillow. The bed underneath her was warm from Jane's body.

Time passed, imperceptibly. Winter stayed with her face pressed against the tear-soaked pillow. She must have dozed, because she didn't hear the floorboards announce Jane's return, only felt the delicate touch of a finger at the small of her back, tracing a shivery trail up her spine.

"Don't say anything," Jane said. Winter felt the bed creak as she sat down beside her. "It's my turn to apologize."

"I didn't mean for it to work out like this," Winter tried to say.

"I didn't catch a word of that," Jane said. "You're talking into the pillow."

Winter rolled over. "I didn't—"

She didn't get to say it this time, either, because of something Jane did with her fingers. She gave a little yelp instead, and Jane laughed.

"It's all right. I've worked it out." Her smile turned wicked. "But I hope you weren't planning on getting any sleep."

In fact, Winter slept better than she had any right to. The sun was well up by the time she opened her eyes and stretched, savoring the pleasant ache in her body and the unaccustomed sensation of the bedsheets against bare skin. The bed was empty except for her. She could hear a distant clatter and clamor of voices that was presumably the girls fixing breakfast. Jane would be down there, presiding.

If we win . . .

Winter shook her head. She just *didn't know.* Janus had said the Black Priests would come after her, for bearing a demon. *But if Orlanko's beaten, they won't have any allies in the city. Would Janus still need me?*

She sat up, got out of bed, and found a fresh basin of water waiting on the table to replace the one Jane had smashed the night before. Her clothes were there, too, in a rumpled pile. She splashed some water on her face in an effort to bring herself a bit more fully out of sleep, and dressed in yesterday's creased, sweaty outfit, wrinkling her nose a bit before doing up the buttons.

How quickly we forget. In Khandar she'd worn the same uniform and even the same underclothes for days at a time, and counted herself lucky if she had enough water to drink, let alone wash with. *Too much city living is making me soft.* She ran her hands through her hair, shook her head, and went down to see if there was anything left of breakfast.

On the way she saw a couple of girls, idling unconvincingly in the corridors, who hurried ahead of her and out of sight as she approached. Other than that, the corridors were empty, and Winter frowned as she came closer to the dining room. *Is that a* drum*? What the hell's going on?*

She opened the door to find that the tables—and all the debris of the previous evening—had been pushed to the edges of the hall, leaving a broad clear space in the center. In that space, lined up in nearly even ranks, were Jane's girls. There were about two hundred of them, Winter guessed, in a ten-deep formation, with one young woman on the end holding a child's drum. When she caught sight of Winter, she beat a simple pattern, and every one of the girls straightened up and *saluted*. They had obviously been practicing this, and while they didn't quite have the parade-ground snap, Winter had to admit they did a better job than most of the Patriot Guard.

Jane stood by one side of this formation, grinning in a way that Winter didn't like at all.

"Good, aren't they?" she said, catching Winter's slack-jawed expression. "I thought we should get in a little practice before heading down to the Triumph."

"What?" Winter shook her head. "Jane, what in Karis' name are you doing?"

"We're going to volunteer." She looked over her shoulder. "Isn't that right?"

"Yes, *sir*!" the girls said, in a soprano chorus. Clearly they'd practiced that as well.

"You're going to *volunteer*," Winter repeated, feeling sandbagged.

"To fight," Jane explained patiently. "Vhalnich said he needs every man he can get to carry a musket. So I thought, why not us?"

Winter crossed the room, grabbed Jane's arm, and dragged her without a word toward the door. Jane came along willingly enough, shouting over her shoulder as she went, "Chris! Get them to practice the salute a few more times!"

Once the door had closed behind them, Winter pushed Jane against the wall and looked her in the eye. "Have you gone totally out of your mind?"

Jane, still grinning, shook her head. "I don't think so."

"Why would you put them up to this?" Winter glared. "Is it supposed to be a *joke*? If so—"

"It's not a joke."

"Then you really want to take them to a *battle*? Some of those girls should still be playing with dolls, and you want to give them *muskets*?" Winter took a step back and shook her head. "I think you *have* gone mad."

"They wouldn't all fight, obviously." Jane straightened her shirt and brushed herself off. "Just like with the Leatherbacks. But the younger ones could still make themselves useful somehow."

"You're really serious about this." Winter drew in a long breath. "God above, where do I start?"

"I don't see why you're so shocked. We've been fighting Orlanko's tax farmers for years."

"This is not the same thing. A little brawl in an alley is one thing, but these are Royal Army troops. You don't know what it's like."

"*You* did it, didn't you? Why can't they?"

Winter paused, temporarily thrown by this line of reasoning.

Jane crossed her arms. "Besides, your colonel seems to be taking any *men* who are willing. My girls may not be soldiers, but they'll do a better job than some of the boys I've seen going to sign up."

"But—" Winter gritted her teeth. "This is about me, isn't it? You want to follow *me*."

"That's what it was, at first—"

"You can't be serious. I don't care *how* you feel—marching two hundred people into harm's way just so you can be near me is wrong. It's *wrong*, Jane."

"I said *at first*." Jane took a deep breath. "Listen. Last night I thought, all right, Winter ran away and joined the army, so why don't I? I'll just go after her and keep her safe. I got up early so I could make sure everything was arranged here for the next few days. But when I came downstairs, Chris told me she'd caught four of the younger girls trying to sneak out, because *they* wanted to try the same thing."

"I would have thought you'd put a stop to that," Winter grated.

"I was about to," Jane said. "But I thought, I can't tell them not to do what I was about to do myself, can I? And by then news had gotten around, and some of the others said they wanted to go as well. They want to *help*, Winter. They hate the tax farmers, and they hate Orlanko, and they want to help defend this city."

"I don't—they're not thinking straight, then. None of them know what it's like, either."

"And the men who're signing up do? You're fine with every butcher's boy and apprentice fisherman in the city carrying a musket in the ranks, but not us?"

"It's . . ." Winter stopped. She wanted to say, "It's not the same." *But it is the same, isn't it?* She remembered watching the recruits at Fort Valor, thinking how *young* they were. Raw boys, enticed into the king's service by the promises of recruiting sergeants, and thrown willy-nilly across thousands of miles of ocean to fight people they'd never heard of. *These are girls*—people—*who want to defend their own home.* "I don't know."

"Neither do I. But I didn't think that was good enough to tell them they had to stop."

Winter lowered her voice. "Even if it means some of them won't come back? Because that *is* what it means. Even if we win."

"You don't think they know that?" Jane shook her head. "Our battles may be just 'little brawls' to you, but the tax farmers and their thugs aren't fighting with cushions. Everyone in there knows what it's like to lose someone."

"But . . ." Winter paused, still not quite believing she was being talked into this. "Look. Even if I agreed with you, Janus would never allow it. There's no way we could sneak them *all* in as boys. Even getting you in"—Winter glanced at Jane's chest, and blushed slightly—"might be difficult. If we tried it with more than a few, someone would give the game away."

"You're right," Jane said.

"Then you don't think we should do it?"

"I don't think we should do it in disguise."

"You want to just . . . what? Walk up to the colonel with two hundred girls, and say you want to sign up to fight?"

Jane nodded. "Exactly."

"He'll think you're mad."

"Everyone already calls me Mad Jane."

"But he'll never agree to that!"

"He might," Jane said, "if *you* were the one asking."

An hour later, crossing Saint Vallax Bridge to the North Bank, Winter could still hardly believe what she was doing.

"Remember the deal," she said to Jane, under her breath. "If Janus says no, that's the end of it. For *all* of you."

"I remember," Jane said. She looked over her shoulder. "Jess! Keep 'em moving!"

The girls had started out in a column, and even tried to keep in step, but by the end of the first street they'd devolved into a mob. They'd passed over the Island like a gang of tourists, pointing at the grand buildings and laughing with one another. For most of them, this was the first time they'd been over the bridges from Southside, and they were as new to the city as country children, for all that they lived only a few miles away.

Jane's lieutenants kept the group together and in motion. They still drew stares as they passed by, and the occasional shout. Some of these were obscene, and were answered cheerfully in kind, but most people just wanted to know where they were going. Every time this happened, one of the girls would sing out, "We're going to join the army!" and everyone around them would start laughing.

Once they crossed Bridge Street, Winter quickly located the Twin Turrets by its distinctive silhouette and the squad of Mierantai guards outside. Two of these trotted over as soon as they saw the small army of young women coming, which led to a tricky situation. Winter didn't want to reveal her male persona, not here, but the Mierantai sergeant was equally reluctant to let the troop onto the grounds. Eventually Jane convinced the guards to send someone to tell Janus that Winter Bailey was here with Mad Jane, and a few minutes later the reply came back. The Mierantai escorted the girls out to the back lawn and sent Winter and Jane up to the house itself.

"The colonel," Jane whispered, as they passed through the elegantly appointed hall and climbed the main stairs. "He knows who you really are, right?"

Winter nodded. "He knows everything. And I mean *everything.* Don't try to lie to him."

For a moment, she felt a pang of conscience. She'd told Jane about her history with the army, but not that her original task had been to spy on the Leatherbacks. It didn't matter, she told herself sternly, because she'd never actually *done* any spying to speak of, or made any reports.

"He must really be something," Jane said. Her tone was dismissive. "The whole city seems to have gone mad for him."

"He's . . . you'll see."

They reached the oak-paneled door to a study. Another guard stood outside it, and he exchanged salutes with their escort, then knocked politely.

"Yes?" Janus said.

"It's the . . . young women I mentioned, sir," said the sergeant, with a gravelly mountain accent. "You said you'd see them."

"Of course. Let them in."

The Mierantai opened the door. The study was neatly furnished but obviously unused. Bookshelves lined the walls, full of volumes with neatly matched bindings. A desk stood in front of a window, empty except for an inkpot. In the center of the room was a large table, and here Janus had spread out a pair of maps: a large-scale one of the city, and a smaller one showing the surrounding area.

He was looking down at them as the two women entered, making notes on a scrap of paper and occasionally picking up a pair of steel dividers to measure a distance.

Winter closed the door behind them, straightened to attention, and saluted. Janus looked up.

"Lieutenant Ihernglass. It's good to see you again." He laid his pen carefully aside where it wouldn't drip on the maps. "I understand I have you to thank for the recent events in the Deputies."

Winter felt herself flush. "No, sir. At least, not only me." She gestured Jane forward. "This is Jane Verity." *As you well know.* "Sometimes known on the streets as Mad Jane. She's been of enormous assistance throughout."

"Of course. My thanks to you as well, Miss Verity. I understand that you have something to talk to me about?" He cocked his head toward the window, gray eyes gleaming. "Presumably something to do with the company of young women who are currently engaged in defoliating my back garden."

Winter winced. "Sorry about that, sir."

"Don't trouble yourself. Making the house our headquarters ensured that we would have soldiers tramping all over the grounds, and the gardens were bound to be casualties. Better that the flowers be picked before they're stomped into the mud. So why have you brought me these young ladies?"

"They want to volunteer, sir." Winter took a deep breath. "They're Jane's people." *The group you sent me to "infiltrate."* "The Leatherbacks."

"I see." Janus smiled. "I'm certain we can find work for them. In the medical services, or transport—"

Jane cut in. "No, *sir.* We want to fight."

Janus' smile faded slowly. He looked from Jane to Winter, and Winter found herself shrinking before that cool gray gaze. Then, abruptly, he turned away from both of them and went to the window. He looked down, and said nothing for a long moment.

"We've been fighting Orlanko's tax farmers since before you arrived," Jane said, nervously, eager to fill the silence. "Some of my girls even know how to handle a musket. We've been protecting ourselves in the Docks since—"

"I have three conditions," Janus said, turning back from the window.

"What?" said Jane.

"What?" said Winter.

"The first is that your people will be evaluated by their commander, once they've had some training. Anyone that commander judges as not strong enough to use a weapon properly, or not fit to stand in a firing line, will remain behind, without argument."

"Fine," Jane said. "Provided you promise that your commander will give us a fair chance."

Janus nodded. "Second, you will form a unit of your own, both in camp and in the field. You will take responsibility for keeping your people apart, and keeping others away." He paused. "I will not have a unit in my command becoming a glorified brothel, understood?"

"A *brothel*?" Jane's lip twisted. "If you knew what we've been through in the Docks—"

"I *don't* know," Janus said. "In fact, I know nothing about you, save for what Lieutenant Ihernglass has told me. Her recommendation counts for a great deal, which is why I'm willing to agree to this . . . experiment. That, and the fact that we are going to need all the help we can get." He shrugged. "Primarily, this condition is for your protection. Whatever the moral qualities of your young ladies, you can be certain that there will be those who will assume they intend to provide that kind of service. And some among them will be willing to take by force what is not offered freely. Keeping you together will help, but you must be prepared to set watches and guard yourselves closely."

Jane still looked unhappy, but she nodded slowly. "I understand."

"You will be mocked. Laughed at. Then, when it becomes clear you really mean to go through with it, you will be insulted, slandered, attacked from all sides. You understand what this means? To all of you?"

"Yes." Jane faced Janus' piercing stare head-on.

"And then there are the risks of the battlefield. Your 'girls' will be shot. Some of them will die. Others will make it back to the cutters, and have their limbs taken off with bone saws."

"Just like all those *boys* you're rounding up."

"Some of them may be captured by the enemy," Janus continued remorselessly. "In which case I doubt they will be accorded the usual status of prisoners under the rules of civilized war."

"I understand," Jane grated. "We all understand that. What's your third condition?"

"You will be second in command of the unit, under one of my own officers."

"Who?"

Janus smiled, just for a moment, the ghost of an expression. "Lieutenant Winter Ihernglass."

"Wait," Winter said. "Wait a minute."

Jane, slowly, grinned. "I think we can accept that."

"Sir!" Winter said. "What about the Seventh? What about my men?"

"Captain Warus has made appropriate assignments to fill the gaps in the Colonials during the voyage home," Janus said. "First Battalion, Seventh Company has a new lieutenant. Lieutenant John Marsh, if I recall correctly."

"You . . . but . . ." Winter's throat was thick. "Sir. Those are my men. I'm . . . responsible."

Janus' expression softened. "I understand, Lieutenant. Once the emergency is past, I will see what I can do. For the moment, however, it's best for discipline if the Colonials go into battle under the officers they've had for the past three months, and in the meantime Miss Verity's command requires your attention."

"I . . ." Winter shook her head, and her fists clenched. "Would that be my attention as Lieutenant Ihernglass, or as Winter Bailey?"

"The former. This unit must be seen to be commanded by an officer of the Colonials." Janus paused. "I assume that most of Miss Verity's companions are aware of your real identity?"

"Yes." *Whatever that is.*

"In that case, I suggest you impress on them the need to keep it to themselves. If this experiment is a success, perhaps in time you can dispense with the charade. But until then . . ."

"They can keep a secret," Jane said. "Sir."

"Very well." He looked from Winter to Jane and back again. "Was that all?"

Jane glanced at Winter. "I . . . think so."

"Could I have a moment with the colonel?" Winter said. "Please."

"Sure. I'll be outside."

The door opened and closed with a soft click. Janus waited patiently. Winter took a deep breath.

"I have to know," she said. "You sent me to Jane."

"I did," Janus said. "I wasn't one hundred percent certain, of course, that she was the friend you told me about, but the balance of probability seemed to indicate it."

"And then . . . all the rest. Jane stormed the Vendre. I ended up in the

Deputies. And getting you out of prison . . ." She hesitated. "Is that why you put me there? So I could do what I did?"

"Did I know what was going to happen, in other words?" Janus chuckled. "Ah, Lieutenant. You have no idea how easy it would be to cultivate a reputation for genius, simply by taking credit for things after the fact."

"But—if you didn't know, then why . . ."

"Do you play chess?"

Winter blinked. "Not very well."

"As a game, it has never interested me," Janus said. "But it is useful as a metaphor. In chess, against a strong opponent, one can never plan with certainty. A good player does not claim to predict exactly what will happen, and position his pieces just so. Rather, he puts his pieces in the places where they will have the most *opportunity* to help him, whatever his opponent does."

"And I'm just a piece in your game?"

"You're a soldier under my command. A valuable asset. I guessed that having you by the side of the notorious Southside gang leader Mad Jane would be more likely to be a good use of your talents than, say, keeping you at court. As it happens, I was right, and Jane proved pivotal. But can I say I knew that would happen? No. Much as I might like to."

"I understand." Winter let out a long breath. "I wanted to thank you. For . . . keeping your word, about Jane."

"Of course."

"And what about the Black Priests? It was one of them who assassinated Danton. You must have had the Colonials bring the tablets back from Khandar, but—"

"One thing at a time, Lieutenant," Janus interrupted. "Right now Orlanko is the opponent in front of us. Once he is dealt with . . . we shall see."

CHAPTER TWENTY-TWO

MARCUS

"Fitz!" Marcus said, grabbing his ex-lieutenant's hand. "Damn, I'm glad you're here. The extra stripe suits you!"

"Thank you, sir," Fitz said. His blue uniform was immaculate as always, and the two silver stripes that marked him as a captain gleamed bright. "It's only provisional, of course, until it's confirmed by the Ministry."

Marcus laughed. "If we win, I don't think that will be a problem. And if we lose . . ."

"My thoughts exactly, sir."

"You can dispense with the 'sir' now, you know."

Fitz looked almost offended. "Oh no, sir. You still retain seniority."

Oh well. At least some things never change. "You're here to see the colonel?"

"To pick him up, actually." They were standing outside the front door of the Twin Turrets, and Fitz indicated the two-horse carriage parked in the drive. "He wanted to see the Triumph, where we're doing the public training. I imagine he'll want you to come along."

"Glad to hear it." Marcus fingered the hem of his coat, self-consciously. "It's a little odd, living in a house where the queen wanders in to breakfast in her bathrobe."

"I can imagine, sir."

There was a long pause, and Marcus felt strangely awkward. He'd spent two years with Fitz, and during that time the lieutenant's presence had become an organic part of his life. He'd hardly had to issue orders—Fitz had anticipated him and done what needed to be done, as easily as breathing.

Now, though, he didn't know where he stood. Fitz was captain of the First Battalion, Marcus' old unit. Marcus had no doubt he was up to the task; it was his own position that was unclear. He didn't *have* a real position, except that of captain of the now-defunct Armsmen and general assistant to the colonel. In the old days, Marcus would have been quizzing Fitz on the state of the troops and what preparations had been made, but now it felt as though that would be infringing on the new captain's prerogative.

Fitz frowned. At first Marcus thought he was feeling the same awkwardness, but he said, "Sir. I hate to be the bearer of the bad news, but there's something you need to know."

"Bad news?"

Fitz nodded soberly. "It's concerning Miss Alhundt. I know the two of you were . . . close."

"Ah." Marcus swallowed, mouth suddenly dry. "And?"

"She didn't survive the crossing, sir," Fitz said. "I'm sorry. The doctors tried their best, but in the end they couldn't even get her to take water. We had to bury her at sea."

Marcus nodded distantly. He wasn't sure if he should be grieving or relieved. He could remember Jen in the ancient temple, wielding a cracking, spitting sorcery that tore stone to shreds, mocking the time they'd spent together. But he could also see her in his tent, huddled tight against him to fit on the narrow camp bed, her chin resting on his shoulder and her slow breathing tickling his ear. There had been a gentleness there, a vulnerability that he couldn't reconcile with the vicious creature who'd attacked him.

Which one was the real woman, and which one was the mask? Now, he supposed, he'd never know.

"Thank you for telling me," Marcus said, eventually.

"I'm sorry," Fitz said again. "I thought you'd want to know sooner rather than later."

"Yes." Marcus took a deep breath, past the knot in his throat. "What about the others?"

"Everyone's doing well, sir. We had a few rankers come down with a fever, and we left them in Vayenne, but otherwise it was a quiet voyage." He made a face. "The men didn't appreciate having to wait an extra week in the transports, though."

"An extra week? What do you mean?"

"We docked downriver at Ohms a week ago, sir. The colonel's instructions were to wait there for a message from him, then to make our best time up the Green Road to the city."

"And you did an excellent job, Captain Warus," Janus said, opening the front door. Two of his Mierantai followed, long rifles resting on their shoulders. "I didn't want the Colonials to march into the city without being sure of their reception," he explained to Marcus. "So I left instructions for them to wait. And a good thing, too. No telling how the deputies would have reacted to an army regiment turning up unexpectedly."

"No telling," Marcus murmured, remember the couriers riding in all directions as soon as Janus had been released. *I wonder what else he had waiting.*

"Shall we?" Janus said. "It's going to be a busy day. Messengers from the duke arrived this morning."

"Messengers?" Marcus said, as they started toward the carriage. "With what sort of message?"

"His Grace demands our surrender, of course. Having defeated Deputy Peddoc's force, he assumes we are at his mercy. His representatives were very surprised to get the news that the Colonials had arrived."

"That should give him pause, I should hope."

"The longer the better," Janus said. "We need time more than anything. Unfortunately, I suspect the duke realizes that as well."

"What did you do with them, sir?" Fitz said. "The messengers. I assume they wanted to open negotiations."

"Oh, I imagine they're negotiating as we speak." Janus flashed a smile. "I told them I was only empowered to defend the city, not to engage in any discussions, and that they would have to talk to the deputies. I last saw them heading toward the cathedral."

Marcus barked a laugh. "That ought to keep them busy for a few days."

"What if the deputies agree to the surrender?" Fitz said.

"The deputies," Marcus explained, "can't agree on *anything*."

"It may buy us a brief respite," Janus said, opening the carriage door. "Let's see what we can do with it."

"This isn't the lot, surely," Marcus said, looking out at the drilling recruits.

"No, sir," Fitz said. "We've made our main camp at Ohnlei. Plenty of space in the gardens there for drills, and it's good to get the volunteers out of the city. Keeps them from wandering off at night. But the colonel requested that we have a company or two take their instruction here in the Triumph so that everyone could see what it was like. It might encourage a few more to sign up."

"They've certainly got an audience," Marcus said. "But I'm not sure it's going to convince anyone."

A stream of blistering curses drifted up from one of the Colonial sergeants, in a mixture of Vordanai and Khandarai. The foreign obscenities seemed to make quite an impression, and there was even scattered applause from the onlookers. The recruits were in two long lines, about a hundred men in all, ununiformed but sporting army-pattern muskets. They were being attended to by two blue-coated sergeants, one of whom called out the stages of the Manual of Arms while the other prowled the ranks, looking for shirkers.

It took Marcus back in time, not even to Khandar, but to his childhood. None of the boys who went to the War College were going to be rankers, but the instructors considered it important that the future officers understand what it was they were ordering their men to do. So the first three months of every cadet's instruction had been identical to what a newly arrived ranker would get in one of the army training camps, albeit with a bit more attention to the niceties and less summary corporal punishment. Marcus remembered long afternoons in the sun, miming the steps to load, ready, level, and fire until his arm went numb.

He'd been sixteen, younger than most of the boys here in the square, but he thought that he and his classmates had caught on faster. *Though I suppose they've only been at it a few hours. And having half of Vordan City staring at them can't help their concentration.*

Janus was watching the drilling men from beside the coach. Fitz had wandered over to exchange a few words with one of the sergeants, and Marcus had followed him. Now they stood together, but once again Marcus had the feeling of being *apart*, separated from the unit that had been the only family he had for all of his adult life. He cleared his throat.

"Yes, sir?" Fitz said. He hadn't lost his knack of picking up on Marcus' tiniest hints.

"How many new men have you got in total?"

"I don't have the latest counts. They're still trickling in, and the sergeants are culling out those who won't be able to fight. But I'd guess we'll end up with at least six thousand."

Marcus raised his eyebrows. In one sense, that felt like an enormous number—more men than the Colonials had ever had at any one time. *On the other hand, only six thousand came forward, out of how many hundreds of thousands in the city?* He shook his head. *We work with what we have.*

"Have you got six thousand muskets?"

"No, sir," said Fitz. "We brought about two thousand spare up the river with us, mostly captured from the Auxiliary's armory in Ashe-Katarion. Mor has been working to scrounge up whatever he can find here. There's the stocks of the Armsmen and the palace guards at Ohnlei, but unfortunately it looks like this Peddoc already stripped those pretty clean. The colonel pointed us to a few private sources, but Mor doesn't think they'll amount to more than another thousand. Plenty of powder, though, and we've got men working on making cartridges."

"What about the other half of the recruits?"

"We're giving them pikes. I don't know if it'll be worth anything, but . . ." He flicked his eyes at Janus. "I think the colonel has a plan."

"I'm sure he does."

"You see how we've got them doing the Manual of Arms before anything else?"

"Yes." Marcus frowned. "That is odd. When I was at the College, we started with formations and marching."

Fitz nodded. "Colonel's explicit orders. When I asked why, he said that we might be able to teach them to shoot a musket in a few days, but we haven't got a chance of getting them to march straight, so we shouldn't bother to try. I can't say that I disagree, but I still don't follow his reasoning."

"The joys of serving under Janus bet Vhalnich," Marcus said, carefully under his breath.

Saints and martyrs. Pikes and men who can't march. He tried to imagine being on the battlefield with a pike—little more than a long pole with a spiked blade at one end. The boom of guns, the rattle of musketry, smoke and flashes everywhere, men falling in screams and blood. *And you out there with a pointy stick, like it was two hundred years ago.*

And as for marching, any infantry that couldn't reliably form square would be decimated if it was caught in the open by enemy cavalry. At least one cavalry regiment had been quartered at Midvale, he knew, and Orlanko might have been able to scrape together more.

"Hell," he said aloud. "I hope he's got a *good* plan."

"We'll get through it, sir. The Colonials have faced worse odds than this."

Marcus winced. The sentiment was well meant, but the last time they'd faced well-equipped troops, it had been General Khtoba's Auxiliaries. That engagement had cost the lives of hundreds of men, and it had cost Adrecht—Marcus' best friend—his arm, and possibly his sanity as well. *Let's hope we do better this time.*

"Very good, Captain," Janus said, coming over to the two of them. "I want you to take them to live rounds as soon as you feel they're ready. Every man should feel the kick of his weapon before he takes it into battle, and I don't know how much time the duke will give us."

"Understood, sir." Fitz saluted.

"I'm going to look in on things at Ohnlei," Janus went on. "Fitz, I'll need you with me. Marcus, I'd like you to check in with our artillery contingent and see how things are progressing."

"Understood, sir," Marcus said, with a salute of his own. He was relieved to be assigned a definite task. "Where can I find them?"

"Captain Vahkerson is at the University, working with the crews. Captain Solwen is looking for tubes, so he'll be out in the city, but I imagine Captain Vahkerson will know where to find him."

"Yes, sir. Anywhere in particular at the University? It's a big campus, if I recall."

Janus' smile flashed across his face. "You can just follow the noise, I expect."

Boom. It was odd how the sound of a gun going off changed as you got closer to it. At a distance, only the bass thump of it was clear, like thunder growling far away. As you got nearer, the higher tones became audible, until it was a full-throated *bang* that resonated at the back of your teeth and in the pit of your stomach. And when you thought it was so loud you must be nearly on top of it, you found that you were still a couple of hundred yards off. Get closer and it grew louder still, until your ears rang like cymbals in the silence that followed each detonation.

Marcus was able to find the Preacher, not only by walking toward the booms but by following the crowds of curious, nervous University students. They looked very somber in their black scholar's robes. Most of them were young men, but there were a few older students and even a couple of women among them.

The University itself consisted of low, ancient stone buildings, veiled with climbing ivy, tile-roofed and rambling. Additions, extensions, and new construction had gone up over the centuries without any plan, dividing the grounds into a set of irregular courtyards whose grass was maintained to exacting perfection by the famously dictatorial University gardeners. Most of the windows were the old lead-lattice sort, filled with warped, bubbly glass, so as Marcus walked by he got distorted, fish-eyed views of rooms and students within.

At the back of the campus, the University grounds blended imperceptibly into the Old Woods, a tag end of ancient trees that was the last remnant of the primeval forests that had covered the valley of the Vor before the city had been founded. Between the tree line and the manicured lawns was a large field of tall grass, a kind of no-man's-land between natural antiquity and modern perfection. It was here that the Preacher had set up his cannon, aiming it south so that any stray balls would splash into the Vor or hit the uninhabited slopes of Thieves' Island.

Marcus paused at the edge of the grass as the company of young men by the gun, perhaps thirty in all, simultaneously ducked and put their hands over their ears. Only Captain Sevran Vahkerson remained stolidly upright, shading his eyes with one hand to observe the flight of the ball. The cannon bucked and roared, spitting a momentary gout of flame and a huge cloud of powder smoke, and a moment later a puff of dirt downrange marked where the shot had struck. There was a square of red cloth there, Marcus noticed, a dozen yards past the point where the ball impacted.

"Short," the Preacher said, shaking his head sorrowfully. "Far too short. You sprayed a bit of dirt in their faces, but that's all, and now they're going to come over here and gut you with bayonets." He turned to the young men, who were slowly straightening up. "Can anyone tell me what Ranker Quilten did wrong?"

"He must have fucked up the angle—" said one student, in the front of the crowd, only to be pinned to the spot by a furious glare from the Preacher. "Sorry. He must have gotten the angle wrong."

"I had the angle dead-on!" said a powder-blackened young man, presumably Quilten. "And Tart checked it."

"It did look right," another man admitted.

"I think," Quilten said, turning on the Preacher, "that your godda—that your *darn* cannon is broken." He held up a sheet of paper. "My calculations were quite precise! At that arc the ball should have landed precisely on target."

"And," the Preacher said, "in the course of your calculations, did you examine the cannonball?"

"What?" Quilten looked down at where a small pyramid of cannonballs stood beside the gun. "Why?"

"Because *that* ball was at least a quarter inch smaller than the last one."

"That's not fair!" Quilten said. "You can't hand me a dud and expect me to make the shot."

"You think cannonballs are all the same?" the Preacher roared. "You think they get finished by master artisans in some china shop? You think, in the field, you've got the luxury to pick and choose?" He shook his head. "Be grateful to God if you have *enough* balls, let alone good ones. You'll get shot that's too small, too large, misshapen, scored, or worse. You'll capture the enemy's ammunition, and only Karis knows where *he* gets it. You need to be able to feel a ball, and know what to do with it. If it's too small, you'll get more windage, which means you need a bigger charge to get the same force! But give thanks to God if your balls are too *small*"—he ignored a chorus of sniggering—"because if they're too *big*, and you cram them in, this gun will explode in your face!"

At the end of this monologue, he caught sight of Marcus and acknowledged him with a nod. Glaring at the young men, he said, "I want you to go through this stack of shot and tell me which ones are heavy and which are light."

"Can we have a balance?" one of the students said, doubtfully.

"You think you'll have a balance with you in the field?"

"We might be able to rig one up," said another man, "with a rock and some sticks. We could use a known-good ball to calculate the mean error—"

The Preacher sighed and stalked through the long grass toward Marcus, shaking his head. Marcus suppressed a smile.

"Karis preserve me from boys who think they know what they're doing," the Preacher said. "I liked it better working with rankers straight from the farm. At least it was easy to put the proper fear of the Lord into them."

"I assume this was the colonel's idea?" Marcus said.

"Yes. And it's not a bad one, in truth. You can teach anyone to load and fire a gun, but being able to lay a shot properly takes a bit more skill. This lot"—he waved at the young men clustered around the cannonballs, now arguing about how to make their decision in the fewest number of trials—"gives everything strange names and talks a lot of rubbish about parabolas and acceleration, but at least they know what goes up must come down. We might make a couple of decent gun sergeants out of them."

"Will you have enough time?"

"That's the big question, isn't it?" The Preacher shook his head. "If I had even a week, I'd be thankful, but the colonel tells me we might not get that long. We'll manage, I expect, with the Lord's help." He paused. "It's good to see you again, Senior Captain."

"Likewise. I hope you had a pleasant voyage."

"I don't know about pleasant, but we're here, by the grace of God. And none too soon, it seems." The Preacher scratched his nose. "Are you going to be taking over the First, then?"

"No," Marcus said. "Fitz is doing a fine job, I think. I'll be assisting the colonel."

"Too bad. Fitz is a good boy, but a bit too clever for his own good. I'll miss having your hand on the tiller." He shook his head. "God's will be done, of course. And the colonel's."

"I'm supposed to give him a report on the artillery."

"We'll manage something here, if we can find enough metal. I've got men pulling guns out of the water batteries, but those are siege pieces. If we go into the field, it'll be a hard job getting them in place. Val is out rounding up everything he can find."

"I'll check up on him. Do you know where he is now?"

"On the Island, somewhere near the cathedral. Someone said there were old guns out in front of some of the big buildings there. Shouldn't be too hard to track him down."

"Right." Marcus looked at the squabbling students and shook his head. "Anything else I should tell the colonel?"

"Not from here." The Preacher hesitated. "You'd best know, about—"

"Jen? Fitz told me."

"Ah." The Preacher coughed. "Well. I'd better get back to it before someone drops a ball on his toes. God's grace go with you, Senior Captain."

"And you," Marcus said. He turned about and went in search of Val.

The eastern end of the Island felt strangely empty. Marcus crossed over the Saint Uriah Bridge and walked through the Exchange, where the great multistory trading houses with their rooftop cranes and pulleys were all shuttered and silent, the crowd of frantic traders in hiding. Crossing one of the little shop-lined bridges that separated the Exchange from the Island proper, he could see the spires of the cathedral looming up like stone masts amid the surrounding buildings.

The square in front of the cathedral—where the deputies were entertaining

Orlanko's messengers—was nearly empty, with the crowds having moved a few blocks west to watch the recruits drilling in Farus' Triumph. There were carriages and cabs about, though, and a few pedestrians. Marcus, conspicuous in his blue uniform, collared the nearest and asked where there was a Royal Army party looking for cannons.

A few minutes later he'd tracked down Val, who was accompanied by Lieutenant Archer of the artillery, a dozen rankers, and another dozen burly civilians waiting by an empty wagon. They were clustered around a tiny cannon, only a few feet of gleaming bronze with iron-bound wheels, standing on a small plinth outside an impressive-looking building. One of the rankers had one hand on it, looking as proud as a boy with a new puppy, but Val was shaking his head. Marcus caught the tail end of his remarks.

"I know we're looking for cannon, Ranker Servus," he said, "but you have to realize that not everything that *looks* like a cannon is, in fact, a cannon. This, for instance, is a statue."

"But it's got wheels, look! And it looks old!"

"Look at the barrel, Ranker. A cannon needs a *hole* in the barrel. Otherwise where are we going to put the balls?"

Servus looked crestfallen. He rapped the solid muzzle of the little gun with his knuckle, and sighed.

"Right," Val said. "Where next?"

"Fellow I talked to said he thought there were two or three down on the riverfront," one of the rankers said. "He said he used to eat his lunch there, and they were so covered in pigeon shit he didn't realize they were cannon for years."

"I hope you're up for scraping off some pigeon shit, then." Val turned around, and his eyes widened at the sight of his long-absent senior captain. "Balls of the Beast! Is that really you, Marcus?"

"Last I checked." Marcus grinned, and Val grabbed his hand and shook it with unnecessary force, slapping him on the shoulder with his other hand for good measure. He had quite a grip. Captain Valiant Solwen had been one of Marcus' longest-serving companions in Khandar, and probably his best friend after the dead Adrecht Roston. He had the florid face of a serious drinker and a pencil-thin mustache of which he was inordinately proud. "Good to see you, Val."

"And damned good to see you," Val said. "Damned good to see the old city, too. Though truth be told, I was just happy to see solid ground after all those months with nothing to look at but blue. I'm never getting on another ship as long as I live, I swear it by Karis the Savior."

"That bad?"

Val rolled his eyes. One of the rankers sniggered and said, "The captain gets seasick."

"That's enough of that," Val said. "Archer, take them down to the waterfront and see if those are guns or stones under all the guano. I'll catch up after I have a word with the senior captain."

Archer nodded and started barking orders. The wagoneers got on the bed of their vehicle and rumbled off, followed by the soldiers.

"Have you seen the others?" Val said.

"Briefly," Marcus said. "Fitz and the Preacher, anyway."

"Mor's tearing the city apart looking for muskets," Val said. "And Give-Em-Hell has been culling out anyone who says he can ride from the recruits, and trying to turn them into cavalry."

"Small hope there," Marcus said. "It takes more than a few days to make a trooper."

"What about you?" Val said. "The way I hear it, you're the colonel's right-hand man now. Has he got you on some secret errand?"

"Just checking up on the guns. Are you getting anywhere?"

"There's some siege pieces in the water batteries," Val said. "And so far we've pulled maybe a dozen smaller guns from places like this." He gave the little gun sculpture a kick. "A lot of banks have them out front, for some reason. Popular decorations, or at least they were a hundred years ago. Some of the pieces we've got have to date back to the Civil War."

"Are they still serviceable?"

"That's the big question." Val pulled absently at his mustache, first one end and then the other. "Preacher says he's going to scour them, load them up, then set them off with a torch on the end of a long pole. Anything that doesn't explode, we'll keep."

Marcus chuckled and shook his head. The ingenuity of the Preacher and his men when it came to cannons and explosives was notorious; he trusted they'd come up with something.

"Is it true the colonel made you captain of Armsmen?" Val said abruptly. "Before all this started up, I mean."

Marcus nodded. "He landed me right in the thick of it. I don't know if you've heard what happened at the Vendre."

"Only rumors. You were there?"

"I'll tell you the story, when we've got more time."

"Right." Val sighed. "Hell of a thing, to spend three months at sea and then pitch back into it as soon as we get here."

"You think the men are up for it?"

"Oh, they're up for it, just a little ticked off. I feel sorry for whoever gets in their way. Some of them aren't crazy about fighting Vordanai, but after Khandar . . ." He shrugged. "I think every man of them would follow the colonel if he told 'em to march into the river."

"Does that include you?" Marcus said. Of all the Colonial officers, Val was the one who had retained the most connection to home. He was a nobleman of sorts, the younger son of a lesser branch, but those kinds of ties went deep. *He probably has cousins on the other side.*

"I don't know about the colonel," Val said, "but I'd follow *you* if you said we were going to storm the moon. If you say this is the right side to be on, then it is." He coughed to cover this moment of unexpected candor. "Besides, I hear we have the queen with us, so that makes it all right."

"We've got her," Marcus confirmed. "I saw her at breakfast this morning, in fact."

Val blinked. "You're *staying* with the *queen*?"

"Actually, she's staying with me. Or we're both staying with the colonel, I suppose." He didn't mention that he'd helped the queen escape her own chambers and led her personal guard into an ambush. Val might have fainted.

"Now, *there's* something I never thought I'd hear. What's she like?"

"A bit odd. She looks younger than she is. Smart, pretty in an awkward sort of way. I'll introduce you when we get the chance."

"After the battle, please," Val said. "If we're getting ready to fight, the last thing I need to worry about is a royal interview."

He spent a bit longer with Val, catching up on the regimental gossip and relating a few choice tidbits from his time in the city. At first they were able to banter as though nothing had changed, but something uncomfortable gradually crept into the conversation. It took a moment for Marcus to realize what it was. Val had *work* to do, and Marcus was keeping him from it. When Marcus had been in command, whatever he'd had to say to his subordinates was by definition the most important thing in their lives at that moment, at least as far as their duties were concerned. Now he could sense Val's nagging feeling that he ought to be off with Lieutenant Archer looking for cannon. Marcus eventually let him off the hook with a promise that they'd finish their catching up sometime later, and rustle up Mor and Fitz for cards as they had done in the Ashe-Katarion days.

What the hell has Janus done to me? Marcus walked, hands in his pockets, back toward Cathedral Square. If the Colonials were a single living thing—and Marcus often thought of them as one—then Marcus was a tiny piece of that creature excised by a surgeon and carried across the sea. The regiment had survived, and even thrived, but the place where he'd been had scabbed over and turned to scar tissue, and he didn't fit back into it anymore.

It'll be different, once we win. If they *lost,* of course, none of it would matter. At best they'd be fugitives, on the run from Orlanko's secret police. And at worst . . . well, that was always a risk on a battlefield. *But if we win . . . then what?* He couldn't picture it. But the queen would find *something* for him to do, wouldn't she?

It was well into the afternoon by now, and he decided his aching legs weren't up to the long walk back to the Twin Turrets. Instead he hailed a cab, which turned out to be occupied by two other men also headed north across the bridges.

"We're all doubling up these days," the cabbie told him. "Half the boys have hidden their rig and taken their horses to the countryside until all this is over. It's only a few minutes out of your way."

The man was eyeing his uniform, and Marcus probably could have evicted the other passengers with a word of command and a pointed look. But he was in no hurry, so he climbed in and took his seat beside two young men wearing the restrained but expensive clothing of professionals or successful merchants. The door closed, and the horses started *clip-clopping* up the cobbled street.

"It's true," one of the men said to the other, taking no notice of Marcus. "One of my kitchen boys has a cousin who's a carter, and he's been making the run up to Ohnlei. He said he saw them in the field, muskets and trousers, bold as brass."

The other man snorted. "Whores drumming up business. Girls acting like men does it for some people, I suppose. I can see the appeal. It's cute, like putting a little coat and hat on your dog and pretending he's a gentleman."

"This carter talked to some of the new soldiers," the first said. "They said one of the men asked for a price, and got a kick in the fork for his troubles."

The other laughed. "Probably tried to lay a hand on the merchandise without paying cash up front. I met this girl in a Southside tavern once, and she would slit you as soon as look at you until you crossed her palm with gold. After that, well, it was a different story . . ."

Marcus pressed his head against the window and tried not to listen. He was certainly no stranger to prostitutes—no soldier was—and he'd had his share in Ashe-Katarion, before the Redemption. There were always girls willing to fawn over the Vordanai soldiers in those days, for the status and protection from the prince's law, but Marcus had preferred the honesty of a straightforward commercial transaction. Then there had been Jen, and after she'd betrayed him . . .

And now she's dead. He still wasn't sure how to feel about that. There had always been the wild hope, in the back of his mind, that she'd wake up and beg forgiveness. Janus said whatever Ihernglass had done had stripped her of the demon she'd borne for the Church, so she'd be no further use to them. *She could have stayed with me, and—what? Marriage?* His mind balked at the idea.

It doesn't matter now. He swallowed a lump in his throat and shook his head. *Fantasies never helped anybody.*

After letting the two young men off at a fashionable town house south of Bridge Street, the cab rumbled around to the Twin Turrets. The sun was still up, but already the house was ablaze with light, torches burning beside the doors and candles showing in the windows. Marcus paid the fare, exchanged salutes with the Mierantai guards, and went inside.

Janus was in his study, still going over the maps of the ground between Vordan City and Midvale with a pencil and dividers. The usual stack of folded papers, weighed down with books, inkwells, and whatever else was handy, stood at his elbow. The colonel always insisted on thorough reports from his subordinates.

Marcus saluted again, then relaxed at Janus' vague wave. He closed the door behind him.

"Good afternoon, Captain," the colonel said. "What news from our officers of artillery?"

"They're making progress, sir." Marcus related what he'd seen at the University, and what Val had told him.

"It's something, anyway." Janus sighed. "If I were truly the all-seeing genius they call me in the streets, I would have had a cache of cannon secreted somewhere in the city in preparation for this moment. Take note, Captain. Preparation has its place, but there is no substitute for improvisation. And a great deal of hard work."

"Yes, sir." Marcus hesitated. "You were up at Ohnlei today?"

"Briefly," Janus said. "Captain Warus and I decided to keep the headquarters here. If the duke moves quickly enough, it's possible Ohnlei might come within his reach, and it's poorly suited for defense. We'd have to abandon it."

"I see."

Janus looked up, big gray eyes skewering Marcus. "Why do you ask?"

"I . . ." Marcus paused, his face reddening a little, but there was no turning back now. It was hard to hide anything from Janus. "I heard something on my way back. Just a rumor, I'm sure. They said a gang of women had taken up residence there, and were . . . practicing their trade. I wondered if you knew about it."

Marcus wouldn't have put it past Janus to hire a bunch of prostitutes for the use of his newly recruited soldiers, now that he came to think about it. For all that he was a nobleman, he lacked delicacy in such matters, though as far as Marcus knew he himself never indulged. He wondered if Janus had a woman, back in Mieran County. *Hell, or a wife. I've never asked, and he never talks about himself.*

"Ah." Janus laid his pencil down and straightened up. "I suppose word was bound to get out."

Now I've put my foot in it. Marcus' cheeks were flushed under his beard. "If this is something you've arranged, I don't mean to imply—"

"It is indeed something I arranged, Captain, but it's not what you think. This morning I had a visit from a group of young women who wished to volunteer as soldiers."

Marcus barked a laugh, automatically. Then, as he put this together with what he'd heard in the carriage, his forehead furrowed.

"You sent them on their way, sir, I should think," he said.

"On the contrary, I told them their services would be welcome. Their spokesman was the notorious 'Mad Jane,' with whom I think you may be familiar."

"You told them . . ." Marcus shook his head. "I don't understand. What are you hoping to accomplish?"

"I am *hoping* to defend this city and my queen against the Last Duke," Janus said, a touch of harshness entering his voice. "I will accept the assistance of anyone who wishes to offer it."

"So you sent them to be—what? Nurses? Washerwomen?" Marcus' frown deepened. "I don't like it, sir. A few girls, out among so many young men. People are going to make assumptions."

"You don't seem to understand, Captain. I sent them to be *soldiers*. As for their safety among so many men, I think Miss Verity and her companions have adequately demonstrated their ability to care for themselves, don't you?"

"You sent them to be soldiers," Marcus deadpanned. "A bunch of girls."

"Yes."

"To carry muskets."

"Yes."

"And to march—"

"Yes. Captain, what is it about this concept that you find so difficult to understand?"

"But that's ridiculous, sir! You can't—I mean, they would—"

Janus said nothing, eyes hooded. Marcus took a deep breath.

"If they're dead set on it, maybe we could use them for recruiting," he said. "But you can't seriously think of sending them into the fighting."

"Why not?"

"Because they might get killed!"

"And I suppose you think all the *boys* we've recruited have steel skins?"

"But—"

"Forgive me if I sound callous, Captain, but from my experience I am reasonably certain that a woman can stop a musket ball as well as any man. If she can load and fire her own weapon as well, I see no reason to stop her."

"The other recruits will never stand for it. *Nobody* will stand for it."

"You'd be surprised," the colonel said. "'Mad Jane' is quite popular, and many of our new soldiers come from the Docks. And if anyone does object, they'll have their officers to answer to."

"But . . ." Marcus turned even redder. "I don't think you've thought this through, sir. What if they're captured by the enemy?"

"Then I suspect they will be raped," Janus said, pronouncing the ugly word with a deliberate bluntness. "A fact of which they are certainly well aware. These are not noble girls from the Fairy Castles, Captain. It's a threat they've lived with all their lives."

"But how can we send them out if we *know* that might happen to them?"

"We fought the Redeemers, who liked to burn their prisoners alive and, some said, to eat them. There was also the option of impalement, which I understand involves a wooden spear inserted via the anus and positioned in such a way as to leave the victim alive for days while he's mounted on the city wall. The Desoltai tortured, gelded, and murdered our scouts and left them for us to find. Against any of these enemies, did you hesitate to order your men forward because you were worried about what might happen to them?"

"But these aren't *men*. They're—"

"Captain d'Ivoire," Janus growled. Marcus had only heard the colonel raise his voice in anger once, in a temple on Ashe-Katarion's sacred hill. This was only a shadow of that violent outburst, but it carried an echo that made Marcus' skin crawl. "You seem to be laboring under a misapprehension, and perhaps I am to blame. Our victories in Khandar have made many in the Colonials overconfident, and their estimation of my own abilities has risen to frankly unjustified heights.

"I know my worth, Captain, but I have no magic trick to pull out of my bag here. Orlanko has more trained men than we do, and they are well equipped. He has more guns, and he has a regiment of cuirassiers to our few hundred light horses. All I have to set in our side of the balance pan is the assistance of the people of Vordan City, to whatever extent they are willing to offer it. If we lose, you and I, not to mention the other officers of the Colonials, will almost certainly lose our heads, and our queen will become a slave in all but name. Under the circumstances, please believe I mean what I say when I tell you I will take *any* help I can get. I am not going to turn away two hundred highly motivated volunteers because *you* have scruples about their gender. Is that understood?"

"Yes, sir." Marcus drew himself up and saluted. "I understand, *sir*."

"Good." Janus' expression calmed, as though the brief burst of anger had never been. A moment later, he flashed a smile. "If you have any further objections, I suggest you take them up with Her Majesty. I have no doubt she would be happy to listen."

WINTER

Putting on her uniform, straight from Janus' laundry, felt more comfortable than Winter could have imagined. Her specially tailored undershirt, tight across the chest in the right places, tucked into blue trousers with razor-sharp creases.

A proper lieutenant's jacket, with a double row of gleaming buttons and the white stripes sewn on the shoulders. And the brimmed cap, which sat differently than she was used to. Winter puzzled at this until she realized she hadn't had her hair trimmed in weeks, and her usual close-to-the-skull cut was getting distinctly shaggy.

It was all as familiar and comfortable as an old glove, but during the walk across the palace grounds she found herself tugging nervously at the seams and sleeves. The problem was Jane's unaccustomed gaze. In Khandar she'd managed to forget that her disguise *was* a disguise, but with Jane watching she couldn't put it out of her mind.

Finally, out of earshot of the outer ring of sentries, she muttered, "You don't have to *stare* at me like I was a dancing bear."

"Sorry," Jane said, with a smile that was anything but. "I'm still getting used to this. Do you know you even walk differently?"

"This is going to be awkward enough," Winter said, "without you making me nervous."

"All right, all right. But promise me something?"

"What?"

Jane's grin turned wicked. "Wear that outfit to bed sometime? I can't look at it without thinking about how I'd peel it off you."

Winter rolled her eyes but couldn't help a little blush. *So now I have* that *image to keep me company.* She started off again, and Jane fell in behind her. Winter could almost feel her leering gaze. Jane could out-ogle any tavern full of sailors Winter had ever encountered, when she put her mind to it.

The First Colonial camp was laid out directly in front of the palace itself, split by the broad main drive and occupying the grass lawns that spread out from the cul-de-sac with its fountain and statue of Farus IV. Farther down the drive was the space they were using as a drill field, and the new recruits, lacking tents, were bedding down in the offices and hallways of the various ministries. The notorious Cobweb had been mostly gutted by fire, started by Orlanko's minions as they'd fled. The drill sergeants had been using targets chalked on its facade for target practice, so the once-smooth columns and frontage were now scored and pitted as well as black with smoke.

All the drills thus far had been with weapons, without even a token effort to teach march discipline or camp skills. Jane's girls, given a hallway of hastily abandoned offices in the Ministry of War, had organized a cooking schedule and set watches on the doors with the thoroughness of long practice, but the rest of the recruits were not nearly so organized. Fires burned at random among the once-perfect grounds, and carefully trimmed trees and shrubs were hacked to bits for wood. Rough-looking men filled their buckets from the ornamental fountains, and the specially bred black-and-white carp in the Ministry of State's reflecting pool were quickly captured and eaten.

The First Colonial camp was far more organized, with the familiar torchlit avenues between rows of faded blue canvas tents. One ring of sentries surrounded the camp, and patrols with lanterns walked around the palace, protecting it from looters. There weren't enough men to guard the entire vast estate, but Janus had asked that the royal residence, at least, be spared wanton destruction.

Once they were among the tents, Winter was at least spared Jane's continued attention. The familiar scene of an army camp was entirely new to her, and she looked around eagerly at the tents, the stacked arms, and the big kettles where the men were cooking dinner. Her stares were returned from every quarter, and as they passed, men poked one another and whispered. Rumors had obviously started to spread about the girl soldiers. For a moment, Winter felt the familiar urge to shrink in on herself, but a glance back at Jane steadied her. She straightened up and walked a little faster.

When they found First Battalion, Seventh Company, the first few men they passed looked up and froze, unable to believe their eyes. Before she'd taken a dozen steps, though, Winter found herself at the center of an instant crowd, drawing soldiers out of their tents with almost magnetic force into a narrow circle around her and Jane. They were all shouting at once, greetings, questions, gossip, and Winter had to hold up her hands for silence. She could hear Jane laughing.

"It's good to see you all," she said, when they'd calmed down a little. "No, I'm not back for good. Not yet. The colonel said he would see what he could do. For now, can you tell me where I can find the corporals?"

A young man with a peach-fuzz beard and a pip on his shoulder was pushed forward. Winter recognized him vaguely but couldn't recall his name. He saluted, nervously, and said, "I'm Corporal Morraz, sir. But I think you mean Sergeants Forester and Folsom. They're with the lieutenant. Follow me, sir."

The corporal pushed his way through the crowd, and the men made way as Winter and Jane followed. He led them to a tent, marked out from the others only by the light of a candle burning inside.

"Shall I introduce you, sir?" the corporal said. Then, glancing at Jane, he added, "Miss?"

"I can manage, Corporal," Winter said. "Thanks."

Morraz saluted and scurried off. Jane looked at the tent, whose highest point was barely above her nose, and gave a low whistle.

"You *lived* in one of these?" she said, quietly.

"For two years," Winter said. "You get used to it. Eventually all you care about is having a dry spot to sleep."

"And I thought we had it hard in the swamp."

Winter knocked at the tent pole. An unfamiliar man's voice said, "Yes?"

"Um," Winter said, disconcerted. "It's Lieutenant Ihernglass."

"Ah yes. I thought it might be, from the commotion. Come in!"

Winter pulled up the flap and went inside. Jane followed, walking stooped. A folding table was strewn with papers and ledgers, the sight of which gave Winter an instant, instinctive feeling of guilt. Two people sat on opposite sides of it, pens in hand.

The man facing Winter was in his shirtsleeves, but Winter guessed he was the lieutenant. He was blond and blue-eyed, giving his face a vaguely Murnskai cast, and he had a jawline you could have cracked rocks on. Winter guessed he was a few years older than she was, in his mid-twenties.

His companion was Rebecca Forester, also called Robert Forester, known in both guises as Bobby. *Senior Sergeant* Bobby Forester, Winter saw, from the three pips on the shoulders of her jacket. Fitz had evidently done more than move a few lieutenants around in terms of getting the units sorted out. She looked somehow older than when Winter had last seen her, more adult. Winter still couldn't see her soft, round face as a boy's no matter how hard she tried, though it had fooled her well enough when they first met. As soon as Winter entered, Bobby popped to her feet. Before she could rush to embrace Winter, however, Jane came in, and Bobby stopped uncertainly in her tracks. The lieutenant raised an eyebrow.

Winter stepped forward into the uncomfortable silence, head slightly bent, and offered her hand across the table. "Lieutenant Winter Ihernglass."

"Lieutenant John Marsh," the man said, returning a firm handshake. "I think you know Sergeant Forester?"

"You might say that." Winter shot Bobby a conspiratorial grin. "This is Jane Verity. I don't know if you've heard that I've been placed in charge of one of the new companies—"

"I think everyone in the camp has heard by now," Marsh said.

I was afraid of that. "Jane is my second in command."

"I see." Marsh glanced, for some reason, at Bobby, who gave a tiny shrug. "Well. Welcome, Lieutenant, Miss Verity. How can I help you?"

"I just wanted to have a few words with my corporals. My former corporals," Winter corrected. "If it's all right with you."

Marsh, again, looked at Bobby. Winter thought she saw the girl nod very slightly.

"Of course," he said. "I expect you have a lot of catching up to do!" He got to his feet, slapping dust and drying sand off his thighs. "Shall I fetch Junior Sergeant Folsom?"

"I'll get him later," Bobby said, and smiled at Winter. "Graff isn't here, though. Fitz made him a lieutenant for the Third Company."

"I'll have to congratulate him," Winter said.

She and Jane stepped aside, letting Marsh slip past them with a polite nod. He ducked through the tent flap and let it fall behind him. Bobby gestured for the two of them to sit, and gathered up the paperwork to pile it out of the way. Winter settled herself onto the cushion in front of the old, familiar low table, with Jane at her side.

There was a long pause. Bobby looked from Winter to Jane and back again, not sure what to think, and Winter couldn't figure out how to begin the conversation. It was Jane who finally broke the silence with a laugh.

"Look at the two of you." She shook her head, trying to fight her grin and failing. "I'm sorry, but it's funny. You're so tangled up in your secrets you can barely move!"

"I . . ." Bobby hesitated. "I don't know what you—"

"This is *Jane*," Winter said. "From Mrs. Wilmore's. I found her."

Bobby's mouth opened, silently, and her eyes went wide.

"*I* didn't go anywhere. You were the one who disappeared," Jane said. "What kinds of stories have you been telling about me?"

"Winter told me the truth about herself," Bobby said, "and about how the two of you were friends before she ran away."

"Friends." Jane shot Winter a tiny smirk.

"And Bobby's story is . . . complicated," Winter said. "I found out—"

"That she's a girl?" Jane said. She shrugged at Bobby's shocked look. "She didn't tell *me* anything, but it's not exactly a stretch to figure it out once you start thinking in those terms. Just look at you!"

"Nobody else has guessed," Bobby said, defensively.

"I doubt anyone else is looking," Jane said. "Now. We've established that everybody knows everybody else's secrets. Can we all relax?"

Not all *our secrets,* Winter thought. There was no way for Jane to know about the *naath* Feor had gifted to Bobby, or the patches of her skin it had replaced with living marble. *No need to break that to her yet—*

"Actually," Bobby said, "I have one more."

"Bobby," Winter cut in. "Are you sure you want to—"

"I can't keep secrets from you," Bobby said. "It feels wrong, after everything. And you may need to know."

Winter paused. "From me?"

Bobby nodded. "It's Lieutenant Marsh. He knows . . . about me."

"*What*? How did he find out? Has he told anyone?"

"It's not like that," Bobby said. "He's a good person, honestly. He and I . . . I mean, we're . . ."

"You're what?"

Jane rolled her eyes and put one arm around Winter's shoulders, pulling her close enough to speak into her ear.

"They're fucking," she stage-whispered, turning Bobby's face instantly beet-red. "You know. Like men and women do, at times?"

Winter blinked. *Oh.* Several conflicting emotions assailed her at once. Fear, for Bobby and for herself, the old terror of being discovered. Irritation that Bobby had exposed them like this. And, she realized, just a hint of jealousy.

She bit her lip and shook her head. *Don't be ridiculous.* She had Jane now, and that was all she'd ever wanted. *Besides, if she and Marsh are . . . I mean, she's not . . . like me.*

"He's not blackmailing you, or anything like that?" Jane said while Winter fought through her confusion.

"No, no." Bobby's blush deepened. "I told him myself. It was a stupid thing to do, but we were in a storm at sea, and there was something . . ."

"It's all right," Winter said. "I don't need the details."

"Speak for yourself," Jane said.

"The point is, you think you can trust him?" Winter badly wanted to ask about the *naath* and the traces it had left on Bobby's skin—*which Marsh must have seen, obviously*—but didn't want to bring it up in Jane's presence unless Bobby mentioned it first. She felt a burst of frustration. *Jane's right. We do have too many damned secrets.*

"I'm sure I can. And I haven't told him anything about you."

"All right." Winter shook her head. "See if you can clue him in to the fact that I know. That might make things a bit less awkward."

"Right." Bobby gave a little sigh of relief. "God, I've been so worried what you would say."

"It's hardly my place to disapprove," Winter said.

Jane laughed again. "I can't tell if you're the father or the mother in this little allegory. Maybe both."

Winter managed a chuckle, and a little bit of the tension seeped out of the tent. She settled herself more comfortably on the cushion. "Bobby was at Mrs. Wilmore's, too, you know. I think she ran away just before you came back."

"You went back?" Bobby said. "I wouldn't have thought *anyone* would go back there on purpose."

"It took me a while to nerve myself up to it," Jane admitted.

"She marched the girls out of there!" Winter said. "Right under the old hag's nose, too."

Jane looked embarrassed. "Something like that."

"Wow." Bobby gave Jane an admiring stare. "How did you manage that?"

"It's not actually all that much of a story," Jane said. "The really interesting parts happened afterward."

Winter sat back while Jane told the story of what had happened to her exodus after leaving the Prison—their time in the swamps, and then with the Leatherbacks. By the time she got to a considerably exaggerated version of Winter's storming of the Vendre, Bobby was clapping her hands in delight. Winter retaliated with stories of the fighting in Khandar, which Bobby embellished with lurid details. Before Winter knew it, the sky had darkened entirely and the torches outside were faint glows through the tent walls.

The only awkward moment came when Bobby was filling in what had happened after they left Ashe-Katarion. She and Folsom had been promoted to sergeant as Fitz worked to fill out the ranks of the junior officers, while Graff, because of his long experience and against his fervent objections, had been made a lieutenant. Of their little circle, that left only Feor, and here Bobby hesitated.

"She was on the ship with us," she said. "I even saw her, once or twice. But I think Fitz kept her under guard. There were a couple of cabins none of us were ever allowed to visit, with sentries on every watch, and she slept in one of those. I didn't see her again after we transferred to the riverboats." Catching Winter's expression, she tried to be reassuring. "I'm sure she's here, though. You can ask Fitz when you see him."

Winter nodded. She had a pretty good idea of where Feor was, and what had been in that guarded cabin. Janus would not have left the steel plates bearing his precious Thousand Names in Khandar without the Colonials to guard them. Feor was certainly here, but whether the colonel would ever let her out again was uncertain. *He has to let me* in, *at least. He owes me that much.*

Eventually Folsom arrived, huge and taciturn as always, and Winter made another round of introductions. The big sergeant was happy to see Winter, but curiously shy in the presence of Jane, and the fact that he wasn't privy to the secret made the conversation a bit more circumspect. Shortly thereafter, Winter and Jane excused themselves, and Bobby promised to send Graff over to visit when she tracked him down.

More shouted greetings followed them away from the row of tents, and Winter turned to wave over her shoulder to the rankers. She and Jane walked together in silence for a while, through the rest of the Colonial encampment and out past the line of sentries, on to the darkened lawn that separated the palace from the Ministry of War.

"They all love you," Jane said, after a while.

Winter winced. "It took me a while to get used to it. It's not even about anything I've *done*. Just that we went into battle together, and they survived. I'm like a . . . a lucky charm."

"You don't sound happy about it."

"Not everyone survived." Winter bit her lip. "They tend to forget about that. I can't blame them, but . . ."

Jane snaked her arm through Winter's and crooked it at the elbow. Winter went stiff.

"Don't," she said. "Someone might see."

"It's dark," Jane said. "Besides, you think you're the only lieutenant who keeps a girl?" She laughed. "We know Marsh does."

"Marsh." Winter sighed but left their arms linked. "I don't know what Bobby was thinking."

"She was thinking that he was handsome, and she was lonely. How old is she—sixteen? Seventeen?"

"Seventeen, probably."

"You must remember what it was like to be seventeen and have your head turned by a pretty face." Jane's fingers found her hand and squeezed it. "I know I do."

"Is he handsome, then?" Winter said, glad the darkness hid her flushed face. "I've never been able to tell."

"Sure. At least, *I* thought so, and Bobby seems to agree. But there's no accounting for taste."

"I suppose he does look a bit like those old paintings of Mithradacii gods, with that hair. Do you remember those old storybooks we found in the Prison library? They were always turning into boars or swans to get women to fall in love with them."

"I never quite understood how *that* worked," Jane said. "But I recall you being very interested in the woodcuts of nymphs and dryads without any clothes on."

Winter rolled her eyes and gave Jane's arm a tug. "Come on. We had better make sure your girls haven't killed anybody."

Chapter Twenty-Three

RAESINIA

"My queen," said Count Vertue, bowing low. "I beg you. We have one last opportunity to avert this bloodshed. Let us act, before it is too late."

Raesinia stood on a hillock beside the north road from Ohnlei. It was another beautiful August day, though a breath of cooler air carried the hint that summer would not last forever. Count Vertue, dressed in a "simple" riding outfit embroidered with silver and gold thread, stood beside his mount with two blue-uniformed soldiers at his side. Raesinia stood alone, but there was a squad of Colonials waiting at a discreet distance, in case Orlanko's emissary tried something desperate.

"I agree," Raesinia said. "Let me extend you one final offer. Tell your master that if he orders his troops to return to their camps, his noble followers to disperse, and offers himself into our care, I personally guarantee that he will receive no punishment, and will be free to live out his days in the duchy. You may assure your fellows that none of them will be punished, either. Only members of the Ministry of Information who directly participated in the plot against the Crown will be brought to trial."

"It grieves me to hear you say that, Your Majesty. I have no 'master,' as you put it, only a good friend in His Grace the duke, around whom all the right-thinking gentry of the kingdom have come together. He does everything in Your Majesty's interests, whatever these traitors may have told you." Vertue glanced scornfully at the Colonials. "If you would only appeal to them yourself, I feel sure they would throw off the orders of Vhalnich and the so-called deputies and return you to your proper place. How can you ally yourself with a pack of rabble-rousers and treasonous thinkers who have disgraced the sacred halls of the cathedral and Ohnlei both?"

"I am the queen, Count Vertue. It is for me to say who is a traitor, and who is not, and I tell you the traitors are in your own camp."

"If you will not think of the nation," the count said, "at least consider the men who will die to no purpose if you throw this mass of beggars and frontier soldiers against the pride of the Royal Army. You must know they cannot stand the test of battle."

"Whatever deaths there have been"—Raesinia gritted her teeth—"and whatever deaths are still to come, all of them fall on Orlanko's conscience, not mine. Not that I imagine it bothers him. His hands are well stained already."

"I see that you have been led completely astray." Vertue sighed. "So it must be. God sends us these trials to prove we are worthy of His continued grace. When the slaughter begins, remember that you hold it in your power to end it at any time." His eyes narrowed. "And when you do choose to surrender, seek me out. I will make certain you and your companions are well treated."

"Allow me to extend you the same courtesy, my lord," Raesinia said.

Vertue snorted and turned to his horse. His guards mounted up as well, and the trio wheeled about and rode away, down the slope of the hill and north along the road. The cavalry pickets parted, reluctantly, to let them through.

Somewhere up that road—not far up it, if the latest reports they'd received were correct—was Orlanko's army. Not a large army, by historical standards. Not even larger than Raesinia's, if every last pike-wielding teenager was counted. But of course the point was that the pikes and the teenagers didn't count for much, in the eyes of men like Vertue. *Rabble, he says.* They certainly met the description. Janus had done wonders to gather and arm so many in a week, but it was still only a week, which didn't allow for much in the way of training.

Another horse climbed the slope. Janus bet Vhalnich himself dismounted and stood beside his queen, looking south down the road instead of north after the retreating emissaries. He was head-and-shoulders taller than her, but that was something Raesinia was used to ignoring.

"They've gone," she said. "Vertue and his minders." Janus had been certain that the "soldiers" had been Concordat spies in Royal Army uniforms.

"I saw," Janus said, without looking back at her.

"Was it really wise to let them leave? They'll tell Orlanko we've marched."

"We can't expect to keep that information from him. Frankly, I expect he has a complete picture of our forces by now. The city is too big and too open to keep anything secret for long, and we don't have enough men to post a screen and intercept his couriers. Surprise is not where our advantage lies."

"Where *does* our advantage lie?"

"Numbers and will," Janus said. "And the faith that comes with fighting on the right side."

"And superior generalship?"

"Under ordinary circumstances, modesty would require me to deny that. But since the opposition is commanded by either Duke Orlanko or Count Torahn, 'superior' is a low bar."

"I thought you respected Orlanko," Raesinia said.

"In certain arenas. He has a genius for analyzing information and organizational structures, and a crude but instinctive feel for human nature. None of that translates into battlefield competence, however, and his chief defect is his overconfidence. He does not know enough to leave things in the hands of more capable men." Janus shrugged. "On the other hand, he has a great many cannon. That can make up for quite a few character flaws."

"You don't think we can win?"

Janus was looking at the road again. "If I didn't think there was a chance, I would never have given the order to march. But as to how *much* of a chance . . . we shall see." He smiled briefly. "Here they come."

A rising cloud of dust had been visible around the curve of the road for some time, but now Raesinia could see the first blue-coated ranks coming into view. The First Battalion of the Colonials had the lead, behind the wide-flung cavalry screen, marching in a long, thin column to the cheerful accompaniment of drums, flutes, and fifes. Janus had ransacked the city's theaters for any man who could play and walk at the same time to provide bands for the troops. Whether anyone could hear *anything* among the clatter of boots on the dusty road and the creaks of the wagons, Raesinia was uncertain, but she hadn't argued.

After the First Battalion came the Second, its head marked by its pair of battle flags. Alongside the steady river of blue-coated troops were the wagons, a motley collection of farmers' wains, two-wheeled carts, and even converted cabs and carriages. At intervals among the slow-plodding vehicles were batteries of artillery, hitched to their limbers, muzzles pointing backward and down toward the dusty ground.

Behind the Second Battalion was the endless river of new recruits, still in their civilian clothes. For the most part they were a drab mass of gray and brown, but here and there a nobleman who'd thrown in his lot with the deputies stood out as a splash of color. Blue specks at regular intervals were the sergeants borrowed from the Colonials to try to impose order. Each man had *some* kind of weapon, but for every musket there was a long-handled spear or pike, fashioned in haste or dragged out of Grandfather's closet.

It did Raesinia good to see them marching. She'd spent the week at the Twin Turrets, and while Janus had brought her regular reports, she hadn't been up to Ohnlei to see it with her own eyes. It was too dangerous, the colonel had argued; among so many men, Orlanko had no doubt inserted a few of his own agents. She'd had an odd fantasy that all the volunteer soldiers were a myth, that Janus was only humoring her, and that when the day finally came to face the duke, she'd find herself alone.

Militarily, though, she had to admit they did not inspire confidence. The only hint that they were soldiers instead of a mob was that every man sported a black armband, a nod to the so-called rules of war that prescribed reasonable treatment for "uniformed troops." It couldn't hurt, though Raesinia had her doubts that any rules would constrain Orlanko if he won. They'd chosen black to respect the passing of her father, or to show their allegiance to the deputies, or—she thought this the most likely—because, with Ohnlei still decked out in mourning, black cloth had been readily available in unlimited quantities.

The column marched slowly, and an hour later they were still coming. Raesinia had moved to the edge of the hill, where they could see her easily, and she waved her hand at the recruits as they came by. For the most part they didn't recognize her, but whenever someone did, they raised a cheer. *I should be closer,* she thought. *If they're going to die for me, they should at least know what I look like.*

The sound of a horse approaching at speed brought her attention back to the hilltop, where Janus was conferring quietly with the Colonial officers. The rider, a cavalry trooper in weather-beaten blues, trotted up the slope, reined his mount around, and saluted. Raesinia drifted over.

"Sir!" the trooper said. "Give-Em-H—" He noticed the queen standing nearby, paused, and went on. "Captain Stokes sends to say that he has located the enemy. We've sighted their main body, and engaged their outriders."

He dug in his saddlebag and produced a folded note. Janus took it, read it gravely, and nodded.

"As expected. It's the logical place, from his point of view." He turned to the captains standing nearby. The only one Raesinia recognized was Marcus, in Royal Army blue now instead of Armsmen green. She couldn't catch his eye.

"You may proceed as we've discussed, gentleman," the colonel said. "Good luck!"

They saluted and headed for their own horses.

Janus turned to Raesinia. "Your Majesty. You know what I advise."

"I'm not going back, if that's what you mean." Raesinia set her jaw. "I started all this, and now I feel so helpless. The least I can do is watch." She lowered her voice. "Besides. You know the danger is . . . not entirely relevant."

"I am, of course, Your Majesty's humble servant. Lieutenant Uhlan and his men will accompany you." Janus matched her whisper. "If we lose, Your Majesty—"

"Don't."

"If we lose," the colonel continued remorselessly, "I have given Lieutenant Uhlan orders to place his entire complement at your disposal. I trust them implicitly. While I don't anticipate being in a position to offer further advice, I might suggest that you allow him to conduct you to Mieran County. It is a remote place, and you would find it easy to disappear, even from the likes of Orlanko." He smiled, briefly. "Of course, that is only a contingency plan."

WINTER

The march was a mild one, as marches went. The day was warm, but there was a breeze to cut the heat, and the fertile green countryside they passed through was a pleasant change from the endless rocks and sand of Khandar. Jane's girls carried no packs—there weren't enough tents and bedrolls for all the new men, and the wagons carried their food and extra ammunition. It would make for miserable camping, but for the moment it meant not having to lug anything heavier than their muskets.

Jane walked at the head of the column, and Winter near the back, encouraging any of the girls who flagged and making sure none of the men around them did more than stare. There had been plenty of *that* during their training at Ohnlei, and a fair bit of name-calling and whistles as well, but Winter had been impressed at the girls' stoicism. Here on the road, things had gone surprisingly well. By accident or design—with Janus in charge, Winter suspected the latter—the groups directly ahead and behind were mostly made up of dockmen, who had a healthy respect for Mad Jane and the Leatherbacks.

Another worry had been resolved the day before, when Abby had turned up at the training ground. She'd been reluctant to talk about her errand, other than to say that her father was all right.

"He's a rotten old coward," she said, and refused to say any more on the matter. Now she was walking up and down the column, exchanging a few words with the girls, smiling and keeping up a brave front. It was needed, Winter thought. The faces she saw around her were the faces of young women wondering what the hell they had gotten themselves into. They whispered together, walking side by side for a few steps and then throwing an anxious glance up at Jane or back at Winter. No one dropped out of line, though.

Abby fell back until she was next to Winter, looking worried.

"Word from the head of the column," she said. Rumors traveled down the length of the marching army like sparks along a powder trail. "We're turning off the road. Give-Em-Hell is taking the rest of the horsemen out front." The recruits, imitating their veteran comrades, had adopted the nickname for the cavalry commander.

"Then Orlanko's just ahead," Winter said. She glanced overhead, where the sun hung near its zenith. "We'll fight today. Maybe tomorrow, but probably today. Orlanko can't afford to wait around, and our supply situation can't be good."

"Right. Today." Abby swallowed hard. Her hand was tight around the butt of her musket, the barrel resting on her shoulder. "You think we can win?"

"It's not our job to think about that," Winter said. "We signed up for this army, and that means we agreed to fight where and when Colonel Vhalnich and the other officers think we ought to. *Whether* we should fight is their decision, and we have to trust them. Letting every ranker think about that for himself is the first step toward a rout."

"Right," Abby repeated. "Right." She looked at the backs of the marching girls. "Do you think they'll do all right?"

Winter nodded. "I think so. As well as any of the rest."

"Right." Abby took a deep breath and blew it out slowly. "All right."

Winter wondered if her nerves had shown so clearly the first time she'd gone into a real fight. *Probably they did, and I was too scared to notice.*

Up ahead, the road turned to the left, but a blue-coated lieutenant was directing the column off to the right. They broke through a thin belt of trees and tramped across a field of cabbages, cutting a muddy brown trail through the rows of ripening green vegetables. A low wall of unmortared stone had blocked the way here, but the leading battalion had dismantled it and left an opening wide enough for the wagons and guns to pass. Beyond, a low hill sloped up toward a grassy crest, where a few milk cows grazed peacefully and watched the marching intruders with incurious eyes.

On the near slope of the hill, the army of Janus bet Vhalnich was forming up. The First and Second Battalions of the Colonials were already there, assembling around their twin flags into a battle column. Sergeants screamed orders at the recruits as they came up, directing the pike-armed men into a great mass milling behind the two Colonial formations, while those with muskets were sent farther up, just below the crest of the hill. The wagons remained down at the base, while the guns were wheeled farther on, over the top of the hill and out of sight.

Winter saw Jane paused up ahead, talking to Marcus. She hurried forward, Abby at her side.

"Ihernglass," Marcus said. "I wanted to . . ." He looked at the young, female faces, gathered in a semicircle and staring at him, and rubbed at his beard distractedly. "Come here, would you?"

Winter stepped forward, and Marcus turned his back on the rest and spoke to her quietly.

"Look. The colonel has put you right in the center of the line. It's the safest place, in some ways, but the fire is going to be hot. I don't want . . . if you want me to reassign your company to the reserve, I will. They've made their point. Nobody would think less of them."

"They're not here to make a point, sir."

"You can't be any happier with a bunch of *girls* getting shot than I am," Marcus hissed. "We ought to do the honorable thing."

Winter couldn't help smiling. What was it Janus had once told her? *Captain d'Ivoire missed his calling as a knight-errant.* "They wouldn't agree with you, sir. As I think you know, or else you'd be willing to say it to their faces."

"All right." Marcus looked over his shoulder and shook his head. "All right. You remember the plan."

"Yessir."

He pointed up the hill, to a spot directly in front of the two formed battalions. "Up there. Take about a hundred yards of line and wait for the signal."

Winter saluted. "Yes, *sir*!"

After Marcus had walked off, shaking his head, Jane tapped Winter on the shoulder.

"What did he want?"

"To offer us a last chance to back out," Winter said.

Jane laughed. "You think he would have learned better than that at the Vendre."

The guns began to roar as the army finished its deployment.

It was a simple enough formation. Up ahead of where she was standing, on the descending slope of the hill, the artillery had set up in a long line. The Preacher's field guns were directly ahead of them, while the flanks were occupied by a motley collection of smaller cannon gathered from the city. Somewhere down below were the siege guns pulled from the river defenses, but manhandling those into position might take all day.

Behind the guns, and just far enough on the near side of the slope that they were not yet exposed to the enemy, the musket-armed volunteers had formed a long, loose line. It wasn't the shoulder-to-shoulder line of battle Winter had marched in against the Auxiliaries in Khandar, but a thinner formation with plenty of space between each man and his neighbor. Winter herself stood in the center of the stretch of line occupied by Jane's girls, with Jane a dozen yards in one direction and Abby about the same distance in the other.

Below this cordon, the regular infantry of the Colonials waited in double-company columns, four battalions strong. There was a considerable empty space between them, enough room for each column to fold out into a line if it needed to, or alternatively to provide a killing ground swept by musket fire if they had to form square and hold off enemy cavalry.

Finally, another hundred yards back, there was the mass of pike- and spear-armed volunteers. Their officers, borrowed from the Colonials, had herded them like sheepdogs into a squat block, dozens of men deep, with polearms waving slowly overhead like the legs of an overturned centipede. What they were supposed to *accomplish* like that wasn't clear to Winter, since without training in disciplined marching, any formation would dissolve as soon as they tried to move. But, as she'd told Abby, it wasn't her job to worry about that sort of thing.

The first cannonball passed over the crest of the hill with a weird whining, woofing sound, overshooting the entire formation and burying itself wetly in the cabbage field below. Every head in the army turned to follow its flight, and every soldier flinched in unison a moment later as the *boom* of the gun's report drifted over the field. It was followed by another, and another, the single blasts gradually merging into a solid wall of sound, a roll of thunder that went on and on without end. The duke's cannoneers could see nothing except the Colonial artillery, over the crest of the hill, so the shots were aimed at these guns and mostly invisible from Winter's position. The occasional ball ricocheted up and over the hilltop, or overshot like the first and screamed over their heads.

So far, so good. The girls hadn't broken for the rear at the first sound of firing, not that Winter had expected them to. A cheer rang from the volunteers as the friendly artillery took up the challenge. Their close and louder reports were accompanied by the gradual appearance of a column of smoke from each gun as though two dozen small bonfires had been kindled along the ridge. Instead of rising into the sky like woodsmoke, though, the powder smoke hung in wreaths over the field, twisted and shredded into strange shapes by the breeze. Winter caught the burning tang of it in her nostrils.

Time passed, ludicrously slowly. Nervous tension tied Winter's shoulder muscles into knots. It was a sensation she'd grown all too familiar with—the battle had begun, men were already fighting and dying, but there was nothing *she* could do but wait. It could drive you mad. Orlanko's guns roared in their distant, hidden positions, the Colonial artillery responded with sharp barks, and balls smashed through the air or raised fountains of dirt where they struck the ground. Once or twice she heard screams, as a well-aimed shot plowed through an unlucky gun crew. Before long the first wounded men—the fortunate ones, those who could still walk—were hobbling or dragging themselves back from the firing line.

It wouldn't be long now, if Winter understood Janus' plan correctly. She beckoned to Abby and Jane, and they hurried over. Tension showed on both faces, but to Winter's surprise Jane's was especially pale. She flinched visibly at the blast of each nearby cannon.

"Remind everyone of what we're doing here," Winter said. "We're *not* going to let the regulars get too close. Keep shooting, and keep falling back if they move up. And make sure they're all waiting for the two signals."

The two of them nodded, wordlessly, and started down the line in opposite directions, exchanging a few words with each of the girls. Farther on the flanks, Winter could see the other volunteer companies milling as their officers performed the same task. As the wounded passed through their line toward the rear, here and there they were joined by one or two volunteers whose courage had utterly failed them. They skulked away, hoping to join the trickle of injured, or simply tossed their muskets away and ran, ignoring the jeers of their erstwhile comrades. In the army, such behavior would be punished, possibly by summary execution, but the officers among the volunteers were too busy to do more than shout curses.

None of hers were leaving, Winter was glad to see. If they weren't half-brave and half-stupid, they wouldn't be here in the first place.

An officer on a horse—Fitz—trotted out from the waiting columns of Colonials and waved his hat for attention. He slashed his hand forward, his shout nearly lost amid the roaring cannon.

"First line, forward! Advance to range and open fire!"

He wheeled away, headed down the line to make sure everyone had gotten the message. Winter filled her lungs and repeated, "Forward! Walk, don't run!"

Company by company, the volunteers began to move. They had none of the precision of the drum-measured advance of a regular army unit, looking instead more like a heavily armed crowd out for an evening stroll. The natural tendency of the men was to bunch up for mutual support, and every officer was quickly engaged in hurrying up and down his line breaking up these clots with the warning that larger groups would present better targets to the enemy. Winter, Abby, and Jane followed suit, pulling the girls apart with their hands when the cannonade grew too loud to speak.

As they came over the crest of the hill, the friendly artillery went quiet, perspiring gunners flopping to the ground beside their pieces to make the most of the pause. Orlanko's guns kept firing. The thick pall of smoke hid everything farther away than a few yards, but the flash of the distant guns was visible, like a barrage of lightning, followed moments later by the booms and the scream of the balls. Human screams joined the chorus, too; the loosely packed volunteers made a poor target for artillery, but here and there the hurtling metal found flesh. The shroud of smoke hid the casualties from view, leaving only the shrieks, moans, and curses of disembodied ghosts.

Then, as if a curtain had been drawn aside, they stepped through the leading edge of the cloud and got a clear view of the descending slope of the hill and the valley beyond. Up and down the line, officers shouted, "Forward!" as men stopped to stare. Winter lent her voice to the general roar. She split her attention between watching the ground to keep her footing and trying to make sense of what she could see up ahead.

There was another hill, perhaps eight hundred yards distant, taller than the one they'd just crossed but less steep. At the top of it the duke's artillery formed a long line, the mirror image of their own, and similarly hidden by its own cloud of smoke. His advantage in weight of metal was obvious from the volume of muzzle flashes.

Coming down the slope in front of his guns were the six battalions of Orlanko's infantry, marked out by their fluttering battle flags. They had started moving before the volunteers, passing through their own line of artillery and making their way to the bottom of the hill. As Winter watched, they were deploying from column into line, companies folding out neatly from their positions behind the leading units and taking up their assigned places in the line of battle. The spaces between battalions were small, and when the maneuver was completed the enemy presented a single thin ribbon of blue, three ranks deep and more than a thousand yards long.

Waiting in the wings, well behind the advancing infantry, the squadrons of cuirassiers had formed into loose wedges. They had split into two groups, one on the left and one on the right, advancing at a walk to stay roughly behind the flanking infantry battalions. At this distance it was impossible to make out individuals from the mass of blue uniforms and horses, but the steel breastplates that gave the heavy horsemen their name flashed in the sun as they came forward. Their path forward was marked by the occasional splash of blue and red, where cannonballs had struck down horse, rider, or both together. A few of Give-Em-Hell's troopers were visible, too, retreating across the valley in the face of the advancing infantry.

"Come on!" Winter waved her arm, beckoning the girls forward. "Come on, come on!"

The valley floor was broken by a small, rocky streambed, too shallow to be an obstacle. The slopes of the hills were all knee-high grass, tall enough to conceal an ankle-breaking rock, but not enough to provide any sort of cover. As the volunteers moved forward, the friendly guns started up again, raising fountains of dirt at the edges of the enemy lines and among the cuirassiers. Orlanko's cannoneers were concentrating on trying to knock out Janus' artillery—a difficult task at best, requiring precision gunnery—while their opponents went for the far more tempting target of the densely packed heavy horsemen.

As the volunteers descended, reaching the relatively flat ground of the valley floor, the drums of the regulars became audible. The steady *clomp-clomp-clomp* of the cadenced march, like the ticking of some enormous clock, grew until it was louder than the cannons. The wall of blue uniforms made an intimidating sight, each with musket held against the shoulder just so, officers on horseback behind them with drawn swords, battle flags flapping in the breeze. Their own troops, brown and gray with black armbands, made a pathetic comparison. The range closed steadily.

At seventy-five yards, Winter called for a halt. The ragged line of volunteers grew more ragged still, as each company commander judged the moment for himself. The girls stopped, eyes glued to the steady advance of the blue line as if they were watching an oncoming avalanche.

"Ready!" Winter shouted. Jane and Abby repeated the order. Muskets came up to shoulders, and hammers clicked.

"Aim!" They'd stressed this in training. An ordinary infantryman, packed shoulder to shoulder, could normally fire nowhere but straight ahead. In the looser formation, they would have to make their shots count. On the other hand, it was hard to miss. The advancing regulars were slightly below them, fifty yards away, a wall of blue stretching out of sight in both directions.

Muskets started to crackle, somewhere else along the line. Winter swung her arm down before the roar made her inaudible. *"Fire!"*

It wasn't a proper volley, discharged in a single deadly blast. The sharp reports were spread out over a half minute, as individuals stepped forward, found their balance, or lined their weapons up on target. Pink-white muzzle flares were instantly blotted out by billowing clouds of smoke. The pall was not yet thick enough to obscure the enemy, though, and Winter could see the effect of the shots. Men went down, all along the line, crumpling sideways in heaps, falling backward, tumbling out of rank or clutching suddenly at their wounds. The neat perfection of the oncoming regulars dissolved, for a moment, then reformed like the surface of a lake closing over a hurled stone as the line continued its relentless advance. The soldiers stepped over the dead and wounded, closed their ranks, and came on to the beat of their drummers.

"Load!" Winter shouted. Most of her girls were already working on it, fumbling with cartridge pouches and ramrods. She heard squeaks and curses where someone had dropped a ball or spilled the powder. The rattle of ramrods in barrels mixed with the beat of the drums as the regulars approached. "Fire at will!"

No point in readying another volley. Muskets were already firing to either side, and each member of Winter's company brought her weapon up as soon as it was ready and sighted through the shredded smoke. Muskets began to flash again, and more blue-coated regulars fell. Winter could see her people making mistakes—firing too high, or before they'd brought the musket level, so the ball raised a miniature burst of earth and grass only a few yards on. At least one ramrod, left sticking out of the barrel, went pinwheeling out like a stick hurled for a dog.

Here it comes. Winter kept her eyes on the enemy lieutenants, walking or riding behind their soldiers. It was too loud to hear the orders at this distance, but she could recognize the gestures. And everyone in the volunteer line could see the regulars halt, their first rank kneel, and the muskets come up to their shoulders.

"Down!" Winter screamed, with all the lung power she could muster. At the same time she threw herself forward, spread-eagled in the grass and pressing her face into the dirt. From the sudden lack of fire to both sides, she thought her command had been followed—*God, I hope they have the sense to follow*—

A *real* volley rolled out from the regulars, tight and precise, hundreds of simultaneous musket blasts coming together into a wall of sound that rolled over Winter like a wave and set her ears to ringing. She could *feel* it, through the ground, along with the *thwack, thwack, thwack* of balls hitting the earth. On her stomach, she made a hard target, but she was hardly invulnerable, and it took a few moments to convince herself that she hadn't been hit. She pushed herself up on her elbows and raised her head, but the enemy was still invisible inside the roiling fogbank of their own discharge.

"Up!" Winter shouted. "Fire at will!"

She could hear Jane and Abby repeat the command, which eased her mind a fraction, but now the shrieks and curses rising from the battlefield were not only coming from the enemy. It was impossible to tell, from a scream of pain, whether it came from a man or a woman, but when Winter climbed to her feet, not everyone in her company did likewise. Whether those who remained still were wounded, dead, or simply frozen in terror, she had no way of knowing.

Muskets fired again, and the smoke was closing in. The rest of the line became vague figures in the fog, periodically outlined against pink-white stabs of flame. With their first volley spent, still under fire, the regulars had gone from organized volleys to the old soldier's standby of shooting off rounds as fast as they could manage, at whatever they thought they could hit. Winter's company, and the whole line of volunteers, were doing likewise.

This was where the real killing began, the two forces working each other over at close range like boxers drawn into a clinch. There was nothing for Winter to do but shout "Hold and fire! Hold and fire!" over and over, until her throat went raw and her voice was a ragged croak. Every breath tasted of powder smoke, and her heart slammed painfully hard in her chest.

The irony of the battlefield was that neither side could see what effect their fire was having on the enemy, who was hidden behind the billowing smoke, but both could easily tell how badly they themselves were being hurt. Winter, stalking back and forth between smoke-shrouded figures, heard balls *zip* and *zing* as they went past, and watched silhouettes crumple and fall around her. A girl two yards to her front gave a quiet "Urk," dropped her musket, and doubled over. Another screamed, clutching her leg and rolling back and forth in the grass. Other figures passed her by, shuffling wounded to the rear, or unhurt and running away—there was no way to tell.

The enemy, she knew, was having it worse. They *had* to be having it worse. Her own people were spread out, able to kneel, or to step forward out of their cloud of smoke and take aim at enemy muzzle flashes. The regulars, trapped in their line, could only load and fire blind, while their tight-packed ranks made for a wonderful target. But there were more of them, more muskets that could be brought to bear and more bodies to throw into the grinder.

"Pull it back!" Winter said. "Back up the hill! Open the range!"

She started backward, not running but walking slowly, keeping her face toward the enemy. Jane was still shouting—*thank God*—and the girls of the company followed. They emerged from the gray-white fogbank one by one, like ghosts, muskets clutched with white knuckles darkened to black by powder grime.

"She's dead," someone screamed. "I saw her—"

"Has anyone seen—"

"My sister, it hit her foot, she's still—"

"Keep firing!" Winter screeched, banshee-wild. "Load! Fire!"

Hesitantly, the rattle of musketry rose again. Winter could see their faces now, tense and determined, or crying, tears cutting through the black grit as they brought the muskets to their shoulders. One girl jerked, a fountain of blood blooming high on her chest and blood soaking her shirt. She raised her musket to her shoulder, fired, then collapsed backward into the grass.

A new sound thrilled through the firing. A skirl of drums, not the low, steady beat of the march but the rapid heartbeat-fast pace of the charge. Winter pictured six thousand bayonets coming out of their sheaths, wicked-sharp points gleaming as they snapped home.

"Back! Up the hill!"

Standing to receive the charge would be suicide. A formed body of troops would go through the thin line of volunteers like a rock through fog. But the regulars, packed tight, would have a hard time running down their more nimble opponents.

A few muzzle flashes came from the enemy line, men firing as they ran. Winter backpedaled as her company turned and ran, searching the smoke for laggards. Balls twittered and zipped overhead, but she didn't turn to run herself until the leading rank of Orlanko's men emerged from the cloud of smoke, trailing streamers of gray fog from their uniforms. Then she sprinted up the slope and after the girls of her company, catching sight of Jane well ahead.

Here and there along the line there was a clash of arms, as some volunteer who'd been too slow turned to fight or tried to defend a wounded comrade. The regulars charged like lancers, spitting these unfortunates on their fixed bayonets, then carried on up the hill with a cheer. Winter saw one thin figure—whether it was a boy or a girl, she couldn't be certain—jump up from the grass like a pheasant taking wing in front of a hunter, only to be brought crashing down by a blast of musketry from the advancing line.

The majority of the volunteers escaped their pursuers, however, and the regulars quickly realized the chase was futile. They slowed down, then halted, sergeants shouting furiously to dress their ranks. The men cheered at the sight of their enemies in panicked flight.

"Halt!" Winter shouted. "Halt and fire!"

This, she knew, was the moment of truth. Conventional military wisdom said that, once a body of men had broken formation and started to run, it was impossible to get them to return to the fight until they'd fled out of sight of the enemy and their ingrained discipline and fear of their officers could overcome the terror of battle. If that was true, the volunteers would keep running, down past the guns and the Colonials, and likely panic the formation of pikemen along the way.

On the other hand, as Marcus had explained the plan, this was a different sort of army, with a different sort of soldier. They didn't have a complicated formation to maintain, and more important, they had a *cause*, something beyond their immediate survival or possible punishment by their officers to motivate them. Janus was gambling that this would make them tougher than the time-serving rankers who opposed them.

Whether it was true of the volunteers in general Winter couldn't say, but her heart lifted when it became clear that Jane's girls, at least, were going to confound the tactics manuals. They stopped running at her command, and as she jogged up toward where they were gathered, they went back into their loading and firing, their shots cutting short the cheers among the surprised regulars. More muskets cracked along the line—while some had no doubt continued to run, it seemed as though the volunteers had justified Janus' faith. For a few minutes, the enemy was dumbfounded, as balls zipped over their heads and men fell in place. Then, ignoring the shouting officers who were still trying to reorganize the ranks, they began to fire back. The smoke grew thick once again, and the nightmare of dimly seen figures firing and falling in spasmodic flashes began anew.

Winter could well imagine the enemy commander's consternation. The roar of musketry was continuous, but the return fire from the volunteers did not seem to be slackening. If they couldn't be broken with firepower, they had to be shifted with cold steel, but when his troops stumbled forward they found their opponents flitting back out of their reach like ghosts, only to stop when the attack had spent itself and return to their constant, galling fire. Twice more the regulars worked themselves into a frenzy of cheers and charged, and both times they caught only a handful of stragglers.

Among the volunteers, confidence was steadily increasing. Balls struck home, and men fell here and there along the line, but their loose formation made for a much harder target than the disciplined shoulder-to-shoulder ranks of the enemy. Janus' artillery had joined in as well, switching its fire to the infantry and arcing balls to bounce through the enemy line. And when the breeze tore gaps in the wall of drifting smoke, they could see the damage they were inflicting. A carpet of blue-coated bodies marked the slow progress of the regulars across the valley floor and up the slope, mounding in drifts in some places where they'd halted to exchange fire.

Whoever was in charge over there—Orlanko, Torahn, some army colonel—had one card left to play. *How long will he hold it back . . . ?*

"Abby!"

Jane's shout jerked Winter's attention back to the here and now, amid the skeins of drifting, powder-scented smoke. She saw a knot of her girls gathering, and hurried in their direction, trying to listen through the earsplitting din of musketry.

"Spread out!" Winter croaked. Her voice was almost completely gone, and she resorted to grabbing the clustered girls by the arm and pushing them to either side. "Don't make a target! Spread out!"

"Winter!" Jane was bending over Abby's prone body. Her voice was as raw as Winter's. "I think she's hit, but I can't find where."

"We should—"

"*Help* her," Jane said. Her eyes were very wide, and her dark crimson hair had faded to dull gray under a layer of grime. The hand that reached out for Winter was gray as well, cut by streaks of sweat.

Damn. Winter looked down at Abby, then up at the enemy. *Damn, damn, damn.* She knelt beside the girl, curtly waving for Jane to back off.

Abby lay on her side. Winter took her shoulder and pushed her onto her back, limp arm flopping into the grass beside her. *No time for half measures. If she's dead . . .* But taking a pulse was impossible amid the constant crash and jar of muskets and cannon.

There was a crust of blood and a sticky trail, right at Abby's hairline. Winter probed it tentatively with one finger, anticipating the soft, sick shifting that meant a shattered skull. Instead she found only a narrow ridge of torn flesh. Abby's mouth opened, and she gave a low moan.

"She's alive." Jane put her arms around Winter and squeezed tight, as though *she* were somehow responsible. "We have to get her out of here."

"We can't leave the others," Winter said. "Find a couple of the taller ones—"

She stopped. Another sound was barely audible, under the blasts and concussions of the battle. More shouts, not the cheers of excited troops but screams and warning. And, beyond that, the rumble of hooves.

"Run," Winter said. She tried to raise her voice, but it came out as a hoarse squeak. "Run! Jane, tell them to run!"

"I'll take Abby—"

"No!" Winter jumped to her feet and grabbed Jane by the arm. "Come *on*. There's no time!"

It was a few moments before Jane realized what was happening, and she allowed herself to be dragged a half dozen steps before digging in her heels. "What are you doing? We can't just leave her!"

"No *time*," Winter gasped. Another couple of figures loomed out of the smoke, two of Jane's girls. Winter grabbed one with her free hand, eliciting a squeak of surprise.

"Help me with her!" she said, nodding at Jane. "We have to run. Back to the Colonials!" From somewhere, she found the energy to raise her voice one last time. "Run! Over the hill!"

Gradually—*thank God*—the cry was taken up, passed down the line by those who still had the voice to spread it. The two girls took Jane by either arm and dragged her up the hill, away from where Abby had fallen, heedless of her orders and protestations. By the time they'd gotten clear of the smoke, the need for haste had become obvious to everyone.

The cuirassiers, sweeping around the ends of the line of regulars, were converging on the volunteers from both sides. Even if they'd had fixed bayonets, without a tight formation there was no way to halt the cavalry charge. That was, after all, *why* the shoulder-to-shoulder line had made its way into the military textbooks—without a solid front of bristling steel, infantry was always vulnerable to a sudden rush by enemy horses.

The volunteers ran for it. This wasn't the steady jog they'd used to retreat from the regulars, but a true, panicked flight, streaming up the hill and over the crest. Some men tossed their muskets away in the panic, while others fell to the ground and lay still, hoping to be passed over. The cuirassiers were in among those who'd reacted slowly, sabers rising and falling in sprays of blood, cutting men down and trampling them into the dirt.

Winter's company, in the center of the line, had more warning than the others. They ran—even Jane, who'd fought free of her minders—and reached the line of artillery before the horsemen caught up with them. The artillerists waved them on, standing beside their pieces with flames in hand, ready to fire. Up ahead, over the crest of the hill, Winter could hear the steady beat of the Colonials' drums. *Square, square, form square.*

The riders ought to have pulled up, once they'd sent their prey running. But they'd spent the day being hammered at long range, and their thirst for revenge combined with the fox-hunt spirit of the chase to drive them onward. In the smoke, it was easy to keep going, chasing the next fleeing figure, hacking him down, and moving on to the next. By the time they broke out of it, they were too close to the guns to stop.

One by one, the cannon *boomed* and belched loads of canister in the ranks of the oncoming cavalry. Swarms of iron balls buzzed and stung like hornets, blasting great gaps in the squadrons and tearing horses and riders apart. The remaining cuirassiers broke into a vengeful charge, but most of the artillerists had already joined the tide of running volunteers, and those that remained ducked beneath the smoking tubes of their guns, leaving the cavalry to slash at them impotently with too-short sabers.

The momentum of the charge was too strong to stop. It came on, over the crest of the hill, following Winter and the others toward the formed ranks of the Colonials. The four blue-coated battalions had reshaped themselves into four diamonds, edges fringed with bristling steel. Sergeants behind the line were bellowing at the oncoming volunteers, shouting for them to *get down* and clear the field of fire. Others beckoned them forward, into the interior of the squares.

Winter, legs burning, took the lead and led her company toward the First Battalion flags. Someone recognized her, or else had orders to let the volunteers in, because a couple of ranks of bayonets moved aside just in time to prevent the girls from skewering themselves. They poured through the gap, tumbling into the clear space beyond like broken dolls, spreading themselves across the grass and gasping for air.

Jane. Winter found her on her hands and knees, sobbing and coughing all at once. She knelt to help her, but Jane looked at her, eyes furious, and waved her away. Winter stood up, blinking, and rubbed her eyes with a filthy sleeve.

The gap in the square had closed behind her. The cuirassiers were coming, big men on big horses, breastplates gleaming on their chests and sabers unsheathed in their hands. There was the familiar pause as they closed—seventy yards, fifty, forty—

Then, from a dozen throats at once: "First rank, *fire*!"

MARCUS

We let them get too far ahead, Marcus thought, fists clenching tight as he watched the volunteers streaming over the ridge. *Karis' mercy. It's going to be a slaughter.*

But the charging cavalry were not as close behind as he'd thought. Some clearheaded officer had ordered the retreat well before the cuirassiers had actually made contact, and they'd cleared the line of guns in time to allow a last thudding volley of canister to sweep away huge swaths of the enemy. The thinned ranks that came over the hill were moving at a full gallop, spurring madly and waving their sabers, but their formation was broken and there weren't enough of them.

They're not going to break the squares. The volunteers were still streaming past on all sides, or making their way through the ranks, but Marcus permitted himself a smile, and a moment of pity for the advancing horsemen. *Those poor, brave bastards.*

Their impetuous pursuit of the fleeing volunteers was going to cost them dearly. A volley stabbed out from the squares as the horsemen closed, toppling horses and punching riders from their saddles. It was suicidal for them to try to charge home against the wall of bayonets, and equally suicidal to rein up and try to turn about in the face of all those muskets. They had no choice but to keep riding, splitting like a stream around a rock, taking fire from the sides and rear of the squares as they went. By the time they'd made it out of musket range, they were no longer a formation, just a scattered band of panicked men and animals, curling out to either side in flight.

"It's a rare cavalry captain who can rein in his men when the enemy is before them," Janus commented. "I hope your Captain Stokes makes a note of the potential consequences."

"I doubt he will, sir."

Janus' lip curved in a slight smile. "I suppose not."

Marcus looked around the square. None of his men had done anything more dangerous than fire their muskets at a cuirassier as he went past, and the ranks were still in good order. The grassy interior of the formation was crammed with volunteers, sitting or lying wherever they'd fallen and breathing hard after their desperate flight. He caught one blue uniform amid the dull-colored mass, and recognized Lieutenant Iherngiass, which meant that at least *some* of the men sprawling around him were actually women. There was certainly nothing feminine about them now, and they'd been liberally smeared with blood and grime. Marcus could see several nursing wounds, and he felt a sudden stab of guilt. *I shouldn't have let them go out there—*

"Captain," Janus said.

"Sorry, sir. What was that?"

"I said that we must seize the moment. I want you to take the volunteers and attack. The artillery will support you."

"Attack?" Marcus looked back at the exhausted citizen-soldiers. "I don't think—"

"The pike formation is still fresh," Janus snapped.

"Perhaps the Colonials should lead—"

"Captain," Janus interrupted, "I have no time for argument. You will lead that attack *now*, or I will find someone who will."

"Yessir." Marcus drew himself up and saluted. "At once, sir!"

He ran to the edge of the square, edged sideways between the surprised rankers, and hurried across the killing ground toward the pikemen. These volunteers, still formed into a rough block, had done nothing but bristle and cheer as the horsemen swept past. Marcus waved his hat at the blue-uniformed lieutenant in charge.

"Captain!" The man—Bosh, Marcus recalled—snapped a salute. "Do you have orders?"

"We're to attack, on the double." Marcus pointed up the slope, at an angle that would let the pikes edge around the still-formed squares. "That way. Follow me!"

"With this lot, sir? They don't know how to march! We'll just be a mob."

"It's what we've got," Marcus said, trying to emulate Janus' peremptory demeanor. He raised his voice. "We're going at them! Follow me!"

An enthusiastic cheer came from the ranks of the volunteers. There was nothing for raising men's morale, Marcus thought, like watching a battle without actually being shot at. He waved his hat in the air again, chopped his hand in the direction he wanted, and set off.

Lieutenant Bosh's prediction came true almost immediately. As soon as they started to move, the ranks the sergeants had so painfully constructed dissolved, and the formation started to look more like a blob than a rectangle. He heard the clatter of wood and the occasional shocked screech as men tangled their long-hafted weapons, trod on one another's feet, or fell over.

"Keep those pikes up!" Bosh shouted, walking backward and waving his arms frantically. "Keep together!"

"Double time!" Marcus said, and then broke into a trot himself. The sound of confusion behind him increased, but he could hear the thud of many boots climbing the hill. The Colonials gave him a cheer as he went past, and to either side the cannoneers were running back to their guns.

Crossing the crest of the hill, he was confronted with an immense bank of smoke, just starting to break up in the feeble breeze. Through a few gaps, he could see the enemy line, still putting itself back together after its last attempt to catch the fleeing volunteers. The reason for Janus' haste was suddenly obvious—until the line got back into shape, and the men reloaded their muskets, there would be no volley of deadly, coordinated fire to break the momentum of the pikemen's charge. *But how the hell could he know that, from the other side of the hill—*

Marcus shook his head. One day, he thought, he might learn to stop second-guessing Janus bet Vhalnich. He drew his sword as the leading edge of the mass of pikemen came over the grassy top of the hill behind him. From either side, the *boom* of cannon resumed as the artillery picked up its attack.

If this works, it's going to be one of those things that get written down in the history books. He wondered, briefly, what he should say. *Oh well. I can always think of something clever later to tell the historians.*

"Come on!" He chopped downward, toward the enemy. "Let's get the bastards!"

Marcus broke into a run. Behind him, the volunteers let out another cheer and followed. They made it halfway to the enemy line before someone with a loaded musket spotted them through the smoke, and a crackle of musket fire came to meet them. Marcus heard balls zipping overhead, and men jerked and tumbled behind him, but for the moment he was untouched. He didn't dare stop, for fear of one of his own men skewering him from behind.

He expected an awful collision, the crash of body on body and weapon on flesh, but it never happened. The men in the thin line of regulars watched the pikes come on, three thousand strong, and made a rapid assessment of their chances. First one by one, then all in a flood, they broke and ran, sprinting down into the valley, desperate to stay ahead of the vengeful mob. In spite of the shouts of the officers, the panic was contagious, as the companies to either side of where the line had been breached decided they were better off following their companions.

In a few seconds, the solid-looking line of blue had shattered around the charge of the pikes like a pane of glass hit by a stone. The regulars were in full flight, scattered across the valley, and the volunteers whooped and went after them. Marcus slowed to a trot, then finally halted, his sword still unbloodied. He couldn't have brought his cheering men under control if he'd wanted to, but it no longer mattered. High on the other hill, he could see rearing horses and frantic motions, as Orlanko's officers and cannoneers also decided on the better part of valor.

The battle was over.

Now what?

Chapter Twenty-Four

MARCUS

The greatest challenge the new government had faced so far was staging the victory parade. The military officers had wanted to hold it in the traditional spot, on the main drive at Ohnlei, while the Deputies-General had insisted it wind through Cathedral Square on the Island to pay proper respect to the representatives of the people. In the end the queen had arranged a compromise—the procession would begin at the palace and make its way through miles of countryside, to finally enter the city and finish at the cathedral. A reviewing stand was hastily erected by the side of the Ohnlei Road, roughly halfway along the route.

Marcus thought it was a bit hard on the soldiers, who had done all the marching and fighting and would now be required to march a few miles more. When he'd mounted the reviewing stand, however, he began to perceive the wisdom of Raesinia's solution. The side of the road was lined with people, cheering and waving blue-and-silver flags. They stretched in an unbroken line toward the city as far as he could see, as though the entire population of Vordan had turned out to bear witness to their triumph. Trying to cram all of the spectators onto either the palace grounds or into the square would have been a disaster.

He was used to thinking of the queen as a passive participant in the plans of the likes of Janus or Orlanko. *But she's smarter than we give her credit for, isn't she?*

At the moment, Raesinia sat at the front of the stand, in a dress that, while elaborately laced and ruffled, was nonetheless black. Recent events might have blotted out the memory of the king's death for some, but not for her. The officers present had added black armbands to their uniforms, which served a nicely doubled symbolic duty of representing their mourning and expressing solidarity with the volunteers who'd fought and died only a few miles north of here.

She was surrounded by a mixed flock of courtiers and army officers, the former in brightly colored finery and the latter in dress blues trimmed with silver and gold. It was, as yet, a small flock. Proclamations had gone out immediately following the victory, calling on the great nobles and the colonels of all the army regiments to come and swear loyalty to the new queen and the Deputies-General, but so far only a few had answered. Some noblemen and -women, younger sons and daughters for the most part, had arrived bearing excuses for their families, but few of the counts and almost none of the colonels had turned up. They were frightened by the Deputies-General and its rhetoric, and in spite of the queen's triumph they were hedging their bets. An aristocrat's first allegiance was always to survival. The officers who had come were younger men, captains and lieutenants who'd come up through the college and were eager to spit in the eyes of their higher-born colleagues.

No one came to dance attendance on the new Minister of War. They'd offered perfunctory congratulations, but Marcus suspected that most of the officers hoped to persuade the queen to reject the country nobleman in favor of one of their own. After all, they told each other, he'd only gotten lucky, and happened to have his men on the spot in the moment of crisis. And Khandar, well, whipping a troop of gray-skins wasn't such a great feat when it came down to it, was it?

Marcus almost felt sorry for them. The queen was *definitely* a great deal smarter, and more stubborn, than *they* gave her credit for. And, having worked with Janus for the past week on drafting his plans for a reorganization of the Royal Army, he knew that these men were about to have their world turned upside down.

"May I ask a question, sir?" Marcus said.

"Certainly, Colonel."

For a moment Marcus nearly looked over his shoulder to see who Janus was speaking to. He fingered the silver eagles on his shoulders uneasily, as if to confirm they were still there.

"I think I've puzzled out most of what you did during the battle. Using the volunteers as a skirmish screen was inspired."

"I guessed it would confuse the enemy," Janus said. "The Desoltai used similar tactics, if you recall, and they certainly caused problems for me."

"And you knew they would eventually have to commit their cavalry."

"Indeed. It was Orlanko's misfortune that he had only a regiment of heavies available. A few squadrons of hussars or dragoons would have been better suited to the task."

"I even," Marcus said, "understand why you launched the final attack when you did. The enemy were still in disorder from their own charges."

A smile flickered across Janus' face. "None of this amounts to a 'question,' Colonel."

"Why did you send in the volunteer pike? Why not the Colonials? It seemed to me that a charge by regular troops would have made success more certain."

"Ah," Janus said. "Truthfully, there were a number of reasons. The Colonial formations were still tied up with the fleeing skirmishers, and it would have taken time to get them shaken out and moving. I judged that a single concerted assault, delivered promptly, would be more likely to succeed than a more traditional attack by lines. There was also the matter of keeping something in reserve—if the attack had failed, the Colonials could be relied on to hold their ground, whereas the volunteers would likely have panicked. The proper use of reserves is crucial. If the Last Duke had kept a few of his battalions in reserve to launch a counterattack, things might have gone very differently."

"I think I understand that, sir."

"Also," Janus said, lowering his voice slightly, "there's the matter of replacement."

"Sir?"

"Casualties among the volunteers will be easy to replace." He waved a hand at the crowds. "A call from the queen would no doubt produce a groundswell of support. Whereas well-trained, *reliable* troops are in very short supply. It seemed prudent to preserve the Colonials, as much as it was practicable."

There was a long pause. Marcus looked away from Janus' face, following his gaze down to the passing lines of volunteers. One company, marching with a slightly larger gap ahead and behind than usual, was just passing in front of the reviewing stand. Marcus recognized the slim figure of Lieutenant Ihernglass in the lead, and though the soldiers behind him wore trousers instead of skirts, there was no concealing their true identity. A mutter ran through the gathered officers, and the crowds on either side of the road fell silent for a moment as they passed.

Then the queen, rising from her seat, offered the female soldiers a wave. Cheers rose again, louder than before, and the company marched on.

"Then," Marcus said, "you don't think this is over?"

"It's a long way from over, Colonel. This may only be the beginning. Given time, we may be able to bring the army and the nobles into line, but . . ." Janus sat back in his chair, eyes hooded. "Don't forget the matter of our prisoner."

Marcus winced. The Guardhouse had been critically undermanned since the fall of the Vendre, a skeleton of a skeleton crew, and no one had even noticed that Adam Ionkovo was gone until long after it had happened. *Gone, from inside a locked cell, with no evidence of violence.*

"One of the guards is missing as well," Marcus said. "It's quite possible that Ionkovo or his allies got to him, and now he's either gone to ground or been disposed of."

"It's possible," Janus said. "But I doubt it. Ionkovo let himself be captured because he knew he could escape. My guess is he was the one who shot Danton, and he pulled the same disappearing act there."

"Then you think he's one of *them*. The *ignahta*." The Elysian word felt alien on Marcus' tongue. "Like Jen."

Janus nodded. "*That* is the true face of our enemy, Captain. Don't forget it."

Marcus shook his head, but said nothing. The enemy that *he* cared about was still out there. *Orlanko.* The duke had fled north after the defeat, to meet with his Borelgai allies. *He'll tell me the truth about what he did to my family. Even if I have to choke it out of him.*

"You intend to press the issue?" Marcus asked, after a moment.

"I have no choice." Janus tapped a finger on the arm of his chair. "Even if I have to lead an army to the gates of Elysium itself."

WINTER

Marcus had given Winter's company a hall in the former barracks of the imprisoned Noreldrai Grays, now that the Ministry of War was gradually being reopened for its proper function. It was considerably more luxurious accommodations than they'd enjoyed before the battle, or even back at Jane's building in the Docks. The girls had to bunk four to a room, but they were big rooms with proper beds, glass windows, and clean linen. Winter, somewhat to her embarrassment, had the suite that had belonged to the mercenary captain, which was closer to a nobleman's apartments than a soldier's barracks.

It was the morning after the great victory celebration, and the hall outside was quiet. After the parade, the volunteers had returned to their chaotic encampment at Ohnlei, and a great crowd of citizens had accompanied them. At the queen's order, the cellars of the palace had been thrown open and barrel after barrel of wine rolled out for the grateful, thirsty crowds. Vendors from the city sold food, with special discounts for anyone wearing a black armband, and enthusiastic entrepreneurs hawked keepsakes, souvenirs, and celebratory woodcuts. One image in particular was everywhere—an artist's impression of the queen's surrender, with Raesinia bowing her head in submission to the triumphant Deputies-General while her guards and officers looked on, aghast. Until the small hours of the morning, Winter heard cheers and shouts of "One eagle and the Deputies-General!"

She'd posted sentries around the hall, as before, to protect her soldiers' notional virtue, but they were to keep people out, not in. Small groups of girls kept slipping away to join the fun, and while Winter was certain some of them were going to do things they might regret in the morning, she didn't feel she had the moral standing to try to stop them.

For herself, she'd stayed in the great bed with Jane. Any carnal desire could be satisfied out there, she was sure, for at best a nominal fee, but it held no attraction for Winter.

She awoke, naked and warm under the sheets, with Jane clinging to her arm like a limpet. Winter kissed her on the forehead, and Jane's brilliant green eyes flickered open. She let out a low groan.

"I am not getting out of bed today," Jane said. "And neither should you."

"I have to," Winter said. "And so do you. They're coming back from the hospital today, remember?"

Winter rolled out of bed, went to the basin to wash, and started buckling herself into her uniform. She caught a raised eyebrow and a lewd look from Jane as she did so, and gave an exaggerated sigh.

"What?" Jane pulled on her own trousers, trying to look innocent.

At the outer door of their apartment, Winter could hear shouts of happiness and cheering from outside. *They must have arrived.* As she reached for the latch, Jane caught her sleeve.

"What am I supposed to say to her?" Her eyes were glued to the inlaid woodwork, refusing to meet Winter's.

"What do you mean?"

"I mean, 'Sorry about leaving you to die, glad you didn't!' That sort of thing?"

"It wasn't like that," Winter said, putting an arm around Jane's shoulder. "You know that, and so does she. So does everyone out there."

"I was the one who got them into this in the first place," Jane said. "It's my responsibility."

"You know that's not true, either. You told me yourself it was their idea."

"I know."

Winter moved her hand to the back of Jane's head, pulled her down, and kissed her thoroughly. When they finally broke apart, Jane let out a long breath.

"I love you," she said.

Winter smiled, cheeks only a little pink. "Likewise. Now, I think we have work to do."

The newly released patients were gathered in the barracks' small dining room, along with the girls who were sufficiently clearheaded to leave their beds. The half dozen bandage-wearing wounded were led by Abby, who had a strip of clean white linen wound around her skull but seemed otherwise unhurt.

These were the lightly injured, of course. There were more who were still under the surgeon's care. After the horrors of the hospital and the bone saw had taken their toll, some few of those would return, and some of them would do so on crutches or with an empty sleeve pinned up. And then, of course, there were those who had never returned from the battlefield at all. For a moment, looking at the happy, laughing girls, Winter felt a flash of anger and was tempted to remind them of what they'd lost.

The thought passed quickly. They knew. Of course they knew. It was in every embrace, every shared glance. They were happy to see Abby and the others in part because they all knew who *hadn't* come back. Winter remembered the Seventh Company, cheering for her after she'd brought them out of d'Vries' horrible mistake at the Battle of the Road. At the time, she'd thought it ghoulish to cheer, dwelling on all the men she *hadn't* been able to save. But a proper soldier's attitude was the other way around, and somehow, over the course of the past week, these girls had become proper soldiers.

Jane came in, and Abby ran to her at once, wrapping her in a fierce hug. As it turned out, no words were necessary, on either side.

After a while, things settled down enough that breakfast could be served. Jane sat at the head of the table, as always, with Winter on her right hand and Abby on her left. Winter caught Abby's eye when Jane leaned forward to shout something, and they both smiled.

I wonder if she knows what happened. Probably not, Winter decided. Abby had said she'd only awoken the next day, in the cutter's tents, where they told her that she'd been very lucky. A ricocheting ball had creased her forehead, but without enough force to shatter bone. *Anyway,* Winter thought, *we only did what we had to.*

A girl in a black armband came in, one of the sentries. She had a musket under her arm and wore a puzzled expression.

"Sir?" she said, looking at Winter. "There's someone who wants to see you."

"Who is it?" Winter said.

"I don't know her," the sentry said. "She said she heard that this is where they were keeping 'Mad Jane's Army' and that she wanted to join up."

"To *join up*?" Jane chuckled. "And they called *me* mad."

"You can tell her," Winter said gently, "that we're not recruiting at present."

"Yes, sir. Should I say the same thing to the others?"

"Others? What others?"

"There's quite a few more saying the same thing," the sentry said, glancing back toward the front door. "We're trying to get them to form a queue."

Winter met Jane's eyes. One corner of Jane's lip quirked, in her familiar, maddening smile.

RAESINIA

Raesinia had been expecting to return to her old rooms in the Prince's Tower, but after the parade and the interminable audiences, the servants had conducted her to the royal apartments instead. It was impossible to fight the feeling that she was being taken to see her father, and she had a brief fantasy that he would be standing there when she opened the door, waiting to tell her that she'd passed an elaborately contrived test.

Or else his ghost, telling me that I've disappointed him with my failure and now he's going to haunt me for the rest of my days. It was hard to say what he would have thought of recent events. She'd beaten Orlanko, fair enough, but much of the country was still beyond her grasp, and the Deputies-General was issuing orders in the name of the people.

God only knows what happens next. She had Janus, and that redressed the balance of power enough that she was no longer actually a prisoner, but now that the crisis had passed the deputies were clamoring that Janus was more of a threat to the government than a protection. She'd named him interim Minister of War as a stopgap solution, so he would still be around but with no official capacity to command troops. But that was a fig leaf, and both sides knew it. If Janus gave orders, the Colonials would obey, regardless of his official role, and so would many of the volunteers.

She ghosted through the anteroom, the presence chamber where her father had received important guests, the private dining room where he'd entertained his friends. There was very little of *him* left in the place. Some kings had worked hard to put their stamp on Ohnlei, but Farus VIII had been willing to let the unfathomable palace bureaucracy have its head. His rooms were richly furnished, but somehow *anonymous*, without a soul, a place where someone had stayed but not really *lived*, like the world's most expensive hotel.

Liveried servants waited beside every doorway, bowing as she approached. Raesinia passed into the bedroom, told the footman inside to get out, and shut the door behind him.

At least the week's interval had given them a chance to freshen the place up. When her father was well, Raesinia had met him in the outer chambers, so her only memories of *this* place were from when it had smelled of sickness and death. The sick-sweet stench of the doctor's concoctions, the reek of the royal bedpan, and the too-strong perfume the servants sprayed to cover it up. Now it smelled of starch and fresh linen, and the four-posted bed was decked with a different canopy and set of covers than she remembered. *Hell, I bet they had to burn the mattress.*

Paintings stared down at her from the walls. There was her father's favorite family portrait from when Dominic had been twelve and she herself had been an infant. Her mother, Elizabeth, a pale, dark-haired woman of whom Raesinia had no memory, stood holding the baby by her father's side. The next portrait over was her grandfather, Farus VII, and on the other wall was one of the slender, sickly Farus VI. More women she didn't recognize, great-aunts and great-great-aunts, clustered around the great golden-framed portraits of the kings.

How did Father sleep with all of them staring down at him? Raesinia shook her head. *It's a good thing I don't sleep, I suppose.*

She went to the bed and tossed herself into it, sinking deep into the feathery morass. Her dress wasn't designed for lying down, and she could feel it tugging and pinching her skin, but the pain barely registered.

What happens next? She hadn't really devoted any thought to it. For all that she'd worked and schemed to get here—because it was the right thing to do, because it was what her father would have wanted, because she couldn't stand to let Orlanko win—now that she'd made it, she wasn't at all sure what to do. If she let it, Ohnlei would devour her, sinking her days in mindless ritual and spectacle designed to give a sense of purpose to an essentially purposeless existence. Some of Vordan's kings had delighted in it, and given themselves completely to the Court; others, like her father, had resisted, and applied themselves to the business of the state. Raesinia wanted to be one of the latter, but she didn't know how to start, or whether they would let her.

It's been a long day, is all. She couldn't sleep, but there were other ways to rest the mind. *A hot bath, a book, and out of this damned dress.* Raesinia sat up, ready to call for the maids—she couldn't even get *out* of the dress herself—and froze.

There was a figure in one dark corner of the room, away from the braziers. As Raesinia's eyes fell on it, it bowed low.

"Your Majesty." A familiar voice. *Very* familiar—

"Sothe!" Raesinia crossed the room at a run, heedless of her dress and her dignity. When she was nearly there, she tripped on a trailing flounce and stumbled forward, but Sothe caught her one-handed before she hit the floor. Raesinia threw her arms around the woman and hugged her tight.

"Your Majesty," Sothe murmured, "please mind the arm."

Raesinia blinked and let go. Looking more closely, she could see that one of Sothe's arms was bound in a sling, and belatedly remembered the pistol ball the maidservant had taken in the shoulder during their escape from the Grays.

"Sorry!"

"It's all right," Sothe said, straightening her sleeves fastidiously and wincing slightly. "It's healing, but slowly."

"That's good," Raesinia said, then shook her head wildly. "But where have you *been*? I thought you were dead. When you didn't come back after that night . . ."

"I was able to lure the Concordat agent into an ambush and kill him," Sothe said, as though this were as simple as going down to the bakery for morning bread. "Afterward, though, I was very weak, and my wound needed tending. I spent several days in the company of a doctor of my acquaintance, fighting off a fever." She gave a little shudder. "Thank God the wound was too high in the shoulder for him to amputate, or I would certainly have awoken without the arm. By the time I was able to move about, you were in the Vendre."

Raesinia nodded. "But once Janus let me go . . ."

"I must apologize for not coming to you then, Your Majesty. But it would have been difficult while you were surrounded by Vhalnich's Mierantai. I wanted to keep him unaware of my presence."

"Marcus met you," Raesinia said, feeling puzzled. "He may have said something to Janus."

"If the subject arises, you should tell them I died at Concordat hands that day. It will give me greater freedom of action."

"Don't be ridiculous. You're going to be living here with me, so I can't very well tell them you're dead—"

"No, Your Majesty."

"What?" Raesinia blinked unbidden tears from her eyes. "What are you talking about? I *need* you."

"I know. And, someday, I will be able to stay by your side as long as you wish. For the moment, though, I think it would be better if I remained in the shadows."

"But why?"

"Because I do not trust Janus bet Vhalnich."

There was a long pause.

"He did save the city from Orlanko," Raesinia said. "I don't know if anyone else could have done it. And just afterward . . . if he'd declared the deputies dissolved and himself king, I'm not sure anyone would have been able to stop him." Raesinia had been half hoping he *would*. She couldn't let him, of course, not in good conscience, but at that moment she'd been as helpless as the rest. *And then I wouldn't have to worry about "what next?"* "He's done nothing to draw suspicion."

"On the contrary," Sothe said. "If he had made some move to take power for himself, or wealth, or even pressured you to increase his holdings or his title, that would make some sense. But he's asked for nothing, has he?"

Raesinia shook her head. "Not yet, at any rate."

"And that is suspicious. What is his *motive*? He saved the city, he saved the deputies, he saved you, but *why*?"

"You don't think he simply wishes to serve his country?"

"If he does, I owe him an apology." Sothe frowned. "He knows something that very few people know—that there is still magic in the world, if you know where to look. He knows about your . . . condition. And I have been investigating what he did in Khandar. I think . . ."

"What?"

"I can't say. Not yet. But I don't think he's a simple patriot. He wants something, not wealth or even the throne, but something else. I intend to find out what that is."

There was a long silence.

"I understand," Raesinia said. "And you're right. It would be nice to have someone around here that I could really trust, but you're right."

"I will make regular reports," Sothe said.

"Be sure that you do. I'm certain I'll have other need of your talents, aside from Janus bet Vhalnich."

Sothe bowed her head. "Of course, Your Majesty."

She slipped to the doorway, one leading off into a servants' hall, silent as a shadow. Before she could leave, Raesinia cleared her throat.

"Sothe?"

"Yes, Your Majesty?"

"I'm glad you're not dead."

"So am I, Your Majesty." Her lip curved, just slightly, in what was very nearly a smile. "So am I."

EPILOGUE

IONKOVO

In the silent corridors of the darkened Royal Palace, a shadow rippled like black ink. Ionkovo stepped out of it, dressed in his working outfit of loose, dark leathers. He had a long knife in one hand, its shine dulled by lampblack.

There would be at least one guard just outside the queen's room, he was certain, but he'd slipped past the outer perimeter. With the palace practically shut down, it was easy to move about without running into any stray servants.

He eased a door open and slipped into a long corridor, lined with large-paned windows on both sides looking out onto grassy courtyards. The moon was high, throwing a silver light that stippled the floor with shadows. Outside, the wind was picking up, and the manicured flowers along the walkways dipped and nodded.

The pontifex had been specific about what to expect. A simple assassination would be insufficient. Accordingly, there was a leather bag attached to Ionkovo's belt, big enough to contain the young queen's head. His instructions were to convey that grisly trophy all the way to Elysium. He wondered if the poor girl would be awake for the whole bumpy journey, and what it would be like to be reduced to a disembodied head.

I don't suppose it matters. But he couldn't help feeling a pang of sympathy. *After all, she might have been one of us, had things gone differently. If she had kept faith.*

Something tinkled gently against the window to his left. He glanced in that direction, but there was nothing but moonlit grass and flowers, whipping back and forth in the violence of the wind. Ionkovo shook his head and continued down the corridor, moving noiselessly over the marble floor.

Tink. Tink, tink, tink—

He spun, backing away. Tiny objects were bouncing off the window, like hailstones wildly out of season. As he watched, a thick cloud descended into the garden, and the impacts multiplied. The sound rose to a roar like the ocean crashing against rocks.

Then the glass started to crack, a spiderweb of thin white lines splaying from one side of the pane to the other. Ionkovo stepped backward, knife raised, a deep shadow underfoot.

The window exploded inward in a spray of glass and—

Sand?

The sand was everywhere, rushing into the corridor from the courtyard like water pouring into a holed ship. When he tried to breathe, Ionkovo got a mouthful of flying grit. The only thing that kept him from diving into a shadow at once was the knowledge that he would have to report this to the pontifex. *What in the name of the Savior is going on?*

The sand swirled, pulling together into a tall whirlwind. It began to shrink, and through the drifts a human figure became visible. A few moments longer and it solidified completely into a tall, thin man wearing odd, baggy clothing. His skin was a chalky gray that marked him as Khandarai, but his face was invisible behind a steel mask, featureless except for three thin slits.

"You wish to harm the queen," the apparition said, in accented Vordanai. "I cannot allow this, *abh-naathem*."

Ionkovo blinked dust from his eyes. "And who are you?"

"I was Jaffa-dan-Iln." The steel mask tilted slightly. "You may call me the Steel Ghost."

"You're a long way from home," Ionkovo said. "What is this queen to you?"

The Ghost's voice was flat. "The enemy of my enemy."

There was a long pause.

"You're one of *them*, aren't you?" Ionkovo said. "Even the pontifex thought your cult had died out long ago."

The Ghost only raised a hand. The wind rose to a shriek, filling the corridor and rattling the windows, and a blast of sand stung every bit of Ionkovo's exposed skin.

He exerted his own power, and the floor rippled underneath him, dropping him neatly into the shadow realm. Safe in the darkness, he considered his options. It would be interesting to test his power against this demon, and that would give him the chance to complete his mission—

But no. More important to report this information to Elysium. That, across the sea, the ancient enemy had survived.

There are still servants of the Beast.

THE PONTIFICATE

The council chamber of the pontificate was a dusty triangular room, deep in the bowels of the great fortress-city of Elysium. It had once been richly appointed, and some vestiges of the finery still remained. The heavy, three-sided table was carved from fine hardwood, and under its coating of grime, gold and silver inlay glittered.

No servant had cleaned the room in years, because it was no longer necessary. Following the Great Schism and the subsequent reforms, one of the three pontificates had ceased to exist. The remaining leaders of the Church, the Pontifex of the Red and the Pontifex of the White, met up above, in daylight and full view of their followers. Elysium was riddled with chambers like this—whole wings that had lost their function centuries ago, closed up and abandoned to silverfish and cobwebs.

The leaders of the Red and the White entered together. The Red took his seat casually, while the White pulled his out, then carefully wiped it down with a silk cloth, lest the dust stain the perfect purity of his robes. They exchanged a look and settled down to wait for their colleague, the one who no longer officially existed.

The Pontifex of the Black was a man in his middle years, with a broad, powerful build. His face was concealed behind the mask of his order—black cloth, covered with hundreds of facets of black, volcanic glass, so the light seemed to ripple across him as he moved. His voice was a thick, unhealthy rasp.

"Brothers," he said, taking his own seat. "Thank you for answering my call."

"It seems to me that *you* have much to answer for," said the White. He was an old man, with hair as snowy as his robes of office under his tall cap. "This entire situation is the result of your meddling."

"I am afraid I must agree with my Brother of the White," said the Red. He was a younger man, round-faced and ruddy-cheeked, with bushy eyebrows and a squashed bulb of a nose. "This is not the result you promised, when you proposed to intervene in the matter of the Vordanai princess."

"The concept was a sound one," the Black rasped.

"Placing a demon on the throne of one of the great powers of the world?" said the White. "A considerable risk to the souls of every one of her subjects, as I believe I said at the time. *This* is a sound concept?"

"As I said at the time," the Black returned, "those souls are in grave danger, cut off from the true Church as they are. A compliant monarch, who might lead her people back to the faith—"

"Enough," the Red snapped. "It is done, and there is no undoing it now."

The Black inclined his head. "Indeed. And our problem stems not from the girl, but from . . . unanticipated factors."

"Vhalnich," said the Red.

"Vhalnich." The Black's rasping voice turned the name into a wet, ugly cough, as though he wanted to spit. "He is the most dangerous heretic we have faced since ancient days."

"So you say," said the White, querulously. "I have seen only slim evidence to that effect. You *say* he is the Demon King come again, but all we have is a single vague report."

"Vhalnich returns victorious from Khandar," the Black said. "He sets this child queen on the throne. And now we find her protected by the *enemy*."

"Vhalnich may simply be a pawn," the Red said.

"Not Vhalnich. He has studied the arts. And now he has control of Vordan." The Black crossed his arms. "We must move against him, or face the greatest loss since the Schism. No simple heresy, but a true apostate, a whole nation under the sway of the enemy such as we have not seen since the Demon King. Such a step backward might threaten the Grace itself, and unleash the final judgment."

The White's lip twisted, unconvinced. "Or Vhalnich may be a man like any other. He should simply be eliminated."

"Difficult," said the Red, "under the present circumstances."

"I have set events in motion toward that end," the Black said. "But careful preparation is required. And, regardless, broader action will be necessary. Even if Vhalnich is removed, we cannot allow Raesinia to rule . . . unguided."

"True," the Red said. "It may be that this represents an opportunity."

"It is a great risk," said the White. "But if the prize is the restoration of the true faith to Vordan . . ."

"Then we are agreed?" the Black said.

The White nodded, and the two of them turned to the Red. He shrugged, crimson robes rustling.

"I will make the arrangements," he said.

The hand of the Church moved slowly, almost invisibly. It tightened its grip in easy stages, as messengers rode to and fro, and news of what had happened in Vordan spread through the civilized world.

The agents of the pontificate knew their business. In Holy Korslavl, capital of Imperial Murnsk, the Priests of the White began to whisper of the opportunity presented by a girl queen and a popular revolution. The chance to stamp out the heresy of the Schism, after so many years. And darker rumors spread, apparently without a source, hinting of demonic forces at work at the heart of the new government and the so-called deputies.

In Viadre, seat of the Borelgai Court and the pulsing heart of world commerce, the Priests of the Red met with nervous bankers in their tall houses along the market streets. Vordan's debt to Borel was great, and the queen had left her financial policy in the hands of demagogues and rabble-rousers. If they took it in their heads to repudiate the loans, heads would roll in the Exchange.

And in Hamvelt, high in its mountain fastness, angry currents among the burghers started to come together. Sworn Priests were banned there, but the agents of the Pontifex of the Black still moved in secret, spreading Elysian gold where it would do the most good. They spoke of the long-disputed border between Vordan and the League, the coastal counties over which so much blood had been spilled over the centuries. And to Hamvelt's ancient nobility, ever jealous of its privileges, they spread the word that the queen intended to finally dissolve the Duchy of Orlanko, just across the mountains, and subordinate the old families of Vordan to the new "representatives of the people."

At length, couriers set out from these three great cities, hastening by stagecoach and riverboat across the length and breadth of the continent. In their diplomatic bags, secured by the wax seals of the world's most powerful men, they carried messages addressed to the new Queen of Vordan. The letters were in three different languages, couched in elaborate diplomatic circumlocutions, citing ancient legal precedents and disputes generations old. But when all the curlicues and embellishments were stripped away, they all carried the same deadly simple meaning:

War.